3 Novels of Questions
Unanswered
Since World War II

*The*

# *Lost Loves*

## OF WORLD WAR II

# COLLECTION

## Bruce Judisch & Sharon Bernash Smith

AMHERST PUBLIC LIBRARY
221 SPRING STREET
AMHERST, OHIO 44001

**BARBOUR**
PUBLISHING

© 2014 by Barbour Publishing, Inc.

*Katia* © 2010 by Bruce Judisch
*For Maria* © 2012 by Bruce Judisch
*The Train Baby's Mother* © 2013 by Sharon Bernash Smith

Print ISBN 978-1-62836-245-9

eBook Editons:
Adobe Digital Edition (.epub) 978-1-63058-067-4
Kindle and MobiPocket Edition (.prc) 978-1-63058-068-1

All rights reserved. No part of this publication may be reproduced or transmitted in any form or by any means without written permission of the publisher.

All scripture quotations, unless otherwise noted, are taken from the King James Version of the Bible.

Scripture quotations marked NKJV are taken from the New King James Version®. Copyright © 1982 by Thomas Nelson, Inc. Used by permission. All rights reserved.

This book is a work of fiction. References to real people, events, establishments, organizations, or locales are intended only to provide a sense of authenticity and are used fictitiously. All other characters, incidents, and dialogue are drawn from the authors' imaginations.

Published by Barbour Publishing, Inc., P.O. Box 719, Uhrichsville, Ohio 44683, www.barbourbooks.com

*Our mission is to publish and distribute inspirational products offering exceptional value and biblical encouragement to the masses.*

 Member of the
Evangelical Christian
Publishers Association

Printed in Canada.

# CONTENTS

# KATIA

by Bruce Judisch

# Dedication

To the *Unbekannt*
1961–1989

# Chapter 1

## March 22, 2004

"Maddy, sit down. You will wear a hole in our carpet."

I quit pacing and dropped onto the edge of the bed. "Oh, Greta, I just don't know what to do!"

She settled back in her chair and peered at me over her small wire-rimmed glasses. "You should accept the assignment."

"You really think so?"

She nodded. "You know you want to. And perhaps it would give us a chance to see each other more. It seems like only yesterday you came to Berlin."

Greta Döring had become a best friend the moment I arrived in Germany last August. The only daughter of my sponsor family, she also proved to be a lifesaver as soon as classes started in October. Three semesters of German at the University of Michigan plus the Freie Universität's six-week intensive-German course were barely enough to keep me afloat in my journalism studies. And I wasn't alone. Another exchange student boarding at the Dörings', Shiloh Mackey, from Ohio State of all places, and I both kept Greta awake well into the night more than once with panic attacks on tough assignments. We valued her friendship as much as her German-language expertise.

My dilemma now, though, had nothing to do with translating German idioms. This wasn't school. This was real.

"I'd go for it, Maddy." Shiloh leaned against the doorjamb with her thumbs hooked into her jean pockets. "I think you really lucked out. I'd love to stay in Berlin, but there's not much chance for a chemistry major to get a follow-on assignment like yours. I'll miss visiting you back in the States, though—even if you do go to Michigan." She wrinkled her freckled nose at me.

I returned their smiles. "Yeah, I'm going to miss you guys, too. You've been an awesome host, Greta, and I'm so glad we met, Shiloh—despite your unfortunate choice of schools." I wrinkled my nose back at her. Then my smile faded. "But this is kind of scary. Moving in with an elderly German lady and writing her memoirs? You know my language skills aren't all that great. What if I find I'm in over my head?"

Greta rolled a blond curl around her forefinger, an endearing habit I teased her about at every opportunity. "Your German is better than you think. And if you need help, you can call me."

"Thanks." I squeezed her hand. "But what about my parents? They don't know anything about this. They expect me home in three weeks."

Shiloh slid her small frame down the wall and sat cross-legged on the floor. "Think they'll mind? My folks would jump at the chance to keep me out of the country a little longer."

We laughed, and Greta raised an eyebrow at me. "You came to Germany to study journalism, *ja?*"

"Yes."

"And your parents, they gave their blessing?"

"Sure. In fact, my dad was the one who talked me into this whole exchange-student thing."

"*Na schön*, so how can they object?"

"Okay, okay." I grabbed my head and scrunched fistfuls of red hair. "Ach! I'm so nervous!"

Greta smiled. "See, you sound like a German already."

I took a deep breath. "I guess I'd better write my parents. I think a letter might smooth the news better than an e-mail."

"Ja, I will leave you alone."

"Me, too." Shiloh pushed up from the floor. "My first final is Monday, and I am *so* not ready."

"Ugh! Don't remind me." I slumped my shoulders. "Thanks, guys. You're great."

Greta kissed me on the cheek and left.

Shiloh gave me a thumbs-up. "Sorry, no kiss. Wolverines have nasty teeth." She smiled sweetly.

"Yeah, and buckeyes have nastier prickles." My smile dripped honey, too.

Shiloh stuck out her tongue and scurried from the room, but not before my pillow hit her in the back.

⊷∞⊷

*March 22*

*Dear Mom and Dad,*

*I can't believe finals are next week! Berlin has been fantastic. Thanks so much again for talking me into this exchange program. The Freie Universität has been awesome. In fact, it looks like I may have a chance to stay on a little longer.*

*An extra-credit opportunity has come up that can apply to my journalism certificate and will transfer to Michigan. A Herr Schultmann contacted the school on behalf of an elderly woman who wants her memoirs written. Professor Müller recommended me, for some reason. I can use the course credit, so I'm going to accept the assignment. He says the lady is fluent in English, which is a relief. I'm going to need all the help I can get.*

*Herr Schultmann picks me up at school on Wednesday, the 31st. I'll send you the new address when I get it. Don't worry. Professor Müller knows Herr Schultmann well and says he's a fine man.*

*That's it for now. I need to get back to studying. I hope you're not too disappointed I won't be home right away, but this opportunity is too good to pass up. If you need to contact me before I get you the new address and phone number, we can use e-mail. I understand the lady lives somewhere in the eastern part of the city. Her name is Katia Mahler.*

*Love,*<br>*Maddy*

# *Chapter 2*

*I hope I'm not calling too early.*

"Mom? Hi, it's Maddy. . . . No, nothing's wrong. I just wanted to call to—. . . Really, everything is fine. You got my letter, right? . . . Good. It explains everything I know so far. Look, I'm running a little low on funds and need you to send me some money from my savings account, please. I'll send you the address tomorrow. . . . Brendon? No, he doesn't know anything about this. I don't think he'll care, Mom. He stopped writing me two months ago."

*The jerk!*

"Well, I'm not so sure about that, but I don't want to get into my love life right now. . . . No, I don't know how long the project will take. I should find out over dinner at her house this evening."

*Two minutes left.*

"Mom, I've really got to go. Herr Schultmann is waiting in the car. I might be able to call tomorrow with the address, but I don't know what arrangements we'll come to over calling international long distance from her home phone. . . . I love you, too, Mom. Say hi to Dad for me."

                                                    ❧

I leaned forward and peered down the bicycle lane as Herr Schultmann turned right onto Fabeckstraße. His quiet voice startled me. "They are everywhere, *nicht wahr?*"

I straightened in my seat. "Yes, true. I'm sorry. A habit, I suppose."

"But a good habit, ja?"

I nodded. "There have been a lot of accidents on campus this year. Sometimes drivers don't see the bikes; sometimes cyclists don't see the cars."

"Do you think if we all pedaled the streets, there would be not so many accidents?"

"No, I expect we'd still find ways to run into each other." I smiled. "It's in our nature."

He echoed my sentiment with a chuckle.

Herr Schultmann's gentle manner set me at ease the first moment I met him in Professor Müller's office. I judged him to be in his mid-sixties, maybe a little younger. His dark gray hair was battling a receding hairline and betrayed the telltale crop marks of an amateur barber. Thick-rimmed glasses perched high on his ruddy nose framed clear blue-gray eyes that disappeared into slits the first time he smiled at me. Deep crow's-feet stretching well into his temples testified that such smiles were frequent. Only a few inches taller than I, he carried his weight well on a stocky torso with broad shoulders. Large callused hands suggested a life acquainted with manual labor, a suspicion confirmed when he hefted my two large suitcases and backpack seemingly with little effort and carried them to the car. He kind of reminded me of my Grandpa McAllister. . .only German.

"Herr Schultmann—"

"Please, you may call me Oskar. I am not so old that I would not like a *schönes Fräulein* to use my given name."

"Oh, a pretty maiden, am I? My, you are a charmer, aren't you. . .Oskar?" I cocked my head at him.

His eyes disappeared behind another broad grin. And did a touch of pink tinge his pale cheeks? I believe it did.

"Oskar, I'm puzzled. Why did you and Professor Müller choose me to interview Fräulein Mahler? There must be plenty of native German-speaking journalists who are more

9

experienced at this sort of thing than I am."

"Katia—Fräulein Mahler was pleased when I told her of you."

"What did you tell her?"

"That you are a fine young American journalist."

"That's all?"

"It was enough."

He maneuvered the vintage Audi onto Unter den Eichen and into heavy traffic. Leaving him to drive, I scanned the familiar stretch that had become a favorite street of mine shortly after arriving at the university. I had often window-shopped beneath the stately oaks that lined the wide boulevard and filled the median. The store owners may not have known me by name, but I'm sure they recognized my nose, so often was it pressed up against their display windows. I take that back; the owner of the chocolate shop definitely knew my name.

A sudden thought returned my attention to Oskar. "Why does Fräulein Mahler want her memoirs written? Is she famous?"

He smiled. "*Nein*, she is not famous. Quite the opposite. It was difficult for me to persuade her to tell her story."

"You had to persuade her? Why?"

"I thought it to be important."

"But—"

"*Enschuldige*, a moment, please. This is not a safe street."

He paused the car then picked his way across Wolfensteindamm and entered the access road to the A103, the inner-city autobahn. A red S-bahn train clattered past on my right, slowed, then stopped to disgorge its diverse load of tourists, skinheads, and young professionals at the Rathaus Steglitz station. The street-train station served the Steglitz City Hall and the Kreisel, a towering glass-and-steel office building that seemed out of place amid the more traditional architecture of the Steglitz district. I stared up through the windshield at the behemoth, thinking it would be more at home on the Kufürstendamm—the "Ku'damm"—at the center of western Berlin's bright-light district.

Oskar broke the silence. "It is a monster, nein?"

Apparently he felt the same way about the Kreisel.

I adjusted my purse on my lap. "Where does Fräulein Mahler live?"

"Karlshorst, in the house where her family lived. Until last year, her Tante Frieda was with her. She is alone now."

"Aunt Frieda?"

"Ja, she was eighty-nine years old. A strong woman. A difficult life."

"Where is she now?"

"She was riding to market. An automobile crossed the bicycle path. The driver did not see her."

I winced, fearing I had struck a nerve with our earlier conversation about bicycle accidents. "I'm so sorry. But, riding a bicycle? At eighty-nine years old?"

His smile returned. "A strong woman."

The sounds of the city faded as the A103 coursed beneath the old sedan. I lost myself in curiosity over what the evening, and perhaps the next few weeks, might bring in the company of the enigmatic Fräulein Mahler. My reverie broke when Oskar slowed and nudged the car onto the entrance ramp to the A100. The Audi's engine shimmied as he kicked the speed back up on the freeway. Soon, the expansive grounds of Tempelhof Flughafen broke the solid ranks of apartment buildings along the far side of the railway tracks that paced the autobahn. I peered through the rear window at the massive terminal and hangar complex built in the shape of the German Eagle.

"The airport seems quiet."

"Ja, flights into Tempelhof are fewer and fewer. The city wants to close the airport in favor of Tegel and Schönefeld."

"I heard protesters were trying to keep it open."

"They argue over the land. If it closes, the airport may be preserved as a landmark, but I do not know by whom."

"Probably the taxpayer," I smirked.

He nodded. "Ja, probably."

Oskar exited onto the A113 then took the first off-ramp at Späthstraße. We crossed an arm of the Teltowkanal, one of the many man-made waterways that sliced through the city. He glanced at me. "In Berlin are more canals than in *Venedig*, you know. Almost two hundred kilometers."

I surveyed the dark brown water and traced the wake of a garbage scow clawing its way against the current. A smug smile curved my lips. "Perhaps Berlin has more canals than Venice, but it lacks the romance."

A chesty laugh tipped back his head. "Now, where is the charmer in you, Fräulein?"

I hunched my shoulders. "I'm sorry. That was a terribly rude thing for a guest of your city to say."

"Not at all." He chuckled. "Well, perhaps a little rude."

I dipped my duly chastised head, but his infectious smile tickled the corners of my mouth. I glanced back up at him. "Oskar, please call me Maddy. Everybody does."

"Hmm. 'Maddy.' We shall see."

I raised an eyebrow, but he offered nothing more.

We continued along Späthstraße, which suddenly became Baumschulenstraße. My seven months in Berlin still hadn't accustomed me to the seemingly random naming strategy of the streets. I'd read that ninety-five towns and villages had merged into the twelve boroughs that made up the great metropolis. This kluging created a hodge-podge of highways and byways, many of which retained their original names. So the same stretch of road could change names without warning three times in less than a mile. Giving directions—worse, getting directions—in Berlin always gave me a headache. I was glad Oskar was driving.

He cleared his throat. "I must stop before our next turn. Fräulein Mahler requires medication that is prepared at a certain, how do you say, *Apotheke?*"

"Drugstore."

He grimaced. "Drugstore? And you say Germans lack romance?"

I laughed. "Okay, how about pharmacy? Does that sound better?"

*"Ein bischen."*

"But only a little, huh?"

He politely ignored my jab. "There is a pharmacy on this road near the S-bahn station. I will not be long."

Oskar veered into an empty spot next to the curb. With a nod, he slipped out of the car and hurried around the corner. I lowered my window and inhaled the brisk air of the early spring afternoon. The pungent odor of exhaust from passing cars mixed with the heavenly aroma of fresh bread wafting from a nearby bakery. Together they created a curious, but not unpleasant, ambiance only the big city offers.

Rosebushes trellised to the red-brick fronts of apartment houses and businesses had recovered from their early pruning and now sprouted buds of bright pink, yellow, and white. Flower boxes suspended from second-story window ledges promised summertime splashes of pansies, begonias, and a dozen other color spots I couldn't name. My thoughts turned wistful at my own failed attempts to cultivate the flowers in the box outside my upstairs window at the Dörings'. I tried everything to keep their spindly stems from turning brown and keeling over. I fed them, watered them, talked to them, sang to them. . .wait, maybe that was it. My mom's green thumb could grow almost anything back in Saginaw Valley's silty clay. My thumb was so brown it could kill a plastic plant just by being in the same room with it for ten minutes. And the only thing more deadly than my gardening thumb was my singing voice.

The click of the driver's door interrupted my thoughts. Oskar slid onto the seat and handed me a plastic bag. I set it on my lap and rolled up my window while he buckled in and started the engine. We turned right at the next corner and soon crossed the Teltowkanal again. Oskar signaled a left turn, but not before the street name changed to Schnellerstraße. I rolled my eyes and gave up trying to memorize our route.

"We come soon to Karlshorster Straße. It is not far now to the house."

I turned toward him. "You say Fräulein Mahler is not famous, so who exactly is she, then?"

He kept his gaze on the road. "It is better you discover that from her."

"But that's hardly fair. She must know something about me, or else why would she let me move in with her?"

His voice quieted. "*Fair* is a word that will mean something different to you before long, I think."

The cryptic comments were beginning to grate on me. "Can you at least tell me if I'll like her?"

"That is up to her."

I frowned. "Oskar, this is frustrating. Why do you refuse to tell me anything about Fräulein Mahler?"

"Because we have arrived."

The car pulled to a stop in front of an aged single-story house nestled in a small copse of linden trees. Ten meters of broken concrete limped from the curb, wriggled under a crooked wrought-iron gate, then collapsed against the bottommost of three tilted steps that fronted a shallow porch. Two wide boards, slightly warped and beveled at the ends, ramped the steps from the porch to the walkway. The deck sagged nearly even with the topmost step, its gray wooden planks scarred and split from the combined assault of weather and time. A brown plastic chair with a scrawny calico curled up on its seat perched at an uneven angle to the right of a wooden door, itself hung slightly off center in the rough red-brick wall. The only other feature on the facade was a gray window separated into two upper and two lower panes with a sheer white scrim just visible through the cloudy glass.

I swallowed, wondering what I'd gotten myself into.

When I reached for my door handle, Oskar touched my arm. *"Bitte."* He lifted the pharmacy bag from my lap and opened his door.

I remained on my seat while he stepped out of the car, retrieved my bags and backpack from the trunk, and set them on the narrow sidewalk. He opened my door and offered me his hand. The cat lifted her head and yawned when I stepped onto the curb. Oskar glanced at the house then at me. Determined not to betray any concern, I smiled. He reached for the gate.

The screech of the wrought-iron spindles across the ancient concrete raised the hair on the back of my neck and the cat from her chair. It reminded me of the times my little brother, Carson, scraped his fingernails across the blackboard in our home-school room—only ten times worse.

Oskar held the gate for me. "Entschuldige. There is some need of repair."

"No need to apologize." I tried to look nonchalant, despite the ringing in my ears. My gaze flitted to the window when I stepped through the gateway. Was it my imagination, or did the curtain move? Oskar picked up my bags and led the way toward the house.

I stepped carefully along the uneven pathway, watchful of turning an ankle. When I reached the porch steps, I smiled at the cat. "Hello, kitty. What are—"

The calico's back shot into an arch that would put a well-endowed camel to shame, and a low hiss whistled through more teeth than I thought possible to fit into a feline mouth. I stepped back, wide-eyed. She leaped onto the porch and disappeared under a low rosebush at the side of the house.

Oskar mounted the steps between the ramp boards. "She lacks charm, also."

Before I could retort, he smiled and knocked on the door. "Katia?"

A thin but firm voice filtered through the doorway. *"Komm herein."*

He opened the door. "Please follow me."

I took a deep breath, mounted the stairs, and stepped across the threshold into another world.

# Chapter 3

*Dear Mom and Dad,*

*I arrived at Fräulein Mahler's today. You should've seen the place. The yard and outside of the house were a disaster, so I braced myself for anything when I walked in the door. Boy, was I shocked.*

*Even as fastidious a housekeeper as you are, Mom, you'd have been impressed. The inside was everything the outside wasn't. The main living area was sparsely furnished but tasteful. A Turkish rug covered most of the rustic hardwood floor, its intricate design still vivid despite obvious wear. On the left wall, a built-in bookshelf rose from the floor to the ceiling, not an empty space showing among the orderly bindings. The opposite wall hosted a fireplace, swept but darkened with coal residue. A neatly arranged grouping of framed pictures stood centered on a dark wood mantel over the fireplace. Over the mantel hung a large cross that appeared to be carved from a single piece of rough wood. Aside from the door, the front wall was bare, but for a double window covered by lacy white scrims. Beneath the window rested a worn floral-print settee, a crocheted cream-colored afghan draped over its backrest. A dim hallway stretched along the inside front of the house to my right, which I would discover led to three small bedrooms and an even smaller bathroom.*

*The far side of the front room opened into a dining nook furnished with a dark-wood table and four matching chairs. A mosaic bowl with freshly cut flowers served as a centerpiece for two crisscrossing embroidered runners. Each runner terminated at a place setting, three of which were occupied with a plate, a tumbler, and a set of silverware precisely arranged on a cream-colored cloth napkin.*

*The faint aroma of baked apples—oh, how I hoped it would be strudel!—floated through the doorway leading to the kitchen and blended with the scents of lavender and roses wafting through the open windows beyond the table.*

*I don't know how long I stood by the door taking all this in, but the next thing I heard was. . .*

⚬

"*. . .und* bitte, *mach die Tür zu, Oskar.*"

Oskar nodded and closed the door.

"*Danke.*"

The soft voice came from a corner of the front room to my left. In an old-fashioned wooden wheelchair sat a slight woman—what, a hundred and ten pounds, maybe? No, probably not even that. She wore a navy-blue dress with a gentle print of petite white flowers and ivy tendrils cascading from a lacy white neckline and trailing beneath a tight-knit sweater unbuttoned at the front. Anklets, the same blue color as the dress, gloved feet tinier than I thought possible on a human being. Visible through the sheer anklets, knotty toes on both feet curved toward each other as though yearning to touch. Blue veins scurried upward from the top of the anklets beneath cellophane skin and disappeared under the modest hemline of her dress. Her lower legs appeared barely thicker than the bones supporting them—which I doubted they could do, had she attempted to stand. I fought the urge to stare, but with little success.

"Fräulein McAllister?"

The quiet voice coaxed my gaze to her face, an artisan's study in contrast. Pale age-lined skin stretched over pronounced cheekbones that sheltered hollows dark in shadow. Her thin lips underscored a narrow nose tipped up at the end. A neck that looked too frail to support a head even as slight as hers sprouted from her rounded shoulders. Hair still dark but frosted with subtle streaks of gray gathered itself into a tight bun, not an errant wisp in sight. She sat erect with her hands folded on her lap, a caricature of primness.

I began to respond but stopped short when my eyes encountered hers. Amid her fading visage shone two crystalline chips, crisp and clear as alexandrite, their color equally defying definition. So clear, they seemed to emit their own light rather than reflect the light around them.

"You are Fräulein McAllister, *nee?*"

"Yes. . .yes, I'm sorry." I lowered my gaze, but only for a moment. Her eyes seemed to call to me, and I lifted my head again.

"Why are you sorry to be Fräulein McAllister?" Her voice perked, but no smile softened her pursed lips.

I knit my brow. "No, I meant—"

She lifted a delicate finger from the arm of her wheelchair. "I know what you meant, Fräulein. Bitte, *setzen Sie sich.*" She nodded toward the sofa beside her.

"Thank you." Nonplussed, I slipped my purse from my shoulder and set it beside me as I settled onto the cushion. I shifted toward her and pondered which of my many questions to ask first.

She cocked her head at me. "Are you prepared to begin?"

"I. . .begin?"

"*Natürlich.* Begin the interview."

I glanced at Oskar, who had set my bags against the wall and pulled a chair away from the dining table. He sat down and returned a blank look.

"Well. . .it's just that. . .I have some questions." I cleared my throat.

"Questions?"

"Yes. I understand I am to interview you, but that's all I was told. I don't really even know who you are. . .at all."

"Is that not the purpose of the interview, to learn of me?"

"Well, I suppose so—"

"You are a journalist, *nicht wahr?*"

"Yes. I mean, I'm still in school, but I have done a little professional work. Actually, that leads me to my first question. Why me? How did you hear of me? Surely there are others more qualified than I am to interview you, aren't there?"

"That is three questions."

I slumped my shoulders. "Yes, ma'am, I know. I only meant—"

"Bitte, sit straight, Fräulein. If you are to interview me, you must be precise in your posture and your language."

My mouth snapped shut. I found myself lost between an indignant retort and an apology, like the proverbial mule dithering between two stacks of hay. That was surely a rebuke, but her face remained expressionless, likewise her tone.

I straightened my shoulders on impulse, which rankled me. "Yes, ma'am. Still, I wonder why you selected me to interview you."

"If you interview me well, perhaps that will come out."

I averted my eyes. This wasn't going to be as easy as I thought.

"Bitte, look at me, Fräulein McAllister. I must see your eyes to understand what you mean."

My forehead warmed. I refused to be treated like a child, no matter how important the project might be to my college degree.

"Yes, ma'am." I made a concerted effort to blunt the edge in my tone. Apparently not concerted enough.

"You are—how do you say?—*irritiert* with me."

I set my jaw. "No, Fräulein Mahler, I'm not irritated with you. I must confess I'm heading that direction, though." I bit my lip at what I'd just blurted out to my new hostess. *Well, that should pretty much kill this project.* I braced myself for a tongue lashing.

Instead, a slight curve touched the corners of her mouth. "*Sehr gut.* And at last you speak my name. I did not know how long you would allow me to push at you."

I shook my head. "I don't understand."

"You show spirit. That is important. I will push at you, if you allow me. You must not allow me."

"But—"

She straightened her shoulders. "Our dinner is ready. We begin the interview tomorrow."

I eased back on the sofa, the realization dawning that I had just undergone the oddest—and perhaps most astute—job interview of my young career. Fräulein Mahler was not the decrepit invalid she appeared to be. Like her house, her outside was in decline, but inside she was immaculate. I glanced at Oskar. He nodded and smiled.

I paused before standing up. Maybe it was time to try a little initiative. "Fräulein Mahler, if we are to work together, it would be nice if you'd call me by my first name."

Across the room, Oskar cleared his throat.

She remained silent.

I dared a half smile. "My name is Madeline, but my friends call me Maddy."

"*Was ist das?* Maddy?" Her brow sank into a furrow deeper than I thought it had the skin to support.

My smile faltered. "Yes, Maddy."

"You have the beautiful name of Madeline, and you destroy it with Maddy?"

I shot a look at Oskar, who appeared to be struggling against another grin. Then I remembered his veiled remark in the car about my nickname.

She shook her head. "*Um Himmels willen*—Maddy?"

Oskar trembled with suppressed laughter then forced a straight face as Fräulein Mahler addressed him. "Oskar, show Fräulein McAllister where she will sleep, *bitte*."

He retrieved my bags and stepped to the hallway. Red-faced, I fumbled for my purse and lurched up from the couch. Oskar nodded for me to follow, and I escaped down the hallway chased by Fräulein Mahler's muttering.

"Maddy? *Lieber Himmel. . .*"

# Chapter 4

## April 1

Dear Mom and Dad,

I don't have much time to write. I'm pretty tired. Today was my first full day on the job. I don't believe the stamina this woman has! She can go hours without a break. I think she might have been done in by dinner, though, as the meal passed in near silence.

I spent the evening preparing my materials for the next day. She nestled into what appears to be her favorite spot in the corner of the front room, read, and meditated—on what I have no idea. She keeps a small leather-bound book by her wheelchair. I haven't had a chance to look closely, but I think it's a Bible. She paged through it last night just before bedtime and took it with her when she retired to her room.

Today we mostly sorted through old photos, letters, and some family papers. Fräulein Mahler took her time with each photograph. She started to comment on one or two then shook her head and set them aside. I guess the explanations will come as the interview progresses. The other papers she merely read and reread quietly.

Oskar dropped by this afternoon with a few groceries and another bag of some kind of medicine, I think. He didn't stay, just asked if we needed anything. I didn't see her pay him for the groceries or meds. I'm not sure what kind of arrangement they have. Maybe that will come out in time, too.

Anyway, this morning was a near disaster. I almost blew the whole project before we even got started. . . .

⤙⤚

Morning arrived with a thunderstorm. I yanked my laptop plug from the wall socket, concerned it might take a power surge through wiring that had to be at least twice as old as I was. I snuggled deeper under the puffy *Federdecke* that draped the thin mattress of the old bed. The air hung heavy with the mustiness of chalking paint, aged wood, and poor ventilation.

A solid overcast visible through the small window next to my nightstand drenched the tiny bedroom in charcoal gray, the house in sweeping sheets of rain. Rolling thunder rattled the loose casement, but no lightning flashes pierced the granite cloud cover to disturb the dimness enshrouding the room. The early morning cold neutered any thought of abandoning my toasty feather comforter, although the oversized red numbers on my digital alarm clock advised me that lingering in bed would soon be only a fond memory. Fräulein Mahler had called for an early start to the day before she wheeled off to her room yesterday evening.

The creak of a floorboard outside my door affirmed the clock's suggestion that I roust out of bed. My hostess was already up and about, probably muttering about the sleepyhead American. Releasing a heavy sigh, I rolled over and squinted into the gloom.

My rose-colored terry-cloth robe—normally cheery, warm, and inviting—sprawled sullenly over the chair by my nightstand, clearly disgruntled at having left the cozy bedroom at the Dörings' modern townhouse. My furry white slippers slouched beneath the chair, assuming a sickly gray in the murky dankness.

A gentle tap on the door broke my muddled thoughts.

"Fräulein McAllister? *Frühstück*."

Breakfast! Well, in that case. . . "Coming!"

I groped for the dour robe and dragged it under the comforter to warm up. A shiver raced through me as soon as the chilled terry cloth touched my body. It seemed to have absorbed half the humidity in the room and now shared every soggy molecule with my thin cotton pajamas. I lifted the cover and frowned at the twisted jumble of fabric. The only thing missing from the delinquent robe was a smirk.

Giving the housecoat time to warm up, I flipped onto my back, blew a tangled auburn wisp from my eyebrows, and pondered the day ahead.

Today we would begin to chronicle Fräulein Mahler's story. True to my rigorous training, I first planned to outline the project, dividing major sections by the decades of her life. Each decade would be subdivided into years, or months, depending upon the amount of activity worthy of note. I would devote segments of my tablet—pre-tabbed and color-coded, of course, for quick reference—to each era.

I'm proud to have developed a homegrown shorthand since Pitman's notation system successfully eluded my intuition my freshman year, and Gregg's symbology had proven equally evasive to me as a sophomore. I could get the main points down on paper and let my digital recorder pick up the details for later review. At the end of each day, I would transcribe the session with follow-up questions into my laptop. Everything was ready to go. We just needed to get organized and all should proceed very—

"Fräulein McAllister?"

I jumped at the now-not-so-gentle tap on the door.

"Coming! Coming. . ."

I sat up and wrestled my arms into the half-warmed, still-grouchy robe then swung my legs over the side of the bed and squirmed my toes into the grumpy slippers. Wobbling to my feet, I pulled the housecoat around my waist and flipped the belt into a loose knot. I shook my rebellious bangs away from my eyes and opened the door. After a quick stop in the bathroom, I plodded past Fräulein Mahler's room. Reaching the end of the hall, I stepped out into what was surely the next best thing to heaven.

The soft glow of lamplight bathed the front room in melted butterscotch and chased the chilly gray of my bedroom into faint memory. I closed my eyes and inhaled a tantalizing olio of strong Colombian coffee and fresh *Brötchen*, the chewy bread rolls that had enraptured my taste buds shortly after arriving in Berlin. Oh, I didn't want to exhale!

I peeked around the fireplace to the dining table, already laden with glass containers of fruit compote, a block of butter, and a flask of orange juice. As at dinner the evening before, matched place settings of Dresden china lay opposite each other, framed perfectly by heavy Solingen silver and crowned with Stölzle crystal goblets. The lady had class, I had to give her that.

Expectantly, I donned a broad smile and padded across the soft Turkish rug toward the table. At that moment, Fräulein Mahler wheeled in through the kitchen doorway with a plate of steaming soft-boiled eggs balanced on a towel across her lap. We stopped short at the sight of each other.

I stared at her prim white sweater, freshly ironed navy skirt, and lace-trimmed blouse, clasped modestly at the neck with a lovely cameo brooch—no doubt a priceless family heirloom. Her hair, meticulously brushed, was pulled so tightly into its bun you could have bounced a one-euro coin off it.

She surveyed my disheveled robe, gaped open above the belt to reveal an equally crumpled purple-and-pink-striped pajama top missing its uppermost button. My crushed shoulder-length curls splayed in every direction, their lesser tendrils plastered against my unwashed forehead and unmade-up cheeks.

Our eyes reengaged for an awkward moment, during which I mentally searched for a hole to crawl into, and which, I suspect, she prolonged for optimum effect.

I attempted a smile.

She did not.

"Umm. Excuse me a moment, please."

"Ja."

Twenty minutes later, properly dressed and brushed, I returned to the dining nook to cold eggs and tepid coffee. Her place at the table had been cleared, and she was in the corner by the front window with a small brown hardback propped between her slender fingers. I slipped into my seat and began to wolf down whatever was still edible.

"Fräulein McAllister, may I speak with you, bitte?"

"Certainly," I mumbled around a crust of Brötchen.

Silence.

I paused mid-chew and glanced toward the corner. Her book lay open in her lap, her hands folded across it. She looked at me with that. . .that expressionless expression she seemed to have perfected. I choked down the morsel of breakfast roll, dabbed my mouth with my napkin, and pushed back from the table. I stepped across the room and stopped three paces in front of her, my hands clasped at my waist. She eased a tiny pair of reading glasses from her nose.

"I have retained you to interview me, not as a house companion. However, there are some—how do you say?—common courtesies for us to observe."

I closed my eyes and nodded. "I know what you're going to say. I apologize for my tardiness and my appearance this morning. It won't happen again."

"It is impossible for you to know what I am going to say until I have said it, Fräulein McAllister. If you anticipate me during our interview, you will lead my story astray—just as you are astray in assuming I refer to your performance this morning."

My eyes blinked open, and my cheeks tinged pink. "Performance?"

"Is that not the correct word?"

"No, that is not the correct word. I do not *perform* for anyone." I knew I was going to regret this, but I never could completely tame my Irish blood. "I was late and not properly dressed, and I've made the gesture of apologizing."

"Gesture."

"Yes. I would expect common courtesy to have you accept that gesture. But apparently the responsibility for courtesy extends only to me in this relationship." The head of steam was building.

Her tone remained infuriatingly even. "Relationship? We have a business arrangement."

My tone ratcheted up a notch. "Business arrangement? I have heard nothing of business discussed. In fact, I still don't understand exactly what you want from me, other than to be interviewed—whatever you believe that to mean. I have no idea what I'll walk away with at the end of this, or what you expect to walk away with."

"Fräulein McAllister, if you have not noticed, I will not walk away at the end of this."

"Oh, stop it! You know what I mean." My eyes began to blur, but I refused to let her see tears.

"Na schön, let me be clear."

I folded my arms across my chest. "Please do!"

"Without interruption, bitte."

I clenched my jaw if for no other reason than to force my mouth shut.

"You will help me gather together my history. You will produce a written document—*ein Buch*, ja?—for me. In return, you will have food and a place to sleep. You will also receive payment."

"And if I decide to quit?"

She narrowed her brow. "Quit?"

I had no intention of quitting, but it was the principle of the thing, and I had gone too far to back down now. "Yes, what if I decide I don't want to do this after all?"

"That would be rude, Fräulein McAllister. You have already agreed."

"Why would it be rude? In my country, people can quit if they decide they don't like the business arrangement."

"It may serve you well to remember you are not in your country."

I drew my head back with another retort poised at the tip of my tongue, but her words pricked a faint memory, and I paused. The memory strengthened and whispered to me that she was right. I had violated the foremost promise I made to myself before coming to Germany: that I would never become the Ugly American and forget that I am a guest in a foreign land at the pleasure of its people. Short of compromising moral principle, I would meet the Germans in Germany, not in Michigan.

I dropped my arms to my side and drew a deep breath. A slight waver wrinkled my voice, and it annoyed me. "You're right. Please forgive me. Sometimes I lose my head. I suppose it's the Irish in me."

The hint of a smile shaded her mouth. "Nee, it is the American in you."

I sputtered a laugh. "Yes. You're right again. I can't blame the Irish for the Americans, can I?"

"No more than you can blame the other *Volk* who make up your America."

The laugh relieved the pressure in my forehead, and I nodded, trying to subdue another smile. "Very well. If there's nothing else, I'll clear my dishes, and we can begin."

"There is one thing. It is the courtesy I mentioned a moment ago."

I steeled myself, determined to curb my emotions. "Yes, ma'am?"

"I wish to apologize to you and offer the courtesy to permit you more time to rise and prepare for breakfast. Your appearance was to be expected. I failed you as your hostess."

My jaw slackened. "That was the common courtesy?"

"Ja."

I closed my eyes and sighed. "And if I had kept my big mouth shut. . ."

Her voice carried a smile. "Your mouth is not so large, Fräulein McAllister. And perhaps these things needed to be said, nee?"

⟫⟪

So, after that inauspicious start, we settled down to work. The stack of photos and documents dwindled as we sorted them into chronological order. My German was sufficient to figure out most of them, and any clarification I needed could come later. Toward the end of the afternoon, though, my eyes began to glaze over. Apparently, she noticed.

"Is this too much? Do you need to rest?"

"No, thank you. I just want to make sure my notes will be organized."

She sighed. "There is much to say and perhaps little time."

I glanced up at her, the question begging. Oh well, I couldn't get a worse reaction than I did with the please-call-me-Maddy suggestion. Maybe it was time to test the waters again.

"So little time? Are you. . .going somewhere?"

"I am not a young maiden like you, Fräulein McAllister. At my age, we are not promised another tomorrow."

I chanced a little informal banter. "But that is true of all of us, regardless of our age, isn't it?"

She eased the photo she was studying onto the table and folded her hands. "Ja, what you say is wise. But tell me, do you ever wake up in the morning surprised that you have done so?"

My smile faltered. "I suppose not."

"One of the gifts of age you will discover is the awareness of time. We receive a number of mornings at birth. The more that slip our grasp, the tighter we cling to those that remain."

I set down my notepad. "But surely you have many mornings ahead of you. What little I do know of you from these documents puts your years only around sixty. Your mind is very sharp. Your body is, well. . ." Needles of panic pricked my forehead, and I hesitated. I hate it when I find myself stuck in a sentence and can't get out.

"Ja?"

She wasn't going to let me get away with this one.

I lowered my voice. "I'm sorry. I know nothing of your condition, and it was presumptuous of me to comment."

She knit her brow. "Presumptuous?"

I wracked my brain for the right word. *"Anmaßend?"*

"Ja. But I think it is not so much presumptuous, as it is probing, nee?"

I winced. That would be the last time I tried subterfuge with this lady. I expected a rebuke but was shocked when a smile broader than I believed her capable of overtook her. More astounding was the transformation it brought to her face—as though she had gathered up all the beauty she possessed into an urn hidden behind her eyes and the smile tipped the vessel, splaying its glorious contents from brow to neck. Gone were the hollows of her cheeks, the gray pallor. Her skin seemed to smooth and shimmer at the same time. My breath caught at her sudden radiance.

She misinterpreted my reaction. "Do not be embarrassed, Fräulein McAllister. You are a journalist. It is your job to probe—if a good journalist, your nature to do so."

I couldn't let the moment pass.

"It's not that, Fräulein Mahler. It's your smile. You're positively beautiful!"

I should've let the moment pass.

As quickly as they had separated, the clouds rolled back in. She tipped her head forward. Her hands fidgeted in her lap then groped for the photograph she had laid on the table. The snapshot trembled in her fingers as she pulled it close to her face and blinked at it.

Confusion numbed me, puzzlement at what I'd said that could have discomforted her. I chanced another look at her. "Fräulein Mahler?" I whispered. "I'm sorry. Did I say something. . . ?"

She didn't respond.

# Chapter 5

## April 5

*Dear Mom and Dad (and yeah, you, too, Carson),*

*I wish I could e-mail you, but there's not even a telephone in the house, let alone a computer, and the nearest Internet café is five kilometers from here. So it looks like we're stuck with snail mail and the times I can get to a public phone. That reminds me—my calling card is nearly out. I hope you sent the money I asked for.*

*The pace of life here is really different from school. I think the serenity might drive me nuts. I'm used to getting out to a dance club on the Ku'damm or just walking around the Europa Center mall once a week. I'm really going to miss Fridays with the gang at the Irish Pub—not that I ever developed a taste for Guinness, but they have a great salmon on toast. (Sorry, how did I get off on that?) Anyway, there was something of the real world back at the university, but here it's so quiet. Oh well, I'm not here to party. I'm here to work.*

*Yesterday morning Oskar drove us to church; then we relaxed for the rest of the day. She still attends services where her father served as a pastor. He was ordained in the Lutheran Church and actually attended the Barmen Conference in 1934, where Dietrich Bonhoeffer founded the Confessing Church. The service is a little different than I'm used to at St. Luke's, but the church is beautiful. Anyway, we won't be working on Sundays. She's adamant about that.*

*Today was the first full day of the actual interview. You won't believe what happened. Remember I wrote you how I was going to approach the project? Well. . .*

❧

"...so I've tabbed my notebook, as you can see. Now what I'd like to do first is block the story. We'll start with the year you were born. You can brainstorm all the major events in each of the decades from that point on, and we'll organize them by year. Then we can match your photographs and documents to the exact year and event. That should help you recall the details. Then—" I glanced up from the table and met a blank stare. "Fräulein Mahler? Is everything okay?"

After a moment, she blinked then surveyed her dining table. I followed her gaze. Not a square centimeter of the polished wood was visible through the orderly stacks of documents and photographs, two tabbed writing tablets, my Dell laptop and Sony digital recorder with extra batteries, an array of color-coded sticky-note pads matched to the colored tabs on the tablets, and assorted pens and extra pencils.

"Fräulein Mahler?"

She raised her eyes and blinked again.

"Is something wrong?"

Without a word, she pivoted her chair and wheeled slowly to her spot by the front window. She backed into the corner and gestured toward the sofa with her hand.

Puzzled, I set my pen down and rose from the dining table.

She patted the cushion closest to her. I crossed the room and eased myself onto the couch. Then, to my shock, she lifted my left hand from my lap, laid it on the arm of the wheelchair, and rested her hand over it. With a gentle smile, she leaned her head back and closed her eyes. Her forefinger began to brush back and forth across my wrist.

"I was born on 23 November 1943 in a bomb shelter in Karlshorst, Germany. . . ."

The house lay still, aside from her hushed voice and the faint *tick-tock* of an alpine clock on a wall near the dining table. She spoke of her father, Helmut, and her mother, Anna, but gave only a little of their backgrounds. I also learned more about Tante Frieda, her mother's sister. I wanted to ask for details but hesitated to break the flow of her narrative. There would be time for questions later.

The detail of her recollections surprised me. She must have learned some of the facts secondhand, as she would have been too young to pick up on them herself. Still, she recited dates, days of the week, often even times of the day. All the while she rested her head against the back of her chair and spoke with a gentle lilt.

"British bombs fell on Berlin the day I was born, I am told. It was the beginning of the end of the war, although we did not know it then. My father did what he could for his—what is in English *Mitglieder?*"

I searched my mind. "I don't know the word."

"People of the *Kirchegemeinde*, the Church."

"Oh, congregation."

"Ja, congregation. He did what he could for his congregation, but it was very difficult. It would get worse.

"My mother, Anna Schiller, was beautiful and intelligent. She attended the university in Leipzig, rare for a woman. She could have had any man, lived a life of wealth. But, in her third year, she met my father, a poor theology student on holiday from seminary. They married in eight months, and she left the university. Her father, my Opa Georg, was so angry. He never forgave my father. He said Papa ruined Mama's life."

I studied her face as she spoke. Her eyes remained closed even when she paused to question an English word. She held my hand the entire morning and stroked my wrist. The gesture was soothing, but, at the same time, unnerved me. The intimacy was such a departure from the otherwise formal manner in which she treated me. I wondered if it helped her to focus, or maybe she gauged my response through her touch. Perhaps both.

I glanced at the dining table where my recorder and notepads lay out of reach. I was desperate to record her story but reticent to remove my hand from hers for fear of breaking her train of thought. I hoped I could remember all this.

As she unfolded the tale of her early childhood, I couldn't help but reflect upon my own. The contrast couldn't have been greater. Hers was ravaged by war and the aftermath of war. Deprivation was a part of life, daily existence defined by the struggle to survive and to protect oneself from others struggling to survive. For me, deprivation was my Netflix DVD arriving a day late.

She spoke of ordeals I was unequipped to comprehend, yet her demeanor remained calm, her face serene. There would be moments of tension, though, when her grip would tighten around my fingers. The first of those moments came just before lunch as she recounted an early memory of her brother.

"It was late on a Saturday afternoon. . . ."

". . .and Friedrich, mind your sister."

*Mama pulled her coat over her shoulders and stepped out the door. Tante Frieda patted me on the head, then pulled on her own wrap. She threw a sharp glance at my brother, who slouched on the sofa immersed in a copy of Hans Fallada's* Young Man—What Now?

"*Friedrich, did you hear? Watch after your sister. And mind what you read. You are too young for such a man as Fallada.*"

*He ignored her.*

*She frowned, glanced back at me, then hurried after Mama. The door banged shut behind her.*

*Friedrich sighed and tossed his book onto the side table. He stretched his arms over his head and yawned. "So, Katia, what is it you draw, eh?"*

*"A cat."*

*"Ah, today it is a cat. Was it not a rabbit you drew yesterday?"*

*"Yes."*

*He slid off the couch onto his knees and crawled to where I sat with my slate board and colored chalk. His finger tipped the slate back toward his face.*

*"You are quite the artist, young lady. I can see it is a cat even upside down." He smiled and tugged on my pigtail.*

*I blushed. "No, it is not so good, I think."*

*"Of course it is. But you will get even better."*

*I set the slate down. "Where is Papa? I have not seen him today."*

*"Who knows? He has meetings with his deacons. They plan Sunday service, I guess."*

*"Service is the same all the time. Why do they need to plan?"*

*He shrugged. "Do not ask me, Katia. The world falls apart while we sing songs and recite prayers. Instead, we should fight those who keep us poor so they can be rich."*

*"But Papa says we fight against things we cannot see. He says—"*

*He slapped the floor with his hand. "I know what he says! But there is plenty we can see that we should fight against. Our prayers and songs do nothing against hunger and Soviet machine guns."*

*"But—"*

*"Ach, forget it, Katia. You are young. There will be enough life ahead of you to forget these times."*

*My eyes began to tear. "You are not so old yourself, Friedrich."*

*"No, but I do not want to forget."*

Fräulein Mahler's grip eased. "I was only five years old, but I still remember the times. Berlin was torn apart. At the end of the war, the Soviets took the eastern half of the city—which included our Karlshorst—and the Americans, British, and French divided the western half. In 1948, the Soviets blockaded us, trying to force the other *Alliierten* out, but the Americans flew supplies into Berlin. Tempelhof Flughafen was only three kilometers away, and the distant noise of aircraft filled the air day and night for almost a year. Many of my neighbors watched the sky, their faces pale at the deep hum of the engines. I was too young to remember the sound of bombers, but I could see their fear."

I thought back through the documents we had sorted the day before. "I didn't know you had a brother. Is he in any of your pictures?"

"Ja. Friedrich was seven years older than I. I loved him so much. He was—how to say, *unruhig.*"

"Restless."

"Danke, restless. In the years before I was born, his friends began to join the Deutsches Jungvolk, the younger boys of the Hitler-Jungend, but he had no interest in this. His friends became fewer and fewer until only those who shared his opinion of the Nazis remained. In the last days of the war, Hitler forced old men and young boys to take a final stand against the invading Soviet army. Friedrich refused to serve the Nazi cause and hid when the Waffen Schutzstaffel—the regular soldiers of what was called the 'SS'—came to our neighborhood looking for those who could fight."

"What happened to him?"

"We will come to that, ja?" She blinked her eyes open. Releasing my hand, she urged her wheelchair away from the corner.

"Fräulein Mahler?"

"It is time for *Mittagessen.* We eat now."

"But what about your brother? I was just getting—"

"All in good time, Fräulein McAllister."

# Chapter 6

*I think there's enough time left on this calling card.*

"Hi, Dad! I didn't expect you home at this hour. I'm on a pay phone at the Karlshorst S-bahn station. It's not too far from Fräulein Mahler's house. Where's Mom? . . . Grandma McAllister's? What's wrong? . . . Oh, no."

*Poor Grandma. It's just one thing after another for her.*

"Yes, I got the money. Thanks. . . . The interview is going well so far, I think. This was only the fourth day. It's been really interesting. Fräulein Mahler is so—I don't know how to describe her. . . . Yeah, fascinating is a good word. She's mostly told me about her family, so far. . . . No, just the immediate family. Oh, and there's an Aunt Frieda, too—or was. She died last year. Anyway, I just wanted to touch base with you and say thanks for sending the money. I'll let you—what? . . . Oh, we're up to the early fifties—around 1952, I think. . . ."

⟶⟵

". . .May, it was. Friedrich was now sixteen years old. Some of his friends came to celebrate his birthday."

We sat in the front room, I on the divan and she, of course, in her wheelchair. Again she held my left hand, leaving my right hand free to write and shuffle through the memorabilia I brought with me from the dining table.

"Is this a photograph from the party?" I picked up a faded black-and-white print, creased with age. A small cluster of teenagers stood on a dirt path in front of what appeared to be the Mahler's house. A scruffy-haired youth, Friedrich I surmised, anchored the group. His arms were wrapped around a young girl in a light-colored dress standing in front of him, her head cocked at a shy angle.

"Ja. His friends and I."

"Do you remember them?" I handed her the snapshot and shifted closer so I could see it, too.

She tilted her head back and peered through her reading glasses. "I am in front of Friedrich, here. He hugged my shoulders just before Tante Frieda snapped the picture. His girlfriend, Evvie Wagner—he called her Ev-Ev—is on his right. A beauty, nee? Such curls she had, and eyes the color of the sky. Aidan Zeller, his good friend, is on the other side with his elbow on Friedrich's shoulder. It is difficult to see here, but Aidan was never without a— how do you say, *schelmisch*?"

I frowned. "Hmm. I'm not sure."

"He liked to tease, to play his jokes on us."

"Okay, mischievous, perhaps?"

"Ja, that is it. Aidan was never without his mischievous smile, so much fun."

I tapped my chin with my pencil. "Aidan isn't a German name, though. Isn't there an approved list of names Germans use for naming their babies?"

"Ja, but he was born across the border in Czechoslovakia. His family moved to Berlin when he was four years old. His father was German, his mother Irish. She insisted on the namesake of her own father."

I nodded and squinted back at the photo. Behind Evvie slouched a boy with close-cropped light hair. He was the only one in the group without a smile. I pointed to him. "Who is this?"

Her smile faded. "Franz Schindler. Such a serious boy. His father, Günter, was a deacon in our church."

25

I jotted the names down on my pad then peered again at the photograph. "There is one other person. There, behind Aidan."

Her voice dropped. "Elke Heuer. She was not a close friend of Friedrich's. Her family came to church sometimes. They were quite poor. Papa asked Mama to invite Elke to the party. She was very nice but seemed to have few friends."

"The picture is faded, but she seems to be smiling."

"Ja, she wanted to please, but it was difficult for her. She did not seem able to clean herself. There was an odor. People were not always kind. I felt sorry for her."

I nodded and scribbled Elke's name beside Franz's. She handed the picture back, and I focused on the young girl in Friedrich's arms. Her bright eyes beamed life into the glossy print. I smiled and began to write the date and place above the names on my pad.

"You look very happy, there with your brother—"

Her next words stopped me midsentence.

"Ja. It was the last day I was able to use my legs."

*"Evvie, move closer to Friedrich. I cannot get you in the picture." Tante Frieda fumbled with the old Speedex camera.*

*"Hurry, Frieda. I felt a drop of rain." Mama cast a nervous glance at a dark cloud overhead.*

*As if to answer her, a low rumble rolled across the sky. The thunder chilled me. I loved rainstorms but was always fearful of the lightning. I wanted to be in the house.*

*"Everyone! You must be still for the picture. Aidan, take your hand from Friedrich's face. Do not be so silly! Ready? One. . .two. . .three!"*

*As soon as the camera clicked, the first large raindrops began to splatter around us. Laughing, we turned and stumbled over each other in a race for the house. I held the door for Mama and Tante Frieda.*

*Mama crossed the room to the dining table while Tante Frieda scurried into the kitchen for plates and silverware. We gathered around the dining table, where a small chocolate-glazed cake and glasses of apple juice were ready to be divided. What a wonderful treat! Chocolate and sugar were still not plentiful after the war. Papa must have saved his money a long time for such a feast.*

*"Mama, where is Papa?"*

*She did not look at me as she began to cut the cake. "At a meeting. He will be here soon."*

*"A meeting? What kind of meeting? Did it have to be on Friedrich's birthday?"*

*"Quiet now, Katia. These things cannot always be helped."*

*Friedrich patted my shoulder. "Yes, meetings are most important, Katia. Be sure in your life never to miss a meeting."*

*"Friedrich, that was not necessary." Mama stopped slicing the cake, and the room became quiet.*

*"Forgive me, Mama. I know how important it is to choose just the right songs for Service. One must not take such things lightly."*

*Mama's face grew very stern. I thought I saw her eyes moisten, but she looked down. She said nothing more and began again to slice the cake.*

*"Friedrich, take the first piece. Then go see to your friends." Tante Frieda's voice was hushed. My brother began to speak, but then he stopped. Perhaps it was her frown. I had not seen such a look on her face before.*

*Friedrich turned away from the table. He did not take a piece of cake.*

*"Mama?" I wanted to cry.*

*"Hush, child. It is all right."*

*But it was not.*

*Aidan stepped up behind me and put his hands on my shoulders. He told a funny joke, and everyone laughed. Then he slapped Friedrich on the back and pushed a plate of cake into his hands. "Eat, or I will eat it for you!"*

*Tante Frieda tsk'd, but Mama smiled at Aidan and continued to cut the cake. I handed plates and juice glasses to each of our guests then took my own.*

*In an hour, Friedrich's friends began to leave.*

*At the door, Aidan tugged my ponytail and kissed me on the cheek. "You are very beautiful, little Katia. Perhaps I shall wait for you before I marry."*

*I blushed, and his smile grew wider.*

*Tante Frieda propped her hands on her hips and frowned. "Aidan, let the girl be."*

*"Never! Not as long as she is this pretty." He winked at Tante Frieda, who, I think, almost smiled. He tapped me on the nose with his fingertip and sauntered out the door.*

*Elke followed behind Aidan. "Thank you so much, Fräulein Schiller. It was a wonderful party."*

*Tante Frieda smiled and nodded to her. Elke stepped close to me and cupped my face in her hands. I also smiled but held my breath as she kissed me on the cheek, too. "Aidan is right, Katia. You are very lovely."*

*My aunt patted my back. "Good-bye, Elke. We hope to see you again soon."*

*"Good-bye." She turned her head. "Thank you, Frau Mahler. Bye, Friedrich!"*

*I released my breath when the door closed behind Elke.*

*Tante Frieda patted me. "You should say 'thank you' at such a compliment."*

*"I am sorry. Elke is very nice, but her smell upsets my stomach."*

*"Yes, it is unfortunate, I know. But still, we must not forget our manners."*

*"Yes, Tante Frieda."*

*Friedrich was quiet the rest of that evening. Just before dark, he left the house. Tante Frieda called after him as he closed the door, but he did not answer. Mama and she sat at the table, drank tea, and spoke softly. I laid on the couch and finished Heinrich Hoffmann's* Struwwelpeter *children's tales yet again. Papa gave me the book when I was five years old, and I had worn the pages thin over the years. I never tired of the colorful pictures and silly stories. Finally, at nine o'clock, I could not stop yawning, so I set aside my book.*

*"Mama, I am going to bed now."*

*"Good night."*

*"Good night, Mama. Tante Frieda."*

*I prepared for bed and peeked one more time into the front room before closing my bedroom door. Papa was still not home. I missed him so, when he was gone all day. I thought there must be a lot to being a minister, to plan services so much. I lay in bed and tried to think of the party, but Papa would not leave my mind. I fell asleep after dark.*

*I awoke sometime later, still in the dark. The air was cold, but my body felt hot. I kicked off my feather comforter, shivering and sweating at the same time. My head ached, and I thought I was going to be sick.*

*"Mama?" I could hardly speak. It hurt to swallow.*

*"Mama!" Tears came to my eyes and I tried to sit up, but my back ached so. I rolled to my side. My stomach cramped, and I turned my head. I emptied what little was in me onto the floor. Although I had nothing else in my stomach, I could not stop. . . .*

❧

"...but you probably do not want to hear more of this, Fräulein McAllister." She had opened her eyes and was studying me, her head slightly cocked.

I broke my stare at her, but not easily. The sentence I had begun on the pad remained unfinished.

"No—I mean, yes, please. If you don't mind telling me."

"My illness did not leave me for days." Her finger slowed its stroke on my wrist. "Some of it never left me."

"I don't understand."

She shrugged and dropped her gaze to her gnarled ankles. "In three years, Doktor Saulk would discover a medicine, but it was too late for me."

I gasped. "Polio? You contracted polio? Fräulein Mahler—"

"I will never know for certain how. The disease is carried through poor cleanliness—I think in English you say hygiene."

"But polio is very contagious. Did anyone else at the party become infected?"

"Aidan fell ill the next day, I remember, but he recovered quickly."

"How? I didn't think polio could be cured."

"There is no cure, only Doktor Saulk's—how do you say, *Impfung*?"

"Probably immunization, if you're talking about Jonas Saulk's work."

She nodded. "Ja, immunization. But the disease does not affect everyone in the same way. Only a small number have *paralytische* polio."

"I thought all polio caused paralysis."

"Nee. Most people infected never show any signs of the disease. Others only seem to have *die Grippe*, like Aidan."

"Influenza. The flu."

"Ja, the flu. If the polio becomes paralytische, the back, the arms, or the legs cannot move. Sometimes it takes the whole *Nervensystem*, and the lungs cannot work. Then there is death. I have been blessed with the use of my arms. Only my legs and sometimes my back fail me."

"*Blessed*?" I sputtered. "How can you even use that word? I think it would be terrible."

"Of course, blessed. And, nee, terrible would be death, which many suffered. God spared my life, and I am thankful."

"I don't know that I could handle paralysis at all, let alone find something to be thankful for—" I blanched as I realized what I had just said in front of my infirm hostess.

Her mouth twitched into a slight smile. "Perhaps the blessing is still to come in my story, nee?"

# *Chapter 7*

*F*ourth *ring. C'mon, guys, somebody pick up.*
    "Hi, Mom. It's Maddy. . . . Yeah, I know it's been over a week. Sorry, I've been really busy. How's Grandma McAllister doing? . . . Good. The interview is going well. Yesterday we took a break and went to a nearby public park, the Volkspark Wuhlheide. It's absolutely beautiful. They've laid walking paths through the trees and even built a miniature train that tours the park. Everything has greened up so nicely since winter. Oskar drives us there and walks behind us while I push Fräulein Mahler's wheelchair. She's a better interviewer than I am, I think. She asks me one question, and before I realize it, I'm spilling everything about family, school, what I like and don't like."
    *I wonder how she does that.*
    "Speaking of not liking things, Mom, I got a letter from Brendon yesterday. Did you talk to him? . . . Then how did he get this address? . . . That's what I thought. Look, I know you like him, but if Brendon can't find time to write me just once in over two months, there can't be much there. . . . Sorry, but schoolwork is a bad excuse. I know what his course load is, and it's pretty light this term. Finals should be a breeze for him."
    *Mom, you're not listening.*
    "Please just let it alone. Things are fine without him. . . . I don't know if I'll answer his letter or not. I haven't read it yet. Look, I have to go. It's getting late, and I'd like to be home before dark. . . . Yes, we start again right after breakfast tomorrow. Fräulein Mahler wants to fill in some thoughts she left out yesterday. We're in the mid-fifties, somewhere around. . ."

⁂

    ". . .1956, when Andropov's tanks appeared on the streets of Budapest. Life became more difficult as the Soviets tightened their grip on the nations of the Warschauer Pakt."
    "Andropov? Wasn't Nikita Khrushchev the Soviet premier in 1956?"
    "Ja, Yuri Andropov was the Soviet ambassador to Hungary when those who resisted Communist rule began their demonstrations. He convinced Khrushchev to invade, even while he promised the Hungarian government that the Soviet Union would take no action against the dissidents. Later, he left Hungary to lead Soviet State Security, the KGB. From there, he directed the invasion of Prague twelve years later. He was—how do you say, *rücksichstlos?*"
    "Ruthless."
    "Ja, danke. Ruthless. He was determined to crush dissent."
    "How did that affect you here in Berlin?"
    "Thousands of Hungarians became homeless, refugees to other lands. Some settled in East Berlin, like the Szabó family, who came to live across the street from us. They brought news of terrible things in Hungary. Execution and torture. They also brought other news. . . ."

⁂

*Mama rushed into the house. "Helmut! Did you hear?"*
    *Papa sat by the dining table scraping a large piece of oak with his knife, while Friedrich and I played a hand of two-player* Schafkopf *on the floor. Papa looked up as Mama stopped by the table, out of breath.*
    *"What is the matter?"*
    *"I tell you what is the matter, Helmut." Her face broke into a wide smile. "The Communists have released Cardinal Mindszenty from prison."*

*Papa set his knife on the table. "Released? How do you know this?"*

*"Sófi Szabó told me. They are the new family in the Richters' old house."*

*"Yes, I have met Miklós Szabó already. Where did they hear such a thing?"*

*"A cousin has just arrived from Dunakeszi, outside Budapest." She fanned her face with her hand.*

*"Sit, Anna. Take a moment to breathe, then tell me what you know." He set the wood aside and helped her into a chair.*

*I pushed myself up and leaned against the couch.*

*Friedrich tapped my arm. "Katia, it is your turn."*

*"Please, Friedrich. I want to hear."*

*He sighed and tossed his cards onto the floor.*

*Mama caught her breath. "They released him last week, on Tuesday. By Friday he was already with the demonstrators. On Saturday, he denounced the Communists on the radio."*

*Papa frowned. "He must be careful. They need little excuse to imprison him again."*

*"Papa, who is this man?" I leaned my crutches against the couch and hoisted myself onto a cushion.*

*"An old friend, Katia. Just an old friend."*

*"Why was he in prison?"*

*Mama smiled. "József Mindszenty is a Roman Catholic cardinal who was imprisoned for treason seven years ago by the Communist regime in Budapest. He and your father—"*

*"Anna, please." Papa touched her hand. "We were once friends. That is all."*

*Friedrich propped his head in his hand and looked at Papa. "He is Catholic and spoke out against the Communists? I thought good Christians did not do that."*

*Mama's smile faded. "Friedrich, that is enough."*

*"No, I want to know." He sat up. "Is it fear of prison that keeps us from speaking out?"*

*"Friedrich!"*

*"Anna, it is all right." Papa turned and met my brother's look. "Son, not everyone called into battle carries the same weapon. Some lead, some dig the trenches, others tend the wounded."*

*"And still others hide in the rear echelon."*

*"Friedrich!"*

*"Anna, let the boy speak—"*

*"No, I will not let the boy speak until he learns how to address his father! Friedrich, you do not know as much as you think you know. You will respect your father!"*

*Friedrich nodded. "Very well." He stood and crossed to the front door. "Fight however you wish. But as for me, I stand with the Cardinal."*

*I flinched as the door slammed shut.*

*"Papa?" My voice quavered.*

*Papa rose and limped across the room to my side. He eased himself onto the sofa and took my hand. "Pay this no mind, Katia. Your brother is strong-willed and carries as his cross the zeal of youth. He is a good boy—no, he is a good man. He will learn how to properly carry this cross soon enough. Until he does, it will be painful for him. And sometimes it will be painful for those around him."*

*"I am afraid."*

*He smiled at me. "There is no need to be afraid. We are a family. That is what is important."*

*I leaned my head against his chest. "I love you, Papa."*

*"And I love you, Katia."*

*Papa patted my head then stood and returned to his chair. He picked up his knife and began once again to carve on the wood.*

# Chapter 8

*April 12*

*Dear Mom and Dad,*
*    This will be another short letter. I have a lot on my mind. Mostly just information overload.*
*    I've read about the Iron Curtain in history books, but the accounts all seemed so sterile next to the stories of someone who actually lived through it. It makes me reevaluate my approach to journalism. We're taught how important verifiable fact is—and it is, of course—but I wonder about the value of anecdotal evidence, too. There is always so much more to the story. Objectivity is the goal, and anecdotes are rarely objective, but I think they add important color to black-and-white facts that carry no attraction, give you no reason to care.*
*    I mean, I know East Berlin's population was over a million people, but my mind stumbles over the "million" and stops short of the "people." Does that make sense? Can you truly lose sight of the trees for the forest?*
*    Enough for now. Again, sorry this is so short—and not very cheery, now that I look back over it. We get another early start tomorrow. Fräulein Mahler ended Saturday's session with kind of a cryptic comment, something about. . .*

❦

". . .the year that changed everything for us."

As usual, she held my hand, but, with these words, she reached across her lap and covered it with her other hand, too. Her fingertip trembled on my wrist. I double-checked the RECORD light on the Sony and laid aside my pencil as she continued.

"February was a very cold month in 1960. Coal was scarce for us, and the chill hurt my legs. I pulled the comforter from my bed to the couch to stay warm. There were other health problems, but what I remember was the cold."

She shifted in her chair, as though the memory brought the pain back with it.

"Friedrich spent less time at home and often came in late. From my bed I could hear Mama question him. His voice was too low for me to hear. Their conversations were never long. I would hear the door to his room close, then Mama's. There were more nights Papa did not return home before I fell asleep."

I frowned. "Where was your father so late at night?"

She patted my wrist but ignored my question. "In the middle of the month, Oma Marta died."

"Grandmother Marta? I don't remember seeing any mention of her in the family records so far—no photographs or anything."

"Ja, Marta Schiller. She and Opa Georg lived in Potsdam. Opa laid cobblestones for the streets, and Oma made—how do you say, *die Stickerei?*"

"Oh, I know that word. Let me think. . . ."

"It is many colors of thread. She would sew cloth—"

"Embroidery! That's it. I knew it; I just couldn't remember."

"Ja. She made the embroidery on Mama's dress for her wedding. It was so beautiful." She cracked open her eyelids and glanced at a cabinet near the dining nook. "I have some things she made here. . .somewhere."

31

"May I ask how she died?"

Fräulein Mahler closed her eyes again. "Oma was not well for many years, never the same after we lost Tante Maria. One night she fell asleep and did not awake in the morning."

"Tante Maria? I didn't know you had another aunt." I grabbed my pencil and jotted down the new names.

"Ja, she was two years younger than Mama. I did not know her. She was taken before I was born."

"Taken?"

"Tante Maria married Izaak Szpilmann, from Szczecin, Poland. In Germany we called it Stettin. Opa was in the Party and became upset that she married a Jew."

I glanced up. "Your grandfather was a Nazi? That surprises me."

"Do not judge too quickly, Fräulein McAllister. It was necessary for him to join the Party to keep his job in the *Verein*—what you call the union. He was wounded at Verdun in the Great War and could do little with his hands without much pain. It was difficult for him to lay the cobblestones, but he worked hard and became a master. To lose his job was for his family to starve. He feared Tante Maria's marriage could threaten his job, his means to provide for Oma."

I thinned my lips but kept my sentiments to myself.

"Opa—how do you say?—ach, I do not know if we have a word for it. *Er wollte mit ihnen nichts zu tun haben.*"

"He wanted nothing to do with—oh, he disowned them. He disowned Maria and Izaak?"

"Ja. Oma could say nothing to change his mind." Her voice shuddered and dropped to a whisper. "He was a good man, but sometimes he would not listen."

I looked down at my pad to hide my skepticism. She took a deep breath, and the evenness returned to her tone.

"To tell you of Tante Maria, I must go back to 1939. The Gestapo came for them in the winter—"

I jerked my head up. "The Gestapo?"

She nodded. "Mama said Izaak tried to send Maria away, to save her, but she refused to leave him. She did not understand what they would do. There were rumors of camps, but she did not know what they were. Izaak and Maria had twin daughters—Lilli-Anna and Kammbrie—only three months old then. The Gestapo left them behind."

I hesitated to voice the question. "What. . .what happened to them?"

"There was a church, the Bekennende Kirche, led by a man called Bonhoeffer."

"Yes, Dietrich Bonhoeffer. I wrote a report on him once. He was a Lutheran clergyman, an outspoken critic of Hitler. He founded the Confessing Church and a seminary there in Stettin, if I recall correctly. The Nazis arrested Bonhoeffer then executed him at the Flossenbürg camp in 1945, just before the war ended."

"Ja, Dietrich Bonhoeffer. A great man. A family in his church, the Dudeks, found Lilli-Anna and Kammbrie the next day and took them into their home."

"How did you find this out?"

"They had no children of their own, so Herr Dudek returned to my aunt's house for the babies' clothes and food, anything he could find for them. He found a letter Tante Maria wrote to my mother but did not have the chance to post. Our address was on the envelope. He wrote to Mama about the arrest. He said he would bring my cousins to us in Berlin."

"Did he do that?"

"Nee. The war did not allow it. Adolf Hitler had invaded Poland two months earlier, and Stettin is near the German border. We did not receive the letter until February. He wrote that he and his wife were trying to escape to Österreich, to Salzburg, where they had relatives. He would try to get the twins to Berlin from there. But he never came."

I paused writing, wanting to ask a question, but she went on.

"After the war, Mama traveled to Austria to look for them. One woman remembered Frau Dudek—that she seemed very protective and private about the children. She thought perhaps they moved on to Frankreich. But she was not sure."

"Did your mother go to France to look for them?"

"Nee, she did not know where to begin looking, and Papa needed her back in Berlin."

I jotted down the names and places. Perhaps there would be some follow-up work.

"Do you know what happened to Uncle Izaak and Aunt Maria?"

"The Gestapo broke them apart. We know, because she wrote to us after the war. Mama cried, she was so happy to know her sister survived."

I frowned. "Broke them apart?"

"Ja, at first they went to the Ravensbrück camp then to Auschwitz. At Auschwitz they were separated and never saw each other again. Then in January 1945, the Nazis forced Tante Maria and thousands of others to march west to the camp at Bergen-Belsen. She became sick there. *Der Typhus.* You know this word?"

"Yes, it's the same in English. Bergen-Belsen was decimated by typhus. Thousands upon thousands died there, including Anne Frank and her sister."

"Many, ja. Then in April, the English and Canadians freed the camp, and Maria went into the hospital. There she met a medical soldier from Canada. When she recovered, he asked her for marriage. At first, she refused, although she felt love for him, too. She could not marry when she did not know about Izaak. But when Auschwitz fell to the Red Army, survivors began to arrive in the West. Many met up with those the Nazis forced to march to Bergen-Belsen. On a small chance, she met a man who was looking for his wife. The man knew Izaak. He had fallen ill a year earlier. Too weak to work, he went to the gas chamber." She quieted. "The man said he was very sorry."

I dropped my pencil on the pad and rubbed my temple. I couldn't comprehend tens of thousands of people dropping around me from sickness, starvation, and execution. I'd seen photos of the camps, bulldozers scraping piles of emaciated bodies barely recognizable as human into open pits. Over six million Jews, their sympathizers, and political prisoners died in the camps. Thousands of others were left without their families, their health, their hope.

But, as horrific as it was, the Holocaust didn't fit into my reality. The numbers were just too big, like a trillion-dollar trade deficit that should surely concern me but that had no discernible impact on the five-dollar bill in my purse. Of course I knew in my mind each number was a real person: someone's daughter, someone's husband, a baby once held in someone's arms. But now I knew in my heart one of their names. She was Maria Schiller, daughter, sister, and aunt. Maria Szpilmann, wife and mother. Her niece, through whose veins her shared blood flowed, sat beside me. The surge of realization clogged my throat and flooded my eyes.

"Fräulein McAllister?"

"I'm sorry," I whispered.

She patted my hand. "Perhaps we stop now for tea, ja?"

⬥

I resumed my seat on the couch and picked up my pencil. She laid aside her book.

"The walk outside was good for you, nee?"

I nodded while I fidgeted with the Sony. "Yes, thank you. I'm sorry we lost the time from the interview, but it helped me clear my mind." I pressed the RECORD button and set the device on the cushion beside me. "Now, where did we leave off?"

She cocked her head but said nothing.

My eyes widened. "Oh!"

I laid my hand on the arm of her wheelchair. She covered it with hers, and the smile returned to her lips as she leaned her head back and closed her eyes.

"Tante Maria did recover. Strength returned to her mind and her will, but not so much to her body."

I smiled. "I know someone just like that. Her spirit defies her body—wait, you said recovered. Is she still alive?"

Her brow creased. "I do not know. She married the soldier and went with him when he returned home. There was no chance to see her before they left. She wrote from the hospital ship that she would try to return to Germany and visit, but she never came back." She tipped her head forward and glanced over at the table. "Her letters are here. . .somewhere."

"Do you know why she never returned?"

"Perhaps she was afraid to see Opa again, or she was not strong enough. I know nothing of her now."

I wrestled with a delicate question for a moment then decided to ask. "And her children, Lilli-Anna and Kammbrie? Were they. . .did you ever hear anything more about them?"

"Nee. Mama wrote to the special European commission for children who were lost during the war, but there were many thousands of inquiries. She received no reply from them. I know in my heart that Tante Maria wrote, too."

"It seems she'd have done everything possible to find her children."

"I am certain she did, but she was ill and now across the ocean. I know she prayed they survived, but there were too many years, too many miles. Many families broke apart, especially in the camps. I am sure she prays the Dudeks loved and cared for her girls, but perhaps we will never know. It is difficult, but it was the war."

I set my jaw and put two exclamation points beside the twins' names. *Follow up.*

"Before I asked about Tante Maria, you mentioned 1960 was a pivotal year for you."

"Pivotal?"

"I'm sorry. It means very important. You said everything changed for you that year."

"Ja." Her voice quieted. "In 1960, Friedrich and I discovered a family secret. But the cost of the secret was great."

# Chapter 9

*Postscript: I know I've already signed off in this letter, but I tore it back open to add a few things. I'll post it tomorrow.*

*This project is becoming more difficult. I accepted it for the school credit, and when I first met Fräulein Mahler, I figured it would be easy to stay detached. I'm not so sure now. I don't know why. Maybe it's because she holds my hand while she talks—did I tell you that?*

*She told me about her father this afternoon. Dad, I couldn't get your face out of my mind. I'm not sure I can handle too many more days like today. . . .*

✣

"...and it was a day like we should never have again." Her hand trembled.

"Fräulein Mahler, are you okay? We can stop—"

She silenced me with a lifted finger. "Nee, I must tell you. Tomorrow there may not be the strength."

✣

"Mama? I hear something at the door." I reached for my crutches. "Mama?"

She came into the front room from the kitchen, wiping her hands on a towel. "Stay there. I will see to it."

When she opened the door, my brother rolled through the doorway against her legs and sprawled onto the floor.

"Friedrich! What is—"

I screamed.

"Katia! Be still!" Mama bent over my brother. She peered outside briefly before pulling him in and closing the door.

I began to cry. "He is dead!"

"He is not dead. Calm yourself." Mama stretched Friedrich out and probed his head with her fingertips. "There is a bump on his head and some scrapes." She rose and hurried into the kitchen.

I was not able to stop staring at my brother's pale face.

Mama returned with a wet cloth and began to dab his forehead. "Friedrich, Friedrich. In heaven's name, what have you done?"

After a moment, he moaned and his head rolled to the side. She twisted the cloth over his face. "Wake up, Son!"

He sputtered and shook his head. "Mama?"

I could barely hear his voice.

"Yes. Hold still. I need to look at your head."

"I am okay."

"You do not look okay."

He rolled onto his stomach and pushed himself to his hands and knees. Mama helped him sit, but he wobbled and grabbed the couch. I thought he would fall over again.

"Katia, move aside. I want to put him on the sofa."

I slid to the side and wrung my hands as she steadied him onto the seat. Then she went back to the kitchen with the cloth. I threw my arms around Friedrich and squeezed his neck.

"Ach! Katia, please!"

"I am sorry. I was so worried. I thought you were dead."

35

*"I was not so sure myself."*

*Mama returned with a glass of water and the dripping cloth. "With that lump on your head, it is fortunate you are not." She held the glass out to him and pressed the cloth against the back of his head. "Drink."*

*He took a sip then held the cold tumbler against his forehead.*

*Mama lifted the cloth and frowned at a splotch of blood on the white fabric. She inspected the lump. "There is an explanation, yes?"*

*"I do not want to—"*

*"No, you do not have that choice. You have met danger and perhaps have brought it to our house."*

*He sighed then nodded. "I was. . .at a meeting."*

*"What kind of meeting?"*

*He averted his eyes. "A dissidents' meeting."*

*"And?"*

*"The Stasi found us."*

*"The Stasi? Where did you meet? Was no one watching?"*

*"No, we did not think it necessary. We all knew each other—"*

*She shook her head. "You never know who will speak to the Stasi. There is no group that is safe from infiltration. None, no matter who you think you know. You must never—"*

❧

I broke in. "The Stasi were the East German police, is that right?"

"Nee, the national police were the Volkspolizei, the People's Police. The Stasi, the Ministerium für Staatssicherheit—you would say Ministry for State Security—were the secret police of the Sozialistische Einheitspartei Deutschlands, the Socialist Unity Party of Germany. The Stasi and the Volkspolizei sometimes worked together, but the Stasi was larger and more fearsome."

I scribbled the terms at the top of my pad. I'd heard of the Stasi, of course, and something of the ruling SED but knew little of how they worked. I wanted her to continue, though, so I deferred further questions about the East German authorities until later.

She shifted in her chair and picked up the story again.

❧

*Mama peered into Friedrich's face. "How were you hurt? How did you get away? Who brought you here?"*

*He hung his head. "I do not know."*

*"How can you not know?"*

*"When they broke down the door, somebody smashed the ceiling light. The windows were covered, so the room went dark except for the light coming through the open door. There was shouting and scuffling. Karl and I—"*

*"Who?"*

*"Karl Werner. We met at a café two weeks ago. He was easy to speak to, and we became friends. He was the one who told me about the meeting."*

*"Hmph! He would be my first suspicion. What do you really know of him?"*

*"I know him—"*

*"Ach, Friedrich! You are going to get yourself killed."*

*"Mama—"*

*"What happened then?"*

*"Karl and I crouched by the wall, and when the doorway cleared, I ran toward it. I reached the hallway, and someone hit me from behind. That is all I remember until you woke me up."*

*"Who else was there? Who else that I know?"*

*"I will not—"*

36

*"Yes, you will! You do not understand what you have done. I must know everything."*
*His voice dropped. "Franz Schindler and Willie Brenner."*
*"Franz Schindler? Günter's son?"*
*"Yes."*
*"Oh, my—!"*

❦

"Fräulein Mahler, your hands are cold. Do you need a blanket?"
"Nee, danke. It is painful to remember these things."
"We can leave out the parts that upset you."
"Nee, that is what we cannot leave out."
She squeezed my hand and continued.

❦

*Mama hurried to her bedroom and returned with her coat and hat. "Stay here with Katia. Your head may be hurt more than you think. Drink your water. If you feel sick or dizzy, lie down. I will come back soon."*
*I held my brother's arm. "Where are you going, Mama?"*
*"To find your father."*
*Friedrich stared at the floor. "I am sorry. I did not mean—"*
*"I know, Son. We will talk later."*
*Mama reached for the handle but jumped back when someone knocked. She looked over at us then straightened and opened the door.*
*A man wearing the green uniform of the Volkspolizei with Leutnant insignia on his epaulets stepped into the house.*
*Friedrich jumped to his feet then grabbed his head and fell back onto the couch.*
*I sat still, not able to speak.*
*The man turned and closed the door behind him. "Good evening, Anna."*
*Mama sounded relieved. "Horst, it is you. Praise God!"*
*Friedrich narrowed his eyes. "Mama?"*
*"This is Leutnant Klein. He is a friend."*
*"A friend? But he is—"*
*The policeman turned to me and smiled. "Hello, Katia." Then he glanced at my brother, and his face grew serious. "Friedrich, I am sorry I had to hit you."*

❦

I set down my notepad and covered her trembling fingers with my right hand. "Fräulein Mahler, I'm worried about you. Your hands are freezing."
She opened her eyes but didn't seem to focus on me right away. Her breath came in short gasps. "I am fine, danke."
"Let me at least get you some more tea."
"In a moment. I must finish now what I have started."
She took a deep breath.

❦

*Leutnant Klein turned back to Mama. "Anna, we must talk."*
*She nodded. "Please, sit."*
*"Thank you. It is a difficult day."*
*Mama led Leutnant Klein to a chair at the dining table. He unbuttoned his overcoat and laid his hat on the table.*
*"I can make tea—"*

*"No, thank you. There is little time."* He sat down and glanced over at Friedrich and me. Then he looked back at Mama.

*"It is all right. They can hear what you have to say."*

Friedrich scowled. *"What do you mean, you hit me?"*

Leutnant Klein focused his gaze on my brother. *"It was the only way for you to escape the Stasi. You were fortunate I was there."*

*"Fortunate? I do not think—"*

*"Friedrich, you will remain quiet, and you will listen."* Mama stood with her hands on her hips.

He glared at the policeman but said nothing more.

Leutnant Klein leaned forward and rested his elbows on his knees. *"As your mama knows, I am a liaison officer between the Volkspolizei and the Stasi. Although it is the Stasi who handle cases of sedition like dissidents' meetings, I make sure to hear when there is going to be an operation. This afternoon we received a call that they were going to raid such a meeting. They had a tip from an informant when and where it was to take place. There were too few of their men available, so they called us for help. I went along, just in case."*

*"Just in case?"* Friedrich asked.

Mama warned him with a look.

*"Yes, in case you were involved."*

*"How do you know me?"*

Mama spoke up. *"Leutnant Klein is a member of our church, although he does not come to open services. His position with the Volkspolizei has been. . .very valuable, and it was important that he not be associated with us."*

He shook his head. *"Very valuable?"*

*"Hush and listen."*

Leutnant Klein cleared his throat. *"When we arrived at the apartment, two of us positioned ourselves in the hallway. When the Stasi broke down the door, the lights went out, and it was too dark for me to see who was there. Their own men went in to bring out prisoners. We were to help take them to the van. When the struggle began, I edged closer to the door. I prayed you were not there—or, if you were, that you would not be killed."* His voice lowered. *"They beat to death two of your friends who resisted."*

Friedrich paled. *"Who. . ."*

*"Willie Brenner and a girl, Helga Altmann."*

My brother covered his face with his hands.

Leutnant Klein continued. *"When you appeared at the doorway, my partner reached to grab you. I stepped in front of him and hit you on the head with my club. I told him I would carry you to the van and that he should watch for others who tried to escape. It was the only way to take charge of you and not betray that I knew who you were. I dragged you down the hallway, but when we got outside, I took you to the Volga I drove from the police station. I prayed that, in the confusion, my comrade would not remember you."*

*"For a policeman, you pray a lot."*

*"For the son of a good pastor, you seem to pray very little."*

Friedrich snorted, but the policeman raised a hand when Mama stepped forward. Her face was red.

Leutnant Klein leaned back in his chair. *"My comrade was injured in a scuffle, and he did forget you, thank God. He rode back to headquarters in the van and left me to take the car alone. Fortunately, it was nearly dark, so I brought you here and propped you up against the door. It was necessary I return quickly before I was missed. It was there I learned of Willie and Helga. But I learned something much more important. It is what brings me back here."*

He looked at Mama. *"While I was checking on the prisoners, the senior Stasi officer pulled a boy aside. He spoke with him for a moment then pointed down the hall to the rear door. The boy left. It was Franz."*

Mama closed her eyes. *"Günter's son?"*

"Yes."

"I feared that. I was leaving to find Helmut when you knocked on the door."

"I thought so when I saw you had your coat on. I already sent word to Helmut. I just hope it is not too late."

Friedrich frowned. "What do you mean too late?"

Leutnant Klein turned toward us again. "Your father—"

We all jumped at a loud bang on the door. Mama hurried to open it, and a man I recognized as one of Papa's deacons stumbled in. He was out of breath.

Mama's face went white. "Waldemar?"

The man wrung his hat in his hands. "Anna, I am so sorry. They have taken Helmut!"

# Chapter 10

*. . .and then I insisted we take a break. Her hands shook, and she sounded short of breath. I brought her some tea and shortbread, thinking a little sugar might help. It seemed to do some good. I sat beside her and rubbed her hands until they warmed up.*

*Dad, I think I was shaking almost as badly as she was. I can't imagine what it would be like to be taken away like that. Not knowing where or for how long would be bad enough. But not knowing why. . .*

⤝❦⤞

I held Fräulein Mahler's hands in mine. "I don't understand. Why would they take your father? Because of Friedrich's involvement with the dissidents?"

"Nee. My brother and I discovered something that day that never before entered our minds." Her eyes went distant for a moment, then they closed again as she resumed her narrative.

*"Papa? Why have they taken Papa?" I cried.*

*Friedrich whispered, "It was because of me."*

*The deacon crossed the room and grasped Leutnant Klein's hand. Then he turned back to Mama. "Horst and I must speak. Please stay with your family, Anna. Nothing can be done right now."*

*The men stepped into the kitchen. I could hear their hushed voices but could not make out their words.*

*Mama sat on a chair next to the couch. Her face was pale, but her voice remained steady. "No, Friedrich. It was not because of you."*

*"Then why?"*

*She gazed at both of us, as though not sure what to say. "What I tell you now you must not repeat to anyone. Do you understand?"*

*We nodded.*

*"Papa helps people who hide from the Stasi—those who try to escape to the West. I do not know everything. He kept much to himself, so that if he was taken and I was questioned, I could truly deny knowledge of names and places."*

*Friedrich slumped against the back of the sofa. "But. . .how long. . ."*

*"Always. I do not know a time when Papa did not fight those who stand against Christ and His Church. Papa's ways are peaceful, quiet, and have never interfered with his ministry. Many have been helped by him and those in our church who labor with him."*

*"What other people?" It was all so confusing to me.*

*"I would not say even if I could. I know only of Leutnant Klein and Waldemar Schmidt because they chose to reveal themselves to me. They have watched our family and protected us from discovery."*

*Friedrich jerked his head. "Watched us? Then that is why the policeman—"*

*"Yes, Leutnant Klein has watched to ensure you do not get into trouble, and if you do, that you do not to bring the authorities to us, to your father. His vigilance has saved us more than once." Her voice caught. "Today, though, our time has run out."*

*"Then it was because of me."*

*"No, when I heard you say Franz Schindler was with you, I began to suspect. Franz betrayed you to the Stasi, and I am sure his father betrayed Papa."*

*"But Herr Schindler is a deacon. He would not—"*

*Mama's look cut off Friedrich's words. "Son, you never know who will talk to the Stasi. Some break under interrogation, some are blackmailed, others hope to gain by informing. I do not know Günter's reasons, and now they do not matter."*

*My brother shuddered. "They will force Papa to tell more."*

*Mama shook her head. "He will say nothing."*

*"But Mama, they do terrible things to make prisoners talk."*

*"Yes, but this is not the first time for your father under torture."*

⌒❧⌒

"What?" I stared at Fräulein Mahler. "Not the first time?"

She opened her eyes, now glassy with tears. "There was so much we would learn of Papa that day."

⌒❧⌒

*Friedrich shook his head. "I do not understand."*

*Mama reached out and touched my brother's cheek. "You have never asked your father why he limps?"*

*"I did ask once. I do not remember his answer."*

*Her smile was sad. "You know your father so little, Son. Do you remember going to Hamburg on the train with Tante Frieda when you were five years old?"*

*"Yes, but—"*

*"Papa sent you away to protect you. He and I hid Jews from the Nazis before and during the war. They would come to our church, referred by others we trusted. We would begin them on a journey out of Germany. Your father and others built a network of homes to shelter them. He would determine which route would be the best for each man, woman, or family. Often he would travel with them as far as he could, to ensure their safety, but he would always be home in time for the next service. Papa knew prayer was as important to their well-being as food and shelter."*

*"But why did you send me away?"*

*"Papa received word that the Gestapo was watching our house. He knew they would come soon. He tried to convince me to go, too, but I refused. I agreed to hide if they came, to continue the work, but I would not leave him alone in Berlin. One night they did come. They took him to their headquarters on Prinz-Albrecht-Straße and interrogated him for two weeks. They released him because he would tell them nothing, they had no proof of subversion, and there was still some sensitivity to the clergy in the regime. He came home bruised, with cracked ribs and his leg broken in two places."*

*I put my hands over my ears, but Mama's words still came through, soft and low. "No, he will tell the Stasi nothing."*

*"Mama?" Friedrich had tears in his eyes. "Why did he never tell me? I could have helped. He knows I want to fight the Communists."*

*"He would have, Son, but he delayed for two reasons. First, he needed to see maturity in you. You are too hotheaded, and that leads to being careless—as it did today. He owed protection to many others, as well as our family."*

*Friedrich flinched but said nothing.*

*I uncovered my ears as Mama continued. "Second, he wanted you to understand why he did what he did. It is not for pride, not for ourselves. It is to follow the example of Christ, to help those who are in need, those unjustly accused and persecuted. We pray on our knees and act on our feet. A balance between the knees and the feet is most important. You had not yet shown any desire to achieve that balance."*

*Friedrich hung his head.*

*I touched Mama's arm. "Mama?"*

*"Yes?"*

*"When will Papa come home?"*
*She did not answer.*

Fräulein Mahler fell silent. I looked at my watch. Four forty-five. Enough for today.

I whispered, "Why don't you let me prepare dinner this evening?"

She gave a gentle sigh, and her breath dropped into a steady rhythm. I slipped my hand from beneath hers and thumbed the STOP button on the Sony.

# Chapter 11

*I* *hope somebody's there. I forgot it's Saturday, and—*

"Hey, Carson! What are you doing home? Don't you have a soccer game? . . . You quit? Why? . . . Well, I know Coach Hawthorn is a little tough to get along with sometimes, but. . . C'mon, Squirt, you love soccer. There's gotta be another reason. . . . Who? You're kidding! Moira O'Brien? Aha! Now it's becoming clear. I told you she had her eye on you! . . . Yeah, I did, don't you give me that!"

*You little schemer, you!*

"Hey, is Mom or Dad home? . . . Grandma McAllister's in the hospital again? Why? . . . Brill's disease? I've never heard of it, either. Okay, I can call later. . . . Yeah, it was good to talk to you. I hope everything goes well with Moira, lover boy. . . . Hey! Don't you hang up on me, you little—"

⟨≈⟩

". . .and so we hung it above the fireplace."

I inspected the rough-hewn cross mounted over the mantle with renewed interest. "So, that's where it came from. I noticed it the day I arrived. It's beautiful. Did your father carve anything else?"

"Nee, not that I know. It took two years, perhaps more. He had little time to work on it."

I was careful how I referred to Fräulein Mahler's father from this point on. The story of his arrest seemed to take a lot out of her. I know it took a lot out of me.

This morning, Oskar drove us to the park for another outing. The air was warm, and sunbeams filtered through the branches of the oak trees like undulating klieg lights illuminating a thousand miniature dramas along the pathway. We needed only to stop and trace one beam to see a column of ants scurrying about in their daily scramble for survival, another to spot a snail racing across the pressed dirt for the safety of the thick grass.

"Do you see the worm, Fräulein McAllister?"

I nodded. "A shame."

The shriveled remains of an earthworm caught in the open air too long without moisture lay a few centimeters from the edge of the path. Behind it, a trail of slime faded over the pebbles.

"What is the saying, 'So near, and yet so far'?"

I smiled. So sharp a mind trapped in so frail a body. "Yes. If he could have persevered a little longer, he would've made it."

"I wish very much to complete our interview. Do you think we will make it?"

"Of course we will."

She dipped her head but did not respond.

The question unnerved me, so I changed the subject. "Listen to the birds. Isn't it lovely today?"

Her voice perked. "Ja, the birds have their stories, too."

"Really? How so?"

She leaned her head back and closed her eyes. I nudged the wheelchair ahead.

⟨≈⟩

*"See what, Tante Frieda?" I hobbled into the kitchen on my crutches.*

*"Look. On the ledge." She nodded toward the window.*

*"Oh, he's beautiful!"*

*"Hush!" she whispered. "You will scare him away."*

*"What kind is he?"*

*"A Blaumeise. See his color?"*

*"I have not seen such a beautiful bird before."*

I gazed at the white and gray blue tit. His small head, capped with a light blue swath, swiveled to and fro on a soft yellow breast, ever vigilant for signs of danger. We remained still so he wouldn't notice us through the window. The petite bird hopped along the ledge and began to peck at a rose stem tied to the trellis on the back of our house.

Tante Frieda's face wore a big smile, something not usual for her. She so loved her birds. *"They are good for the garden. They clean the roses of insects, although sometimes their beaks injure the flowers."*

At that moment, Friedrich sauntered into the kitchen with his arms stretched above his head and a big yawn on his face. *"Where is Mama?"*

The startled bird flitted from the ledge.

Tante Frieda frowned. *"Your mama is where she always is this past five months. She has gone to Prenzlauer Berg to ask the Volkspolizei about your father."*

Friedrich sliced a thick piece of Vollkornbrot.

Tante Frieda grumbled, *"You slept late this morning. Breakfast is past."*

*"It was a late night,"* he mumbled around a mouthful of the whole-grain bread. *"Aidan is now twenty-five. We celebrated."*

*"I did not know he was home from the university."* I tried to hide the excitement from my voice.

Aidan was special to me. He never changed his teasing or his compliments, even with my illness and my crutches. He had not yet married. I thought perhaps he waited for me, as he once said.

*"Yes, he finishes as a mechanical engineer from Technische Universität Dresden this month."*

I was certain Aidan would be a wonderful engineer. He was always so good at fixing things, and he loved to work with his hands.

*"Perhaps he will visit?"* I did not look into Friedrich's face as I asked.

He shrugged. *"He returns to Dresden tomorrow afternoon. He has exams next week and—"*

A sound at the front door cut off Friedrich's words.

*"Mama?"* I turned and tottered out of the kitchen.

Mama had taken off her coat by the door. I could see her eyes were red even across the room.

*"What is wrong?"*

She laid her coat over the arm of the couch and sat. I hobbled to the sofa and dropped onto the cushion beside her. *"Mama?"*

She tried to smile, but her lip quivered. Tante Frieda came in from the kitchen and sat on a chair in the corner. Friedrich stood by the kitchen door.

*"It is Helmut?"* Tante Frieda whispered.

Mama nodded and started to speak then leaned forward and began to cry. I tried to hold her, but I did not know what to say. Tante Frieda left her chair and knelt on the floor by Mama's feet while she sobbed. Her whole body shuddered, and I was afraid. I had never seen Mama cry like this.

Tante Frieda looked at me and shook her head.

A few moments later, Mama straightened. Tante Frieda gave her a handkerchief, and Mama dabbed her eyes. She took a deep breath and held my hand.

*"Leutnant Klein has finally received news of. . .your father."* Her chest heaved with another sob, but she did not let it escape.

*"And?"* Tante Frieda put her hand over Mama's and squeezed it.

*"He has been sent to the East. To the Soviet Union. There are camps they call 'the Gulag,' where they send political prisoners. I do not know which camp."*

*"But he is alive,"* Tante Frieda offered.

*Mama sniffed. "Yes."*

*"We will not give up, then, will we?"*

*Mama shook her head. "No. There is still life, so there is still hope."*

*"And where there is suffering, there is oneness with Christ, no?"*

*Mama's eyes filled again. "Yes, Frieda. I know this in my head, but my heart does not want Helmut to suffer. Is this wrong of me?"*

*"No, Anna. Christ will tend to the suffering. You will tend to the hope."*

*Mama and Tante Frieda held each other for a long time. I stroked Mama's mussed hair and cried with her.*

*The front door clicked shut behind Friedrich.*


I stopped next to a bench and sat down. Oskar stood quietly behind the wheelchair.

"Fräulein Mahler, do you believe Jesus wants us to suffer?" I asked.

"Nee. He Himself did not want to suffer. He prayed in the garden that He would be spared the cup He would drink. But He knew only He could drink of it, so He prayed for strength from the Father. And the Father gave Him strength." She shifted in her chair and grimaced as she straightened her back. "We who follow Christ know, too, that we need not seek suffering. Trouble is always before us, and it will come, as He told those who would listen. We pray for the strength of Christ to endure, and He gives it to us, because He knows what it means to suffer."

I shook my head. "It all seems so harsh."

"But it is a mercy, nee? Tante Frieda said the Blaumeise pecks the harmful insects from the rose, and, though he bruises the flower, it heals and is better than before. Perhaps it is the same with us, ja?"

# Chapter 12

*April 10*

Dear Maddy,

 *Carson told us you called today. Sorry we missed you.*

 *Just a quick note to send along with this money order. Your account was pretty low after the last withdrawal, so I thought I'd help out a little. Hope it's enough.*

 *I know Mom usually does the writing, but she's not home. Grandma McAllister is doing better, but not all of her hospitalization is covered by insurance, so Grandpa went back to Terrebonne to sell some property. Mom is staying with Grandma until he gets back.*

 *We miss you. Can't wait for you to get home, but I understand how important it is, what you're doing. Will write again soon.*

              Love, Dad

❧

"...but it's not important. I don't need a break, if you want to continue."

"Nee, to walk is good. Oskar will soon be here. He loves the walk, too. Perhaps we can interview in the Volkspark."

I smiled, happy for the chance to escape the closeness of the house for another afternoon. I could carry my recorder in the pocket of my Windbreaker but would leave behind the notepad so my hands would be free to push the wheelchair.

Oskar knocked at the door fifteen minutes later, and soon we were all packed into the Audi and headed for the park. Although nearly midday, the sky remained overcast, and the morning chill lingered beneath the oaks bordering the street. Oskar pulled the car into a parking space and cut the engine. Fräulein Mahler tucked her sweater collar around her neck as he lifted her from the car. I steadied the chair, and he eased her onto the worn padded seat.

"I am sure you must tire of toting me around, Oskar."

The ever-waiting crow's-feet claimed his eyes. "It is the highlight of my day, Katia. When else can I sweep such a *liebliches* Fräulein into my arms with no fear of having my face slapped?"

"Oskar Schultmann, *schäm dich!*"

"Shame is a small price to pay for such a privilege." He touched her shoulder and stepped back.

That glorious smile lit up her face as she smoothed a crocheted afghan over her spindly legs. When Oskar turned to close the car door, I'm sure I noticed the corner of his eye glisten.

I unlocked the brake on the wheelchair and smiled at the two old friends with renewed curiosity over their relationship, wondering how they may have met. Surely that story would come in time, too. Fräulein Mahler gestured to the left, and we started down a different path from the one we normally walked, this one more heavily shaded. As usual, Oskar followed a pace behind me.

"What do we start with today?"

She hesitated. "I wish for Oskar to speak."

His voice edged over my shoulder. "Bitte?"

I glanced back at Oskar.

A smile colored Fräulein Mahler's tone. "I have spoken of my life for hours. I would like to listen now."

"I have no story, Katia."

"Of course you do. In all these years you have told me so little of your life before you found me at the cross. I would like to hear of it."

"Nee, there is nothing—" Oskar protested.

"Oh, c'mon," I teased. "You could make something up. We'd never know."

"I do not want—"

"Komm, Oskar. Enough of your protest." Fräulein Mahler half turned her head, her voice still light but taking on an edge.

"You may as well give up," I chided. "She's not going to let you get away."

Silence.

She raised her hand for me to stop. "Oskar?"

When he spoke, his voice was more distant. I turned. He had stopped in the pathway several paces back, where he stood stiffly, his face flushed.

"I have forgotten something. Excuse me for a moment. I will catch up to you." He turned and set a brisk pace back toward the car.

Fräulein Mahler resumed her gaze straight ahead. Her fingertips stroked the smooth wooden armrests, much like they did my wrist during our interview sessions. A minute later, she waggled her finger, the signal to move on.

Neither of our voices disrupted the muffled crunch of twigs and gravel under wheel.

# Chapter 13

*April 24*

*Dear Mom and Dad,*

*I think we've reached a milestone in our interview. The number of photos and documents so far has been small. Judging by the next stack on the floor by the table, though, that's about to change. There are letters, newspaper clippings, and some official-looking correspondence. The photos appear to be mostly of shots around the city: some construction, some crowd scenes, a few with a smaller group of people I didn't recognize. Hopefully, she'll be able to put some context to them.*

*Our last walk in the park was a week ago. Oskar has been pretty scarce since then. I think he's only been by two times to drop off groceries and medicine. He doesn't stay very long, and while he is here, he's quieter than usual—which is saying something. I don't know what happened. He hasn't invited any inquiry on the matter. Fräulein Mahler hasn't mentioned it, either. I have no idea. . . .*

⏤⊷∾⊶⏤

". . .do you have any idea? It doesn't seem to make much sense in my notes."

Breakfast was over, and I was flipping through my notepad from the previous day's session. Fräulein Mahler dabbed her lips with her napkin. "Of course I have an idea, Fräulein McAllister. It is my story, nee?"

I smiled, still scanning my notepad, and shook my head. Over the past couple of weeks, I'd grown accustomed to her candor. The matter-of-factness that irked me at first I now considered humorous—even endearing. Such knifelike honesty from Fräulein Mahler was as natural as the drum-tight bun perched on her head. That comment coming from anyone else? Well, I would've slapped them silly.

She folded her napkin over her plate and wheeled back from the table. When she reached her corner, she turned and beckoned to me. I looked at the table, still neatly cluttered with breakfast dishes—Fräulein Mahler being the only person I ever met who could achieve neat clutter. She gestured again, this time with a touch of impatience.

"The dishes will keep."

I rose from my chair with my supplies and left my crumb-strewn plate on the table. Except for the hand-holding, this was the first display of informality I had glimpsed since moving into her house. Before this time, I had invited any opportunity to be casual, but now something as benign as a couple of unattended breakfast dishes left me strangely ill at ease.

A minute later, I was again established on the divan, my left hand listless in her slender fingers, my right hand doing the work. The recording indicator on the Sony showed steady.

"As to your question, you will recall that my brother was now twenty-five years old and had no career. Nor was he in school. He worked at small jobs and brought some money into the household but never for long. That was soon to change."

*"What happened this time?" Mama folded her hands on the dining table, a cup of herbal tea and a half-finished letter in front of her.*

*A crumpled wad of Deutschmarks lay on the table. Friedrich fidgeted next to a chair with his hands in his pockets. I sat on the couch, my own tea now cooled, and paged through a book that promised to teach me to crochet.*

*"Ach, it is unfair, Mama," he fumed. "Herr Wilheit expects too much for the pay."*

*"The government sets the pay, not Herr Wilheit. Did you not know both what he expects and what the pay would be from the beginning?"*

*"Yes, but the railcars are now fuller with lumber than when we began. There is more work, more difficulty."*

*"You receive a set pay for the time you work, not by the railcar load, do you not?"*

*"Yes, but. . .you know what I mean!" Friedrich's face went red.*

*"No. I am trying, but I do not understand what you mean."*

*He raised his hands. "Never mind! No one understands, not even you!" My brother turned and stalked over to the couch. He crossed his arms and dropped onto the cushion beside me.*

*"Friedrich! Your elbow—"*

*My teacup, once balanced on the arm of the divan, crashed onto the floor. I covered my ears at the words my brother found to use. Many of them were unfamiliar to me.*

*"Friedrich! That is enough." Mama rose from her chair and fetched a broom propped in the corner of the dining nook. She began to sweep the pieces together. I tried to help, but it was difficult to reach the floor from the couch.*

*Friedrich sat with his head in his hands.*

*I peered at my brother then reached over and touched his shoulder. "It is okay. Please, do not worry."*

*But he did worry. He leaned with his elbows on his knees and covered his face with his hands. I felt his shoulder shaking. Although I heard no sound, I knew he was crying.*

*Mama set the broom aside and knelt in front of him. She put her hands on his cheeks and kissed his forehead. Even sitting next to him, it was difficult to hear his voice.*

*"I am sorry, Mama. I am so sorry. . . ."*

Fräulein Mahler sighed. "I love my brother, but he did not always choose well."

I selected my words carefully. "Do you think losing his father may have had a more serious effect on him than anyone suspected?"

"It is possible this is true. But we may never know, nee?" She leaned her head back. "This was in July 1961. In three weeks, life would change forever."

*A knock at the door startled me. I looked through the window. "Come in, Tante Frieda!"*

*She opened the front door and stepped into the house. "Good day, Katia. It is hot, no?"*

*"Yes, it is a Berlin August." I stretched on the couch and massaged my legs.*

*She closed the door. "Your therapy?"*

*I nodded. "I do not know if it helps. Sometimes it feels good. Sometimes it hurts me."*

*"You are young. Perhaps you will yet get better." She smiled at me but only with her lips. Her eyes did not seem to focus.*

*"Perhaps. Is there something wrong? You have a worried face."*

*"Where is your mama?"*

*"She is in the garden. There are herbs ready to pick."*

*"I must speak—"*

*The back door to the garden creaked open and then closed. Mama came in from the kitchen and set a basket on the table. "Hello, Frieda." She wiped her forehead with her sleeve.*

*"Anna, the city is in turmoil."*

*"Turmoil? Come and sit. I will heat some tea."*

*"No, thank you. I cannot stay. Have you heard about the barrier?"*

*"Barrier? No."*

*"Chancellor Ulbrecht has closed Berlin, the East from the West."*

*Mama sat down at the table. Tante Frieda took the chair across from her.*

*"Yesterday we could travel from the Soviet sector to those of the Western Allies, but today the roads between them have closed. Overnight, the Volksarmee has put up wire fences and barricades. All traffic stops. No one may pass."*

*"How can this be? Why have they done this?"*

*"Ulbrecht says to protect the true Germany from the evil and espionage of the Western Allies. But we know many from the East have left for the West, where there is more opportunity. Doctors, engineers, those who he needs to build up the country are fewer every day. The people say the barrier is not to keep the Allies out, but to keep us in."*

*"But all in one night?"*

*"Yes, it was not expected. Those from the East who worked in the West can no longer get to their jobs. Families are cut off from each other. Already there have been shootings when people try to cross the barrier."*

*"Shootings?" Mama grew pale.*

*"Yes."*

*She turned to me. "Katia, where is Friedrich?"*

*"I do not know."*

*"Have you seen him this morning?"*

*"No. I did not hear him come in last night. But, perhaps while I slept—"*

*She jumped up. "I must find him. He sometimes goes to Treptow and Neuköln. I do not know where the barriers are. Could he be on the other side?"*

*Tante Frieda rose. "I am sure he is fine."*

*"No, we both know Friedrich. If he is across the barrier, he will try to get back." Mama steadied herself against the table.*

*"Mama?"*

*She did not answer me. Her face was now white. "I have already lost Helmut to the camps. I do not know if I would survive losing my son, too."*

*"But we have no idea where to look. Is it not better to wait for him to come home?"*

*"I cannot wait. I cannot sit here while he may be in danger." Mama hurried to the fireplace and took her small purse from the mantel.*

*Tante Frieda followed her. "I will come with you. Katia, watch for your brother. If he comes home, tell him to stay here until we return. Do you understand?"*

*I nodded.*

⌘

Fräulein Mahler shifted in her chair. "I was so happy when Friedrich came home at sunset. Mama and Tante Frieda were still gone. I told him they were looking for him and that he should stay here. He was quieter than usual. He said he would fix something to eat, if I was hungry. I said, 'Yes, thank you.'"

"When did your mother and aunt return?"

"A little later. Mama hugged Friedrich. Tante Frieda scolded him, but with a kiss and a smile. He did not seem upset."

"I'm glad he was safe."

"Yes, for now."

# Chapter 14

NEW

*To: Ian.McAllister@ftr.net*
*Subject: Quick Hello*

*Hey, Dad—*
  *My first time at this I-net café. Oskar drove me. Can't take long. He's in the car. Don't know how often I'll get back here but wanted to try it out. My Inbox was crammed. One flamer from system admin for overloading the mail server. Rest was spam, including from Brendon. LOL. I wore out the DELETE key.*
  *Took the afternoon off from the interview. F. Mahler was tired, took a nap. Saturday she talked about when the Berlin Wall went up in '61. Scary time. Read about it in school, saw pix, but not the same as hearing it firsthand. You know.*
  *Don't know where she'll go with this tomorrow. We'll see, I guess.*
  *Enuff for now. Go ahead and reply, but not sure when I'll check e-mail again.*
                                                    *Love ya! Maddy*

SEND

⤜∾⤛

We had finished our morning meal and were back at our places by the front window. An overcast sky cast a gray pallor over the day outside and dulled the ambiance inside, despite the lamps' best efforts to cheer up the dining nook and the front room. I slipped off my flats and curled my legs onto the couch against the humid morning chill that even a hot breakfast and steaming coffee couldn't seem to deter. Fräulein Mahler must have felt it, too. She pulled her sweater tight and fastened all its buttons instead of leaving it open as she normally did. She sipped her tea then paused for an instant with her hands wrapped around the warm cup before easing it back onto the saucer.

Without a thought, I reached over and rested my left hand on the arm of her wheelchair. Her fingers glided over mine, patted me twice, then settled. I glanced up. She was smiling.

"You put up with my silliness, to hold your hand."

I smiled back. "It's not silly. I admit it seemed odd to me at first, but now I find it comforting. I like it."

She dipped her head.

I scanned my notepad. "You were telling me yesterday about the Berlin Wall. It must have been a shock to see it appear so quickly."

"We did not know then what this barricade would mean to our lives. We hoped it would not last long, that the Allies would protest. But it did not go away. It became stronger."

"How did it affect your family?"

Her fingertip quickened its stroke on my wrist. "It was now February of 1962. . . ."

I glanced down at the recorder, and my eyes widened at only one tick left on the battery indicator. There was no way to break her narrative now, even if my spare batteries were within reach. I fingered my pencil and smoothed the page of my notepad, hoping I'd be able to keep up if the recorder dropped out.

*Technology. We get so spoiled. You're a journalist, Maddy. Figure it out.*

"...when Friedrich burst through the door."
*What did I miss? Focus, Maddy!*

⤜⤛

*Friedrich waved a crumpled piece of paper, his face livid. "Mama! Where is Mama?"*

*I paused my crocheting halfway through a stitch. "She is—"*

*"What is it, Friedrich?" Mama appeared in the kitchen doorway.*

*"Ulbrecht has begun conscription! I am to report to the Volksarmee at the end of the month. The Volksarmee, Mama! I cannot do that, not after Papa—"*

*"Quiet, Friedrich. It does not help to shout. Is that the summons?"*

*"Yes."*

*She held out her hand. "Please."*

*Friedrich gave her the paper and propped his elbow on the fireplace mantel. He leaned his head on his forearm while Mama read.*

*In a moment, she laid the letter on the mantel. "It is for ages eighteen to twenty-six. You are twenty-five, so it appears there is nothing you can do, Son." She looked up from the paper. "But it is only for eighteen months."*

*He covered his eyes. "Why now? I am finally in a good job. I have worked for Herr Baumgartner four months now. Longer than for anyone. It is good work, Mama. I cannot leave."*

*"I suspect Chancellor Ulbrecht does this because the barricade remains in place, and he can strengthen his power. He could not do so before, while still under pressure from the Western Allies."*

*"The barricade not only remains," he fumed, "they strengthen it every day, make it taller."*

*She sighed. "Yes. I had hoped it was temporary—Ulbrecht rattling his Soviet-made saber. But it seems now as though it will be with us for a while."*

*I set aside my crocheting. "What will you do in the army, Friedrich?"*

*"I do not know yet. There are four parts to the Volksarmee: the land forces, the navy, the air force, and the Grenztruppen. The border guards are the second-largest part after the land forces. Perhaps if I am assigned as a border guard, I can remain in Berlin."*

*Mama's voice was quiet. "With your father arrested, you likely will not be a Grenztruppe. They would consider you a risk to escape."*

*"I will try anyway, if I have any choice. Perhaps they will not see the records."*

*"Who else of your friends has received this letter?"*

*"I do not know. I only just checked the post."*

⤜⤛

Fräulein Mahler cleared her throat. "Friedrich did report to the Volksarmee at the end of March 1962. He entered into service with Heinrich Schwerer, an old friend from school, and his new friend, Karl Werner. I knew Heinrich but had not met Karl. Friedrich liked them both very much."

I jotted down Heinrich's name. "What branch of the service did your brother enter?"

She paused. "What is 'branch'?"

"Did he go into the land forces, navy, air force, or the border guards?"

"Strangely, he was indeed placed in the Grenztruppen as a border guard. Heinrich, also. Karl went to the land forces and, after training, was sent to the Potsdam caserne. Friedrich supposed Karl's arrest at the dissidents' meeting did not permit him to guard the border."

I laid down my pencil and took another glance at the battery indicator. The recorder was still alive but not for much longer. "May I get you another cup of tea?"

"That would be nice."

⤜⤛

I settled back onto the sofa and slipped a new pair of AAAs into the Sony. She balanced her teacup in her lap, her head tilted back at rest. I doubt she opened her eyes the entire time I was up.

I had taken the opportunity to clear the breakfast table while the tea water reheated. Her food was hardly touched. She normally ate well for such a petite woman, but this morning's plate only showed signs of nibbling. She did seem to be thirsty, having downed three cups of coffee and two glasses of juice. I glanced at her face. She breathed easily, and her color was good—well, as good as it ever was. A summer holiday on the Spanish coast sure couldn't have hurt.

"How are you feeling, Fräulein Mahler?"

She tipped her head forward and opened her eyes. "I am fine. Do I look unwell?"

"No, not at all. I just wondered. . .well, you hardly touched your breakfast. I thought maybe. . ." The notion that I had overstepped again began to cloud my mind. But it was an honest question. No reason to feel awkward. So why did I, then?

She laid her head back. "I was not restful last night. Perhaps a nap this afternoon would be good."

"We'll plan on it. I have a lot of notes to transcribe into my computer. There's plenty to keep me busy."

"You will have more before we finish. One terrible morning in February of 1963, my dear brother changed forever."

I stopped writing and glanced up at her. She had closed her eyes again.

⁂

*"Friedrich! We did not expect you until next weekend."*

*My brother closed the door quietly, and I reached up for my hug. He squeezed my shoulder but did not bend over to hug me. His face was pale.*

*"What is wrong?"*

*"There is something wrong?" Mama stepped in from the kitchen, wiping the blade of a small knife with a wet cloth.*

*The fragrance of rosemary and sage floated into the room behind her. Dried herbs from last autumn's garden filled the room with delicious aromas. Mama always enjoyed curing herbs, but now her brow furrowed with her first glimpse of Friedrich's face.*

*He sat on the couch next to me, his army hat in his hands. He did not lift his gaze from the floor. Mama set the knife and the cloth on the table and crossed the room. She knelt at his feet and peered into his face. "Friedrich?"*

*He shook his head. "I cannot go back."*

*"Why? What happened?"*

*"I have deserted."*

*"What? Why would you do such a thing?"*

*He cleared his throat. "We had our inspection formation this morning. There was a new officer with our commander, a Soviet colonel of the KGB, Polkovnik Chernov. He arrived from Moscow a week ago. Rumors among the soldiers were that, as a junior lieutenant, he was with the Soviet forces who fought in the Battle of Berlin in 1945. He carries scars on his face from battle. They say his family was in Leningrad during Operation Barbarossa when Hitler's army besieged the city, that they were among the million Russians who died there. He is very severe."*

*Mama put her hand on his arm. "What has he to do with you?"*

*He swallowed. "The ranks had formed, and inspection was ready to begin. Heinrich was not yet there. He was often late but always arrived before inspection. This time he rushed into his place beside me just after we were called to attention. Colonel Chernov stopped the inspection and came over to us with our commander. I could hear Heinrich trying to control his breathing after his run from the barracks."*

*Friedrich's voice grew weak, and he coughed. He sounded like he was going to be sick. "Colonel Chernov eyed Heinrich up and down but said nothing. Then he pushed between Heinrich and me. I*

53

*could not see what he was doing, but suddenly my commander stiffened. I heard him say, 'Polkovnik Chernov, what—' and then the explosion deafened my ear."*

*Mama's eyes grew wide. "Friedrich—"*

*My brother shuddered, and his voice cracked. "Something splattered against the side of my face, and Heinrich fell to the ground. The back of his head was. . .gone."*

*She put her hands to the sides of my brother's face and pulled him to her shoulder. He began to sob. She stroked his head, and tears ran down her cheeks, too. I did not know what to think, what to do. I did not cry, for it was not yet real to me. I could only watch my brother and mother hug each other.*

*Finally, Friedrich sat back and rubbed his eyes with his sleeve. "Colonel Chernov stepped over Heinrich's body and replaced his pistol in its holster. He stood toe-to-toe with my commander. I heard him say, 'Proceed with the inspection, Herr Oberst.'" Friedrich's voice caught. "That was all."*

*Friedrich's next words tumbled out. "I told him to hurry. I told Heinrich he would get into trouble, but he would never be dressed until the last minute. I always stayed with him to make sure he was on time, but I became angry with him this morning and told him I was going on ahead, that he could be late all the time if he wanted to. I should have stayed with him. I should have hurried him. I did not, and now he is dead."*

*Mama shook her head. "You must listen to me. This is not your fault. Heinrich was a grown man, a soldier. He was responsible for himself, as you are for yourself."*

*"But—"*

*"No, there is no but. You are not to blame."*

*Friedrich's voice dropped to a whisper. "But he was my friend."*

⤜⊰⊱⤛

Sometime during the session, Fräulein Mahler's left hand joined her right hand over mine. She massaged my wrist until I thought she would rub it raw. I set down my pencil, reached over, and covered her frail fingers. She jerked her head and stopped stroking.

When she opened her eyes, a tear escaped down her cheek. "I am sorry. I am hurting you."

"Not at all. I was concerned about you, that's all."

She nodded and lifted her left hand to wipe away the tear. She took a deep breath.

"What happened then? Did Friedrich return to his unit?"

She shook her head. "Nee. During the inspection, the Soviet colonel gave him demerits and put him on extra duty for having blood on his face and uniform. Later, Friedrich went back to the barracks and scrubbed his face, but he could not rid himself of the feel or the smell of Heinrich's death. He slipped away when they prepared to go to their duty stations. He said if he went back, he was sure Colonel Chernov would shoot him, too."

"Where did he go?"

"He changed his clothes then packed his uniform and some other belongings into his bag. He kissed us good-bye but would not tell us where he was going, so the police could learn nothing from us. He said he would see us when he could but that he would have to be careful. They would watch the house and us, too, when we went out."

"Was he ever able to come and see you?"

She shook her head.

# Chapter 15

*Dear Mom, Dad, and Carson,*
    *Today's session was pretty heavy. I learned more about Fräulein Mahler's brother. If I ever say another mean thing to you, Carson, just pull this letter out and show it to me, okay?*
    *She was exhausted by lunchtime. She refused any food but had another cup of tea. Then she went back to her room for a nap. I nibbled some cheese and crackers, but my appetite was gone, too.*
    *I spent the afternoon typing up notes. I think I got up every fifteen minutes to listen at her door, hoping to hear her moving, or breathing—anything.*
    *Around four-thirty, I heated up more water and looked around in the refrigerator for something easy to make for dinner. She needed to eat something, or I was afraid she was going to get sick. When I tapped on her bedroom door, she told me to come in. She was already awake and in her wheelchair in a corner of the room. It was very dark, but for one lit candle on her bedside stand. She was looking at a framed photograph. I didn't ask. . . .*

⌘

". . .and I meant to ask if dinner is okay."

We sat at the table with bowls of vegetable soup, rolls, and cheese. I was determined to keep the conversation light. I had pulled the curtains back from the windows to let in the late afternoon sun, although the sheers afforded little shade even when they were closed. Fresh flowers adorned the centerpiece with bright whites and yellows—some kind of daisies and pansies, or something, I think. I also stashed the photos and documents, plus all my note-taking materials, out of sight. This evening there would be no reminders of the interview. Or tomorrow, for that matter, if I didn't see some improvement in her eating.

"It tastes very good. Danke schön."

I prattled on. "You're welcome. I'm glad you like it. I didn't make it from scratch, of course. It was in the fridge, but soup is tastier a day or two after it's made, don't you think? The flavors have more of a chance to blend—at least that's what my dad always says. I think he's right, don't you? I like to melt my cheese in it. It gets all stringy and stuff and sticks to the spoon. Would you like another roll?"

"Ja, it is very good. Thank you." She didn't look at the bread basket.

"Fräulein Mahler?"

She sipped the broth but said nothing.

I hesitated then went for the jugular. "Katia?"

Her eyes jerked up midsip. She lowered her spoon. "You become familiar, Fräulein McAllister."

I hoped I hadn't made a mistake.

"It was the only thing I could think of to get your attention."

I had made a mistake.

"I ask you to think longer the next time."

The Irish—American—whatever!—heat rose again. I set down my spoon. "Fräulein Mahler, I do apologize for becoming familiar, but I've been talking to you for the past ten minutes, and I don't think you've heard a word I've said."

Her voice maintained that frustrating evenness my own has ever yet to achieve. "It is not necessary always to talk."

My shoulders slumped.

"Bitte, Fräulein McAllister—"

"I know! I know! Posture. Excuse me, please."

I pushed out of my chair and cleared my dishes to the kitchen. When I returned, she was still sipping. I crossed to the couch, pulled my laptop from its hiding place in the corner, and jabbed the POWER button.

Ten minutes later, Fräulein Mahler wheeled in from the kitchen, the dining table now cleared. She assumed her place in the corner and picked up a blue hardback from the bookshelf next to her. She began to read aloud:

*"Call on the present day and night for nought,*
*Save what by yesterday was brought.*
*The sea is flowing ever,*
*The land retains it never.*
*Be stirring, man, while yet the day is clear;*
*The night when none can work fast draweth near."*

She laid the book in her lap. "Johann Goethe. From his *Book of Proverbs.*"

I didn't look up. "Yes, ma'am, I know."

"Fräulein McAllister, do you think we will finish?"

"Please stop asking me that."

# Chapter 16

*P*icked up on the first ring!

"Hey, Mom. It's me. . . . Yeah, I had to get out of the house for a while. This evening was kind of the pits. We had a little tiff over names, of all things. I shouldn't have let her get under my skin. So, how's Grandma? Doing any better? . . . Good. Dad mentioned Grandpa is selling some land. I didn't know he owned any. How much did he sell? . . . Wow! And where was this again? . . . Terrebonne. Not familiar with that. Where is Tere—what? . . . Okay, I can wait a minute. . . . So, who was that? . . . Oh, really? You let Carson borrow the car? Man, I forgot he got his license. . . . Yup, he's growing up all right."

*He'll always be a squirt, though!*

"Well, sorry this is such a short call, but I have to sign off. I just wanted to hear someone's voice not picking at me. . . . Sorry, I didn't mean that. I'm just feeling sorry for myself. It'll be fine. . . ."

⤜⤏

". . .really, it's fine, thanks, Oskar. Did I give you enough money?" I sat at the dining table and sorted through the supplies I asked him to pick up: a pencil sharpener, more batteries, a couple of hair bands, and a few other girl-junk things. After yesterday evening, I should've had him pick up some Excedrin, too.

"Ja, and here is the change."

"Keep it for your trouble."

"Helping a friend is never a trouble, Fräulein McAllister. Please take." He dropped a couple of euros into my hand.

I looked him in the eye. "If we're such good friends, why do you still call me Fräulein McAllister? It's supposed to be Maddy."

He shrugged and smiled as he tucked his change pouch into his pocket.

I took a deep breath. "Oskar, I'm a little concerned about Fräulein Mahler."

He glanced up at me. "Ja?"

"Her appetite is way down, and she seems to tire more quickly. She said she was restless and didn't sleep very well a couple of nights ago. I don't know how many other rough nights she's had. I never thought to ask."

"Does she drink water during the day?"

"Well, not water, so much. We do go through a lot of tea. Come to think of it, she has been drinking more hot tea lately."

He frowned. "She must drink to avoid—what is *Entwässerung*?"

"Oh, I'm not sure. You mean dehydration, when she doesn't get enough liquids?"

"Ja, there is also *Dehydration* in German. I did not think of it."

"I'll try to get her to drink more, but I don't think she'll listen to me. In fact, I'm trying to think of any time she has taken my advice."

He smiled. "You have discovered our Katia."

"Oh no, sir! I called her Katia yesterday, and I thought the world was coming to an end."

He raised his eyebrows. "You called her Katia?"

"I didn't mean to be disrespectful. She was so distracted, and I thought it was the only way I could get her attention. I won't do *that* again."

His smile returned. "Well, if you called her Katia and you are still living in her house, she must like you very much."

I laughed. "It's that important, huh?"

He shrugged again.

I sobered as a thought came to mind. "The last thing we talked about seemed to trigger her mood."

"Ja?"

"Yes, it was about the last time she saw her brother, Friedrich."

He paused then glanced toward the door.

"Oskar?"

"Ja, I must go now. Enschuldige, bitte."

He bumped into the arm of the sofa on his way out the door. Puzzled, I watched him leave.

"Where is Oskar?" Fräulein Mahler wheeled through the kitchen doorway with a paper bag on her lap.

"He left. Rather suddenly, in fact." I listened to the sound of the car engine as it faded up the street.

"He was to take some Brötchen. I baked them this morning."

I mimicked his shrug.

❦

We settled into our usual places. She took my hand, more tenderly, I think, than normal. I pressed the RECORD button and straightened my writing pad. Her first words threw me for a loop.

"You are a very lovely girl. Where is your boyfriend?"

"Excuse me?"

"*Ein fester Freund.* Surely you have a boy interested in you, nee?"

"Umm." I laughed, and my cheeks flushed. "No, I—what brought that on?"

She cocked her head. "Brought on?"

"Why do you ask about a boyfriend?"

"Because I wonder who it is I am keeping you from."

I laid my pad down. "You're keeping me from no one, Fräulein Mahler. I can't think of anyone I would rather be with right now than you." Even with all our missteps, my words sealed their truth in my own mind.

She dipped her head. "And I with you."

❦

To my surprise and minor confusion, the morning passed amid small talk. We didn't delve into her story at all. I started to switch off the Sony then decided to leave it on, in case something interesting did come up. Her lead-off question about a boyfriend put me off balance. I had no idea why, but I couldn't drain the color from my cheeks. What was the big deal? She had asked a simple question, nothing more. Maybe she hit a nerve I didn't know was there, given my recent falling-out with Brendon.

It occurred to me that if so simple a personal issue niggled at me that much, how must the memories of such intense events from her past have affected her? I studied her face as she sat, her head in its characteristic tipped-back position, her eyes closed. She betrayed no anxiety, but she did seem more wan than when I first arrived, perhaps even a little thinner, if that was possible. It was as if a reserve of—what, strength? vitality?—inside her body ebbed little by little with every word she spoke. Her preoccupation with finishing the interview rose in my mind. I wondered if she perceived an emotional-physical spillage in recounting the events of her life and tried to gauge it with the flow of her narrative.

Oskar's advice about her health returned to me, and I resolved to monitor her more closely. The full glass of water I placed on the bookshelf beside her chair after breakfast was the start of that. She ignored it.

"Do not nag me, Fräulein McAllister. You are my scribe, not my nurse."

"I nag you as your friend, not your nurse or your scribe."

She cracked open one eyelid and peered at me. "Friend?"

"Yes, ma'am. Whether you like it or not."

# Chapter 17

*Dear Mom and Dad,*

*I think I'm finally getting the hang of this interview. How embarrassing is that for a journalism major after a whole month? I'm so glad you guys bought me the Sony for Christmas last year, because I get so wrapped up in her story that I forget to take notes.*

*The weekend was a bust as far as any work goes. I think it was a break we both needed, though. We spent Saturday afternoon in the park. It was more crowded, since it was May Day, a big holiday in Germany. The air was chilly, but it felt good. Once again, Oskar played the silent partner.*

*I'm beginning to wonder about Oskar more and more. He's always there when you need him, never when you don't. He never comes to the house empty-handed, and once he's there, he seems to dissolve into the woodwork and you almost forget about him. I need to ask. . . .*

⌘

". . .how you met Oskar, Fräulein Mahler? You mentioned something about a cross the other day in the park."

She patted my hand. "It was interesting, how we met. But that story is yet to come, ja?"

I nodded and curled my legs up on the divan. Over the past week, the stack of photos and documents I brought into the front room for our sessions grew shorter. Her descriptions of events were so vivid that I found little need to consult them while she spoke. In the evenings, when I did glance over some of the material, it was as though I had already studied them, so thorough were her recollections. What an incredible memory. All I needed was my trusty recorder, a pad and pencil—and the ubiquitous cup of tea, of course—and we were good to go.

"And what is that little machine you have, Fräulein McAllister?"

I raised my eyebrows. "Machine?"

"Ja, the little box with the buttons next to you."

"Oh! That's my recorder. Do you like it?" I picked it up and turned it proudly in my hand, as though I had something to do with its sleek design and modern features.

"So small. Do recorders not have tape?"

"Not this one. It's digital."

"Digital?"

"Yes, it stores sound in tiny memory circuits instead of on tape. Here, take a look." I handed her the Sony.

"Tiny memory circuits." She squinted at the liquid crystal display. "I have many words for you. Will this machine keep them all?"

I smiled. "Oh, yes. It can record hundreds of hours of sound. Besides, I upload our sessions every couple of days."

"Upload?"

"Yes. Into my laptop."

Her gaze dropped to my jeans. "Laptop?"

I stifled a chuckle. "My computer. It stores our sessions as MP3s."

"Empee—"

"Never mind. We won't lose any of your story. Trust me on this."

She gave the recorder one more skeptical glance and returned it to me.

I held up my pad and pencil. "And there's always these."

She nodded, appearing reassured. "Gut. We can continue."

"Okay, I think we were still in 1963. Somewhere around springtime?" I punched the RECORD button.

She nodded and leaned her head back.

⤳⤳

*Tante Frieda opened the front page and dumped the morning's coffee grounds onto the official newspaper of the Socialist Unity Party. "Anna, I have finally found a good use for the* Neues Deutchland.*"*

*Mama smiled at her sister's nasal snicker. She sipped the last of her coffee and pushed back from the dining table. "How are you coming along, Katia?"*

*"Very slowly, it seems to me." I held up a wool sweater, minus the left sleeve. "My fingers tire too quickly."*

*"You have become very good with your crocheting." She patted my arm.*

*"Thank you, Mama. I enjoy it. I am making Friedrich something for his birthday."*

*Her face sobered, but she nodded. "That is good."*

*Tante Frieda sat down at the table. "Have you heard from Friedrich?"*

*"Not yet."*

*"Do you have any idea where—"*

*"No. Please do not ask." Mama gathered our empty teacups and went into the kitchen.*

*Tante Frieda shook her head. "No woman should have a time such as this. Her husband and her son both gone. She does not know where."*

*I held up my hand. "Please, I ask you, too, not to speak of these things. They are very hurtful."*

*She shrugged and rose from her chair. "I go to the shops now," she called out.*

*"Yes, Frieda." Mama's voice trickled through the kitchen doorway. It sounded tired.*

*After Tante Frieda closed the front door behind her, I set aside my yarn and reached for my crutches. When I hobbled to the kitchen, Mama's back was to the window. She held a towel to her face.*

*I touched her arm. "Mama?"*

*She started at my voice. "Katia! I did not hear you come in." She lowered the towel and turned toward me. Her eyes were red and moist. She began to put away the breakfast dishes.*

*"It will be okay. Friedrich is only being careful."*

*She nodded but did not lift her head.*

*I moved around her to the end of the narrow kitchen. "If you give me the juice glasses, I can put them up."*

*"It is all right. You should rest."*

*"The doctor says I must exercise my legs or they will shrivel up. And I want to help. I do so little around the house." My throat began to tighten, I was not sure why. "All I do is sit on the couch. I am just another burden for you—"*

*"Katia!" Mama spun toward me, fresh tears on her cheeks. "Never say such a thing again!"*

*I looked down.*

*She stepped toward me and tipped my chin up until our eyes met. "You are. . .all I have left. You are never a burden to me." Her voice caught in her throat. "Never say such a thing again," she whispered.*

*"I am sorry." I sniffled. "I did not mean to—"*

*"Quiet, child." When she caressed my cheek, it was as though her touch tipped over whatever holds the tears behind our eyes, and I could not stop them from flowing. She drew me to her and held me tight.*

*I do not remember how long we hugged. When I wiped my eyes, a movement at the window startled me. "Look, a Blaumeise. Careful, or we will scare him away."*

61

*Mama smiled and brushed a tear from her own cheek.*

*Together we watched him hop along the window ledge toward the rose trellis. As he began to peck at a pink rosebud, a flash of white caught my eye.*

*"What is that?"*

*The bird stood on a piece of paper, its corner just in sight over the lip of the window frame. We moved closer, and he flew away. Where he had stood lay an envelope. Mama opened the back door and reached over to the sill. She pulled back two letters tied together with string. The top envelope had "Mama" written on it. My name was on the other.*

*We took the letters to the dining table and sat down. Her hand trembled as she traced the letters with her fingertips.*

*"Friedrich's writing," she murmured.*

*I stared at my letter but did not open it. She eased open the flap of hers and drew out a folded piece of notepaper. She read it slowly.*

Mama,

I am sorry I have not been able to visit you as I promised. I have come to the house but saw men in cars along the street. I am sure they watch for me. Please know that I have tried to see you, and I miss you very much.

Karl and I escape to the West tonight. I have met with him twice since I left home, when he had a pass from the caserne in Potsdam. There is a place where people have crossed over with success, and we have a good plan. I will not say where, in case someone finds this letter. Our uniforms will help us get close to the barrier, and the dark will hide my face from those who look for me. Please do not be afraid.

I will work hard to bring you, Katia, and Tante Frieda over. There is much opportunity, and I will not have to hide anymore.

I love you. I will not fail you this time, as I have so many times before.

Your loving son, Friedrich

*Mama reread the letter, her lips moving silently. After several moments, she looked up at me.*

*"What does Friedrich write to you?" I said. I looked at the envelope but was afraid to open it. I wanted to know what he wrote, and I did not want to know.*

*"Katia, please."*

*I looked up at her. She clutched her letter against her chest, her eyes moist. I nodded and slipped my finger beneath the flap.*

Dearest Katia,

I have written about my intentions to Mama. I will not repeat them here. Please know that I am going to take care of you, some way. I am certain I can succeed in my plans.

You have always been the greatest joy to me. I look forward to playing Schafkopf with you again, this time in freedom.

Today is 15 April, dear Sister. Remember it well. It is the day of a new beginning.

Your loving brother, Friedrich

*I gazed at Mama. Her face was pale.*

*"What is it, Mama?"*

*"This Karl Werner. I still do not know him. After the dissidents' meeting, I am afraid. . ."*

*"You do not trust him?"*

*"No."*

*"But he wants to escape to the West, too."*

*She shook her head. "We do not really know what he wants, do we, Katia?"*

❧

I glanced at the dining table. "I think I saw the envelope with your name among the documents, but I didn't see your mother's."

"Mama said we should destroy our letters, that if the Stasi found them, it would endanger Friedrich."

"But he planned to cross over that night. Surely you could hide them until he escaped. It would be very difficult to destroy a letter like that, it seems."

She nodded. "Ja, it was very painful. Mama cried as she held a match to it over the kitchen sink. But, though Friedrich planned to cross that night, he could be delayed and might have to try another night. To have the letters was a danger to him. I was to burn mine, too, but Tante Frieda came home at that moment and interrupted us. I slipped my letter into my sweater pocket. Later, I could not bring myself to destroy it."

"Did Friedrich. . .did he make it?"

"I do not know."

"How could you not know?"

Her finger resumed caressing my wrist, and her voice quieted.

❧

*The next morning Mama and I ate breakfast in silence. I had not slept well that night. I do not think she slept at all. Our morning chores also passed with little conversation. When I finished, I sat down on the couch and picked up my crocheting. Friedrich's sweater was nearly finished, but I wondered now if he would ever wear it. After only one or two stitches, I could no longer concentrate. I set the yarn aside and stared at the floor, for how long I do not know.*

*At midday Mama asked if I was hungry. I said no. She did not eat, either. That afternoon Tante Frieda came to visit. She was very excited.*

*"Did you hear, Anna? There was an escape to the West last night. They swam the River Spree behind the Reichstag."*

*Mama steadied herself against the dining table. "They?"*

*"Yes, two men. A patrol boat fired at them. One was shot, but the other made it to the western bank. . . . Anna? Is something wrong?"*

# Chapter 18

*Dear Carson,*

*I want you to read something when I get home, letters someone wrote to his mom and sister a long time ago. I can tell you the story about them later. They've made me think a lot.*

*We've always gotten along pretty well, wouldn't you say? Except for the times you deliberately annoyed me, of course. Not that I've ever done the same to you. (Teasing, Squirt!) I guess I just want to say I appreciate you, and, in spite of some of the things I've said, I love you. You'll know why when you read the letters and hear the story.*

*Stay out of trouble, and say hi to Moira for me, okay?*

*Love, Maddy*

~⁊⁊⁊~

Fräulein Mahler sipped her tea then set it on its saucer. "We discovered the next day that it was indeed Friedrich and Karl who swam the Spree."

I jotted the date 16.4.1963 on my pad. "How did you find out?"

My pencil lead snapped against the pad at her reply.

~⁊⁊⁊~

*A crash at the door woke me from my nap. Before I could clear my mind, three Volkspolizei officers burst into the house. One man stayed by the door and one went to the kitchen. I heard the back door squeak open. The other policeman turned down the hallway.*

*In a moment, I heard Mama's voice. "What do you want here? Do not touch me!"*

*A man cursed.*

*Then Mama called louder, "Katia! Do not touch my daughter!" Something crashed, and I heard a louder curse.*

*The policeman came back into the room with Mama. She struggled, but he pinned her arms against her side. When she tried to come to me, he held her tight. The slamming shut of the back door echoed through the kitchen doorway.*

*"Mama?" I groped for my crutches, but the policeman by the door kicked them across the room.*

*"Unterwachtmeister Messner, that is not necessary! She is no threat."*

*The shout came from the man who had gone to the kitchen. I stiffened when I recognized him. It was Leutnant Klein, the man who'd brought Friedrich home from the dissidents' meeting. But he now wore the insignia of an Oberleutnant. He did not look at me.*

*Instead, he turned to Mama. "Anna Mahler, you are under arrest for crimes against the State."*

*"Why? What is it I have done?" Her eyes were on fire.*

*"Your son and another man violated the border yesterday. They left their uniforms by the barrier, so we know it was him. Surely you are aware of this. You must have known of his plans."*

*"I have not seen Friedrich for weeks. I do not know what you are talking about."*

*"We shall see what you know." He gestured toward the door. "Take her to the car."*

*The policeman called Messner stepped forward. "Oberleutnant Klein, we have not searched her or the house."*

*The man holding Mama smirked. "Do not worry. I will search her thoroughly in the car."*

*"Wachtmeister Heuler, you will not abuse the prisoner unless you wish reassignment to cell*

*duty at Hohenschönehausen Prison."*

*Heuler frowned but said nothing.*

*Messner pointed at me. "What of the girl?"*

*"She is a cripple, Messner. Even you can see that. There is no extra room in the Volga, and she is of no use to us." Oberleutnant Klein barely glanced at me. "Take the prisoner to the car and place her in the backseat. Wachtmeister Heuler, take the front seat. Messner, you will drive. I will sit next to the prisoner."*

*Heuler opened his mouth, but Oberleutnant Klein cut him off. "I am responsible for the prisoner, so I will take charge of her. Go. I will come as soon as I get my hat from the kitchen."*

*Heuler sneered. "You want a moment with the Fräulein, no, Oberleutnant?"*

*I do not think the policeman saw the back of the officer's hand until it struck his cheek. "I will deal with you later. Go! Now!"*

*I reached out. "Mama!"*

*Mama's face was calm. "Do not worry, Katia. They have no cause to arrest me. I will be back—"*

*The two policemen pushed her out of the house.*

*"Mama!"*

*When the door swung shut, Oberleutnant Klein slipped his hat out from beneath his overcoat and hurried across the room. He retrieved my crutches from against the bookcase and brought them to me. I shrank back when he knelt on the floor in front of the couch.*

*"Listen very carefully. There is no time. I will protect your mama from the Stasi as best I can. I will also call for Tante Frieda. Be brave, Katia. I will send word to you soon."*

*"Herr Klein. . . ?"*

*He smiled and touched me on the cheek. "No tears now, eh?"*

*Then he was gone.*

⟡

It took three attempts to hit the Stop button on my recorder, and as many swallows to get past the lump in my throat. I shuddered, and my vision blurred. "My God, Fräulein Mahler—"

Her finger stopped its caress. "Fräulein McAllister, this house has not heard a curse in over forty years. It will not tolerate one now."

My cheeks flushed. "I'm sorry. It. . .it just slipped out."

"If it slips out again, the interview will end. My Lord's name and my mother's memory are above all to be respected."

Her voice was quiet, but her words cut deep. At any other time, or with any other person, my ire would've taken over. But she was right. God's name had become too easy for me to trivialize over the past couple of years, especially after I left home for school. I took a deep breath. "Please accept my sincerest apologies. The last thing I want to do is offend you."

Her tone dropped to a whisper. "It is not the offense to me that should most concern you."

I looked down. "Yes, ma'am."

Her finger twitched on the back of my hand. I chanced a glance at her face. Her eyes searched mine for a moment, then the gentle smile returned. She patted my wrist. "Perhaps some tea."

*Dear Mom and Dad,*
      *This letter will be short. Yesterday morning, I learned what happened to Fräulein Mahler's mother. The police took her away when Fräulein Mahler was only nineteen years old—and crippled, no less. It boggles my mind that things like this can happen in a modern world. I have been so sheltered.*
      *I've seen documentaries about the Cold War, but to me that was just Hollywood. And I've read scads of articles and books, but they were just black print on white paper, something to plow through for the next exam. They even used the same photographs book after book. I guess I became inured to it after a while.*
      *But to sit here and listen to a first-person account is really sobering. It makes me want do something—I don't know what. I mean, the Cold War is over, and there's nothing I can do to change history. Maybe as a journalist, though, I can have some small part in the future, to keep events like this fresh in our minds so they won't happen again. Do you think they could?*
                                                                                *I love you, Mom.*

⤲⤳

"...who is this Ian and Avery McAllister?"

Fräulein Mahler squinted at an envelope lying on the dining table as I was slipping my arm into my Windbreaker for an evening stroll to the Bundespost box.

"Oh, that's my dad and mom."

"You address your parents by their given names?"

"My goodness, no!" I coughed a nervous laugh. "Only on envelopes. For the post office. You know, to make sure it gets to the right McAllisters...and everything." I'm sure the stammering didn't help my case any.

She cocked her head. "I read where in America it becomes common for children to address their parents and other adults by their given names. Is this true?"

I hesitated. On campus at Michigan, I would overhear students refer to their professors by their first names, sometimes to their face. Even in church I heard adults insist that kids be familiar with them, as Fräulein Mahler would put it. I was never comfortable with that; I'm not sure why. Maybe it was my dad's influence. I could hear his voice now. *"Children need parents, not pals; role models, not roommates. Familiarity breeds contempt, and there is a lot of contempt in youth today."* Boy, would he and Fräulein Mahler get along!

I cleared my throat. "Some of what you read may be true, but perhaps since you read it in the newspapers it's not so common, or it wouldn't be news."

"But you—"

I held up my hands. "I wouldn't consider such a thing, in spite of the other day when I used your given name. Honest. That was a mistake and, now that I look back on it, I think it surprised me as much as it did you."

Her forehead smoothed. "Gut."

⤲⤳

I was almost afraid to begin the session after breakfast the next morning. I had tossed and turned all night amid dreams of broken-down doors, green overcoats, and black river water. It seemed I jumped at each little creak and bump in the night. I'm sure I glanced at my alarm clock at least once during every hour of darkness. I finally dozed off sometime after six o'clock. The next thing I knew, a thin streak of bright yellow sunlight shimmered on the wall above my bed. I jerked my head up and glanced at the clock. Eight thirty!

*Oh, no.* I groaned and threw the cover off.

Fifteen minutes later, I was at the breakfast table shoveling down a bowl of muesli. Fräulein Mahler occupied herself in the corner with a book. When I finished, I hurried to clear my dishes then grabbed my recorder and my pad. I covered a yawn with the back of my hand as I plopped onto the sofa. She laid her book in her lap.

"You did not sleep well?"

I shook my head to dislodge the cobwebs from my sluggish brain and tried in vain to curtail another enthusiastic yawn—the healthy kind that waters the eyes. "My goodness! Excuse me. No, not a restful night." I glanced at her book. "What are you reading?"

"Poems by Alexander Pushkin."

"Really? Is it in Russian?"

"Nee, I have not used my Russian in many years. I have probably forgotten it. This is a German translation of his poetry."

*"Nu, khorosho."* I smiled.

*"Da, Aleksandr Pushkin napisal otlichnuyu poeziyu. Mnogo lyet tomu nazad, ya mogla chitat' ego sovsyem' po russki, no teper'—"*

"Okay! Okay!" I laughed. "I surrender! So, you've forgotten your Russian, have you? I exhaust my entire vocabulary with 'well, good' and you return fire with the first half of *War and Peace*!"

"Pushkin did not write *War and Peace*, Fräulein McAllister. Tolstoy wrote it." She turned toward her bookshelves. "I have a copy here. . .somewhere."

I hesitated. "I know. I meant that—"

She turned back to me with a smile, her fingertips touching her lips. "I know what you meant. I make a joke with you."

*A joke? From Fräulein Mahler?*

I grinned and pulled my pad onto my lap. "Oh, so it's going to be *that* kind of a day, is it?"

"Ja."

The morning session passed quickly, mostly amid small talk. Her mood was light, such a contrast from yesterday afternoon. I didn't see how I would ever be able to recover from so horrific an event as my mother's arrest, let alone bring myself to recount it in such detail. But she did, and now it was almost like it never happened, as though to verbalize it somehow emptied it from her, or maybe released her from it.

I reflected on a psychology course I took my freshman year. The textbook's author averred that it was therapeutic to express a trauma verbally, or depict it in writing or pictures—that it aided the healing process. But Fräulein Mahler witnessed these events over forty years ago. Had it been bottled up inside her all this time, along with all the other things she'd told me about over the past month? How can a person survive that kind of pressure? I'd explode.

In any event, when we broke for lunch, she said she wanted to prepare the meal. And it was fantastic. She brought out crusty rolls with shaved ham and cheese, assorted pickles and relishes, a platter of fresh fruit, and, of course, tea. She stunned me when she wheeled out of the kitchen with a dusty bottle of wine and two small stemmed glasses propped up on her lap. She held the wine out to me.

"Would you please open it? I am not so strong anymore."

"Sure. What kind is it?"

"It is Trockenbeerenauslese."

"I'm not well versed on wines. What's Trockenbaus. . .Trockbeer-laus—what did you call it?" I held the bottle up and scanned the label.

"Trockenbeerenauslese. It means the wine is made from dried grapes selected by hand. Very good wine, very rare. We drink it with *Nachspeise*."

I squinted through the glass. "Oh, a dessert wine. Is it sweet?"

"You will see." She tapped her finger on the table. "But you must open it first."

I laughed then went into the kitchen and groped around in the utensil drawer until I found a corkscrew with a handle made of a section of grapevine cane. The brittle wax seal over the cork scored easily with a paring knife and the corkscrew bit through the wax with little effort. A gentle tug and the bottle was open. Unfortunately, the aged cork didn't fare very well. It broke apart as soon as it cleared the opening. A quick peek through the clear glass confirmed I hadn't left any cork bits floating in the wine.

I returned to the table and set the bottle in front of Fräulein Mahler then brushed the dust from my hands. "This looks like you've had it for a while."

She nodded and poured the honey-colored liquid into the glasses. "Ja, since 1959. Papa received it as a secret gift from a man he helped escape to the West. Trockenbeerenauslese is very expensive, and he felt so honored. Mama and Papa would have been married twenty-five years in July of 1960. We were to open it on their anniversary."

She held a glass toward me. I stared at her, my mouth agape. "I can't—"

"Take! Take, bitte, my arm is weak."

I accepted the wine but didn't remove my stare from my hostess. She smiled and raised her glass. "*Prost!* To a good interview."

The delicate crystal rang when she reached over and clinked her glass against mine. She tipped it toward her lips then stopped. Her eyes peered at me over the rim of the wineglass. "*Trink*. What is wrong?"

I set my glass down. "This wine must be very special to you. I can't. . . Why are you opening it now? Shouldn't someone important to you, like Oskar, be here to share it? It seems like. . .I don't know, too important."

She lowered her glass, and her soft eyes searched mine. Her words came quietly. "You are important to me, Fräulein McAllister."

My eyes misted, and I had difficulty swallowing. "Thank you. I just—"

She didn't raise her voice, but her tone was firm. "It is rude if you do not drink the toast with me."

My cheeks warmed, and I lifted my glass and took a sip. Now, I'm no connoisseur, so I have no idea if it was technically good wine or bad wine. All I know is that it was the smoothest liquid that ever flowed across my tongue. My limited experience with wine normally involved a slight gag at the first sip, as the alcohol burned a path down my throat to condition it for the next assault. There was nothing of that in this nectar. It didn't bully my taste buds into submission; it coaxed them to their feet.

"Wow. This is incredible."

She nodded. "It is gut, nee?"

"Oh, saying this is good is like saying the *Mona Lisa* is cute."

A pleased smile settled on her lips.

I took another sip then set down my glass. "Why the feast?"

She shrugged. "I sensed it was time."

The afternoon passed quietly. She retreated to her corner, and I cleared the dishes and covered the table with interview material. I looked over at her occasionally while I organized my notes and uploaded the past couple of sessions into the computer. She sat with her rust-colored Bible turned over on the arm of her wheelchair, her head tipped back in graceful repose.

At five o'clock, I sat back from the laptop and rubbed my eyes. Another glance across the room showed her still to be at rest. As I rose from my chair, a thud from her corner startled me. I crossed over to her corner. Her leather Bible had slipped off the arm of the wheelchair and lay facedown on the floor. Her hand hung loose at the wrist.

"Fräulein Mahler?"

I leaned over and touched her shoulder. My pulse quickened.

*"Fräulein Mahler!"*

# Chapter 20

*Oh, please be there!*

"Mom? It's Maddy. I'm at the hospital. Fräulein Mahler passed out this afternoon! I panicked, Mom. I had no idea what to do. I banged on some neighbors' doors, shouting—I don't remember whether in English or in German. The next thing I knew, the Polizei and an ambulance were there. The policeman was kind enough to give me a lift to the hospital. . . . Oh, Dad! I didn't know you were on the line, too. . . . Yeah, I'm okay. Just a little shaken up."

*A little shaken up?*

"Yes, I called Oskar just before I called you. He should be here any moment. Dad, I have no idea what's wrong with her. We were having a great day. Next thing I knew, she was out. . . . No, I didn't even check to see if she was breathing. How stupid is *that*? You went to all the trouble to teach Carson and me first aid and CPR, and I totally spazzed out. If I weren't so worried, I'd be embarrassed."

*Oh, there's Oskar!*

"Hey, Oskar just got here. I have to go. I'll call you back as soon as I know something. . . . Yeah, I'll be all right. . . . Love you guys, too."

⟛

I paced around the waiting room while Oskar consulted with the hospital staff. He had arrived only ten minutes earlier, but it seemed like he was taking forever. I jumped when he touched my shoulder from behind.

"Perhaps we can sit?"

"Oh, I don't know if I can sit, Oskar. I'm going crazy. What did you find out?"

He gestured toward a row of plastic chairs against the wall and took my arm. I let him lead me to a corner near the front window and ease me onto a seat.

"She is in—how is it said, *Intensivstation*?"

"Intensive care. The ICU."

"Ja. There is no news yet. I brought a list of her medicines for the doctor."

"What meds was she on? She must've kept them in her bedroom, because I never saw any pills in the bathroom or the kitchen. I should've asked, in case she needed help with them."

"She would not have told you. But it is good you think of it."

"Yeah, but a little late, don't you think?" I put my head in my hands. "Oh, Oskar, I don't believe how stupid I've been. Here I've lived with an infirm elderly lady for over a month now, and I have no idea what her condition is, what medications she's on, if there's a routine I should ensure she follows—nothing!"

"You are not her nurse, Fräulein McAllister."

"I know, I'm her scribe. We had that discussion." I shook my head. "I should've been more assertive."

He smiled. "Nein. If you had been more assertive, you would no longer be her scribe, either."

I peered at his face. "What's wrong with her? Why the meds?"

"She has poor sugar in the blood. The polio also haunts her."

"I didn't know polio could recur."

"It is, they say, *Postpolio Syndrom*. The disease does not really return. When it first comes, it kills many of the nerves in the muscles. Now that she is older, the nerves that remain do not

70

work so well. Her legs and back are weaker now than even before, when the disease was new to her body. She takes medicine for pain, but. . ." He shrugged.

"She's in pain? She doesn't show it. How much pain?"

"Katia will not say."

I looked toward the double doors into the hallway that led to the ICU. "Will we be able to see her?"

"I do not know." He glanced at his watch. "It is late. I will take you back to the house."

"Thanks, but I'm not going anywhere. Not until I find out how she is."

He reached for my hand. "We wait together, then, ja?"

I squeezed his fingers. "Yes."

⋘⋙

*"Herr Schultmann?"*

The nurse's voice jolted me from my stupor. I glanced at the wall clock. Two fifty a.m. I grimaced at a crick in my neck left over from my head lolling on my shoulder.

He was already on his feet. "Ja?"

I joined Oskar at his side, and the nurse looked at me. *"Sie sind auch mit* Fräulein Mahler?"

"Yes, I am also with her."

She smiled and nodded. "Ach, *Amerikanerin.*" She continued in English. "Fräulein Mahler rests now. Her signs are stable, but she has not awakened. We are testing for the cause of her coma."

"Coma? She's in a coma?" I gripped Oskar's arm.

He patted my hand and nodded to the nurse. "May we sit with her?"

"I will ask Doktor Frühling. There is no reason to sit with her, though, as she is not conscious."

"Please ask if we may visit anyway."

She nodded and disappeared through the double doors.

I lapsed into a blank stare, my mind whirling through a fog of anxiety and fatigue.

Oskar turned his head toward me, his smile apologetic. "Fräulein McAllister, forgive me. My hand requires blood."

"What—oh! I'm so sorry!" I released my vice grip on his arm.

The crow's-feet claimed his eyes as he flexed feeling back into his numb fingers. "I waited as long as I was able. It is rare I have such a lovely Fräulein on my arm. I did not wish to disturb you."

I laughed and slapped him on the shoulder. "You're incorrigible!"

"What means 'incorrigible'?"

"Guess!" On an impulse, I rose onto my tiptoes and kissed him on the cheek. "You really know how to ease tension, don't you?"

He stiffened, and the most remarkable shade of crimson spread across his face.

I giggled. "Why, Oskar, one would think you'd never been kissed."

His fingertips touched the spot where my lips met his cheek, and his ruddiness deepened, if that was possible. "As I say, it is rare." He cleared his throat and focused on the double doors.

My smile broke when the nurse returned.

"Herr Schultmann, Fräulein—?"

"McAllister."

She nodded. "Doktor Frühling asks you to return at regular visitor's hours, one o'clock this afternoon. She would like her patient to have complete quiet. If she is stable, you may sit with her then."

Oskar dipped his head. "Danke schön."

I added my thanks.

"Bitte schön."

The drive back to Karlshorst passed in silence. I peered out the side window at the sprinkle of night lights hinting at Berlin's skyline. A high red beam pulsed atop what I supposed was the Fernsehturm, the television tower at Alexanderplatz. I diverted my mind from worry over Fräulein Mahler's coma by trying to remember what I could about the tower. The Turm peaked at over twelve hundred feet, making it the tallest structure in the city. It not only served as an antenna tower but also hosted a restaurant near the top that rotated 360 degrees twice each hour. I had resolved to eat there at least once before I left Berlin, but I rarely had the time and never had the money.

On my first tour of the city, Greta Döring explained that the East German leader, Walter Ulbrecht, approved its construction in 1965 to be a hallmark of the atheist German Democratic Republic. Ironically, the design featured a massive stainless-steel globe that reflected sunlight in the shape of a brilliant white cross. So, the people of Berlin dubbed it the Rache des Papstes, the Pope's Revenge.

Thoughts of the pope nudged my mind back to Fräulein Mahler's Bible lying on the floor beside her wheelchair. I tried to erase the mental image of her still, pale face and her limp wrist. The remembrance would not deny itself, though, try as I might to close my mind against it. My tortured reverie snapped when Oskar pulled up to the curb in front of the house.

"I shall see you to the door."

"That's not necessary. I can—"

He silenced me with an upraised finger. I sat with my hands in my lap while he came around and opened my door. I accepted his hand and climbed out to the curb. He lifted up on the wrought-iron gate to minimize its screech across the concrete and took my elbow as we navigated the broken walkway. When we reached the door, I turned and hugged his neck.

"Thanks, Oskar."

*"Gute Nacht."*

"Good night."

Yawning, I stumbled through the doorway and headed down the darkened hall toward my room.

As tired as I was, the remaining hours of darkness crawled by, few of them spent in sleep. I dragged myself out of bed at first light and threw my robe on over my pajamas, letting the belt hang loose from the loops. Ignoring a scraggly tangle of hair clinging to my face, I reached for the door handle. Then I stopped.

Twenty minutes later, properly dressed and brushed, I turned the heat on under the coffeepot. The new day blossomed through the kitchen window in cumulus ochre and cirrus magenta, the first bulge of a brilliant sun just visible above the jagged row of trees opposite the road. In the waxing dawn, a flutter caught my attention. A petite bird sporting a light blue cap and a pale yellow vest skittered across the window ledge.

"Hey, little guy," I whispered. I was sure he looked back at me before he hopped to the rosebush and began pecking away.

I lifted the slice of bread from the toaster as soon as it popped up and slathered it with strawberry compote. Toast and coffee in hand, I stepped into the dining nook.

The table was just as I had left it—in disarray. Amid the tipped stacks of photos and letters sat my open laptop, now dark in sleep mode. The Sony rested against the keyboard, its USB umbilical still connected to, appropriately, the computer's motherboard. They snoozed, tucked into bed by Energy Star.

"Sure glad at least you guys got some sleep," I muttered through a yawn.

I settled onto the chair, propped my chin on my hand, and dipped a corner of my toast into my coffee. While I chewed, my eyes scanned the paperwork cluttering the table.

*So, where do I go from here? Organize what I've done so far and wait for Fräulein Mahler to recover, I suppose.*

*Recover.*

I blinked back an annoying swell of moisture rising toward my eyes at the mental image of her still body in the wheelchair. Another nibble of coffee-toast, and I began to shuffle the paper stacks back in order. She would never tolerate such a mess. Maybe I would clean the whole house before—what was this?

The edge of a black-and-white snapshot protruded from the last envelope I had shifted. Three torsos dominated the lower half of the glossy. I pulled the photo out and held it up to the early morning light.

The soldiers grinned at the camera with their arms draped over each other's shoulders. Their uniform coats hung open at the front, and their hats tipped forward at a cocky angle. On the white border at the bottom of the photograph was scrawled the date 17.12.1962. I turned the photo over and hoped someone had captioned it. No such luck.

I flipped it back to the front. The soldier on the far left looked like Friedrich—older, of course, than the teenager in the birthday picture, and his hair now short. Fräulein Mahler mentioned Friedrich entered the service with Heinrich Schwerer and Karl Werner, so I assumed them to be the other two soldiers. Something odd struck me, and I squinted more closely at the men's faces.

I laid down my toast and took the photo into the kitchen, where I held it up to the bright sunlight that had just burst through the window. My breath caught.

❧

"Ja, you may go in. Doktor Frühling will be along shortly."

I stepped quietly past the nurses' station and bowed my head against the sterile white glare of the overhead fluorescent lights. The odor of antiseptic and floor cleaner assailed my nostrils, a stark reminder of why I went out of my way to avoid hospitals. Oskar paused before the second door on the right then entered. I rubbed my bare arms against the chill as I followed him into the dimly lit ICU.

My throat constricted at the sight of Fräulein Mahler's small head lying motionless on the light green pillowcase. The muted overhead light cast deep shadows over her face and accentuated the hollows of her cheeks. Thin wires snaked down from an array of electronic equipment behind her railed stainless-steel bed and disappeared beneath the sheets. Equipment panels sparkled with tiny red, yellow, and green lights, their digital screens flickering with numbers and trace lines that monitored her pulse, blood pressure, and probably a bunch of other vital signs I knew nothing about. A bag of clear fluid hung from a tall stand beside her bed and fed a tube attached to an IV needle taped to the back of her right hand. Stillness pervaded the room but for an occasional beep or click from the monitors or a muffled telephone ring from the nurses' station outside the open door.

Oskar scooted a chair away from the wall to her bedside and settled onto it. He reached for her hand and slipped his beefy fingers beneath her frail palm. I was sure his gaze hadn't left her since we entered the room.

I moved another chair next to him and watched his face. "Her color is good. She looks peaceful."

"Ja." His whisper was hoarse.

"I'm looking forward to having her back home to continue our interview."

He nodded.

I laid the photograph on the blanket next to his hand. "Perhaps you can help with that. . . Herr Werner."

# Chapter 21

*. . .and I bet you've never seen a look like that come across a man's face. He went so pale, I thought I was going to have to call for a nurse. Oskar stared at the photograph for the longest time. I sat back and waited for him to say something. He didn't.*

*I've turned this over in my mind again and again, wondering whether I had been too abrupt. I was taught that it's important to control the conversation when you interview someone. Some interviewers advocate surprise as a good technique to do that. If you're too subtle, your subject can stall for time to develop a defense. Surprise puts him off balance and makes him easier to lead. Well, Herr Werner was definitely off balance, and I feel guilty. I'm not sure I like the technique so much.*

*He's across the waiting room from me as I write this, the photograph still in his hand. When the nurse asked us to step out so Fräulein Mahler could be bathed, I had to jostle his arm to get him to stand. He didn't look at me. I hope I haven't ruined our relationship, but if he is Karl Werner, an explanation is due. It's not like he's been completely honest.*

*The doctor should be here soon. She's supposed to tell us what she knows at this point—oops, here she comes. More later, gotta go.*

Doctor Frühling sat beside Oskar. I slid my chair over to them and introduced myself. Oskar didn't acknowledge my presence. I learned later that Doctor Frühling had spent two years at Johns Hopkins in Baltimore and her English was superb. I was relieved, since my German medical vocabulary was pretty weak.

The doctor folded her hands on her lap. "Fräulein Mahler rests well. Her breathing, pulse, and blood pressure are not strong, but acceptable. Our tests indicate what is called a hyperosmolar nonketotic coma. It is most common in the elderly who have diabetes."

"Diabetes?" I turned my head and stared at Oskar. "She has diabetes?"

He didn't respond.

The doctor continued. "Who has been with her the most often?"

My face flushed. "I have."

"You did not know of her condition?"

I threw a frown at Oskar. "No. Absolutely not."

"How did she seem the day of her seizure?"

"It was actually a pretty good day. We had a wonderful lunch, and she seemed happy—better than most days."

"How is she most days?"

"More tired lately, a little bit distracted maybe."

Doctor Frühling nodded. "Did she drink much water?"

"No, not so much. She doesn't like plain water. She drank a lot of tea, though."

"Did she have sugar with her tea?"

"Sometimes, but she usually takes it with honey."

"What else was there for lunch yesterday?"

"Bread, ham and cheese, more tea. She prepared a fruit platter, and we had wine."

Oskar shifted in his chair at the mention of the wine.

The doctor pulled a small pad from the pocket of her white jacket and jotted a note. "And after lunch, how was she?"

"She read quietly. I worked on other things, so we didn't talk. Late in the afternoon, I thought she had dozed off in her wheelchair, but she didn't respond when I tried to wake her."

Doctor Frühling laid down her pad. "Many things can combine to produce this coma. High sugar levels in the blood—here probably elevated by the fruit, wine, and honeyed tea— and dehydration are the most common factors."

My throat tightened. "I tried to get her to drink. She wouldn't take just water, so I kept making tea. I didn't know about the sugar—"

"It is not your fault, Fräulein, if you did not know of her diabetes." She patted my arm. "This type of coma—how do you Americans like to say?—sneaks up on you. There are other signs, like weakness in parts of the body, but that would hide in her post-polio condition. There is sometimes fever, a loss of vision, and sleepiness or confusion. If you were not with her in the afternoon, you would not have noticed these, unless she told you of them. The medications she takes could also have confused the symptoms."

"Will she be okay?"

"She should recover. We will treat her with insulin and hydrate her intravenously. Her dehydration has come too far, so simply to drink water will no longer help. She must be hydrated through her veins."

My shoulders relaxed, and I exhaled my relief.

Oskar spoke for the first time, his voice gravelly. "How soon will she awaken?"

She smiled. "It should not be long. We appear to have caught the coma early. You were very good, Fräulein McAllister, to get help so quickly. And the list of her medications, Herr Schultmann, was very helpful to guide a quick diagnosis and start treatment." Her tone quieted. "This kind of coma can lead to death."

❧

"Why didn't you tell me she was diabetic, Oskar?"

He turned the car onto the street leading to Fräulein Mahler's house. "I told you of her poor blood sugar."

I crossed my arms. "But that was only yesterday, and just a blood-sugar problem doesn't necessarily mean full-blown diabetes. How was I supposed to know—"

"You will not scold me, Fräulein McAllister."

An edge I had never before heard in his voice brought me up short. "But—"

He pulled to the curb. "I will return in one hour. Bitte, have your bags packed. I will take you back to the university. The interview is over."

A wave of hurt and confusion prickled my forehead. "Now wait just a minute—"

"One hour." He got out of the car.

By the time he walked around and opened my door, the confusion had given way to irritation. I refused his hand and pushed past him out of the car. On the walkway, I spun around. "You can't just kick me out like this!"

He scraped the gate open and did not reply.

"Oskar! Talk to me. What's going on?"

He lifted his head but did not meet my eyes. "I am sorry, but you have become a threat to us."

*A what? A threat?* I stood at the gate, mouth open but useless. A myriad of words crowded my mind, but none of them could locate my voice.

He climbed back into the Audi and drove off.

My redheaded blood began to percolate and took only a moment to boil over. I glared at the car as it turned the corner at the end of the street. "Oh, no you don't, mister. It's not going to be that easy."

❧

I paced the front room, afraid even to think about my next move until I cooled down. One thing was certain: I wasn't going anywhere. I had a job to do, and I was going to finish it.

Besides, Fräulein Mahler had retained me, not Oskar—Karl—whoever he was! She would be the one to fire me, nobody else.

On the fifth pass by the dining nook, my blood finally dipped below the boiling point, and I stopped pacing. I surveyed the uncountable hours of effort and emotion represented by the equipment and paperwork strewn across the table. Memories of meals and conversations—the missteps, the subtle confidences, and especially her captivating smile—fueled the emotion, and my blood temperature began to climb again.

*No, I'm not finished, Herr Werner. I've barely begun.*

I tightened my jaw and set to work. The laptop, recorder, and documentation went on the floor against the wall. The centerpiece and embroidered runners were banished to the kitchen. I pushed two of the dining chairs against the wall near my equipment and files. All that remained were two chairs opposite each other across a bare table. My mind flew back to an interrogation scene I once saw on a *Law & Order* rerun. A mirthless smile flirted with my lips as I settled onto the chair facing the front room, my back to the window. My face would be shadowed against the glare of the afternoon light. Herr Werner's would not. I folded my hands on the table and waited.

≈≈≈

The Audi's familiar sputter grew then choked off at the curb. I narrowed my eyes at the door.

*Brace yourself, Herr Werner. The Nürnberg Trials were a sideshow compared to what you're about to go through.*

I didn't respond to the rap on the door. Or the second rap.

The door creaked open, and Oskar's sturdy silhouette filled the doorway. He stepped across the threshold and squinted into the dim room. "Fräulein McAllister?"

"Yes?"

My voice drew his focus. He frowned. "You have not prepared."

"On the contrary, Herr Werner, I am quite prepared."

His tone sharpened. "Karl Werner is dead. He must remain that way."

"Why don't you have a seat and tell me about it?"

"I have nothing to tell."

"Then I will guess, and you can tell me where I'm wrong."

He glanced behind himself at the door. When he turned forward again, his face was hard. "It is most important to both Fräulein Mahler and myself that you let this be."

"If it is most important to Fräulein Mahler, then it is most important to me. She has retained me to chronicle her life, and that is what I intend to do. It appears you are a larger part of the story than I realized—and, I'm guessing, than she realizes, too. Right so far?"

"I told you the interview has ended."

"She has the deciding vote on that, not you, Herr Werner."

"She cannot speak for herself. Surely you can see that—and stop calling me Herr Werner!"

"Then we wait until she can speak for herself, and you only become Herr Schultmann again when you sit down."

He glared at me and shot one more glance at the door. After a moment, he heaved a frustrated sigh and pulled the chair away from the table. He dropped onto the seat and laid his hands on his lap.

I leaned forward. "Why is it so important that Karl Werner is dead?"

"For reasons you cannot comprehend."

"I'm a pretty quick study. Try me."

He clenched his jaw and stared at the tabletop. Just as I began to fear he wouldn't budge, his eyes flicked up to mine. He took a deep breath.

≈≈≈

*"Karl! Here!" Friedrich signaled from the top step of the Friedrichsfelde U-bahn station.*

76

"Friedrich! What are you doing?" I looked over my shoulder then hurried to the stairs that led down to the subway platform.

"Come, quickly." He turned and took the steps two at a time.

I followed.

A train pulled up to the platform just as we reached the bottom of the stairs. He thrust a ticket into my hand and slipped through the door of the first car. I stepped in behind him, and we took a bench seat at the front of the car.

"You are in uniform, Friedrich! What are you thinking?"

"I am thinking they will not expect me to be dressed like this in public. Listen, there is not much time." He glanced around. A young couple had sprawled out on a seat at the rear of the car, but they were too tangled up in each other to notice us.

His voice dropped to a whisper barely audible above the rattle of the train. "Do you still want to go to the West?"

"Yes, of course. But it becomes more difficult every day."

"That is why we must go soon. I know of a place we can cross. Others have done so. I am sure we can make it."

"Where is this place?"

"The barrier is not yet strong along the River Spree."

"The river?"

Friedrich leaned his head closer to mine. "The fence is close to the river across from the Reichstag. I have heard of no obstacles in the water, although there are patrol boats. I know their schedule, at least a little—"

"A little?"

"Enough to know how to watch for them, what the interval is between patrols. We can get close enough to the barrier in our uniforms not to raise suspicion. Once in the water, we can swim most of the way beneath the surface."

"Friedrich, it is March. The river will be freezing!"

"Then they will not expect an attempt. It is perfect."

I rolled my eyes.

He grinned. "It is almost April. . ."

"Ach! It will still be cold!"

"Come, Karl. It is now or never. How long do you think I can continue to hide? And you said your unit may deploy to Magdeburg soon. Your chance will be lost then."

I rubbed my forehead. "I do not receive another pass for three more weeks."

"That is good. It gives me more time to watch and to plan."

I closed my eyes. Everything was happening so quickly.

"Karl?"

"Okay, okay. We will meet where we used to near the Brandenburger Tor. Fifteen April. I can be there by ten o'clock at night."

"Good!" He slapped me on the shoulder.

Friedrich stood up as the train approached the Bahnhof Lichtenberg station. "I get off here. Stay on the train until the next stop."

We shook hands, and he pounded me on the shoulder again, the broad smile still on his face. "Fifteen April, ten o'clock, near the Brandenburg Gate. Don't be late!" Then he was gone.

I sat alone as the train moved away from the platform and picked up speed, wondering what on earth I had just agreed to. Another furtive look around the car revealed that the young couple had still not come up for air.

❧

Oskar fell silent, and I studied his face. "I know there were many who escaped to the West after the Wall went up, but why you? Why did you want to leave?"

"If you have to ask that question, you would not understand the answer."

# Chapter 22

## May 15

*Dear Mom and Dad,*

*Things are pretty shaky right now. Fräulein Mahler is still in a coma, and Oskar has become stiff and perfunctory. I know how I feel about Fräulein Mahler, but I'm not sure how to feel about Oskar.*

*I hate the thought of losing a friend, but stepping back may help me approach the interview more objectively. He has to understand why I'm doing this. I owe it to Fräulein Mahler, and he appears to be a huge part of her story. I don't know; how would you feel? What would you do?*

*I got spoiled with him bringing groceries by so often. It's been four days now since he's brought food, and the fridge is just about empty. Looks like I'll be doing some shopping. How about another money order, Dad? (Kidding)*

*He's agreed to pick me up every morning to visit the hospital. The ride in this morning was r-e-a-l-l-y quiet. I may have to coerce him to spend the afternoons at the house to fill me in on his side of the story. Well, if I have to force him, I will. Whatever it takes. . . .*

⊰≫⊱

". . . it takes a lot out of you, doesn't it?"

He didn't shift his gaze from Fräulein Mahler's face. "Takes a lot out of. . . ?"

"I'm sorry, Herr Schultmann, that's not going to work anymore. I think your command of English is better than you let on."

His mouth twitched. "No. I do not like to see Katia—Fräulein Mahler—in such a condition. Does it not take a lot out of you, too?"

"Of course."

"Na schön. . ."

Very well, indeed.

I sat back and swallowed through a tight throat. The chilled edge to his voice was such a contrast to the easy warmth I'd come to love. I missed how his eyes disappeared behind his contagious smile, his. . .humility. That word fit him best, now that I thought about it. The old Oskar was the warmest, most unassuming man I had ever met. The new Herr Werner-Schultmann was stiff and detached. I wondered when—if—I would see Oskar again.

Doctor Frühling's voice startled us both. "She still sleeps." She stood at the foot of the bed and studied the chart in her hand.

"Is that bad?" I asked.

She arched her eyebrows. "I thought she would revive by this time."

Oskar returned his attention to Fräulein Mahler. He brushed a wisp of hair from her forehead. "I hoped so, as well."

The doctor stepped around the bed and inspected an electronic monitor. She lifted a stream of paper that fed from a box beneath the equipment stand and scanned the jagged trace burned over the graph lines. Her expression wasn't encouraging.

"Doctor. . . ?" I was unsure exactly what to ask. "Is it abnormal?"

"Nein, that is the problem. Everything looks normal."

Oskar looked up at her. "Then why does she still sleep?"

"I do not know. I will order some more tests."

I pressed for something—anything—to cling to. "Do you have any ideas, or even guesses, as to what it might be?"

Doctor Frühling glanced at me. "Guessing is not a recommended way to do business in my profession, Fräulein McAllister."

I reddened. "I'm sorry. How about any theories?"

She smiled. "Not yet. The tests should tell us more."

⟡

The Audi edged from the hospital parking lot into traffic. I studied Oskar's face. He kept his eyes to the front.

"Yesterday you told me of planning your escape. What happened then?"

He narrowed his eyes at the road. "I am not certain I want to continue this discussion. I do not see how it could become—how do you say, constructive."

"Well, Herr Werner, let's just see where it leads."

"You are not to call me Herr Werner."

"Oskar Schultmann talks to me. Karl Werner does not."

His knuckles whitened against the steering wheel. "You do not understand. Katia must never know I am—I was Karl Werner. What will happen if you let it slip out in front of her after she awakens?"

I dropped my gaze. "Gee, you're right. That would be a bad thing, wouldn't it?"

The idea of emotional blackmail was abhorrent to me, but I needed that story, and Oskar's deception was not worthy of protecting at the expense of what I owed Fräulein Mahler.

I glanced over at him. His taut jaw told me I had scored.


We settled at opposite sides of the dining table. I laid my pad and pencil on the table, but when I pulled out the Sony, he shook his head. I shrugged and slipped it back into the flap of my backpack—but not before I pressed the RECORD button. I was beginning to feel more like a spy than a journalist.

He focused on the table. "Friedrich and I met at the appointed time and place. . . ."

⟡

*"Karl!"*

*"Quiet, Friedrich!" I glanced over my shoulder. "Why must you talk so loud?"*

*I could sense his grin through the darkness as I ducked into the narrow doorway.*

*"Listen. The river behind the Reichstag is less than fifty meters wide. We can swim most of it under the water. You know that."*

*I shrugged, my skepticism masked by the night.*

*"The patrol boats vary their schedule, but I have not seen an interval of less than fifteen minutes. We will wait for the boat to pass then shed our uniforms and slip into the water. You go first. I will follow."*

*"You should go first. If something happens, the second man will more likely be caught than the first."*

*"Nonsense! Do not argue. I have thought this through. We do it as I planned, okay?"*

*I sighed. "Okay."*

*"When you need air, you know how to break the surface of the water with no noise. We have both been trained on this."*

*"Yes."*

*"Try to make it at least halfway across before you rise for air."*

*"Okay."*

*He grasped my arm. "I am so excited. This will work. I know it!"*

*I patted his hand absently, while my mind raced over what lay ahead.*

*He tightened his grip. "I need to ask you something."*

*"What is it?"*

*"I have told you of my family."*

*"Yes, of course."*

*"You know I go to the West to prepare a place for them."*

*"I know this. You have spoken of it many times."*

*"If something happens to me—and it will not—but if it does, remember your promise to continue what I have started. You must somehow get my family across to the West. Especially Katia. I know there are doctors who can help her. Maybe she can go to America."*

*"I do not know—"*

*"You have promised. It is all I ask."*

*"Okay, okay. I will do what I can. But I do not want to fulfill this promise. If it comes to a choice, you must succeed rather than I. You have a family. I do not."*

*"We will do what we need to do."*

*We clasped hands then settled into the doorway to wait.*


Tiny beads of sweat glistened on Oskar's forehead.

I set down my pencil. "If you need to rest, we can take a break."

"Nein, I have begun, and I will continue. Perhaps then you will understand."

⚙


*The night hours seeped away one minute at a time. I huddled into the back corner of a covered doorway with my overcoat pulled around me. Friedrich sat near the open front, watching and listening. He decided we would wait until after midnight before we moved closer to the river. The guards would be less alert at that time, and there would be fewer patrol boats. I trusted him, as he was in the Grenztruppen and should know these things.*

*At two o'clock in the morning, he nudged me. It was time to go.*

*We kept to the shadows as we worked our way toward the river. The water was black and still. I wondered if I would be able to endure its cold, but it was too late to think of that now.*

*Fifteen minutes later, we crouched by the corner of a building closest to the water. Two barrier wires stretched from an iron peg in the brick to the first crossbeam stanchion. The brace sat far enough from the wall that we could squeeze between the wires and remain hidden. Friedrich told me that the engineers had paid little attention to this part of the barrier yet. They considered the river enough of an obstacle, and there were other places that needed more urgent attention. So, only these two wires marked the death zone and there was no sign of alarms. Still, we tried not to disturb either wire when we slipped through.*

*The air was heavy with mist that obscured the moon and stars. A dull yellow halo circled a streetlight not far away, but it did little to push back the darkness. I thought of my warm cot in Potsdam and was surprised that it did not beckon to me in my mind. I was ready for the escape. I just did not know if I was ready for the freezing river.*

*We edged along the building until the growl of a diesel motor suddenly echoed across the water. Friedrich tapped my shoulder. We stretched out on the ground and tucked ourselves low against the cold brickwork. A patrol boat chugged by only thirty meters away. Its searchlight scanned the river, but the guard did not raise his light high enough to spot us.*

*I squinted past the boat but could not see the Reichstag across the river through the mist. I swallowed, still unsure if I had done the right thing in agreeing to this. The patrol boat rounded a bend downstream, and the sound of its engine faded.*

*Friedrich turned his head. "Now!"*

*We wriggled out of our overcoats and threw our hats onto the ground beside them. Then we jumped up and ran.*

"Herr Schultmann, you're shaking. Are you all right?"

I wondered if I should have pushed him into this, but at the same time, I didn't want him to stop. His every word enthralled me. I could almost feel the cold brick scuff my back as I shrank back from the patrol boat's searchlight, the chilly night air biting my face and burning my lungs. But there my imagination failed me. I had never known mortal danger or the fear it engendered like what Oskar must have felt. I tried to picture myself bent low in a frantic race across concrete and dirt, my teeth clenched against the exertion and the fear—then my next gasp of air cut short as a bullet hissed out of the darkness and smashed into my spine. I'd crash to the ground, the coarse concrete scraping my face bloody. Pain and cold would shudder through me as I lay there, immobile. Numbness would gradually extinguish the fire burning through my chest then deaden my mind. The last thing my dulled ears would hear would be pounding feet, hoarse shouts, and profane congratulations between the men who had killed me. The hazy glow of the streetlight would become fuzzier then finally die as my eyelids shut out this world forever.

Then nothing.

*Nothing?*

I forced a deep swallow. "Herr Schultmann?"

His eyes had closed.

# Chapter 23

*It's late enough they should be home from church.*

"Hi, it's Maddy—who is this? . . . Umm, why are you answering our phone, Moira? . . . Mom and Dad just left? And you and Carson are at the house? Alone?"

*This is weird.*

"What's going on? . . . Which movie? . . . Okay, my parents are going, too. That's cool. Hey, since Carson is indisposed at the moment, can you do me a favor? In the desk drawer there by the phone is my mom's address book. Would you pull it out, please? . . . Purple flowers on the cover—yeah, that's the one. I need my Grandpa and Grandma McAllister's address. Grandpa's birthday is coming up, and I want to send a card or something. . . . Are you still there?"

*M comes right after L, Moira. C'mon.*

"Oh, sorry. I should've warned you. There's more torn envelope corners with return addresses jammed in that book than there are addresses actually written down. I've had to pick them up off the floor, too. Are you at the M's yet? . . . You should have an entry for a J & M McAllister. . . . Two addresses? . . . Terrebonne? . . . No, I need the one in Detroit. . . . One six three Thompson. What's the zip? And pass me the phone number, too, please. . . . Okay, thanks, Moira. You have fun with Squirt at the movies. . . . Yeah, be sure to ask him why I call him Squirt. He'll get a chuckle out of that. . . . See you, too. Bye, Moira."

<hr>

I set my backpack against the ICU wall and stepped over to the bedside while Oskar checked in with the nurses' station. Fräulein Mahler looked comfortable, like she would open her eyes any moment and say, "*Guten Morgen*," with that wonderful lilt. I didn't realize until now how much I missed that. Her face appeared serene, younger, it seemed. Her color was better, the wrinkles not so pronounced. I reached out to touch her hand but jerked back at Oskar's voice.

"There is nothing new." He moved to the other side of the bed and gazed down at her face.

I glanced up at him. "She looks good."

He didn't reply.

The afternoon crawled by with no words between Oskar and me to hurry it along. Doctor Frühling was not on duty, so there was no chance of an update. I sat against the wall and watched him. I don't think he took his gaze from her the entire time.

An inspiration struck me, and I reached for my backpack. I had taken an art class a couple years ago, which only taught me that I had no talent for drawing. Still, I thought the composite of Oskar and Fräulein Mahler against the backdrop of the ICU cluttered with sensors and cables was an interesting study. Perhaps I could get at least an abstract sketch. It was worth a try.

I pulled a clean pad from the main pocket then groped around in the front compartment for a pencil. My fingers brushed an object jammed against the left side of the pocket. I lifted it from beneath the nylon flap. A pink-covered *New Testament with Psalms* lay in my hand, curled at the corners from lying cramped in my backpack for who knew how long. My grandparents gave it to me when I graduated from Confirmation classes at St. Luke's. I think I was twelve or thirteen years old; I don't remember for sure. Neither did I remember putting it in the backpack when I packed my bags for Germany. I rubbed my thumb against a dark smudge obscuring the gold-embossed title. Some of the discoloration came off, but it still looked a bit worse for wear.

I flipped it open and stopped at a color illustration of the Crucifixion inserted among the pages of the twenty-seventh chapter of St. Matthew's Gospel. Although I had seen the depiction countless times through the years, the figure of Christ struck me, His head bent under the weight of perfect submission and indescribable pain. The image forced my eyes back to Fräulein Mahler. Here were two examples of defeated suffering I had yet to comprehend, yet her serenity stood in such stark contrast to His agony. Somewhere in the back of my mind, the vision loomed of her seated in her wheelchair with her fingers stroking the worn cover of her Bible, her head tilted back, her smile subtle. She ended each day in such peaceful repose, her heart and her mind focused upward. I glanced back at His head canted downward. Somewhere during those evenings, I fancied, His gaze and hers met.

My throat tightened, and I thumbed through a few more pages—awkwardly, it seemed to me. A voice from the hallway pulled me from my reverie.

"It is time for Fräulein Mahler's bathing. Would you please excuse us?" The nurse stood in the doorway with an apologetic smile.

Oskar nodded and brushed Fräulein Mahler's forehead with his fingertips, a parting ritual he adopted from our first visit. I replaced my pad and hoisted the backpack to my shoulder. We headed toward the door, then I paused. I glanced back at the bed then at the Bible in my hand. I looked up at the nurse. As though she perceived my thoughts, she nodded.

I moved back to the bedside and tucked the precious book beneath Fräulein Mahler's listless fingers.

Oskar did not look back.

⚬⚬⚬

Back at the house, we sat again on our respective sides of the dining table. "You left me hanging yesterday, right in the middle of your escape."

His brow furrowed. "Some things cannot be hurried."

⚬⚬⚬

*At the embankment, we flattened ourselves against the dirt. We kicked loose our boots and tore off our shirts but left our trousers on to be presentable when we crossed into the West, as silly as it seems now.*

*Friedrich swung his legs over the edge of the low wall reinforcing the embankment.*

*I stooped beside him and stared at the black water, its surface shimmering with wavelets from the patrol boat.*

*"Remember, swim as far as you can before you surface for air. Then, do it quietly. Go!"*

*I laid on my stomach and eased myself over the lip of the retaining wall. When my feet slipped into the river, I did not feel the cold, only an ache, like when ice touches bare skin. I lowered myself to my waist and jolted as water poured over my beltline and filled my trousers. My leg muscles cramped."*

*"Karl, hurry!" Friedrich hissed.*

*I tried not to gasp aloud when my shoulders reached the level of the water. My chest convulsed, and I did not think I would be able to breathe at all, let alone gulp enough air to swim halfway across the river. Friedrich slid in beside me. He grabbed my shoulder, took a breath, and disappeared. I followed him.*

*We kicked off from the wall into blackness. I did not open my eyes, since there would be nothing to see and I feared the icy water might blind me. The current ran stronger than the surface of the river betrayed, so I angled upstream against the drift. I stroked and kicked as hard as I could and must have moved ahead of Friedrich, as twice his arm hit my leg.*

*When my lungs felt ready to burst, I arched my back toward the surface. I reached above me to feel the surface silently with my fingers. Suddenly, I hit my head on something hard. I tried to kick upward, but the back of my neck caught on what felt like a cable. They had begun to construct a barrier in the river!*

*I pushed away from the cable and flailed my arms. Friedrich and I broke the surface together with a splash and gasped for air. The noise shattered the stillness of the night. Stealth was no longer possible. Now there was only speed. Friedrich must have realized the same thing, and we floundered through the water side by side. Suddenly, he grabbed the collar of my undershirt, and I looked up. We had become disoriented when we surfaced and were swimming back toward the East!*

*We turned, and I tried to see the western bank, but it was too dark. I guessed where it must be and stroked in that direction. Friedrich paced me at my side.*

*I do not know how much time passed before I heard the shouts. A searchlight flashed from the eastern bank, and we ducked under the surface. I knew the border guards would see the broken water and guess where we would come back up, but there was no other choice than to keep swimming.*

*My hand hit the soft rise of the western embankment just as I ran out of air. I reached forward and clawed at the muck for a handhold and kicked my legs against the current. Then I surfaced directly into the beam of the searchlight. Friedrich splashed up to my left, just out of the light. The first shot sounded across the river, and I jerked at a sharp burning in my shoulder. A second bullet kicked water into my face, and another splattered the mud just above the waterline. I ducked back under the water.*

*For some reason, I turned and swam upstream against the current. I do not know if I thought they would assume I would float downstream, or if I thought anything at all. I only wanted to get out of that cursed light. I heard more plops and three bullets hissed through the water around me. I had lost track of Friedrich.*

*When I resurfaced, it was dark. I looked over my shoulder. The searchlight beam swept the water's edge ten meters behind me. I jumped as a hand grabbed the waistline of my trousers. Friedrich sputtered into the chilly air at my side. "Go now, up the riverbank. It is our last chance!"*

*We lunged for the slope and pulled ourselves halfway out of the water. Pain from the wound in my shoulder melted into the aches and cramps seizing all my muscles. The mud and grass gave us no handholds, and my wet trousers felt like an iron weight chained to my body. I was exhausted. I did not think I could make it.*

*Both Friedrich and I cleared the water but then slipped on the wet riverbank halfway back into the river. It was then I heard the roar of the patrol boat's engine. Over my shoulder I saw the prow turn the bend in the river less than one hundred meters away. Its searchlight traced the bank upstream toward us.*

*Friedrich's hoarse voice choked in my ear. "Karl, go! I will push your feet. Go! Now!"*

*"Friedrich, I cannot. You will—"*

*Friedrich slapped me in the face and yelled, "Go! Do not forget your promise!"*

*He grasped my trousers and pulled me up ahead of him. I dug my feet into the mud and pumped my legs as fast as I could. As he slid back toward the water, he grabbed the bottom of my foot and shoved upward. The searchlight found us just as I grasped the trunk of a small sapling near the top of the slope. A burst of gunfire churned the dirt around me. I pulled on the tree and threw myself onto the top edge of the bank. When I turned around, Friedrich was halfway up the slope. Shots from the patrol boat tore up the embankment and splashed geysers of water up from the river's edge.*

*I reached for his hand as a line of bullets crossed his back.*

⊸⧉⊷

"Herr Schultmann?" I covered his trembling hand with my own. "We can stop now. You don't need to do this."

His eyes, wide and tear-brimmed, met mine. He shook his head then coughed and continued his story.

⊸⧉⊷

*Friedrich tumbled backward into the river. Then there was nothing. I stared at the water until the patrol boat's spotlight blinded me. Another barrage of bullets threw dirt into my face and cut down the small tree next to me. I rolled back and pressed to the ground, barely able to breathe.*

*Shouts came from the direction of the Reichstag, and two flashlight beams bobbed through the darkness toward me. The searchlights blinked off, and everything went black. A pair of hands pulled me up and dragged me away from the edge of the riverbank. A moment later, I was shivering on the concrete sidewalk behind the Reichstag.*

*A deep voice asked, "Are you hurt?"*

*I raised my head and stared into a man's bearded face bent close to mine. "Only a small wound," I gasped. "But my friend—do you see my friend?"*

*He shook his head. "There is no one but you."*

*Someone threw a coat over me. I laid my head back, and tears flooded my eyes.*

⤳

I sat back and let Oskar relive the tears until his trembling shoulders settled and he wiped his eyes on a sleeve. His words came in rasps. "And so you see why it is so important that my name remains Oskar Schultmann."

"Forgive me, Herr Schult—Oskar." I leaned forward and took his hand again. "I still don't understand. Why can't you resume your real identity? This all happened over forty years ago."

His eyes searched mine with an intensity I'd never before seen in them. "There are two reasons. I mean this with no disrespect, but try hard to understand what I am about to say."

I nodded.

"First, Katia clings to the hope that her brother survived. The hope is small, because she has never heard from him. But she has now lost her entire family, and that small hope is all she has. If she discovers I am Karl Werner, she will know it was Friedrich who was killed that night. Her hope will die, and I fear so may she."

"I understand. What's the second reason?"

"I was a deserter from the Volksarmee and an escapee to the West. Either one of those things could have me killed, or worse yet, have me sent back to the East. The two of them together would certainly do so. I have built a fine life as Oskar Schultmann. It makes no sense to disrupt that life."

"But it was so long ago. Surely you don't still fear retribution."

"That is the part that will be most difficult for you to understand, Fräulein McAllister. Life in the East during what you Americans call the Cold War was something you cannot understand without experience. After Germany reunified, the government opened what official records were not destroyed after the fall of the SED. They proved what we who lived in the East already knew. Almost two hundred fifty thousand people worked for the Stasi. Their own officers admitted they had recruited at least two million informants, both unofficial collaborators and regular spies. This means one out of every seven East Germans worked with or for the Stasi as an officer, worker, or informant."

I sat back, unable to grasp these kinds of numbers.

"You trusted no one. The son spied on his father, the pastor on his church, the postman on his neighbors. You began to regard your pet dog with suspicion. A coworker would drink to your health one evening, and the next day betray you for a slip of a tongue too loosened by the next beer. Cameras, hidden and open, covered the streets in East Berlin and monitored every move of every person. Never in history has there been such tight control over a people as there was in East Germany."

"But you were free now. You had made it to the West."

A sad smile thinned his lips. "Before the Wall opened, West Berlin was already overrun with Soviet and East German spies. I tried to disappear, but I could never be sure of my safety. I looked over my shoulder at every street corner, changed apartments after only a few months. Today I had a beard, tomorrow a mustache. The changes puzzled my new acquaintances and coworkers. I quit jobs, gave excuses. There was no rest, Fräulein McAllister, no rest."

I shook my head. "But the Stasi collapsed with the Wall over twenty years ago. Why did you still fear them?"

He set his face. "Think for a moment. Try to place yourself in Berlin in the months following November 1989. A former Stasi spy now walked the same streets as the newly released prisoner he betrayed. An ex-Stasi officer now rode the U-bahn across from a person he tortured and imprisoned. More than one spy disappeared; more than one officer died in a dark backstreet. Then there would be revenge. The stalker would be stalked, the killer killed. The institutions that built this way of life vanished, but the way of life did not. Who knows how many generations it will take for the fear, confusion, and hate to go away? In your own country, there are those who still fight your Civil War in their hearts and it ended over 150 years ago."

I closed my eyes and massaged my temples with my fingertips.

His voice tightened. "You must understand: ours was a confused generation. We were lost in time. After the war, the Communists assumed control of our lives with no time for us to recover from the Nazi propaganda that had vilified them. Overnight the enemy became the friend. We were to embrace this friend with our whole hearts. Not to do so was to risk fortune and even life. Those who created the Deutsche Demokratische Republik denied any flaws. They demanded a perfect image of it in the hearts and the minds of the people. It became our forced reality. Western imperialism was now the enemy. Our children were taught from the earliest ages that you, American Fräulein McAllister, were the new evil and to revile you."

I flinched at the personal inflection. He didn't appear to notice.

"For forty years the SED pressed the East German people into the mold it needed to stay in power. Then, almost without warning, the Wall collapsed. The Party and the Stasi disintegrated. There was no more German Democratic Republic. Our perfect reality vanished, our identity dissolved. We were now the nameless half of a united Germany allied with a West we had been conditioned to hate. Once again, the enemy became the friend overnight with no time for us to understand how or why."

I nodded as the first glimmer of understanding flickered to life. "And you, Oskar?"

He stared at the table. "And I still ran. The Wall, the only barrier that gave me even a little protection from the East, was gone. Not only could former Stasi now walk into the West, but so could those of the Volkspolizei and Volksarmee. When would I sit at a café and look up to see former comrades-in-arms staring at me from the next table? When would I be in a shop and see a former neighbor—perhaps one I knew as an informant, or one who thought me to be a spy—putting my groceries into a sack?"

I shook my head. "But over time you must have begun to relax. No one can survive that kind of pressure for so many years. Besides, you grew older. Your appearance changed, and you would become more difficult to recognize."

He reached into his shirt pocket and flipped the black-and-white snapshot onto the table. "You recognized me from a faded forty-three-year-old photograph, and we have just met."

I slumped and closed my eyes. "Oh, Oskar, I am so sorry. . . ."

His hand gently touched mine. "It was only a matter of time, Fräulein McAllister. It just happened to be you." Then his voice lightened, and a trace of the old Oskar smoothed its tone. "This makes you a good journalist, nein?"

When I opened my misty eyes, his disarming smile was back. Something pushed me to my feet and around the table. I dropped to my knees by the side of his chair. "I've missed you, Oskar," I whispered.

We embraced, my head pressed against his chest, for how long? Who knew?

# Chapter 24

*Dear Mom and Dad,*

*Oskar told me the rest of his story this afternoon and we've reconciled. I didn't realize how much I had hated calling him Herr Schultmann until the first "Oskar" rolled off my tongue again. I'll fill you in on what I left out of my last letter. I can't imagine living like he did. They'd have committed me to an asylum years ago.*

*It didn't occur to me until later, though, that his personal safety was a secondary reason he kept his identity a secret. His primary concern was to shield Fräulein Mahler from the loss of hope over her brother. I'm not sure exactly how I'm going to handle this when she awakens. Of course, I'll honor his wishes.*

*Karl Werner is indeed dead. . . .*

*. . .and we rejoice and thank God you have survived, Maria. We must see each other. Please, write back soon. I remain,*

*Your loving sister, Anna*

I laid the letter on the table and rubbed my eyes, physically and emotionally drained. Oskar left after we shared what little remained in the fridge—two stale Brötchen, a small lump of butter, a slab of swiss cheese I had to scrape the mold from, and one soft apple. He apologized and said he would be by in the morning with breakfast and a resupply of groceries.

"I'll be happy to pay for the food," I said and reached for my purse.

He patted my arm. "Fräulein McAllister. . ." His smile lingered in my mind's eye long after he walked out the door.

I grinned and shook my head. *I love that man.*

The afternoon sun filtered through the lace sheers over the window. I glanced at my watch. Five fifteen. A yawn I'd been wrestling for the last half hour finally pinned me, and I surveyed the documents littering the tabletop. The letter to Tante Maria was among those I hadn't sorted on the first day. There was no date to pinpoint it, but it must have been in the mid-1940s, since it appeared they had just discovered she was still alive. It had never been mailed; it hadn't even made it into an envelope. I wondered why. Maybe Fräulein Mahler could clear that up when she revived.

*When she revived.*

I leaned back and stared at the ceiling. "What's going on with you, Fräulein Mahler? Everybody but you thinks you should be awake."

Shuffling the letter into the "Uncertain" pile, I returned to the stack of documents. Two aged envelopes tied together with twine lay at the top of the stack. I tugged at the bow and slipped off the twine, but the glue from the top envelope flap stuck to the one beneath it. I didn't want to damage any of the family records, so I took a deep breath and peeled the first envelope slowly from the bottom one. Thankfully, with a little urging, the yellowed papers separated intact.

I held the topmost letter up to the light. A faded *Juli 1945* struggled through the smudged postmark, but the precise date was beyond salvage. I eased the letter from its sheath. The German was fairly simple, so I could read it without much difficulty.

*Dearest Sister,*

*I know you received my first letter, as I have your reply here beside me. I was over-joyed to hear from you. There were days in Auschwitz and Bergen-Belsen that I believed I would never see any of my beloved family again. Praise God you survived the war! We must plan a reunion, whenever that may be.*

*My health continues to improve. Many of the women and children from the camp who have come to this hospital have not survived. There are burials every day. I was fortunate to be at Bergen-Belsen for only a few months. The typhus did not ravage me as it did so many others.*

*I have met a man, a Canadian soldier. I did not tell you in the first letter, because I was not sure how he felt about me, nor I about him. He is quiet, gentle, and very kind. He has hardly left my side, on or off duty. His name is Jim. This morning, he asked me to marry him, Anna! I said no, but not happily. Is it wrong to have such feelings for a man when I do not yet know the fate of my own husband? I feel as though I am being unfaith-ful, although Izaak and I did not see each other after leaving Ravensbrück. My gracious, that was five years ago! How do the days drag by so slowly, while the years race by so quickly?*

*I pray each day for Lilli-Anna and Kammbrie. They must be little ladies now, almost seven years old. I pray they reached safety, now that you have told me of the Dudeks, praise God for them! It tore my heart from me when the Gestapo dragged us out the door, my baby girls asleep in the nursery. I hope yet to find them, but they were too young to remember me now. I wonder if they know, if they understand. Please pray with me that they understand.*

*I hope I will soon be strong enough to leave the hospital. Perhaps Jim can bring me to you. You will love him, too.*

*I must stop now. It is late, and they are calling for lights-out in the ward.*

*I remain always,*
*Your loving sister, Maria*

I sat back and studied the writing. The script was strong, although a little shaky, not at all what I would expect from a concentration camp survivor. Tante Maria was another spirit I will never be able to comprehend. What kind of woman can endure such horror and still write "praise God"—two times, no less—in such a short letter? I thought of my pink gift Bible snuggled into Fräulein Mahler's hand, then of her brown leather Bible shiny not just with age but with use. The thought pulled me from my chair.

I set the letter down and crossed to the corner of the front room, where I dropped to my knees. Her Bible lay facedown, a few of its pages creased and protruding to the side. I'd forgotten completely about it in the flurry of activity when the ambulance arrived. As I eased it up from the floor, the binding separated where the fall had broken the spine. I gasped. She would be devastated at the damage to the precious book. I carefully closed it and examined the torn leather. The split along the spine was almost from top to bottom, with only a few threads of the binding matte holding the cover together.

Carefully, I aligned the covers over the pages and carried the Bible to the dining table. I pulled two thin rubber bands from the side flap of my backpack and stretched them over the cover. Then I laid the Bible on a sheet of legal-size paper and folded the sides of the paper over the book. Another four rubber bands to stabilize the parcel and I set it aside. Perhaps Oskar could repair it, or have it repaired.

I returned my attention to the tabletop, and the second envelope captured my eye. The postmark on this one was better preserved.

*31 Juli 1945.*

I eased the fragile page out of the envelope and opened it.

*Dearest Sister,*

*I have not received your reply to my last letter, but I must write quickly. There was a refugee in the ward yesterday seeking his wife. When we spoke, I discovered he was from Auschwitz. He knew Izaak, but the news is sad. My Izaak fell ill last winter, too weak to work. They took him away. I am sure I know where. Please pray for his soul for me. I do not know if God will accept my petitions, as I married outside the faith. But I will pray anyway.*

*Jim has been told his unit returns home next week. He wants me to go with him. He has asked me to marry him again. I said yes, Anna! I know Izaak would want me to remarry. I would wish it for him.*

*I so wanted to come and see you, but there now appears to be no time. I hope to be strong enough to cross the Atlantic. We travel in two days to Bremerhaven, where we will board a hospital ship for Nova Scotia. I must go to a refugee camp when we arrive until I receive my papers. Another camp, Anna! Jim promises me it will not be like Auschwitz or Bergen-Belsen, but I am still afraid. He promises we will be able to go to his home in Montreal very soon after that.*

*My letters to Mama and Papa in Potsdam have not been answered. Do they still live there? Did they survive the war? Is Papa still angry with me? I am afraid to learn the answers to my questions.*

*I will return to visit you as soon as I have recovered. I promise you, if it is in God's will. I pray this letter reaches you soon. Perhaps you can come to me before we leave. I am so excited! I love Jim so much. Pray for me. Pray for us.*

*I will write from the ship, although it will not post until we reach land.*

*I remain,*
*Your loving sister, Maria*

I sifted through the stack of documents, but these appeared to be the only two letters from Tante Maria. I sat back and reread the letter.

Something bothered me, but I wasn't sure what it was.

# Chapter 25

*...and you would love to read through these things, Dad, being such a history buff.*
*Especially the letters and photos from the '40s. The memories they capture are so vivid, I*
*almost expect to hear a vintage Mercedes chug by outside.*

*Oh, by the way, I've got a couple of questions for you. Some things have been bother-*
*ing me, and these letters have made the itch a little worse. I'll try to get to the Internet*
*café soon to do a little research. Maybe I'll send you a quick e-mail.*

*Gotta go. Oskar will be here shortly.*

*Love, Maddy*

Oskar closed my door then took his place behind the wheel. Several questions cluttered my mind as the car pulled away from the curb, and I was frustrated at the lack of answers. I thought the ride to the hospital might better be spent in conversation.

"Oskar, what did you do in West Berlin before the Wall came down?"

He shrugged. "Some things I would prefer not to discuss. Mostly I found odd jobs. My first steady job was with the American Army at Clay Headquarters as a *Hausmeister.*"

"You mean janitor?"

"Ja, janitor. I swept the floors and the sidewalks, ran small errands inside the compound. As my English improved and I grew in their trust, I drove to other parts of the American Sector: Andrews Barracks, McNair Barracks, the housing quarters in Düppel. In 1975, I began to work full-time. The pay was good, and the Americans were kind to me."

"Did they know you had escaped from the East?"

"Not that I know. I learned of ways, legal and illegal, to obtain papers. To use the government was better, but slower. Also, I feared the authorities might send me back to the East, as had happened to others. I discovered a private group of sympathizers who made documents for escaped East Germans for no fee. It was with this group that I became Oskar Schultmann."

"I thought the Americans would have investigated you before they hired you."

"I am sure they did what they could. Records on many Germans were not complete after the war. They did not spend too much time checking the history of those of us in low jobs. As I said, there were many spies in West Berlin, and I think the Americans assumed some were among us. They did not investigate closely until we applied for full-time jobs. By then, I had made a good name for myself and had friends among the Americans. They spoke for me, and my application for employment passed through quickly. If anyone suspected my past, they did not reveal this to me."

"Didn't West Germany give a stipend to East Germans around the time of Reunification?"

He smiled. "Ja, very small, but a nice gesture. I could not claim the money, though. I no longer had East German papers, and I could not risk being discovered for a few Deutschmarks."

"It must have been fascinating to be here in 1989. I read that when Egon Krenz opened the Wall, it caught everybody by surprise."

"Ja, not the least surprised were the Stasi. They had little time to destroy records before their buildings were taken over."

"Did you foresee the opening of the Wall?"

His voice dropped. "There were signs. The Hungarians loosened their border in August. This began the flow of East Germans through the frontier into the West. In October demonstrations flared up in Leipzig. The protesters took over Stasi headquarters in the city. This was the biggest sign for me. There would be no recovery after that for the Stasi, and the SED could not survive without their secret police to control the people."

Oskar signaled a right turn and pulled into the hospital parking lot. I lifted my backpack from the floorboard. "Did you know any of Friedrich's other friends?"

He nodded and switched off the engine. "Some."

"Do you know what happened to them?"

"Aidan Zeller finished the technical university in Dresden as a mechanical engineer. He took a job in Eisenach, near the border with West Germany. He disappeared in 1971."

"Disappeared?"

A smile crept over his face. "I heard the story of an escape to the West by some mechanics. They built a ladder with hinges that would extend by pulleys and ropes. They used it to bridge a part of the border fence that was not so closely watched because it was electrical."

"What—oh, electrified."

"Ja. It is said a paper was left at the foot of the ladder on the eastern side, an invoice for the materials used to build the ladder." His smile broadened. "It included instructions to send reimbursement to the museum near Checkpoint Charlie dedicated to those who challenged the Berlin Wall. Now, I did not hear for certain that the witty Aidan Zeller was among those who escaped, but I suspect. . ."

I grinned. "I wish I had known him. I think we would have gotten along."

"Friedrich's girlfriend, his Ev-Ev, moved with her family to Erfurt in 1959. I do not know if she heard of his death. I think she married a doctor, or dentist."

I nodded and thought it might be interesting to try and locate some of Friedrich's old friends.

Oskar sobered. "Franz Schindler we did not hear from again." He glanced at me as he reached for his door handle. "And you alone know more than anyone about his friend Karl Werner."

"Karl who?" I asked with my coyest smile.

⤜⥈⤛

We checked in at the nurses' station but found no change in Fräulein Mahler's condition. The nurse was busy preparing medications, so Oskar and I sat in the waiting room. He excused himself for a moment then returned with thick paper cups of what was supposed to be coffee from a vending machine. One sip and I was wired.

"Whoa, this is some serious java!" I coughed. "Did it come with forks?"

He smiled. "Nein. Some liquids you dare not put plastic into."

"I hope the cup holds out long enough for me to finish this." I squeezed my eyes shut and took another sip.

"You do not need to finish. It will not hurt my feelings if you do not."

"Ah, but my ego insists." I raised a haughty eyebrow. "I do have a reputation to maintain, you know."

"Somehow I do not think the reputation of such a schönes Fräulein should rely upon a cup of Colombian diesel fuel."

I sputtered a laugh, the third sip of sludge halfway down my throat. "Oskar?" I set my cup on the floor between my feet. "How did you meet Fräulein Mahler? She said something about a cross."

His eyes went distant. "For you to understand this, you must first know a little more of Friedrich."

"Oh?"

He nodded. "Friedrich and I had many opportunities to talk after we first met at the café and before he deserted the army. I told him of my parents, who died in the fire-bombing of

Dresden in 1945, then my life with my Opa and Oma Werner until 1957, when I went out on my own. They are no longer alive, and there was not much I could remember. He told me of his father, taken away by the Stasi and then east to the camps. He spoke more of his mother, a strong lady. He loved her very much. He had fewer words for Tante Frieda. They did not get along well, although I am sure he loved her as family. Mostly, he spoke of his sister, Katia. . . ."

*". . .and you know how precious she is to me, Karl. Although I know that her polio was not my fault, I remember it was at my birthday party she was infected. It is very important to me that she receives the best medicine. I will see to that. Somehow." Friedrich gulped the last of his Schultheiss and signaled for another beer. He wiped his mouth on a sleeve.*

*"Friedrich, it is difficult enough for you to pass inspection without beer on your uniform."*

*"Ah, but if I am going to receive extra duty, what better reason than for beer?"*

*I laughed and lifted my own glass in a mock toast. "How is your sister's health now? She still walks, no?"*

*"Yes, but with difficulty. She has mastered her crutches, but her legs are so weak. She does not complain. I have never heard Katia complain about anything, I think."*

*"Someday Germany will be one again. You know that. This cursed barrier will be no more. Then there will be better medicine for Katia."*

*Friedrich clenched his fist. "They strengthen the barricades every day. They even replace the barbed wire with concrete walls in places. No, it does not look good, at least for a long while."*

*"But it cannot last."*

*"Perhaps I will be surprised, and it will be removed. But I cannot wait for that. Katia cannot wait."*

Oskar sighed. "And so Friedrich was certain from the beginning that he would try to escape to the West to help his family, but especially for his sister. Deserting the Volksarmee after Heinrich was shot decided for Friedrich when he would escape, not why he would escape. Our discussions no longer questioned whether to defect. Now we planned how to do it. It was during these talks that Friedrich first made me promise to tend to his sister if anything happened to him."

I shook my head. "It's such a shame he didn't succeed. He was so positive in his letters, so intent on not failing like he said he had before."

"But he did not fail. He succeeded in the only way he could."

"What do you mean?"

His voice grew thick, and he dropped his gaze to the floor. "If Friedrich had not fallen back and pushed me to freedom, if we both had tried to climb the slope, we both would have been cut down. He sacrificed himself so that I would live—not only for me but also that his sister would be cared for. I know this to be true." He looked up at me. "Nein, Friedrich did not fail. It was his greatest success. In fact," his voice quieted, "I sometimes think his plan was always that I would be the one to survive. Perhaps he believed I could take better care of Katia than he."

"Well, you certainly have done that." I smiled, and a new appreciation for the troubled young man who was Friedrich Mahler took seed in my heart.

Oskar grimaced through another sip of coffee then shook his head and emptied the cup into the drinking fountain next to his chair. I picked up my own cup and handed it to him. He chuckled, and my coffee followed his into the drain.

I giggled. "Well, so much for the plumbing in *that* fountain."

We settled back in our chairs, and I shifted to face him.

"Go on with your story, please."

"After our escape, I tried to think of some way to contact the Mahlers, but if the Stasi discovered a communication from me, it would go very badly for the family. The years went by. I worked hard, invested my money, and prayed the Mahlers would survive the Communists. When I had nearly given up hope, the borders across Eastern Europe began to weaken. Czechoslovakia. Hungary. East Germany. As I said, the frontier in Hungary was the first to loosen, this in August of 1989. Thousands of East Germans streamed to the West until there was no purpose for the Wall to remain. So Krenz suspended border restrictions in November, one month after the Leipzig demonstrators toppled Stasi headquarters."

"What did you do when you heard the Wall had opened?"

"I took the first U-bahn train I could squeeze onto going to the Kochstraße station, despite the fear that I might still be recognized. Kochstraße was the closest subway station to Checkpoint Charlie, where many of the people were coming through from the East. Oh, there were celebrations like you have never seen! Trabants—we called them Trabbies—the small wooden cars of the common East German, and Soviet-made Ladas poured through the checkpoint. People lined the road and pounded on the cars, waved, and greeted their fellow Berliners. People hugged, kissed, danced, and prayed, all at the same time."

I smiled. "It must have been exciting."

"Ja. Men beat on the western side of the Wall with large hammers. A hole would break through and a man would press his face to the opening to see the glazed eye of a Grenztruppe peering back at him. I know, for I also chanced a peek through. At the Brandenburg Gate, the Wall was thicker, lower, and did not have the dangerous roll bar on the top. People climbed onto the barrier, danced and drank and shouted. Where one day earlier there would have been gunfire at such a scene, champagne corks popped and fireworks exploded. My mind was numb. Everything happened so fast. Then I remembered Katia and my promise to Friedrich."

"How could you possibly hope to find her in such chaos?"

"There was very little hope, but I had to try. I hurried to a small store across the street and purchased a writing pad and a red marker. In the largest letters I could fit on the paper, I wrote her name: K a t i a.

"I stuffed the marker into my shirt pocket, tore off the paper, and rushed out of the shop, leaving the pad on the floor behind me. I had no idea where to go with my sign, or if what I did even made sense. Since Friedrich's family lived in Karlshorst, and there could only be a few openings in the Wall this soon, it might make sense that she would come to this place, if she came at all. If I did not succeed here, I would find some way to get to Karlshorst even if it meant discovery.

"I found a street corner most people seemed to pass after they came through the checkpoint. Although it was late in the day, I held the sign above my head and searched for a woman I supposed would be on crutches. People jostled past me, and some looked up at my sign. From the corner of my eye, I saw a man snap my photograph. A sudden panic overtook me, as fears of the Stasi rose again. But the man, who looked like an American, reached down and took a young girl by the hand. A woman with an older boy and girl joined him, and they walked away. I could breathe again.

"I stood at the corner for perhaps thirty minutes. Then I decided to go to the Wall across from the Brandenburg Gate, where the crowds were larger. I held my sign and walked the Straße des 17. Juni as far as the Soviet War Memorial and back. A young woman with a paper cup of warm *Glüwein* bumped into me and sloshed the spiced wine onto my jacket. She hugged me and kissed my cheek then staggered off. I am sure it was not her first drink of the day. Still, I scanned the people for someone on crutches.

"I decided to move north along the Wall, I am not sure why. It was growing dark, and the sign was now too difficult to read, so I folded it and put it into my pocket. I stopped when I saw the Reichstag loom through the trees at the edge of the Tiergarten, and my mind flashed back to the horror of my escape so many years ago. I turned to walk away, but a sudden thought stopped me. Here, at the end of communist East Germany, it seemed right to salute with a toast my friend Friedrich, the man who saved my life."

Oskar paused, and an odd expression overtook his face. The creases in his forehead smoothed, and the crow's-feet deepened with a spreading smile.

I cocked my head. "What are you thinking?"

He turned in his chair and looked me in the eye. "A strange thing happened when I set my mind on honoring the man who had given his life for me. My fear of discovery began to fade away. For the first time in years, I no longer felt compelled to look over my shoulder for someone watching me. It was like a baptism of my mind, clean and pure, and I savored the relief it gave me. I did not know if the fear would return, if this relief was only a reaction to the celebrations erupting around me. I did not care. It was precious to me, if only for the moment."

"Did the fear return?"

"There were moments, for we do not easily let go of such fears. But a peace I had not known before entered my life that moment. It grew slowly, but it did grow." His eyes glistened. "The joy of this peace is still fresh to me. Freedom is a wonderful thing, do you not think so, Fräulein McAllister?"

I wanted so much to share the enthusiasm in his sentiment, but I couldn't reach his level of joy. There had never been hidden cameras tracking the pedestrians on Court Street in Old Town Saginaw, armed patrol boats with machine guns and spotlights patrolling the Saginaw River, or barbed wire and watchtowers in Rust Park. If a man in a trench coat approached me on the Michigan campus and warned me never to question the U.S. government, I'd have laughed in his face. To me, the freedom to come and go as I wished, to speak my mind, was as natural as breathing. Liberty was so easy to take for granted, as terrible as that sounded to me now that I knew Fräulein Mahler's and Oskar's stories.

I nodded at him and smiled, but somehow I felt like I was standing on the outside and looking into my own privileged life. My voice sounded small in my ears. "What happened then?"

"There was a small kiosk by the street where a man sold Glüwein. I bought a cup for the toast and walked through the trees to the plaza in front of the Reichstag."

A woman's voice broke Oskar's narrative. "Herr Schultmann? Fräulein McAllister? You can go in now." The nurse held the doors open for us.

I followed Oskar into the ICU, and we paused at the foot of the bed. Not much had changed, although I fancied a little more color in her cheeks, perhaps even a slight curve to her lips. I glanced down and was startled to see my *New Testament* in her right hand. I had tucked it into her left hand the day before. They must have moved it when they changed her bedding.

Oskar pulled a chair to his usual place at her bedside. I laid my backpack against the wall and pulled another chair up. We sat quietly for several minutes. I studied Oskar's face, though I tried not to be obvious. An acute intensity that seemed to appear only when he looked at her filled his eyes, as though nothing else in the world existed. At that moment, a startling truth crystallized in my mind.

Oskar Schultmann loved Katia Mahler. It was all over his face.

I knew he was fond of her, of course, dedicated to her well-being. That much was obvious. But the tenderness in the touch of his fingertips on her still hand, the sheen of moisture in his eyes reflecting pinpoints of light from the equipment displays, the total concentration as he scanned her face for signs of hope—the symptoms were unmistakable. He loved her as a man loves a woman. Purely and without reserve.

As much as I wanted him to continue his story, I couldn't violate the moment. I sat back in my chair and listened to the hum and occasional beep of the machinery, the whir of their cooling fans, the rustle of paper as another segment issued from the monitor and settled to the floor.

The quiet lulled me into a daze. Better to leave them alone, anyway.

# Chapter 26

*Should be just about dinnertime. I hope they haven't gone out to eat.*

"Hi, Mom. . . . Yeah, it's a little late here, but I couldn't sleep, so I thought I'd take a walk. . . . Sure, it's dark, but the streets are well lit, and it's a safe neighborhood. Hey, is Dad around? I have a question for him. . . . Yeah, I know it's a workday. I just thought maybe—well, never mind. . . . Fräulein Mahler is still not conscious. The doctor can't figure out why she hasn't come around. . . . No, Doctor Frühling is great. She's doing everything she can, but Fräulein Mahler just isn't cooperating. Oh, speaking of doctors, how's Grandma McAllister doing? . . . Still a little weak, huh? . . . How about Grandpa? . . . Oh, is he? How long will it take for him to finish the paperwork on the land sale? . . . Yeah, that's actually one of the things I wanted to ask Dad about, but it can wait. . . . Sure I can—whoa, Mom, I just got beeped that there are only five minutes left on my calling card. I need to go. . . . Yeah, I should keep a few minutes on it for emergencies until I can buy more time. . . . I will. . . . Love you, too. Bye!"

<hr>

". . .and we can take this in case of emergency."

"Emergency?"

"Sure. You don't want to ingest any more of that diesel fuel, do you?"

Oskar smiled as I handed him the Thermos of fresh coffee. I had prepared some food to take to the hospital for a light lunch, something like an inside picnic, I told him. In truth, my motive was mostly one of self-preservation. The vending-machine goodies that had made it past the walls of my arteries were still sticking to my ribs. One more cellophane-wrapped delicacy and they would have another candidate for the ICU. Yes, a small loaf of fresh bread, block of Münster cheese, fresh fruit, and assorted veggies to munch on would be oh-so-much better.

We had just pulled away from the curb when I planted my foot firmly in my mouth. "So, does Fräulein Mahler know how you feel about her?"

"I do not know what you mean."

I attempted a look of nonchalance. "Come now, Oskar. It's obvious you love her. And don't try to deny it. The way you look at her, speak to her, touch her hand—"

I realized I had blundered as soon as the words were out of my mouth. The car rolled to a stop. I looked sideways at him. *Uh-oh.*

"Fräulein McAllister—"

I put my hands over my face. "Oskar, wait. Please forgive me. My comment was uncalled for."

The last thing I wanted was to damage our newly restored relationship, but, once again, I had forgotten I wasn't sitting around the dorm with my girlfriends. I had poked fun at a mature German gentleman about a fifteen-year love commitment like I could only hope someday to experience—and even then, in my thickheadedness, it would probably go right past me.

I turned and peered at him through spread fingers. "Please. . . ?"

He smiled, an effort that must have herniated his face muscles, but he was that gracious. "You are a difficult woman to become angry with."

I lowered my hands and murmured, "Oh, I don't know. For a couple of days there, I did a pretty good job of putting you off."

"I was not angry with you, Fräulein McAllister. I was fearful of you."

I flinched. That he feared me bothered me much more than if he'd been angry. I touched his arm. "I don't ever want you to be fearful of me again. Please trust me, in spite of that last comment about you and Fräulein Mahler. I respect you and her more than any two people alive."

His eyes flicked toward me at that last sentence. "Danke schön."

The Audi resumed speed.

"And, no."

I glanced over at him. "Excuse me?"

"It is. . .as you say. But, no, she has no idea of my feelings for her."

*Hmm, I think I'm on thicker ice to comment on that one.*

"Forgive me," I said. "It's none of my business, but why do you assume she doesn't know?"

"How could she? I have said nothing."

"Take it from a woman, Oskar. She knows."

This time the car screeched to a halt. He stared at me. "That is impossible! I have said nothing, made no overtures."

I hid my smile at his beet-red face. "How long do you think it took me to notice?"

"But I—she couldn't—"

"C'mon, you know how perceptive that woman is. I read the signs in a heartbeat, and I'm a brick compared to her."

Horns blared behind us. The car crawled forward, and Oskar's whitened hands guided it into a parking space. The car bumped the curb twice before it shuddered to a stop.

"This cannot be," he muttered. "You must be wrong."

"Pretty sure I've got this one nailed, my friend." I leaned forward and looked into his face. "Why is it so terrible that she should know how you feel?"

"Himmel! It would ruin everything!"

"Why? I don't get it."

He pressed his forehead against the steering wheel and closed his eyes. When he spoke, his voice was barely audible. "I do not deserve Katia. I live because her brother is dead. I promised Friedrich I would take care of her. There can be" —he swallowed—"no other reason."

I laid my hand on his shoulder. "Doesn't she get a vote on that, Oskar?"

He shook his head. "Nein."

<hr />

Nothing had changed. She lay still, her ever-vigilant electronic guardians pulsing and beeping away. We sat at her bedside. Oscar leaned over her, his mouth close to her ear. Out of respect, I forced myself not to try to overhear what he whispered, not to study his face while he studied hers. Finally, he sat back and sighed.

"Oskar?" I spoke softly, but the word shattered the tranquility of the room like a thunderclap.

"Ja?"

"You didn't finish telling me how you met Fräulein Mahler. Where was this cross she mentioned?"

"It was very much a miracle, I think."

"A miracle?"

"Ja. I sipped my Glüwein and walked toward the plaza in front of the Reichstag. The crowds continued to grow, although it would soon be dark. The Quadriga reflected spotlights in brilliance atop the Brandenburg Gate. I could see three or four silhouettes against the sky, daring souls who had climbed the Gate and danced with the four horses and their chariot. Someone cut the hammer-and-compass crest from the center of an East German flag and waved the flag from the Wall. It was now just a red, yellow, and black German flag with a large hole in the middle. I saw in it the first ragged symbol of Germany's reunification, a dream that would come true in less than a year."

I closed my eyes and tried to picture the scene. He continued.

"White traces arced toward the Gate, fireworks aimed at the flag of the failed regime. I tapped a man on the shoulder and pointed to his woolen cap. It was smoldering from the sparks of a rocket that had just flown low over our heads. He jerked the hat off his head, laughed, and pounded my shoulder as he beat the hat against his coat. I smiled back but wondered how busy the hospitals would be that night.

"I held the cup of Glüwein above my head as I struggled through the crowd toward the Reichstag. The throng of people thinned and finally died out by the time I reached the shadows of its great walls. I pulled my light coat up to my neck against the chill and trekked along the wall to the back of the building. When I rounded the corner, I stopped.

"There was now a chain-link fence at the top of the riverbank where the man from the West had dragged me away after my escape. Flat white crosses hung on the fence with words in black centered on them. I squinted into the dusk and read the name "Klaus Schröter" and the date "4.11.1963" inscribed on one cross. I started to walk toward the fence when I saw her.

"A fine young lady on crutches moved out of the shadows to my right. I paused and watched her hobble toward the fence. She stopped in front of the cross next to the one with Herr Schröter's name. She began to waver, so I dropped my Glüwein and hurried forward. Just as I reached her, she collapsed against the fence, her forehead pressed against the cross."

"Well, Oskar, it was not exactly that way, now was it?"

We both jumped at the voice. I spun and stared at Fräulein Mahler. Her pale lips thinned into a gentle smile, and her half-opened eyes—her glorious eyes—shined in the fluorescent light over her head.

"Fräulein Mahler!" I leaped up from my chair.

"Katia!" Oskar's voice broke.

I grabbed the cord suspended on the wall next to her bed and punched the button. A nurse rushed into the room, and everything became a blur.

# Chapter 27

## May 12

*Dear Mom and Dad,*

*I wish you could've been there when she revived. Oh, it was awesome! The nurse ushered us to the side of the room while Doctor Frühling, who had just come on duty, fussed over her patient. I didn't know one person could do so many things at once. She held the narrow strip of graph paper in one hand and pressed the fingertips of her other hand against her patient's wrist. One eye was focused on the electronic monitor screen, and the other one winked at us. All the while she issued a nonstop stream of orders to the nurses and orderlies who had suddenly filled the room from I don't know where.*

*I wanted to cry. I think I did. I know Oskar did.*

*At the doctor's request, we left for the day to give Fräulein Mahler a chance to recuperate and for the hospital to run a couple more tests. If her signs were good and the test results showed no problems, they would move her to a recovery room the next morning.*

*Before we left, the doctor gave us a moment to say good-bye. Oskar smiled, his face still wet, and touched Fräulein Mahler's shoulder. She tsk'd at him. I leaned over the bed rail and kissed her on the cheek. I didn't know what she'd make of that, but while she was captive in the hospital bed, I wasn't about to miss the opportunity. She'd just have to deal with it.*

*We forgot all about lunch, so I grabbed the basket on the way out. Oskar said he would pick me up at five o'clock and treat me to a celebration dinner. The next celebration, he said, would be with the three of us.*

*He just now dropped me off after an incredible meal of* Jägerschnitzel *and* Spätzle. *I'm stuffed.*

*Going to bed. Good night.*
*Love, Maddy*

G ood night! What next?" I grumbled as my bread broke into pieces in the toaster. I love Vollkornbrot, but its grains are so large, once they start coming unglued, it disintegrates beyond repair. I pulled the plug from the wall and tried to pry the chunks out with a butter knife. No joy. I finally turned the toaster upside down and shook the debris onto the counter then scooped a couple of the larger pieces into the palm of my hand and tipped them back into my mouth. Still tasty!

I glanced out through the kitchen door at the alpine clock in the dining nook. Eight o'clock. *Where are you, Oskar?*

As though to answer, his familiar knock sounded at the front door.

"It's open!"

I pinched a couple more pieces of bread off the counter and washed them down with the last of my orange juice. I had just brushed the remnants of the crumbly disaster into the trash can when Oskar appeared in the doorway.

I stared at his puffy face and dark circles. "You look terrible!"

"My sleep was not restful."

"Would you like me to drive?"

"I am not *that* tired."

I narrowed my eyes. *Jerk! Lovable, but still a jerk.*

⤙⤏

The recovery room was wonderful. Light, cheery. A linen curtain separated Fräulein Mahler's bed from the other one in the room. I resisted the urge to peek through at her roomie.

The head of her bed canted up, and she looked comfortable, her hands folded on her lap.

"Fräulein McAllister, are you prepared to continue the interview?"

"You just came out of a coma!"

"What better time? I have had plenty of rest."

I shook my head and smiled as I pulled a notepad and the Sony from my backpack. "As you wish."

She cocked her head at Oskar, who sat erect on the edge of his chair, his gaze glued to her. "Oskar, you were in error in your account of our meeting."

He raised an eyebrow.

She leaned her head back onto the pillow and closed her eyes.

⤙⤏

*After Mama was taken, Tante Frieda moved into the house with me. She worked as a clerk in a small shop near Alexanderplatz, and I had my crocheting I could sell privately. We would get by until Mama returned. Tante Frieda inquired many times with the Volkspolizei about Mama. Oberleutnant Klein told us that she had been taken by the Stasi for questioning. He tried to object, but they would not change their minds. He could no longer protect her, only watch and wait with us. One day became the next. I do not remember all the years. We did not hear from Mama again.*

*By 1989, hope for Mama had faded, hope for Papa barely a memory. Tante Frieda and I settled into a quiet routine, thoughts of the past revered and thoughts of the future avoided. My life passed one crochet stitch at a time.*

*One Friday afternoon, a knock at the door broke our silence and our routine. Frau Szabó stood at the door, breathless.*

*"Frieda, Chancellor Krenz has opened the Wall!"*

*"Opened the Wall?"*

*"Yes. Late last night. People from the East go to the West. People from the West visit the East. My country opened the border two months ago. Your country does that now."*

*Tante Frieda shook her head. "I knew the border opened in Hungary but have not heard these things about Berlin. Are you sure?"*

*"Very sure. Go and see for yourself."*

*My aunt reached for her coat. "Come, Katia! We will see if this is true."*

*Tante Frieda had traded a basket of vegetables for an old Trabbie belonging to a neighbor widow who could no longer drive. She helped me out to the car and settled me onto the passenger seat. I leaned my crutches against the backseat. We had little money for fuel, but the tank was over half full. I was not sure the car would start at first, but finally the engine sputtered and caught. Gray smoke poured out the back, and the smell hurt my nose, but I was too excited for it to bother me.*

*She steered the Trabbie onto Am Tierpark, and we rattled up the street while I pulled my coat around me. Another left on Alt-Friedrichsfelde put us behind a long line of cars belching their own fumes into the autumn air. We decided to follow them, since we would not know which streets to the West had been opened.*

*The traffic crawled and stopped then crawled again. We finally reached the checkpoint into the American Sector to the shocking sight of cars and people streaming both ways past the raised barrier bars. Tante Frieda's face was taut as we approached the barricade. She looked both ways, as though she expected to be challenged. The border guards stood in clusters at the side of the street and offered no challenge. We edged past the Wall into a different world. People surrounded our car as we drove through the checkpoint. They slapped our hood and roof with their hands, waved to us, and blew kisses through the window. I shrank back, a smile on my face but afraid of all the people, all the eyes. I pulled my coat over my thin legs and looked down.*

*Tante Frieda squinted through the windshield. "I do not know where to go from here. I have not been to the West in so many years."*

*A thought struck me. "Turn right at the next street. I want to find the Reichstag."*

*I remembered the important landmarks of Berlin from my school lessons. If we could find the tall Brandenburg Gate, we would find the Reichstag. It was important to me to see the building that was the traditional seat of the German government, although it was not an interest in civics that motivated me now. I said nothing of my secret intentions to my aunt.*

*She turned onto Niederkirchnerstraße, which too late we discovered was a mistake. The narrow side street was nearly impassable with people overflowing the sidewalks and darting into traffic. A man clutching an open bottle of Schnapps scooted across the hood of our car on the seat of his pants and grinned at us through the windshield. Tante Frieda frowned back at him.*

*We finally reached Stresemannstraße after twenty minutes of inching forward through the chaos.*

*"Turn right again, Tante Frieda."*

*"Yes, yes," she grumbled.*

*We followed on the bumper of the Lada in front of us until I saw a sign for Potsdamer Platz. My excitement grew. "Keep going. This is the right direction."*

*In another fifteen minutes, we stopped at the edge of the Tiergarten. I recognized the Quadriga atop the Brandenburg Gate.*

*"We are almost there! Go on."*

*Tante Frieda shook her head. "I can go no farther. Our fuel is low, and the crowds are too thick."*

*"I will go, then." I reached toward the backseat for my crutches, and she grabbed my arm.*

*"What are you doing? You will be killed out there!"*

*"There is something I must see."*

*"What is to see?"*

*"I must go to where Friedrich crossed over."*

*"I cannot let you—"*

*"You have no choice!" I pulled my arm free and opened the door.*

*She called to me as I stumbled onto the sidewalk, but I could not hear her words through all the noise. "Wait for me here," I yelled over my shoulder. "I will come back soon." I shut the door and pushed off through the Tiergarten. I did not look back.*

❧

Oskar remained quiet as she spoke. I recognized the poker face, undoubtedly perfected through the years at any mention of Friedrich. He nodded at the appropriate times but seemed determined not to betray too much interest in her tale. I realized his greatest fear was to be drawn into the conversation and let something slip. My thoughts flew back to our walk in the Volkspark, the suppressed panic in his voice and the look in his eyes when she asked him to share his history. It puzzled me then. No longer.

I took advantage of a moment when she paused for a sip of water. "How did you make it through all the people? It would be difficult on crutches."

She nodded. "I became tired, ja. But it was important to me. Yet there is more. . . ."

❧

*When I reached the Reichstag, I sat on a bench to rest my arms and legs.*

*The sun had set, and the air was cold. I pulled my coat tighter and pushed to my feet. I could move more quickly now, free of the people mobbing the streets behind me. When I reached the end of the building, the sight of the white crosses stopped me. I was not prepared to see such icons. I set off toward the fence until I could read the words on them by the lights of the Reichstag. I saw first Herr Schröter's name and breathed a prayer for his memory and his soul. Then I looked to the right. It read "Unbekannt," "Unknown." Beneath the word was the date "16.4.1963."*

My temples began to pulse, and my eyes filled with tears. I fought the urge to look at Oskar, lest my emotions betray him. My promise would stand.

Fräulein Mahler looked at Oskar. "This was where you made your first mistake. You described a fine young woman on crutches. I was crippled and broken, my friend, but you are kind in your words."

He shook his head. "I stand by my words, Katia. You have never been broken."

They quietly exchanged looks for a moment. I averted my eyes and lifted an unobtrusive finger to brush a tear from my cheek.

She cleared her throat and continued.

*As I approached the Unbekannt cross, my crutch caught on a break in the pavement. I teetered then fell forward.*

Fräulein Mahler narrowed her eyes at Oskar. "That was your second mistake. I most certainly did not collapse. I tripped." She lifted her chin at him.

He broke into a smile and dipped his head. "In that, my dear Katia, I do stand corrected. Please forgive my lack of precision."

She sniffed but was unable to subdue a smile. "Forgiven."

I grinned. "Please go on."

*Two strong hands grasped my shoulders and eased me back from the fence. A handsome face appeared at my side.*
*"Fräulein, are you hurt?"*

Oskar chuckled. "Now it is you who loses precision, Katia. Strong hands? Handsome face?"

She frowned at him. "*Stille*, Herr Schultmann! This is my story, and I tell it as it was. Kindly do not interrupt."

I pressed my hand to my mouth, but I'm sure a giggle squeezed through.

*I could not take my eyes from the cross. The date 16.4.1963 burned itself into my mind. The word* Unbekannt *burned itself onto my heart.*

*I gazed into the face of the handsome man. "Do you have a pen, please?"*

*"I have a marker. Will it do?"*

*"Yes, thank you."*

*He handed me a large red marker and steadied me as I pulled off the cap. I drew two lines through* Unbekannt. *On the left crossbeam I wrote the name* Friedrich Mahler. *On the right,* Karl Werner.

*The man's voice was tender in my ear. "The Polizei will not like what you have done to the cross, Fräulein."*

*"They will become used to it, mein Herr."*

"It was at that moment I fell in love with Katia Mahler." Oskar guided the Audi through the late afternoon traffic.

I sat back and smiled as my mind replayed the morning's events. The story was coming together in ways I never expected, and I was disappointed when the hospital staff cut short our visit. Doctor Frühling was apologetic, but her patient needed rest. We left behind a promise to return tomorrow with Brötchen and honey. Fräulein Mahler smiled. Doctor Frühling did not.

*"You will clear her diet with me, Fräulein McAllister."*

*"Yes, ma'am."*

I glanced out the window at traffic that seemed thicker than usual. "When do you think she'll come home?"

"I do not know. I hope it will be soon."

I lowered my eyes. "I'll take better care of her this time, Oskar. I promise."

He reached over and patted my hand.

# Chapter 28

## May 14

*Dear Mom and Dad,*
*Fräulein Mahler comes home tomorrow! I can't wait. It seems like I've been alone in this house forever. Doctor Frühling is still a little niggled at why the coma lasted so long, but she says the tests look good. She gave me a stack of homework and made me promise to read it before she releases her patient. Fortunately, it's all in English. Medications. Dietary restrictions. Physical therapy. When the doctor said there could be more exercise in the routine, Fräulein Mahler frowned at her. Doctor Frühling frowned back. I think Fräulein Mahler may have met her match.*
*Oskar said our dinner celebration will wait until Tuesday to make sure we don't tire her out the first day home. He won't tell me where we're going. Honestly, I don't really care, as long as all three of us are together. . . .*

"Where are you going?" I looked over my shoulder at Oskar, who had stopped at the door. "I have things to prepare for Katia's return. I will come for you after breakfast."

I set my backpack against the wall. "Okay. I've got some cleaning to do around here anyway."

He leaned in and glanced around the front room. "Ja."

"Hey, it's not that bad—"

His smile cut me short. I swatted at him. "Go on, get out of here!"

It embarrassed me to discover that it really was that bad. I went over the place twice that afternoon and still wasn't sure it was up to Fräulein Mahler's standards. In the early evening, I perused her bookshelf and finally invited William Faulkner to join me over a light dinner of fruit and yogurt. The full-length mirror I dusted in her bedroom had rudely reminded me that nine months of German cuisine hadn't done my hips any favors. *It's probably a good thing Brendon can't see me.*

*Brendon.*

I sighed. We'd had a pretty good thing going—at least, I'd thought we did. Apparently absence can make the heart grow fonder. . .or fainter. I set my spoon down, my appetite suddenly gone. I reflected over our relationship, which had sparked to life my first semester at Michigan. He seemed so different from the other guys, like maybe he actually had his head together. I guess I was way wrong on *that* one. I ran a mental comparison of Oskar's years of steadfast commitment against Brendon's apparent inability to focus more than a few months. Needless to say, Brendon came up short in the contest.

Yet, even Oskar had erred, in my opinion. I tried to define his situation: an inexpressible devotion denied any chance of expression, his adoration sublimated to obligation by self-inflicted guilt. How many years had he sacrificed love on the altar of honor? There's nothing wrong with honor, but as Mom would say, good things become bad things when they keep us from the best things.

I rested Herr Faulkner on the side of the table and took my dishes into the kitchen. The change of venue did nothing to derail my train of thought, though. I flashed back to the hospital room and replayed the morning in my mind. What was that little tit for tat over the story of how they met? Strong hands? Handsome face? If it weren't Fräulein Mahler, I'd suspect her of flirting.

I slapped my hand to my forehead. *Omigosh! Maddy, you really* are *a brick!*

She's as nuts about him as he is about her! How ironic is *that?* For heaven's sake, she was throwing around hints big enough to inflict injury, and he just sat there. Is he dense, or what? And what about her? She has to know how he feels, I'm convinced of that. Why don't they just come out with it? What's up with these two?

*Like, this is just so not right!*

But what to do about it. . .

❧

"So, today's the big day, eh, Oskar?" I bounced onto the passenger seat and slammed the car door.

He nodded.

"Just a nod? Aren't you excited?"

"Of course I am excited."

I peered at him. "Well, tell your face. It seems confused."

He lifted his chin. "I wore a tie this morning, if you have not noticed."

"You wore a—oh, be still, my heart!"

He cleared his throat. "It is not often I wear a tie."

I buried my face in my hands.

He started the engine, and we pulled away from the curb. The ride to the hospital went quickly—I was lost in my thoughts, Oskar likely also lost in his. When we arrived, he cut the engine and pulled the release lever for the trunk. I jumped out of the car before he had a chance to protest and fidgeted impatiently on the sidewalk while he opened his door and emerged at a snail's pace. Then he walked to the back of the car and lifted a dozen of the most beautiful pink roses I've ever seen out of the trunk.

"Okay, now that's more like it." I nodded my approval. "Shouldn't they be red, though?"

His face flushed. "Fräulein McAllister, red roses imply romantic intentions."

I cocked my head and smiled. "Your point being. . ."

"We have discussed this!"

"Okay! Okay!" I pulled an imaginary zipper across my mouth. "Not a word shall pass my lips."

He closed the trunk lid. "I suspect that to be an impossibility."

"Touché, Herr Schultmann. Touché." I bowed in mock defeat.

❧

"Danke schön. They are lovely." Fräulein Mahler accepted the roses with a nod, but there were sparkles in her eyes. She glanced up at him. "You appear flushed, Oskar. Would you like for the doctor to—"

"Nein, danke. I am fine."

I hid my smirk. *Now,* there's *an understatement, if I've ever heard one.*

"They are indeed *wunderschön,* Fräulein Mahler."

The voice came from behind me. I turned to see the curtain pulled halfway back, revealing an elderly lady in the other bed.

"Danke schön. Oskar, Fräulein McAllister, this is Frau Tischner. She was admitted yesterday evening."

We exchanged greetings. She smiled but appeared weak, and her skin looked mottled. I wondered why she was in the hospital. At that moment, Doctor Frühling entered the room with a file folder. After we exchanged pleasantries, she got down to business.

"Have you read the literature, Fräulein McAllister?"

"I have."

"Gut, and you agree to abide by the instructions."

"Yes, ma'am. I have no desire to see Fräulein Mahler back in this building."

She turned her attention to her patient. "Fräulein Mahler, it has been a pleasure to attend to you. You will understand if I say I hope we will not meet again."

Fräulein Mahler nodded. A smile clung to her lips, but I don't think it was due to the doctor's wit. I'm pretty sure it was left over from the roses.

"You will be discharged this afternoon, after you have used the toilet one more time."

Fräulein Mahler's face went crimson. "Doktor Frühling! That is better a private instruction, not a public announcement, do you not think?"

The doctor appeared unfazed as she jotted a note in the file. "Please remember you are in a hospital. Such a comment is quite at home here."

"Ach!" Fräulein Mahler fluttered her hand.

I turned my head to squelch my laughter.

Doctor Frühling tore off what I assumed was a page from her prescription pad and handed it to Oskar. She turned her attention to Frau Tischner. "How are you feeling this morning?"

"*Besser*, danke."

"I can see you are better. Your color is returning." She moved to the woman's bed and lifted the chart from the metal footboard.

"I hope you are well soon, Frau Tischner," I offered.

"Danke. I became infected with typhus many years ago, during the war. It comes and it goes."

"Typhus? I didn't know it could recur."

Doctor Frühling nodded while she scanned the chart. "Ja, it is called Brill's disease."

"Brill's—" My vision tunneled.

She glanced up from the chart. "Fräulein McAllister? Are you ill?"

⌘

I tapped a drumroll on the floorboard with my foot as Oskar turned the Audi onto Frankfurter Allee. "Can we make a quick stop on the way home, please?"

He cast a concerned look at my pale face. "Do you need a pharmacy?"

"No, an Internet café. There's one on the next corner."

"Ja, certainly."

"I won't take long."

⌘

*www.google.com*
*Brill's Disease.*
ENTER.

*"Results 1–10 of about 539,000."*

*Good old Google overkill.*

*"Brill's Disease—Brill-Zinsser Disease—mild reoccurrence of epidemic typhus years after the initial infection; caused by Rickettsia bacteria persisting in body tissue in an inactive state; non-contagious, non-epidemic."*

I swallowed and clicked the search field again.

*Terrebonne.*

*ENTER.*

*"Results 1–10 of about 290,000."*

*"Terrebonne is an off-island suburb of Montreal, in western Quebec."*

I sat back and rubbed my forehead. Then I set my jaw and called up Web Mail.

*NEW*

*To: Ian.McAllister@ftr.net*
*Subject: Question*

*Dad—*
*What is Grandma McAllister's maiden name, please?*
*Maddy*

*SEND*

# Chapter 29

*To: MMcAllister12@umich.edu*
*Subject: RE: Question*

*Maddy,*
    *You wouldn't be asking about Grandma's maiden name unless you already knew the answer. You've become quite an investigative journalist, young lady. Well done.*
    *I suspected you were close. There's a letter on the way. We'll talk when you've read it.*
                                                                    *Dad*

I made my excuses when Oskar arrived at two thirty that afternoon on the way to the hospital to pick up Fräulein Mahler. I had a couple more things to do around the house to prepare for her homecoming, and I thought they might like to be alone anyway.

"*Yes, Oskar, I'll have her wheelchair ready to bring to the curb when she gets home. Of course the tea will be steeping. Sweetener for her this time, though.*"

Meantime, I needed to be alone with my own thoughts. And what thoughts they were. *Grandma McAllister is Tante Maria?* I must have voiced that question to myself a hundred times in the last hour. How could I have taken so long to figure that out? *J & M McAllister*: James "Jim" and Maria. *Returned home to Montreal*: Terrebonne. I cut myself some slack on the Brill's disease thing, but I could've followed my instinct and looked it up when Carson first mentioned it on the phone. That shows how well connected I am to my own grandmother. I didn't even know her maiden name, for heaven's sake!

My mind churned while I adjusted the heat under the metal teapot. I'd never really spent much time with Grandma McAllister, or even developed much interest in her or Grandpa. She was so reserved, and Grandpa was usually out on business when I visited. I remember being curious about a nasty scar on her forearm, but I never asked about it. It suddenly came to me; *I wonder if she had the number that would have been tattooed on her arm at Auschwitz removed.* I hung my head at how self-absorbed I must be to know so little about my relatives.

*Your grandmother is a survivor of the Holocaust, Maddy. You're a twenty-one-year-old college student and a journalist, no less. How could you not know something like that?*

I recalled that Dad had offered to show his family's photo album to me a couple of times, but I was too busy with my own present to concern myself with my family's past. What did I really know of my heritage? Apparently nothing.

Fräulein Mahler's words flooded back. "*You are a journalist; it is your job to probe—if a good journalist, your nature to do so.*"

I sniffed. *Well, good journalism apparently isn't in my nature.* I also thought of Fräulein Mahler's—wait! I covered my eyes. Another news flash, Maddy.

If Grandma McAllister was Fräulein Mahler's aunt, that would make her what? My cousin! Or my second cousin. Or was it once removed? I never could figure out those distant-cousin things. But no matter, we were still family. I blinked through an unexpected sheen of tears and dabbed at my eyes with a dish towel while I sputtered a chuckle at myself.

*You've cried more this month than you have in the past ten years, Maddy. Are you getting mushy?*

Then another thought brought me up short. Who else knows about this? Fräulein Mahler? Oskar? He had made the initial contact with the school, after all. And what were those cryptic comments Dad made on the phone, that Fräulein Mahler was fascinating and that what I was doing was important, as though he knew all along? Well, of course he did! He said as much in his e-mail. And what was it Fräulein Mahler said when I asked why I was selected to interview her?

*"If you interview me well, perhaps that will come out."*

Two plus two had just reached three and a half, and my forehead began to heat. Was this some kind of game? Are they all laughing behind my back? I was being toyed with, strung along. How dare they—no! I squeezed my eyes shut and held my breath.

*Slow down, Maddy. You've seen what happens when your mind gets ahead of the facts—and your mouth gets ahead of your mind.*

I let loose a slow exhale. Okay. So, should I say anything to Oskar? To Fräulein Mahler? No, I'd wait until Dad's letter arrived. And that had better be really soon!

The Audi pulled up outside, and the engine cut off. I poured the hot water into the ceramic teapot, dropped the tea ball in, and pulled the crocheted cozy down over the pot. After one more quick scan of the front room, I brushed the lint from my blouse and retrieved her wheelchair from the corner.

I took a deep breath before opening the door. Well, maybe my journalistic prowess had taken a hit, but I'd spent a little time on the stage. We would see if my acting abilities were any better.

I steeled my mind and forced a smile.

⁂

"Ach! Was ist das?" Fräulein Mahler grimaced and set her teacup onto its saucer.

"What's wrong?" I set my own cup down.

She puckered her lips. "The tea. It tastes strange."

"Oh, it's near-sugar. Sweetener. Doctor Frühling says we have to back off your sugar intake."

She frowned and peered into her cup. "Near-sugar? Someone is indeed a poor judge of distance."

I stifled a smile. "Wait until you taste the diet orange juice."

"It is for your good, Katia. You must be careful, or you will become ill again." Oskar lifted his cup in a mock toast.

"And what is in your tea? Do you have this near-sugar?" she asked.

He straightened in his chair. "Well, I . . ." He glanced at me.

I avoided eye contact.

"I thought as much. Fräulein McAllister, I will have honey with my tea tomorrow. We will reduce my sugar in other ways. My tea, however, will suffer no more indignities such as this."

"Yes, ma'am."

⁂

Oskar paused at the door and handed me a large bulging envelope. "*Guten Abend*, Fräulein McAllister."

I looked at it with a question in my eyes. "Good evening, Oskar."

He smiled and left.

Fräulein Mahler was paging through a book in her favorite corner. I crossed to the dining table and lifted the flap on the envelope. Tucked inside was her leather Bible. I tipped the envelope, and the book slid into the palm of my hand. It looked perfect. I couldn't detect where the repair had been made. It even appeared the binding had been cleaned, although its luster was undisturbed. I was glad. The sheen from years of loving use lent it character.

"Fräulein McAllister?"

"Yes, ma'am?"

"Bitte." She beckoned to me. When I came to her side, she pulled my *New Testament* from her sweater pocket and held it out to me. "It was thoughtful of you. Danke schön."

I took it. "Oh, you're welcome."

"It is quite lovely."

"Thank you. It was a gift from Tant—from my grandparents." I glanced at her face, but she betrayed nothing.

"What did you have for your quiet times while this was with me?"

"I. . .made do." I swallowed and changed the subject. "And I have something for you."

I laid the restored Bible in her outstretched hand. That wonderful smile filled the room with a glow.

"I wondered what had become of it. It was not by my chair. It has been there for years."

I told her how the sturdy book hitting the floor alerted me to her condition that afternoon. Oskar had been kind enough to repair it. "He did a wonderful job. I can't even tell where the break was."

She brushed through the pages deftly with her slight fingers. "Oskar is a good man." I noticed her gaze flit to the vase of pink roses centered on the fireplace mantel.

"Yes, he is. He. . .cares for you very much."

Her brow twitched. "He is a mystery, nee?"

*Not so much anymore.*

I smiled. "Yes, he is."

She cleared her throat and laid the Bible on the arm of the wheelchair. "Perhaps *mein Schutzengel* will have use of it again."

"Excuse me?"

"My, I think you say, guardian angel. Surely you do not think it an accident that my Bible fell to the floor at the very moment I needed you?"

A chill pricked the back of my neck. "Why, I guess I hadn't thought of that."

She smiled, leaned her head back, and closed her eyes. "You should think of such things, Fräulein McAllister." Her fingers stroked the cover.

I stepped away, trying to shake off the chill.

Back at the table, I settled onto a chair and studied the peaceful woman meditating across the room. My head felt thick as I turned the day's revelations over in my mind. I was dying to continue the interview, wondering if the connection between our families would come out. But it was late, and I didn't want to tire her out her first day home. From this point on, I would have to be careful that the questions I asked didn't become leading ones, now that I had inside knowledge of the story. The job could actually become more difficult because of that. I pulled my notepad from the stack of material on the floor, detached the pen clipped to the cover, then began to write.

# Chapter 30

*Dear Mom and Dad,*

*I'm a little tired, so this letter will be short. I'm saving all my questions until I receive your letter, Dad. Then expect a long reply.*

*Fräulein Mahler picked up her routine as though she had never left it. She sat in the corner until around nine o'clock, where she read and meditated. Then she wheeled herself to her bedroom. She looked happy to be home.*

*I fear breakfast in the morning. I could sure use a set of body armor for when she takes that first sip of diet orange juice. . . .*

"...impossible! I cannot drink this!" She held her juice glass up to the light and squinted at the pale yellow fluid.

I put my head in my hands. "Fräulein Mahler, you've rejected sweetened tea, fresh water, now your orange juice. The only liquid you've taken is your coffee. You're going to end up in the hospital again."

"Ja, but I will be asleep and will not taste such bitterness through the needle in my hand."

"It can't be that bad."

She thrust the glass toward me. "Trink."

"I've tasted diet—"

The glass shook in her hand. "Take. Take!"

I sighed and accepted the orange juice. "Look," I said and chugged a full swallow. *Omigosh! What in the world do they put in this stuff?*

I tried not to cringe. "See?" I choked. "It's fine."

"Then why do your eyes water?"

*Drat it!* I frowned at her. There's nothing more annoying than the glint of victory in a geriatric German's eye.

"Okay, okay. But you have to drink something. No way am I going to take a chewing out from Doctor Frühling."

She crossed her arms. "I will drink *Zitronwasser.*"

My shoulders sagged. "Lemonade has sugar in it."

"Nee, you bring me water, and I will add lemon to it."

"Really? Yuck!—I mean, great! Stay right there."

I hurried into the kitchen. *Give the woman her lemon water, Maddy. It's perfect. You don't have to drink it.*

⚜

"Did you take your medication?"

Church services were over, and we had just enjoyed a light lunch with Oskar. After he excused himself for the remainder of the day, I recharged Fräulein Mahler's glass of lemon water and settled onto the couch.

"Do not mother me. I am not so old as to forget my pills." She straightened her sweater and brushed a crumb from her lap.

"Pills. What about your insulin?"

She sniffed. "I could not find my syringes, so I will look again later. I wish to resume the interview as soon as possible."

I rolled my eyes. "Doctor Frühling prescribed a new oral insulin for you, don't you remember? You don't need to give yourself shots anymore. Wait here."

I went into the kitchen. A box with a prescription label sat unopened next to the flour canister. I pulled the lid off the box and brought the spray dispenser into the front room.

"Here. The doctor showed you how to use this yesterday afternoon, do you remember?"

"Of course I remember." She took the small mister and inspected it. With a skeptical lift of the eyebrow, she opened her mouth and sprayed one shot onto the inside of her cheek. She grimaced. "That is terrible!"

"I can get you some lemon to squirt on it, if that will help."

She ignored me.

I took the dispenser and started toward the kitchen. "We'll bring the rest of your medications into the kitchen, too, and keep them all together."

"Nee, we will take the insulin into my room and keep my medications together there."

I pivoted in the kitchen doorway. "Fräulein Mahler, why do you argue with everything I try to do for you?"

Her voice dropped. "Why do you take my privacy?"

I stiffened and prepared a return shot then stopped. She was right. . .again. Well intentioned but poorly executed, I was attempting to retool the delicate balance of her life with a crowbar and a sledgehammer. My lungs deflated. *When am I ever going to do anything right?*

I dropped my hands to my side. "I'm sorry. Again, you are right. I'm just so concerned about you."

"Are you not more concerned about Doktor Frühling and your pride?"

The heat shot back to my forehead. Pride? After everything I had done, everything I was trying to do to ensure her well-being. *Pride?*

"Now, wait a minute!"

"It is true, is it not?"

"I—there's. . .well, of course, I don't want Doctor Frühling—or Oskar—or *you* to think poorly of me. But that isn't why I'm doing this. You're not being fair."

Her voice maintained its even timbre. "Fairness bows before truth, Fräulein McAllister. Do not rely on such a vapor as fairness."

I shook my head. "What do you mean? What more can we hope for other than fairness?"

Her voice softened. "Truth. Our hope must be in what is true, not fair. Fair too often means merely what favors us. The same thing may not be fair to the next person. What is true, is true to all."

"I'm not sure what you mean. Hope on what truth?"

"We hope on the Christ, the One who is truth itself. If our hope is in Him, we need not concern ourselves over what the world thinks is fair."

I took a deep breath. "I think I understand what you're saying, but I really am trying to help. I just feel that my efforts here—"

"—are most appreciated. You have become very special to me, Fräulein McAllister, but you lack the wisdom of years. Such wisdom will only come if you trust the truth and not so much the fairness."

"And this wisdom might start with respecting your privacy?" I murmured.

She dipped her head.

"Fräulein Mahler, I do honestly care for you and am concerned about your welfare. I believe your coma to have been mostly my fault, and I am selfish enough to not want to lose you. You are also correct that I desire the approval of Doctor Frühling and Oskar, and that your well-being somehow reflects on me. I'm not sure yet whether or not to be ashamed of that."

"Perhaps the wisdom of years is coming early for you, nee?"

I glanced into her piercing eyes and gentle smile. My face warmed, and a sudden feeling of unworthiness overtook me. "Thank you."

She folded her hands on her lap. "Now the interview. Where did we end?"

"But it's Sunday."

"This is not work. It is conversation."

I raised my eyebrow. "Isn't that kind of stretching it?"

Her eyes twinkled, but she forced an even voice. "Do not be silly, Fräulein McAllister—and do not argue with your elders. Come. Sit." She patted the sofa cushion.

I grinned and set the insulin on the dining table. My backpack rested against the dining nook wall, and I grabbed the Sony from the front flap before taking my place on the couch. "I believe you had just met Oskar at the cross."

She lifted my hand to the arm of her wheelchair and closed her eyes. "Ja, the cross. . ."

*"My name is Oskar Schultmann. And you, Fräulein?"*

*"I am Katia Mahler. I suppose it is proper that we introduce ourselves, since you are carrying me in your arms."*

*It was the first time I saw his wonderful smile. Oskar smiles with his whole face. His eyes disappear, and his cheeks puff out like that of a chipmunk. He probably would not like to hear me say that, but it is what I think of. I cannot help it.*

*The tip of my crutch had splintered, and I hurt my knee when I fell to the ground. I was not sure if I could make it back to the car. Before I could protest, Oskar lifted me and cradled me in his arms, seemingly without effort. I held my crutches and my breath as he walked along the wall of the Reichstag toward the front plaza. The air was cold, but my cheeks were very warm. I am sure I was quite red in the face. I had not been carried for many years, and never by a man other than my father or Friedrich. I found it wonderfully unsettling.*

*"Really, Herr Schultmann—"*

*"Oskar, please."*

*"Yes. . .Oskar. I can manage. You do not need to carry me."*

*"I am quite sure you can manage, Fräulein Mahler—"*

*"Katia, please." My own words shocked me. He must have thought me very forward to be so familiar. His smile was gentle, though.*

*"Yes, Katia, I am sure you are quite capable, but your knee is scraped and your crutch is broken. Because you can walk does not mean that you should have to."*

*His warm breath—smelling vaguely of Glüwein—caressed my cheek. His arms were strong and his chest sturdy. If I were not holding my crutches, I think my arms would have been around his neck by the time we reached—*

I was grinning. Her eyes were open, their dreamy gaze locked onto the vase of pink roses. Suddenly she stopped and glanced sideways at me.

I straightened my face. Too late.

She blushed. Fräulein Mahler actually blushed! "Why do you smile, Fräulein McAllister?"

"Oh, was I smiling?" The corners of my lips quivered with the urge to curve upward again. Her brow narrowed. "Ja."

"I'm not sure. I must have thought of something funny. Please continue." I made a show of poising my pencil above the pad. The gesture's full effect was blunted by the fact that the page was still blank, but I couldn't help that now.

"Perhaps you should remove my last words from your little machine."

"Oh, that's a drawback with digital recorders, I'm afraid. You can't erase the sounds like you can from tape." I'd have to pray forgiveness for fibbing, but there was no way I was going to delete that last little gem from the Sony. I was only afraid that if she got any dreamier, I might have to attach a PG rating to the session.

She settled back into her chair, threw me a suspicious look, then closed her eyes. The smile reappeared almost immediately.

⤙⤐

*As we approached the Trabbie, Tante Frieda stared at us through the windshield. She shouldered her door open and nearly fell onto the street.*

*"Katia! What happened? Are you hurt?"*

*"Not badly. I scraped my knee and my crutch is damaged, but Herr Schultmann was kind enough to help. Oskar, this is my Tante Frieda Schiller. Tante Frieda, Oskar Schultmann."*

*Her eyes narrowed. "Thank you very much, Herr Schultmann, but we can manage from here."*

*Oskar bowed his head in greeting. He was quite the gentleman.*

*I gripped my crutches more tightly. "Please open my door, Tante Frieda. Oskar, you can please set me down now."*

*Tant Frieda crossed her arms. "Yes, you can put my niece down now."*

*"No, I insist to put her on the seat."*

*She frowned and trundled around the car to open my door. When he carried me past her, she hissed, "Katia! Stop smiling so!"*

*I tried but discovered I could not.*

*Oskar eased me onto the seat. Before he straightened, he took the damaged crutch from me. "I would be honored to repair this and return it, if you will allow me."*

*Tante Frieda put her hands on her hips. "That will not be necessary. We can—"*

*"Thank you. That is very kind."*

*"Katia!"*

*He nodded, and his smile broadened. "And, of course, I will need your address to know where to return it."*

*Tante Frieda huffed, "You can leave it at—"*

*"We live in Karlshorst." I gave him the street and the number then reached for my purse on the floorboard. "Perhaps you should write it down. I have a pen here. . .somewhere."*

*"That is not necessary. I will have no trouble remembering it." He bowed. "It was a pleasure to meet you, Frau Schiller."*

*"Fräulein Schiller."*

*"Of course. I should have guessed. Good evening."*

*I smiled at him while Tante Frieda got in and started the car. We waved to each other as she pulled into traffic. I looked out the rear window until he had disappeared from view.*

*Tante Frieda scolded me all the way home. At least, I think she did.*

# Chapter 31

## May 8

*Dear Maddy,*

*By the time you receive this, I expect you will have discovered Grandma McAllister's connection to Katia Mahler. If not, you're close enough that the news shouldn't come as a surprise to you. I also expect you wonder why all the secrecy. It's really not as mysterious as it may seem. Let me first qualify what I'm about to write.*

*More than anything I want you to know that you couldn't be more precious to your mother and me. We love you so much and are very proud of the young lady you've become. Let that be clear. Having said that, though, we've had some concerns watching you mature into that young lady. Let me explain.*

*Your involvement with Brendon, as much as we like him, has worried us. Your expectations of him have exceeded his obligations to meet outside of marriage, and now that there has been a gap in his writing, you seem to have discarded him as quickly as you snatched him up. Over the past couple of years, your involvement with your family has taken a similar track, your patience has grown thin and the road to frustration short. Even your faith, once vibrant, seems to have dwindled since you left for school.*

*Wow, where did all this come from? I didn't realize I was such a disappointment. Lousy girlfriend, lousy daughter, lousy Christian. Thanks for the eulogy, Dad.*

My trembling hands rattled my teacup in its saucer as I stood from the dining table and carried it into the kitchen. I started to refill it but stopped. It would be too difficult to swallow past the lump in my throat anyway. I set the cup in the sink and stared out the window at nothing in particular.

"Something troubles you?"

Fräulein Mahler looked at me from the kitchen door, her own cup balanced in her lap.

I turned back to the window "No, I'm fine."

Silence.

I glanced back at her. She studied me, her face expressionless. I didn't like it. "May I pour you some more tea?"

"Bitte."

I refilled her cup, adding a little less honey than I knew she liked.

She nodded. "Danke."

I averted my gaze. "You're welcome."

*Now leave me alone.*

When she returned to her corner, I settled back at the table, hesitated, then picked up the letter.

*What does all this have to do with Grandma McAllister and Katia Mahler? Please bear with me.*

*You're also very special to your grandmother. You probably didn't know that, partly because she is so quiet, and partly because you've devoted little time to get to know her. You now understand the kind of life she has led, and where it has brought her.*

*She was thrilled when she learned of your decision to study journalism. She wanted to share her experience with you not just for your personal benefit but to help expand your worldview as a journalist. She also hoped you would chronicle her life, maybe put together some pieces that she hasn't been able to sort out herself. But time is running out.*

*We fear Grandma McAllister is dying. I didn't tell you that because I wanted you to take on her project out of an honest desire, not guilt or pity. When you declined, I took up the effort myself with what little time and skill I have for this sort of thing.*

*To make a long story short, what I was able to piece together from her, plus a little research, turned up Katia Mahler. I contacted a business associate in our Berlin office and asked him to track her down for me. His efforts led him to Oskar Schultmann. Over the next few months, I corresponded with Oskar via letters and telephone.*

*Okay, so Oskar was in on it from the beginning. Great. Let's see, that makes Dad, most likely Mom, Oskar, Grandma, and probably Fräulein Mahler. I feel like a marionette on a string.*

The seed of a headache sprouted behind my forehead. I threw a sidelong glance at Fräulein Mahler.

She sat in her corner, the ubiquitous book in her lap—probably Chinese or Swahili this time, who knew?—and her fingers stroking that silly Bible cover.

I massaged my temples with my fingertips, but the seedling of pain sprouted tendrils that wound through my head. When I glanced back, she was watching me as though she could read my thoughts. I tried halfheartedly to keep the irritability out of my voice. "Do you need something?"

"Nee, danke. Is there something I can do for you?"

*You're probing. Sorry, I'm not giving you this one.*

I swallowed back a smart-aleck comment. "No thanks."

She smiled and returned to her book.

I frowned and returned to my letter.

*When you came home with the flyer on foreign exchange studies, I was excited to see the Freie Universität among your choices. I thought it would be a great opportunity to help with Grandma's story if you could touch bases with Oskar and Katia during your stay. Hence, my encouragement to apply for the Berlin opening.*

*Before I mentioned it to you, I discussed it with Oskar. He agreed but suggested you conduct a full interview with Katia without knowing the family connection. He thought your objectivity would be compromised if you knew you were interviewing a relative. He didn't tell Katia for the same reason. I believe he was wise in that advice.*

*I confess I also hoped that exposure to a world and a time like the ones your grandmother and her family lived through would give you a renewed sense of perspective and awareness of life, which seemed of late to have shrunk to Brendon, your sorority, and your cell phone.*

*Ouch! Was that* necessary?

My forehead burned, and the sapling blossomed into a full-grown headache. I rose from the table and went to my room for a couple of extra-strength Tylenol. In the bathroom, I washed the tablets down with a gulp from the faucet.

I lifted my head and stopped short at my reflection in the mirror. At first I didn't recognize who was staring back. Her face was puffy, and dark circles accented tiny red webs that clung to the whites of her eyes. Wispy auburn tendrils dangled from her half-combed bangs, their split ends snagged on unplucked eyebrows. If she had bothered to put on any makeup this morning, it would probably be smeared.

Mostly, her frown seemed glued in place. I tried to get her to smile, but she refused. She just tossed her head and glared at me. Still, she could've been worse.

*You're not so bad, Maddy. Nobody's perfect. In fact. . .in fact. . .*

...in fact, I was a mess. My face painted the thousand words my father's letter left out. I shook my head at the mirror, and the girl probably shook her head back at me, but her face was too blurry for me to tell. I plucked a Kleenex from a box on the shelf and dabbed at my eyes. What Fräulein Mahler wouldn't have to say about the girl cluttering her bathroom mirror. Then it hit me. She'd already had her say.

*"Are you not more concerned about. . .your pride. . ."*

The girl in the mirror recalled my response: *"I'm not sure yet whether or not to be ashamed of that."*

Well, Dad's letter was clearing that matter up for me. Had I been that self-absorbed? Had my world really become that small? Okay, I did go through some serious withdrawals when I discovered my cell phone plan didn't include Europe. Dad didn't tell me it wouldn't; he let me drag the stupid thing along and find out for myself. I substituted the clubs on the Ku'damm for my sorority parties. I thought I had made some progress in growing my appreciation for my family through Fräulein Mahler's story, but my faith hadn't reawakened in my mind or in my heart. And as for Brendon, well, Dad covered that situation pretty well, too—although that still didn't excuse Brendon's neglect in writing.

I studied the bland face of the mirror-girl studying mine. "So, Dad's little experiment appears to be pretty much a bust, doesn't it, Girl-in-the-Mirror?"

*"Why?"*

"What do you mean why? Take a look at yourself."

*"I am. Are we finished, then?"*

"Finished?"

*"Yes, are we giving up?"*

"Do you mean on the interview?"

*"No, on us."*

"Well, I. . ." The mirror-girl had a point. "I don't know. Do you think it's too late?"

*"Would I be having this conversation with you if I did?"*

My shoulders sagged. Even my reflection was a smart aleck.

"No, I guess not." I paused then sniffed.

She sniffed back.

I cocked my head.

She did, too.

I stuck my tongue out at her.

She ignored me.

Okay, maybe she was a smart aleck, but, unlike me, Girl-in-the-Mirror was right. Neither Fräulein Mahler's story nor mine were over. Fräulein Mahler had a firm grip on hers, but how much influence would I have over how mine would end? Well, that appeared to be up to me.

*"Up to us."* Then Girl-in-the-Mirror stuck her tongue out at me. Belated, but at least now we were back in sync.

As I wiped my face with the washcloth, I was surprised to find that my headache had subsided. Now, Tylenol is pretty good, but it doesn't work *this* fast. I glanced back up. The girl winked at me.

I turned the light out on her and headed back to the dining table. And the letter.

*Your letters have been encouraging, Maddy. We see an awakening in you. We're eager to read Katia's story. Grandma will want to read it—or better yet, hear it from you. Mom and I are very interested in the parts that seem to have affected you so strongly. I fully expect we'll learn something ourselves, too.*

*I know I've been brutally honest, sweetheart. I hope my words haven't been too painful. I only offer them in the hope that you'll be better for them. I'm sorry they came in a letter, rather than face-to-face. You just seemed ready now to hear them.*

*Let me share one last thing—something I think pertains to what you're going through in learning Katia's story and in what I've tried to communicate in this letter. Do you remember Valie Anderson from church? You knew she's a psychologist, a family counselor, right? I was in Dr. Anderson's office a couple of years ago, and a poster on her wall caught my eye. It depicted a Raggedy Ann doll squeezed halfway through the rollers of an old-fashioned ringer washing machine. The caption read, "The truth will set you free, but it will make you miserable first." I sense you're discovering just how true that is.*

*Seek the truth, embrace the pain, cherish the freedom.*

*We love you more than you'll ever know.*

*Dad*

❧

The house lay quiet. Fräulein Mahler's corner was empty. She didn't disturb me when she went to bed. A single lamp burning in the dining nook cast dark shadows behind the hands of the alpine clock. Four fifteen.

My third cup of tea sat cold and untouched by my elbow. I blinked over the grit in my eyes as I read and reread the letter. With each reading, something new materialized from the bold text. Truth, pain, freedom. A Raggedy Ann doll. A Blaumeise. A wheelchair.

I sighed, and my gaze wandered to the corner of the front room. Every evening, Fräulein Mahler took her Bible with her when she retired to her bedroom. Now, though, it lay on a narrow shelf of the bookcase. A worn suede bookmark draped over the smooth cover and dangled from the edge of the bookshelf. Although the room was still, it seemed like the bookmark wavered as though beckoning to me.

*Seek the truth.*

A tired smile settled on my lips as I submitted my mind. My bruised heart still lagged behind, but it was a start.

I reached back and lifted the front flap of my backpack against the wall. My hand dug around in the front pocket and returned with my *New Testament.* A pink ribbon marker, crimped and frayed, protruded from between the pages. I stared at it for a moment and recalled my thoughts over Christ's agony and Fräulein Mahler's serenity. I lifted the ribbon, and the book opened at the sixth chapter of St. Matthew. I scanned the page then stopped and smiled at a familiar passage. I closed my eyes.

*Our Father, who art in heaven. . .*

# Chapter 32

## May 17

*Dear Mom and Dad,*
  *I'll call you this evening.*

*Love, Maddy*

I giggled. Of course it was a silly letter. I wasn't going to mail it; I just wanted to write it. Fatigue makes me giddy. Always has.

"Fräulein McAllister?"

Fräulein Mahler peered at me from her wheelchair at the entrance to the hallway.

"Good morning!" I gave her the sunniest smile my exhausted face could muster.

"Guten Morgen. I smell coffee." She cocked her head at me. "You have not slept."

I feigned an indignant look. "Is it that obvious?"

"Ja."

I laughed. "Breakfast is ready. Please, come."

She wheeled to the opposite side of the table while I went into the kitchen. I returned with coffee, soft-boiled eggs, a couple of thin slices of fried ham, and toast. I had apple juice; she sipped her lemon water.

*Eww! Lemon water for breakfast. Lemon water anytime!*

I tipped my head toward the far corner of the room. "You left your Bible out last night. You normally take it with you when you go to bed."

She glanced at my own Bible lying on Dad's letter at the edge of the table. Her voice remained even, but I fancied a lilt to it. "I sensed it was time."

I paused buttering my toast and smiled at her. "Thank you."

"Bitte schön."

"Tonight Oskar takes us out to dinner." I picked up my fork and glanced back at her face. A slight pink tinged her cheeks; I was sure of it.

"Ja."

"Has he told you where we're going?"

"Nee."

"He's a stinker, that man."

She paused. "What is 'stinker'?"

I grinned. "It means a joker, that he's ornery."

"Oh, I do not know that I have observed such a thing in him."

Then it slipped. I blame the fatigue.

"Fräulein Mahler, I doubt there's anything you haven't observed in—" I froze at my own words, my fork halfway to my mouth.

She eased her toast onto her plate, her gaze fixed on her coffee cup. "And you mean by this...?"

Painful memories reminded me not to try to evade this woman. May as well let it out and face the music.

I set my fork down and leaned forward. "Oskar thinks a great deal of you. Surely you know this."

She straightened her back. I could hear her measuring her words. "Herr Schultmann is a good friend, ja."

*Oh, it's "Herr Schultmann" now, is it?*

She raised her eyes. "He has been a good friend for many—"

I cocked my head and smiled.

More red poured into her face in the next two seconds than a year's worth of ink in my checkbook. Her voice took on a flustered waver. "What are you implying?"

I reached for my coffee. "Nothing. I was just thinking. Forget I said anything."

"Nee, I will not forget. I see something in your face that disturbs me. What is it you wish to say?"

"It's none of my business, but you asked me the question, so I will answer. The man is in love with you."

I grimaced at my bluntness, remembering the promise I made to Oskar that not a word would pass my lips. But I was convinced this was more important than either of them realized. Besides, it was too late now.

"Fräulein McAllister! I do not—"

A slight smile forced itself on me. "And don't you tell me you had no idea, either. You're way too perceptive."

For the very first time—I'm absolutely certain—in her adult life, Katia Mahler stuttered. "H–he has told you this?"

"He didn't have to. It's all over his face every time he looks at you."

She turned away. "I do not know what you mean. Kindly—"

"Kindly what? Since we're on the subject, it's obvious you feel strongly for him, too."

She clutched her napkin and narrowed her eyes at me. "That is enough. I have given no such indication—"

"Oh, but you have. You're forgetting our interview the other day. I have it in my recorder, if you'd like me to play it back. My goodness, when you described him carrying you to the car, I thought I was going to have to fan both of our faces."

"That was fifteen years ago."

"And you were gazing with stars in your eyes at the roses he gave you just four days ago."

She stared wide-eyed at her plate. Her mouth moved, but no words escaped.

I lowered my voice. "I will drop the subject if you tell me to. But, if Oskar feels the way he clearly does for you and if you feel so strongly for him, why don't you tell each other? Why aren't you together?"

She raised her head and went still. She said nothing for a few moments, and I began to fear I had overstepped worse than ever. But the horses were already out of the barn, and I would see it through until she closed the door. "Fräulein Mahler?"

My eyes widened as hers filled with tears.

"Surely you understand. I. . .could never be a proper wife to Oskar. He deserves. . .a whole woman. Men have needs. . ." Her shoulders shuddered, and her hands went to her face.

I sat back in my chair, my mouth agape.

*Omigosh! What a waste of—*

"Fräulein Mahler, Oskar *loves* you. If he wanted another woman, don't you think he would have one by now?"

She sniffed and dabbed her eyes with her napkin. "If he wanted me, do you not think he would have me by now?"

*Oh, no. Tread carefully, Maddy.*

My sleep-deprived brain scrambled for safety. "Maybe there's something stopping him. If you were to ask—"

"Ach, think what you are saying! I cannot ask him."

"You're right! I know. I'm sorry." I grabbed my head. "It's just so sad. You say nothing because you don't think you deserve him, and he says nothing because he doesn't think he deserves you."

Her voice quieted. "Why does he think that? It is not because he is Karl Werner, is it?" My jaw dropped.

⟨⟨⟨❦⟩⟩⟩

"You saw the photograph."

She nodded. "Ja, and there were other things."

"What other things?"

"How he spoke Friedrich's name the few times he dared, the haunted look in his eye. I saw the bullet wound on his shoulder when I measured him for a sweater I crocheted years ago. Although there are other ways to become wounded, I read of the shooting that happened during his escape in what official Stasi records were not destroyed after the East fell. It made sense."

I shook my head and smiled. *She'd make some journalist herself.*

"That day in the park when you wanted him to share his story, you knew he wouldn't talk, didn't you?"

She shrugged. "Ja, but I held a small hope that there would be something he might say. There is much of his life that has nothing to do with Friedrich, and I hoped he would share some of it." She flashed a rueful smile. "I surprised him. That was not fair of me, was it?"

I smiled. "No, but we've had our discussion on fairness, haven't we?"

"Ja, but I did not intend to be cruel."

"I don't think you were cruel. Oskar is very important to you. I don't know how you've gone this many years without telling him how you feel. I would've blurted it out a long time ago. Why haven't you ever told him you know his real name?"

"It needed to come from him. There were surely reasons he became Oskar Schultmann, and the reasons were his own. I had no right to interfere with them. I understood how he might feel threatened by the past, by his life as Karl Werner. I would not take the chance of hurting him with it."

I hesitated then took another cautious step. "Do you know why he doesn't want you to find out that he's Karl Werner?"

"I suspect it is guilt."

"Yes, but there's more. He fears that if you discover it was Karl Werner who survived the escape, you would know it was your brother who did not. He believes you hold out hope that somehow Friedrich survived and that you may yet see him again. If you knew Friedrich died, the loss of hope may kill you. That is his greatest concern."

She smiled and dabbed at a spot of moisture on her cheek. "Ah, but we have had our discussion on hope, too, have we not?"

"Yes, we have."

"And I do know that I will see Friedrich again, if not in this life then in the next. My hope does not die because the One with whom we will rest lives."

"I'm just reawakening to that, I think—wait a minute. You said 'if not in this life.' Do you still think he may have survived?"

She nodded. "I also discovered from the official files that my brother's body was never recovered. The patrol boats, even divers, searched the river but were not successful. The Spree is not so deep there, nor the current so swift that he should not have been found. I can see Friedrich wounded but fighting the river as he fought so many other things. He was a determined man. I have not lost hope that he may have survived and eluded the border guards."

"Then why did you write his name on the white cross if you think he may have survived?"

"When I first saw the cross, the Stasi records were still hidden, so I did not know whether it was Friedrich or Karl who was shot. I wanted the memory of their brave act preserved." A fire kindled in her eyes, and her voice strengthened. "*Unbekannt* was not true. Friedrich and Karl swam the Spree. They conquered the Berlin Wall. Friedrich is not only my brother, he will always be a hero to me."

Then a gentle smile overtook her lips, and her eyes moistened. "Karl—Oskar—is special to me not only because of the wonderful man he is, but because he was the last one to be with Friedrich, to see him alive, to speak with him. Friedrich trusted him to share his greatest adventure."

"Oskar told me Friedrich saved his life during the escape and lost his own as a result." I searched her face for a reaction.

She nodded. "That would be the reason for his guilt. I also suspect it is this guilt that keeps him attending me. He should have a life—"

"Oh, no, ma'am. It's not guilt I see in his eyes when he looks at you or hear in his voice when he speaks your name. I may be young, but I'm still a woman. He's got it bad, trust me on this."

She wrinkled her brow. "What is 'got it bad'?"

"He's good and hooked."

She shook her head. "I do not understand. Is he bad or good?"

I laughed, and a yawn I'd been holding at bay suddenly contorted my face. "Oh my! Excuse me, please."

"Ah, but you are tired, certainly. We will not interview today. You are to sleep. I will clean up."

"Thank you, that sounds good." I thought of the morning dose of medication sequestered in her room. "Oh, and you won't forget—"

Her jaw twitched.

"—to wake me up in time to dress for dinner, will you?"

"Nee."

# Chapter 33

## May 17

*Dear Mom and Dad,*

*This interview has taken a turn I never expected. I find myself thinking more about Fräulein Mahler's future now than I do her past. I want so much for Oskar to be a part of it in the way he should—not just filling her pantry and her medicine chest, but filling her life. It's just not right, the way it is. I shouldn't get involved, but you know how painful it is for me to keep my mouth shut.*

*I can't get over how cultural nuances can do so much to affect people's relationships. We pile so much junk on ourselves, so many assumptions and expectations, and we bury so much of value in the process. I don't know; it's hard to explain.*

*Oskar's due any time now, so I'm going to set this aside. Fräulein Mahler is still in her room. I don't think I've seen her take this much time getting ready for anything. It should be an evening to remember.*

⚬⚬⚬

Fräulein Mahler? I think Oskar's here."

Her muffled voice slipped beneath the bedroom door. "Ja, I am hurrying. I cannot get my hair right." Her voice dropped to a mutter. "Ach, *du lieber. . .*"

"Do you need any help?"

"Nee, stay and talk to Oskar. I will be out soon."

I reached the door at the first gentle tap. "Come on in, Oskar."

"Danke. You look lovely this evening."

"Why, thank you." I curtsied and spun a three-sixty on my heel. "Do you like my dress? You so rarely see me in one, and I haven't worn this one to church."

"I can see why."

"Hey, I pinned up the neckline. Don't tell me—"

He chuckled. "I am teasing. You look very proper."

"Well, I don't want to look *too* proper." I batted my eyes at him and grinned at the lovely shade of red it brought to his face. "Fräulein Mahler will be out soon. She's having a little trouble with her hair."

He nodded then glanced past me. "Ach, the flowers. They did not last as well as I hoped."

I turned. Now on their fifth day, the pink roses looked as tired as I had that morning. They drooped on their stems, and a couple of brown-tinged petals littered the floor beneath the mantel.

He stepped toward the fireplace. "Perhaps I should discard them."

I raised a hand. "If you touch that bouquet, you'll be taking your life into your hands."

"Was?"

"You scored big-time with the roses, my friend. She has hardly stopped looking at them. I don't think she'll ever throw them away."

He blinked at me then looked back at the roses.

I thought for a too-brief moment then stumbled into yet another rash decision. "Oskar, you need to know something."

He looked back at me.

"Fräulein Mahler knows you're Karl Werner."

The look that crossed his face when I showed him the photograph at the hospital reappeared. His voice grated through his throat. "How—you *told* her?"

I shook my head. "She saw the photograph a long time ago and put other hints together. She's known for years."

"This is impossible! It cannot be—if she had known, I would have been able to tell." He staggered to the couch and dropped onto the cushion.

"Huh-uh. No offense, Oskar, but guys are bricks compared to *me* when it comes to this kind of stuff."

Oskar put his head in his hands.

I glanced at the hallway then hurried to the couch and sat down beside him. "Listen. There's no time for me to explain. She loves you. She always has, even knowing you are Karl Werner. She has never let on because. . .well, to be blunt, she didn't want to burden you. She thinks you should have a 'whole' woman."

His head jerked up, and his eyes flashed. "She is not a burden! Katia Mahler is the most complete woman I have ever known!"

"Yes, I know that and you know that, but she doesn't know that. Look, we can't discuss this now, but she thinks you two aren't together because of her physical condition, that she couldn't be what she considers a proper wife to you. She didn't realize the weight you were carrying over Friedrich's death."

He covered his face with his hands. I grasped his arm.

"Oskar, you breached the Berlin Wall. Now break down the wall between you and a life with the woman you love. The freedom you gained escaping to the West will never be complete until you're sharing it fully with her."

He looked up at me. His eyes were red, and his breath came in short gasps.

I pecked him on the cheek and whispered in his ear. "Don't blow it!"

"And what is this, Fräulein McAllister?"

We jumped at her voice coming from the hallway entrance. Oskar lurched to his feet, his face scarlet, his hat crushed in his hands. I stood up beside him, my breath taken away at a Katia Mahler I had never seen before.

She sat erect, a vision of beauty. A silky navy-blue dress draped softly over her knees and fell to a gentle kiss against her ankles. Matching thin-strapped shoes dignified her atrophied feet, which she forced straight against the footrests of her wheelchair, not without pain, I was sure. A beautifully crocheted loose stole replaced the usual white knit sweater, and her hair, minus the bun, flowed gracefully over her ears and caressed her half-bared shoulders. Just the right touch of makeup accented her already remarkable eyes and softened her skin. Her appearance was almost perfect—the "almost" being her stony expression.

"Oskar?"

He answered hoarsely, "We were just—"

"What you were doing is clear."

"It's not what you think." I flashed a look at Oskar and flinched at the streak of lipstick on his cheek.

"Once again, Fräulein McAllister, you presume to know what I think." Her face twitched, and I was horrified to see her eyes begin to brim.

Oskar's voice squeezed through a throat that sounded tighter than my own felt. "Katia, surely you do not suspect—"

"What is to suspect, Herr Schultmann? It should not be my concern over what. . .over who. . ." My heart broke at the catch in her voice.

Her chin raised, but her eyes remained locked on her hands folded in her lap. "Enschuldige, bitte. I am more tired this evening than I realized. Please enjoy dinner without me." She pivoted her wheelchair back down the hall toward her bedroom.

"Fräulein Mahler, this is nothing! You're making a mistake!" I elbowed Oskar's arm. "Say something!" I hissed.

She stopped but didn't look back. "Perhaps such intimacy is nothing to you. Und ja, it appears I have made a mistake." A moment later, the bedroom door latched behind her.

Oskar teetered on his feet, his gaze locked on the hallway. He cleared his throat and took a step toward the front door.

"Where are you going? You can't leave! She can't believe that—"

He opened the door. "It is perhaps best to let it go for now. There has been too much, too quickly. I. . .I must think." He hunched his shoulders and stepped outside.

I collapsed onto the couch at the click of the door.

# Chapter 34

## May 18

*Dear Mom and Dad,*

*The world exploded yesterday evening. I'm still in shock. I mentioned in my last letter about my discovery of Oskar's and Fräulein Mahler's feelings for each other. Well, all bets are off, and it's my fault. All because of an innocent kiss on the cheek.*

*I can't believe this! I told Oskar he should tell her how he feels about her then gave him a little kiss for encouragement. She saw it and came unglued. You guys know me; it was just a friendly gesture. How could anybody think anything of it? One minute we were on top of the world, and the next minute the world had disappeared and we were free-falling. Over what? A peck on the cheek between friends?*

*She went into her room and hasn't come out for breakfast this morning. I don't know if she's taking her medications. I'm afraid she'll do something in there. Oh, I don't know what I'm saying!*

*I can't let this go on, but I have no idea how to fix it. It's all so stupid. I've got to talk to her.*

⊷∾⊶

I steadied the breakfast tray and tapped the bottom of the door with the tip of my shoe. "Fräulein Mahler?"

Silence.

I pressed my arm against the door handle. Locked. "I've brought you some breakfast."

A floorboard creaked. I sighed in relief to know she was awake—alive—and apparently out of bed.

"We've got to talk. This is all a horrible misunderstanding. Please give me a chance to explain."

Silence.

I leaned my forehead against the door. "Please. I don't ask because I deserve a chance to explain. I ask because you deserve an explanation. I honestly believe you want to hear what I have to say."

After a moment, the floorboard creaked again and the door clicked. I stood back, ready for it to open. It didn't. I stepped up to the door and chanced another nudge on the handle. It moved.

I swallowed and pushed down on the lever with my elbow. The door swung ajar. I peered into the room. "Fräulein Mahler?"

"Komm herein." It came in a whisper.

My throat tightened as I stepped into her sanctuary. "I have some coffee, juice, and toast. It's real orange juice. We'll watch the sugar later."

"Danke."

I set the tray at the foot of her bed. "May I turn on a light?"

She didn't respond. I reached over to the bedside stand and tugged on the chain of a small lamp.

She sat in the corner of the room near her dresser. Her bed was undisturbed. She was still dressed as the evening before. The careful strokes of liner beneath her eyes sagged to a blur and disappeared down her cheeks. Her right hand clutched her Bible, squeezing it until her knuckles shone white. It was all I could do to swallow past the rock in my throat.

I stood on the opposite side of the bed and clasped my hands at my waist. My words stumbled over one another in their rush to get out. "First, please accept the most heartfelt apology I have ever offered to anyone for anything I've ever done. I truly mean that." I waited. If my apology was rejected, there would be no point going on.

She nodded but kept her gaze on her lap.

I swallowed again. "I don't know what it looked like to you yesterday evening, but, yes, I did have my hand on Oskar's arm. I did whisper in his ear. And I did kiss him on the cheek. I realize now I should have done none of those things. What I really want you to understand is that I was not trying to seduce Oskar."

Her voice did not raise. "Fräulein. . .McAllister. Such gestures of intimacy are significant."

I flinched. "I don't intend intimacy when I do these things. I grew up understanding such gestures to be signs of friendship. I do the same to all my friends at home and at school. We all do."

"Touch. . .and kiss. . .are important. Did you not see the look on Osk—Herr Schultmann's face?"

I nearly spilled out that the real reasons for his flushed face and agitated demeanor were his feelings for her, not me. But I had intervened too much already. Those words would have to come from him.

Her next question brought me up short. "Was this the first time you kissed him?"

I hesitated at the memory of a similar peck on his cheek in the hospital waiting room while she was still in the coma.

Her voice dropped further. "Your silence answers."

"Oskar is almost old enough to be my grandfather! I have no designs on him."

"I have read the newspapers. I read that in America foolish old men take for themselves silly young women as wives and lovers." She cleared her throat. "Herr Schultmann is a very handsome man."

My cheeks warmed. "First of all, don't believe everything you read. And second, I'm not that kind of a girl."

"I have given you most of my life story. You have given me only a little of yours. I do not know what kind of a girl you are."

The heat rose. "Now, wait a minute—"

"Have you known a man? Are you yet a virgin?"

I reddened. "That has no bearing—"

"Fräulein McAllister, when you first taste of such things, the mind and body beckon for more. With one man, then maybe with others. It does not know how to stop itself. Only love and commitment within a promise can control it."

I searched for something—anything—on which to build a defense, but there was no arguing her point. "I assure you—"

"You are young, beautiful, and. . .whole. I cannot compete with you."

My eyes widened. "Compete? Okay, this is *so* not right! I have explained and apologized for my behavior. Honestly and completely. If I have implied intimacy with Oskar, then it was unintentional. You must believe that. If I owe him an apology, too, then I'll apologize with you as my witness. This has to be made right, and I'll do whatever it takes to make it so."

Something in my heart moved me around the bed. I wrung my hands and beseeched her with my eyes. "You must understand how terrible I feel about what I've done. You must believe that I will never behave that way again." I paused. "You also must give Oskar another chance."

She sighed. "There appears to be much I must do."

"He's completely innocent. I alone am to blame. I respect you and Oskar so much, and—" my voice caught—"and I love you." My own words shocked me with their truth. She had become more important to me than I ever thought possible, and the notion I was losing her dropped me to my knees. She stiffened as I grasped her hands, but I didn't let go.

Her voice quieted. "Love? Why should you do so, child?"

My tone lowered to meet hers. "Because you are more than just my dear friend." I touched my forehead to her hands, and my shoulders began to tremble.

"I do not understand—"

The words pushed out between stifled sobs. "Fräulein Mahler. . .the day you came home from the hospital, I. . .I discovered that my Grandma McAllister is your Tante Maria. We are. . .family."

*Family.*

Never in my life did I have so much trouble containing my emotions, or understanding them, as in the moments that followed those words. Everything in my self-centered life suddenly took a backseat to the approval of a frail woman from a vanishing era sitting in a wheelchair half a world away from Saginaw, Michigan. I'm not sure how long I cried with my head on her lap, but the next thing I became aware of was my hair being stroked. Her voice remained a whisper, but it was now breathy, full of wonder—and perhaps a little amusement.

*"Tante Maria wohnt? Wir sind Verwandten?"*

I laughed between sniffles. "Yes, Tante Maria is alive, and you and I are related. I think we're cousins—well, some kind of cousins."

"But how—?"

"It's a long story, but one I really look forward to sharing with you."

The smile in her voice lifted my head from her lap. "I do not know how this could be, but on the day you came to my house, I saw something in your face, something familiar. I was not sure, but then, from her photograph on my dresser, I believed I saw Tante Maria in your eyes."

I wiped my tears on my sleeve. "Really?"

"Ja, but I thought it—what is the English, *ein Zufall?*"

"A coincidence."

"Ja, a coincidence. A silly notion, but I liked seeing her in you anyway." Her voice quavered. "It now makes sense. Tante Maria is your Oma, and so she lives in you."

I smiled. "Whew! I'm so glad to get that off my chest. Keeping it inside has been killing me."

"Why did you say nothing of this?"

I sat back on my ankles but refused to let go of her hand. "At first, I didn't know if you already knew. I thought it might come out in your story, and I was afraid knowing that we are relatives might disrupt the interview. Oskar knows, though. He's known from the beginning."

She raised an eyebrow. "Ach, this is the 'stinker' you spoke of."

I sputtered a laugh and nodded. The mention of Oskar's name brought another thought to mind. "Fräulein Mahler—"

"Who do you say?"

I searched her face. The words came tentatively. "*Kusina* Katia?"

Then my smile faltered. Something sounded wrong with that. In my mind, a cousin was someone you romped with in an inflatable kiddie pool on the front lawn, a sleepover buddy you clobbered over the head in pillow fights. It may have been the age difference or the profound respect I had for her, but as excited as I was about being related to her, I just couldn't see her through that lens.

She noticed my hesitation. "There is something wrong?"

"I'm sorry, but Kusina Katia sounds strange to me. Do you think—" I glanced up at her. "Ja?"

"Both of my parents are only children, and you are my ideal of a dear aunt. Would you mind if I called you Tante Katia? It sounds so much better to me."

"That would be very nice, Madeline."

*Madeline.* The music of my name floating from her lips for the first time robbed me of my breath and blurred my vision again. I swallowed against the resurgent emotions then thought again of Oskar.

"Tante Katia, what about Oskar?"

Her smile faded. "He hurts, nee? Today he is to bring more food and medicine. I am not sure now that he will."

"Oh, he will, all right." A sly smile crept onto my lips. "And he still owes us dinner out."

"Nee, I do not think—"

"No, no. He did promise, you know." I winked at her. "We need to stick together on this."

She paused then looked down at her lap. I noticed a similar smile struggling for birth on her face.

"Oh, your breakfast!" I stood and turned toward the tray. "I'm afraid the coffee and toast are cold."

"Ach! Forget coffee and toast. Bring me the juice."

We laughed.

# Chapter 35

*. . .and I felt so much better, like a veil was lifted when Tante Katia—I still can't get used to saying that!—learned about Grandma McAllister. She had hoped Tante Maria was still alive, but she had no knowledge of our connection. Oskar did a good job of keeping the secret.*

*Speaking of Oskar. . .*

After breakfast, we resumed our usual places in the front room. I asked a few questions to fill some gaps in her story, but it was difficult to concentrate on the memoir. An interesting change took place, though, I think without either of us noticing. Now, when we held hands, I stroked her wrist with my fingertips. She seemed to like it.

My scattered thoughts rushed back into place at a knock on the door. We released hands, and I straightened against the back of the sofa.

She cleared her throat. "Komm herein."

The door opened, and Oskar entered, hunched at the shoulders. "*Tag*, Katia."

"Guten Tag, Herr Schultmann."

He winced at the formal address. I dropped my eyes to my pad, ostensibly out of respect, but more truthfully so he wouldn't see the grin pushing its way onto my face. He crossed to the kitchen. The rustling of paper and closing of cupboard doors echoed through the doorway.

I threw a helpless look at Tante Katia, whose lips were fighting their own battle against a smile.

"I can't do this," I whispered. "I'm going to lose it; I know I am!"

She puckered her quivering lip and narrowed her eyes at me. "Do not dare lose anything, Fräulein!"

I snorted, and my eyes began to water. I bowed my head again when Oskar came back through the doorway, his shopping tote folded under his arm. I glanced at Tante Katia but kept my head down. She sat with her hands folded on her lap, her patented expressionless expression planted firmly on her face as she held Oskar in her narrow gaze. Her performance was awesome.

*She deserves an Oscar—oh! Did I really say that?* The inadvertent pun nudged the grin closer to the surface, and everything went blurry.

His voice was hoarse. "May I help with anything else, Fräulein Mahler?"

"Ja. There is one more thing you owe us. Do you not know what it is?"

I raised my eyes without lifting my face.

He stared at the floor for a moment then cleared his throat. "Ja. I would like to apologize for my behavior—"

"Nee, nee. Do not be silly, Herr Schultmann. We do not want apologies."

He lifted his head and looked from her face—which was still playing an award-winning role—to mine. I began to tremble. I was going to ruin everything. I think she sensed that.

"You still owe us dinner. We cannot eat apologies!"

That's when I lost it. My face exploded into a grin, the painful kind you feel for days afterward. Oskar disappeared through my tears, and I snorted again. That triggered her. She brought her fingertips to her lips and came as close to giggling as I think she was capable.

Oskar straightened, his eyes wide and mouth agape.

She beckoned to him. "Komm, bitte."

He took two faltering steps toward her wheelchair, and she waved him down. He bent over, and she cupped his face in her hands. To my shock—and obviously his, too—she planted the most beautiful kiss in the history of the world on his cheek. The kiss blossomed into a marvelous hue of crimson that radiated across the rest of his face.

His eyes rounded, and he straightened, although a little wobbly. He wrung the tote in his hands. "I do not understand."

She cocked her head. "Perhaps we can discuss it over dinner?"

"Tomorrow evening?" I added.

He nodded, and the first trace of an uncertain smile tickled his lips. "*Bis* Morgen."

We smiled and, in unison, nodded. "Until tomorrow."

# Chapter 36

*I*t's late enough Dad should be home from work. He's gotta hear this!
   "Hi, Dad! I'm so glad you're home. . . . Yes. I got the letter. . . . Sure it hurt—for a while. But I couldn't fault what you said. And, well, it kind of turned a corner for me. . . . Yeah. There is so much I want to tell you, but not on the phone. . . . What's that? . . . Brendon? What's *he* doing there? . . . Dad, I don't know if I want to talk to— Oh, hi, Brendon. How are you? . . . I know I haven't answered your e-mails. . . . No, I haven't read the letter. Brendon, I was so upset that you hadn't written for months. You just disappeared on me. Then I got caught up in this project and. . . Okay, I'll read it. But can't you just tell me what— Oh, nuts! I thought I had more time left on this stupid calling card. . . . Brendon? . . . Brendon? Are you still there?"

⌘

I knocked on the bedroom door. "Are you ready yet? Oskar will be here any minute."
   "It is my hair again. Himmel!"
   I fingered the door handle. "Open the door. Let me help."
   "Nee, stay and wait for Oskar. I will be there—"
   "You're kidding! After the last time? Not in a million years! He can fend for himself. Open the door."
   The latch clicked. I pushed the door open and gasped.
   "You look incredible! Where did you get that dress? I've never seen it before."
   "Oh, I do not remember." She fluttered her hand. "It has been in my *Kleiderschrank* for ages." I glanced at the new sales tag dangling from the back of her collar by a safety pin and smiled.
   *Right.*
   I picked the brush up from her bed and pulled it through her freshly shampooed hair. "Your hair looks fine to me. What's wrong with it?"
   "Ach! It never works for me."
   "You're being silly. It looks beautiful. Oh, and let me get this for you." I unfastened the pin and dropped the sales tag on the bed. "So, that's where you went this afternoon while I was on the phone with my dad. You know the shops near the S-bahn station pretty well, then, huh?"
   She frowned up at me in the mirror. I smiled, feigning concentration on her hair. "I just want to know how you hid it from me all the way home."
   She sniffed. "I did no such thing."
   A tap came at the front door. "Fräulein Mahler? Fräulein McAllister?" Oskar's gentle voice echoed down the hall.
   "He's here. Get your wrap. Your hair looks great."
   I left her to her wardrobe and hurried to the front room. He stood by the dining table, his hat in his hand.
   "Oskar, is that a new suit?"
   He shrugged.
   I stifled a grin and lowered my voice. "Wait until you see her."
   He began to speak but then stopped, as his eyes focused past me.
   She sat at the entrance to the hallway. Today's perfect put the perfect of two days ago to shame. The navy blue had bowed out to a subtle floral print on azure that wisped over her slight frame as though its designer had only her in mind. The exquisite cameo she wore that morning so many weeks ago protected a graceful neckline, and a scalloped hem just touched

132

a stunning pair of off-white strapped sandals. A tiny matching clutch lay in her lap atop her crocheted stole.

I could hear Oskar swallow even across the room. "Fräulein Mahler—"

She cocked her head.

He hesitated. "Katia?"

The warmth of her smile melted me, as it clearly did Oskar. His voice went hoarse. "You look. . .you are. . .very. . ."

Her smile faded. "There is something wrong?"

I held my hands up and laughed. "No, no. That was one for the record books. Another word would only ruin it. Trust me on this."

Oskar dropped his gaze to the floor. Tante Katia looked at her lap and fingered her clutch.

"Well, I don't know about you two, but I'm hungry." Leave it to me to shatter a poignant moment.

Oskar cleared his throat. When he offered me his arm, I stiffened and glanced at Tante Katia. She nodded with a smile. "It is proper."

I took his arm, and together we eased the wheelchair through the door.

"I can't believe it! The Fernsehturm!" I bobbed up and down on my toes like a middle schooler. "I've wanted to come here ever since I arrived in Berlin. Have you dined here before, Tante Katia?"

"Nee. This is very special."

Oskar stared at me. "*Tante* Katia?"

"Yes, Oskar. My dad explained the whole thing. I know, she knows, and you're sneaky."

He lifted his chin. "Enschuldige, do you think I was wrong to keep it from you?"

"I didn't say you were wrong; I said you were sneaky."

Tante Katia tapped her finger on the arm of her wheelchair. "But we will discuss why you kept it from *me*, Oskar."

He was literally saved by the bell when the elevator dinged our arrival at the restaurant level. The door opened, and we ushered the wheelchair onto the deck of the revolving restaurant. The host showed us to our table, and we settled in to enjoy the view. Berlin spread to the horizon, its skyline bedecked with self-lit emeralds, rubies, and diamonds. Our table faced west, and I could just make out the dark Tiergarten on the other side of the Brandenburg Gate. Vehicle lights streamed through the glittering Ku'damm a distance beyond. It was more beautiful than I ever imagined it would be. The movement of the restaurant around the tower was almost imperceptible, but for the window frame crawling past my left shoulder.

Oskar ordered a bottle of Spätzlese, and we decided to share an appetizer of veal and lime tartare with lettuce, capers, and an incredible balsamic vinegar dressing. He protested that we should select our own appetizers, but Tante Katia would only nibble, and I wanted to save room for my entrée. I promised him I'd make up for it there.

I tried not to be rude by staring out the window, but I don't think my fixation on the panorama was even noticed. Oskar was having his own struggle with fixation, and it wasn't at the outside scenery. The color in Tante Katia's cheeks betrayed her awareness of that struggle—at least it did to me. I suspect he was clueless.

My entrée of veal roulade in mushroom sauce with apple-honey cabbage and potato dumplings was as heavenly as the view. Tante Katia picked at a tasty-looking dish of duck smoked over tea, and served on a bed of Asian vegetables and basmati rice. Oskar selected Geschmorte Ochsenbacke with a cream of celery and pearl onion sauce. I instantly regretted it when I asked him what that was.

*Braised ox cheeks? Great choice, Oskar. She'll never kiss you now.*

For dessert, I zeroed in on the house specialty: the Cup TV Tower, a chocolate ice-cream sundae with coconut cream and passion fruit sauce. Oskar selected the assorted French cheese plate with figs and little slices of nut bread. It came with port wine, which I think is what tipped the scales for him. When Tante Katia ordered hot poached chocolate cake with mango, we both looked at her. I was about to say something about sugar, but a twitch of her jaw invited me to mind my own business.

*Easy for you. You're not the one who has to call the ambulance.*

My mind wandered back over our feast, and I grimaced inwardly at the bill I knew Oskar would face. But he was stuck. A dine-and-dash would be tough enough to pull off with one of us in a wheelchair, but when you're a thousand feet up it's pretty much out of the question.

After dessert, we all settled back with small cups of coffee. I'm sure my sigh of contentment could be heard all the way to Frankfurt. I gazed out the window, mesmerized by a thunderhead to the south throbbing with pulses of heat lightning. I didn't notice Oskar's voice until it tripped over an interesting word.

"...marriage."

My mind snapped back to the present.

"Ja, of course, I know of this opera, but Figaro is not a favorite of mine."

My shoulders slumped.

"But surely the theme would interest you, Katia?"

"And why would that be so?"

He fumbled for a response, his eyes glued to the table and his cheeks ruddy.

*Oh, Oskar. You didn't try the indirect approach, did you? That never works.*

A standoff between jumping into the conversation and hiding under the table nailed me mutely to my chair.

He cleared his throat. "I only thought..." He glanced at me.

I widened my eyes at him. *Get to the point!*

"Ja?" Tante Katia took a sip from her coffee.

"It is just that..." He lifted his napkin and dabbed at the sheen of sweat on his forehead.

I frowned and jerked my head toward her.

She set her cup down but kept her gaze on her coffee.

I moved my napkin from my lap to the table. "Will you two excuse me, please? I need to go to—"

"Katia, please marry me." His voice broke.

I buried my face in my hands.

When I chanced another peek she had straightened her back. "Oskar?"

To my surprise, he assumed a tone of confidence I didn't know he possessed. Maybe it was that the question was finally on the table, or maybe he just felt he had nothing to lose. All I know is I wish I'd had my Sony with me for what followed.

"Katia Mahler, you are the only woman in my life whom I have truly loved. I have withheld my proposal of marriage not because of who you are, but because of who I was. I understand now that nothing has been hidden from you these years, and I have been the greatest fool for allowing them to pass without you at my side."

Her eyes—and mine—went to the size of saucers when he slipped from his chair and dropped to a knee. He placed his hand over hers on the pure white tablecloth.

"You are the highest desire of my humble life. I cannot offer you leisure, only love. Please honor me above all men by becoming Frau Katia Schultmann."

I wanted to cry, sing, and disappear all at the same time.

Katia stared at their hands, her eyes brimming. Her voice came at a whisper. "I cannot... I am...incomplete. How can I be a wife to you?"

"Katia, there is only one thing incomplete about you."

Her shoulders stiffened.

He reached out with his other hand and tipped up her chin. "You lack me as your husband. I am also incomplete in that I lack you as my wife. I no longer wish to live incomplete. Do you?"

She squeezed her eyelids closed.

He reached up and stroked her cheek with the back of his fingers. "Please say you will honor me."

She opened her eyes, and twin rivulets of joy spilled down her face. She nodded. "Ja."

I hadn't registered the utter silence that had descended over the restaurant until a thunderclap of applause burst out around the table. Waiters frozen in midstride and neighboring diners stared respectfully at the only two people in the restaurant who I'm sure didn't hear a thing.

I forgot all about my mascara and streaked a gray-tinged tear away with my knuckle. Oskar and Tante Katia deserved both the grandest celebration and the quietest solitude. I suspected they would prefer the latter, so I tucked my hands in my lap and remained silent.

I glanced up when the couple at the next table rose to leave. Only when the man squeezed Oskar's arm and the woman caressed Tante Katia's shoulder in passing did they break their gaze into each other's eyes. Oskar resumed his seat but did not release her hand.

I cleared my throat. "I really shouldn't be here. . . ."

Oskar smiled as he studied his love's face. "This would never have happened if you were not here, Fräulein McAllister." Tante Katia reached over and squeezed my wrist with her free hand. Neither did she remove her gaze from her. . .her fiancé.

*Her fiancé.*

I rolled the word across the tip of my tongue and cherished its taste.

*Dear Mom and Dad,*

 *Oh, you should've been there! It was the most awesome proposal in the world! I don't know how long we sat after she said yes. Things quieted down around us, and the restaurant got back to normal. Several couples looked over at our table as they left, and at least two of the men got an elbow in the ribs from their dates.*

 *Tante Katia spent the next couple of days in her corner, where she read her precious Bible and meditated. This afternoon she asked if I could wheel her back to the shops near the S-bahn station. As soon as I agreed, I got an idea. . . .*

O*h, you've just got to be home. Please pick up!*

 "Grandpa? Hi, it's Maddy. . . . It's wonderful to hear your voice, too. How is Grandma? . . . Good. Is she there? . . . Can you put her on the phone, please? . . . Hi, Grandma. . . . I miss you, too. You have no idea how much. I have someone here who would like to speak with you. Can you hang on for just a minute?"

 I placed my hand over the mouthpiece. "I put plenty of time on my calling card, so there's no hurry."

 Tante Katia stared nervously at the phone. "I do not know what to say to her."

 "You'll think of something. How long has it been since you've spoken with her?"

 "We have never spoken. I have only read letters from her to Mama." She dropped her gaze to the sidewalk.

 "Well, you're engaged to be married. That's always a good leadoff."

 She shook her head. "I do not know, Madeline. Perhaps this is not so good an idea."

 "Of course it is. Here. Take the phone. Just say hello and go from there. Even if you don't find that much to discuss, it will be nice to have heard her voice. Trust me on this."

 She nodded, and I handed her the phone. She gripped it with both hands and lifted the receiver tentatively to her ear. One more glance at me and she murmured, *"Allo? Tante Maria? Es ist ihre Nichte Katia."*

 A broad smile broke over her face.

⎯⎯⎯⎯⎯

I leaned against the aging brick wall of the train station with my arms crossed. The street lamp across the road flickered to life, and I checked my watch again. I looked over at Tante Katia and held up two fingers. She didn't notice.

 Two minutes later, her voice stopped. She looked at the receiver with a puzzled frown then up at me. "She is gone."

 "You ran my calling card out of time. You've been on the phone for over two hours."

 She shook her head. "Nee, it cannot be. We only began to speak of things."

 I smiled. "And you were worried you wouldn't have anything to talk about."

 She looked wistfully at the dead receiver. When she raised her eyes again, they glistened. "It was Tante Maria. *Meine Tante Maria*," she whispered.

 I swallowed thickly and lifted the phone from her hand. After I hung it up, I knelt in front of her. "We will call her again soon. Have you finished all the shopping you needed to do?"

She nodded. I stood and released the brake on the wheelchair. The walk home passed in silence.

❦

"You're getting some great mileage out of that dress." I stroked the brush through her hair.

I glanced up at the mirror to see a puzzled look on her face.

"I mean you're getting to wear it at some really important times. First at the restaurant for Oskar's proposal, and now to your wedding."

She smiled. "He asked me to wear it. It seems to please him."

"Well, duh!" I looked back up and froze. "Oh! It means of course he does; you look beautiful in it. It's just an expression."

Her jaw twitched.

My cheeks warmed. "I'm sorry. I guess I never thought about how disrespectful that sounds. Please forgive me. You won't hear it again."

She nodded, but her smile was a little slower in returning.

I smoothed her hair onto her shoulder. "Well, that should do it. You look fantastic." I laid the brush on the bed.

"Danke schön."

"You're welcome." I glanced at my watch. "Well, we have over an hour before the taxi comes. I told Oskar he wasn't allowed to see you before the ceremony. It's bad luck."

She smoothed her dress over her lap. "I do not believe in luck. It is too easy an excuse."

"I'm beginning to believe in it less and less myself. Let's just say it's a fun tradition."

I turned her wheelchair from the mirror and eased her through the bedroom door into the hall. "What are you going to do for the next hour?"

"I will have quiet time. It seems a proper thing to do."

"I think it's the perfect thing to do."

After I wheeled her to her corner, I settled at the dining table and hoisted my backpack to my lap. I dug around in the bottom for spare batteries to the recorder. This was one ceremony I wanted to save forever. My hand brushed over what felt like a crumpled wad of paper. I pulled it out. It was Brendon's letter. I set the backpack down and flattened the envelope against the tabletop with the palm of my hand. I fingered the flap, undecided whether to read it.

"What is that you hold, Madeline?"

I looked up. She nodded at the letter.

"Do you remember asking me if I had a fester Freund?"

"Ja."

I held up the envelope. "Well, Brendon was my fester Freund."

"I see on your face that he is no longer a boyfriend, nee?"

"Nee is correct."

"I see in your eyes that does not please you."

I stayed focused on the letter. "Oh, I don't know. I think I'm over him." Her pause lifted my gaze from the wrinkled envelope. "I mean I'm okay with him not being my boyfriend anymore."

"Why are you over him?"

"Because he is apparently over me. Except for this letter, he stopped writing last January. If he truly lov—if he was at all serious, he would have found time to write."

"What did he do for those months, do you think?"

I sputtered a mirthless laugh. "I can only imagine."

"It seems you expect loyalty from your Brendon. Does he not deserve more from you than imagination?"

My forehead warmed. "Tante Katia, this really doesn't concern—"

"It was in my imagination that you wanted my Oskar. If I listened only to my imagination and not to your words, would we know of each other what we know now? Would we. . . love each other as we do?" Her voice dropped. "Would you have brushed my hair for a wedding this day?"

I couldn't explain the pressure behind my eyes, and it annoyed me. I was over Brendon. I really was. "That's different."

"How is it so?"

"It just is." I laid the letter on the table.

"Madeline, read the letter from your Brendon."

"I. . .oh, I don't know, Tante Katia." I leaned my head on my hands.

"There is a time to listen to your head and a time to listen to your heart. After you kissed Oskar's cheek, my head let you explain when my heart would not."

"You really think I should read it, then."

The smile in her voice defeated me. "What is it you say: 'Trust me on this'?"

I sat on the back step of the house. A light breeze stirred the herb garden and swirled heady aromas of rosemary and lavender with the tender fragrance of tea roses on the trellis next to the steps. The aromatic symphony washed over my senses and rinsed away the last of my resistance. I turned the envelope in my hand and slipped my finger beneath the flap. In a moment, a single page of text lay across my palm.

*Hmph. Typewritten. Always the romantic, huh, Brendon?*

I pursed my lips and began to read.

*Dear Maddy,*

*First, I need to ask your forgiveness for taking so long to write. As much as it sounds like an excuse, I'm afraid I haven't been in much condition to do so.*

I sniffed. *I bet. Too much partying, Brendon?*

*Last January, I was on the way home from school for the weekend. As I turned onto Main Street near the coffee shop, a pickup ran the light and broadsided me. I was in the ICU for six weeks. I still don't remember waking up. Everything is kind of a blur.*

My jaw dropped. *Omi—!*

*They're rebuilding my left shoulder. I would write this by hand, but you know how lousy my handwriting is with my right hand. I'm poking the keys of my laptop with two fingers. It looks pretty silly. You remember how fast I used to type.*

*Rebuild your shoulder? Forget the stupid typing, Brendon! What on earth—?*

*Maddy, there's something else. It's my left leg. When I came out of the coma, it was gone. They told me they couldn't save it. They said I should be able to walk again with therapy and a prosthesis. I guess my power-walking is a thing of the past.*

I put my hands to my face. The words were too blurry to read until I regained control. After a couple of moments, I took a deep breath and wiped my eyes.

*Your parents didn't know about the accident until I asked my mom to call yours after I woke up. I made your folks promise not to say anything, that the explanation should come from me. I wanted to call you, but they said you're not at the Dörings' anymore and there's no phone where you're living now. I'll try when I get home. This letter will have to do for now.*

*Anyway, I don't know yet how much mobility I'll get back. As John Lennon wrote, "I'm not half the man I used to be." (Sorry, trying to joke.)*

*I only want to say one more thing before I close. I don't know how much I can offer you. I'll be in a wheelchair until my shoulder heals and I learn to use the prosthesis. I have no idea how long that will be. If you decide to move on, I'll understand. You deserve more, and I don't want to saddle you with a cripple. Pity doesn't make very good glue for a relationship. If you don't reply to this letter, I'll take it as your answer. No hard feelings.*

*Love you, Maddy. Always will. I'm really sorry.*

*Brendon*

The page fluttered to the grass at my feet. My carefully brushed hair was tangled around my clenched fingers, and the tears wouldn't stop.

"Madeline?" Her voice wafted over my shoulder.

I heaved a sob in reply.

"Are you. . . What can I do?"

I only shook my head, my voice buried in my chest. I leaned over and groped for the letter with trembling fingers.

She eased it from my grasp when I held it back over my head. After a few moments, she gently cleared her throat. "He loves you very much to let you go."

She wheeled back from the door when I turned and crawled up the steps. I knelt on the kitchen floor with my head in her lap. She stroked my hair while I sobbed.

"You should answer the letter, Madeline."

I nodded.

# Chapter 38

## June 6

*Dear Mom and Dad,*

*There's so much to tell about the wedding and not nearly enough time. I finally read Brendon's letter. I wish you had told me, even though I know he asked you not to. I'm such a dork.*

*Needless to say, I was a mess. I cried on Tante Katia's lap until she whispered in my ear that I only had fifteen minutes left to get ready. The taxi arrived just as I finished redoing my makeup and putting my hair back together. I don't remember much of the trip to the church. I do remember that, when the cab driver opened my door, I had to steel myself against the leftover emotions from the letter before I got out. This was her day, and I wasn't about to ruin it with my own stupidity.*

*Tante Katia had told me that, under normal circumstances, the bride and groom would have a six-week waiting period after applying for the marriage license to allow the wedding notice to be publically posted, should anyone want to protest it. Then there would be a small civil ceremony at city hall before a Standesbeamte, or registry official. Technically, they were married at this point, but neither Tante Katia nor Oskar considered themselves married until they had exchanged vows dedicated before God, so Oskar scheduled the church wedding the day after the civil ceremony.*

*Oskar had a friend at the registry office who attended church with them. Although Oskar didn't request it, his friend fudged the date on the application out of respect for the elderly betrothed couple and Tante Katia's physical condition. Since neither of them had been married before, there was zero chance anyone would challenge the union on legal grounds. So, here we were, only two weeks after Oskar's incredible proposal in the Fernsehturm. I hoped the ceremony would be worthy of the proposal. I wasn't disappointed*

*We arrived in the narthex of the church before Oskar did. I fussed over her hair and dress while we waited. . . .*

"Oh, no!"

"What is it, Madeline?"

"I've ruined your dress!" I stared at a large tear stain smudged with mascara at the center of her lap.

She smiled. "Nee, it is for me to cherish. I will not wear this dress again. It will remind me of this day for the rest of my life."

"Oh, Tante Katia. . ."

*Don't, Maddy! You'll run your makeup again.*

The front door clicked, and Oskar stood in the entryway wearing the same dark suit he wore to the Fernsehturm. My heart went to my throat when I saw him beaming at his bride. I couldn't see her face from behind her chair, but I'm sure her smile matched his. It was a good thing she didn't believe in luck, because the intensity of the gaze he caressed his beloved with now, before the ceremony, would've shattered any lucky chance they may have had. His sole attendant, Herr Leitner, a distinguished-looking gentleman who appeared to be maybe a year or two younger than Oskar, stood to the side and, like me, allowed them their moment. He glanced at me and flashed a smile so much like Oskar's—the crow's-feet, the disappearing eyes—that I could easily imagine him being a brother, or at least a cousin.

When the first strains of "Hornpipe" from Handel's *Water Music* filtered through the heavy double doors to the sanctuary, she looked up at me with that heart-melting smile. "It is Oskar's favorite music."

"Wait until you hear what I picked out for the recessional." I winked at her.

An attendant eased open the doors, and the music swelled, filling the foyer with glorious stringed overtones. German tradition bade the groom to accompany the bride down the aisle, rather than waiting for her at the front, so Oskar took his place at her right. I moved behind the wheelchair, and Herr Leitner took his position at my right. On cue, the wedding party stepped forward, and I ushered her chair through the doorway and onto the rich burgundy aisle runner. The hall was modest, but beautifully decorated—and full! There had been so little time between Oskar's proposal and the wedding that I didn't think anyone would find out about it. I kept my eyes ahead, but my peripheral vision didn't spot a single empty seat. I had no idea so many people knew Oskar and Tante Katia, until I remembered that her father was once the pastor of this church. I wondered how many of those in attendance remembered him.

The ceremony was simplistic and dignified, the love between its principal actors palpable. At one point, the betrothed couple lit candles from a common flame on the altar table and held them during the pastor's address. During the brief sermon, I glanced at Tante Katia. My eyes widened as her head tipped forward and her candle slowly canted back toward her body. Worried something was wrong, I looked at Oskar to see if he had noticed. He watched, too, as she tapped two drops of white wax onto the stain of tears and mascara on her dress. Then she righted the candle, and Oskar smiled. The now-familiar lump returned to my throat.

During the exchange of vows, I found my gaze lingering on Tante Katia's wheelchair, envisioning Brendon in a similar one. As much as I tried to concentrate on the ceremony, the shock from reading his letter only a couple of hours earlier still numbed the fringes of my mind.

At the conclusion of the rite, Oskar took my place behind the wheelchair, and I took Herr Leitner's offered arm for the recessional. The congregation rose, and I melted as the string quartet that had so gracefully accompanied the processional and colored the ceremony floated the notes of my request, "It's All I Ask of You," from Webber's *Phantom of the Opera*.

From behind Oskar, I saw Tante Katia's arm extend to the side. Her hand beckoned. Oskar turned to me and nodded. I lifted a half-questioning, half-apologetic glance up at Herr Leitner. He smiled, eased my hand from his arm, and ushered me in front of him.

I moved up to her right side and laid my hand on the arm of the wheelchair. She covered my hand with hers, her ring finger now flashing a beautiful, but modest, diamond setting in traditional yellow gold. It took only a moment for her to begin stroking the back of my hand.

Normally, a grand celebration followed the ceremony that would last well into the evening. Due to the abbreviated preparation time, though—and, I fully suspect, this bride and groom's personal preference for quiet dignity—a brief reception in the narthex replaced the extended festivities. To me, it was a blur. Many faces, many smiles, but I don't remember a single name. My mind was already at the Deutsche Telekom booth by the Karlshorst S-bahn station, punching in Brendon's home number. I prayed it wasn't too late.

Yes, I really prayed.

The drive back to the house eludes my memory. When Oskar pulled up to the curb, I let myself out of the backseat. He cut the engine and stepped out of the car.

"Oskar, what are you doing? I have a key."

He walked to the back of the car. "We are home."

"But, aren't you going somewhere? You know. . ." My cheeks pinked.

He opened the trunk and pulled out the wheelchair. "Where else would we go, Fräulein McAllister?"

The pink went to crimson. "Well, I don't know. Anywhere."

He opened the passenger-side door and lifted his wife from the front seat. "Would you please open the gate and follow us with the chair? I intend to carry my bride."

Tante Katia's eyes narrowed at her husband. "Oskar, you will do no such thing. Put me in my chair."

He ignored her. "The gate, please, Fräulein McAllister."

"The neighbors, Oskar! Madeline, bring the chair."

"The gate, please."

"The chair."

"Fräulein McAllister?"

"Madeline!"

"You guys are on your own. I have a phone call to make." I escaped around the car and set off toward the S-bahn station. As I rounded the corner three houses up the street, I heard the gate screech across the walkway. To this day I have no idea who won.

❧

*Please be home, Brendon.*

"Hi, Meghan. It's Maddy. Is Brendon there? . . . I know. I don't blame you for feeling that way. If I were his sister, I'd feel the same way about me, too. I'm such a dweeb, Meghan, and I'm so sorry. I didn't read the letter until just today. I had no idea. . . . Please give me a chance. Or at least let Brendon know it's me, and if he doesn't want to talk, then okay. I'll understand. . . . Thanks."

*Oh, Lord, please don't let me mess this up any more than I already have.*

"Brendon? . . . Hi, how are you feeling? . . . Listen, I have no idea where to start except to ask you to forgive me for being such a jerk. I was so sure you had lost interest in me when I didn't hear from you. Nice of me, huh? . . . Yes, I read it today. I've been clueless in so many ways. Obviously, your letter explains everything. . . . No, and I know exactly what you're going to say, but a wheelchair means absolutely nothing to me. I understand about your leg and it is *so* not an issue, believe me. I have such a story to tell you when I get home. I can't wait to see you. . . . I'm editing the memoir now, so it won't be long. Probably the end of next week. . . . Of course I'd love you to come to the airport. . . . You sound really good, Brendon. I didn't realize how much I've missed hearing your voice. . . . I'll call again when I buy my plane ticket. . . . Love you, too. I really do."

❧

I hung up the phone and lingered on the S-bahn platform, submerged in my thoughts. On an impulse, I bought a ticket and boarded a train on the S3 line. It didn't matter where it was going or when it got there. I sat at the back of the last car, oblivious to everything. At first, my mind defaulted to the memoirs, where it had spent its time almost nonstop over the past couple of months. Much still remained to be done. But my notes were organized and—

*Oh, who cares about your silly notes, Maddy? You have a life to put back together.*

Thoughts of the interview faded into images of my cozy bedroom back in Saginaw, Dad and Mom at the kitchen table sharing coffee and ice cream, my upcoming senior year at Michigan, and my faith and what it really meant to me. When my thoughts got to Brendon, they stopped wandering.

I reached the S3 terminal point at Ostbahnhof and crossed to the other side of the tracks to take the westbound train. I rode the evening away, unmindful of the stops, the transfers, the people. It was midnight before I realized how low I was on ticket money. Train service on the S3 ended at one o'clock in the morning, so I caught one more ride back to Karlshorst.

The station was quiet, awash in the sterile glow of fluorescent bulbs flickering with the tiny shadows of frenzied moths circling and diving. I paused before exiting the platform and took off my heels to give my ankles some relief. The pavement felt cool beneath my feet as I ambled back toward the house. At ten minutes after one, I turned the corner at the top of Fräulein Mahler's—no, Herr and Frau Schultmann's—street, and a moment later stood at the gate. The house lay dark, except for the soft glow of a single lamp visible through the left side of the front window. My hand reached for the gate then paused.

*You can't open this thing, Maddy. It'll wake up half the neighborhood. Besides, even if you opened it quietly, there's no way you're going into that house.*

There I stood in my evening dress from the wedding ceremony, my hair piled on my head like I never wear it, my white heels and sequined purse dangling by their straps from my fingers. All dressed up and nowhere to go. I was just tired enough to giggle at that.

I stepped back from the gate and bumped into Oskar's car parked against the curb. I turned and peered into the dark interior. The rear door was unlocked.

⌘

A gentle rap stirred me from my shallow slumber and forced my eyes open to slits. Through the rear window of the car, the eastern sky shone a bright azure, the yellow halo of a glorious sunrise splaying cheerfully across a pristine sky above the roofline of the house next door. Birds chirped their welcome to the new day, twittering life into the sleepy neighborhood. I had opened the rear windows to a slight gap, admitting cool morning air that wafted in and encircled me with the delicate fragrance of flowers and hearty breakfasts being prepared near open kitchen windows along the quiet street. There, the beauty of my morning ended.

I felt like I'd been poured into an Audi. My legs, bent double, were propped up against the back of the seat, and my spine had molded itself to every seam and lump of the cushion. I shifted my back and grimaced at a crick in my neck, courtesy of the door's armrest, which had served as my pillow. My chin had embedded itself into my breastbone—permanently, I feared. A Bavarian pretzel would have been impressed at the shape I managed to get myself into.

The second rap at the window came more urgently. I squinted past whitened knuckles into Oskar's concerned face. He frowned. I reciprocated.

I reached up, grasped the top of the driver's seat and pulled. With the least ladylike grunt I've ever produced, I pivoted on the seat and collapsed my legs onto the floorboard.

He opened the door. "Fräulein McAllister, what are you doing in here?"

"Which part of me are you asking?" I rubbed the back of my neck.

He offered his hand. I groped the air for his fingers and emerged from the car with all the grace of a half-awakened brown bear in March. I arched my back and groaned, while he retrieved my heels and purse from the floorboard. "Why did you not come into the house last night? Katia wanted me to search for you. She insisted there was no reason for you to stay away."

I raised my eyebrow at him. "I suspect Tante Katia underestimates herself."

He began to reply then stopped. His smile was thanks enough. I stepped through the open gate, and he took my arm as I limped to the front door.

"Madeline, where have you been?" Tante Katia had just set a third place at the table.

"I called Brendon from the S-bahn station."

She cocked her head at me.

I smiled.

She nodded and wheeled into the kitchen. I knew a fuller accounting would be expected, but, mercifully, she deferred it for the moment.

"Who is Brendon?" Oskar asked.

I sucked in a deep breath. The aroma of fresh eggs, coffee, Brötchen, and—was that bacon?—chased everything else from my mind. "Can we hold that question until breakfast?"

Tante Katia returned with a container of fresh strawberry compote. We took our seats, and she glanced at my evening dress. "You have for once overdressed for breakfast."

I sputtered a laugh. "Maybe so, but my robe sure sounds good right about now." I paused. "There's something different about you, too. What is it—oh! You're wearing your hair down."

She straightened her shoulders, and her gaze flitted to Oskar, whose eyes had disappeared behind his smile.

"Oh, I see. Oskar, do you—"

"Stille, Madeline. Oskar, offer thanks, bitte."

I hope it's okay to grin during grace, because I was helpless.

# Chapter 39

## June 15

*Dear Brendon,*

*My calling card is low, but I'm too close to leaving to buy more time. I'm saving the few minutes I have left in case I need them on the trip back home. The couple of times this past week we've been able to talk have been great. I can't wait to see you!*

*Tante Katia's memoir is at the bookbinder shop. It should be ready to pick up on Friday. She insisted I include Oskar's story, too, since she was in the coma when he shared it with me. Oskar still looks a little nervous when the subject comes up. He'll probably hover behind her shoulder the whole time she reads—well, at least for as long as she puts up with it.*

*I can't believe it's almost over. In one way, I've been here forever. In another way, time has flashed by. It's time to leave, though, for both me and the Schultmanns. Oh, that sounds so cool to say!*

*Anyway, I get in on Northwest Airlines just short of nine o'clock in the evening on the 22nd. I ran a print of the itinerary at the Internet café. I'll enclose it. See you soon!*

*Love, Maddy*

Well, that does it." I thanked the clerk and slipped the two nine-by-twelve, two-inch-thick volumes into my tote. The bell over the door tinkled behind me when I left the printing and binding shop on Schloßstraße for the final time. Oskar had been kind enough to drive me halfway across the city to this particular bookbinder. The store did a lot of business with the university, and I knew the quality of their work. I wasn't about to take any chances with this precious document. He met me at the curb and opened my door for me, then took his place behind the wheel.

"Here it is!" I lifted the flap of the tote to reveal the parcels wrapped in brown paper.

"Very nice." He nodded.

I laughed and elbowed him. "No, you can't see it yet. You'll have to wait until we get home. Let's go. I can't wait to see what she thinks."

"And your school, Fräulein McAllister?"

My eyebrows shot up. I had completely forgotten to contact Professor Müller regarding credit for the project. Oskar suggested that we might swing by the Journalism Department before heading back home, since we were so close to the university. Fortunately, Professor Müller was in his office. He rose and shook hands with Oskar, while I stood aside and fingered the handle of my tote.

He turned to me. "So, what do you have for me, Fräulein McAllister?"

I hesitated and glanced at Oskar then eased one of the wrapped tomes from the bag and laid it on his desk. Professor Müller noticed my hesitation.

"There is something wrong?"

"I'm sorry. It's just that. . .well, I wanted Tante—Frau Schultmann to be the very first to see this."

He smiled and nodded. "I understand. I will accept a softcopy on CD, if you prefer, and a letter indicating your satisfaction with her work, Herr Schultmann."

"That will not be a problem, Professor." Oskar winked at me.

Relieved, I tucked the memoir back into the bag and said my final thanks and farewell to my instructor. The ride back to Karlshorst was a restless one. So much work, love, and uncountable tears had gone into the project. I had edited the narrative, resized the graphics, and tweaked the formatting at least a dozen times before I grudgingly handed the materials over to the printer. I knew it was the best job I could do, but a pang of insecurity pricked my brow. What if she expected something else? What if I disappointed her?

In a surge of panic, I swiveled my head toward Oskar. My voice quavered. "I'm scared to death. What if she doesn't—"

The Audi bumped the curb in front of the house. Oskar turned off the engine, smiled, and patted my hand.

⁂

She sat with the memoir on her lap. Oskar stood behind her wheelchair, his hands resting lightly on her shoulders. Her fingertips traced the cord that bound the folds of heavy paper. I threw a nervous look at Oskar. He cleared his throat. "Katia, it will not unwrap itself."

"Patience, Oskar."

"I am patient, but I wish to view Fräulein McAllister's work before my old eyes fail me completely." Her frown didn't fade his smile a bit.

I tried not to fidget as her fingers pinched the ends of the binding twine. *Please, Lord, let her like it.*

She tugged at the bow and slipped the cord around the package. The paper cover slid to the side with a nudge. Her eyes watered in an instant. Embossed on the faux leather cover was their wedding photo. The caption, in old German script, read, *Der Anfang*, The Beginning. She brushed her fingertips over the textured surface and reached up to grasp Oskar's hand with her other hand. She raised her eyes and nodded at me. I exhaled for the first time since entering the house.

She slipped her frail fingers under the front cover and eased the volume open. The title page hosted the same photo as the embossment, but in sepia matte on thick antiqued paper. Even the subdued brown tones couldn't dim the crystalline glint in her incredible eyes. Their glimmer seemed to levitate over the photo and lend the memoir life of its own. Oskar knelt at the side of her wheelchair, his hammy fingers cupping her delicate hand, his own eyes reduced to slits nearly indistinguishable from the wrinkles etched into his temples. It was one of those rare scenes that in an infinitesimal slice of eternity captured everything that could have been right with the world.

Her voice came as a breath. "Oskar, *das Fotoalbum*, bitte."

He reached over and pulled a small loose-bound book from a low shelf of the bookcase. He laid it on her lap, and she opened the booklet to the last page. She removed a snapshot Oskar had taken during one of our walks in the Volkspark. Tante Katia and I posed on the dirt path in the shade of a massive oak tree. I stood behind her wheelchair, my hair tousled by the morning breeze and a silly look on my face in a futile attempt to dissuade Oskar from taking the picture. I never considered myself to be photogenic under the best of circumstances, and the goofy grin sure didn't help any. I grimaced at the image.

"Und, bitte—"

Before she could finish, he handed her a roll of adhesive tape from a small drawer. She smiled at him then tore a strip of tape from the roll and positioned the snapshot beneath the sepia photograph.

"Oh, Tante Katia, please don't. It'll ruin—"

She narrowed her eyes at me, but their sparkle remained. "This is my memoir, is it not, Madeline?"

"Yes, but—"

"Then kindly be still."

I watched her affix the glossy print to the page then gently glide her fingertips over its surface. She tipped her head back and appraised the page through her reading glasses. She smiled. Oskar winked at me and returned the tape to the drawer.

Tante Katia browsed through page after page. The text flowed in precise German thanks to Oskar, who rescued my courageous, but flawed, attempts to translate my notes. She paused at the pages with embedded photographs and studied them carefully. She was so quiet, I began to worry. I shifted on the sofa and studied her face while she read. Oskar caressed her shoulders.

When she finally turned over the back cover, she stroked it like she had the front. The tactile gesture took me back over the hours we sat with my hand in hers, her finger stroking my wrist. I think she communicated more through a single touch than did all the words and pictures in the memoir.

I held my breath for the judgment. She looked up at me, her eyes twinkling. "It is beautiful, Madeline. There were some errors in the German—"

"There certainly were no errors in the German!" Oskar blurted. "You will understand, Katia, that I—"

The second almost-giggle I ever heard from her stopped him short. She touched her fingertips to her lips and glanced up at her husband. That big of a smile had to be painful. I covered my mouth to stifle a laugh of my own.

He shook his head. Then his famous smile broke loose, and he leaned forward and kissed her on the forehead.

Oskar looked up at me. "You had two packages, Fräulein McAllister."

"I made a copy for Grandma McAllister. Although, with all the time you two spent on the phone, Tante Katia, she probably already knows everything." I winked at Oskar.

I reached into my backpack and pulled out a box of CDs. "I'm also going to make a couple of these."

She stared at the box.

"It's a CD, a compact disk."

Silence.

*Uh-oh. Here we go again.*

"I'm going to burn your memoirs onto this."

Her eyes widened, and she hugged the book to her chest.

"No, not really burn them. That means I'm going to save copies from my computer onto these disks."

She looked at the tome in her lap and then back at the CD. "How does it fit?"

"It's digital. It uses a laser—" Her look shut me down again. "Never mind. Let's just say there's no way I'm going to let this memoir get lost."

She smiled, but her eyes were still glazed over.

On Tuesday morning, nothing seemed to go right. It took an hour and a half to pack. I didn't have that much stuff, but it seemed every sweater and sock reached out and grabbed the sides of my bag as I tried to stuff them in. I didn't have the heart to scold them.

Breakfast passed amid awkward smiles and small talk that trailed off to nowhere. Tante Katia's eyes seemed a little red to me, but I didn't ask. I knew my eyes were puffy. Oskar insisted on serving the food. I think he spent more time out of his chair and in the kitchen than normal. It seems the moments I want to remember the best always seem to turn out the worst, and the times I want to last the longest pass the most quickly.

My plane was scheduled to depart Berlin Tegel at 12:45. It was only a thirty-minute drive to the airport, but Oskar thought I should be there by eleven, just to be sure I'd get my bags checked, clear Security, and make it to the gate in plenty of time. At the moment, honestly,

I preferred to miss the flight. Still, at ten fifteen, he carried my suitcases and backpack to the car.

Tante Katia sat in her corner, her memoir on her lap. I stood in the middle of the front room, my hands clasped at my waist, swallowing at a stubborn tightness in my throat. She kept her eyes on the book. Then she reached over and patted the divan. I sat down. She folded her hands on the memoir.

"You have done fine work, Fräulein McAllister."

"You have been wonderful to interview, Frau Schultmann."

"There is another thing."

"What could that be?"

Her words came softly. "Oskar and I will set aside money. It is for another airplane ticket for you."

I raised my eyebrows. "Another airplane ticket?"

"Of course. You agreed to interview me for my life story, nee?"

"Yes, ma'am."

"My life is not yet over."

I smiled. "You saw the blank pages I left at the end of your memoir."

She nodded. "Your work is incomplete."

"Yes, it is."

"Therefore, I must withhold final payment until you return and finish."

"Agreed."

≈≈≈

Ten minutes later, Oskar cleared his throat from the doorway. I lifted my head from Tante Katia's lap and rose from my knees. She rested her head back, her eyes closed, her fingertips massaging the smooth cover of her Bible perched on the arm of the wheelchair. The memoir was propped up on a book stand centered on a ledge of the book shelf. I sniffled and smudged what was left of my mascara and eyeliner with the knuckle of my forefinger. With a final look back, I slipped my purse over my shoulder. Oskar held the door for me.

The Audi's engine sputtered to life, and he shifted into gear. I glanced at the ramshackle house. It looked the same as the day I arrived, minus the calico.

I stifled a smile. "Some repairs are still needed."

He nodded, his face serious. "Katia has given to me what in America I think you call a job jar."

I grinned.

We pulled away, and I took one more look over my shoulder. I was sure I saw the curtain move.

The drive to the airport along the inner-city autobahn passed wordlessly. My mind floundered in a warp between the past and the future. Karlshorst had become home so quickly it felt strange to leave, as though I were going on a trip rather than returning from one. When I did switch to the future, I found myself anxious to get back and share my experiences with my family and friends.

Before I knew it, Oskar pulled up to the curb in front of Tegel's passenger terminal. I kept my hands in my lap. He walked around the back of the car, retrieved my bags from the trunk, and turned them over to a Northwest Airlines luggage porter. He turned and opened my door. I accepted his hand and stepped onto the sidewalk. With great effort, I peeked up into his face.

"I want to say something really meaningful right now, but words fail me. And for a journalist, that's not good."

He smiled. "Words are not always necessary."

We hugged, and as I watched him get back into the car, a sudden urge struck. I hurried around the front of the Audi, leaned down, and gripped the driver's side window.

"*Onkel* Oskar?"

He kept his head forward and dropped his gaze to his lap.

"Since you are, well, sort of my uncle now, don't you think at least once you should call me Madeline?"

He looked up. His watery eyes sought refuge once again behind a full smile, and a droplet squeezed through the crow's-feet. He patted my hand. I stood and watched as he shifted into gear and drove away.

⁂

The line to the Northwest counter was short, the queue to the security checkpoint not so short. Boarding pass in hand, I shuffled mindlessly along with the rest of the cattle until I felt a tap on my shoulder.

"Fräulein McAllister? Fräulein Madeline McAllister?"

Two men stood behind my right shoulder. One was tall, serious looking, with hawkish features. The one who had addressed me was a bit shorter, balding, and had a nondescript face.

"Yes?"

"I am Herr Wilmer with Interpol. This is Herr Brecht of the Bundeskriminalamt. We must ask you to step out of the line and come with us, please."

I frowned. "What on earth for?"

"It concerns your association with an Oskar Schultmann. Please, come this way."

"But my flight—"

Herr Brecht reached for my arm. "This way, Fräulein."

# Chapter 40

Herr Wilmer punched the buttons on the cipher lock and led us into a short hallway. We entered a small room with two chairs and a table. I shook my arm loose for the third time as Herr Brecht tried to guide me along. We glared at each other.

"Please, sit." Herr Wilmer pulled a chair back from the table.

I put my backpack on the floor and dropped onto the edge of the seat. Herr Brecht stood at the door with his arms folded across his chest. Herr Wilmer took the chair opposite me and clasped his hands on the table.

"I apologize for the inconvenience, but we have some serious concerns about Herr Schultmann. I am afraid we require information you are in the best position to provide."

I folded my hands on the table likewise, determined not to be intimidated. "Serious concerns? Why? How do you know of my association with him?"

"Herr Brecht and I are assigned to what you Americans would call a counterintelligence unit. Interpol and national authorities of various countries—here with the Bundeskriminalamt, the German Federal Criminal Police Office—work together to identify and bring to justice former agents and criminals of the communist East who have gone underground, in this case from East Germany."

"What could that possibly have to do with Oskar Schultmann?"

"Herr Schultmann's file reached my desk early this year. There are some disturbing aspects in it. We have watched him now for three months."

"Watched him?"

"Ja, we began surveillance on him just before he contacted you at the university."

"Surveillance?"

"You ask many questions, Fräulein McAllister. It was my intention to question you."

He attempted a half smile. I did not.

"I have nothing to tell you."

Herr Brecht spoke up. "You will tell us what we ask, that is what you will tell us."

I glowered at him. "I will tell you what I know. What you ask and what I know may not match."

He bristled. "We are German law enforcement officers, Fräulein McAllister. We can detain you. I suggest you remember that."

"I am an Irish-American journalist, Herr Brecht. You may detain more than you've bargained for. I suggest *you* remember *that*."

"*Fräulein*—"

"This gets us nowhere, Hans." Herr Wilmer looked up at his colleague. "There is a café near the entrance to the terminal. Could I ask you to buy us some coffee perhaps?"

He frowned. "I do not think—"

Herr Wilmer silenced him with an upraised finger. "Bitte, Hans."

Herr Brecht shot me another withering look and left.

A sardonic smile curved my lips. "So, we do the good-cop-bad-cop routine?"

"Nein, there is no bad cop here. In 1984, Herr Brecht lost his parents to the Stasi. He is very. . .I would say, zealous. . .to track down spies of the former regime."

"Let me share something with you." I took my grandmother's copy of the memoir from my backpack, removed the paper wrapper, and set it on the table. I pointed to Tante Katia's likeness on the cover. "This woman lost her parents and her brother to the East German regime. She, however, has retained a measure of grace and civility. Herr Brecht could use more lessons and fewer excuses."

His tone matched mine. "But we all react differently to such trauma, do we not?"

I stifled another retort and sighed. "You had some questions, Herr Wilmer?"

He nodded. "What is your relationship with Herr Schultmann, bitte?"

"Why do I suspect that you already know the answer to that?"

"Perhaps you will surprise me."

"You said you had Herr Schultmann under surveillance. Doubtless, that surveillance included me."

"Doubtless."

I leaned forward. "How closely? Is there any privacy in Germany?"

His eyes darkened. "Now let me share something with you, Fräulein McAllister. Two weeks ago you took a late-night ride on the S-bahn. You left the Karlshorst station on foot between midnight and one o'clock in the morning."

My eyes darkened in return. "It appears some things have not changed since the fall of the Berlin Wall."

"You are a very eye-catching young lady. Especially in a lovely evening dress."

"Why, thank you," I replied icily.

"You caught the eye of two skinheads, who followed you from the train."

My eyes rounded, and I stiffened against the back of the chair. "I—"

"Hans cut them off two blocks from the station. I recommend greater vigilance on your part."

A collage of horrible images piled through my mind, and I swallowed back a wave of nausea. "I–I'm sorry. Thank you."

Herr Brecht came back into the room with three steaming cups in a cardboard caddy. He set a cup in front of me. I nodded to him.

Herr Wilmer leaned his elbows on the table. "We have no desire for an adversarial interview with you. However, we have a job that requires a certain amount of probing. As a student of journalism, I am sure you can appreciate that."

"I do."

"I would still very much like for you to make your flight. I think you can do that if we abandon this battle of wits and concentrate on the issue at hand."

I took a deep breath. "Okay. What is it you need?"

He took a small notebook from his pocket and flipped it open. "Oskar Schultmann came to our attention because of an incomplete history file. It appears his background can only be traced to the early 1960s. His profile fits that of what we call a sleeper, an agent who lives a normal life in the target country until activated by his organization. I am interested in anything you may have picked up during your time with Fräulein Mahler—Frau Schultmann—and Herr Schultmann, that may shed light on his life before that time."

I smiled. "I believe I can help you with that." I pulled the memoir toward me and opened it. I paged partway through the book then laid it open and turned it around to face the Interpol officer. Herr Brecht leaned over his superior's shoulder.

"This is a photograph of Oskar Schultmann from his employment with the American Army."

Herr Wilmer nodded. "We have that photograph. It is the earliest one we have found."

"Study the face."

He exchanged glances with his partner then looked back at me.

I turned back two pages. Embedded in the document was the photograph I confronted Oskar with at the hospital. "Take a look at—"

"I see." Herr Brecht's eyes focused on the middle subject of the trio of soldiers.

"You're perceptive, sir."

He glanced up at me as though expecting sarcasm, but I only smiled.

His gaze returned to the photograph. "But I also see a Volksarmee uniform."

"Yes, sir, you do. Let me continue. The man on the left is Friedrich Mahler, Frau Schultmann's brother. The man on the right is Heinrich Schwerer, a friend of Friedrich's. In February 1963, Heinrich was summarily shot by a KGB colonel for being late to formation."

Herr Wilmer shifted in his chair. Herr Brecht's jaw twitched.

I pointed to the center figure. "If you check whatever Volksarmee records there may remain from 1962, you'll find a Soldat Karl Werner assigned to the Potsdam caserne. You will also discover that Private Werner deserted on April fifteenth, 1963."

Herr Wilmer jotted a note in his pad.

I continued. "Early in the morning of April sixteenth, Karl and Friedrich attempted to escape East Berlin by swimming the Spree River. Friedrich was killed while pushing Karl to safety. You will find a white cross on the fence near the Reichstag that reads '*Unbekannt, 16.4.1963*.' That was Friedrich."

Herr Wilmer sat back, and Herr Brecht straightened.

I sat back, as well. "Oskar Schultmann breached the Berlin Wall and survived, gentlemen. He has dedicated the remainder of his life making good on a promise to care for the infirm sister of the man who sacrificed himself so Karl Werner—Oskar Schultmann—might live."

Herr Wilmer smiled. "And his proposal of marriage to Herr Mahler's sister was quite moving."

"You were there? In the Fernsehturm?"

"Although I serve as the director of this investigation, I wanted to observe our subject firsthand. My wife was delighted when I told her we would dine in the Turm that evening. Perhaps you will recall a man and woman congratulating the newly engaged couple with pats on the shoulder as they left."

"Vaguely—" I stared at him. "That was you?"

He chuckled. "Ja, my wife sniffled all the way home."

"I didn't recognize you, but then my attentions were elsewhere."

"Understandably."

"Do you always make such personal gestures to suspects you tail?" I asked.

Herr Wilmer leaned forward and rested his arms on the table. "Fräulein McAllister, when you have been in my business long enough, you develop a sense. I did not believe Herr Schultmann to be a threat then, nor do I now."

Herr Brecht interrupted. "But we must still investigate."

I nodded. "I understand."

"May I?" Herr Wilmer extended a hand toward the memoir.

"Certainly." I nudged the book toward him.

He scanned through the pages. "This is very thorough work. You are to be commended."

"Thank you. I think of it as a labor of love."

Herr Brecht stroked his chin. "It is valuable information, but it must be verified, of course."

"How do you intend to do that?"

"We will search the Volksarmee records, as you rightly suggest. We may also have to question Herr Schultmann, and perhaps Frau Schultmann."

I stiffened. "Oh, you can't do that! Oskar has worked hard to put that life behind him, and Tante Katia is too frail. They've just married, and they're so happy. This could disrupt everything for them."

They both looked at me. "*Tante* Katia?"

"Yes, I discovered during my research that my Grandmother McAllister is her Tante Maria Schiller, her mother's sister, a survivor of the Holocaust. Katia Schultmann is a relative of mine, and she has become very dear to me. Herr Brecht, please. Isn't there any other way to verify this?"

He took a deep breath. "I do not know—"

"Hans?" The Interpol officer raised his finger.

"Ja."

"Look here." He pointed to a spot on the page.

Herr Brecht squinted at the book. "Horst Klein? *Oberst* Horst Klein?"

"What?" I looked back and forth at both men.

"You have an Oberleutnant Horst Klein here as a Volkspolizei officer who knew the Mahlers."

"Yes, do you know him?"

Herr Wilmer smiled. "Colonel Klein was an undercover agent for the West German government the entire time he was in the Vopos—what we in the West called the Volkspolizei. Until his retirement, he led our school for counterintelligence officers. Hans and I both studied under him at different times. He is something of a legend among us."

My eyes pleaded with Herr Wilmer's. "Perhaps he could help and you won't have to bother the Schultmanns. If he knows Katia Mahler is involved, he'll verify my story. I know he will."

Herr Brecht nodded. "If Oberst Klein vouches for your story, as far as I am concerned, the case will be closed."

Herr Wilmer echoed the sentiment. "He lives in Spandau now. I am sure he will agree to an interview."

I sighed in relief.

Herr Wilmer tapped the memoir. "We may have to keep this until we have finished our investigation."

I shook my head. "Sorry. That's for my grandmother."

Herr Brecht frowned. "Fräulein McAllister—"

"But you can have this." I reached into my backpack and pulled out a CD case. "It's all on here along with my contact information, in case I can be of any further help."

Herr Wilmer shook his head with a wide smile. "Hans, you bait too easily."

Herr Brecht ran his fingers through his hair. "Fräulein McAllister, I am glad this turned out well. We would not like to take such an Irish-American journalist as yourself to headquarters. They would never forgive us."

I laughed.

He glanced at his watch. "But you must hurry. You have a plane to catch."

I looked at my own watch. "I don't think I'm going to make it. Not with that line at Security."

Herr Wilmer rose from his chair. "I do not think Security will be a problem. Please, allow us."

❧

*Yes! My cell phone works! The battery is nearly dead, but—*

"Dad? It's me. I'm in Detroit. Almost missed my plane out of Berlin, but I'll tell you about that later. . . . I can't wait, either. You'll pick me up at the airport? . . . Really? Brendon, too? . . . Thanks, Dad—oh, and, by the way, this is probably going to sound silly, but could I ask a favor? I know everyone has called me Maddy forever, but—I don't suppose you could call me Madeline from now on, could you? . . . Thanks, Dad."

# Epilogue

*Six years later*

"And that, young lady, is how you came to be named Katia. Now you and your sister get ready for bed. It's late."

"Was she pretty, Mommy?"

Madeline smiled. "Tante Katia was the most beautiful bride I've ever seen, sweetie. Absolutely the most beautiful."

"I wanna see the pictures again."

"Maria, you're stalling. Time for bed." She kissed her twins' foreheads.

"Brendon, would you tuck the kids in, please? I'm on a deadline, and I've already used up most of the evening."

Her husband leaned over her shoulder and kissed her cheek. "Sure, Hon. The *Times* loves your column." He whispered, "There's word on the street it's up for a Pulitzer."

She frowned at him. "Now how would you know that?"

" 'Cuz I'm the one who put the word on the street."

Madeline laughed and swatted at him.

He smiled. "Who'd have thought Aunt Katia's story would have struck such a chord?"

"I'm glad it did, and not just for the income."

Brendon squeezed her shoulder. "I know. You've got your reasons."

"Yeah."

"Okay, girls, story time's over. Upstairs."

Madeline rubbed his hand. "Thanks. I hate to ask you to make the climb with the new leg."

"It's okay. I'm getting used to it. The technology is better."

"The girls' devotional is on Maria's bedside table."

"Got it."

Brendon herded the twins up to bed, and Madeline leaned back in her easy chair.

"Well, little guy, you've been quiet this evening. Not much longer now, Oskar." She massaged her thirty-seven-week belly with her fingertips and smiled. "Yeah, I know. Your dad's just going to have to get used to the name."

Madeline lifted her new Dell onto her diminished lap. "All right, then. Your turn this week, Lilli-Anna and Kammbrie. Let's see what we can turn up." She sifted through the pages scattered across the coffee table.

"Now, I know those notes are here...somewhere."

# FOR MARIA

by Bruce Judisch

# Dedication

To the 1,500,000 children

# *Prologue*

## 1 March 1940

*Frau Mahler,*

*I hope this letter finds you well. I have received no response to my letter of last December regarding your sister's baby girls. I can only hope it reached you and that your response is en route. I fear, though, that there may not be time to await its arrival.*

*Our apartment is being watched, as are so many others in this district. Rósa and I leave for Salzburg tomorrow evening. . . .*

". . .and they hide in the shadows like rats."

"Stay back from the window, Rósa. If they see you, they may come before we're ready."

Rósa Dudek eased the curtain closed and rubbed her thin arms against the damp cold permeating the front room of their tiny second-floor apartment. The chill crept inward from the tips of her frail fingers and numbed her bony hands, triggering a dull ache in her arthritic joints. She shivered and pulled a threadbare woolen shawl tighter around her shoulders. Her wistful gaze flicked to a small fireplace, empty but for the powdery residue of last month's coal, now too costly to replace.

"What are you writing, Gustaw?"

Her husband laid his pen on the table and ran his fingers through thinning black hair. Cupping his hands around his mouth, he blew into them then flexed his stiff fingers next to three stubby candles sprouting from a triple brass candleholder on the table. A weary halo shrouded the sickly yellow flames and cast weak shadows across peeling floral wallpaper and a pockmarked tabletop. The jaundiced glow accented the deep creases in Gustaw's lean, tired face. He coughed.

"I write again to the Mahlers in Berlin."

"But why? They didn't respond to your first letter."

"I know they didn't respond, but I don't know why. The post is slow since the Germans invaded. There could be many reasons." He lifted his gaze. "And we must do everything we can to return the girls to their family."

Rósa clutched her arms around her slight waist. "Perhaps they've left Berlin. Or maybe they don't want the children."

Gustaw paused then rose from his chair and took his wife into his arms. He kissed her forehead. "You understand we must return them, don't you?"

Her eyes brimmed as he caressed her cheek.

"God has withheld children from us for reasons only he knows, Rósa, and lacking a son or a daughter does not lessen my love for you; you know that. I'm becoming attached to the twins, too, but we cannot take another family's children for our own. God would never honor such a thing."

"Of course I know this." She sniffled. "But they're so beautiful, and they look at me as though. . ." Her chest convulsed, and she rested her forehead on her husband's shoulder. He let her release, as he had so often over the past twenty-five years at yet another month's reminder that motherhood had eluded her.

"Rósa, it's time we must—"

They stiffened at a tapping on the wall. Three taps, followed by two. Then silence.

Gustaw rushed to the table and blew out the candles. He stuffed the unfinished letter and envelope into his jacket pocket. "Get the children. Now!"

# Chapter 1

*Saginaw, Michigan*
*Present day*

Madeline frowned at her watch. One hour to deadline, and this week's feature article for the *Times* still had not written itself. Its theme surfaced in her mind days ago, but the words refused to follow. She sighed and pushed back from the breakfast table. Enough procrastination.

A quick refill from the coffee carafe, and she trudged into the study, dropped into the chair behind the desk, and punched the power button on the laptop. She sipped her coffee and lapsed into a blank stare at the far wall, waiting for the computer to wake up.

Muffled giggling from the twins' play table outside the door signaled that her precocious five-year-old daughters were occupied, perhaps only with a misdemeanor, at least for the moment.

"Maria? Katia?"

"Yes, Mommy."

"Have you straightened up your room yet?"

"No."

"Yes."

Madeline narrowed her eyes at the doorway. "Which is it?"

"Yes."

"No."

"Get it done, girls."

More giggling, and juvenile footsteps clattered across the living room's wooden floorboards.

"And keep quiet, please! Oskar's still asleep upstairs."

" 'Kay, Mommy." The footsteps faded up the carpeted stairway.

The monitor flashed on, and Madeline pulled a legal pad and pencil from the desk drawer. She gathered her scattered research notes together into a tidy stack, as if their orderliness would imbue itself into her own fragmented thoughts. She fingered the mouse, clicked an icon on the screen, and flinched as her worst nightmare exploded onto the screen: a blank text file.

*Lord, I'm stuck. Please give me the words.*

Madeline drew a deep breath, counted to ten, and began to type.

*"Tante Katia's Story"*
*By Madeline Sommers*

*My time with Katia Schultmann, though short, spanned an eternity in emotion. I've related many tales of her life behind the Iron Curtain over these past few months, stories that opened an unknown world to me. I still don't think I fully appreciate them. New thoughts, deeper impressions, creep in each time I write. New emotions, too. But the story that evokes the strongest feelings is not of Tante Katia, but of someone she never even met.*

*In December 1939, the Gestapo, Hitler's dreaded secret police, dragged Izaak and Maria Szpilmann from their home in Stettin, Poland, and herded them into a railroad boxcar bound for the Ravensbrück concentration camp. When the Nazis relocated the Szpilmanns to Auschwitz a year later, the couple was separated and never saw each other again. In late 1943, Izaak fell too ill to work and was taken to the gas chamber. Maria survived the forced march from Auschwitz to Bergen-Belsen in January 1945, where she fell victim to the typhus epidemic that decimated the camp.*

*British and Canadian forces liberated Bergen-Belsen in May of that year, and Maria, barely alive, convalesced in a military hospital. There she met her future husband, Corporal James McAllister, a Canadian medical soldier. After they married, they returned to James's home near Montreal. What remained behind, though, is the focus of this week's story—not what, but who.*

*When the Nazis arrested Izaak and Maria, they left the couple's infant twin daughters, Lilli-Anna and Kammbrie, behind to die. Neighbors, the Dudek family, found the girls and took them into their home. Here, the trail fades.*

*The Dudeks wrote Tante Katia's mother in Berlin of their intent to escape occupied Poland to the home of relatives in Salzburg, Austria. There, the trail dies.*

*Although Mr. Dudek promised to bring the twins to Berlin, they were never heard from again.*

*Why among all of Tante Katia's stories is this so close to my heart? You see, Maria Szpilmann was not only Tante Katia's aunt, she's my grandmother. She was also a loving mother to two precious girls who, like thousands of other European children, disappeared into the vortex of a horrific war.*

*I still believe that somewhere I have two long-lost aunts whom I would very much love to meet. Lilli-Anna? Kammbrie? Are you out there?*

Madeline clicked the SEND button, launching the latest installment of "Tante Katia's Story" into cyberspace.

*The most important one so far.*

A glance at the miniature dome clock on the desk reassured her that she'd beaten her deadline, but not by much. She settled back to await her editor's acknowledgment, an impish smile playing on her lips. Hadn't been late yet, although she'd tempted fate a few times.

Madeline swiveled toward the wall and surveyed the four-month calendar hanging by a corkboard covered with clippings of her previous articles. She uncapped a red marker and added to a crooked column of slash marks decorating the Mondays, deadline day. As she recapped the pen, her gaze flicked up to a circled slash mark three months earlier, the day of little Oskar's birth, and her smile warmed. She'd squirmed through irregular contractions all morning polishing off that week's article. Then, as if on cue, her water broke the moment she clicked the SEND button. A frenzied speed-dial call to Brendon at work, and the rest was a blur that only came back into focus seven hours later when the midwife snuggled the Sommers' firstborn son into his mother's trembling arms.

The unslashed Mondays above that date returned a less joyful recollection that the news-paper column had been nearly as painful to birth as her son. It seemed she'd shopped the story around to every major newspaper and magazine in the country for ages, an inch-high stack of rejection letters stuffed into the bottom drawer of the desk testifying to her tenacity—and her frustration. Didn't anybody in the newspaper business know a great idea when they saw one anymore? More than once she threatened to quit this whole journalism thing and open a florist shop somewhere. If it hadn't been for her mom's sympathetic ear and her dad's gentle coaxing not to give up, the calendar would bear no slash marks at all.

The thought of her parents refocused her attention to a row of photographs lining the front of her desk, and the joy returned. Ian and Avery McAllister returned their daughter's gaze from the center frame, a few years younger, but not greatly changed. Madeline touched a dimple on her cheek, a legacy from her mother's lovely face beaming from beneath a tight coif of auburn hair—another legacy. But Madeline's deep hazel eyes were clearly compliments of her dad. So was her stubbornness, or at least she blamed him for it. When aggravation peaked, and she announced her intent to abandon the search for publication, his eyebrow would arch. The simple gesture muted her, a conditioned response from childhood she couldn't seem to shake—a fact that irked her, frankly. Everybody's entitled to grump now and then. Unless Ian

McAllister was around.

But her dad was right. After he suggested she leverage the upcoming anniversary of the fall of the Berlin Wall, the hallmark event of the story, she tweaked her pitch, albeit without much hope. A week later an enthusiastic response arrived from the *Times* feature-article desk, and "Tante Katia's Story" became more than just a dream.

She perked when the computer beeped an incoming e-mail. Her editor's reply carried a single word of text: *Excellent.* Smiling again, Madeline closed the laptop.

Renewed focus on the article shifted her attention to the frame sitting to the right of her parents'. Katia and Oskar Schultmann's wedding portrait, the one Madeline had embossed on the cover of Tante Katia's memoirs, lay sheltered in a brushed-pewter frame, a perfect setting for their warm, but dignified, personalities. Wedged into a corner of the frame was a snapshot of herself standing behind Tante Katia's wheelchair in a Berlin nature park, the silly grin on her face intended to dissuade Oskar from snapping the picture—a failed strategy like so many others sprinkled through her surprise-laden and emotionally exhausting interview with Tante Katia six years earlier.

Madeline's gaze flitted over the other photos on the desk: her brother Carson with his fiancée, Moira O'Brien, lounging in canvas chairs in Rust Park; a group shot of her sorority sisters at the University of Michigan during graduation. Her gaze halted at a burgundy-enameled wooden frame, where her grandparents glowed almost lifelike from a color glossy. She leaned forward and lifted the portrait, grazing the tip of her finger over the glass.

James McAllister's confident smile mirrored that of his son's, Ian. Yes, there was little doubt who had salted the family's gene pool with her dad's rock-solid demeanor. Her attention shifted to her grandmother, whose head rested against her husband's shoulder, her wrinkled hand pressed to his chest.

Maria McAllister's careworn visage never failed to mist Madeline's eyes when she reflected on what her grandmother had endured: the terror of Nazi concentration camps and the loss of her dear twin daughters. Her grandmother's stoicism bore witness to her harsh past, but an underlying gentleness evidenced a persistent faith in the mercy of a loving God. Both of those traits had granted her a life far beyond that expected of a body tortured by man and ravaged by disease, and a psyche battered by such intense personal loss. But Maria McAllister's ninety-second birthday loomed only a couple of months away, and despite occasional trips to the hospital for recurring bouts of Brill's disease, remnants of the typhus she contracted at Bergen-Belsen, and other nagging symptoms of life abuse, her spirit betrayed no intent of surrendering her body. It was as though she perceived something left undone, one thing more to hang on for, although she never spoke of it.

That notion returned Madeline's thoughts to Lilli-Anna and Kammbrie. She replaced the frame and leaned back, stroking her chin with her fingertips.

*I wonder if it could be. . .*

Madeline drummed her fingers on the desktop. How much more time could her grandmother's stoicism buy her? How loving might God's mercy be?

The *Times* would publish her article in tomorrow's edition, and the first broad appeal would be on the street. But that didn't mean she had to wait for an answer.

She straightened her shoulders and flipped up the computer's lid. When the screen sprang to life, she launched her web browser and fingered the keyboard.

*This is for you, Grandma.*

# Chapter 2

Brendon glanced at his watch as he stepped from the upstairs bathroom into the hallway. Nine fifty-six p.m. He leaned through the doorway of his twin daughters' bedroom and broke a smile, despite a lingering annoyance at having to squelch the girls' chattering three times in the past half hour. Characteristically, Katia had kicked off her covers and now lay curled around her bunched-up pillow. In contrast, a twisted cocoon of linen and loose-weave polyester engulfed Maria, a twitching bare foot protruding from one end the only sign of life.

He shuddered. Clearly his daughter hadn't inherited his claustrophobia.

Treading lightly to Katia's bed, Brendon retrieved her coverlet from the floor. She sniffed and shivered when he tucked it around her. Turning, he inspected the elongated lump of material on Maria's bed. His fingers traced the bundle's contours in search of an edge of fabric to grasp but stopped when the cocoon jerked.

*How can she possibly move in there?*

Brendon resumed his gentle probing, found a hem, tugged, and Maria's cherubic face appeared in the faint glow of the hallway ceiling lamp. He stretched open a vent wide enough to give his daughter's pixyish nose plenty of space then drew a deep breath. *That's better.*

Once back in the hall, a quick peek into Oskar's nursery confirmed his son lay submerged in whatever dreamland three-month-olds might conjure, and that door clicked closed, too. He descended the stairs, favoring his prosthesis and nudging aside a toy or two with his toe.

Lamplight streamed from the doorway of the study into an otherwise dark house. Faint tapping grew louder as he navigated the living room, then met him full force when he turned the corner.

Madeline squinted at the laptop's screen, her graceful features exaggerated in elongated shadows from its backlight. A legal pad lay to the right of the machine, her lipstick-smudged coffee cup to the left. She clenched a pencil in her teeth while her fingers attacked the keyboard.

"Hey, you. It's ten o'clock."

She looked up.

"I know—"The tooth-dented pencil freefell onto her lap.

Brendon grinned. "Tasty? I hear No. 2s have more fiber."

"Funny."

"You coming to bed?"

Yawning, she stretched her arms over her head. "Yeah, in a couple of minutes. I have one or two more websites to check."

"You've been at it all evening."

"Have I?"

"Uh-huh."

She shrugged. "I'll be up soon."

" 'Kay." Brendon pushed away from the door and plodded back upstairs.

⬡

Oskar's lusty cry startled Brendon from a deep sleep. He cracked open an eyelid at the digital alarm clock. One fifty a.m.

"Madeline, it's your turn to get him," he murmured.

Silence.

"Madeline?"

He rolled onto his back, and his arm flopped onto her side of the bed.

Empty.

The vibrato in Oskar's wail increased in frequency and intensity, pulling his father upright. Brendon grunted and rubbed his eyes then fumbled his prosthesis onto his leg and trudged to the nursery.

He whispered his son's cries into whimpers while he changed the soiled diaper then hoisted the hungry baby up from the changing table. "The rest is up to your mother, little guy. I'm not equipped."

Pressing his squirming son to his shoulder with one hand and gripping the banister with the other, he descended the dark staircase to the living room. The same stream of light stretched across the hallway from the study. He crossed to the doorway, patting Oskar's trembling back, and flipped up the hallway light switch.

Madeline's head rested on arms crossed over the legal pad, her hair splayed over her face. Crumpled wads of paper littered the desk, and the coffee cup teetered on the edge by her elbow. The laptop lay silent in sleep mode, as did his wife.

Brendon rounded the desk and rescued the imperiled mug. "Madeline?"

She rolled her head onto her other cheek and released a sigh.

"Hey!"

Her body jerked. "What?" She peered up through half-open eyelids. "Why did you wake up Oskar?"

"It's two o'clock in the morning. He woke *me* up."

"Two o'—" She blinked at her watch.

"Your son is hungry, and your husband is lonely. Only you can remedy either of those situations."

She nodded, and Brendon helped her up. He surveyed the cluttered desk, shook his head, and snapped off the lamp.

<hr>

Brendon gulped the last of his orange juice and checked his watch. Creighton was due to pick him up any moment, and Madeline had not yet made an appearance. Oskar coughed and wriggled in his infant seat.

"Mommy will be here any minute, Son. Hang in there."

He grimaced as Katia slurped the last of her chocolate-cereal-flavored milk from her spoon and dropped it into the plastic bowl. Maria tipped her bowl to her lips and gulped.

"Maria, are you supposed to do that?" Brendon raised an eyebrow.

She lowered the bowl, cheeks puffed full, and looked up at him with rounded eyes.

He fought a grin, but the battle was quickly lost. Then he sobered when her helpless expression told him they were both in trouble.

"Hurry up and swallow!"

Maria's chin quivered.

"Maria, don't you dare laugh!"

Her lips stretched tight.

He stiff-armed away from the table. "No—!"

His open blazer did little to shield his white shirt from the spray of milk-sodden cocoa-flavored cereal. Small consolation came from the fact both her quilted yellow place mat and the artificial daisy centerpiece shared the misery.

Katia burst into a giggle fit, her palms pressed to her mouth. Maria hunched her shoulders and stared up at her father, a trickle of milk dripping from her puckered chin. "Sorry, Daddy."

Brendon reached for a napkin and dabbed his spattered shirt without removing his narrowed gaze from his daughter. After a moment, he snorted a chuckle and shook his head.

Maria dared a tentative smile then joined in her sister's giggling.

"Go on, take your bowls to the sink. Maria, bring me a dishcloth, please."

More sniggering as the girls slipped down from their chairs.

Brendon wiped the table as best he could then consulted his watch again. *Madeline better get up pretty—*

A car horn sounded from the driveway at the same moment Oskar's patience dissolved. He whimpered then broke into a throaty howl.

"Okay, okay." Brendon lifted his son from the seat, shushed him, and beckoned to the girls. "C'mon. We've got a job to do."

The four of them crowded up the stairs and halted in the doorway of the master bedroom. Madeline snoozed facing away from the door, her arms tucked up under her pillow.

Brendon bent close to his daughters' ears and whispered, "Pretend it's Saturday morning and that's me. You know what to do."

Katia and Maria raced to the foot of the bed and scrambled onto the rumpled bedspread. They pounced on their mother with a renewed round of laughter and tickled her ribs.

"Hey! What—" Madeline shot upright, wide-eyed and gasping for breath. The twins fought for position on her lap and hugged her neck.

"G'morning, Mommy!"

Brendon handed Oskar to his shell-shocked wife. He brushed a splay of curls from her forehead and gave her a quick kiss. "Cray's here. Kids have been fed, except Oskar, of course. Gotta go."

"But—"

The car horn sounded again, and Brendon turned toward the door. As he exited, he glanced over his shoulder. "Oh, and sorry about the kitchen table."

"What about the kitchen table?"

"You'll see."

❧

Creighton pulled the Impala out of the driveway and glanced at Brendon. "It looks like you were shotgunned by the Keebler elves."

Brendon tucked in his chin and surveyed the front of his shirt. "Maria did her imitation of Mount Vesuvius at breakfast. I dabbed up what I could."

"And smeared the rest." Creighton grinned.

"It's not that bad, is it?"

"Uh-huh. You were holding Oskar, too, weren't you?"

"Yeah, how can you tell?"

"Look at your shoulder."

"Oh, no—"

# Chapter 3

Madeline scraped the last of the toast crumbs from the breakfast table into her open palm and brushed them into the garbage disposal. Leaning over to put the twins' cereal bowls and spoons in the dishwasher, she called, "Maria! Katia! Remember to wipe off the sink when you finish rinsing your hands."

High-pitched giggling answered her, then a squeal from Maria. "Kat! Now look what you did."

Madeline straightened. "Okay, what's going on?"

"Nothing, Mommy."

Her march down the hallway was cut short by a ringing telephone. She narrowed her gaze at the partially open powder-room door then retraced her steps to the kitchen and lifted the cordless phone.

"Hello? . . . Oh, hi, Susan! . . . You saw the article online already? What do you think? . . . Thanks. I hope we get some results, too. . . . Yes, I really do believe it's possible to find them. . . . I know it's been a long time, but I just have this feeling. . . . Well, thanks again. I'll let you know if anything turns up. . . . You, too. G'bye."

As Madeline hung up, a splash and another burst of juvenile glee pulled her attention back to the bathroom. She hurried down the hallway and pushed open the door.

"What on earth—Katia!"

The giggling stopped.

⤜⧉⤛

Creighton pulled into a parking space and killed the engine. "Seriously, bro, you gotta do something about your wardrobe. Ferguson's called a staff meeting for nine o'clock, and you look like a Dalmatian."

"Thanks, pal." Brendon unfastened his seat belt and opened his door. "I don't supposed Clarissa ever decorated you like this."

"My little angel? How could you even suggest such a thing?" Creighton broke into a grin. "Ever notice I keep a sport coat hanging by my desk?"

"Yeah."

"Well, there's a clean shirt and tie on a hanger behind it."

Brendon chuckled then surveyed his shirt again. "Let's hope Ferguson has little kids."

"I doubt it."

"Then let's hope he has a sense of humor."

"Yeah, good luck with that one, too."

Creighton stepped out of the car and thumbed his electronic lock. "Speaking of Ferguson, I heard you got the Anderson account."

"Yeah, neat, huh?" Brendon smiled. "I thought it was going to Dale."

"Neat? It's huge! Maybe the boss is grooming you."

"Yeah, right. Dale's probably swamped. Still, it's a great chance for a little visibility."

The two men swiped their entry badges and pushed open the glass door to the office building's side lobby. Brendon began rubbing at the colicky wet spot on his shoulder with the heel of his hand.

Creighton shook his head. "Wear the stain, my friend. You're just gonna make it worse."

"I didn't have time to change. Madeline was still in bed when I left."

"Late night?"

"For her, yeah. Remember that column she's doing on her Aunt Katia?"

"You bet. I've read 'em all so far. Your wife's really talented."

Brendon punched the UP button on the elevator. "Thanks. She's convinced herself that a couple of her relatives are still alive, although it's been like seventy years since anybody's heard from them. And once Madeline gets something in her head, nothing short of a nuclear blast or a broken fingernail can dislodge it."

"Really? What relatives?"

"It's complicated. You'll understand when you read the latest column. Anyway, she stayed up until two in the morning checking websites and online database archives on families separated during World War Two."

"World War Two? Man, that *is* a cold trail."

The elevator doors opened, and they stepped inside. Creighton jabbed the fifth-floor button. "So, you're left picking up the slack with the kids."

"It appears so. This better not last long, though; I've got enough to juggle without her tossing more balls into the air."

"Maybe it'll pass."

"You don't know Madeline."

The elevator door slid open. Clive Ferguson, chief of the special accounts division, stood in the hallway conferring with a junior vice president. The two men looked up, and Brendon's boss froze, his gaze locked on his subordinate's chocolate-spattered shirt and smeared blazer.

"One of yours?" asked the VP.

Brendon could only muster a lame smile before slinking off toward the men's room.

Fran Tucker leaned into Brendon's cubicle and tapped him on the shoulder. He looked up. "Hey, Fran. What's up?"

"Mr. Ferguson wants to see you. He said to bring the Anderson account file."

"Now? It's spread all over my desk. The capital expenses are done, but I still have to finish the depreciation schedule. It's not ready for a status review."

She shrugged. "I'm just the messenger."

"Okay, thanks."

Brendon gathered the loose paperwork into a green account folder. Pulling his still-damp blazer over as much of his sponged-off shirt as possible, he made his way through the maze of modular cubicles to the account manager's office. Two raps on the door, and a voice bade him enter.

"Fran said you wanted to see me, sir."

"Right." Ferguson pushed back from his desk and wiped his balding head with a handkerchief. "That the Anderson file?" He nodded at the folder under Brendon's arm.

"Yes, sir."

Ferguson held out his hand. Brendon slowly surrendered the paperwork. "I don't understand."

"This was supposed to go to Dale."

Heat crept into Brendon's cheeks. "I wondered about that when it ended up in my box, but I thought. . .maybe you were giving me a chance to broaden a little."

"Sorry about the mix-up."

"But I'm already into it. The preliminary spreadsheets are—"

"E-mail them to Dale."

"Have I done something wrong?" Brendon asked.

"No, you're doing fine."

"Then why the change?"

"This is Dale's account. He handled it last year."

"I know, but we trade projects all the time."

His boss folded his hands on the desk. "This is a big account, and it's complex. Dale's got the experience."

"And how am I supposed to get the experience if I never get a chance?"

"You'll get the chance."

Brendon hesitated. "This isn't because of my shirt, is it?

"Your shirt?"

"My daughter had an accident at the breakfast table this morning, and I didn't have time to change. I know it put you on the spot with the VP, and I'm sorry, but—"

"Oh, that." Ferguson returned his attention to the file on his desk. "Not impressive, Sommers, but not the reason, either."

"I mean, it's not like I always come in with a messy—"

The account manager exaggerated a sigh and lifted his gaze. "I bet you have some work to do."

Brendon stifled a retort, pivoted, and left the office. Back at his desk, he dropped onto his chair.

"What's wrong?" Creighton asked.

"Ferguson took back the Anderson account. Said to e-mail the work I've done so far to Dale."

"Did he say why?"

"He doesn't have to; he's the boss." Brendon yanked on the sliding keyboard tray and grabbed the mouse. "So much for being groomed, huh?" He glowered at the nearly completed spreadsheet on the monitor.

"Sorry, Bren. I don't know what to say. Maybe there'll be another account—"

"Yeah, right." He jabbed the mouse button and closed the file.

The Recycle Bin salivated in the corner of his screen, its wide-open mouth a mere inch beneath the spreadsheet icon. Scowling, Brendon stroked the mouse button, his pride locked in combat with his integrity.

Dale would never know.

*But I would.*

He sighed and launched his e-mail program.

# Chapter 4

Madeline perked at the click of the front door. "Bren, can you watch the twins for me?"
No reply.

She glanced up. "Bren?"

Her husband traipsed into the study, tossed his briefcase onto the love seat, and shrugged out of his blazer. She began to repeat her request then paused. "What happened to your shirt?"

"Don't ask."

She refocused on the computer. "I'm in a chat session with a man at the Hebrew Immigrant Aid Society in New York. Katia's in her room, but Maria's been bugging me to go outside. Can you do something with her?"

"I just got home—"

"I know. Sorry. I can't break at the moment." Her fingers pounded the keys as she spoke.

"It's been a lousy day, Madeline. I don't know if—"

"Please. Only for a couple of minutes." She cast a sidelong look at the legal pad. "Nuts! Now I'm getting things mixed up."

Brendon tossed his blazer onto the briefcase. "Maria's accident at the breakfast table ruined my shirt—"

"Just a sec." Madeline grabbed her pencil and scribbled on the pad.

He loosened his wrinkled tie, looped it over his head, and tossed it onto the blazer. His collar button tussled with his fingers as he struggled to release the tension on his neck. "Mr. Ferguson took a promising account away—"

"Daddy!" Maria pounced through the doorway. "Can we play ball?"

He half turned, still wrestling with the button. "Sweetheart, I don't think I'm up to it at the moment."

"Please, Daddy?" She grabbed his belt from behind and tugged.

The button popped off his shirt and flew into a gap between the cushions of the love seat. "Oh, for Pete's sake."

Maria wrapped her arms around his waist and pulled. "Dad-deeee!"

"Can't Katia play with you?"

"She's grumpy because she lost her baby doll's shoe. She said she'll never ever stop looking 'til she finds it. Oh, please, Daddy."

"Maybe in a few minutes. I need to change—"

Madeline stopped typing and slumped her shoulders. "I really need to concentrate."

Brendon released a slow exhale. "Okay, Maria."

"Goodie!" She raced from the room.

Madeline renewed her attack on the keyboard, barely glancing up as her husband trudged out of the room.

❧

"Daddy, catch!" Maria side-armed the Wiffle ball into the street.

Brendon mustered a tired smile and crossed the sloping front yard to the curb. He scooped up the hollow plastic baseball as it bobbled down the asphalt. "Maria, you throw like a girl," he teased.

She propped her hands on her hips. "I *am* a girl."

"Here, start by throwing underhand. Then when you get the release right, you can try it overhand. I'll show you. Are you ready to catch?"

She nodded and stiffened her arms in front of her, hands overlapped and fingers curled upward. He lobbed the ball. It bounced on her fingertips, and she trapped it against her chest.

Her daddy clapped. "Good catch! Now, throw it like I did."

Brow furrowed and tongue protruding between thinned lips, she arced the ball skyward. It landed three feet behind her. "Where'd it go?" She scanned the ground by her feet.

"Umm, look behind you." He stifled a laugh.

As Maria retrieved the ball, a shout from across the street stole her attention.

"Maria, look!" Her best friend, Alisha Sheldon, careened around the corner of her house, bouncing on her father's shoulders, her arms wrapped around his forehead. He ran circles in the front yard, gripping her legs around his neck and neighing. She screamed her laughter.

Maria dropped the ball. "Ooh! Daddy, can we do that?"

Brendon's smile faded. "I don't—"

"Oh, please, Daddy!"

"I—I can't really run like that, sweetheart."

"That's okay. We can go slow." She ran to her father and lifted her arms.

He hesitated then looked back across the street. Don Sheldon had collapsed onto the lawn, gasping as his daughter straddled his chest and tickled his neck. Brendon took a deep breath.

"Okay, turn around." Brendon hoisted Maria to his shoulders.

"Go, Daddy!" Maria hugged his head.

Brendon clutched his daughter's legs against his chest and started up the slope. Maria giggled and pressed against the back of his neck. "Faster, Daddy!"

He winced at a sharp pain shooting through his left thigh and turned back down the slope.

"Look, Alisha!" Maria yelled. She wriggled on her father's shoulders and waved at her friend. Her other arm slipped down over his eyes.

"Maria—"

The toe of his prosthesis snagged on a tuft of grass, and he pitched forward. Reaching up to protect his daughter, Brendon slammed onto the turf. He lost his grasp on Maria, pulled into a fetal position, and fought for breath. But worse than the shock to his abdomen was Maria's scream in his ear.

"Bren, are you all right?" Don's voice barely penetrated the pain.

"Maria. . ." Brendon clenched his teeth.

"She's okay. Madeline's got her."

Brendon rolled onto his back and tried to sit up, but his stomach muscles failed him. Don eased him up by the shoulders.

Madeline sat on the grass five feet away with her daughter on her lap, wearing a puzzled frown. Maria cupped a skinned elbow in her hand, her cheeks wet with tears. Alisha stooped at her side and stroked her hair.

Brendon nodded. "I'm okay. Thanks."

"Sure." Don straightened. He glanced at Madeline then back at Brendon. "Time to go home, Alisha."

Alisha patted Maria on the head then took her father's hand. She peered back over her shoulder as they crossed the street.

Brendon grimaced as his twisted prosthesis ground into his thigh. He grasped the socket and straightened it.

"Brendon?" Madeline held him in her gaze.

He sighed with another wince. "I know. I shouldn't have tried it. She saw Don and Alisha and wanted so badly to ride. . ." He slumped and propped his head in his hands.

"She could've really been hurt."

"I know," he whispered. His eyes watered, and he shuddered as Maria's scream echoed through his mind.

"Daddy?"

He looked up.

Maria tottered toward him then sat beside him on the grass. "I'm sorry we fell."

"Me, too, sweetie. I'm so sorry—"

"But thank you for the ride. It was fun." She hugged his neck.

Brendon held her tight and squeezed his eyelids closed.

⚭

"I suppose you're still upset with me." Brendon leaned in the doorway of the study.

Madeline looked up from her computer. "I never was upset with you. Just scared."

"Thanks for taking care of Maria's elbow."

"She wanted you to do it."

He stared at the floor. "I know. I felt so guilty about the whole thing."

She smiled. "Well, I think the extra scoop of ice cream you gave the girls for dessert repaired any leftover damage."

He shrugged and returned a half smile.

Madeline folded her hands on the desktop. "You don't have anything to prove, you know."

"Prove?"

"You know what I mean."

"I wasn't trying to prove anything. I was trying to play with my daughter."

She nodded. "I know. But I want you to know you don't have to do everything other fathers do. You're already a terrific dad."

"You really think so?"

Madeline rose and rounded the desk. She draped her arms around his neck and looked him in the eye. "The best." She kissed him.

When she backed away, he slipped his hands around her and pulled her against him. He smiled and brushed the tip of her nose with his. "While we're on the subject, is there anything else I'm best at?"

She arched her brow, but her next kiss lingered.

"Should I feel encouraged?" he asked in a husky voice. He began to nuzzle her neck when the laptop beeped an incoming e-mail.

Madeline pulled back and peered over her shoulder. "That might be the one I've been waiting for."

"Can't it wait?"

"I'll only be a second. Stay right here." She hurried around the desk and punched a key. Her face lit up. "It is! It's the Archives Department of the Holocaust Museum in DC. Oh, finally!"

Madeline dropped into her chair and began punching keys.

Fifteen minutes later, Brendon backed quietly out of the study and limped upstairs.

⚭

Brendon arched his back at another jagged pain. He massaged the stump of his leg for the fourth time since turning off his bedside lamp. Asleep beside him, Madeline shuddered with a light cough. As he turned his head toward her, she shifted onto her back and nestled her head into her pillow.

"Madeline? Are you awake?" he whispered.

A shallow sigh formed her only response.

His gaze traced her delicate features. Outlined against the milky wash of moonlight flowing through the open window, a silver-lined nose tipped up above the graceful curves of partially open lips, and an eyelid fluttered, waving long lashes like tiny reeds in an evening breeze. A gust of cool air ruffled the curtains and fluttered a wayward curl from her bangs onto her forehead. He smiled.

*As beautiful asleep as she is awake.*

He brushed her cheek with the backs of his fingers, and her lips twitched in response. His fingertips traveled across her bare shoulder then caressed the wavy tresses splayed across her pillow. A surge of passion swelled through him, tightening his throat and gripping his chest. Brendon lifted his head and leaned toward her still face. As his lips grazed her cheek, another twinge bolted through his thigh. He grimaced and dropped his head back onto the pillow. Madeline jerked at the movement then shifted away from him. A stiff gust billowed the curtain, flapping their lacy hems only a few inches from her face. The distant rumble of thunder broke the stillness, and the moonlight wavered then strengthened again.

He ground his teeth and kneaded his thigh with a fist, his mind fighting the ragged memory of the traffic accident in Ann Arbor as it did so often late at night. He squeezed his eyes shut against it.

*Cram backpack, extra books, laundry bag into '94 Corolla for two-hour drive home to Midland; stop at Café Verde and grab a cup of coffee for the road.*

He crooked his arm over his eyes.

*Bump arm getting back into car; stupid coffee leaks around plastic lid; snatch wad of crumpled McDonald's napkins off floorboard, scrub at hot spot on jeans; pull onto East Ann Street; grumble at lousy traffic.*

He ground his teeth.

*Stop at North Main; take first sip of coffee; light turns green, enter intersection; car behind blares horn, look left; red pickup runs light, idiot driver thumbing buttons on a cell phone.*

He shivered.

*Veer away! Crash, coffee explodes over dashboard, pain—*

An earsplitting crack of thunder yanked him upright. The moonlight had vanished, replaced by multiple flashes of lightning. The curtains flailed in the wind, and the first drops of rain pelted the side of the house. Madeline murmured something unintelligible and rolled onto her back.

Brendon stumbled from the bed and hopped to the window. Rain spattered through the screen and onto his face, as he wrestled with the stubborn sash. He turned his head away when a crackling filled the air, followed by a brilliant flash and a deafening roar. Grasping the windowsill, he squinted through the glare burnt into his vision at the wreckage of a transformer spewing sparks and smoke on a power pole across the street.

"What was that!" Madeline's startled voice barely pierced the ringing in his ears. A wail from the nursery rose over the storm, and bumps sounded from the girls' bedroom.

Brendon slammed the window shut, lost his balance, and fell backward against the bed. He hit the floor, sending another searing jolt through his hip.

"Brendon?" She grasped him by the shoulder and slid out of bed to his side. "Are you all right?"

She hugged his head to her shoulder and stroked his hair while sheets of rain swept the window and lightning stabbed the darkness. The softness of her touch renewed a twinge of desire, but the throbbing in his leg and the nagging sense of inadequacy his disfigurement induced suffocated it.

Brendon gripped her arm, his chest convulsing. His left fist pounded the floor where his leg should have been. *Please God, one more chance to be whole, that's all. Just one more chance.*

Madeline whispered, "Brendon, it's okay. It's okay."

Tears mixed with the residue of rainwater while the remainder of the story forced itself on him for the thousandth time. He had revived to a dull headache six weeks later at the university hospital, minus his leg, his torso entombed in a mound of plaster and bandages, tubes and wires protruding from everywhere. The doctor told him it would take at least three operations over the next year to rebuild his shoulder. He added apologetically that recovering from the loss of his leg might take a little longer.

So far, it had taken six years.

# Chapter 5

"Not another one!" Madeline rolled her eyes and punched the DELETE button.

Brendon peered over the Sports section. "Another what?"

"Another weirdo. Since the column on Lilli-Anna and Kammbrie ran, I've been inundated with e-mails from people claiming to know them or to be one of them. Some have offered to sell me their story; some have offered. . .other things."

"Didn't you expect that when you—wait a minute." Her husband lowered the newspaper. "What do you mean 'other things'?"

"You don't want to know." She jabbed the key again, declining yet another proposition to chat over dinner sometime soon.

He chuckled. "Maybe you shouldn't have let the *Times* post your photo with the column. You are a cutie, you know."

"Don't be silly."

"Apparently your Inbox is being silly, too." He flipped the paper back up.

Madeline leaned back and rubbed her eyes. "I'm about done in. You ready for bed?"

Brendon folded the newspaper and grinned. "Always."

"Down, boy. I'm exhausted."

He tossed the paper onto the couch. "You're exhausted a lot lately."

"Was that a complaint?"

"Maybe."

She closed the laptop and turned toward him. "Okay, out with it."

"We haven't had a night out without the kids for weeks. I miss you."

She tucked a loose strand of hair behind her ear. "We've both been busy. It's not just me."

"I didn't say it was just you."

"You do think it's me, though. I spend too much time on the computer, or I'm preoccupied with the *Times* column, or I'm too tired from minding the kids."

"It's not your fault, Madeline. We simply haven't had any time for ourselves—"

"Brendon, I can't help it! Look at all this." She gestured toward the legal pad, several of its pages already filled with notes, most of them lined out. Wads of paper lay strewn about, and sticky notes clung to the stem of the table lamp and decorated the desk blotter. "I feel like I'm spinning my wheels, and I can't seem to. . ." Her voice quavered.

Brendon leaned forward. "What's wrong?

"There's nothing. . . It's just not. . ." Her words caught in her throat.

"Sweetheart?"

She buried her face in her hands, and a half-stifled sob escaped between her fingers.

Brendon rose and hurried to her side. "Hey, it's okay."

Madeline shuddered a breath and shook her head. "It's *not* okay. I've got to find them. Grandma may not have much time left."

"But it's been so many years. They could be anywhere in the world, or. . ." He softened his tone. "I think you need to prepare yourself for the possibility that—"

"Don't say it!" She held up her hand and turned her head away.

He folded her upraised hand into his and kissed her fingertips. When she turned back, he cocked his head.

She wiped the moisture from her eyes and steeled her voice. "They're alive. I know."

"Okay."

# Chapter 6

### San Antonio, Texas

"Mother, please take a sip."

"What is it?"

"Chicken-noodle soup."

"I'm not hungry."

"You need to eat something or your medication will upset your stomach."

"What medication?"

Karen's shoulders slumped. "This one is for your blood pressure. The little white one is a diuretic. This one helps your memory."

"There's nothing wrong with my memory."

"I know, but the doctor says the pill will help keep it that way. You need to eat something first, though."

"I don't want anything."

"Take a little. Please." She squeezed her mother's hand. "Besides, I made it myself, and it'll hurt my feelings if you don't eat some."

"You made it?"

"Yes."

Her mother coughed. "What time is it?"

Karen nudged the pills into a neat triangle with a fingertip. "Twelve thirty. Lunchtime. Time to eat."

"When is my hair appointment?"

"Not until two thirty. There's plenty of time." Karen stirred the soup and tested its temperature with a knuckle.

When she glanced back up, her mother sat staring out the window. Her silver hair lay in wisps over the collar of her plain white blouse, obscuring a flesh-colored hearing aid that protruded from her left ear, cockeyed, as though bent on escape. Hollow cheeks and glassy eyes in deep sockets accented the gray glare of an overcast sky slinking in through the kitchen window. A shallow breath rattled from her throat and dissipated into the still air.

For a moment, Karen's memory morphed the frail elderly lady into a lissom middle-aged woman slicing through the choppy waters of Canyon Lake. Karen's swarthy father splashed furiously behind his wife, but he never had a chance. She reached the channel marker five lengths ahead of him and rolled onto her back. A grin curved her delicate mouth when he caught up to her. He puffed to her side and rolled into a float, his chest heaving. Straightening, she leaned forward and kissed his cheek.

*"Race you back!"* She giggled and lunged forward with a powerful breaststroke.

*"Hey!"* He righted himself, gasped for another breath, and wallowed after her.

Tony Romano, Karen's father and the only man her mother ever loved, died of congestive heart failure five years later. Her mother began dying the next day.

Piercing laughter, bright ice-blue eyes, and wavy blond tresses crowded together in a collage now dimming with time. Karen tightened her hands into fists, as though grasping every detail. *Please, Lord, don't take my memories. They're all I have left.* When she reopened her eyes, a slight woman fragile beyond her years reappeared, though blurred now through a teary film.

Karen lifted the soupspoon from the bowl with trembling fingers and whispered into the tiny beige amplifier, "Mother, please take a sip of this."

"I'm not hungry."

# Chapter 7

Karen settled her mother into a chair at the hair salon then stepped back as Wendy eased a burgundy nylon cape over the older woman's shoulders and fussed over her corn-silk hair. "How are we doing today, Mrs. Romano?" The hairstylist winked at Karen and nodded toward the door.

*God bless Wendy.*

Taking her cue, Karen slipped out for a precious half hour of vegetating in the SUV with a dime-store romance novel, anything to kill the temptation to think.

Despite her best effort to relax, her fatigued mind traipsed back over the morning. Gray days affected her mother more lately, dragging her demeanor even lower than its norm, and today was no exception. She usually emerged from her bedroom by eight o'clock, but today Karen had to rouse her out of bed at nine thirty. She found her lying atop the bedcovers, staring at the overcast sky through her bedroom window, barely breathing, it seemed. Any suggestion beyond a cup of coffee for breakfast met with resistance, and lunch wasn't much better. No telling what kind of a struggle dinner would—

A tinny calypso tune jolted her back to the present. She dropped the still-closed paperback onto the passenger seat and groped in her purse for her cell phone. The display read: UTHSC. University of Texas Health Science Center.

She took a deep breath and poked the OK button. "Hi, Nedra."

Nedra Robinson's perky voice fairly skipped through the receiver. "Hey, girlfriend! I tried your home phone. Where are you?"

Best friends since high school, Karen and Nedra were inseparable; two peas from the same pod, her father used to joke. The only commonality it seemed they didn't share was their marital status. Karen married Frank Donovan, a business major, upon graduation from the University of Texas at San Antonio, and they moved back to his home in New England. Nedra, a confirmed bachelorette, dove into her career as a medical technician at the Health Science Center after UTSA and never came back up for air. Now an administrative executive with a master's degree in healthcare administration, her expertise, and especially her friendship, proved invaluable when Karen needed to vent frustration from full-time caregiving.

Normally a joy to talk to, this afternoon her friend's bubbly voice grated in Karen's ear. She struggled to answer in an even tone. "Just dropped off Mom at the hairdresser's."

"Oh. So, how's she doing?"

"There've been better days."

"Sorry. Hey, your mom is actually why I called."

"Really?"

"Do you remember that feature story in the *Times* I told you about? The one about the lady from East Berlin?"

Karen rubbed her forehead against a headache that had sprouted shortly after lunch. "I think so—oh, yeah. Madeline-somebody writes it, right?"

"Madeline Sommers. Have you read any of her columns? I'm hooked on 'em."

"One or two. Last month, I think. What about them?"

Nedra paused then lowered her voice. "Grab today's newspaper and take a look when you get the chance."

"Why?"

"It made me think of something you told me awhile back."

Karen stopped rubbing. "What?"

"It's probably nothing, but. . .I don't know. Just read it."

"Can't you tell me any more than that?"

"Wait a minute. . . Hey, sorry. A call's coming in from the front office. Gotta run. We can talk after you read the article."

"Wait—"

"I'm really sorry, Karen. I've gotta take this call. See you later."

The line went dead.

Frowning, Karen snapped the flip phone shut and dropped it back into her purse. *What was that all about?*

❧

After the hair appointment, her mother retired to her bedroom for a nap, and Karen stole out to the corner store for a newspaper. Scanning the periodicals, she found a single remaining copy of the *Times* cringing between two tabloids, one featuring yet another trove of lost prophecies by Nostradamus and the other. . .well, it wasn't quite clear what the other one was featuring. The *Times* huddled to itself, its pages curled inward, as though loathe to touch its garish neighbors. Was it her imagination, or did the paper release a sigh of relief when she rescued it from the rack and purchased its freedom?

Home again, Karen eased onto the couch and set her diet soda on the tile-inlaid end table. Unfolding the *Times*, she searched the table of contents for feature articles. "Tante Katia's Story" by Madeline Sommers—page D1. She peeled off the first three sections and folded the paper over. The column stretched half the length of the page down the right margin.

*"My time with Katia Schultmann, though short. . ."*

What was the last thing she'd read in the column? Something about a Lutheran pastor being arrested, someone else who had polio—oh, right, that was this Katia person—but that was about all she remembered.

*"In December 1939, the Gestapo, Hitler's dreaded secret police. . ."*

When did the story jump back to World War Two? Wasn't it supposed to be about the Cold War? Some backstory, apparently.

*"British and Canadian forces liberated Bergen-Belsen. . ."*

Karen shook her head. The Holocaust: the ultimate failure in the human experiment. That modern man could conceive such an atrocity, let alone act on it, lay far beyond comprehension.

*"When the Nazis arrested Izaak and Maria, they left the couple's infant twin daughters. . ."*

Karen reached for her soda then froze.

*". . .Lilli-Anna and Kammbrie. . ."*

She leaned forward.

*"The Dudek family. . ."*

Her fists crumpled the edges of the newspaper.

# Chapter 8

Frank Donovan trudged the sidewalk from the driveway to the front porch. The granite-hued sky drained a heavy mist, gluing the cotton-polyester shirt to his rounded shoulders and ample paunch like a second skin. He tugged the open collar away from his fleshy neck with a forefinger and wrestled a full breath from the bloated afternoon air. Hoisting himself up three concrete steps, he twisted his wide frame between two baskets of begonias hanging from the eaves. Grumbling, he shook tiny drips from his umbrella then collapsed it and dropped it tip-first into a clay pot beside the door. The third muggy day in the high 90s this week. Whatever possessed him to relocate from temperate New Hampshire to sweltering Texas...

...oh, yeah. Karen's mom.

He shifted his briefcase to his left hand, muttering as he groped in his pocket for the house key. What was it, four years now? Five? He had come home with the news of his promotion to sales supervisor for a specialty tool company outside Boston, and Karen responded that they needed to move back to San Antonio to take care of her mom. Couldn't they bring her mom to live with them in Nashua? No, she refused to leave Texas; it was home, and her husband was buried there. Sure, home to *her*, not to him. But San Antonio was home to Karen, too, and so, hopelessly outnumbered—one wife against one husband—he quit his job and started over with a small appliance firm in the Alamo City.

He found the key and prodded the lock on the front door. But what about *his* home? And what about the kids? Their daughter, Mandy, and her husband had renovated a historic bed-and-breakfast in Rangeley, Maine, only a few hours north. Their son, Phillip, and his wife had settled in Buffalo, a little farther away, but still a lot closer to New Hampshire than to Texas. Besides, it was hot in Texas, for heaven's sake!

Frank pushed open the door and winced as an invigorating blast of hyper-conditioned air enveloped him, sending shivers racing through his sweat-drenched body. The frosty breeze affirmed his conviction that Texans apologized for their climate by super-cooling their buildings—and his wife had stepped right back into the mold with their home thermostat even after all those years in New England. Why weren't there more cases of pneumonia in San Antonio? This place was going to kill him.

He dropped his keys in the wicker basket on the hall table and traipsed toward the kitchen, where the aroma of homemade chicken enchiladas met him instead of his wife—not an altogether bad substitute, given Karen's superb culinary skills. His stomach rumbled its agreement.

"Honey?"

Frank laid his briefcase on the dining table then poked his head into the family room. A nearly full glass of what looked like cola sat in a small puddle of condensation on the end table, and sections of a newspaper lay strewn across the couch.

"Karen?"

Slipping off his damp loafers, he plodded down the hall. Pale lamplight shone from the mother-in-law suite, prompting him to lean through the doorway. Karen's mom sat in her favorite recliner by the window, a book in her lap, her gaze focused outside the window.

"Mom?"

She turned her head. He gave her a tired smile.

"Where's Karen?"

"Karen?"

"Yes."

She squinted at her feet then returned her gaze to the window.

Frank sighed and continued down the hallway toward the master bedroom. As he passed the staircase to the second floor, a scuffing stopped him. He retraced his steps and turned a corner into the utility room. Beside the linen shelf, a low door leading to a storage compartment beneath the stairway stood ajar.

"Karen?"

"In here." Her muffled voice squeezed through the opening, followed by a sneeze.

Frank squatted and pulled open the door. A bare 60-watt bulb cast wedged shadows along narrow walls of unfinished gypsum board and dusty two-by-four studs, illuminating a scattering of Christmas decorations and gray cardboard boxes with warped lids and peeling gummed labels. He cast a wistful look at an old fly rod leaning in the corner, one he hadn't used since their blessed days in New England. A rustling pulled his gaze to the right. His wife rocked on her hands and knees, half buried beneath a row of plastic-bagged clothes hanging from a galvanized water pipe. Visible only were the bottoms of dirty bare feet and the backs of denim-clad legs.

"Nice view."

"What? I can't hear you."

He raised his voice. "What are you looking for?"

"Just a minute." Karen grunted then crawled backward. Frank stood as she emerged, sweaty and dusty, dragging a small wooden trunk. He helped her to her feet.

"What in the world are you doing in there?"

She brushed a shock of brown hair from her eyes, smearing muddy perspiration across her forehead. "Looking for Mom's memory chest."

"Whatever for?"

"I'll show you. Take this into the family room, would you, please? I'll be out after I rinse off." She turned toward the laundry sink.

Frank shrugged and picked up the chest.

⁂

"Read this." Karen thrust Section D at him.

"What?" He scanned the paper while she downed a couple gulps of soda.

She tapped her forefinger on the feature column then began working on the trunk's hasps. Frank swept the scattered pages of the newspaper from the sofa onto the floor, sat, and began to read. Karen glanced at his face from time to time, and smiled as he reacted to the story.

He lowered the paper. "You're kidding. Can this be a coincidence?"

"It would be a really big one."

Karen tugged on the dry leather handle, and the lid creaked on its rusty hinges. When the rounded cover reached half-open, the brittle grip snapped and the top slammed shut, exploding a billow of dust into their faces. They coughed, and Frank fanned the air with his newspaper.

"When was the last time this was opened?" He stifled a sneeze.

Karen laid the broken strap on the end table. "I have no idea. It was in Mom's attic when we cleared out her house. She's never mentioned it other than to say it had some old childhood things in it."

"Here, let me help. You lift the other side." Frank grabbed his side of the trunk.

They eased the lid up and peered into the box.

"Not much here." He reached in and lifted out a couple of yellowed envelopes. She retrieved an old cardboard shoe box bound with two strands of dirty-white cotton string.

"Ever read any of these letters? The address on the first one looks like it's written in German."

She shook her head. "I've never opened this before. Mom was always private about it, and after we moved back to Texas, I forgot we put it in here."

"Think she'll mind you getting into it?"

"No choice. That newspaper column freaked me out. I need to see if there's a connection."

"What's in the shoe box?"

Karen slipped the cords off and lifted the lid. Several small booklets lay stacked side by side, each with a year penned onto the binding: 1948, 1949, 1950, and so on. "They look like journals or diaries."

He peered over her shoulder. "Maybe they can shed some light on this."

"There's only one way to find out."

Frank laid his hand on hers, his expression apologetic. "No offense; I'm intensely interested, but it's dinnertime and those enchiladas are screaming for attention."

Karen smiled. "Oh, all right. It can wait—but not for long."

# Chapter 9

After breakfast the next morning, Karen settled onto the couch and laid her German-English pocket dictionary on the end table. She took a sip of coffee then set the mug beside the lexicon and picked up the first letter.

Her two semesters of college German were a distant memory, but hopefully she could still remember enough to sort through the text with the dictionary. Pad and pencil in hand, she sat back.

The envelope, addressed to an Anna Mahler in Berlin, lacked a return address and a stamp. Why had it never been mailed? Karen slipped the letter from beneath the unsealed flap, eased open the brittle page, then picked up her pencil and began to transcribe.

*1 March 1940*

*Frau Mahler,*

*I hope this letter finds you well. I have received no response to my letter of last December regarding your sister's baby girls. I can only hope it reached you and that your response is en route. I fear, though, that there may not be time to await its arrival.*

*Our apartment is being watched, as are so many others in this district. Rósa and I leave for Salzburg tomorrow evening. . .*

⊷⊷

". . .and they hide in the shadows like rats."

"Stay back from the window, Rósa. If they see you, they may come before we're ready."

Rósa Dudek eased the curtain closed and rubbed her thin arms against the damp cold permeating the front room of their tiny second-floor apartment. The chill crept inward from the tips of her frail fingers and numbed her bony hands, triggering a dull ache in her arthritic joints. She shivered and pulled a threadbare woolen shawl tighter around her shoulders. Her wistful gaze flicked to a small fireplace, empty but for the powdery residue of last month's coal, now too costly to replace.

"What are you writing, Gustaw?"

Her husband laid his pen on the table and ran his fingers through thinning black hair. Cupping his hands around his mouth, he blew into them then flexed his stiff fingers next to three stubby candles sprouting from a triple brass candleholder on the table. A weary halo shrouded the sickly yellow flames and cast weak shadows across peeling floral wallpaper and a pockmarked tabletop. The jaundiced glow accented the deep creases in Gustaw's lean, tired face. He coughed.

"I write again to the Mahlers in Berlin."

"But why? They didn't respond to your first letter."

"I know they didn't respond, but I don't know why. The post is slow since the Germans invaded. There could be many reasons." He lifted his gaze. "And we must do everything we can to return the girls to their family."

Rósa clutched her arms around her slight waist. "Perhaps they've left Berlin. Or maybe they don't want the children."

Gustaw paused then rose from his chair and took his wife into his arms. He kissed her forehead. "You understand we must return them, don't you?"

Her eyes brimmed as he caressed her cheek.

"God has withheld children from us for reasons only he knows, Rósa, and lacking a son or a daughter does not lessen my love for you; you know that. I'm becoming attached to the twins, too, but we cannot take another family's children for our own. God would never honor such a thing."

"Of course I know this," she sniffled. "But they're so beautiful, and they look at me as though..." Her chest convulsed, and she rested her forehead on her husband's shoulder. He let her release, as he had so often over the past twenty-five years at yet another month's reminder that motherhood had eluded her.

"Rósa, it's time we must—"

They stiffened at a tapping on the wall. Three taps, followed by two. Then silence.

Gustaw rushed to the table and blew out the candles. He stuffed the unfinished letter and envelope into his jacket pocket. "Get the children. Now!"

A crash echoed through the apartment building.

Rósa raced into the small bedroom adjoining the front room. With strength born of terror, she swept the sleeping infants and their blanket into her feeble arms and stumbled from the room.

The muffled thud of heavy boots grew louder.

She staggered into the kitchen where a double window gaped open, its tattered curtains fluttering in the frigid night air. Gustaw hefted a duffle bag from behind a cabinet and threw it through the window. It bounced onto the cobblestones of the small courtyard separating a quad of old apartment buildings.

Footfalls pounded onto the second-floor landing and stopped outside their door.

Gustaw lunged through the window onto a slate overhang that sheltered the back door of the apartment beneath theirs. He reached back through the opening and grabbed the bundled twins. Clutching them to his chest, he leaped three meters to the pavement.

Fists pounded. Muffled shouts penetrated the hallway door and echoed through the front room. Somewhere in the building, a door slammed.

Rósa wriggled through the window. Once clear of the opening, she leaned forward then jerked back as her shawl snagged on the window hasp. She tugged, but it wouldn't release.

A loud thud sounded through the empty apartment then the crunch of splintering wood.

From below, Gustaw rasped, "Leave it, Rósa! Jump!"

She threw a panicked look over her shoulder.

A crash of the door slamming to the floor, and flashlight beams darted over the wall outside the kitchen.

She pulled away from the window and the button on the shawl popped. The wrap swung back and dangled from the window frame.

"Hurry!" Gustaw hissed.

Rósa took one step on the canted slate shingles, and her hard-soled shoes slipped on the damp surface. Her feet shot out from under her, and she slammed onto her back.

The men's shouts grew louder, and a flashlight beam shot through the glass over her head.

Rósa slid over the edge of the narrow overhang and braced for the impact. Gustaw broke her fall, and with muffled cries, they collapsed into a heap. She gasped for air as her husband scrambled to his feet and pulled her beneath the overhang.

Wrapped in their blanket, the infants squirmed and whimpered. Gustaw gathered them in his arms and whispered for them to hush while Rósa regained her breath.

Curses and flashlight beams spilled into the courtyard, both rebounding from mist-soaked redbrick walls. A few faintly lighted windows in the surrounding apartment buildings blinked out. The flashlight rays splashed across the pavement then converged on an archway leading into an alley. A voice shouted an order, and the lights disappeared.

Gustaw pushed the girls into his wife's trembling arms and pulled off a woolen hat he'd donned in the kitchen. He leaped to his feet and flung it into the archway then turned and rapped on the first-floor door. It opened, and two sets of arms pulled the Dudeks inside. The door clicked shut as soldiers poured into the courtyard.

The Dudeks and their rescuers peered through a small window by the back door, keeping low at the sill. A beam of light swept over Gustaw's discarded hat, and a sharp voice rose an alarm. A black-gloved hand yanked the cover off the ground and turned it over. The same voice barked a terse command, and the soldiers raced into the alley.

A hoarse voice wheezed, "Gustaw, Rósa, you must go. Out the front. Quickly!"

They pushed away from the window, collected the twins and the duffle bag, and wended their way through the darkened apartment to the hallway to the front door. A scan revealed no watchers in sight. Gustaw turned and grasped his neighbor's hand. Rósa hugged the man's wife, and the Dudeks slipped from the building and into the night, clutching Lilli-Anna and Kammbrie Szpilmann to their chests.

❧

*. . .where my sister, Zusa Bloch, lives. From there I will contact you. When it is safe, I will. . .*

Karen set down her pen and turned the page over. Nothing.
*What happened?*

# Chapter 10

That's really curious. Something must have interrupted them. Have you read the other letter yet?" Nedra sipped her strawberry lemonade and leaned back in the cafeteria chair.

Karen shook her head. "Didn't have the time. I had to get Mom ready for her one-thirty appointment with Dr. Feldstein."

"They've diagnosed her, then?"

"No." She poked at the lemon wedge in her iced tea with a straw. "Mom refuses to take the tests. This was only a consultation. I asked the doctor to talk to her, maybe convince her to be tested. I thought coming from him it might make a difference, but no dice."

"What did he think? Was he able to make any judgments after talking to her?"

"He didn't say, and I couldn't read his face one way or the other." Karen sipped the last of her drink and set the cup on her tray.

"Well, Feldstein is an excellent diagnostician. He'll normally give you some kind of impression, even with disclaimers. If he hasn't said anything to you, he may not be convinced it's Alzheimer's."

"What else could it be?"

Nedra rested her arms on the tabletop. "There are many types of dementia. In fact, dementia isn't really even a disease. The term describes a range of symptoms that fit a number of conditions. Alzheimer's is the most common type, but it's only one of them."

"But we need some kind of a diagnosis to get any state or federal help in treating it. Her insurance only covers so much, and Frank and I can't afford continuing care. One thing's for sure: we can't go on like this."

"What did Feldstein say? Where do you go from here?"

"We have another appointment next Monday. I guess he wants to consult with some of his colleagues."

Nedra nodded then glanced toward the ladies' room. "She's been in there awhile."

Karen sighed and pushed back from the table. "Yeah, I should check on her. She can't be lost. The restroom is only thirty feet away."

She trudged across the floor and pushed through the door.

Nedra pulled her purse onto the table and rummaged through it for her Blackberry. Three voice messages awaited her, one of them flagged as urgent. As she began to retrieve the message, Karen's choked voice startled her.

"Nedra! She's gone!"

Nedra jammed her telephone back into her purse and jumped up. She grabbed Karen's purse and hurried to her friend's side.

Karen scanned the cafeteria from the restroom doorway, her fingers clenched. "What now? Where could she have gone? She's driving me mad!"

Nedra thrust Karen's purse into her hands. "This way. There's a door around the corner that leads to the parking lot. She may have taken a wrong turn coming out of the restroom. It's the only way she could have gone that we'd have missed seeing her."

They rushed down a short hallway to a double glass-door entryway. The doors parted automatically, and they jostled each other as they squeezed through the slow-moving panels.

"I'll check this way." Nedra pointed up the sidewalk. "You look in the parking garage."

She hurried up the pathway to a concrete staircase that climbed to the emergency-room entrance. A groundskeeper mulching a flower bed looked up when she yelled, "Did you see an elderly woman pass this way in the last ten minutes?"

He shook his head.

Nedra pivoted toward the parking garage when the screeching of tires stopped her short. Then came Karen's scream.

&

"What are you *doing*?" Karen flailed her arms at her mother, who stood beside the crosswalk. "You could've been killed! Why did you leave the cafeteria?"

A man stood beside the open door of a silver Lexus and stared at the two women, his chest heaving.

Tears streaked Karen's beet-red face. "Why do you do these things?"

Nedra raced up and halted at Karen's side. "Karen, it's not her fault."

Karen ignored her. "Why can't you *think*! Where were you going?"

Her mother's tiny voice barely covered the distance between the two women. "I was going to the car."

"Why? You knew we were waiting for you at the table."

Her mother stared at the ground. "I'm tired. I want to go home."

The man cleared his throat. "Ma'am, it's okay. No harm done."

Karen jerked her head around. "No harm done? How can you say that? You almost killed my mother!"

"Now, wait a second, lady—"

Nedra stepped forward. "Karen, everything's fine. Get a grip."

Karen spun on her. "Get a *grip*? You don't have to live with this! You have no idea—"

"Karen! That's enough!" Nedra grasped her friend's arms. "Chill. Just chill."

Karen glowered, her shoulders trembling. She opened her mouth, but a hoarse sob choked off her words. The sob opened a floodgate, and she broke down in Nedra's arms.

The door of the Lexus slammed, and the engine revved. The driver glared through the open window as he edged past.

Nedra half smiled. "I'm sorry, sir. She's just—"

"—nuts, that's what she is. Get your friend some help." He rolled up the window, and the car turned the corner to the exit kiosk.

Karen shuddered and took a deep breath.

Her mother hunched her shoulders and stared at nothing.

# Chapter 11

Karen shook aside the curtains and blinked at the brilliant sunshine flooding the breakfast nook. Although the splay of golden heat would raise the room temperature despite the air conditioner, the deep blue sky was too gorgeous to hide behind draperies. Perhaps some granola and strawberries on the patio would start the day well.

A weak cough from the doorway interrupted her thoughts.

"Good morning, Mother," she said, forcing cheerfulness.

Her mother returned a nod, her gaze fixed on the empty table. Karen stepped away from the window.

"What sounds good for breakfast?"

Her mother sniffed. Karen gestured toward the patio door.

"I thought cereal and fruit outside would be nice. Care to join me?"

"Is there coffee?"

"Not yet. I'll put some on now."

Her mother turned and shuffled back down the hall.

Karen sighed as she filled the carafe with water.

After a light breakfast on the veranda, Frank excused himself to the bathroom with the newspaper, and Karen went to check on her mother. A cartoon show prattled chaos from the sitting-room television, but the recliner sat unoccupied. Karen peeked into the bedroom. Her mother perched on the edge of the bed, half dressed, staring into her dresser mirror. A half-full cup of coffee sat next to an untouched slice of toast on the nightstand.

"Mother?" she whispered.

No response.

"Do you need any help?"

Her mother lay back on the bed and curled into a fetal position.

Karen fought despair for the thousandth time since moving back to San Antonio. Would she ever be able to callous herself to her mother's decline, to not care so much in defense of her own sanity? Would her mother be better off in a home, where she'd have round-the-clock care and opportunities for peer relationships? And again, for the thousandth time, she shook her head. *I've heard too many ugly stories about those places—at least the ones we'd be able to afford.*

She draped a coverlet over her mother, collected the dishes from the dresser, and tiptoed from the room.

Karen set the dishes in the sink, poured herself a second cup of coffee, and pulled a chair away from the kitchen table. The German-English dictionary lay facedown beside a white legal pad that hosted a half-finished transcript and a circular coffee stain. She picked up the second German letter and squinted at the faded scrawling. Taking a deep breath, she pressed the pencil to the pad and began to write.

Thirty minutes later, a voice from the hallway disrupted her concentration.

"You still working on that?" Frank leaned against the doorway with the folded paper under his arm.

She sat back and rubbed her forehead. "Yeah, this one's tough. The German isn't very good, and the handwriting is even worse."

He pulled out a chair and sat down with a grunt. "Why don't you contact the *Times* journalist? Maybe she can fill in some blanks."

"Not yet. I want to finish going through this documentation first."

"Seems pretty certain to me that Mom's connected to the story." He swiveled the legal pad toward himself. "Hmm, this is kind of sketchy."

"Think you can do better?"

"No, I'm not talking about your translation. I mean the content of the letter. It looks fragmented, like whoever wrote it was in a hurry."

She nodded. "That's what I thought. It's not the same handwriting as the first letter."

"This wasn't mailed, either?"

"No. It was still in its envelope, not even addressed."

"It's written to the same person as the first letter, though."

"Yeah."

Frank picked up the pad and read aloud.

*2 April 1940*

*Dear Frau Mahler,*

*I write to [inform?] you of the twin girls. They are safe with me. I am in Salzburg now. There is [illegible word] here and I cannot remain. Much has happened. . .*

⁓⁓⁓

". . .and give me yours, too. We'll keep them together."

Rósa handed her identification papers to Gustaw. He slipped the documents into his inner jacket pocket then turned his attention to the platform outside his window. The smudgy glass exaggerated the dusky train station's gloom and mirrored his frame of mind. He massaged his stiff neck and grimaced at another pang from a blossoming migraine. A quick look at his watch revealed the train wouldn't depart for another half hour—plenty of time for things to go wrong.

So he watched. And he listened.

Thirty minutes later, the train pulled away from the Wolsztyn station, and Gustaw finally slumped against the hard wooden seatback. His wife's head lolled on her shoulder, betraying a fitful slumber. The Szpilmann twins huddled to her side, also asleep. Closing his eyes against the burgeoning throb in his temples, Gustaw diverted his thoughts to the series of events that had led him to this train compartment.

The tickets he'd procured back in Stettin were dated for the day after they'd fled from their apartment, but the risk of remaining in the city was too great. The train station would likely be watched anyway, so he guided his family through the silent alleyways to the road leading southeast toward Stargard. Ten kilometers from the city, they forked south toward Wolsztyn, where his brother, Stanislaw, lived.

The two-hundred-kilometer trip consumed five days on rutty back roads, sprawled in straw-laden ox carts or trudging on foot. The third day of their journey, they chanced upon an ancient Fiat camionnette, one of the few motor vehicles not yet commandeered by the invading Germans. The cargo van provided welcome relief from the open oxcarts, but their ride lasted only two hours until the driver signaled his intent to turn west. The Dudeks thanked him, clambered out of the vehicle, and slogged southward through the early spring mud. Twice that day they barely made it into hiding as German convoys rumbled past.

Restless nights passed in haylofts of old barns and on bare wooden floors huddled close to dying coal fires of sympathetic Poles. The last night of their journey, they sheltered in a dense copse of birch trees, where Gustaw chanced a small fire to ward off the frigid air and to heat the remainder of their thinly rationed food supply. They arrived in Wolsztyn at noon the next day, exhausted, half starved, and nearly frozen, but thankful for God's protection.

Gustaw's brother rejoiced at the unexpected visit then hardened when he discovered the reason for it.

"Have you lost your mind? You know what the Germans do to Poles who harbor Jews." Stanislaw paced and smoked while his older brother sat at the kitchen table, hands cupped around a tepid mug of tea.

"Would you have me leave them to die?"

"Better two lives than four."

"And yet none have died, have they?"

Stanislaw whirled. "Not yet. But you've brought them here, and that endangers my family."

"No one here knows they're Jewish. To Wolsztyn, we're merely a family of four visiting relatives." Gustaw sat back. "And soon we leave for Salzburg, if that relieves your fears."

Stanislaw pulled a chair from the table and labored his heavy frame into it. Jamming the spent cigarette butt into his empty tea cup, he sighed then softened his tone. "There's no need to leave so soon. You know we love you and Rósa. I'm fearful for you, that's all."

Gustaw smiled. "Thank you, and I know you love us. But we must move on."

"Do the girls have documents? You'll need them for the Nazi checkpoints."

"I found no papers for them at their home. Perhaps we can appeal to their young age, say that proper documentation was not completed because the war began so soon after their birth."

"They'll never believe you."

"Then God must provide."

Stanislaw flicked his hand. "Bah! Bonhoeffer has deluded you like he has so many others. What is this 'Confessing Church' anyway? The only confessing you'll do is under torture before the Gestapo shoots you."

"Then we'll be with Christ. What more could we ask?" Gustaw drained the rest of his tea and pushed back from the table. "But until we're shot, we will do what is right."

Stanislaw rose. "I can lend you the money for train tickets. I suppose that's why you came to us."

"That's very kind of you. It's not why we came, but I'll accept your offer and repay you as soon as I'm able."

The brothers grasped hands. Stanislaw pulled his brother into an embrace. "I'll purchase tickets for the evening train to Prague and give you enough money for a connection to Salzburg. They may try to route you through Munich. Avoid that. You don't want to go into Germany if you can help it."

Gustaw slapped his brother on the back and released him. "You forget the Sudetenland belongs to Germany now, so Prague is no safer than Munich. And, after the *Anschluß*, neither is Austria."

"Then why do you go there?"

"Zusa and Kurt can keep us until we find safer refuge."

Stanislaw gripped his brother's shoulders. "I hope you know what you're doing."

"So do I. But I must do something. . . ."

❧

The train jolted, and Gustaw cracked open his eyelids. The migraine had subsided, leaving behind a dull residual ache. He squinted into a predawn gray filtering through the window as the train slowed. A wooden sign bearing the name *Walbrzych* slipped past his window. He patted Rósa's arm when she stirred and covered a yawn. The twins still slept. He returned his gaze to the window then stiffened.

German army helmets and rifles slung over gray-uniformed shoulders crowded the platform at eye level. A billow of steam obscured them as the train groaned to a halt.

"Rósa! Quickly, take the girls to the toilet and lock the door."

"What—?"

"Just go! Now!"

Gustaw pulled Kammbrie to his chest while Rósa struggled to her feet and lifted Lilli-Anna to her shoulder. He herded them to the rear of the car, pushed Kammbrie into his wife's arms and closed the door. The lock clicked, and he hurried back to his seat. Crossing his arms over his chest, he dipped his head to his chest as the first jackboots sounded in the corridor.

"*Papieren!*" The soldier's order for documentation bellowed from the adjacent compartment.

Gustaw feigned sleep until the blunt toe of a boot dented his ankle. He raised weary eyelids and blinked.

"Papieren!"

"Oh, yes." He groped through his coat pocket and produced a sheaf of folded papers.

"*Du bist allein?*"

He was about to affirm that he was alone when the soldier's gaze settled on the duffle bag. Rósa's sweater lay atop the jumble of clothing, its dainty white neck visible in the early morning light. Gustaw forced an even tone. "My wife travels with me. She must have gone to the toilet while I slept."

The soldier straightened and peered toward the end of the car.

"You will not want to disturb her. It is—how should we say?—an awkward time of the month." He chanced a knowing smile at the trooper. The German glanced once more toward the end of the car then frowned and held out his hand. Gustaw surrendered their documents.

After a cursory scan, the soldier thrust the papers back at Gustaw and stomped to the next compartment. "Papieren!"

Gustaw released a slow exhale. Separating the papers, he slipped Rósa's into his left coat pocket, his into the right, then closed the duffle bag and tied it off. At the next document check, he would be a lone traveler.

A few moments later, the cluster of soldiers shifted away from the train. Gustaw's eyes widened at two men and a woman standing against the depot wall, hands on their heads. A squad of soldiers leveled their weapons at the trio. A captain approached the squad and snapped an order at the squad leader, who began his report. Another burst of steam drowned out the officer's reply as the locomotive whistled its intent to depart the station.

The bench beside him creaked. Gustaw turned his head as his wife pushed a twin onto his lap. "Keep them down!" he hissed. "We have not yet left the station. They don't know—"

A staccato burst of rifle fire cut him off. He jerked his head back toward the window as the train lurched forward. The three civilians lay in a grotesque heap on the platform, crimson rivulets streaming down the pitted wall above them. He sat back, swallowed, and groped for his wife's hand on the bench.

The train arrived in Prague late that afternoon. The Dudeks disembarked, and Rósa huddled with the girls on a bench while Gustaw purchased their tickets for Salzburg. They hurried to the connecting train and slipped aboard, but neither relaxed until the train pulled away from the station an hour and a half later.

After two more uneventful stops, they pulled into Freistadt, the first town inside Austria. There would be a document check here, too, so he prepared Rósa and the girls to return to the toilet.

As expected, gray-uniforms with Mauser rifles cluttered the platform. The soldiers swarmed onto the train when it creaked to a stop. A short, fat *Unteroffizier* poked his head into the compartment. "Papieren!" He looked around. "Du bist allein?"

Gustaw nodded through another sleepy demeanor as he groped inside his jacket. "Yes, I am traveling alone."

As he released the papers into the corporal's hand, his heart seized. He had reached into his left pocket! His hand shot toward the papers. "Wait—"

The soldier yanked the documents away. He scanned them then leveled a scowl at Gustaw. "You do not look like a Rósa to me."

"I can explain—"

≈

Rósa slipped back onto their seat as the train whistle sounded, puzzling at the empty bench and unattended duffle bag. After settling the twins onto the bench, she leaned back into the corridor and searched both ways. Failing to see her husband, she edged toward the window. Steam filled the air outside the train car, hiding all but the depot's roof. When the vapor dissipated, a familiar brown coat came into view near a loading ramp at the end of the platform. Gustaw stood before a Waffen SS officer, gesticulating wildly, his face pleading. A soldier stood to one side, his submachine gun trained on the prisoner. The officer jabbed his forefinger onto a piece of paper he was holding, shook his head, then spun on his heel and walked away.

Rósa's scream filled the compartment as the weapon recoiled, and her husband tumbled off the end of the platform.

≈

*. . .so, with Gustaw gone, I have no means to [return?] the twins to you. Please come to the return address when you can. I will try [2–3 illegible words] and then contact you. I remain your friend.*

*Rósa Dudek*

Karen scratched Rósa's name onto the legal pad and dropped her pen. The house lay quiet but for the ticking of the clock over the stove. She sat back and massaged her temples with her fingertips.

Her mother would only have been six months old when Gustaw was killed. Surely she wouldn't remember. Would she?

No, of course not.

# Chapter 12

Karen's mother sat on her recliner with a *Reader's Digest* on her lap, CNN on the TV, and her attention on neither. Karen lingered in the doorway, hesitant to disturb the older woman's thoughts, wherever they might be. She set a glass of ice water on the table by the chair then quietly returned to the living room and the heritage trunk.

Lifting a diary from the shoe box, she inspected its creased cloth cover. A strip of tape covered the binding, its end curled and frayed. On a thin label affixed to the center of the booklet's front cover was scrawled *1950*. Her fingertips brushed over the date, as though to connect through the years with the juvenile fingers that penned it.

When Karen eased open the front cover, a folded reddish-brown document, faded and stained, fell onto her lap. She picked it up. Printed in bold letters beneath an official seal were the words CARTE DE SÉJOUR DE RESIDENT TEMPORAIRE. Below the title appeared the name *Rósa Szpilmann*. Karen set it aside.

She carefully flipped through the diary's off-white pages, noting the entries were written in block printing rather than cursive, but not pausing to read them. As she neared the back cover, another paper slipped out: a gray-green card with two diagonal burgundy stripes stretching from corner to corner. It bore the same official seal as the first document but read TITRE D'IDENTITÉ DE VOYAGE and carried a price of 60 francs. Rósa's name also appeared at the bottom of this card.

"Why Szpilmann?" Karen muttered. "According to the *Times* column, that was the twins' birth parents' last name. But Rósa's surname was Dudek. . ."

⬥

*. . .and so much pain, loneliness; how long will it go on?*

Rósa gazed out the musty second-story window into Salzburg's late afternoon, her heart as heavy as the leaden sky.

She and the twins had arrived midmorning the day after Gustaw's death, although she barely recalled the train halting at Salzburg's central train station. Everything after the horror of Friestadt had crumbled into disjointed fragments in her memory. Events only began to refocus when Zusa and Kurt Bloch met her after receiving a wire from Stanislaw that the Dudeks were coming and when he believed they should arrive.

She stumbled from the train car and trudged along the platform in a daze, the twins clutched to her chest and the duffle bag dragging from a strap slung over her arm. At the end of the platform, the Blochs hurried to her side and Kurt caught her as she collapsed. She scarcely remembered her sister-in-law peering into her face.

"Rósa! Where is Gustaw?"

"He. . .he is gone."

Six months later, the shock of Gustaw's execution still gripped her. The guttural bark of the submachine gun, her husband's bloodied body twitching on the ground, and her scream filling the train car haunted her dreams and numbed her waking hours.

Time passed with nothing to distinguish one day from the next. Rósa helped as she could around the house, but without proper documents, securing a job was impossible. Although she managed to supplement the household income by taking in sewing and cleaning private homes, it was clear she could not remain there indefinitely. But how does one flee occupied Austria with no identification papers?

"You know you're welcome to stay, Rósa, but I fear for your safety." Zusa folded a napkin and laid it on the stack of clean linens. "It's only a matter of time before you are stopped on the street for a document check. What will you do then?" She paused when there came no reply. "Rósa?"

Rósa started then turned away from the window. "I'm sorry. Did you say something?"

"Have you decided what you are going to do, where you will go?" Zusa pulled a chair away from the dining table and settled onto it.

"I met a man last week who can help," Rósa replied. "I embroidered a tablecloth for his wife. He knows of men who smuggle refugees over the mountains to France and Italy. It's difficult to find one who will accept young children, but he will inquire for me."

"And how much will this cost?"

"I don't know yet. Maybe a thousand reichsmarks."

"A thousand reichsmarks! Where will you get such a sum?"

"I've saved some money. I'll save more."

"Rósa, it's nearly impossible—"

"What choice do I have, Zusa?" Rósa snapped then caught herself and calmed her voice. "You said yourself I have no papers. Do you expect me to buy train tickets?"

Zusa sighed. "It's too late in the year now to attempt a journey through the mountains. You'll have to wait until spring."

"Then it will give me more time to save."

"Where will you go?"

"I've heard of a French organization that takes in refugee children, the Oeuvre de Secours aux Enfants. Perhaps they will help us."

"I know of the OSE. It's a Jewish organization. You are not Jewish."

"But the girls are Jewish."

"What about you?"

Rósa fingered the hem of her blouse. "If I offer to work, to volunteer with them, I'm sure they'll keep us together."

"You? A goy?"

"They don't need to know I'm not Jewish. I can change my name, become a Polish Jew. I know of their traditions and rituals. . .at least a little. Perhaps I will become Rósa Szpilmann. Then I can remain with the children." She shrugged. "Besides, my true name may be on a watch list after Gustaw's. . .arrest."

Zusa leaned forward. "It would be safer if you were to turn them over to the French Jews and then get yourself out of Europe. The OSE will know how to take good care of—"

"No!" Rósa jerked her head up. "I will not give them up to strangers. They need a mother." Her voice quieted. "They need me."

Zusa peered at her sister-in-law. "Rósa, did you post the letter you wrote to the girls' relatives in Berlin?" she asked quietly.

Rósa folded her arms and looked away. "Of course."

"Then why haven't they come? It's been four months since you wrote the letter."

She shrugged. "Perhaps they don't want them. I don't even know if they're still alive." Her voice sharpened. "Berlin is not a safe place for the girls anyway. They need to escape Hitler, not move closer to him."

Zusa studied her for a moment then resumed folding linens.

# *Chapter 13*

Karen set her coffee mug on the end table and knelt next to the chest. Selecting the first diary, she removed the temporary identification card and travel authorization and laid them on the coffee table. As she set the box down, the second diary shifted, uncovering the edge of an envelope.

She tugged the envelope from beneath the diaries. It bore the initials *HICEM* in the upper left corner and *Mme R. Dudek* penned at the center. One end was slit, so she tipped it, and several documents slid onto her palm. Two of the items were heavy cardstock, one with a knotted cotton string threaded through two holes at the top. An identical card, but without its string, lay beneath it. Karen unfolded them. Stenciled on the stringed card was the number *71* and on the other, *70*. An inspection of the reverse sides revealed no other identifying markings. The cards joined the papers on the table.

Karen turned her attention to a faded red card with a large white *1* emblazoned on it. The name *Serpa Pinto* appeared at the top, and beneath them, *"D" Vorderer Speisesaal. . .erste Abteilung. . .Tisch nr. 21. . .Bitte diese Karte aufbewahren und dem Tischstewart vorzeigen.*

She retrieved her pocket dictionary from the end table. Most of the words were familiar, but she checked them for confirmation: *"D" Forward Dining Hall. . .First Compartment. . .Table No. 21. . .Please keep this card and show it to the table waiter.* She smiled at the speed with which her German vocabulary was returning.

Setting aside the meal voucher, she picked up a small gray card. Again, *Serpa Pinto* appeared at the top, followed by *Platzkarte für Bett. . .Abteil nummer C13. . .Bett nummer 4.*

*Reservation Card for Berthing. . .Compartment Number C13. . .Berth Number 4.*

Handwritten in the bottom right corner: *R Dudek.*

Setting aside the remainder of the documents from the envelope, Karen reached for her coffee. So, her mother transited the Atlantic Ocean on a ship named the *Serpa Pinto*. But the return of the name Dudek instead of Szpilmann gave her pause. Her finger brushed the card's surface, then she leaned back against the sofa cushions. So many unanswered questions.

What it must have been like for a lone woman to travel across a war-ravaged continent and an ocean with two young children in tow? *I wonder if I'll ever know. . .*

⁓

*. . .and that is that.*

Rósa knotted the cotton thread and tucked it into a seam. Laying the shirt aside, she massaged her aching fingers. She scanned the calendar on the wall then peered out the window at shrunken icicles clinging to glistening eaves and leaking sun-sparkled droplets onto the sill.

The winter of 1940 had passed into 1941 in a blur, her thoughts consumed with amassing enough money to bribe a smuggler to take her and the twins to France. Her current sum fell well short of 1,000 reichsmarks, but time grew short. Austria had become increasingly hostile to Jews, and suspicions ran high over every foreign face or accent. Too many close calls with random document checks had forced her indoors, hampering her efforts to earn more money. Early in the spring, she appealed again to the man who had promised to put her in contact with a guide. Then she could only wait.

In mid-May, an unsigned note wedged into their front door promised a "Herr Johann Schmidt" would contact her within the next week. She was to tell no one and not inquire anymore about passage out of Austria.

The tap on the door came one moonless midnight.

"Who's there, Rósa?" Kurt's drowsy voice crept down the narrow stairway.

She stared at the figure in the doorway shadowed against the glow of a neighboring street lamp. "It's no one, Kurt. Just a man who lost his way. He came to the wrong house."

When the door to the upstairs bedroom clicked shut, she turned back to the stranger. "Herr Schmidt?"

The figure leaned forward and rasped, "You wish to leave Austria? It will cost 1200 reichsmarks for you and the brats."

She flinched as the odor of beer and onions filled the vestibule. "I don't have 1200, only 875. It is all I've been able to save."

He turned to leave.

"Wait!" She groped for his sleeve.

He spun and grabbed her wrist. "Don't touch me!"

Rósa winced. "Please, we'll be no trouble to you, I promise. We must leave as soon as possible. Perhaps I can send more money to you after we reach France."

He pushed her hand away. "And how would you do that?"

"I don't know, but I'll do whatever it takes." She rubbed her wrist.

He stepped back from the covered doorway. Lamplight spilled into the recess, illuminating her from the neck down. She lowered her head as his gaze raked over her thin housecoat.

He closed the gap again. "I'll take no less than 950 reichsmarks—and I've never done this for so little. You don't understand the risk I take. Know that!"

"I'll find the money. Somewhere."

"You have three days. I'll come for you after the sun sets. If you aren't ready, if you don't have the money, you'll never see me again—or any others who guide people over the mountains. I'll make sure of that."

He turned on his heel and disappeared around the corner of the building.

Rósa shut the door and leaned against the foyer wall, her trembling shoulders hunched.

The following day, after confiding in the Blochs of her plans and her dilemma, Kurt handed her the remaining 75 reichsmarks. "This is foolhardy, Rósa. You know that?"

She nodded and thanked him, promising repayment. He shook his head and walked away.

⌘

The evening of her departure, Zusa pressed another 50 reichsmarks into Rósa's hand and hugged her. "Hide this. You will need money when you reach France." Rósa nodded and returned a nervous smile. They hugged, and Zusa went upstairs.

Ten minutes later, Herr Schmidt's slouching figure reappeared at the doorway, his scowl deepened by the night shadows. She held the reichsmarks out with shaky fingers, and he swiped them from her grasp. Without a word, he pivoted and stalked to the street, leaving her with the children and the duffle bag.

They set out beneath the sneer of a slivered yellow moon sulking low over the city. Herr Schmidt set a pace nearly impossible for Rósa to match, and the gap between them lengthened until, just outside the city, she lost sight of him.

When she struggled over the next rise, he stepped from behind a tree, sending her heart into her throat. "You are too slow!" he hissed.

She nodded and shrugged the duffle bag higher onto her shoulder.

The third time she fell behind, he grabbed the duffle bag in disgust but refused to touch either of the twins.

The heightened German presence in Austria forced them away from the main roads to back trails and small villages. When her guide could arrange rides in oxcarts, Rósa stretched, massaged her aching muscles, and did her best to quiet the twins. Once near the Swiss border, when she was unable to hush the restless girls, Herr Schmidt threatened to abandon them altogether. She pleaded with him, finally surrendering the hidden 50 reichsmarks in a desperate effort to stretch his patience.

When on foot, the late spring forced them through meadow valleys and along low forest paths below the receding snow line. They spent chilly nights nodding off around tiny campfires of dry wood devoid of bark to avoid smoke. Rósa huddled the twins close as the fires died, and they were left only with their body heat and a single woolen blanket. Some evenings Herr Schmidt went into a village to procure food. Other evenings he just went into a village.

One night outside Söll, he staggered back to camp well after dark. Rósa lay on her side near the cooled fire pit with the girls tucked against her, the blanket draped over them. He rustled through his pack then went quiet. Rósa perked, uneasiness creeping up her spine. She shifted on the hard ground then stiffened as a calloused hand clamped onto her shoulder and slid toward her neck. The hand covered her mouth and forced her face against the ground. Herr Schmidt slid onto the blanket and pressed his body against her back. Her breath shortened to shallow gasps, and her stomach turned at his bristly cheek scraping her neck and rancid breath scouring her face.

"Make no sound," he growled.

She closed her eyes, her heart pounding. For several moments, he lay still. Then voices and heavy footfalls rose above the night sounds. She opened her eyes to see flashlight beams darting through the trees over their heads.

The voices grew louder.

German voices.

He pressed his hand against her mouth until the crunching of boots on rocky ground faded up the hillside. When he released his grip, she sucked in a deep breath and fought to control her heaving lungs. He moved away.

Rósa patted the twins, thankful they hadn't stirred. She looked over her shoulder at Herr Schmidt, silhouetted against the star-filled sky.

"I thought. . ." Her voice shook.

His guttural slur dripped sarcasm. "You thought I meant to take you?"

She averted her eyes.

"You hold no interest for me, or I'd have taken you long ago," he snorted. "I like women with meat on their bones." With that, he dropped to the ground on the far side of the fire pit and stretched out. Soon, his low snore joined the whisper of the breeze through the pines.

Sleep was longer in coming for Rósa.

❦

Herr Schmidt gestured toward the village. "I go no farther." He turned on his heel and climbed the slope toward the tree line.

Rósa stared at him. "Wait! Where are you going?"

He scowled over his shoulder but didn't reply.

"But what do I do now?"

Again, he pointed toward the village.

Rósa turned and surveyed the scattering of low gray houses tucked into the trees. Traces of smoke curled from stone and metal chimneys, and a dog's hoarse bark echoed up the hillside. The valley seemed suspended in time, no movement apparent along the narrow road winding through the town. Even the smoke hung still in the air as though asleep. Or dead.

"What is this place?"

"You are in France."

"But I don't know where to go, who to find." Her eyes beseeched his but met only ice in return.

"They will find you."

"But the children—"

He pivoted and strode away. In a moment, Herr Schmidt vanished beneath the thick evergreen canopy.

Tears flooded Rósa's eyes, and she slumped onto the grassy slope. Deprived of human companionship even as crass as Herr Schmidt's, her will faltered then died. The twins squirmed onto her lap, but she barely noticed. Weeks of fatigue and disheartenment joined months of loneliness and uncertainty and took their final toll on her body and spirit. Her shoulders sagged, and she slipped into a foggy stupor.

Rósa had no idea how long she'd been sitting on the hillside when a crunch behind her sent a chill racing up her spine. A small rock rolled past, and another bumped against her lower back. Holding her breath, she turned her head. The last thing she saw before she passed out was the muzzle of a double-barrel shotgun.

# Chapter 14

Rósa awoke in murky darkness. A gentle flapping curried her attention, and she tilted toward the sound. Outlined against an open window, loose curtains tickled the sill, their frayed hems quivering in a breeze and fluttering a hazy splay of moonlight across the floor. The breeze ushered in an earthy blend of coal smoke and pine mixed with the faint aroma of freshly baked bread that clenched her empty stomach.

She raised onto an elbow, rubbed her eyes, and scanned her surroundings. The subdued moonlight gave form to a tiny room with a single bed, a small bureau against the opposite wall, and a chair by the window. She squinted at a faint trace of light framing a closed door next to the bureau.

She sat up, and the knot in her stomach tightened, but now from fear. The children! Her widened eyes searched the room, but the girls were nowhere in sight. She threw off her coarse blanket and lurched to her feet, launching a rush of vertigo into her sluggish head. She grasped the bedpost then staggered to the door and fell against it. The cold metal door handle ignored her repeated attempts to budge it.

"Lilli-Anna! Kammbrie!" Rósa pounded on the door.

A scuffing then heavy footsteps preceded a click at the lock. The door opened, and she stumbled into the grasp of a large hand. It steadied her as she shielded her eyes from the glare of a single lightbulb suspended from the ceiling. A voice heavily accented in French hissed a warning in mixed German. "*Stille, Madame!* What are you trying to do, summon the entire gendarmerie?"

"Where are my children?"

"They're here. There's no need to shout."

The hand released her, and deep-set eyes stared at her darkly over a hawk nose. The man straightened, and her eyes widened at the size of her host—her captor? His bald head, perched on broad shoulders, sprouted oversized ears half covered by bushy red sideburns that flared into a full beard. He stepped away, his gnarled hand straightening a threadbare jacket of russet tweed over a thin woolen shirt open at the neck to reveal a thick mat of hair.

Rósa's gaze fell to a double-barrel shotgun leaning against the wall, and she shrank back. "Who. . .who are you? Where am I?"

"You're in a farmhouse, and my name is of no consequence."

The man closed the door to the bedroom and gestured toward a wooden chair set next to a small cast-iron stove. She eased herself onto the edge of the seat, clutching her arms. "Why have you brought us here?"

He leaned against the wall and folded his arms. "I am with the Résistance, something you would have discovered soon enough but that you best quickly forget. We were alerted to your journey soon after you left Salzburg. We've been waiting for you."

"Alerted? Who alerted you?"

"That's also something best left unsaid. It's enough to know you have a benefactor who has arranged your journey to Montintin."

"Montintin?"

"The children's home at the Château de Montintin, near Limoges, where you and your children will go."

"Where are my children? You said they're here."

"*Oui*, they are safe. They've eaten, and my daughter has given them her bed. She sleeps in the barn tonight, as shall I."

"I want to see them."

"In the morning. They rest now, as you must do. We have much to do in the morning to prepare for your journey."

The man crossed to a small table and uncovered a plate of bread and a bowl. "Eat now, then sleep. I will awaken you for breakfast."

The aroma of vegetable broth and bread drew Rósa unsteadily to her feet. *"Danke schön—merci."*

He nodded then retrieved his shotgun and moved toward a door beside the stove. "Turn off the light when you go to bed. There's no need to lock the bedroom door again. That was in case you awoke after I went out to the barn. I couldn't have you wandering about."

She nodded.

He snagged a faded brown beret from a peg on the wall and perched it on his head. "Sleep well."

❦

After a night of spotty sleep, though the most restful since leaving Salzburg, Rósa slipped out of bed at first light. She rummaged in her duffle bag for her sweater and pulled it over her shoulders then opened the door to the kitchen. The subtle glow of a cloudless dawn filtered through the room's double window, elevating the darkness to a light gray. She shivered and reached for a cord suspended from the lightbulb then hesitated. No need to betray her wakefulness to an outside world she knew nothing about.

A glance about the room revealed a door near the table. She stepped across to it and tested the handle. The door creaked open to a tiny bedroom, similar in furnishings to her own. As her eyes adjusted to the dark, she caught the sound of light snoring.

"Mama?"

Her heart leaped at Kammbrie's breathy whisper. "Yes, baby. I'm here."

Rustling blankets interrupted the nasal breathing as Rósa crossed the room and lowered herself to the edge of the bed. She pulled Kammbrie into a snug embrace.

Lilli-Anna's sleepy voice seeped from beneath the blanket. "Mama?"

"Yes, Lilli." The girl pushed herself free of the bedcovers and snuggled against her mama's side. Rósa rocked the twins gently, cooing to them as they yawned and sniffed the new day.

A door latch clicked in the kitchen, jerking Rósa's head up. The bulb snapped on, and she blinked at the off-white light. She hugged the twins closer when a tall, slender silhouette appeared in the doorway.

*"Très bien,"* you've awakened." The voice was young, soft, and the French-German less accented than the man's was the previous evening.

Rósa squinted against the light. "Who are—"

"I will begin breakfast." The silhouette disappeared, and the sound of metal against wood scraped through the doorway. Lilli-Anna shivered and pressed to Rósa's side.

"Stay in bed, girls. I'll come for you when there's something to eat." She stood and tucked the twins back under the covers.

Rósa stepped through the doorway. A girl in a yellow flowered dress stooped by the oven and blew onto a newly revived fire. The iron grate squeaked shut, and the girl straightened. She smiled at Rósa then turned to a small cupboard and gathered cooking utensils.

The girl appeared to be in her early teens, although her loose dress hid any evidence of an adolescent figure. Auburn hair cropped short in a boyish style capped her head beneath a light green scarf. When she turned again, vivid blue eyes shone from a scattering of freckles across her cheeks and nose. A thin scar scored a pale pink trace from the corner of her left eye to below her ear, the only blemish on her delicate features. She hummed a quiet tune as she spread a clean cloth over the rough-wood sideboard.

"May I help you with anything?" Rósa offered.

196

"*Non*, but I thank you." The girl uncovered a baguette and cut it into small slices. At that moment, the outside door swung open and the Frenchman entered. He leaned his shotgun against the wall and squeezed the girl's shoulder. She smiled back at him then returned to her work.

Fifteen minutes later, a simple meal of toasted baguette spread with butter and red currant jelly, slices of cheese, and herbal tea adorned the table. The twins shared a small cup of milk and licked the jelly from their toast. Kammbrie held her soggy crust up for more jelly, but Rósa shook her head. "Eat the bread with the jelly, Kammbrie."

The French girl smiled. "It's all right. She can have more." She scooped a dollop from a glass jar with a pâté knife and slathered the crust with it.

Lilli-Anna stared at her sister's toast, having just downed the last of hers. She peered up at Rósa.

Their hostess giggled. "There is more for you, too, *ma petite*." She dipped the knife into the jar again and wiped the dull blade across two of the toddler's fingers. Lilli-Anna's fingers disappeared into her mouth. The adults laughed as she sucked and slurped until the fingers reemerged spotless.

"Thank you so much for your kindness, Mademoiselle. . . ?"

The Frenchman looked up sharply, and the girl flashed Rósa an apologetic smile.

"I'm sorry. I shouldn't have asked." Rósa lowered her gaze. The girl touched Rósa's hand then rose to clear the dishes.

The Frenchman wiped his mouth on his sleeve. "I'll gather food for our journey. It's best if you and the children remain out of sight. We will be ready to depart by midday." He pushed back from the table. "You have far to go."

"How far?"

"Montintin is nearly six hundred kilometers from here. I'll take you to a certain point then pass you to another. He, in turn, will pass you to another. You will learn no names; it's not important the route you take." He reached into his jacket pocket. "You'll need these. The children are too young to need papers."

He handed her a card bearing the title Carte De Séjour De Resident Temporaire across the top. The second document was a multifold titled Titre D'identité De Voyage. She opened the travel document and gasped. Affixed to the third page was a small black-and-white photo cropped from a snapshot of Gustaw and her taken the year before. "Where did you get this?"

He shook his head and picked up his shotgun. "There is a pen on the sideboard. Be sure to sign your documents."

"*Mon père*, we will need an extra blanket." His daughter nodded toward the twins.

"Oui." Her father snagged his beret from its hook then left the house.

———

They departed before noon in an open cart pulled by the largest horse Rósa had ever seen. The sturdy leather reins in the Frenchman's hands appeared little more than strings against the Percheron's flanks, and she wondered how the massive beast would even detect the lead, let alone respond to it. The animal seemed docile enough, though, and soon they were clopping along a path away from the farmhouse at a steady pace. She looked back to see the man's daughter waving from an upstairs window. A quick smile and returned wave, then the house was lost from view.

Rósa sat beside the Frenchmen on the driver's seat, while the twins played on a blanket laid over a layer of straw in the cart's bed. The morning sun's climb to zenith was nearly complete, and she loosened her sweater from her shoulders. Her guide remained silent for the first half hour, chewing a stalk of hay that protruded from beneath his shaggy mustache.

Rósa shifted in her seat, her mind in search for something to break the awkward silence.

He glanced at her then cleared his throat. "If we are stopped, you are my cousin recently arrived from Poland. We are traveling to visit family in Lyon. Remain silent. I will speak."

"I understand."

"The name Szpilmann is a problem," he grumbled.

"Why?"

"Marshal Pétain, the leader of the puppet Vichy Government, collaborates with the Nazi occupiers to the north." He shook his head. "I will need to convince them you are not Jews."

Rósa considered telling him her real surname and the reason for adopting the name Szpilmann but decided against it. Her travel documentation already bore the assumed name, and to confess the truth to her guide now would only complicate matters.

He slapped the reins against the horse's haunches. "Many Jewish sympathizers escaped south when the Boche invaded through Belgium. Perhaps you will find help along the way. And God must smile upon you."

His comment burdened her mind. How many prayers for safety had she sent heavenward since leaving Salzburg? She'd lost count. In the midst of her supplications, the deceit of keeping the twins, at failing to post the letters to their relatives in Berlin, pricked her conscience but not enough to risk losing the children. After all, she had given her husband for them. God would understand. She shook away the fledgling guilt and sought a safe topic. "Your daughter is a lovely girl."

"She is the joy of my life."

"Where is her mother?"

The man's eyes narrowed, and he barked a short cough. "She is gone."

Rósa fumbled for an apology.

He shifted his weight. "Until last year, we lived outside Reims. When the Boche invaded, they overran our village before we had time to escape. I was in the fields when an advance reconnaissance unit reached our farm. They took my wife and daughter. . ." His eyes brimmed, and he cleared his throat. "My daughter alone survived. The soldier was drunk on a bottle of our wine. His blade missed her throat."

"I'm very sorry," Rósa whispered.

"I found Moni—my daughter—in the barn feigning death, her dress in shreds, her head in a pool of blood. I treated her as best I could."

"You did a fine job. The scar is small."

His tone hardened. "Two of the soldiers remained to loot the house after their unit moved on." He patted the shotgun propped against the seat next to him. "One for each barrel."

Rósa shuddered then offered, "She is very sweet natured to have had such a terrible experience."

"God has healed her heart." His knuckles whitened at their grip on the reins, and his voice dropped to a near whisper. "Now he must heal mine."

At dusk, he pulled the cart into a wooded area south of Saint-Alban. After a cold meal supplemented with blackberries plucked from a nearby bush, he arranged a heavy blanket over the hay for Rósa and the twins. They lifted the girls onto the makeshift bed, and he offered her his hand.

She accepted it. "I have not thanked you for your help."

The Frenchman shrugged.

"I will pray always for you and your daughter."

He drew back his head and stared at her, his expression distant. A moment passed, and a wave of heat surged through Rósa's forehead at the realization that her hand was still in his. He helped her onto the wagon bed, and Rósa nestled next to the sleeping twins. Her guide folded the blanket over them, retrieved his shotgun, and crawled beneath the cart.

Rósa fell asleep, her hand still warm from the Frenchman's touch.

# Chapter 15

They passed through Pont d'Ain late in the afternoon of the second day. At the city's southern outskirts, the Frenchman veered onto a narrow lane through a hedgerow twenty meters from the road. The path led to the foreyard of a two-story stone cottage, its first-floor windows and door boarded shut. They rounded the cottage and halted near a three-sided shed.

Rósa wrinkled her nose at the pungent scent of manure and composting vegetation. "Where are we?"

"Another farmhouse." He climbed down from the bench seat.

She surveyed her muddy surroundings. The shed, its weather-bleached boards warped and split, sagged inward and appeared ready to disintegrate at the least suggestion of a wind. Rusted field implements leaned against the dilapidated structure in a tangle of weeds, skeletal reminders of a once productive farm. Beyond the shed, an overgrown trellis of grapevines and two tangled blackberry bushes laden with early fruit bordered a fallow field that stretched to a wooded slope. A twin-rutted path bisected the field and disappeared into the trees at the base of the hill. Rósa peered at the stumpy remains of whatever crop the field had last borne. Beans? Asparagus, perhaps?

The squeak of rusty hinges and a door slamming startled her. She turned to see a slim woman with waist-length black hair striding toward the cart. Rósa's gaze locked onto a shotgun wedged under the woman's arm, a twin to the weapon resting by the Frenchman's leg.

He lifted a hand. "*Bonjour*, madame." She nodded.

He stepped down from the cart and approached her. They embraced and kissed each other's cheeks. After a few quiet words, the woman peered around his wide shoulders. Rósa attempted a smile but received none in response.

The woman approached the wagon. Her eyes swept Rósa from head to foot, wrinkles creasing her forehead. When she glanced into the back of the cart, she froze. The Frenchwoman spun to face the man. A silent battle of words waged between the two, then the man dipped his head. The woman turned back toward the cart, her face pale.

Rósa's eyes beseeched the Frenchman for an explanation. He ignored her and studied his comrade. The woman leaned her shotgun against the wagon and gripped the edge of the cart, her gaze locked on the twins.

Lilli-Anna stopped playing and looked up. Rósa began to introduce the twins to the woman but fell silent when Lilli-Anna crawled to the side of the cart and held her arms up with a smile. The woman stiffened then slowly reached down and eased the tot up from the wagon bed. As Lilli-Anna hugged her neck, a tear slid down the Frenchwoman's cheek and disappeared into the young girl's blond curls. Without a word, she pivoted and strode back toward the house, Lilli-Anna clutched to her bosom.

Rósa shot a panicked look at the Frenchman. He crossed to the wagon and lifted Rósa's duffle bag from behind the seat. Grasping the Frenchwoman's shotgun, he nodded toward Kammbrie and turned to follow the woman.

Rósa scrambled down from the seat and gathered Kammbrie into her arms. Halfway across the yard, the Frenchman halted and peered back over his shoulder, his eyes dark.

"Speak no German while you are here."

❧

The evening passed in near silence, the Frenchman absent. Rósa's new hostess scarcely acknowledged Rósa's presence, bestowing most of her attention on the twins, especially

Lilli-Anna. Following a light meal of lentil soup and fresh bread, she cleared the table then gestured for Rósa to follow her.

The Frenchwoman picked up Lilli-Anna and walked through a door into a short hall-way. Rósa hefted her duffle bag, took Kammbrie by the hand, and followed. At the end of the hall, a stairway climbed to a cramped garret with two small beds, where the woman knelt and eased Lilli-Anna to the floor. Brushing her fingers through the toddler's hair, she stood, gave Rósa a terse nod, and walked out.

After tucking the children in, Rósa stretched out on the other bed and closed her eyes, but restful sleep eluded her. Fragmented dreams of shotguns and horses melding with machine guns and train stations tossed her on the thin mattress, depriving her body of much-needed rest. At last, sometime after midnight, the rhythm of rain pattering on the roof lulled her into a dead slumber.

She awoke the next morning to weak daylight oozing through the louvers of a small window on the far wall. Rolling onto her side, she squinted at the bed next to her. Kammbrie slept, her chest rising and falling with light snoring. Lilli-Anna's side of the bed lay empty.

Rósa threw the covers off and jumped to her feet. She scanned the room, her heart in her throat. The door stood ajar, and she stumbled toward it, pulling on her sweater. Taking the stairs two at a time, she burst into the kitchen. Empty.

Chest heaving, Rósa lunged across the room, threw open the back door, and sloshed into the rain-soaked backyard. As she opened her mouth to shout for Lilli-Anna, she caught a movement near the shed.

The Frenchwoman knelt on the ground with a small reed basket. Lilli-Anna, her back to Rósa, plucked low fruit from the blackberry bush. The woman held the basket toward the young girl, who giggled and stuffed the blackberry into her mouth. The woman laughed softly then stiffened when she caught sight of Rósa. She dropped the basket and bolted to her feet, her gaze focused downward. When she looked back up, grim defiance darkened her eyes.

Rósa stood ankle-deep in muddy water, shaking and panting. Lilli-Anna plucked another berry and dropped it into the basket then glanced up and spotted Rósa.

"Mama!" She tottered forward. The Frenchwoman grabbed the girl's arm one pace away from a water-filled rut. She pulled the child back from the puddle then stared again at Rósa.

As Rósa fought her breathing back under control, she focused on the woman's expression. A curious mixture of—was it sadness? joy? fear?—shaded her eyes. The perceived emotions, old acquaintances of Rósa's, turned her thoughts inward. When Gustaw first brought the aban-doned girls to their apartment in Stettin, sadness overtook her at the horror that had befallen the Szpilmanns, then joy at the sunshine the beautiful twins brought into her life, and lastly fear at the notion of having to surrender them to their relatives in Berlin. What kindred events could this Frenchwoman have suffered?

Rósa took a deep breath and forced a smile. Then, with all the willpower she could mus-ter, she turned and walked back to the house. When she returned to the garret, Kammbrie had awakened and was sitting up. Rósa brushed the toddler's hair and led her downstairs.

Kammbrie and Rósa emerged from the stairway at the same moment the Frenchwoman and Lilli-Anna entered from the yard. The two women locked gazes. The Frenchwoman gave a slight nod, and the first hint of a tentative smile crossed her lips. Rósa smiled back.

Lilli-Anna ran across the room babbling unintelligibly, most likely something having to do with the purple stains on her lips. Rósa laughed, but Kammbrie eyed her with a puzzled frown. She stroked Kammbrie's hair and groped for words to explain, when a hand bearing two blackberries appeared before the tot's face. Kammbrie's eyes widened. She peered up into the Frenchwoman's smile and held out her hand. The fruit had barely touched her palm before it disappeared into her mouth.

Their hostess straightened and moved to a small table by the stove. She set the basket next to a bowl of thin batter, and soon the aroma of sizzling crepes and eggs filled the air.

❧

Rósa had just changed the girls' clothes when a clattering arose from the front yard. The sound choked off and a door slammed. Gathering the twins, she ushered them downstairs and into the kitchen then crossed to the back door and peered into the yard.

The Frenchwoman traipsed around the corner toward the door, the familiar shotgun wedged in the crook of her arm. A short, swarthy man trailed her, wiping his bald head with a gray cloth. When the woman caught sight of Rósa, she jerked her head toward the house.

Rósa ducked back into the kitchen, moved the girls to the table, and waited. The door opened, and the Frenchwoman and her companion entered. He stopped short at the sight of the twins and cast an annoyed look at the woman. She ignored him.

"Where is the man who brought me here?" Rósa asked in broken German.

The Frenchwoman spun on her heel and stared her down. The Frenchman's caution not to speak German rushed back into Rósa's mind, and she dropped her gaze. The man muttered something in French, and Rósa lifted her head. The woman and her companion exchanged strained looks, then she turned her back and leaned the shotgun against the wall.

The man shook his head and, with a sigh, gestured toward the door. Rósa raised a finger, pleading for him to wait a moment. She hurried up the stairs to retrieve her duffle bag and returned to the kitchen to see the Frenchwoman kneeling in front of the twins, her fingertips tracing the girls' cheeks.

"*Bonne chance, mes petites,*" the woman whispered then kissed them both on the forehead. Her lips lingered on Lilli-Anna's brow. The woman stood, eyes glistening. A final nod to Rósa, and she turned away.

Rósa hesitated then murmured, "Merci." The woman shrugged but didn't turn around. Rósa gathered the twins and her duffle bag then followed their new guide through the doorway.

She led the twins around the corner of the house and stopped. A decrepit truck—at least it looked like a truck—stood in the side yard. Behind it a wispy cloud of gray-black smoke curled into the dank morning air. She picked her way through the muck around the vehicle to where the bald man held open the passenger door then hesitated, staring into the truck bed.

In the middle of the cargo platform, a large metal container perched slightly atilt, sprouting two rusty metal pipes that bent downward and disappeared though a rectangular hole. A small iron box affixed to the base of the tank belched smoke. Scattered piles of charcoal littered the platform around the tank.

The man walked to the back of the vehicle and retrieved a flat scoop. He opened a side panel of the smoking box and shoveled a couple of loads of charcoal into a dirty fire. The door clanged shut, and he tossed the implement onto the bed.

Rósa questioned him with her eyes. He pointed to a hole above the rear fender where the filler tube for the gas tank should have been.

"Boche. *Petrol.*" He sliced a forefinger across his throat. Then he gestured toward the water tank and shrugged, flashing a partially toothed smile.

She nodded.

On their first day's journey, her guide had told her the Germans had assumed control of France's petroleum supply and commandeered serviceable civilian vehicles immediately after the invasion. Judging by the condition of this man's truck, they must have decided they had no use for it. Lacking proper fuel, the resourceful Frenchman had refitted his truck to run on steam power.

She returned an uneasy smile and lifted the girls into the cab. The man climbed behind the wheel and engaged the gears. As the rickety vehicle bounced across the uneven ground, yet another anxious prayer in Polish squeezed through rusty holes in the roof and pressed heavenward through a mist-swollen sooty sky.

# Chapter 16

They left Pont d'Ain under skies as gray as Rósa's mood. She only vaguely noticed the signs for Gévrieux and Dagneux crawl past the smudgy window before being handed off to another escort in Lyon. Byways around Saint-Etienne and Clermont-Ferand passed under the wheels of a similarly powered ancient Citroën piloted by a dour man who spoke hardly a word. The next day's travel put the refugees into a large oxcart hauling hay, whose driver was as talkative as the previous man was mute. He prattled on in French, pausing only long enough for courtesy breaks. She smiled and nodded at various points of his monologue but had no inkling what he was saying. They creaked into the tiny village of La Chapelle after dark, where Rósa spent a restless night in a small inn, her sanguine guide's nasal voice still droning in her mind's ear.

When she awoke the next morning, the house lay quiet. Her restive night had sparked a dull ache behind her eyes that no amount of massaging could extinguish. She rousted the bleary-eyed twins, and they straggled into the inn's front room. A paltry breakfast of day-old bread, dry cheese, and water on a rough wooden table greeted them when they stepped into the dimly lit front room.

The twins fussed during the short mealtime and refused anything more than a nibble or two. After forcing down a few flavorless bites, Rósa pushed her own plate away and dragged herself from the table. Pausing by the front window, she nudged the curtain aside and peered into the yard. A scruffy dog tied to a stake across the street yapped incessantly at who knew what, each yelp piercing her throbbing temple like a hot needle. Behind her, Kammbrie squirmed and whimpered, and Lilli-Anna banged a spoon on the table. When the spoon clattered to the floor, Rósa spun around.

"Hush! Will you *please* be quiet?" She clenched her eyelids shut and stroked her forehead with her fingertips. Kammbrie's whimpering climbed to a wail, soon joined by Lilli-Anna's quavering voice.

The front door slammed, silencing the twins and snapping open Rósa's eyes. A buxom woman in a soiled gardening smock, the innkeeper who had grudgingly received them the night before, glowered at them, her fists on her hips. Lilli-Anna sniffled again then went silent. After a discomfiting minute, the innkeeper stepped from the doorway to reveal another woman as diminutive as the landlady was robust, standing behind her.

The newcomer stood erect, hands clasped at her waist. Small wire-rimmed glasses framed gray eyes over her thin nose, and silver-streaked ash-blond hair pulled itself into a tight bun on the nape of her neck. The woman studied Rósa then turned her attention to the twins. Without a word, the landlady trundled out the door, leaving them alone.

"Pani Szpilmann?" the woman asked.

Rósa's heart leaped at the sound of her native tongue. *"Tak."*

"I am Hana Fuchs. I've come to escort you to the Château de Montintin."

"How do you know my language?"

"I was born in Lodz. I've lived in France six years now, at work in the children's homes."

A dozen questions vied for priority in Rósa's mind. "Where is—"

Hana raised a finger. "There will be time for questions. We must go now. The sooner we reach Montintin, the better for the children. We have many sympathizers in this region, but," she glanced out the window, "many also live here who are not."

Rósa nodded. "I'll get our bag." She hurried into the bedroom and stuffed into her duffle bag the few items she'd removed the evening before. Before returning to the front room, she lifted her gaze toward the ceiling. "Thank You, Lord, for Your protection. I confess I did not trust Your provision at all times during our journey. But You have been faithful, as always. Please forgive me." She took a deep breath and stepped through the doorway.

Hana was kneeling in front of the twins, smiling and stroking their cheeks with the back of her delicate fingers. Lilli-Anna smiled back, but Kammbrie merely stared.

"They are beautiful but so much alike. How do you tell them apart?"

Rósa assumed a smile of stolen pride in the Szpilmann twins. "It can be difficult, but look. Kammbrie has a birthmark behind her left ear."

She brushed the tot's curls aside. Hana peered at her neck then looked up. Rósa glanced down then quickly released Lilli-Anna's hair and brushed Kammbrie's away from her neck. Hana smiled at the chocolate-colored blemish on the toddler's skin.

Rósa's cheeks warmed, and she cleared her throat. "As I said, it can be difficult."

Hana leaned back and pursed her lips. "I wasn't told they were so young."

"Is their age a problem?"

Hana shrugged. "We'll find a way." She helped the twins onto the floor.

"Is it far to Montintin?" Rósa asked when they reached the street.

Hana gestured to her left. She gripped a hand of each child, and they tottered along beside her. "Only three kilometers. The children will walk as far as they are able. Then we will carry them."

"Did you walk the entire way from the home this morning?"

"Tak."

"It seems a long distance."

"When the Germans invaded France last summer, my husband Noach and I fled from Eaubonne, north of Paris. He is an accountant and helped administrate some of the children's homes. We joined others from Montmorency and Soisy and walked to Limoges, then here to Montintin." She offered Rósa a thin smile. "This is no distance at all."

"Where is your husband?"

Hana's smile faded. "Noach was captured while foraging for food near Orléans. He decoyed the gendarmerie away from our group but was not able to escape them. I don't know if he is in a camp, or. . ."

Rósa touched her arm. "I'm very sorry for you."

"And your husband?"

"Gustaw. . .did not survive our escape from Poland."

Her companion nodded, her eyes softening. "Then I'm very sorry for you, for I still have my hope."

Rósa lowered her gaze and shifted the duffle bag to her other arm. Few words disturbed the remainder of their journey.

# Chapter 17

The twins fared well, given the toll their trek from Salzburg had taken on them. Lilli-Anna outlasted Kammbrie by a few minutes before Hana picked her up. Lilli-Anna hugged Hana's neck and stared blankly at the passing farmland, while Kammbrie's head lolled on Rósa's slight shoulder with each tiring step. Finally, the Château de Montintin loomed through the trees as the women and children topped the final rise two hours later. They halted at the edge of the estate to catch their breath.

The Château resembled a castle from a child's storybook. The rough-stone three-story building featured massive turrets at either end, their conical roofs piercing the low cloud cover. Multiple gables jutted from the steep roofline like eyebrows peaked with worry. Rósa could easily imagine a horse and carriage from a Brothers Grimm tale waiting patiently near the front door for the fashionably clad lord and lady of the house to emerge.

Instead, into the empty yard stepped an ordinary-looking woman in a plain black frock. She crossed her arms and scanned the group, her expression terse.

Hana turned to Rósa. "Madame Krakowskie, one of our directresses."

She set Lilli-Anna down and smoothed the girl's wrinkled dress. When Rósa attempted to set Kammbrie on the ground, the toddler grasped her around the neck and wouldn't let go. Rósa straightened and shifted Kammbrie to her other hip. Hana led them across the open lawn.

They halted when they reached the doorway. Hana gestured toward Rósa. "*Je vous présente* Madame Szpilmann." She placed one hand on Lilli-Anna's head and the other on Kammbrie's back. "*Et voici* Lilli-Anna et Kammbrie."

Rósa fidgeted under Madame Krakowskie's silent appraisal. She plucked a bit of leaf from Lilli-Anna's hair and tightened her grip on Kammbrie.

Lilli-Anna smiled and lifted her arms. The woman ignored the girl's overture. Finally, she addressed Hana. "*Elles sont très petite.*"

Hana nodded, her smile undiminished.

The directress turned her attention to Rósa. "*Parlez-vous français?*"

Rósa shook her head.

"*Elle parle polonaise,*" Hana interjected.

Madame Krakowskie drew a deep breath then continued in Polish, "Come with me, please." One more look at the girls, and she pursed her lips then turned on her heel.

The directress led them through a dark foyer into a large dining room. She offered them chairs then crossed to the door that led into the kitchen. A few muffled words, and she returned to the table, followed soon by a young woman with a tray bearing an earthenware carafe, three cups, and a small plate of biscuits. The woman smiled at the twins and set the tray down then excused herself from the room. Hana gave each of the girls a biscuit and poured the adults small cups of ersatz coffee. Lilli-Anna took a big bite, but Kammbrie only nibbled.

Madame Krakowskie clasped her hands on the table. "We only accept children over six years old. I don't know that your girls can remain here."

Rósa paled. "But we've nowhere else to go."

"There's no one here to tend to children so young."

"I. . .I hoped I could remain and work. I can sew, cook, and clean, whatever you need me to do. I do not expect pay, merely to be able to remain close to my. . .children." She forced a light tone. "I abide by all our customs, and I assure you that the children will—"

"You are not Jewish."

Rósa's pulse quickened. "Of course I am."

"Come now, madame, don't you think we can tell?"

"But how—?"

Madame Krakowskie leaned forward. "Jewish homes have small boxes containing scripture attached to the front doorposts. You didn't ask me why there was no *tefilla* on the Château."

Hana shifted in her seat.

Rósa swallowed. "I know this, of course. I assumed. . .that it would be dangerous to have such symbols displayed openly." A bead of sweat trickled down her spine. "With so much hostility toward. . .our people, perhaps—"

The directress settled back. "Madame Szpilmann, the doorpost box is a *mezuzah. Tefillin* are worn on the forehead and the arm."

Rósa's heart sank. "I–I'm sorry. I did not want to deceive you, but I was so afraid you wouldn't accept us if you knew." She perked, renewed hope in her voice. "But the children. . . they are Jewish."

Madame Krakowskie arched an eyebrow.

"Please believe me. My true name is Rósa Dudek. My husband, Gustaw, and I are from Stettin. We took the children in as babies after the Germans arrested their parents, Izaak and Maria Szpilmann." Her voice quavered. "Gustaw was shot protecting the girls."

Hana gasped and touched Rósa's arm. She turned a pleading eye at her superior. Madame Krakowskie kept her gaze on Rósa, her face even, but the first hint of compassion softened her voice. "I'm sorry for your loss."

Rósa dropped her gaze to the table and fought the pressure behind her eyes. She shuddered at the first reference she'd made to her husband's death in such stark terms.

Hana's words came softly. "Madame Krakowskie, La Chevrette's housekeeper left with the first trainload of children for Marseille. Our cook transfers to another home in two weeks. We need help with the chores and watching over those who remain. And I'm sure Ania would love to watch the twins. She so misses her own young sisters."

"Madame Fuchs, there are kosher considerations in preparing the food at La Chevrette. How can you expect a goy—"

"I can learn!" Rósa straightened. "Your cook can teach me before she leaves. I learn quickly. I will cook and clean—whatever you need." Her eyes beseeched the directress. "*Prosze*, do not separate me from my children. Please. . ."

"Allowing a family to stay will create problems. If the other children see you favoring your own, there will be resentment, which will lead to discipline problems. *Hashem* knows we need no more of those."

"I will be careful."

The directress paused, her gaze leveled at Rósa. "If you stay, the twins will not be permitted in the kitchen during the day. You may be alone together only in the evenings and at night. Also, there must be no favoritism, no sneaking treats for them. They must be only two children among many you will provide for. And they must observe all Jewish practices, as this is their heritage."

"I promise."

Madame Krakowskie massaged her forehead with her fingertips. "Okay, we'll try this for a week. If no problems arise, you may stay."

Rósa exhaled. "Thank you."

"But I caution you, there will be many chores. You're a small woman. Are you sure you can keep up with your duties and still mind your children after hours?"

"I'm sure."

"Very well. Madame Fuchs, there's an empty room on the girls' floor at La Chevrette. Introduce Madame Dudek to Naida. She will begin working in the kitchen immediately.

The children's care will be your responsibility. Use Ania as you choose. First, though, ensure Madame Dudek completes her paperwork." Madame Krakowskie rose.

"Paperwork?" Rósa asked.

Hana nodded and gestured toward the door. "Come."

Rósa gathered the children to her side and hoisted her duffle bag. "I don't know how to thank you, Madame Krakowskie."

The directress gave a slight nod and turned toward the kitchen.

Hana smiled and ushered La Chevrette's newest residents from the dining room.

⤸⤹

Rósa's head ached by the time Hana pulled out the final forms in the triplicate stack. Places, dates, birthdays, weight, height, hair color—why did they need to know all these things? Her forms filled in easily, but the twins' were a different matter. What she knew of their history, she recited to Hana, who penned it in French onto the endless sheets of paper. What Rósa didn't know, she made up.

"Birthday?" Hana poised her pen above a blank line on the twins' biographical sketch.

Rósa frowned. "I. . .I don't know."

Hanna twiddled the pen between her fingers and waited.

"They were around three months old when we. . .found them. Let's see: December, November, October—sometime in September. What date is today?"

"The twenty-first of June."

"Twenty-one September 1939, then."

With a stroke of Hana's pen, Lilli-Anna and Kammbrie Szpilmann became twenty-one months old.

"How much more paperwork is there?"

"That's it." Hana laid down her pen. "I've signed the forms for you as Rósa Szpilmann. You will need to learn the signature."

"Finally," grumbled Rósa.

Hana shuffled the forms into a neat pile. "Who knows? These papers may come in handy."

Rósa shrugged.

Hana smiled. "Let's gather the children and settle you in your room."

⤸⤹

"Madame Krakowskie is very severe." Rósa set the twins on one of the beds in the tiny room and laid her duffle bag in the corner.

Hana stood in the doorway. "*Nie*, she is very fair. She fights every day for our survival, ingratiating us with local authorities, begging farmers and merchants for food and supplies, tending to the many problems with the staff and the children. She maintains formality to keep order."

"Does she administer the Château and La Chevrette?"

"Only La Chevrette. The Château de Montintin's directress is away until tomorrow, so Madame Krakowskie assumes responsibility for both homes until her superior returns. The Château once belonged to a doctor, but it now houses nearly 150 children. La Chevrette was the servants' quarters for the Château. Fifty orthodox children displaced from Eaubonne now live here."

"She seemed displeased with the girls' age."

Hana tipped her head. "They cannot carry their weight. Indeed, they will need to be watched while you are working. That will take Ania and others away from their studies and chores. If we need to leave quickly, they will slow us down."

"Leave quickly?"

" 'Free France' is a myth, Rósa. There will be no freedom for these children and their

206

families until the Nazis are vanquished. Until that happens, we must be ready to flee as the persecution moves south. And it will, be certain of that."

Rósa fell silent for a moment then asked, "You mentioned Ania in our meeting with Madame Krakowskie. Who is she?"

Hana smiled. "A very lovely and gifted thirteen-year-old girl who escaped the Warsaw ghetto early last year." Her smile faded. "The rest of her family was not so fortunate. Ania's fluency in Polish and French will help you a great deal. You must learn as much as you can from her."

"If Madame Krakowskie thinks we are such a problem, why does she let us stay?"

"Because she's very fair," Hana repeated, her voice hushed. "Your husband gave his life for two Jewish babies. Perhaps she feels she can risk no less for you. Oh, and I should tell you also that it was not necessary for you to contrive a Jewish identity. The Nazis' hate extends far beyond the Jews. We have Christian children at Montintin, also."

"I see. I can assure you, though, that we'll be no trouble."

"Mama?" Kammbrie broke in.

"What is it, Kammbrie?"

The toddler grimaced. Her eyes widened, and she doubled over and emptied her stomach onto the floor. Lilli-Anna stared at her sister.

Rósa touched the back of her hand to Kammbrie's forehead. "She's warm."

The toddler wretched again but now only bile. She squeaked out a sob. Lilli-Anna sniffled then whimpered.

Rósa tested Lilli-Anna's forehead. "Lilli, are you feeling okay?"

The young girl lifted rounded eyes toward Rósa then looked back at her sister.

"Go sit there." She set Lilli-Anna on the floor and prodded her toward the second small bed.

Hana turned to leave. "I will get cool water and a cloth." She glanced at the floor by the bed. "And something to clean this up."

"*Dziękuję*," said Rósa.

"You are welcome."

The door clicked, and Hana's footsteps faded down the hallway.

# Chapter 18

Rósa's first three weeks at the children's home raced by. Naida condescended to instruct the "goy" in kosher food preparation as she was able, but her own duties demanded most of her time. The terse cook's patience wore thin, although Rósa strove to please her. She learned quickly and was able to wean herself from Naida's reluctant tutelage well before the cook's departure.

La Chevrette's kitchen featured no stove or oven, merely a massive open fireplace that demanded Rósa make significant adjustments to her culinary skills. Her schedule allowed no break between cleaning up after the morning meal and launching into preparations for that day's lunch, then likewise for dinner. When she finally completed her evening tasks, little energy remained for the twins other than to prepare them for bed.

Happily, Lilli-Anna and Kammbrie thrived. The twins' seclusion in Salzburg permitted no contact with other children, no chance to develop their social and verbal skills. But life at La Chevrette more than compensated. Lilli-Anna's open and trusting personality endeared her to even the most reserved of the children. Kammbrie, while quieter and slower to warm up to people, also blossomed in the attention. Both girls picked up a spotty vocabulary quickly for their ages, although their fledgling vernacular assumed a curious hybrid of Polish, French, Yiddish, and even a smattering of Flemish. Rósa's French also improved, thanks to Ania.

One afternoon, Hana offered to help Rósa prepare dinner. The women chatted as they gathered what scarce foodstuffs were available.

"You mentioned a transport the day we arrived." Rósa set a stack of mismatched dishes on the table. "What was that?"

Hana began distributing the plates. "Over the past several years, charitable and activist organizations have saved thousands of displaced and orphaned children, many of them rescued from the camps themselves. Most are Jewish, but not all. Some have found refuge in England, the Americas, and other countries, where they await reunions with their families in orphanages or foster care. This has become known by some as the *Kindertransport*."

"How do they get out of France?"

"The children in the Limoges area have taken different routes. Some cross the Pyrenees into Spain then travel on to Portugal where they board ships for the Americas. With the help of the Résistance and other groups, some have made their way to Switzerland, others to Palestine and even China."

"China? Why so far away?"

"Because the Chinese allowed them to come. You see, the most difficult part is gaining acceptance abroad. Visa quotas in many countries have denied thousands of homeless children safe harbor. Turned away by country after country, many were forced to return to the European continent, like those aboard the MS *St. Louis*."

Rósa paused stoking the fire. "What was the *St. Louis*?"

"It was a German ship carrying nearly a thousand refugees, most of them Jewish. Two years ago, when the ship reached Havanna, the Cubans refused to recognize their tourist visas, nor would they grant them political asylum. They demanded five hundred dollars from each passenger before allowing them to disembark."

"Five hundred dollars?"

Hana nodded. "Only a handful could afford such a sum. The remaining refugees sailed on to the United States, where immigration quotas denied them entry. There is even a rumor the Americans fired a warning shot at the ship to keep it away from the harbor. The Canadians would not accept them, either."

"Where did they go?"

"The *St. Louis* returned to Belgium. At Antwerp, the captain refused to release the ship to Germany until he found refuge for his passengers, bless his soul. He negotiated with emissaries from Great Britain, Belgium, France, and the Netherlands, and finally found haven for all of them." She quieted. "But then came the Blitzkrieg, and many were consumed by the camps they had once evaded.

Rósa shook her head. "Who is it that does this, rescues the children?"

"Several groups, some of whom work together, others who do not. The American Friends Society—the Quakers—selected the children from Montintin for the first transport under visas from the United States Committee for the Care of European Children, the USCOM. The children boarded the *Mouzinho* in Lisbon and were expected to reach New York on June 21st."

"When the girls and I arrived."

Hana nodded and smiled. "*Baruch* Hashem for their good fortune."

"How do they decide which children will go?"

"With heavy hearts, I'm sure. I would not want to choose who is to be saved and who is not. The Americans push for the visas to go to the youngest children, as they are easier to place in foster care."

Rósa's pulse quickened, her thoughts turning to the twins.

"But we know that the older children are at greater risk of arrest, so it becomes a battle between politics and practicality."

A young voice from the doorway interrupted them. "Madame Fuchs?"

Hana smiled. "Yes, Julia."

"Madame Krakowskie is asking for you."

"Thank you."

When Hana excused herself, Rósa eased onto a chair. Hana's mention of the American government's preference for younger children reignited hope in her heart and set her mind racing.

*Perhaps there is yet a chance.*

With renewed optimism, Rósa tackled her duties with fierce resolve. Naida left in mid-July, and affairs did not skip a beat as Rósa redoubled her efforts cooking and housekeeping. Most evenings she dragged herself to their small room with less than a half hour to spare before the twins' bedtime. Often she collapsed onto her bed and dozed off before the girls had quieted down.

Each day she prayed there would be room aboard one of the transports for the twins and her, and that it would be soon. Word had filtered through the community that a purge was coming in Vichy, France—one that would place them all at great risk.

A week after Naida left, rumor became reality.

❦

Rósa clenched her jaw and grasped the handle of the cast-iron pot with a heavy cloth. Wiping the sweat from her forehead with a sleeve, she stirred the pot of *tobinaumbour*, a root that supplemented La Chevrette's food supply when vegetables became scarce, which was often. Normally fed to livestock, the coarse tuber was barely palatable for humans, and its unfortunate effect on their digestive systems made for even coarser jokes from the older children. But it was nutrition.

Rósa raised a silent prayer of thanks for an enterprising former cook who had concocted a stock of vinegar, oil, onion, sugar, and salt that greatly enhanced the tuber's appeal, or at least mitigated its lack of appeal. Still, a nice stew of fresh carrots, potatoes, and—should she even hope?—beef would be such a blessing from the mundane menu she could offer the children.

Today, it would be up to the carrots, apples, and cherries some of the older boys had gathered that morning to cut the stodgy soup's aftertaste.

She had just begun pitting the cherries when Hana burst through the doorway. Rósa dropped the knife and stared at the woman's red face. "Is something wrong?"

"The time has come. We must leave Montintin."

Rósa wiped her hands on her apron. "Why?"

"The Vichy government is bowing to the Nazis' edict to rid the country's economy of all Jewish influence. No Jew is safe; businesses are being taken over, and arrests are on the rise." Hana steadied herself at the side of the table and fanned her face. "The OSE is closing the home at Château Mas Jambot, close to Vichy. We will be next."

"Where will the children go?"

"There is a new facility at Le Couret, hidden in the forests of Haute Vienne." She coughed.

"Please sit down." Rósa pulled a chair from the table.

Hana dropped onto the edge of the seat.

Rósa dipped a cupful of water from a basin and offered it to her friend.

Hana nodded her thanks. "Madame Krakowskie is being reassigned to the home at Le Couret."

Rósa blanched. Would the next administrator be as sympathetic to the twins' and her situation? She took a seat across from Hana.

"And what of La Chevrette?"

"There is one more transport scheduled to leave for Marseille next month."

Rósa gripped her hands. "And. . ."

Hana averted her gaze. "The children have already been selected."

"What of the. . .others?"

"Some may be able to move to Le Couret, but not many. The others will be dispersed to homes throughout France." Hana met Rósa's gaze. "I don't know what will happen to the twins. Of course, we hope to keep them together, but. . ."

"Hope? Surely they would not separate us."

"We try not to separate siblings, but if there's no one willing to take both—"

"You cannot do that!" Rósa jumped to her feet. "They're too young. They need each other. They need me!"

Hana rose. "You must remain calm—"

"Remain *calm*?" Rósa backed away from the table, tipping her chair over. "How can you even consider—"

*"Pani Szpilmann!"* Hana's tone sliced the air.

Rósa stiffened.

Hana leveled her gaze. "This is the danger I spoke of when you first arrived. You recall our discussion, do you not?"

Rósa took a deep breath and nodded. "I–I'm sorry. It's just that. . ."

"Please believe we will do everything we can for the girls' welfare." Hana stepped over to Rósa and laid a hand on her trembling arm. "But you must remain calm for the children as well as for yourself."

Rósa opened her eyes to a blurry room. "Perhaps Madame Krakowskie. . . ?"

"She has all of La Chevrette to consider, Rósa. There is only so much she can do."

"Still, I must speak with her."

Hana nodded.

<hr>

Rósa's whitened knuckles rapped on Madame Krakowskie's bedroom door.

*"Entrez."*

The directress sat behind a makeshift wooden desk, her elbows propped on a smattering of papers strewn across its surface. Her tented fingers tapped against tight lips. "Madame Dudek," she acknowledged.

Rósa cleared her throat. "Hana informed me of your reassignment."

The administrator nodded.

"I was sorry to hear of it. You've been very good to us, to the girls. I'm grateful."

Again, Madame Krakowskie dipped her head.

"She. . .she also told me there's another transport next month."

Silence.

Rósa fidgeted. Surely the directress could hear her heart pounding in the stillness of the room. "I was wondering. . .hoping. . .might there be room for—"

"The manifest has been decided."

"I know. I just thought, the twins are so small. They take so little space, so little food. If—"

"It's not a matter of space or food; it's a matter of paperwork. There are exit, entrance, and transit visas, sponsorship affidavits, medical releases, good character vouchers—you have no idea the number of documents and how fragile they are. A pass is good today but not tomorrow at the whim of some junior official; visas carrying short-term time limits can take years to replace if a deadline is missed by one day. Even shipping companies can decide overnight to stop honoring tickets already purchased by Jews. Such things have happened, and they will happen again."

"Yes, but certainly—"

"Certainly what, Madame?" The administrator folded her hands on the desk. "We are crowded with children who are no less deserving of rescue, children with no guardians, who have been here longer, waited longer." She gestured to the paperwork on her desk. "On the first transport, other relief agencies chose which children would go and which would not. Now that task has fallen to the OSE, to me." Her voice cracked. "For every child I save, I condemn five others. . ."

Madame Krakowskie's voice faded, smothered under the heaviness in Rósa's heart. She dropped her gaze, and the floor wavered through a film of tears. Gradually, the administrator's words reemerged from the buzzing in Rósa's head, their significance now moot.

". . .and you have performed well, Madame Dudek. We are grateful for your service. I cannot, however, give you preferential treatment. We'll do everything possible for the children, but they must wait—"

"Yes." Rósa's voice sounded distant in her own ears. Her hope and a single teardrop disintegrated together in a ragged dark splotch on the scarred hardwood floor. "Thank you."

She turned and closed the door quietly behind her.

# Chapter 19

Rósa watched from the doorway of La Chevrette as the last child clambered onto the truck bound for the train station at Magnac-Bourg. The children carried small bags with a scanty lunch of bread, cheese, and a small apple. Most of them carried nothing else.

She voiced their names silently as each child settled onto the truck bed: Philippe and the older boys who foraged the woods for berries and apples and begged her to make compote, or perhaps some pie; Marta and the girls who cried when they hugged Lilli-Anna and Kammbrie good-bye and left them little gifts—praise God the twins were still too young to understand parting; Georg, Trina, and the younger children who pestered her for leftover scraps between meals, and who hugged her—the boys properly shook hands, of course—before they skipped across the yard to the waiting vehicle.

But mostly she would miss Ania. The sweet young Pole's selection for the transport left Rósa at a loss at how she would manage the twins. She didn't fully realize the attachment she'd formed to the young girl until she climbed onto the truck bed and was lost from sight among the other children. Ania had promised not to shed a tear when saying good-bye to the twins. It was the only promise Rósa ever saw her break.

She wiped her moist cheek against her shoulder as she carried remnants from the packed lunches into the kitchen. Fatigue from too much work, bittersweet emotions at the departure of children she had come to love, and fear at the thought of what her future might hold weighted her steps. She set the scraps in the sink, turned and leaned against the basin, losing herself in a blank stare at the floor until Hana's voice startled her.

"Rósa?"

"Yes?"

"Madame Krakowskie wishes to see you."

"But I must begin meal preparations. The children's departure delayed me, and I am afraid the meal will not be—"

"She wishes to see you now."

An even look neutralized Hana's normally kind demeanor, giving Rósa pause. But before she could reply, Hana turned and walked out the door.

Rósa wiped her hands on a towel and untied her apron. She combed her fingers through her disheveled hair. What was all the fuss about? The twins hadn't gotten into mischief, had they? Smoothing the creases on her dress, she hurried to the third floor.

At the first knock, Madame Krakowskie bade her enter.

As she eased the door closed behind her, the directress rose from her chair and propped her fingertips on the desk. Hana stood in the back corner of the room. Rósa's eyes threw a nervous question at her friend then focused on Madame Krakowskie.

"You. . .wished to see me?"

"You are to gather your children and your belongings. Your services are no longer required."

Rósa's knees weakened. "What. . . I don't understand."

Madame Krakowskie stepped from behind the writing table. She paused then lifted two pieces of paper from the edge of her desk. "I was just informed that two of our girls scheduled to leave on the transport have failed their health examinations. I am giving their visas to Lilli-Anna and Kammbrie."

Rósa's eyes widened, and she shot another look at Hana, whose face now wore a smile. "I. . .I still do not—"

"Of course you understand, Madame Dudek. I cannot be clearer." Madame Krakowskie sniffed. "The American consulate in Marseille will supply—"

Rósa flew at the directress and flung her arms around the startled woman's neck. "How can I ever thank you? I never dreamed we would have this opportunity!"

The administrator stiffened. "Madame Dudek, please control yourself!"

But Rósa refused to loosen her hug. Instead, her shoulders began to tremble, and she clung even tighter. After a moment, a gentle brush of fingertips over her shoulder and a pat on her arms brought back her awareness. She choked back a sob, released the directress, and stepped back. Wiping the tears from her eyes, she looked into Madame Krakowskie's face, now softened with the first smile Rósa had seen her dare to put on.

Madame Krakowskie assumed the role of the administrator once again. "There were two visas released. One for each of the girls." She moved back to her chair.

Rósa paused. "But how. . . What does that mean for me?"

"It's true they are too young to travel alone. For that reason, and others, I selected Madame Fuchs to chaperone them."

Rósa's shoulders sagged.

Madame Krakowskie turned toward her subordinate, still quiet in the corner. "This may be her one chance to escape the camps. So I assigned her to go."

Hana cleared her throat. "Madame Krakowskie. . ."

The directress lifted a finger for silence. She returned her attention to Rósa. "However, Madame Fuchs has"—she lowered her voice—"chosen to surrender her place to you."

Rósa stared at Hana. "But—" Her throat tightened, and she gripped the edge of the desk.

"Do you accept," Madame Krakowskie dropped to a whisper, "her gift?"

Rósa dropped her gaze to the cluttered desktop. The children's visas lay atop the pile of paperwork, so near, within reach. She could accept them, but Hana's chance for freedom, her one true friend at Montintin? The words forming in her mind frightened her, but they needed to be said. She shook her head. "I don't see how I can—"

"How can I leave France, Rósa?" Hana interrupted softly. "Noach might still be alive." She tilted her head.

Hana faded through a blur of tears. Uncounted moments passed before Madame Krakowskie's voice broke through once again. "You must hurry. You have much to do before the truck returns."

Rósa tried to readdress Hana but hadn't the words. She lowered her head. "I don't know what to say. I—"

"Go now. Gather your children." Madame Krakowskie resumed her place behind the desk. She shuffled papers and did not look up as Rósa backed to the door then left.

⚒

Rósa scooped together their belongings and stuffed them into the worn duffle bag. Lilli-Anna sat on the floor and played with a rag doll one of the older girls had fashioned for her before departing. Kammbrie scribbled on a scrap of paper with a broken pencil for the first few minutes then curled up in the corner and fell asleep. When Rósa finished, she sat on the edge of the bed and stared out the window. What would life in America be like? Where would they live? How would she support the girls? Gustaw would know.

*Gustaw.*

The heaviness that oppressed her those months following her husband's death threatened resurgence, but she shook it away. Gustaw now belonged to another lifetime, yet he still haunted corners of her mind and heart. He would want to know.

*We go to America, Gustaw. Do you know this? Can you see—?*

"Mama?"

Rósa struggled against the lump in her throat and turned her head. Lilli-Anna held her doll out at arm's length. A knot forming the toy's right hand had unraveled, and the frayed end hung loose. Rósa reached for the doll and struggled to retie the knot, squinting through a sheen of moisture.

Lilli-Anna climbed onto the bed and peered up at her mama. She touched a wet streak on Rósa's cheek, a question clouding her eyes. Rósa smiled into the young girl's innocent face.

"Ah, Lilli. I pray you will be spared what I have endured. In America we will have such a good life. I promise." She held Lilli-Anna's hand against her cheek then kissed it before tucking the repaired doll back into the toddler's grasp.

Lilli-Anna climbed down to the floor and hugged the toy to her chest but kept her gaze on her mama.

Rósa returned her attention to the task at hand. After a final look around the room, she roused Kammbrie from her slumber, shrugged the duffle bag's strap onto her shoulder, and took Lilli-Anna by the hand.

One thing remained to be done before she departed for the train station.

# Chapter 20

"Why, Hana? Why did you do it?" Rósa settled beside her friend on the kitchen bench. "I told you. How can I leave without Noach?"

"But there would be opportunities for him to come to America, too. Would it not be better for you to await him somewhere safe?"

"The opportunities are not as plentiful as you think, Rósa."

"And I still don't understand Madame Krakowskie's decision. What of the other children who have been here longer, who have no one to look after them?"

"It is better not to question the decision." Hana winked. "Provisions are being made for the others. The Maquis will take some of them. Others—"

"The Maquis?"

"The Résistance. You've noticed we have no children here over fifteen years old? On their sixteenth birthday, they become adults under Vichy law and are subject to arrest. This is the reason we tend to favor the older children with visas. The Maquis come for them before they turn sixteen."

"What happens to those who go with the Maquis?"

"They go to sympathetic families and other hiding places here in France to wait out the war. Some cross the border into Switzerland and beyond." Hana's voice softened. "Some of the boys remain with the Maquis and fight."

Rósa's voice tightened. "What will you do, Hana?"

"I will accompany Madame Krakowskie to La Couret and serve there until I hear news of Noach. If—when he is found, I will go to him."

Rósa grasped her friend's hand. "But there's so much danger in that. What if they take you?"

"It doesn't matter, Rósa. Noach is my life." Hana smiled. "The world stops for my husband."

Rósa squeezed Hana's wrist, further words begging but evading her.

Hana attempted a more lighthearted tone. "You can travel as far as Portugal on the documentation Madame Krakowskie will give you before you leave."

"Where did she get travel documents for us on such short notice?"

Hana smiled. "Do you remember all that irksome paperwork we filled out when you arrived?"

"Yes."

"She sent it to the American consulate in Marseille. It has been working for you these past weeks, in case of such a contingency."

"But Madame Krakowskie seemed so resistant to my request that the twins and I be accepted on a transport. Why would—"

Hana lifted a finger and shook her head. "Why ask? Just be comforted that Madame Krakowskie is so thorough." Then she sobered. "You still lack a sponsorship affidavit for America, which is necessary for your entry visa. But perhaps HICEM can finalize that before you embark the ship for America."

"HICEM?"

"One of the organizations involved in the Kindertransport. They're based in Lisbon, but have a presence here in France, as well."

"But what if nothing comes through?"

Hana smiled and patted her hand. "Trust Hashem."

❧

Rósa stood in front of the Château and watched the truck lumber onto the estate grounds. The driver choked off the engine, and the vehicle shuddered and belched a final puff of black smoke.

"Lilli, Kammbrie, stay close to Mama." She lifted her duffle bag and thrust her arm through its strap. Gasping her hands, the girls toddled along beside her. The driver opened the passenger door and lifted the twins onto the bench seat. His dour expression told Rósa that he was less than pleased with another unscheduled trip to the train station.

She laid her duffle bag at the front of the truck bed then turned for one last look at the Château de Montintin and La Chevrette. At that moment Madame Krakowskie and Hana stepped through the Château's doorway. The directress crossed her arms and nodded. Hana stood a pace behind her superior's left shoulder, the familiar smile adorning her face. She lifted a hand in a half wave. Rósa began to return the wave then paused.

"Madame?" The driver held open the passenger door and extended his hand toward Rósa. *"Un moment, s'il vous plaît."* She began to turn back, but before she could move, the driver tapped her shoulder. He handed her a folded piece of paper with *Mme Fuchs* penciled on the front. Rósa accepted it and hurried back across the yard.

She slowed as she approached Madame Krakowskie. The directress motioned her forward; then, to Rósa's surprise, pulled her into an embrace.

"Bonne chance, mon *amie,*" she murmured.

Rósa hugged Madame Krakowskie a moment longer than protocol might dictate then stepped back.

When she shifted her gaze toward Hana, the tears flowed freely. The two women hugged as though they would never let go. When they broke their embrace, Rósa remembered the piece of paper. "Oh, the driver gave me this. It's for you."

Hana creased her brow and took the note. She unfolded it, read, and her hand went to her cheek. "They have found Noach! He is en route to a new camp at Drancy." She reached for Rósa's hand. "He is alive, Rósa!"

Rósa squeezed her dear friend's arm, but tears of fear now mingled with those of parting. She looked Hana in the eye. "What will you do?"

"I will help establish Le Couret, as I promised. Then I will go north to be with him."

"But Hana—"

Hana shook her head and touched a fingertip to Rósa's lips. "Go. The driver is waiting."

Rósa's shoulders trembled as the women kissed each other's cheeks. A final nod toward Madame Krakowskie, and she turned away. When she reached the truck, the driver helped her onto the front seat then slammed the door. She bent her head through the window and waved as the truck's engine coughed to life. The women of La Chevrette returned her wave then were lost from view through the trees.

# Chapter 21

The truck sputtered along back roads, protesting every kilometer to Magnac-Bourg, its bumping and swaying lulling Rósa into a stupor. Her gaze leveled onto the countryside through the half-lowered window, where wispy ribbons of mist floated over low-lying meadows and scurried into the gaps between fir-treed glens away from the warmth of the sun encroaching from the east. The sight reminded her of her own flight from the heat of war bearing down on them from the north. But she refused to press the analogy any further, knowing the mist fled in vain.

In the cab, the fresh scent of pine struggled for dominance over acrid fumes of spent diesel fuel leaking from the engine compartment. The twins coughed and squirmed in the middle of the ragged bench seat. She pulled them onto her lap and lowered the window farther.

When the truck wheezed into the train station, she perked at familiar faces from Montintin swarming the platform. A few harried adults were attempting to herd the fidgety youngsters into order. As she helped the twins onto the roadside, one of the women hurried toward her.

"Are you from Montintin?" she asked, panting.

"Yes."

"And you have two more children?"

Rósa nodded.

The woman pulled a pad of paper and a stubby pencil from her pocket and began to scribble then stopped. "Oh! I'm sorry. How rude of me. My name is Adele." She flashed a tight smile and extended her hand. Rósa shook it, wincing at the firmness of the woman's grip. "I'm the senior administrator for the American Friends Service Committee."

"You are not Jewish?"

Adele chuckled. "No. It's a political thing. The Vichy government would only acquiesce to the program if a non-Jewish organization administered it." She leaned closer and whispered with a wink, "Don't tell anyone, but the Unitarians are here, too."

Rósa managed a weak smile. *So much intrigue.*

Adele motioned toward the platform. "Please bring your children. We'll need to verify their papers. The train arrives in fifteen minutes. We must be ready to board quickly. They won't delay for us."

With that, Adele bustled back to the platform, on the way snagging a tittering runaway girl and hustling her back toward the station. Rósa helped the children from the truck and had just grabbed her duffle bag when a familiar high-pitched squeal pierced the tumult. Ania burst from the boisterous crowd of children and ran toward the truck. She scooped Lilli-Anna and Kammbrie into her arms and covered their faces with kisses. Smiling up at Rósa, she took the twins by the hand and led them to the platform.

Through no less than a miracle, the children assembled into orderly lines as the train pulled into the station. When the doors opened, they piled on board and scampered through the cars to claim space. Rósa commandeered a bench next to the window and settled Lilli-Anna and Kammbrie beside her. The twins stared at the frenzy, occasionally looking up wide-eyed at their mama, apparently unsure whether to be excited or afraid. Rósa smiled and patted them on their shoulders. The chaos quieted when the whistle sounded and the train chugged away from the depot.

Lacking direct service from Limoges to Marseille, it became necessary to change trains in Toulouse. The six-hour layover stretched what would have been a simple journey into a two-day ordeal. At Toulouse, Rósa and other chaperones struggled to contain the children's restlessness until the connecting train steamed into the station. As they had at Magnac-Bourg, the older children dominated the bench seats. The slower ones among them stretched out on the floor. Several of the smaller children climbed into empty overhead luggage racks and curled up for the overnight leg of the trip.

Lilli-Anna and Kammbrie nestled against Rósa's side and dozed off, lulled to sleep by the swaying of the old train. Rósa stared through her window into blackness, broken by the occasional light of a distant farmhouse or small village abutting the railway. She tried to recapture the events of the past three months since they left Salzburg, but too much had grown foggy, too many details lost. Always prominent in her mind, though, was Hana. Before nodding off, she lifted yet another silent prayer of safety for her friend.

They hissed to a stop at Marseille's Saint Charles station late in the afternoon. Two Quaker representatives met them at the platform and guided them to the Hôtel Du Levant not far from the harbor. Children from homes at Chabannes, Masgellier, Morelles, La Guette, and Chaumont had already arrived and claimed the best rooms, if any of the rooms could be considered good. Rósa soon discovered the title of Hôtel was generous to the point of deceit.

She eyed the derelict building's gloomy interior as they climbed the creaky staircase. By the time she reached the second-floor landing, the banister had deposited a filthy residue on her hand that no amount of wiping on her skirt could dislodge. Peeling wallpaper lined the thinly carpeted path to their room at the far end of the corridor. She grimaced and pushed down on the grimy door handle. They entered, and her shoulders sagged.

Threadbare covers lay askew across sagging mattresses perched crooked on two rusty iron bed frames. A scarred wooden nightstand supporting a small table lamp with a ripped cloth shade separated the small beds. Above the beds, early evening light filtered through the dingy glass of a cracked window, illuminating a stained gray carpet spotted with cigarette burns. All that was needed to complete the ensemble were bedbugs or lice. A slap of the hand on one of the stained mattresses revealed that the ensemble was indeed complete.

After a light meal, Rósa and Ania settled the twins in for the evening, making the best they could of the sleeping arrangements. Fresh air being a commodity lacking at the Hôtel Du Levant, Rósa opted for a stroll along the city streets before retiring.

Marseille's early evening teemed with activity, seemingly oblivious to the threatening conflict building to the north. People hailed friends from open-air cafés, and traffic bustled along the streets. A few children raced by, weaving in and out among the pedestrians. Rósa lowered her gaze to the sidewalk as a pair of Vichy gendarmes strolled past.

She had just turned the corner onto a side street when a slender hand forced itself into hers. Startled, she saw a girl no more than thirteen years old peering up at her. Rósa started to pull away, but the girl's grip tightened. A stiff smile plastered on the youngster's face accented the fear in her widened eyes.

"Please, madame, I beg you," she rasped under her breath. "Tell them I am your child!" The girl released Rósa's hand and wrapped her arms around the startled woman's arm, her wooden smile tightening.

Rósa looked up. Two gendarmes walked slowly toward them, their attention focused on the girl. Without a second thought, Rósa bent and faced the adolescent. She brushed a wisp of red hair from the child's eyes and waggled a finger in her face, feigning a scolding. Then she stood, gripped the child's hand, and guided her across the street away from the militiamen. She cast a surreptitious look over her shoulder before rounding the next corner. The gendarmes had halted on the far sidewalk, their eyes still locked on the girl.

When Rósa stepped around the corner of the next building, the waif leaned against her and released a deep breath. When she pulled her hand loose, Rósa grasped her shoulder. "Wait. Who are you? What is all this about?"

"Let go! They may still be following me." The girl tried to pull away, but Rósa tightened her grip.

"No, I saw them stop." She turned the girl to face her and bent eye to eye. "You're safe."

"I am *never* safe!"

Rósa loosened her hold. "What is your name, child?"

The girl lowered her head but kept a wary eye on Rósa. "Angelique."

"Where are your parents, Angelique?"

"They're prisoners at Gurs."

"But how did you get here?"

"That doesn't matter." She struggled again against Rósa's grasp.

"Where will you go?"

"To my brother, Raul. Please, let me—"

"Who takes care of you?"

"We take care of each other." Angelique finally pulled loose but stood her ground. "Raul and I know how to survive. We have for two years now."

"But—"

"Madame, I thank you very much for rescuing me from the gendarmes, but I have nothing to offer you in return. Please, I must go now."

"Why were they chasing you?"

"They take orphans from the streets and send us to camps." She lifted her chin. "I have been to the camps. I will never go back."

Angelique retreated a step as Rósa straightened. "There must be something, someplace—"

"There is nothing. Thank you, again, but I must go."

"Angelique, please come with—"

Her words fell to the empty pavement as Angelique turned and raced down the sidewalk. She started to follow, but the girl ducked into an alley at the end of the block.

Shaken, Rósa turned to retrace her steps. When she reached the street corner, she froze. The two gendarmes stood directly across the intersection. They stared at her then dropped their gazes to the now vacant place by her side. They gripped their batons and stepped off the curb.

Her heart leaped to her throat. She took a step back as a produce wagon swerved to avoid the policemen, blocking them from her view. Rósa fled back down the sidewalk. People backed away from her as though by instinct, women pressing their children against the storefronts and men diverting their paths across the street.

No cover offered itself in the scattering crowd, and Angelique's alleyway was too far for her to reach before the militiamen reappeared and spotted her. Swiftly, she ducked through a doorway and found herself in a crowded bakery café. Another hurried glance over her shoulder, and she wound her way through the patrons toward the back of the room, trying not to draw attention. She searched frantically for a rear door, but only three large mirrors in gilded frames and a couple of shaded lamps broke the surface of the back wall. A half-dozen small round tables sat beneath the mirrors, three of them occupied. The table in the far corner sat empty, littered with sections of a newspaper and a used coffee cup.

She slipped into a chair at the table, her back to the door, and yanked out her hairpins. Her curled tresses fell across her shoulders, and she shook her head to smooth out their crimps. Snatching up a segment of the newspaper, she hunched over the cup and struggled to control her breathing.

A flurry of movement in the mirror above her table caught her eye. She watched as the gendarmes paused outside the front window and conferred. The taller militiaman moved on, but the other man entered the bakery. She hunched lower as his stocky figure filled the doorway, silhouetted against the glare of the late afternoon.

An eternal moment later, Rósa forced another glance into the mirror. The gendarme's sweeping gaze halted at her table.

# Chapter 22

Rósa scanned the room again, but the only exit was a swinging door leading into the kitchen behind the counter. She slouched lower and lifted her gaze back to the mirror.

The gendarme had only taken one step toward her table when another figure filled the entryway. A hulk of a man barged into the room and shouldered past Rósa's pursuer, knocking him off balance. He strode over to Rósa's table, leaned down, and planted a full kiss on her cheek. He dropped onto a chair and smiled at her, while she recovered from the shock.

The stranger grasped Rósa's hand and muttered, "If you know what is good for you, you will smile back at me." His dark eyes flashed.

Rósa forced a tentative smile, her gaze flitting back toward the mirror. The gendarme had recovered his balance and was wending his way through the cluster of patrons toward her corner.

"Do you speak French?" the man whispered.

"Not well," she replied.

He winced. "*Mon Dieu*, your accent! Say nothing. I'll do the talking."

When the gendarme approached, the stranger rose to his feet and pivoted to face the officer. He crossed his arms over his barrel chest. "What do you want?"

The militiaman took a step backward. "This—this woman. I must question her."

"She is my wife. What do you want with her?"

When the gendarme peered past him, the stranger advanced a pace. The policeman retreated another step.

"We believe she sheltered a runaway urchin—"

"We?" Rósa's "husband" scanned the room. "Who is 'we'?"

"My comrade and I. . .we saw her outside. . .at least I think—"

"You *think*? When did the Vichy begin thinking?"

A chorus of snickers filled the air. The gendarme reddened. "Now see here—"

"See what? My wife has been inside all day. She works here and has just finished her shift. Is that not right, Claude?" The big man didn't remove his glare from the militiaman.

A short bald man wearing a flour-dusted apron spoke up from behind the counter. "Of course." He raised a fresh baguette and smiled at Rósa, who stared at him from the mirror. "Marie, do not forget your bread. You were to take this home with you."

Holding the officer in his gaze, the big man reached back and patted Rósa on the shoulder. "Marie, go get our bread. You remember Henri and Francesca are joining us for dinner this evening."

Rósa rose stiffly to her feet, her knees threatening to give way. She edged to the counter and blinked at Claude. He winked and handed her the baguette then jerked his head toward the door. She complied without hesitation.

Her rescuer's booming voice sharpened. "The next time you make advances on my wife, it will not go well for you."

"Advances?" the gendarme sputtered. "I assure you—"

"Oui, it is clear what you intended. You think you can walk in here and have any woman because you wear a uniform?"

"Of course not! I only—"

"Get out," the stranger snarled. "While you can still walk."

Rósa looked away as the gendarme fled past her, suffering bumps and jostles from customers on his way toward the door. When the door slammed behind him, a burst of laughter filled the bakery.

The big man grinned at Claude. "Merci, my friend. I will pay you for the baguette."

Claude shook his head. "Non, Sebastien. It was a small price for the entertainment."

Sebastien threw back his head and belted a chesty laugh. He received several slaps on the back as he moved toward the door. When he reached Rósa, he tipped his head and gestured for her to follow. Pausing outside, he scanned the street then turned and offered her his arm. She hesitated then accepted it. The feel of a man's arm beneath her hand—and one as muscular as his—sent a startling tingle through her.

"It was a fortunate doorway you chose, madame. There is no love for the Vichy within those walls."

Trembling, Rósa found her tongue. "I don't know what to say, how to thank you."

"There's no need. What you did for the girl earned you our gratitude."

She widened her eyes. "You saw her?"

He nodded. "I observed from across the street when she approached you. I saw what you did, how you foiled the gendarmes. The concern you showed before she ran off was touching." His voice assumed a half-teasing tone. "Your only mistake was in returning the same route from which you came. Surely you considered the possibility that the gendarmes might still be where you left them."

She shook her head. "No, I didn't even think about it. I'm afraid I'm not well practiced at intrigue."

He cocked his head. "Then what are you well practiced at, madame? Why are you in Marseille? Clearly you're not French."

"I am chaperoning a group of children from an OSE home near Limoges. We have just arrived in Marseille."

"Limoges, eh? Perhaps the Château de Montintin?"

"Yes. How did you know?"

"Then you are acquainted with Madame Krakowskie and Madame Fuchs."

"Why, yes. Do you know them?"

He smiled. "Very dear ladies. We watch out for them as closely as we can, but it becomes more difficult to the north."

" 'We'?"

He patted her arm, and this time his hand lingered. The gentle touch belied his raw power and palpable capability for violence, and the tingling resurged. It had been long since Rósa felt this secure.

"Where are you staying?" he asked.

"The Hôtel Du Levant."

He grimaced. "I'm sorry for you. May I escort you there, madame—?"

"Dudek—but I'm traveling as Rósa Szpilmann."

His eyes sparkled. "I see. Szpilmann, but really Dudek. And you are not practiced at intrigue, hmm?"

Her cheeks warmed. "It is. . .of necessity."

"I'm sure it is." He chuckled, and they walked for a few moments in silence.

Sebastien's musky scent accented his powerful masculinity, and Rósa grew heady at their closeness. Her hand shuddered under his, and she fidgeted with the baguette clutched beneath her left arm.

His tone softened. "You care for orphans. It is a command of *le Christ*. You, too, must be a dear lady."

"I have twin girls in the transport."

"I see. And your. . .husband?"

Rósa shook her head. "He didn't survive our escape from Poland."

His hand squeezed hers. "I'm sorry."

By the time they reached the hotel, the sun hung low over the roofs across the street. They halted in the shadows near the front door, and he released her arm.

"Madame Dudek, I salute your courage. I will pray a safe journey for you."

His piercing gaze deprived her heart of yet another beat, and she stammered, "Thank you again for. . .rescuing me. Your. . .prayers will be most appreciated."

He lifted her hand and brushed it with a gentle kiss. "Bonne chance, Madame Dudek-Szpilmann." The twinkle returned to his eye. "Give my love to your precious twins—whatever their names may be."

She nodded, the kiss having robbed her of her voice.

His smile lingered in the air long after he disappeared around the building at the end of the block. Lost in thought, Rósa nearly collided with Adele entering the hotel.

"Rósa! Where have you been?"

"I'm sorry. I was. . .detained for a while. Everything is fine now."

" 'Now'?"

"Yes. . ."

# Chapter 23

Ten days after their arrival in Marseille, the transport split into two. The first group of forty-five children would travel to Lisbon to rendezvous with the Portuguese-registered ship, the *Mouzinho*, which would take them to New York. The second group of fifty-five would follow in a couple of weeks to meet another Portuguese vessel, the *Serpa Pinto*. Rósa, Ania, and the twins would travel with the second group.

When the first group departed for the train station, those remaining scrambled to claim new rooms, some of them a marked improvement over earlier accommodations. Rósa, Ania, and the twins settled into a small suite at the front corner of the hotel, where double windows gave their second-story view a virtual panorama of the buildings and streets to the west. The furniture was newer, the bugs fewer, and the common toilet for this end of the hallway was next door—a blessing whenever the twins moaned their needs in the middle of the night.

Time slowed in restless anticipation of their departure. Then, a week after the first group departed, matters took a turn for the worse. A diphtheria epidemic broke out in the city, restricting the children to the hotel grounds. Not only could exposure endanger their lives, but also even a touch of the disease could disqualify them from continuing their journey to America. As the days crawled by, unspent juvenile energy led to pranks, fights, and other mischief. The chaperones spent most of their days mediating arguments and praying for deliverance as tension continued to mount.

Finally, their day of departure arrived. Rósa ushered the last of the children onto the old train, their restive attention now focused on vying for space in the cars and watching the bustling activity of the station through the dirty windows. She loitered on the platform, harboring a vague notion in the back of her mind.

Adele called to her from an open window. "Rósa, come aboard. It's time to depart."

Rósa nodded then glanced over her shoulder a final time before stepping through the coach's narrow doorway. Although she berated herself for being silly, she had often peeked through the windows of the hotel or scanned the streets while on errands in hope of spotting Sebastien. More than one double take at an oversized figure on this street corner or through that shop window fluttered her stomach. But she never saw the gentle giant of a man who had captured her wounded heart so quickly that first afternoon. The remembrance of his hand on hers transported her unsettled mind to the moment on the road to Montintin, when her hand rested in that of the Résistance fighter's. The warmth that touch brought to her cheeks had embarrassed her, too. What was wrong with her? She was no flighty schoolgirl who flitted from beau to beau with all the speed of a ricocheting bullet and only half the control. She chided herself for such an absurdity of emotion, weakly reaffirming to herself that her heart should belong to Gustaw's memory.

But the power of Sebastien's presence, the breathy softness in his lowered voice, the beguiling twinkle in his eye not only remained but also grew in intensity, as did his words. *"Dear ladies. . . We watch out for them. . . You, too, must be a dear lady."* Perhaps he still watched over her, unseen, as he had during her encounter with Angelique. Though never confirmed, the thought gave her comfort, and she clung to it.

Rósa settled onto the bench seat and tucked her duffle bag behind her feet. Lilli-Anna and Kammbrie played on the floor with Ania, leaving her to her thoughts. A hissing cloud of steam roiled up outside the car. When the train began to move, Rósa pressed her forehead against the window and stared through the smudgy glass. She perked at a movement at the head of the platform. A tall figure emerged through the dissipating vapor, an arm raised in apparent farewell. She rubbed at the glass with her sleeve, but the grimy film covered the outer surface. Latches welded shut with rust foiled her attempts to lower the window. She cupped her hands on the glass and squinted.

*Sebastien?*

A lump rose in her throat, and she fought the urge to jump up and run to the door. As the train pulled away from the platform and the figure receded into the dusky station, she pressed her palm to the window and waved back.

Just in case.

❦

The Quakers divided the children into groups of four, one chaperone overseeing each foursome. Rósa's charge included her twins, Ania, and a younger French girl, Marie-Élise. Four other groups of girls occupied their car, with the boys segregated in the next car. Their chaperones would travel as far as Lisbon then return to Marseille while Rósa continued the journey to America—if she could resolve the bothersome sponsorship issue.

"*Trust Hashem,*" Hana had said. Rósa sighed.

Early the next morning, Adele stepped through the doorway into their car and beckoned to the five adults. Rósa checked on the napping twins then slipped into the narrow aisle. Timing her movement with the swaying of the train, she skirted thin arms draped over the ends of benches and stepped over small feet blocking her path. When they gathered at the front of the car, Adele gathered them close.

"We will make a short detour before we reach Spain."

"A detour?" A chaperone asked.

"Several of the children have parents at the camp at Gurs. I received a telegraph in Toulouse that we have been given permission to make a brief stop there."

Rósa peered into Adele's face, the question begging.

"This will be the last chance for the children to see their loved ones before sailing to America. There they'll await the release of their parents—" A sharp cough erupted from the senior administrator's throat, and she pressed her hand to her chest. "Of course, we pray their reunions will be soon."

"Do the children know?" another chaperone asked.

"They are learning of it now. Would you please inform the children in this car?"

"Of course. When will we arrive at the camp?"

"Tomorrow morning."

After more instructions, Adele proceeded to the next car, coughing into her sleeve. The chaperones moved along the aisle to convey the message. The news met with varying responses, and it quickly became apparent which of the children had parents in Gurs. Rósa fielded more questions than she could answer and left behind more apologies than information.

Once back in her seat, she stared out the window. She had heard of such places as Gurs, but this would be the first internment camp she would witness.

❦

Rósa helped distribute paper bags containing breakfast morsels to the children as the train rolled past Oloron-Ste.-Marie and began to slow for the final fourteen kilometers to Gurs. The children fidgeted on their seats and spoke little, most of their faces pressed to the windows.

As the train decelerated, Adele entered and wended her way down the cluttered aisle toward Rósa's seat, collecting the other chaperones along the way.

"We'll halt on a siding beside the camp." She cleared her throat and took a deep breath. "Their parents will be escorted out of the compound by guards. The children will remain on the train. They'll have three minutes for their. . .visit."

Rósa stared at her. "Three minutes to see their parents? Why can't they leave the train?"

"The camp authorities fear the group will become unruly. And I fear it may become too difficult to retrieve the children if they go to their parents."

"But surely—"

"Madame Szpilmann, this is the children's one chance to escape their parents' fate. I cannot allow their emotions to jeopardize that chance. If the prisoners become agitated, if there's any hint of resistance, the guards may force them back into the camp, including the children—or worse, they may shoot. We cannot control what they do, and we'll have no avenue of appeal if they take the children."

The two chaperones stared at the floor and nodded. Rósa closed her eyes. After a moment, she also nodded. "I understand."

"Eight of the children in this carriage have parents in the camp. Four of the children themselves were rescued from Gurs. We'll lower the windows on this side of the car." She gestured to the left. "The openings are too small for any but the youngest to crawl through. You must ensure that does not happen." She paused. The Quaker escorts nodded again, but Rósa remained in thoughtful silence.

Adele touched her arm. "Can you do this?"

Rósa inhaled. "Yes."

Adele deflected another rattled cough with the back of her hand then looked back up. Her eyes glistened. "It was a difficult decision whether or not to request this visit, but I thought the children should have one last chance to see their families. For closure." She eyed all three chaperones in turn. Her voice quavered. "I hope I haven't made a mistake."

"I'm sure you haven't." Rósa attempted a reassuring smile and patted the administrator's hand. The other chaperones also affirmed their leader's decision.

When Adele left, Rósa gathered the twins onto the seat and gave them their breakfast bags. She stared out the window as the train crawled through the rolling countryside. *Three minutes? To say good-bye to your family?* She huddled the twins against her side. *How can this be? What kind of world—*

A child's shout broke her thoughts. She leaned forward to see a metal fence post with a floodlight mounted on top slip past the window. The sight that followed stole her breath. Endless rows of wooden shacks bogged down in a rutted field of mud filled the barbed-wire enclosure. Gray-tinged laundry waved in the morning breeze on lines strung between the hovels, appearing to pull the overcast sky even closer to the barren earth. As the train slowed, clusters of prisoners, most of them women, rose from beside makeshift cookstoves on which tin buckets roiled faint wisps of steam into the dank morning air. They slogged through the ankle-deep muck and grasped the barbed wire, staring at the young faces peering from the train windows.

As the train slowed to a crawl on the siding, more prisoners emerged from the buildings. All motion in the encampment seemed to come to a halt as the train lumbered past, gazes frozen onto its precious cargo. Rósa turned and peered through the windows on the other side of the car to an identical scene stretching toward the east. Her throat tightened at the camp's immensity and squalor, and her heart ached at the tortured expressions on the dirt-streaked faces of the women, some of whom clung to the wire, some to each other, and yet others who thrust their arms through the fence in a futile attempt to touch the train car.

The children glued themselves to the windows, foreheads and palms pressed against the streaked glass. Rósa could no longer tell which were the eight who had families in the camp; all the children reacted as one.

The chaperones rose from their seats as the train braked. They nodded at Rósa then lowered the windows on the western side of the car. The rusty clasps dug into her fingers as the pane screeched downward along grimy tracks. She gagged and turned her head as a gust of sour air reeking of trash, smoke, excrement, and rancid vegetation billowed through the window.

As the train ground to a halt, a cluster of prisoners—some men, but mostly women—came into view near the main gate. They jostled each other and craned their necks toward the train. The crowd bulged against the cordon of guards, who held their weapons at ready. Rósa jerked back as the children rushed to her side of the car and climbed onto the seats. A few boys from the adjacent cabin burst through the door and plastered themselves to the window among the girls, apparently deprived of vantage points in their own car. Arms were thrust through open windows, and shouts of "Mama" and "Papa" filled the air.

The crowd of children forced Rósa into the center aisle, separating her from Lilli-Anna and Kammbrie, now trapped against the wall. She reached over the end of the bench seat. "Lilli! Kammbrie! Come to me!"

Kammbrie tucked her legs to her chest and stared at Rósa, but Lilli-Anna struggled to her feet, turned, and stared out the window.

"Lilli! Sit down!" Rósa yelled, but the tumult drowned out her words.

The group of prisoners surged toward the train, oblivious to the shouts of the guards. Soiled hands extending from ragged sleeves strained toward the open windows where smaller hands flailed the air in a vain effort for fingers to touch.

Lilli-Anna reached down and tapped Kammbrie on the shoulder. Kammbrie twisted on her seat and pushed herself up beside her sister. Again Rósa yelled to the girls, but again to no avail. The twins stood side by side on the seat, enrapt at the scene erupting around them.

Somewhere to Rósa's right, a child's breakfast bag appeared in one of the hands protruding from an open window. After a moment, the bag dropped into the forest of arms crowding the platform. As if on cue, dozens of paper bags carrying precious crusts of bread, slivers of cheese, and bits of sugar pushed through the windows and dropped into the hands of loved ones.

Lilli-Anna looked at her sister and then at their bags sitting on the bench. Kammbrie followed her gaze then reached down and grabbed the bags. Lilli-Anna yanked on the blouse of a girl at the window, and Kammbrie held their breakfast bags up. The girl wiped tears from her eyes with her sleeve, smiled, and took the bags. They, too, dropped through the window and disappeared into the crowd.

Rósa's throat constricted. Perhaps it was merely borne of a desire to be included in the excitement, perhaps they were only mimicking the others; she didn't care. The girls had given away their food without a second thought. She believed in her heart they knew exactly what they were doing.

The blast of the steam whistle shattered the moment, and the train shuddered. They inched forward, young arms still dangling from windows, older hands still slapping the outside of the car. When the crowd began to move with the train, the ring of guards closed in. Two warning shots into the air prompted as many screams, and the hands fell from sight.

The children remained at the windows long after the train passed the last wire-bound fence post. Then, one by one, they quietly slipped from the benches and returned to their seats.

A round-faced boy with a broad smile dimpling his tear-stained cheeks settled onto the bench across from Rósa and the girls. "Today is my birthday, and I got the best present in the world," he sniffled. "I got to see my mother."

# Chapter 24

The Pyrenees resembled a row of broken teeth, nature's empathic reminder of the bloody civil war that had engulfed the land to the south a few short years earlier and a harbinger of an even more devastating upheaval now building to the north. Rósa squinted into the depths of the mountain range's cuts and rifts, their portentous shadows deepening with each passing mile. Disappearing into one of those forest-green vales, as they surely would, released a conflicting mixture of emotions: trepidation that they might be dashed against the solid granite barrier, but comfort in the notion that neutral Spain lay beyond. Once through, the formidable barricade would lie between Nazi Germany and her family.

She held her breath when the train plunged into the first mountain pass then released it as a curious serenity descended around them. Rushing brooks swirled around massive boulders, surged through narrow ravines, and cascaded over steep waterfalls in startling contrast to the muddy squalor they'd left behind at Gurs. She shielded her eyes against bright sunlight reflecting from lofty snow-frosted crags, their pristine splendor belying the horror of nations warring on its continent.

The children also seemed to notice the change. Voices quieted, hands and faces pressed to the glass, gazes locked onto the surrounding majesty. Ania gasped and pointed toward a low meadow where a small herd of deer grazed beside a crystal-clear pond. The patriarch stag lifted his head but soon resumed feeding, seemingly indifferent to the train's clattering intrusion.

The train entered a tunnel, and heads jerked back in the sudden near-darkness, nervous giggling filling the air. Moments later, startled eyes blinked through streams of sunlight again pouring through the windows as they emerged into another unspoiled pine glen. Lilli-Anna and Kammbrie appeared no less enthralled with the panorama, glancing up with wonder in their eyes as Ania hugged their shoulders and whispered in their ears.

They climbed to meet the clouds, clinging to narrow ledges cut into the mountainsides. Several of the children shrank back from the window when the train took a particularly sharp switchback, leaving nothing in view but a spiked carpet of firs a thousand feet below. At another dizzying turn, animated voices exclaimed and fingers pointed toward a downy cumulous layer spreading over the valley floor. Rósa had never seen a cloud from above, and judging by their reactions, neither had the children.

Finally, they began their descent to the variegated plains of northern Spain. At the border, the train halted. Rósa looked up as Adele swooped through the car, an uncharacteristic scowl darkening her face.

"Gather your children quickly. We must debark and walk to Canfranc."

Rósa scrambled to her feet and hoisted her duffle bag to her shoulder. Ania and Marie-Élise each picked up a twin and followed Rósa to the door. Outside, they found Adele toe-to-toe with the stationmaster, her face beet red. A terse discourse enflamed the air between them, but Rósa couldn't catch their words. Finally, Adele waved the man off and spun on her heel. She stalked over to the group of children fidgeting on the platform.

"This is nonsense!" she fumed.

Rósa adjusted her duffle bag. "What's wrong?"

"Bah! The imbeciles! French trains are built for a different gauge than Spanish tracks, so we must walk to Canfranc to board a Spanish national train."

"How far is Canfranc?"

"Over four kilometers."

"But why did we stop so far from there?"

"Because anti-Semitism knows no borders," she snorted. "This is harassment, nothing less!"

Adele called for the chaperones to organize their groups. When the hubbub quieted, she squared her shoulders and gestured everyone to follow.

The stationmaster leaned against the depot door, his hands in his pockets. The senior escort's eyes shot daggers at him as they passed. He spat onto the platform then turned and entered the building, slamming the door behind him.

The group straggled over the rough terrain, the older children helping the younger ones, until two hours later they stumbled into Canfranc, exhausted and nearly dehydrated. Their reception at the custom house proved little better than their send-off at the train station.

Although the connecting train already sat at the siding, the senior official refused to permit them on board until he checked all documentation. Adele pleaded with the administrator to allow the children to rest out of the heat. He shrugged and pointed toward the partially covered platform next to the tracks then turned and ambled into the station with their documents. The chaperones herded the children onto the platform and tucked them away from the sun as best they could. Rósa waited with the twins for their brief turn at a dribbling rusty water spigot on the side of the building.

A restless hour later, the official gave grudging permission for them to board. Another forty-five minutes passed in the stagnant heat of the passenger cars before the whistle sounded their departure.

The decrepit Spanish train made the French relic that carried them from Marseille look as though it had just rolled off the production line. Straight-backed wooden benches replaced curved smooth seats. Binding wire, not hinges, held the broken door to Rósa's car closed. Sooty hot air gusted through breaches along windows hanging crooked in their frames. The stuffy carriage lurched and swayed, purging the sour contents of several young stomachs onto the floor. Kammbrie's scant meal joined Marie-Élise's on the back of the seat in front of them. Lilli-Anna's face tinged green, but she avoided following her sister's lead. The pervasive dust awakened a nagging cough deep in Rósa's chest and launched spasms into her strained lungs. She covered her mouth and nose with a thin cloth, longing again for the crisp, clean air of the mountains.

Thankfully, their schedule included another train change at Zaragoza. They hurriedly abandoned the limping wreck as soon as it wheezed to a halt, both train and passengers worse for the experience. After rinsing themselves as well as they could at the station, they piled onto the connecting train. To Rósa's relief, the conditions aboard this carriage were considerably better than that of its predecessor.

The transport lumbered on, and Rósa's ease increased with every mile added to those separating her and the girls from Germany. Her greatest relief—and surprise—though, came when they arrived in Madrid at midmorning the following day.

⚜

Rósa peered through the bus window on the way from the train station to a stopover at a local monastery. Either Madrid had forgotten there was a European war under way, or it simply chose to ignore the fact. Modern buildings lined the central boulevard; the pace of life was calm, the traffic unhurried. Women strolled by or lounged on park benches wearing brightly colored dresses and ornate jewelry, stunning vestiges of a more genteel age.

When the priest and several nuns met them, the sisters fussed over the children while he conferred with Adele in Spanish. Rósa had no inkling what they were saying, but their gracious smiles reassured her all was well.

After a plentiful meal, the children were permitted a stroll into the city. Energy and emotions pent up over days of traveling overflowed, and it was all the chaperones and the sisters could do to contain them. The cooler evening air invigorated Rósa, and she stretched muscles cramped from endless hours aboard crowded trains. People they passed smiled kindly at the children, a stark contrast to their official reception at the border. For the first time, she began to relax. *Will it be this nice in America? Nicer, perhaps.*

That evening, the buses returned them to the train station. Rósa settled her small group aboard and gazed longingly out the window at the serene city. She fought a momentary urge to remain behind and build a life for them in Madrid, but the notion died at the blast of the train whistle. She watched the engorged red ball of a sun alight on the tops of the trees between two buildings, having already laced a crimson hem onto a feathery layer of clouds high overhead. She sighed. Could anything be more peaceful, more serene? It seemed impossible.

Sated from the first full meal since Marseille, the children's heads lulled, and a chorus of snores soon floated above the sound of the engine and the tracks. Lilli-Anna and Kammbrie nestled against Rósa, and she pulled them tightly to her sides. She gazed dreamily at the awakening city lights and stroked the twins' shoulders until they fell asleep. Her mind wandered, and, with some surprise, only vague memories of Salzburg returned, although she'd left Austria but a few short months earlier.

More bittersweet was her last recollection of Gustaw. He would forever be in her heart, but the lingering image of his death had grown fuzzy, less painful, which birthed in her a pang of guilt-tinged comfort. Was she healing from the trauma or hiding from it, adapting or avoiding?

Then, unbidden, Sebastien's strong smile and twinkling eyes emerged from the back of her mind, obscuring Gustaw's visage. The mental image brought with it a fresh surge of guilt. Should she have such visceral feelings for a man so soon after the death of her husband? What was the proper amount of time to mourn? She shook both of the men's images away, but not easily. Life had become too complicated, feelings too mixed.

Rósa leaned her head back and closed her eyes. Yes, things would be better—simpler, even—in America.

# Chapter 25

The following afternoon, they quit the train and boarded buses at the Portuguese border. Lush farmland, verdant forests, and orderly white and blue houses scattered along their route defined another country that had declared its neutrality in the festering European conflict. Could the buffer zone Spain offered shield its neighbor from a war consuming more and more of the continent? Rósa prayed it would, at least until she and the children were safely away.

Lisbon's lights beckoned the next evening as their buses trundled toward the bridge spanning the mouth of the harbor. The children craned their necks to glimpse the Atlantic, another new experience for most of them. But the sun had dipped beneath the horizon, leaving only the suggestion of an ocean in the sparse scattering of lights from channel buoys and ships creeping along the coastline.

A chaperone lowered her window on the seaward side of the bus to admit the evening breeze. The scent of the coastline poured into the vehicle, tickling young noses with its unique aroma. Rósa closed her eyes and inhaled the rich sea air, its strong scent leaving a briny taste on her tongue.

Lilli-Anna stirred and sniffed the air then lifted a questioning gaze toward her mama. When Rósa pulled the toddler onto her lap, the movement awoke Kammbrie. Rósa encircled her with her free arm, and the three of them gazed out the window.

When the buses rolled off the northern end of the bridge and into the heart of the city, Rósa caressed the children's shoulders as they took in the metropolitan vista. After several minutes of navigating the urban maze, they left a downtown in transition between the day's commerce and the evening's leisure. Rósa's arms tightened around the twins as the bus clattered across a double set of railroad tracks and turned down a dark street. The invisible ocean's salty ambiance strengthened, joined now by the gentle rumble of waves caressing the shoreline. Kammbrie looked up at her mama and wrinkled her nose. Lilli-Anna giggled.

They pulled to the curb in front of a long two-story building, its dark facade broken by dim lights shining through a few windows. A street lamp sprouting from the paving stones across the sidewalk cast the recessed doorway in shadow like a gaping yawn, as though in sympathy with the drowsy newcomers. The driver stilled the bus's motor, leaving them in startling quietness. Hours of engine and road noise echoing in Rósa's ears slowly subsided to the gentle pulsing of the nearby surf.

A curtain fluttered in a front window, then the door opened, outlining a slim figure whose shadow cleaved a splay of yellow light across the sidewalk. At Adele's prompting, Rósa gathered the girls and her duffle bag then helped the other chaperones rouse the children from their seats. The youngsters stumbled from the bus and stretched their arms and legs.

Adele approached the building, and the figure of a trim woman stepped into the streetlight's glow. The women embraced and spoke quietly while the chaperones arranged their charges into order. When the group quieted, Adele turned and faced them.

"This is Mrs. Stein. She is with the Jewish Joint Distribution Committee, or the Joint, who will administer the remainder of—"

She doubled over in a sudden coughing fit and staggered forward. Mrs. Stein grasped her colleague's arm and whispered into her ear. The Quaker leader nodded and straightened but did not release Mrs. Stein's hand.

"Please forgive me." She regained her balance and cleared her throat. "The Joint will administer the transport from this point forward. Our chaperones will return to Marseille tomorrow morning. Please extend to Mrs. Stein and her staff the same courtesy and attention you have given us." She surveyed the mass of children crowding the sidewalk, and her voice quavered. "We will miss you, dear ones. May your reunion with your families be soon. Bonne chance."

Mrs. Stein peered into the face of her friend and whispered. Adele nodded, released her hand, and stepped back. Mrs. Stein addressed the group in precise French. "You are privileged to be staying at a lovely children's resort, the *Colónia Infantil*, compliments of the Lisbon newspaper, *El Seculo*. Staff members will show you where you will sleep. Please maintain order. Chaperones, stay with your groups. You will retire with them this evening." She paused while some of the escorts relayed her words to those children still struggling with French.

Rósa huddled the twins to her side as the cluster of fatigued children shifted then edged toward the door, prodded by the adults. Rósa followed and touched Adele's arm as she passed. Adele attempted a smile through another cough.

Their second-floor room was small but warm and dry. Clean linens covered the cots, and the children dropped onto them, taking in the strange fragrance of freshly laundered bed-clothes. As Rósa nestled her duffle bag under the bed, a staff member tapped on the door and informed her that a light meal awaited them in the dining room. She and the four children joined the others coursing down the hallway toward the stairwell.

The "light" meal overwhelmed her, and apparently the children, as well. Trays of fried fish and green beans cooked in oil flowed from the kitchen in the arms of smiling servers. Platters of bread rolls stretched the length of the long dining table, accompanied by small plates of butter. No sooner had they taken their seats than several of the children sitting near Rósa began stuffing bread into their pockets.

She laid her hand on the arm of a boy sitting next to her. "There's no need to take bread with you."

He shook his head. "They might take it away."

"Surely they won't. It's meant for you."

"It always happens. There is bread, and then there is not. My stomach has ached too many times to be sure there will be food tomorrow."

Rósa's eyes misted, but she mustered a comforting smile. "You don't need to worry about that anymore."

The boy nodded, but the roll remained in his pocket.

After dinner, the children settled in their rooms for the night. Rósa pushed her bed against the twin's cot and slipped under the coverlet. Sighing, she rested her head on the soft pillow and smiled at the contented breathing filling the room. A rare surge of hope blossomed in her sleepy mind; America seemed closer than ever. She swallowed past an itch in her throat then drifted into slumber.

⋘✑⋙

A brilliant sunrise welcomed them the following morning, its yellow-white beams streaming through gaps in the heavy drapes and warming the room. The Quaker chaperones remained behind to prepare their departure while the children yawned and stretched their way to break-fast under the watchful eyes of their new hosts.

After a full meal of eggs, bread, and fruit, each child received a piece of candy. They stared at the bulging bags from which the staff had distributed the luscious sweets but were told they could have only one for now; there would be more later.

"We made that mistake with the first group," shared a staff member named Leah, who'd taken the seat beside Rósa.

"What mistake?"

"We were so excited to see the children, we distributed candy freely in welcome. It had been so long since they'd had sweets, it made them sick. It nearly ruined their stay with us."

Rósa nodded and glanced down at Kammbrie, whose cheek bulged with a lump of taffy. An intent expression locked her face as she labored at chewing the gooey mass. Lilli-Anna's confectionary morsel was already history, leaving behind only a smile as evidence of their brief encounter.

"We have other surprises, though," Leah whispered. "Watch."

Rósa looked up as Mrs. Stein called the room to quiet. "How would you like to visit the ocean today?"

Several heads bobbed up and down, and a few others shared fleeting looks, apparently unsure what to think. Rósa smiled as the refreshing fragrance of the surf reclaimed her memory.

Mrs. Stein continued. "This morning, we'll take you to a public beach. You'll be free to play, and many of you will have your first view of the ocean. I'm sure you'll enjoy it. First, though, there is another surprise for you in your rooms. You're dismissed." She called out above the sudden scraping of benches and juvenile babbling, "Chaperones, please have your children ready to leave for the beach in one hour."

The children crowded out of the dining room and raced upstairs, where they discovered piles of new and used clothing donated by sympathetic members of the Lisbon community. When Rósa and the twins arrived at their room, Ania and Marie-Élise had already shed their tattered frocks and were pulling on clean dresses. Rósa dodged when Marie-Élise kicked off her cracked wooden-soled shoes and slipped her calloused feet into a new pair of sandals. She lifted her arms and spun in circles, her eyes closed and a wide smile stretching her lips. Ania giggled when the younger girl twirled into the side of her bed and collapsed onto the mattress.

Ania's shoes, little more than thin leather pads strapped to her ankles, soon joined Marie-Élise's clogs under the bed, and she, too, spun about the room.

Rósa helped the twins slip into new dresses, adjusting buttons and ties. When she turned, her eyes watered at the sight of a new garment lying on her bed. Lifting it to her neck, she hugged it to her body, appraising the fit. When was the last time she owned a new dress? The answer lay far beyond memory.

An hour later, the children assembled on the sidewalk and set off for the beach. Almost without exception, passersby nodded and smiled, especially at the youngest members of the group who lagged behind with their mama. At the end of the street, Rósa and the twins caught up with the now stationary group of children. They skirted the crowd and halted. The Joint chaperones stood off to one side.

Rósa and the girls stared with the rest of the children. A 50-meter-wide strand of rippled beige sand spread before them, dotted up and down the coastline with a few small umbrellas. A scattering of native children were already splashing in the gentle waves and piling up mounds of wet sand. She surveyed the immense expanse of the Atlantic Ocean that stretched to a razor-thin horizon against a cloudless azure sky. The midmorning sun sparkled on crests of rolling waves like crystalline chips scattered across the water. She closed her eyes and drew a deep breath of sea air.

Rósa looked over the group of children then creased her brow. No one moved toward the beach. Instead, they huddled closer together, whispering among themselves. Rósa turned a questioning eye toward Leah, who stood nearby.

The escort stepped to her side. "We saw this also with the previous transports. Two problems face the children. They have scratched for survival for so long, their ability to throw off inhibition and enjoy themselves has eroded to nearly nothing. They have simply forgotten how to play."

Rósa nodded then shook her head.

"The second problem is evident in their eyes."

Rósa scanned the children. Nervous glances darted up and down the beach, a few cast over hunched shoulders toward the treed streets behind them.

Leah continued. "There's no place to hide."

"Hide? What do you mean?"

"Do you see the young boy there with red hair?"

Rósa followed the woman's gaze to a boy of about fourteen years hunched in the second tier of children. A girl huddled next to him, gripping his arm.

"Antoni and his sister, Brygitka, walked from Gdansk to Paris. Just the two of them."

Rósa's eyes widened. "How could they survive such a journey?"

"By keeping to forests and back roads, traveling by night, hiding from unfamiliar sights and sounds. Do you see any place to hide here?"

Rósa shook her head.

"The openness we see as beauty, they view as a threat."

A tug on Rósa's hand drew her attention. She looked into Lilli-Anna's wide eyes. "What is it, Lilli?"

The young girl pointed toward the beach.

Rósa smiled and nodded. Lilli-Anna grasped Kammbrie's hand and they tottered onto the beach, their tiny feet slipping on the shifting sand. They giggled, plopped down, and began sifting the fine grains between their fingers.

Lilli-Anna looked back over her shoulder with a wide smile. She pushed to her feet and stumbled back to the group, where she grabbed Ania's hand and pulled. The teenager stepped gingerly behind her.

"And a child shall lead them," Leah whispered with a smile.

Ania knelt beside the twins. Kammbrie scooped up a fistful of warm sand and poured it into the young Pole's outstretched hand. Ania laughed and turned her head back toward the other children.

Her laughter seemed to break the surface tension holding the group together. A few of the younger children tiptoed onto the beach. One brave lad trotted toward the water; then a few more children broke ranks and ventured out of the crowd.

Minutes later, all but Antoni and Brygitka were exploring the sandy expanse and testing the water. The brother and sister stood alone, arm in arm, lost in a blank stare. Rósa stepped over to them and laid her hand on Brygitka's shoulder. The young girl jumped at the touch.

Rósa nodded toward the water. "Tak, *to dobrze*." Her gentle smile reinforced her assertion that everything was okay, and the stiffness in the girl's arm eased. Rósa took Brygitka's hand and led her and her brother onto the beach.

The transport children shuffled over the warm sand and stooped to probe the foamy wavelets caressing the fringe of the beach. Rósa smiled at the carefree Portuguese children laughing and splashing in the gentle surf. But her throat tightened at the grim expressions on many of the refugee children's faces, most of whom remained in groups of two and three. How long before they would act. . .normal again?

# *Chapter 26*

"You wish to see me?"

Rósa stood outside Mrs. Stein's doorway, wringing her hands. The summons had come shortly after she'd returned from the beach. No explanation had accompanied it.

The Joint administrator bade her enter, the expression on her face doing little to relieve Rósa's anxiety.

Rósa closed the door and eased herself onto a chair in front of a small desk. Mrs. Stein fingered a document atop a stack of papers then lifted her eyes. "It appears your papers are not complete. Are you not aware that the American government requires you to be sponsored, so as not to add a burden to the economy?"

"Yes, Madame Krakowski told me this. She said the matter would be resolved, and that I should continue on with the children."

"And did she say how the matter would be resolved?"

"No, she didn't."

Mrs. Stein frowned. "Madame Krakowskie isn't known for shoddy paperwork, but in this case she has left me at a loss as to what to do."

Rósa's pulse quickened. "Perhaps I can travel on the twins' affidavit? After all, they are. . . my children. I'll certainly be staying with them, won't I?"

"I'm afraid that's not possible. The children's sponsorship affidavits are unique, nontransferrable. They usually come from foundations or other well-wishers in America who know they will never actually support the children but sign paperwork to satisfy the official process—generous on the part of the guarantors but nonetheless a formality. When the children arrive in New York, Jewish organizations will distribute them across the country to foster homes."

"How do they decide where to place them?"

"It's our policy, and our genuine desire, to keep siblings together, but that's not always possible. We investigate the foster homes to try to ensure they will be welcoming and will not exploit the children for labor, but, honestly, we've not always succeeded in that."

"Labor? Surely no one would expect children as young as Lilli-Anna and Kammbrie to work."

"We would expect not; indeed the sponsorship paperwork stipulates foster parents won't allow a child to work until he or she is of age. But the rules are not always followed." Mrs. Stein paused. "The twins' ages are the biggest problem. They will consume a great deal of time and resources until they grow older and can mind themselves, let alone contribute to the household. That's a lot to ask of a family not even related to the children."

"But I will be there to help."

"Mrs. Dudek, you don't understand. The children are on a group affidavit through the USCOM. The affidavit cannot be used for anyone over fifteen years old."

Rósa's cheeks warmed at the mention of her true name. "But they're my children. How can I possibly leave them?"

Mrs. Stein retrieved a piece of paper from the side of her desk. She held a handwritten note up to Rósa's view. "This is from Madame Krakowskie. It explains your relationship to the girls."

Rósa's mind scrambled in search of a defense. "But isn't a guardian as valuable as a blood relative in a case such as this?"

"I fear it is not. As the name implies, the Kindertransport applies to orphans and children displaced from their parents by the Nazis, not to families. With the arrest of Izaak and Maria Szpilmann, the twins qualify. You, however, are an anomaly. While we are very grateful for your dedication to the children and for your service at the OSE home, there are no provisions to accommodate you without an individual affidavit."

"But surely there will still be need of chaperones aboard ship."

"The *Serpa Pinto* arrives in port tomorrow with a full complement of volunteer escorts for the voyage to America."

Her fear now bordered panic. "How can you separate me from the twins now that we've been through so much? I lost my husband escaping with the children. Now you would take them from me when they're all I have left?"

Mrs. Stein sighed. "It is not I who take them from you. It is procedure—"

"Procedure?" Rósa cried. "These are children, not projects!"

The Joint administrator bolted up from her chair, her face hard. "Mrs. Dudek! I am very well aware that these are children! You have no idea what we have gone through, how difficult. . ." She closed her eyes and held her breath. After a moment, she slowly exhaled.

Rósa dropped her gaze to her lap, chastised, but mostly fearful her outburst may have cost her any hope of clemency.

Mrs. Stein continued stiffly. "It's not only about sponsorship affidavits. It was very difficult to persuade the US State Department to issue the special dispensation of two hundred visas under which these children travel. In fact, it took the direct intervention of the American First Lady, Mrs. Eleanor Roosevelt—also the honorary chairperson of the USCOM—to release them. The visas are very fragile. There's a time limit on them, and they could be revoked at any moment for any reason. The American government has attached specific rules, and we dare not violate these rules or we could lose everything—including your twins' visas. So, yes, there are procedures. And these children—including your twins, Mrs. Dudek—will be saved or condemned by them."

Rósa winced. "Please forgive me. I know you're doing everything you can. It's just that. . . I don't know what I would do without them." She lifted her head and met the administrator's gaze. "They're my very life."

Mrs. Stein settled back onto her chair. "I understand, Mrs. Dudek. Please believe that I do understand."

"So," Rósa struggled to control her voice, "is there anything that can be done?"

"I have no authority in this matter. I will consult with the group arriving on the *Serpa Pinto*, but please understand, even if they agree to take you aboard, you will still have to satisfy the authorities in New York. It's possible they could turn you away at the port of entry and force you to return to Europe." Mrs. Stein's eyes softened. "There is only so much we can do, and we must be careful. There are many in America who are not sympathetic to the children's plight. Unfortunately, several of them serve in Congress."

"I understand."

"Thank you."

Rósa rose unsteadily to her feet. A spasm gripped her chest, and she leaned on the back of her chair.

Mrs. Stein straightened. "Are you all right?"

Rósa nodded then turned toward the door. In the hallway, she hacked a wet cough then plodded upstairs.

# Chapter 27

Mrs. Stein convened the staff after breakfast the following day.

"The *Serpa Pinto* arrived at dawn. The crew and chaperones are preparing to receive the children."

"When will it depart?" Rósa asked, wringing her hands.

"The day after tomorrow."

Rósa exchanged a look with Mrs. Stein, who then turned her attention to another staff member's question.

While the day seemed to fly by for the children, it crawled for Rósa. Surely, they wouldn't take the twins without her for want of a silly piece of paper. *They wouldn't dare.* The weak self-assurance did nothing to loosen the knot in her stomach.

Lilli-Anna paused playing with her rag doll after lunch and peered up at Rósa, who sat on the edge of her cot lost in a blank stare. The toddler climbed onto her mama's lap, touched her face, then cuddled against her chest as Rósa hugged her tight. Kammbrie followed her sister onto the bed, and Rósa wrapped an arm around her shoulders and squeezed her close.

*I will not leave my children. No matter what.*

❧

The midday meal completed, Mrs. Stein accompanied the group on another excursion to the beach. Most of the children displayed less anxiety, some even whispering excitedly among themselves when they spotted the sparkling blue water. When they reached the access road, several of the refugees rushed onto the beach. The administrator blew a short blast on a whistle and motioned them back. The children clustered around her, and she pointed to a gray and white ship moored down the coastline. Visible even from this distance was the word *Portugal* painted in huge black letters on the side of the vessel.

"That is the *Serpa Pinto*. It will take you to your new homes in America."

The children gawked. "It's not very big," a young voice piped up.

"But big enough to get you to New York," their patroness said. "The *Serpa Pinto* has already carried many children like you across the ocean. You will be quite safe."

Soon the younger children began to fidget. When a little girl tugged on the administrator's sleeve and tipped her head toward the beach, Mrs. Stein smiled and nodded. The girl slipped from the group and ran onto the sand. Her giggle released the floodgate of children, who laughed and kicked up sand in a race toward the water's edge. Only a few hung back, their faces still grim.

Rósa took two hesitant girls by the hand and led them toward the surf. The twins ambled behind her; then the last of the holdouts followed.

❧

The children's evening chores included gathering their belongings in preparation for boarding the *Serpa Pinto* the next day. Rósa spent much of her time fervently praying over her lack of American sponsorship, although she had no idea how such a prayer might be answered. From a murky corner of her mind, guilt at taking another family's children whispered doubt to her, declared that her journey would end here while the Szpilmann twins continued, that this would be a judgment from God. She silenced the niggling voice with the argument that Gustaw's sacrifice earned her the children, that God was doubly blessing her in recompense for unfairly denying her a child of her own. She deserved a family, the right of every woman, and nothing less.

Then why couldn't she sleep?

She tossed and turned the night away, her doubts wrestling with her excuses, the match refereed by the uncertainty of her future. Floating barely beneath the surface of consciousness, her shallow dreams looped through fragmented images of empty ships and overburdened office desks. The children's soft breathing whispered across the ghostly yardarms and rustled the phantom paperwork. Twice she awoke in painful fits of coughing, anxiety and fatigue exacerbating the thickness in her chest and head. After a third spate of hacking into her pillow, she surrendered any notion of rest and through half-closed eyes watched the inky night graduate through predawn gray to the subdued hue of an overcast morning sky.

The summons to Mrs. Stein's office came as Rósa ushered the children into the dining room for their last meal in Portugal.

"Please sit down."

Rósa fingered a small handkerchief on her lap as Mrs. Stein folded her hands on the desk.

"I consulted with the lead escort from the *Serpa Pinto* concerning your passage."

"Yes?"

"She has no authority to circumvent the sponsorship requirements."

Rósa's heart fell. "Then. . .there is nothing—"

Mrs. Stein lifted a finger. "However, when I returned to my office, this had arrived." She hefted a large brown envelope from the edge of the desk.

Rósa fought to control her trembling as she accepted the packet. Addressed simply to *Mme R. Dudek*, the initials *HICEM* adorned the upper left corner. The envelope bore neither postmark nor postage stamp. She eyed the hand-printed address with growing alarm. HICEM should know her as Rósa Szpilmann, not Dudek.

She lifted the flap and tipped two official documents and a typewritten letter into the palm of her hand. The first document was entitled Affidavit In Lieu of Passport from the American consulate in Marseille. Adorning the front page were an embossed official seal and a duplicate of the photo on the travel document she'd received from the Frenchman. Exit, transit, and entry visas stamped in red, blue, and purple ink decorated the front and back. The document bore the surname *Dudek*. Mrs. Stein's voice interrupted Rósa's inspection of the precious documents.

"Don't forget to sign it." The administrator smiled.

Her pulse racing, Rósa laid the immigration permit on her lap. The second document was—a copy of her sponsorship affidavit! Rósa closed her eyes and released a full breath for the first time since she entered the office. She clutched the papers to her chest and whispered a prayer of thanksgiving, as Hana's words rushed back to her. *"Trust Hashem."*

*How little trust I've shown through all my worry.*

She refocused on the Joint administrator. "But how could this be? What happened?"

"Perhaps that will explain." Mrs. Stein nodded toward the letter.

The paper shuddered in Rósa's hand as she read aloud.

*Mme Dudek,*

 *Enclosed you will find the documentation needed to complete your journey to America. A brief explanation, I believe, is in order.*

 *Shortly after your departure, Mme Krakowskie contacted my office to plead your case. At first, I assured her there was nothing I could do to bypass the sponsorship requirement. It was then she told me of your true relationship to the twins and how they came into your care. She also explained why you had adopted the name Szpilmann to escape Austria. She then produced the immigration paperwork you now hold in your hands. When I asked her where she obtained it, she only smiled. Experience has taught me not to pursue such lines of questioning, especially with Mme Krakowskie. The surname on your paperwork, as you see, is Dudek. The children's names will remain Szpilmann. There is a good reason for this.*

*The group affidavit from the USCOM cannot be used for children with parents, only those unaccompanied. Therefore, your identities must be separated. Your affidavit was a bit more complicated. Fortunately, a solution for you presented itself, also.*

*The Edwin Gould Foundation in America has entrusted me with a limited number of affidavits to use at my discretion. When I learned of your husband's sacrifice, as well as your continuing labors, it more than pleased me to exercise my authority on your behalf. I am only sorry I could not so honor your husband, too; may he rest peacefully.*

*I have dispatched this package via trusted courier. The mail is unsafe, and the information in it would endanger people. I ask you to destroy everything but your official documentation immediately, including this letter. I also suggest you destroy any duplicate documents carrying your name as Szpilmann, as they could cause unnecessary difficulties if viewed by the authorities. Please do not neglect this; it is most important.*

*I wish you a safe journey and a good life in America, and I remain*

*Your humble servant,*
*Vladimir Schah*
*Director, HICEM-France*

Rósa lowered the letter and leaned against the back of her chair. She tried to settle the pounding in her chest, but her mind churned out too many thoughts, too many emotions, for her heart to contain.

Mrs. Stein broke the silence. "Madame Krakowskie included a note with the package containing your envelope. Perhaps you would like to read it?"

"Please."

Mrs. Stein produced a small sheet of notepaper carrying the directress' bold handwriting.

*Dear Mrs. Stein,*

*Please ensure Mme Dudek receives the enclosed package. I write from my new post-ing at La Couret. It will be of interest to Mme Dudek that all goes well, but we miss her hard work and dedication.*

*It will interest both of you to know that Mme Fuchs accompanied me to La Couret and has done much to help establish the home. However, when I perceived her heart ached for her husband, I released her with my blessings. She has traveled north to be with him at Drancy. I received one note from her soon after she left, but nothing since.*

*I've also learned that Drancy is a transit camp. Prisoners are held there temporarily then sent to the labor camps—most often Auschwitz. I fear for Hana and Noach. Please join me in praying for them.*

*With sincerest thanks, I remain*

*Your friend,*
*Anna Krakowskie*

Rósa returned the note. "Thank you. I will indeed pray for Hana and Noach."

"As shall I." Mrs. Stein paused. "There is one more thing."

"Yes?"

The administrator handed her a smaller envelope. Opening it, she jolted at the sight of several US dollar bills in various denominations.

"There was more to the correspondence from Madame Krakowskie that will remain in my confidence, but one piece of information applies to you."

Rósa looked at the banknotes then up at Mrs. Stein, who lowered her voice. "Madame Krakowskie notified your benefactor when you left Montintin. The money arrived soon afterward."

The tall Frenchman's cryptic words that first morning in France rushed back to Rósa's mind. "Benefactor?"

"I know nothing more than that a black marketeer has apparently taken an interest in your welfare." She studied Rósa's face.

Rósa lifted her shoulders and shook her head.

Mrs. Stein continued. "In his. . .business dealings. . .he has formed ties with factions of the Maquis. Through them he has monitored your progress since you arrived in France. For obvious reasons, Madame Krakowskie did not divulge his name, but she did say that if I chose to explain anything to you, I should simply mention Wolsztyn."

*Stanislaw!* That explained the cropped family photograph on the French travel permit, but the black market? Stanislaw?

"By your reaction, I assume you understand this."

Rósa nodded. "Gustaw's brother. But I never thought for a moment. . ."

Mrs. Stein reached into an open desk drawer and handed Rósa a box of stick matches. "There's a metal bin in the alley behind this building. Be thorough; scatter the ashes—and try to be discreet."

# Chapter 28

*Shalom*, Rósa. May you have a safe voyage and a wonderful life in America." Mrs. Stein hugged her then stooped, eye level with the twins, and touched their cheeks with her fingertips. "Shalom, dear ones."

Lilli-Anna reached out to hug the administrator's neck, and Kammbrie shyly followed. Mrs. Stein smiled and returned their hugs.

She surveyed the group of refugees waiting to board the *Serpa Pinto*. Each child wore a cardboard identification tag suspended from his or her neck with a unique number stenciled on it. When Lilli-Anna and Kammbrie cheerfully donned theirs, the cards hung below their knees, nearly tripping them when they walked. Lilli-Anna tugged at the string and pouted up at her mama. Ania laughed then lifted their tags to chest level and knotted the string behind their necks.

Rósa gathered the twins to her side and smiled at Mrs. Stein. "Thank you. We'll pray for you—all of you." She paused. "When is the next transport?"

A cloud crossed Mrs. Stein's face. "This is the last one, at least for this year. The expanding war makes it more difficult to safely move the children, and immigration quotas still hinder our efforts. We seek other destinations in South America, Cuba, and Palestine, but not all countries are willing to accept refugee children. I fear many will remain in Europe to wait out the war."

"I will pray for their rescue."

Mrs. Stein dipped her head. "As shall I."

A bump shuddered beneath her feet, and Rósa turned to see a stevedore securing the ship's gangplank to the pier. He checked the walkway's stability then signaled to Mrs. Stein.

The administrator blew her whistle. "Quickly now! Chaperones, you know the order in which you are to embark with your children. Be ready to board at your turn." She turned toward Rósa. "You're first."

Rósa ushered the girls toward the inclined walkway. Ania followed a short distance behind with Rósa's duffle bag. The shore hand lifted the tots over the threshold then offered his hand to Rósa. She eyed the loose ropes and stanchions lining the narrow walkway then cast a nervous look at the man. He nodded, stepped ahead of her, and guided the twins up the center of the ramp, Rósa, Ania, and Marie-Élise following.

A gaunt, taut-faced woman with a clipboard met them on deck. She read the numbers on the twins' placards and checked them against the passenger manifest. After a cursory glance at Rósa's documentation, she handed her six cards. Rósa scanned the first document, which announced in German that her berthing assignment was in compartment C13, bed number 4. The twins received beds 2 and 3. The remaining three cards assigned them to table 21 in the forward dining room. She smiled, comforted by such precise organization. America seemed so close she could reach out and touch its promise. Her reverie evaporated when the escort tapped her clipboard with her pencil and pointed toward another woman waiting near a hatch in the ship's superstructure. Rósa and Ania herded the twins quickly across the deck.

The second escort frowned at the tots then glanced through the doorway. Rósa followed the woman's gaze. Inside the hatchway, a steep ladder with handrails along either side descended into the ship.

Rósa stared into the dark recess. "Down there?" she asked.

The woman nodded. Lilli-Anna smiled up at the chaperone while Kammbrie grasped a fold of Rósa's dress and huddled to her side.

Rósa turned to Ania. "I will go first with my bag. When I call to you, help Kammbrie down, then Lilli-Anna."

"Tak." Ania handed her the duffle bag and grasped the twins' hands.

Rósa managed an awkward descent, the duffle bag suspended from her arm bumping against each rung. Near the bottom of the companionway, an unseen hand relieved her of her bag and took hold of her elbow.

She stepped onto the lower deck and turned to find herself staring into the chest of an immense black sailor. He loomed over her, his bright white teeth reflecting the subdued light through a broad smile. Rósa tensed. She'd never seen a black man until arriving in Marseille, and then only from a distance when an errand took her near the waterfront. Suddenly finding herself alone and in such cramped quarters with one—especially one this size—seized her breath.

He appeared to notice her discomfort and stepped back with a bow, his smile undiminished. She collected herself then nodded her thanks. The sailor gestured for her to follow, but Rósa shook her head and pointed up the ladder. He placed her duffle bag against the bulkhead and waited while she climbed back up the companionway.

Near the top, Rósa called to Ania, who appeared through the doorway with Kammbrie. The young girl gripped Ania's hand and stared down the ladder.

Rósa extended her hand. "Ania, turn her around, and let her step down backwards. Kammbrie, Mama's here. Don't worry."

Ania tried to comply, but Kammbrie refused to release the girl's hand. Impatient clamoring from the other children lining up at the hatchway crowded the small space, and Rósa reached for the tot. "Kammbrie, let go of Ania. We need to hurry."

At no response, she climbed two more rungs and slipped her arm around Kammbrie's waist. The girl whimpered then wailed when Ania broke her grip on her hand and Rósa pulled her onto the steps. One arm wrapped around the squirming toddler, she descended slowly. At the bottom, the sailor eased Rósa onto the deck. When he spotted Kammbrie, his grin broadened. He squatted down as Rósa set the crying girl on the deck and patted her on the back. She turned around, and her sobs died in her throat.

With a deep laugh, the sailor lifted Kammbrie into his arms, rose, and hugged her to his chest. She stared wide-eyed into his ebony face, her breathing abated and her arms stiffened against his broad shoulders. His grin spread until Rósa thought his face would disappear into it.

Ania's voice floated down the companionway. *"Allo?"*

Rósa quickly mounted the ladder and returned with Lilli-Anna. When she set the twin down, the sailor adjusted Kammbrie into one trunklike arm, bent down, and scooped Lilli-Anna up into his other one. Lilli-Anna's eyes widened to match her sister's as she gaped at the seaman.

After a moment's pause, Lilli-Anna lifted her hand. Her creamy white fingers touched the tight jet-black curls of the seaman's sideburn then traced his cheek line down to his chin. Another deep laugh rocked the big man's chest. An uncertain smile appeared on Lilli-Anna's face. She touched his wide lips and peered at the pearly expanse of his grin. He gave her fingertips a playful kiss. Lilli-Anna's smile broadened, and she snaked her arm around his neck and laid her head on his muscled shoulder. Kammbrie's smile soon followed, and she nestled herself into his other shoulder. A glisten appeared in the sailor's eye as he gently squeezed the twins tighter.

At that moment, Ania stepped off the bottom step of the companionway and bumped into Rósa. Marie-Élise scrambled down the ladder behind her into the already crowded gangway, followed closely by two more children. The sailor gestured and stepped off briskly toward the stern, the twins hugged to his chest. Rósa retrieved her duffle bag and followed.

The sailor ducked agilely through bulkhead hatches and deftly avoided pipes and dim lights affixed to the ceiling. Accustomed to the open air, the cramped interior pressed in on Rósa, making it difficult to breathe. She stumbled forward when a sharp cough tightened her chest. Ania touched her back. Rósa turned, smiled weakly, and nodded at the girl's concerned expression.

After what seemed like hours of torturous hiking, they stepped into a large cargo hold. Bolted to the inside of the hull stood rows of narrow bunks stacked four high. Round portholes lined the walls, admitting streams of chalky light.

The sailor halted beside the bunks closest to the hatch. Rósa fumbled for their berthing cards, but he shook his head and nodded at the bunk rack. He eased the twins onto the two middle bunks, relieved Rósa of her duffle bag, and set it on the top mattress. Rósa eyed the distance from the girls' bunks to the deck. She pointed to the lower beds. The sailor lifted a finger to his lips, a slight smile on his face, then patted the three upper bunks. She eyed the bunk again then shrugged.

Rósa began to thank the sailor but hesitated. They had yet to exchange any words, and she had no idea what language he spoke. She touched his arm. "Merci."

He dipped his head then turned away to settle the other children into their bunks.

The ship's engines roared to life shortly before noon, sending low vibrations pulsating through the hull and into the bunk racks' metal frames. Soon, the faint odor of spent fuel oil melded with the salty air permeating the converted cargo hold. The *Serpa Pinto* pulled away, its movement through the calm water nearly imperceptible in the ship's bowels, where the children idled and fidgeted in strange, cramped quarters. At the captain's behest, they stayed belowdecks until the ship was under way. Several of them crowded around the portholes and stared at the cityscape slipping past the ship. Soon they exited the harbor, and the coastline receded, leaving nothing in view but sea and sky.

Call to the noonday meal came in the form of Mrs. Ryle, a USCOM escort who had introduced herself earlier while checking on the children's sleeping arrangements. Rósa helped her and two other chaperones lead the children forward to the dining room. She located their table and settled the twins onto the bench. To her delight, Mrs. Ryle took a seat across from her. Rósa had warmed quickly to the American's calm demeanor, aided by her fluency in German and French.

"You've settled in well, I trust?" Mrs. Ryle folded her hands and winked at the twins, who responded with shy smiles.

Rósa nodded. "Yes, thanks to one of the sailors. He's a very large man, dark."

"Oh, you mean Paulo. Imposing fellow, isn't he?"

"Very."

"Paulo is from Mozambique. Of all the crewmembers on this ship, he's proven the most helpful and loving with the children."

"He doesn't seem to say much."

"I've never heard him speak."

"Is he unable to?"

Mrs. Ryle smiled. "I don't know. He's never told me."

Rósa laughed then scanned the dining room. "I haven't seen him since we boarded. I wanted to thank him for his help with the girls."

The escort lowered her voice. "Paulo has been. . .well, confined to quarters."

"Why?"

"Apparently, one of the new crewmembers made a crass comment about his interest in little children. He overheard it."

"That's shameful!"

"I'm told the ship's doctor attempted to set the crewmember's jaw while he was still unconscious, but without much success. I suspect he'll have a difficult time speaking from this point on, too."

Rósa stared at the American, who shrugged. "Our Paulo has a bit of a temper." Her eyes brightened. "Your girls seem to be doing well. No seasickness?"

"No, they're doing wonderfully. How long will we be at sea?"

"At least two weeks. We'll stop for provisions at the Azores and then again in Bermuda. There's always the weather to contend with, of course—and the Germans."

"The Germans?"

"German wolf packs, their submarine forces, prowl the Atlantic. Although the *Serpa Pinto* is a Portuguese ship and is therefore neutral, that does not guarantee the U-boats will leave us alone."

"You don't mean. . .they wouldn't. . ."

Mrs. Ryle touched Rósa's hand. "I don't mean to alarm you, but it's better that you be aware. The Nazis don't care about nationality or neutrality. In fact. . ." She paused. "Do you know why my organization, the USCOM, was formed?"

Rósa shook her head.

"We were chartered over a year ago to transport British children to the United States, away from the Luftwaffe's bombing. Last September, the Germans torpedoed the *City of Benares* in the North Atlantic." Her voice caught. "There were ninety children aboard that ship. Seventy-seven of them perished."

Rósa covered her mouth as Mrs. Ryle continued.

"Understandably, the British government withdrew support for the program. So we refocused our efforts on rescuing children from the European continent. Baruch Hashem, none of these ships has been lost—although a few have been stopped and boarded. So far, we have transported over four hundred children safely to America."

Rósa shuddered, and Mrs. Ryle patted her hand. "I didn't mean to alarm you, but, as I say, it's better that you know." She leaned forward and whispered, "When you're on deck, watch for periscopes. Rest assured the crew will be watching, too."

At that moment, their servers arrived, and soon the children were tearing into fresh fruit, eggs, cheese, and all the bread and butter they could eat. But the deadly specter of Nazi submarines scuttled Rósa's appetite beyond a nibble or two.

# Chapter 29

Two days into their voyage, Rósa began to relax. The weather remained excellent, their sailing smooth. Food was plentiful, and the fresh air topside spared all but the most fragile of constitutions from motion sickness. The children quickly found their sea legs and occupied themselves improvising games to burn pent-up energy. Rósa's nervous eye spent much of the first day scanning the waves for periscopes, but the children's constant demands soon pushed such fears to the back of her mind. The second day passed uneventfully, and she settled into a comfortable routine. Although her first time at sea, these proved the most calming couple of days she'd experienced since leaving Salzburg. She settled back onto a canvas deck chair and watched the twins playing with Ania and Marie-Élise.

*Perhaps the worst is behind us.*

Their third night at sea shattered that hope.

The gale overtook them in the predawn hours. Rósa woke to the pounding of waves against the outer hull and the sound of young stomachs purging themselves. She gripped the sides of her bunk, her own stomach convulsing as the ship rocked and yawed. The darkness outside the portholes gave her nothing on which to ground her senses; it seemed the entire world was in chaos. The dim light afforded by the few lightbulbs in the compartment revealed nearly every child retching over the edge of their bunks. Those on the lower tiers became inadvertent targets for the bile discharged from above. Paulo's mysterious advice to claim the upper bunks suddenly became clear.

Rósa fought to retain control of her own dinner, her nausea heightened by the sight and smell of the sickness around her. She leaned over to see Kammbrie on the bed immediately below hers whimpering and holding her stomach. Her eyelids clenched shut, the toddler rolled onto her side and curled into a ball. Rósa lowered herself unsteadily over the end of the teetering bunk rack to check on Lilli-Anna and Ania.

Paulo had rigged two straps vertically over the front sides of the twins' bunks to prevent the tots from rolling off their thin mattresses. Rósa gripped the leather strap for support and lifted another brief prayer of thanks for the kind seaman's second act of foresight. She peered into the lower bunk, where Lilli-Anna lay on her side facing the hull. Rósa patted her on the shoulder. Lilli-Anna turned her head, eyes glazed, mouth drawn into a thin line. Rósa offered her an apologetic smile, and Lilli-Anna faced back toward the hull.

Rósa stooped lower. "Ania, how are you—"

She jumped back at a warm splatter on her bare feet. Ania squinted up at her from the bottom bunk, a remorseful glint in her pained eyes. Rósa attempted a feeble smile then began the long trek to the head to wash.

Fighting to ignore her cramping stomach, she stumbled up the swaying passageway. Faint points of light danced across her vision as the thick air pressed in from all sides. When she bumped through the second bulkhead hatch, her lungs clutched and dizziness dropped her to her knees. It subsided, and she staggered to her feet.

The head appeared through the gloom, and she groped for the stiff handle, but her fingers refused to cooperate. Without warning, her chest seized and bent her double in a fit of coughing. She dropped to the deck again, her arm pressed across her mouth. Her vision tunneled, and the last thing she saw before passing out was a faint red stain on her forearm.

❧

"Mrs. Dudek? Are you all right?"

*Soft sounds—words?—seep in, swirl, falter, disintegrate.*

"Mrs. Dudek?"

*Eyelids flutter, try to swallow, throat too dry.*

"I think she's coming around."

"Mama?"

*Kammbrie?* The voice penetrated her stupor, and the void in her subconscious began to fill. A feathery touch tickled her cheek. "Mama?"

*Lilli-Anna?* Rósa drew a partial breath, but a spasm cut it short. She grimaced and gurgled a cough.

"Mrs. Dudek?" Fingertips gently brushed her forehead.

Rósa forced her eyelids open to a slit and met blurry gray. She stifled another cough and widened her eyes. A face began to form—who? Mrs. Ryle?

"Can you sip some water?"

The escort's anxious face assembled itself in Rósa's view. Over Mrs. Ryle's shoulder, another face, round, black, and flanked by two curly blond heads, materialized. Paulo's toothy smile flashed in the dim light. Her gaze flicked back and forth between the blond heads. "Kamm—"

Another spasm gripped the back of her throat, and she pulled her knees to her stomach.

"Can you lift your head? I have some water here." Mrs. Ryle cupped Rósa's cheek.

Rósa tipped her face forward and closed her eyes. The cool rim of a metal cup caressed her parched lips and fresh liquid salved their split skin. When she admitted a few drops of water, the sweet fluid mixed with the rancid coating on her swollen tongue and gagged her. She subdued the urge to vomit then forced down another two sips. Exhausted, she laid her head back on the pillow. "What. . .happened?"

"Paulo found you lying in the passageway early this morning. He carried you back to your bunk and fetched me."

Rósa forced her eyes open and weakly returned the sailor's smile. "Thank you."

"Mama?" Lilli-Anna stretched both arms over Mrs. Ryle's shoulder, her lower lip quivering.

"Your mama needs to rest, sweetheart." The escort patted the tot's hand.

Rósa reached out to Lilli-Anna, but Mrs. Ryle intervened. "Mrs. Dudek, we don't know what's wrong with you. It may. . .it could be contagious. You don't want to infect. . ." She nodded toward the twins.

Rósa shook her head, her voice resolute. "I'm fine. Really. I just need. . .to rest. I'm sure it's nothing. . ."

Her vision faded gray, then black, and her arm went limp.

❧

Two days later, Rósa succeeded in climbing the companionway without help. She eased onto a canvas deck chair and pulled a light blanket over her lap while Ania sat a short distance away, playing with the twins. Rósa smiled and closed her eyes. She had just dozed off when a young girl's squeal awakened her. She looked for her girls. They were gone!

She bolted upright and searched the deck then relaxed when she spotted them among a crowd of children at the gunwale. Ania squatted between them at the railing, an arm around each girl's waist. Rósa pushed to her feet and shuffled over to them.

A girl pointed toward the front of the ship, and the children crowded closer, some of them poking their heads between the rails. Rósa leaned over and scanned the water. Two dolphins broke the surface, twisted their sleek bodies in midair, then disappeared back into the waves. The creatures' graceful forms mesmerized her as they gamboled with the prow of the *Serpa Pinto*. She held her breath more than once, certain they would veer into the hull, so close did they swim. But at the last moment, they peeled away and vanished beneath the waves then reemerged to taunt the hulking ship again.

Mrs. Ryle's voice floated over her shoulder. "We must be close to land."

Rósa turned to see her friend next to the rail. Paulo stood by her side, the usual grin on his face. He tapped Mrs. Ryle on the shoulder and pointed ahead of the ship. A bump broke the horizon, a tan wart on the edge of blue-black water framed against a pale cerulean afternoon sky. Mrs. Ryle clapped her hands and smiled at the black sailor.

"The Azores!"

He nodded.

# Chapter 30

The *Serpa Pinto* steamed into Porto Martins at midmorning. The ship had covered nearly nine hundred nautical miles in six days, delayed only by the storm midway from Lisbon. The children leaped at the opportunity to debark and explore the island, but Rósa declined the invitation to join them, citing her concern for the twins' safety. In truth, she simply hadn't the energy.

She languished in her thoughts at the breakfast table, picking at a crust of bread while the twins nibbled their own meals. At Mrs. Ryle's firm suggestion, Ania had reluctantly moved to a neighboring table, but Rósa refused to surrender her girls.

*"You need to see the ship's doctor, Rósa. Lilli-Anna and Kammbrie—"*

*"I'll take care of my girls! There's nothing wrong with me, save perhaps a cold. Besides, I'm feeling much better."*

Fear of losing guardianship dropped her into an emotional crouch like a mother bear brooding over her cubs. She avoided even clearing her throat when anyone was near, lest it spark a bout of coughing. But she paid the price for her charade in the solitude of the head, doubled over in fits that tore at her diaphragm.

By day, Rósa spent as much time in the fresh air of the open deck as she could. But at night, the oppressive closeness of the sleeping compartment challenged her endurance. She muffled her coughs with a towel, spattering it with flecks of blood. Each morning, the towel disappeared into the bottom of her duffle bag, only reemerging at secret moments during the day to be rinsed in the head. Surely this would soon pass, and all would be normal once again.

Rósa had just lifted her coffee to her lips when a shout at the dining-room hatch nearly caused her to spill it. Ania rushed over to their table toting an odd brown ball with pointed leaves sprouting from its top.

"It's called a pineapple. Have you ever seen anything so funny?" She set the fruit on the table. "Go ahead. Touch it."

Rósa grasped it and flinched as the rough surface prickled the palms of her hand. Lilli-Anna reached up and poked the pointy tip of a leaf with her forefinger. She jerked back and stared at the tiny depression it left in her skin. Kammbrie stared at the strange object then peered up at her mama.

"You won't believe it," bubbled Ania, "but it's delicious!"

Rósa arched an eyebrow then set the fruit back on the table.

Ania pulled a cloth from her pocket and unfolded it to reveal three bright yellow chunks oozing with clear juice. "This is what it looks like on the inside. Try it!" She offered the cloth to Rósa, who took a piece and inspected it.

"Here, Lilli, take one. You, too, Kammie." Kammbrie looked up at Rósa and mimicked her mama's doubtful expression. Lilli-Anna glanced back at Ania's eager face then touched the fruit to her tongue. She smacked her lips, and her eyes widened. In a flash, the pineapple disappeared into her mouth, and she grinned at Rósa, a drop of juice dribbling down her chin.

Rósa tucked her morsel into her mouth. Kammbrie followed her mama's lead.

Ania giggled again at their surprised looks. "Good?"

Rósa smiled and nodded while the twins gestured for more.

"That should be enough for now." Mrs. Ryle's voice came from behind Rósa. She rounded the table and sat, wearing a knowing smile. "We learned on the first transport to ration the pineapple. Several of the children gorged themselves on it, not realizing its sugar disguises its acid. There were some very sick tummies on that voyage—even a couple of blistered mouths."

She lifted Ania's pineapple from the table. "Best have this join the others in the galley."

Ania pouted, her longing gaze locked onto her prize as the escort rose from her seat.

Mrs. Ryle laughed. "Don't worry, young lady. We'll be sure to include some with each meal."

"When do we depart?" Rósa asked.

"This evening. We'll have a longer layover in Bermuda."

"How long is the voyage to Bermuda?"

"Another week, if all goes well."

"What could go wrong?"

Mrs. Ryle began to reply then faltered. "Nothing, of course. Excuse me."

# Chapter 31

The *Serpa Pinto* departed Porto Martins after dinner, skirting southward of the outer islands on a westerly course into a gold-magenta sunset. After the evening meal, the children and escorts gathered on deck and watched the lights of the archipelago sink beneath a cloudless eastern horizon. The cooling evening breeze chilled Rósa's bare arms but invigorated her sluggish lungs. She inhaled deeply, although carefully.

The children crowded the railings, chattered, and pointed to pinpricks of celestial light piercing the cobalt mantle unfolding from the east. Rósa settled into a deck chair and pulled the twins onto her lap. Kammbrie fidgeted, seemingly unable to find a comfortable position. Lilli-Anna laid her head on her mama's shoulder and stared into the star-spangled expanse, so still it appeared she'd fallen asleep.

Soon the escorts herded the children belowdecks to prepare for bedtime. Ania dragged a deck chair alongside Rósa's and lingered, whispering a Polish lullaby to the twins. Had there ever been a more peaceful time? Not in memory.

The breeze picked up, prompting Rósa to get the girls below and out of the chill. As they ambled toward the companionway hatch, a sailor—apparently an officer, by his uniform—crossed to the starboard gunwale and lifted a pair of binoculars to his eyes.

Rósa followed his gaze. A small light flickered and bobbed several hundred meters from the ship. She squinted. It flashed again then disappeared.

The officer lowered his binoculars and crossed their path on his way back to the bridge, a deep frown marring his features.

⤜◈⤝

Silence awoke Rósa. She lifted her head from her pillow and rubbed her matted eyes, struggling for orientation. Something was different. But what?

The silence.

No bass hum reverberated through the hull next to her head. No vibrations energized the bunk frame against her arm.

She pushed onto an elbow and peered through a nearby porthole. A sullen gray sky rode choppy waves that scratched at the hull not far below. Rósa leaned toward the hazy round window then jerked back as a falling body flashed past, followed by a muted splash. She stifled a scream then pressed her face to the glass. A man's head bobbed between the frothy white crests. He turned and swam toward the side of the ship. Before he disappeared beneath her view, she recognized the panicked face of the ship's cook.

Rósa pulled her sweater from its perch at the foot of her bed. Slipping it over her shoulders, she climbed quietly down from her bunk. She winced as the hatch squeaked on its hinges, but a hasty look over her shoulder confirmed she hadn't awakened any of the children.

She stepped through the hatchway and hurried toward the companionway, ignoring the pressure in her chest. The metal rungs dug into her bare feet as she struggled up the ladder, bringing a grimace with each step. At the top, she peeked through the hatchway.

Fifty meters starboard, a gray submarine slouched in the restless water. A man stood on its deck aiming a cannon at the *Serpa Pinto*. Rósa pulled her sweater tighter to her neck.

Nearby, the Portuguese captain stood with a group of his crewmen, their gazes fixed on a gap in the gunwale railing. Rósa ducked back as a man's head and shoulders appeared in the gap. A sailor with a machine pistol slung over his shoulder hoisted himself onto the deck and pulled his weapon to ready. He trained it on the *Serpa Pinto*'s mariners while five more armed

249

sailors clambered aboard behind him.

Rósa blanched at the sight of the machine pistol. Her mind flashed back to the train station in Freistadt where Gustaw's execution, buried in the recesses by time, resurrected itself with macabre clarity. She went lightheaded, as the rattle of automatic gunfire echoed in her mind. Her knees weakened, but despite her strongest effort, she couldn't tear her gaze from the ugly weapon.

She finally broke her stare when another man, an officer by his bearing, climbed onto the deck. The captain of the *Serpa Pinto* stepped forward and halted three paces in front of his crew.

The foreign officer moved to the front of his men and yelled at the ship's captain—in German! Rósa shrank farther back into the shadows. The captain returned an even look at his counterpart. The German officer flexed his fingers and rested his hand on the butt of a pistol holstered at his hip. The Portuguese captain clasped his hands behind his back and held his ground.

The German commander barked an order over his shoulder. Four of the sailors scattered in different directions. Another approached the *Serpa Pinto*'s crewmen.

"Papieren!"

When Paulo approached with his documents, the scowling German stepped back. The black man towered over the armed seaman, his face impassive. The sailor sneered and snatched Paulo's identification papers from his hand. After a cursory review, he tossed them at Paulo's feet. When Paulo bent to pick them up, the German spat on the back of his head.

Paulo slowly straightened and locked gazes with the German, who took another step back and swiveled his weapon level from his shoulder.

*Oh, Paulo, please don't—*

A tap on Rósa's shoulder launched her heart into her throat. She spun to see Mrs. Ryle behind her wearing an apologetic expression. She brought her forefinger to her lips and gestured toward the hatch. Rósa moved aside. As she backed against the wall, a short burst of gunfire stopped her short.

*Paulo—no!*

Mrs. Ryle peeked through the hatchway, but Rósa couldn't bring herself to look. The adrenaline rush dizzied her, and an overwhelming urge to cough clenched her throat. She cupped her mouth with her hands, teetered backward, and began slipping to the floor. A firm arm linked itself under hers, arresting her slide down the wall. Mrs. Ryle's concerned face peered into hers.

Rósa regained her balance. "I'm okay," she rasped.

A shout refocused the women's attention through the opening. Two of the *Serpa Pinto*'s galley crew limped across the deck, hands clasped behind their heads, their backs prodded by the muzzle of a submachine gun. They halted before the German officer. Terse words flew between the officer and the sailor who had arrested the galley hands. The sailor saluted then shoved the cooks toward the gap in the gunwale railing.

The Nazi sailor who had checked the crew's paperwork returned to his commander's side. Rósa forced herself to look over at the group of civilian mariners. When she spotted Paulo's dark head above those of his fellow crewmen, she released a deep breath and grasped hands with Mrs. Ryle.

The remainder of the boarding party returned from their search, and their commander strode to the Portuguese captain, spat words into his face, then turned on his heel and led his men over the side. The sailor who had boarded first backed to the railing, his weapon still drawn, then also disappeared over the edge.

A *Serpa Pinto* crewman pulled a panel across the gap while the captain moved to the gunwale and casually observed the boarding party and their two captives making their way back to the U-boat in a small launch. When the boat reached the submarine, the captain hand-signaled behind his back.

Two crewmen crouched and ran past the companionway hatch to the port side of the ship. They threw a life preserver over the side, and after a tense moment of pulling on the preserver's halyard, they dragged the ship's cook, drenched and shivering, over the railing. The men helped him to his feet and hustled him out of sight.

Rósa and Mrs. Ryle hurried to the dispersing group of seamen. The women stopped at the sight of the wooden gangway at Paulo's feet peppered with bullet holes. He lifted the cuffs of his pants and inspected his damaged shoes. Blood trickled from splinter wounds in his ankles.

Rósa grasped the sailor's beefy arm. "Paulo! Are you okay?"

He shrugged.

Mrs. Ryle knelt and plucked a large sliver protruding from his pant leg. She flicked it aside and reached for another shard when Paulo stiffened and stepped back. He shook his head, his eyes wide. Mrs. Ryle rose, a scolding expression on her face but warmth in her eyes. She poked his chest with her finger. "Hold still." The gentle woman knelt and resumed her ministrations.

Paulo shifted and beseeched Rósa with his eyes, but she only smiled and turned away.

The ship's captain remained at the gunwale, his gaze fixed on the U-boat. She peered past him as the warship's diesel engine roared, and the submarine peeled away toward the north.

# Chapter 32

The *Serpa Pinto* entered Bermuda's Great Sound six days later. The island oasis lolled in an endless expanse of ocean, its unspoiled beauty mesmerizing Rósa. Stretches of pure white sand underscored low green hills festooned with splashes of white, red, and yellow—radiance of unfamiliar flora that beckoned in greeting. Gulls dipped and swooped low over the placid bay and the maneuvering ship, shrieking at others who dared overfly their fishing spot.

It seemed the entire population had turned out to greet the young refugees. Islanders and the media alike doted on them whenever they ventured ashore, snapped photographs, and asked them about their journey. Their second afternoon in port, the governor invited them to a picnic on his estate, where the children gorged themselves on more food than they had ever seen in one place.

Rósa welcomed the singular attention Lilli-Anna and Kammbrie received as the youngest refugees. Less welcome, though, was a visit on board by a small group of doctors and nurses to consult with the ship's doctor and check the children's health. Her coughing had intensified over the past week, becoming more difficult to conceal. But she shook away her concern. Surely the fits were a residual effect of a bug she'd picked up in Portugal; they would subside. Still, she fought a persistent fear that it was more than that when, their third night in port, she awoke chilled and drenched with sweat. Her lungs clawed for a full breath, but it died to a rattle in her throat. She rolled onto her side. *Oh, Lord, please. Not this close.*

On the fourth day in port, the captain gathered the adults on deck. Rósa studied his terse expression as he called the meeting to order.

"German U-boats have been sighted offshore from North Carolina to New England. Therefore, the American Navy and Coast Guard have tightened restrictions on coastal navigation."

"When will it be safe to continue?" asked a chaperone.

"We're waiting for clearance from the Coast Guard. When it comes, there will likely be a very small window of time in which to act. For that reason, any shore excursions must remain close to the port, and the lead escort must check in with the harbormaster at least once every two hours."

He waited for the murmuring to abate. "Actually, I prefer everyone remain on board, but I know that's not fair to the children. They need the respite, and so do you. I advise you, though. . ."

All whispering ceased.

". . .I will not delay departure for anyone who does not heed my instructions."

❧

The Coast Guard notified the *Serpa Pinto* to proceed the morning of their seventh day in port. The captain ordered the restless children to remain belowdecks while his crew bustled to get the ship under way. Soon the ship shuddered awake, the guttural hum of the engines renewing a sense of urgency and determination.

At their first movement, word came that the passengers could go topside to bid the idyllic island farewell. Waving crowds lined the waterfront, and smaller vessels moored in the harbor blasted salutes to the lumbering ship as it yawed toward the open sea. The children crowded the railing to watch Bermuda's outer islands slip by.

The *Serpa Pinto*'s prow sliced through the swells, churning froth on the teal brine and leaving a sun-sparkled trail in its wake. Rósa hunched near the gunwale, her sweater wrapped tightly around her, despite the warmth of the morning sun. She scanned the dark billows cresting with whitecaps beyond the portside breakwater of Ireland Island. Each glint of sunlight off the choppy waves became a periscope to her imagination, and she scoured the sea until her eyes ached.

The ocean breeze picked up and forced Rósa to retreat to a deck chair lee of the bridge. She dropped onto the seat and collapsed against the backrest. After another check that Ania had settled the twins safely away from the railing, she closed her eyes.

The past few days, every move had become an exhausting effort. Climbing the companionway to the top deck winded her to the point of lightheadedness. Her last full breath abandoned her days ago, and her tortured lungs resorted to wheezing gasps. Still, she'd successfully evaded the medical crew earlier that week, despite Mrs. Ryle's objections.

"Rósa, you must let them examine you."

"Nonsense. I just need more rest, and I'll be. . .fine."

She awoke to Lilli-Anna climbing onto her lap. Ania stood beside the chair with Kammbrie. "I let you sleep as long as I could, but the girls wanted their mama."

Rósa pulled Lilli-Anna close and hugged her. Kammbrie extended her arms and leaned down, nearly losing Ania her balance. She settled Kammbrie onto Rósa's lap and sat on the edge of an adjoining chair.

"How are you feeling, Mrs. Dudek?"

"I'm fine. Why do you ask?" Rósa replied more tersely than she intended. Ania looked away.

A shadow fell across the group, and Rósa squinted up to see Paulo's massive silhouette against the sun. He pointed to a squall line darkening the horizon then gestured toward the companionway hatch.

Rósa urged the girls from her lap and asked Ania to get them below. Paulo offered his hand, and she gratefully accepted but staggered into a coughing fit after taking one step toward the hatch. A wave of vertigo overtook her, and she wobbled, groping for Paulo's other hand. Her vision tunneled, and she crumpled to the deck. The last thing she remembered was a strong arm wrapping itself around her waist and another lifting her off her feet.

# Chapter 33

Clinking echoed through Rósa's mind and nudged her to the brink of consciousness. She winced at a sharp chest pain and rolled onto her side. Her eyes opened to semidarkness and struggled to discern their surroundings. The clinking sharpened, undergirded by the familiar tremor of engines.

Rósa pushed onto an unsteady elbow and surveyed her surroundings. A small porthole admitted a narrow stream of gray light into what appeared to be a small compartment. Bolted to the wall across from her cot hung a cabinet, its double doors hooked shut. Beneath it, a metal table tipped in pace with the movement of the ship next to the vague outline of a hatch.

She dragged her stiff legs to the side of the bunk, pushed to a sitting position, and focused toward the noise. Atop the table, next to a folded white towel, a shallow tray lay strapped in place. In it, a glass syringe in a metal casing rolled across the bottom of the tray. The ship dipped toward the bow, and the cylinder hit the side of the tray then began its return journey as the ship overcorrected to stern.

Rósa pushed to her feet. Fighting vertigo, she leaned against the table then edged toward the hatch. It opened to a deserted, rain-wetted deck. She squinted into the overcast sky but, the sun lacking, couldn't judge the time.

Steadying herself against the wall, Rósa worked her way forward. She paused as a low throbbing noise rose over the sounds of the ship's engines. The throb rose to a roar, and she instinctively ducked as two large shadows flashed across the deck. The warplanes buzzed the *Serpa Pinto* from port to starboard, passing so low it seemed they scarcely avoided colliding with the smokestack. On the underside of each wing shone a white star on a blue field radiating from a red circle, and on the tail, horizontal red and white stripes alternated in their climb up the rudder. She perked at what she assumed were American markings but sobered again at the sight of bombs affixed to the underside of the wings.

The coastal patrol continued northward, apparently satisfied of the *Serpa Pinto's* noncombatant status. Rósa continued her trek across the deck toward the companionway. When she was only steps from the hatchway, Mrs. Ryle emerged.

"Rósa! How are you feeling?"

"Better, thank you." She brushed back a wisp of unruly hair with shaky fingers. "What happened?"

"You passed out. Paulo took you to the infirmary, where the ship's doctor examined you." Her pulse quickened. "What. . .what did he say?"

"He ran some tests."

"Tests?"

Mrs. Ryle lifted Rósa's arm and nudged her sleeve back. A faint red prick mark dotting the edge of a low bump on her skin blemished her forearm.

"It's a tuberculosis test."

"Tuberculosis? Surely he doesn't think—"

"Rósa, we both know of your coughing fits, how weak you've become."

"Did you tell the doctor about my coughing?"

"I did."

Rósa glared at her. "Why? Why would you do that?"

"For you and for the children. Of course I pray it's not tuberculosis, but if it is, we must heal you and protect them. The disease is contagious; you know that."

"It's *not* tuberculosis! I just caught a cold, or something. I'm sure it's going away. I feel much better, in fact—"

"Rósa, look at me."

Rósa shook her arm loose, her chest heaving. Another seizure threatened to choke her, but she suppressed it.

Mrs. Ryle hesitated. "Your towel shows blood stains."

"You looked through my bag? You had no right!"

"The towel was hanging from your bunk. To dry, it appears." Mrs. Ryle's deep brown eyes searched Rósa's. "You can't continue like this, Rósa. It's hurting you, and it's not safe for the children."

"I'm not contagious!" She stepped back and focused over the American's shoulder. "I need to see my girls."

Mrs. Ryle didn't move.

Rósa narrowed her eyes. "Get out of my way."

"I can't. I'm sorry."

"You can't keep me from my children!"

"Ania is watching over them. They'll be fine until the test results show. It should only take a couple of days."

"*No—*"

A tap on Rósa's shoulder startled her, and she spun, teetering on her feet. Paulo stood behind her, his expression apologetic. He offered her his hand, but she ignored it and turned back to face Mrs. Ryle.

"I thought you were my friend!"

"I am, Rósa. I truly am—"

Her face taut, Rósa lunged forward and shouldered the woman out of the way. Mrs. Ryle cried out and toppled to the deck. Rósa wobbled again, gasping for breath, then groped for the hatchway. Before she could take another step, a strong hand on her shoulder restrained her. She pivoted on her heel.

"Let. . .me. . .go!" she screamed, her face contorted. She slapped Paulo's hand aside and, in the same motion, arced her other arm upward. Her open hand connected with the sailor's cheek with a loud crack. She stepped back, wide-eyed, her stinging hand now covering her mouth.

His eyes merely searched her face.

"*Rósa!*" shouted Mrs. Ryle.

Her pulse racing, Rósa backed into the senior escort, who had regained her feet. Mrs. Ryle's hand gripped her arm just as the latent seizure broke loose and bent Rósa double. She dropped to her knees, her head low. Tears mingled with the bloody splotches on the deck.

Two strong arms steadied her shoulders, while gentle fingers tenderly stroked her hair. The loving gestures released another flood of tears.

"What. . .what is to become of me?" she sobbed. "Of my children?"

⌘

On 21 September 1941, the *Serpa Pinto* sailed into New York's harbor with fifty-five refugee children from war-ravaged Europe. Together, Jews, non-Aryan Christians, and other "undesirables" crowded the railing and gawked at the Statue of Liberty as the ship maneuvered toward Ellis Island. Among them, Ania squatted and chattered into the ears of Lilli-Anna and Kammbrie, two years old this day.

Rósa lay on the infirmary cot, the sickbay's hatch propped open to the animated scene by the gunwale. Mrs. Ryle sat at her side and held her hand. Rósa fixed a blank stare on Ania and the twins, her head listless on the pillow. Her bare arm stretched out to her side, a blistered pink welt marring her pale forearm where only a needle prick had been two days before.

"Rósa?"

No reply.

"They'll only quarantine you until you're cured."

Rósa hacked a shallow cough.

"The girls will be fine. I'll watch over them at the orphanage until you come."

Across the deck, Lilli-Anna turned. Her eyes widened when she caught sight of her mama through the hatchway. She ambled toward the infirmary, but Ania caught her from behind. With an uneasy glance at Rósa, she hoisted the wriggling tot to her chest then grasped Kammbrie's hand and led the girls toward the bow.

Lilli-Anna's voice quavered through the opening. "Mama?"

They passed from view.

Mrs. Ryle stroked her hand. "Only until you're well, Rósa."

Karen Donovan laid the documents bearing the photo and name of Rósa Dudek on the table. She sipped her lukewarm coffee, pondering again what it must have been like for a lone woman to travel across a war-ravaged continent and an ocean with two young children. What chance could she possibly have had?

# Chapter 34

Satisfied?" Frank popped another chocolate-covered pretzel in his mouth and surveyed the documents littering their coffee table. "Enough to contact this Madeline person?"

"Just about," replied Karen thoughtfully. "I still haven't read any of the diaries." She pulled the shoe box closer and lifted the lid.

"Whose do you think they are? Your mom's?"

"I don't know. I guess so. It makes sense that—"

"What are you doing?"

They both jumped at the thin voice behind them.

"Mother!" Karen lurched up from the couch.

Her mother leaned against the archway, gaze locked on the wooden chest. "Where did you get that?"

"It was in your attic at the old house. We put it into storage when you moved in with us."

"What have you done? Why have you opened it?"

Karen's stiffened hands pressed against her thighs. "I'm sorry, Mother. I didn't mean to pry. But there was this newspaper column, and. . .well, a journalist has written something. . ." Her shoulders slumped. "Oh, I don't know where to start."

Her mother took a faltering step into the room and stared at the paperwork strewn across the coffee table.

Karen cast a guilty look at the mess. "I hope you're not angry. . . ."

Her mother closed the gap to the table, her watery eyes scanning the tabletop. She brought one hand to her cheek then slowly reached down with the other. Her trembling fingers hovered over the placard bearing the number *70*. Hesitating, she moved to the placard marked *71* and lifted it, fingering the knotted string.

Karen's throat constricted as her mother studied the age-dried cardboard, her slight fingertips tracing the numerals. What had come over the elderly woman's face—pain? sadness, perhaps? No, neither of those fit. She focused on her mother's eyes, piquing at a flash, a glint distinct from light reflecting off their ubiquitous sheen of moisture. It awoke a faint memory of something she hadn't seen for years. Could her mother possibly recognize reminders of her early childhood, her near infancy, when she seemed so unaware of her present?

Tentatively, Karen picked up the travel document bearing Rósa Dudek's photograph. She held it out. Drawing it close, her mother stared at the picture. Her hand began to shake, and a whisper escaped through her pale lips.

"Mama?"

Her eyes glazed over, and the document slipped from her grasp.

Frank caught her as she fainted.

"Should we take her to the emergency room?"

"She's breathing okay. Let's watch her a little while longer."

"Are you sure?"

Nedra laid the elderly woman's hand gently back onto her stomach and rose from the edge of the couch. "Her pulse is normal. I'd have some water ready when she wakes up, though. There may be some shock, and you don't want her to dehydrate." She looked up quickly. "I'm not a doctor, of course, so you can certainly take her in if you like."

"You're a licensed practical nurse; that's good enough for me." Karen squeezed her friend's hand. "Thanks so much for coming over."

"Of course, girlfriend! I only live a block away. Oh, and my LPN certification lapsed years ago, so don't hold me to it."

"I'd trust you with my dying breath."

Nedra lifted an eyebrow. "Don't bother."

Karen laughed.

"How soon do you think she'll wake up?" asked Frank.

"It shouldn't be long. Her eyelids fluttered a couple of times, and her breathing is lighter."

As if she'd heard, Karen's mother rolled her head to the side.

Nedra surveyed the paperwork on the coffee table. "So, there's a lot more here than just a couple of letters."

Karen nodded. "Some of the papers were tucked into the first journal, but most were in an envelope hidden under the diaries. When she saw Rósa Dudek's photograph, she fainted."

"Hmm. Sounds like there may be some dormant memories coming alive in a corner of the old girl's mind." Nedra smiled. "I often thought there was more to your mom than what we were seeing."

Karen shook her head. "Is it possible she could remember the Dudeks from so long ago? According to the second letter, Gustaw Dudek died when she was only about six months old. I don't know when Rósa Dudek passed away, or why. Mother has mentioned only snippets of her life in foster care after she came to the States. She's hardly spoken of her mother when I've asked; only mentioned the name Dudek."

"And now you have the *Times* column. Quite a puzzle, huh?"

"Maybe it's time to contact them," Frank interjected.

"Maybe," murmured Karen.

"Well, I'll leave you guys to it. I've got some errands to run." Nedra picked up her purse. "I'll have my phone with me. Call if you need anything—of course, if it's serious, call 9-1-1, not me."

The two women hugged, and Frank saw Nedra to the door.

Karen picked up the article she'd clipped from the *Times*. It carried Madeline Sommers' e-mail address. Frank returned, and she looked up.

"Frank?"

"Yeah?"

"Is our document scanner working?"

# Chapter 35

Madeline slouched, elbow propped on the desk, chin resting on the palm of her hand. She sighed and punched the DELETE key, sending another obvious wild-goose chase into cyber-oblivion. Her gaze wandered over the twenty-seven unread message titles in her Inbox. At least two-thirds of them had to do with the *Times* column. Never in a million years would she have imagined the article on Lilli-Anna and Kammbrie would generate so many responses.

So many weird responses.

Four of the messages carried attachments.

*Oh, no you don't. Never again.*

An e-mail she'd received yesterday seemed genuine, and its attachment carried a promising caption, so she eagerly viewed it. *Ugh! Gross! What a creep!*

Madeline vowed from that point on never to open another attachment—especially one with a file name identifying it as a picture. She clicked the first message header.

Picture. DELETE.

Ditto the second.

The third message text didn't even try to disguise its intent.

*Eww!* DELETE.

She clicked the fourth message. It offered a pdf document file. She scanned the brief message text and noted the sender: kdonovan210@yahoo.com. One more glance at the attachment icon and she shook her head. DELETE.

Madeline yawned then closed the laptop and trudged out of the study to start dinner.

⁂

"Hon, would you pass the corn, please?. . . Hon?. . . Madeline?"

"What? Oh, sorry. What did you want?"

Brendon cocked his head. "The corn."

"Sure." Madeline slid the bowl across the table then resumed her blank stare at the daisy centerpiece and probed her lukewarm ground sirloin patty with her fork.

"Where are you, Madeline?. . . *Madeline!*"

The fork clattered to the table. "What? *What?*"

Katia and Maria stared wide-eyed at their mother. Oskar began to fuss in his infant seat.

Brendon patted his son's arm and frowned. "You've been absent the entire meal. What's going on?"

Madeline sat back in her chair and rubbed her eyes. "I'm sorry, Bren. Something's bothering me, and I can't figure out what it is."

Brendon's jaw twitched. "It wouldn't have anything to do with the newspaper column, would it?"

"Well. . ."

"You can't even eat—"

"Wait!" Madeline raised a finger. "I think I know. Would you excuse me a second, please?" She pushed back from the table.

"Where are you going?"

"I'll be right back." Ignoring her husband's exaggerated sigh, Madeline flipped her napkin onto the table and hurried into the study. She lifted the lid to her laptop. "C'mon, c'mon. Wake up!"

The screen flashed on, and she launched her e-mail program. She clicked the Deleted folder and found the last message she'd discarded. After another suspicious glance at the attachment icon, she scanned the message text again.

*Dear Ms. Sommers,*
*I read last Tuesday's column with great interest. I think I have something for you.*

Madeline tightened her lips. *Yeah, I bet.*

*There's too much to try to cover in this message, so I've attached some documentation that I think will help.*

*Of course you did.*

*It's a copy of Lilli-Anna and Kammbrie Szpilmann's immigration paperwork, and one belonging to Rósa Dudek.*

*Sure it is—wait! That's it!*
Madeline reread the line. She pivoted and searched the corkboard for last Tuesday's column. She traced her finger down the text. When she reached the end, she turned back toward the monitor.

"*Rósa* Dudek."

In her article, Madeline had only referred to "the Dudeks" and "the Dudek family." But this person had given Mrs. Dudek a name. *Rósa.*

Madeline reached for her mouse and moved the cursor to the attachment icon. She held her breath and double-clicked.

The file opened to the scanned image of a document entitled AFFIDAVIT IN LIEU OF PASSPORT bearing the photos and names of two beautiful, curly headed, blond girls so alike in appearance one could scarcely be discerned from the other. Their names appeared at the bottom of the document: *Lilli-Anna and Kammbrie Szpilmann.* Madeline's breath caught, and to her surprise, tears blurred her vision. She dabbed her eyes with a sleeve and advanced to the second page. It carried an identically titled image but a different photograph.

Wavy light hair framed Rósa Dudek's wan face, a pensive half smile curving her pale thin lips. The smile contrasted with the weariness in her eyes, lending the woman a haunted countenance. There seemed to be something behind her enigmatic expression, something that begged to be given voice but for which there were no words. Unfulfilled hope? An unoffered apology? Fearful resignation? All three? She shook her head. What trials had Rósa Dudek endured; when and how had she met her end?

Madeline tore her gaze from the image and closed the attachment. The message text reappeared.

*Sincerely,*
*Karen Donovan*

The cursor nearly tripped over itself in its rush toward the REPLY button.

# Chapter 36

To: kdonovan210@yahoo.com
Subject: Praise God!

Dear Karen,

You have no idea what your e-mail meant to me! I'd nearly abandoned hope of ever finding Lilli–Anna and Kammbrie.

Can we talk? My phone number is below my signature. Or I can call you. Please let me know soonest.

Sincerely and with great excitement,
Madeline Sommers

Karen sat back from her computer and tried to sort through the rush of emotions released by Madeline Sommers's reply. Was this a wise thing to do? Had she overstepped? Her mother still knew nothing of the newspaper column and its revelation about her real parents. Perhaps after witnessing her reaction to Rósa Dudek's photo she should've waited awhile, slept on it, discussed it more at length with Frank and Nedra. But she'd been so excited about the now obvious connection between her mother and the *Times* article, she'd scanned in the documents and fired them off via e-mail almost before taking her next breath. Well, she'd opened the door now, and she was committed to follow through.

Her mother seemed disoriented when she revived from her swoon. She'd lain on the couch and stared at the chest and the documents but made no move to touch them. Karen gently roused her from the couch to wash up for dinner then replaced the paperwork in the chest. She began to carry it to the hall closet but halted at the thought that its sudden disappearance might disturb her mother even more. So she tucked the chest into the corner of the front room then went to check on the casserole and set the table.

A half hour later, on her way to summon Frank and her mother to supper, Karen glanced into the living room as she passed the archway.

Her mother sat cross-legged on the floor, the chest before her, its lid tipped back. She held a diary in her lap, and a couple of the documents lay scattered by her side. Karen stared, her mouth half open. When was the last time her mother sat on the floor—and cross-legged, no less?

As Karen squinted into the shadowed corner, a light gray object against her mother's blouse caught her eye. She stepped into the room. Looped around the older woman's neck by its loosened string hung the 71 placard. Her mother gently massaged its corner with her fingertips. Karen tiptoed across the room and settled onto the floor.

A moment later, Frank's hand came to rest on her shoulder. She covered it with her own. Still, they remained silent.

Her mother released a deep sigh and turned toward her daughter. Karen's breath caught at her faraway look. She nearly missed the older woman's quiet words: "I'd forgotten," she whispered.

Frank extended the *Times* article over his wife's shoulder. Accepting it, she returned her attention to her mother. "Mother, there's something you should read." She held the newspaper clipping out to her.

※

The late-afternoon light squeezed through a gap in the filmy lace-hemmed scrims over the Donovans' living-room window, spotlighting levitating dust motes undisturbed by even the slightest movement of air. A low hum shuddered the ambiance as the air conditioner whirred to life, an event normally unnoticed but now deafening in the utter stillness of the room. A gust issued from the overhead vents and plowed through the ribbon of dust, swirling the motes into a stray wisp of silky hair over the ear of the woman seated on the floor. The clipping held loosely between her fingers fluttered then stilled as the waft of air evened.

Frank and Karen held hands and watched a gradual range of expressions overtake her mother: a furrowed brow, a rosy tint on the cheekbones, then trembling fingertips touched to quivering lips. She lowered the clipping and stared at the floor.

Frank patted his wife's hand, and she shot him a worried look.

Her mother lifted her gaze and stared at Karen, her expression undecipherable. She uncrossed her legs and rocked forward. Frank and Karen stood to help her to her feet, but she shifted to her knees and rose under her own power. Teetering for a moment, she caught her balance. Then, clutching the newspaper article to her chest, she shuffled around the couch and disappeared down the hallway, dinner certainly forgotten.

Karen put her hand on Frank's arm. "What do you think?"

"I don't know. I couldn't read her."

"Maybe I should call Madeline Sommers now."

"Good idea."

"I hope she has some answers."

"She'd better. She started all of this."

⌘

"Bren, can you get the phone? I'm changing Oskar."

Madeline wrinkled her nose and reached for a clean diaper. She pressed the top of the spent disposable to her son's stomach and shook open a fresh one. Oskar gurgled and kicked his feet.

"Oh, no you don't," she muttered. Fountainous experience taught her never to retire the old diaper until the new one was ready to deploy. Boys were so much more trouble than girls. *In more ways than one. . .* "Brendon, the phone!"

"I got it," he called up the stairway. "It's for you."

*That figures.* She rolled her eyes and tugged another lotion-soaked wipe from its plastic container. "Who is it?"

"It's a Karen Donovan. I can have her call back—"

"No! I'll take it! Tell her to hold a sec."

Madeline hurried through her chore, gave her son a quick kiss, and laid him in his playpen. She raced for the phone extension in the master bedroom.

"Hello! Ms. Donovan? Thank you, Karen, and please call me Madeline. . . . I'm so excited! I don't know where to start. . . . I don't know how much more I can add to what you've already read in the *Times*. May I ask which twin is your mother? . . . Really? That is so cool. . . . Yes, my grandmother—I mean, *our* grandmother—is still alive. She's surprised us, frankly. We thought we were losing her years ago, but she keeps hanging on. Tough lady, huh? . . . You bet. Does your mom know about her yet? . . . So, she's read the column, then. How did she react? . . . Oh, Alzheimer's. I'm so sorry. Do you have any idea where her sister might be? . . . I see. Well, there's still hope, isn't there? . . . Fly up here? Sure, that would be great. I'd love to meet you. . . . No, Grandma doesn't know about this. I haven't had time to tell her since I got your e-mail. Maybe we should surprise her. . . . Right. Tell you what: I'll pick you up at the airport, and you can stay with us while you're here. . . . No, it's no trouble at all. I insist. I'll wait to hear from you. . . . You, too. Thanks so much for calling! . . . Bye."

As Madeline eased the telephone onto its cradle, Brendon's voice startled her from the doorway. "What was that all about?"

She spun around and beamed at him. "We found Kammbrie!"

262

# *Chapter 37*

Karen fidgeted on the edge of the love seat. Her mother sat on her recliner, staring out the window into the deepening twilight. The newspaper clipping draped over the arm of her chair, and the number placard from the *Serpa Pinto* pressed lightly against the front of her cotton blouse. Her forefinger traced gentle circles on the fabric of the chair's arm, widening the threadbare spot worn from years of the same absent gesture.

"I don't know what it means."

"What, Mother?"

"This." She tapped the clipping with her forefinger.

Karen smiled. "I think it means you have a mother in Michigan, one who I bet would very much love to see you."

"Mama died."

"The lady—the wonderful lady—who rescued you and your sister died."

"Mama died."

Karen's smile faltered. "I spoke with the woman who wrote this column. She would be. . .your niece. It's all true."

Her mother shook her head.

Karen leaned forward. "I know this must be a shock to you."

"She never came."

"What?"

"She never came for us."

"Who? Do you mean—"

The older woman tapped the clipping again.

"We don't know what happened, Mother," Karen said. "She and your father were taken away by force. They had no choice. It was the war."

"She never came for us. She's not my mama. Mama died."

Karen reached out and laid her hand over her mother's. "I told Madeline, your niece, that we would come visit."

Another shake of the head, this one more vigorous.

"Don't you at least want to see your mother, to find out what happened?"

"No."

"But—"

"No!"

❧

Karen removed a dinner plate from the dishwasher and handed it to her husband. "I don't know what to do, Frank. She doesn't want to go, but I really think she needs to."

"Well, we can't force her." He opened the cabinet and laid the dish onto a stack of its mates.

"Why not? We force her to take her medication, get dressed in the morning, walk the cul-de-sac for exercise, and a million other things. That's all part of caregiving: forcing her to do things she needs to do but won't."

He leaned his back against the counter and crossed his arms. "Really? Caregiving is about forcing?"

"Sometimes, yes." She shut the appliance door more forcefully than necessary and turned to face him.

He arched an eyebrow.

"Don't you give me that look. You don't know what it's like. You go to work every day and I'm left here—"

"That's not fair," Frank objected. "I relieve you when I can, and you know it."

She took a deep breath. "I know. I'm sorry."

"Besides, it wasn't my idea to move down here," he muttered.

Karen's eyes blazed. "Wait just a minute! Now *you're* not being fair. We discussed this at length five years ago. You had every chance to voice your opinion, and you agreed—"

"I know, I know. I'm sorry. My comment was uncalled for. We did the right thing, sweetheart. It's what you do for family." He took his wife's hands into his and kissed her on the cheek. "But are you sure this is one of the things that should be forced?"

She hesitated then nodded. "I think so. Matters like this need closure, don't they? I mean, how can she spend the rest of her life knowing what she knows now and not do anything about it? She'd regret it, and I'd feel guilty for not making her see it through. We don't know how much longer her mother has left to live. According to Madeline, she's already on borrowed time."

"Okay. Do you need me to go along?"

"Can you?"

"I'll check my vacation hours. I ran the balance pretty low last Christmas. Then it took another hit when you got sick in March and needed me home for Mom." He shrugged. "Besides, three airplane tickets on short notice; I'm not sure what our bank account can bear."

"Can you check on prices, please? I'll go talk to Mom again."

"Sure. I'll—"

"No."

They jumped. Karen's mother stood in the doorway, her face set.

"Mother! How long have you been standing there?"

"Long enough."

Karen took a step forward. "We need to talk. This is important."

"No. We will speak no more of it." Her mother turned and disappeared down the hallway.

Karen set off in pursuit, but Frank caught her by the arm. "Karen?"

She spun on him. "What?"

"Have you noticed something?"

"What are you talking about?"

He smiled. "Your mother has communicated more today than she has in the past year."

Karen looked back toward the hallway. "Do you think so?"

"Don't you see it? She even got up off the floor this afternoon with no help. When was the last time she did that? Heck, when was the last time she even sat on the floor?"

"I—I don't know. I was so wrapped up in what's been happening, I guess I didn't think about it." Karen paused then met her husband's gaze. "But you're right. Do you suppose it's the *Times* column?"

"What else could it be?"

"But you can't cure Alzheimer's. It must be a fluke, a temporary lift or something."

He shook his head. "Maybe, but I don't think so. It sure looks to me like some lights are coming on. Why don't you leave her alone for the rest of the evening? Let her digest this a little more. Maybe tomorrow she'll be more receptive to talking about it. We'll see if her awareness continues or if she relapses."

Karen nodded. Frank squeezed her shoulder and left the kitchen. She thought for a moment then reached for the telephone.

"Hello, Nedra? . . . What are you doing for breakfast tomorrow? . . . Good. Plan on waffles at my house. . . . I know you were going to work, but it's Saturday. You can go in a little late, can't you? . . . You need to see something."

# Chapter 38

Frank encouraged Karen and Nedra to sit and visit while he cleared the breakfast table. His mother-in-law insisted on helping. Nedra sat back, sipped her coffee, and watched the older woman brush crumbs from a plate into the trash can.

"You look lovely this morning, Mrs. Romano."

"Thank you, dear."

It was true. The elder woman's hair, normally mussed with stray wisps straggling over her forehead and ears, was brushed smooth and gathered at the nape of her neck, restrained by a green elastic band. A dab of rouge invigorated her normally chalky complexion, and a thin application of liner underscored her blue-gray eyes, now absent their usual glaze. Perhaps the rouge lay a bit heavy and the eyeliner squiggled unevenly, both applied by a hand long out of practice. But they were there.

When Frank excused himself with the morning paper and Karen's mother drifted off to her suite, Nedra crossed her arms. "You could've warned me."

Karen barely suppressed her smile. "Warned you?"

"You know exactly what I'm talking about, girl. She's like a new person."

The smile broke loose. "You noticed something, then?"

Nedra laughed. "Noticed? I'd have to be comatose not to."

Karen set her coffee cup down and leaned her arms on the table. "What do you think? How could this happen? I didn't think Alzheimer's could reverse itself."

"It can't."

"So, how do you explain this?"

"Simple. It isn't Alzheimer's."

"But what about—"

"Karen, Alzheimer's was your diagnosis, not Dr. Feldstein's."

"Well, yes, but I thought, you know, with all the symptoms—"

Nedra leaned forward. "Dementia isn't an easy nut to crack. The only way Alzheimer's can be definitively diagnosed is either by a brain biopsy—imagine how fun *that* is—or an autopsy, even less fun." She paused. "What exactly did Feldstein do during your visit?"

"His office told me before the appointment that they normally do blood work, order a CT scan, and conduct some cognitive, reflex, and coordination testing. Mom refused the lab work and the CT, but I think he sneaked in some diagnostic questions while he was chatting with her."

"And?"

"Like I told you, he didn't give me an indication either way. Our follow-up appointment is on Monday."

Nedra leaned back and grinned. "Oh, I'd love to be a fly on the wall during that one."

"Why?"

"If he gave you no indication, didn't insist on the lab and CT data, but just scheduled a follow-up consultation, I bet he's skeptical that it's Alzheimer's. And now it appears with good reason."

"Really?"

Nedra nodded. "There are two categories of dementia: primary and secondary. Primary dementia covers those types we can do nothing about except try to slow down the decline. Simply put, there's no cure. Alzheimer's claims about 80 to 85 percent of primary dementia cases, the remainder being induced by trauma, such as a stroke."

"What's secondary dementia?"

"Secondary covers a range of maladies that can be treated. For example, depression can bring on symptoms of dementia. But it's reversible. Take away the depression, or the cause of it, and the symptoms disappear, or at least subside."

"Do you think that's the case with Mother?"

Nedra held up her hands. "Whoa, I'm not making a diagnosis here. Don't you dare read one into what I'm saying. All I'm telling you is that what I saw this morning doesn't look to me like Alzheimer's. I'm no doctor, but I've spent a lot of time with Alzheimer's support groups and have done a little research of my own." She winked. "I think Feldstein may have some interesting news for you on Monday, especially if he sees her like she is now."

" 'If'?"

"It's early yet, Karen. The sun has broken through—and brilliantly, I might add—but we can't assume the clouds have rolled away completely. She may relapse, she may not."

Karen thought for a moment. "One thing I don't understand, though. If this is depression related, it doesn't seem the newspaper column would relieve the depression, just the opposite. Mother had a negative reaction to it. She doesn't want to go to Michigan and see her birth mother."

Nedra shrugged. "On the surface, yes. But she probably has a million competing emotions pinging around inside her head: bewilderment, disappointment, excitement, anger. I sure would." She paused. "Even though she says she doesn't want to see her mom, something got her up early this morning. And fixed her hair and her face."

Karen couldn't subdue her smile."I'm so excited, but I'm nervous, too. Should I keep up her medications?"

"Absolutely. Don't change a thing unless Dr. Feldstein tells you to."

Karen nodded thoughtfully. "Maybe she won't be as difficult to get onto an airplane as I thought."

"Maybe not." Nedra smiled and took another sip of her coffee.

⌘

"You want to fly next Tuesday, then?" Frank asked.

"If possible, yes. It's the day after Mother's appointment with Dr. Feldstein, so maybe I'll have a better idea of how to handle her." Karen shook her head. "Boy, do I have a bunch of questions for him!"

"I bet. I'll make the airline reservations now, but you know they're pricier unless you make them at least a couple of weeks in advance."

"I know, but I don't want to delay. We're so close, and if something happens to her mom before we see her, it would kill me. And who knows what it might do to her condition? She could nosedive again."

"Okay. I'm afraid you're on your own, though. I don't have enough vacation time, and it's busy at work anyway. I don't think the boss would let me go except for an emergency."

Karen nodded and rose from the couch. "I guess I'll try talking to Mother again."

"I'll get online and let you know how much damage this is going to do to our budget."

"Whatever it is, it'll be worth it."

He smiled. "Yeah."

Karen strolled down the hallway, her steps slowing as she reached the mother-in-law suite. She took a deep breath then stepped into the sitting room.

Her mother perched on the edge of the love seat, her back straight, squinting though a tiny pair of reading glasses at one of the documents. The wooden chest lay on the end table, its lid propped open. The room seemed dim, despite the sunny day outside the scrim-covered window. Karen reached for the switch of the reading lamp beside the love seat and twisted it. Her mother jumped at the sudden flood of light onto the yellowed page.

"Is this better?" Karen asked.

Her mother glanced up then resumed her attention to the document.

Karen settled onto the seat beside her. "What are you reading?"

No reply.

Nedra's caution about a possible relapse pricked her mind. "Mother?"

"Hush a moment, dear."

Karen released an inward sigh, despite the rebuke. She studied her mother's face while the older woman read. Finally, her mother set the paper aside. Her gaze wandered to a diary lying on the table.

"I wonder. . ."

"What, Mother?"

"I wonder if she still hates me."

"You wonder if who hates you?"

"Lilli-Anna."

# Chapter 39

Madeline rummaged through the bottom desk drawer. "Brendon, where's the AC cord for my laptop?"

His voice floated into the study from the kitchen. "I have no idea. I never use it. Why do you need it now? We leave for the park in a half hour."

"I know. I want to charge the battery before we go."

His head poked around the door frame. "Why?"

"I thought I'd take it along and get a little work done—"

"Madeline!"

She fumbled the computer and barely rescued it from falling to the floor. "What?"

"You're not serious."

"What do you mean?"

"It's the kids' birthday party. You're not taking the laptop."

"Why not? They'll spend most of the time with their friends on the Playscape. I'll be able to watch and still write a little."

He leaned through the doorway. "No."

She straightened and met his glare. "What do you mean, 'no'?"

" 'No' means only one thing. You aren't taking the stupid computer. Susan will be there with Alisha. You can relax and visit with a friend for a change. Besides, you've already found Kammbrie."

"Yes, but there's still Lilli-Anna. Who knows whether she'll—"

"Madeline, you can take it to the church committee meeting afterward if you have to, but for heaven's sake, it's the girls' birthday party. C'mon."

She set the laptop on the desk. "Okay. If that's the way you feel about it."

"It is. You're missing your daughters' childhood."

"Don't exaggerate. I'm just as much engaged—"

"Daddy?" Maria's soft voice preceded her through the doorway.

"What is it, sweetie?"

"Can you fix my shirt? I got the buttons all wrong."

"Sure, honey. Go into the kitchen. I'll be right there."

"I can help, Maria." Madeline rounded the desk.

"That's okay, Mommy. Daddy knows how to do it." She ambled off toward the kitchen.

Madeline's cheeks warmed. Brendon tipped his head to the side.

"Go ahead." She crossed her arms. "Say it."

"Nothing to say." He turned and followed Maria into the kitchen.

❧

"So, how was the birthday party?" Sherry Johnson laid her Bible and committee folder on the library table.

"It was great. The girls were exhausted by the time we got home. I asked our babysitter to watch them so Bren and I could come to the meeting."

Sylvia Weller set her folder and coffee cup down. She peered at Oskar, asleep in his infant seat beside his mother's chair. "Your kids are gorgeous, Madeline. But then, you already know that, don't you?" She winked.

"Of course." Madeline smiled.

"Good thing they take after their dad."

"Hey!"

Sylvia laughed. "I'm kidding!"

Sherry winked. "Oh, I don't know. Bren's a hunk."

"Watch it." Madeline shot her friend a dark look, but the twinkle remained in her eye.

Sylvia smiled. "Well, it's true. You're a lucky girl."

"Looks like someone else thinks so, too." Sherry elbowed Sylvia and nodded past Madeline's shoulder.

Madeline swiveled to see Brendon holding the library door open for Sally Morgan. She laughed and flipped her shimmering ash-blond hair onto tanned shoulders covered only by the spaghetti straps of a wispy floral sundress. Her sky-blue eyes held Brendon in a teasing gaze. She whispered something through full pink-glossed lips into Brendon's smiling red-tinged face.

Madeline's eyes narrowed. *So, what's up with the blushing?*

"Not her again," Sylvia muttered.

Madeline turned back toward the table, hoping her forehead didn't look as hot as it felt. "What do you mean?"

Sherry fingered the corner of her file folder and lowered her voice. "I wouldn't trust that woman as far as I could throw her."

"C'mon, guys. Let's be fair." Madeline opened her own folder. "She's still pretty new to the church. We just don't know her."

"Are you kidding? She all but has *I'm Available* tattooed on her forehead—and she doesn't care who reads it."

Madeline's throat tightened. "Let's not gossip."

Sylvia smirked. "It isn't gossip if it's true."

"Yes, it is." Madeline slapped the folder closed.

"Okay, okay, if you're fine with it, so am I." Sherry shrugged. "He's *your* husband."

"Yeah. Sorry." Sylvia picked up her coffee cup.

Straightening, Madeline threw another furtive look just as Sally twittered another laugh and touched Brendon's sleeve. Madeline gritted her teeth.

Sally turned her head, and she and Madeline locked gazes. Sally's smile faded, but she regained her composure in a flash and hailed someone across the room a little too loudly. She glided across the carpet to a far seat, a stiff smile glued to her lips.

Brendon approached the girls' table. "Hi, Sylvia."

Sylvia sipped her coffee, her gaze fixed through the window.

He hesitated. "Hi, Sherry."

Sherry studied her meeting agenda, her chin propped on the palm of one hand and the fingertips of the other lightly tapping the tabletop.

He frowned. "Madeline?"

Strike three.

He shrugged and dropped into his chair.

∞

"So, what's eating you?" Brendon steered the VW onto Janes Avenue.

"What do you mean?"

"You know what I'm talking about. If I'd sat at that table much longer, I'd be nursing third-degree frostbite."

Madeline sniffed and kept her gaze on the road ahead. "If you'd sat at Sally Morgan's table, you'd be nursing third-degree burns."

"What?"

"You know what I mean. What was that little tête-à-tête you two had going on before the committee meeting?"

"I still don't know what you're talking about."

Madeline winced as the car rattled over the railroad crossing. "Slow down. You're going to wake up Oskar."

"Sally Morgan came out of the ladies' room as I was passing in the hallway. She said hi. What was I supposed to do, ignore her?"

"Would've been fine with me."

"Be serious, Madeline. We walked down the hall. I opened the door for her. End of story."

She turned toward him. "I saw the sultry expression, how she touched your arm—and how she froze when she saw me watching. Oh, and the silly grin on your face didn't escape me, either."

"I wasn't grinning. Besides," he muttered, "at least someone was giving me a little attention."

"I beg your pardon!"

"I don't know what you're worried about." Brendon slowed for the turn onto 23rd Street. "I'm hardly a chick magnet."

"Oh, puh-leeze—"

He jerked his head toward her. "Please, what? You really think someone like Sally Morgan is going to be interested in a gimp like me?"

"A what? A *gimp*?"

"You heard me."

"Oh, for Pete's sake. And what do you mean by 'someone like Sally Morgan'?"

"She can have anyone—"

"Brendon, watch out!"

He hit the brakes. Tires squealed as he yanked the wheel to the left to avoid a car backing out of a driveway. Oskar whimpered.

"Oh, great!" Madeline rolled her eyes.

Brendon set his jaw and accelerated.

"Please slow down, Bren."

"I want to get home."

"Dead or alive?"

"I'm beginning not to care." He veered into their subdivision, and Oskar's fussing graduated to a healthy cry.

Madeline reached back and patted her son's shoulder then glared at her husband. "I don't know what's gotten into you lately."

Brendon pulled the car into their driveway. "Maybe if you were around enough to. . .oh, never mind." He punched his seat-belt release, shouldered open his door, and stalked up the sidewalk to the front door.

"Brendon!"

⁂

Brendon and Madeline tucked the twins in after reading their devotions and singing a couple of Sunday school ditties, tunes from Madeline's childhood she'd carried forward as a bedtime tradition.

> *"Thank you, Lord, for saving my soul;*
> *Thank you, Lord, for making me whole;*
> *Thank you, Lord, for giving to me*
> *Thy great salvation so rich and free."*

She glanced at her husband when he faltered on the second line of the stanza.

The girls reached for their hugs and kisses then grinned in anticipation of their tradition with their daddy. "A zerbert, Daddy! A zerbert!"

Madeline smiled as each girl giggled and squirmed in turn when Brendon wiggled his nose deep into their scrunched necks and blew raspberries against their tender skin. She huffed. "How do you expect them to settle down to sleep when you get them all keyed up right before we turn out the lights?"

He shrugged. "They'd disown me if they didn't get their bedtime zerberts."

Madeline switched off Maria's lamp, and Brendon did the same to Katia's.

"G'night, girls."

Madeline groped in the darkness for Brendon's hand, but he had already moved toward the door. She paused to study his brawny frame filling the doorway, appreciating with her eyes his broad shoulders and slim torso silhouetted against the ambient light of the hallway. He turned his head to the side, and her heart tightened at the rugged contours of his face: strong nose, alluring blue eyes, and oh-so-kissable lips crowning a perfectly dimpled chin. He scratched above his ear, the movement knotting a muscle at the base of his neck. Her gaze permitted itself a visceral journey along his sloping shoulder to a bulging bicep, its precise definition affirming the weight-lifting routine that had replaced his pre-accident power-walking regimen.

She shivered, as a surge of longing, almost debilitating in its passion, traveled up the entire length of her body, leaving a tingle in its wake.

Sherry Johnson was right. Brendon Sommers—Madeline's husband, the father of her children—was a hunk. Her friend's voice echoed in Madeline's mind, whisking her back to the church that afternoon. She began to smile, but the library door opened in her mind's eye, and the vixen Sally Morgan slithered into view, leading Brendon by an invisible nose ring. The silly smile on her husband's face killed the tingle in an instant.

Madeline stepped into the hallway as Brendon rounded the banister and headed downstairs. She sniffed, turned left, and went into the bedroom to prepare for another restless night.

# Chapter 40

Bren, I'm taking Oskar to the nursery. If you don't mind getting the girls settled, I'll be right back."

"Sure. Better hurry, though. The choir is starting to file in." He helped Katia and Maria onto the pew and opened their activity packs. Katia set to work cheerfully defacing her Bible-story coloring sheet with a green crayon, while Maria squinted at the Memory Verse of the Week. She pretended to read the short passage, her lips moving silently, a serious expression on her face. He smiled, opened his bulletin, and began to scan the order of worship when a light touch on his shoulder startled him. He turned his head. Sally Morgan's pearly whites nearly blinded him.

"Hi, Brendon," she whispered, her lips inches from his ear.

"Hey, Sally."

Her hand lingered. "Umm, do you know anything about cars?"

Brendon shifted under her touch. "Some."

"I think my engine is making funny noises, but I have no idea what it is."

"What kind of funny noises?"

"It's hard to describe. Do you think you might be able to take a look at it. . .sometime?"

He shrugged. "I suppose. Why don't you ask Phil Johnson, though? He's a mechanic."

She pouted. "I don't think his wife likes me."

"Sherry? Why not?"

"Who knows?" The sweet smile returned. "Whatever is making the noise, I'm sure you can fix it."

"Well, I suppose—"

A thump against the pew turned his head. Madeline slouched on the other side of the twins, her taut face fixed forward. Sally's fingers slipped from his shoulder, but not before giving it a light squeeze.

His shoulders drooped when his wife pivoted angry eyes toward him.

*"What?"* he mouthed.

❧

Brendon glanced sideways at Madeline as they pulled out of the church parking lot. Her arms were crossed over the purse on her lap.

"Mommy, are you mad at Daddy again?"

Madeline stiffened and turned her head toward the backseat. "Maria! Why would you ask a thing like that?"

" 'Cuz you look mad."

She glanced at Brendon. He kept his eyes on the road.

"I'm not mad, sweetie. Just tired."

"Okay." Maria returned her attention to her doll.

Brendon cleared his throat. "Tired?"

She sniffed. "Yes. Tired of wondering what's going on."

"Nothing's going on."

Madeline snorted. "If Sally Morgan's face had been any closer, she'd have inhaled your ear."

"She just asked if I knew anything about cars. Her engine is making an odd noise."

"You should've told her to turn up her radio if she doesn't like the sound of her engine. She'd probably wonder why she hadn't thought of that herself."

"C'mon, Madeline."

She turned in her seat. "C'mon, nothing! What am I supposed to think? Every time I turn around, she's flirting with you."

"Stop turning around; then maybe she won't. . ." Her expression sent his joke into a tailspin. He sighed. "I'm telling you, nothing's going on. She asked about her car. I tried to refer her to Phil Johnson, but she said Sherry doesn't like her."

"I can't imagine why."

He rolled his eyes. "She's a single woman, so every married woman distrusts her. How fair is that?"

"It's not that she's single, Bren. She's got that look, and she apparently doesn't care who she uses it on."

"What look?"

"The 'oh-am-I-ever-available' look."

"Really? I hadn't noticed."

"Then you might want to check yourself for a pulse."

Brendon slowed the car and pulled to the curb. He set the parking brake then turned and met his wife's puzzled expression. Pulling her hands into his lap, he locked gazes with her. "Listen to me, Mrs. Sommers—"

"*Ms.* Sommers."

"—*Mrs.* Sommers, and don't interrupt. You are an extraordinarily beautiful, highly intelligent, and exceptionally perceptive woman."

Her eyes rounded then softened. "Well, okay. Mrs. Sommers will do for now."

"You're interrupting again."

A smile tugged at the corners of her mouth. "Sorry. Please continue. You've started out so well."

"Yet, with all that intelligence and perceptiveness—"

"Don't forget beauty." Her eyes danced.

"Madeline!"

"Oops."

He leaned forward. "I don't think you have a clue how deeply I love you, how devoted I am to our family, and how committed I am to our marriage."

Madeline sobered and dropped her gaze to her lap.

Brendon waited. *It's your turn. Please say you love me, too, that I'm more important than a newspaper column.*

She remained silent, her head bent.

He held his breath. *Can't you, or won't you?*

"I—I didn't expect that," she murmured.

His chest deflated.

Oskar whimpered, and Madeline turned her head. Brendon released her hands and slumped against the back of the driver's seat. With a sigh, he pulled the brake release and veered into traffic. "We'd better get home."

⚬⚬⚬

"What are you doing? It's after midnight." Brendon loomed in the doorway of the study, his pajama top hanging loose at his waist.

Madeline sat behind the desk, the violated pencil back between her teeth, and the laptop's monitor casting a pallor over her worried face. She let the pencil drop to her lap again but didn't stop typing. "Oh, I'm so stupid! In all the excitement over finding Aunt Kammbrie, I forgot about my deadline. My next column is due first thing in the morning."

"You've been working on it this week, though, haven't you?"

"Yes, but I had to edit it. I added a new ending, and I need to trim the narrative to get back under my maximum word count."

"What ending?"

She sat back and released a weary exhale. "I wanted to update my readers that we found Aunt Kammbrie." She smiled. "I still can't get over it. I remember when Tante Katia first told me the twins' story, and how determined I was to follow up. Boy, I'm glad I did!"

"It is cool. You should be proud."

"Let me read the ending to you. Tell me what you think." She bent back toward the laptop. "Okay, let me find it. . .blah, blah, blah—here it is."

*"My sincerest thanks to all of you who have responded to the recent column on the lost twins Lilli-Anna and Kammbrie—"*

"Well, don't thank all the ones who responded. I seem to recall several who—"

"Don't interrupt." Madeline narrowed her eyes at him, but her smile lingered.

"Sorry."

*"—with tips. You will be delighted to know that in two days, my dear Aunt Kammbrie will be flying to Saginaw to reunite with long-lost family. Yes, we found her! After nearly a lifetime, a 'mother-and-child reunion is only a motion away,' to quote a great Paul Simon song. Now, we just need Lilli-Anna, and everything will be perfect. Don't give up hope!*

*Lilli-Anna, we miss you and love you. Please come home."*

Madeline looked up. Brendon nodded. "Yeah, it's good."

"Thanks." She clicked the SEND button and shut down the computer.

"Do you believe Lilli-Anna is still. . .I mean, you know." He hesitated, searching for the right words. "It's been an awfully long time."

The computer's backlight went out, and her hushed voice probed the darkness.

"I believe now more than ever. . . . I have to."

# Chapter 41

And just what are you smiling at, young man?" Karen's mother frowned at Dr. Feldstein.

He propped his hands on his knees, leaned forward in his swivel chair, and leveled his bright eyes at her. "You, my dear lady, are the reason I come to work in the morning."

"Hmph!" She looked down and shifted in her seat.

"You're also my reason for getting up in the morning, Mother."

The older woman looked up at her, but Karen only smiled.

She turned to the doctor. "Did you get my e-mail? I know I barraged you with questions. I hope that was okay."

He leaned back. "I did, and it was more than okay. It made my day."

"So, where do we go from here?"

"Out for a celebratory meal, if I were you."

"I meant—"

"I know what you meant, Mrs. Donovan. I'm just sharing your joy for a moment. Please forgive my levity."

She smiled. "Help yourself, nothing to forgive."

He returned his attention to his patient. "We won't change any of your medications yet, Mrs. Romano, but I'd like to order a blood test, since you haven't had one in a while."

She shrugged.

"I'll take that as an 'okay,'" he chuckled.

Karen leaned forward. "Is this. . . Do you see this often?"

"Not often enough. I didn't feel comfortable with a definitive conclusion at our last visit—due to its brevity." He cast a teasing glance toward his patient then readdressed Karen. "And truthfully, we still aren't sure of the cause of the condition—or its sudden regression."

"We're flying to Michigan tomorrow to sort that out." She smiled at his puzzled expression. "I'll explain later."

He turned back to Karen's mother. "Speaking of later, Mrs. Romano, I would very much love to chat with you in a week or two regarding your impressions, how you feel, what you're thinking—if you're willing, of course."

Karen's mother nodded.

"Thank you." He readdressed Karen. "The blood test results should be back by Thursday afternoon. I'll leave instructions with the nurse to mail you a copy of the report."

Dr. Feldstein rose, extending a hand to help his patient up from her chair, but she sniffed and pushed to her feet unassisted. He smiled. "The receptionist will give you a form for the blood work. The lab is just down the hall."

Halfway down the hall to the front desk, Karen's mother excused herself and stepped into a restroom.

The doctor touched Karen's arm. "Mrs. Donovan? Take care on your trip; try to keep things calm. Your mother looks quite good, but we aren't necessarily out of the woods yet."

⟨≈⟩

Karen jolted at a roll of thunder that shook the wall of the dining nook. She folded her newspaper and set it on the dining table then rose from her chair and peered between the curtains. Billowing dark clouds loomed over the roof of the house next door. A plastic lid perched on top of the neighbor's overfilled trash can flipped off in a gust of wind and wobbled along its rim across the yard into a hedge of nandina.

A flash of lightning to the northwest backlit a poplar tree across the street, followed by a rush of wind that bent the treetop. Its thin branches flailed the air, and several battered leaves released their grip and skittered across the flapping shingles of an adjacent two-story house. Five seconds later, a clap of thunder rattled the glass against her fingertips.

She grimaced when the lamp over the table flickered, revived, then died. The air issuing from the vent above her head stilled, and the refrigerator's compressor sighed into silence. She groaned inwardly at the memory of their last power failure, a blackout that eluded the utility company's best efforts for two days. How much freezer food would go to waste this time?

The thought of her mother sitting alone in her suite ushered Karen down the hallway. Dr. Feldstein's caution to keep things calm hurried her steps, as her mother did not take well to thunderstorms.

The sitting room cowered from the storm in semidarkness, startling as flashes of lightning pierced its window blinds. By habit, Karen flicked up the light switch. She rolled her eyes at her own silliness when the ceiling light ignored her. "Mother?"

The room lay empty, save an opened suitcase on the love seat, half filled and waiting for the now-stilled dryer to finish with the remainder of her travel ensemble. Karen shook her head at yet another inconvenience thrust upon her routine by a wimpy electrical substation. But then the sobering notion that 80 percent of the world's population would probably kill to have problems like these defused her frustration. "Mother, where are you?"

"Here." The thin voice wafted through the open doorway of the bedroom, sliced off by an explosion of thunder. Karen winced. *That sounded close.*

She skirted the sofa and stepped into the bedroom. Her mother stood at the foot of her bed. Karen's breath caught short at the return of her mother's blank expression. "Are you okay?"

Her mother lifted her head. "Of course."

Karen exhaled. "Why don't you come out into the living room? It's lighter in there, and I can make us some hot tea."

"We have an electric range, dear."

"I know, but. . .oh." Karen sighed. *Who has the memory problem?* "I'll light some candles."

Karen led her mother carefully through the twilight house, settled her on the couch, then retrieved what candles she could find from the pantry. After arranging an assortment of tapers and votives on the coffee table, she touched the flame of a stick match to each. She eased herself onto the sofa beside her mother, the room awash in a peaceful glow and a pleasant blend of vanilla and cinnamon. She smiled in spite of the storm then shifted on the cushion.

"Mother, I've been wanting to ask you about the heritage chest."

"The what? Oh, yes." She cast a quick look at the wooden box in the shadowed corner of the room.

"When was the last time you opened it?" Karen asked.

"I've never opened it."

"Never? Aren't those your diaries?"

"No. They're my sister's."

Karen perked. Whenever the subject of Lilli-Anna came up, her mother either changed it or simply ignored it. "Lilli-Anna's?"

No reply.

She traced the older woman's gaze, fixed on a tall mauve taper left over from a Lenten centerpiece. Its steady flame pointed heavenward, unwavering in the stillness, but for a subtle shimmer near its tip. It brightened as the dusk in the room deepened and the first few heavy raindrops hammered muffled pops on the roof.

"May I ask why you never opened it?"

Silence.

As Karen took hold of her mother's hand, it jerked at another flash of lightning. They both jumped at an immediate ear-splitting crash of thunder, and Karen shot a worried look through the rain-spattered glass, wondering if the neighborhood had just lost a tree, or worse. The wind raged and peppered the side of the house with liquid bullets. The tapping sharpened, suggesting hail mixed with the rain. She glanced back at her mother, who hadn't removed her gaze from the candle, seemingly mesmerized by the steady flame.

The candlelight elongated the shadows across the matron's face, sharpening her features to the point of caricature. It seemed not just to illuminate her face, but also to individualize her essence, give form to the individual threads of her persona, separate yet inextricably interwoven, as the elements of the storm. Gracefulness in the gently upturned Germanic nose, firmness in the slanting arc of her Slavic cheekbones, certainly legacies from her recently disclosed heritage. But most of all, intelligence in the crystalline depth of her aquamarine eyes, intelligence so long denied expression by the unexplained malady from which she seemed to be emerging.

Her demeanor betrayed no concern at nature's tantrum but rivaled the serenity of the gentle candlelight gracing the subdued room. A slight sigh escaped her mother's lips.

"Mother?"

"Yes, dear."

"About Lilli-Anna? Why do you have her diaries? Why haven't you ever opened the memory chest?"

"I promised myself I wouldn't until she came home."

"Why did she leave?"

"Because of me."

"You?"

"Your father and me."

Karen shook her head. "I don't understand."

"It's—"

The overhead light flickered on, devouring the peaceful aura of golden candlelight in its sterile incandescent glare. The gentle shadows defining her mother's features evaporated, leaving her face naked, its careworn pallor again evident, even pronounced. The air conditioner's baritone hum resumed beneath the sounds of the storm, and a rush of air from a vent directly over the table extinguished the taper's flame then evened.

Her mother's gaze traced the slight wisp of smoke from the vanquished wick. She shuddered and said nothing more.

# Chapter 42

Madeline draped the cloth diaper over her shoulder and snuggled Oskar against it. She glanced at the clock as she punched her parents' phone number into the cordless. Wedging the telephone into the crook of her neck, she patted her son's back and paced the study.

"Hi, Mom. Hope I didn't catch you at a bad time. . . . You and Dad are still coming over for dinner, right? . . . Good. I'm picking Karen Donovan and Aunt Kammbrie up at the airport at three fifteen. We'll eat around five thirty. . . . I know, I can't wait, either—what? . . . Oh, sorry. That was Oskar. I'm burping him, and he got a bit enthusiastic with that last one. He's all guy, huh? . . . No, I haven't told Grandma yet. I'd like to keep it a secret. I hope Grandpa managed to hide this week's *Times* column or the surprise will be spoiled. . . . Okay, I'll let you go. Just wanted to make sure we're still on for dinner. Kisses to Dad and see you guys this evening. . . . Bye."

She set the phone down, settled Oskar into his infant swing, and gave her surroundings a critical appraisal. Of all the rooms in the house, this one seemed least able to keep itself in order. Bills, receipts, and other sundry paperwork carpeted the desk, with multicolored sticky notes strewn across them like oversized confetti. Brendon's blazer lay over the love seat's armrest, his Bible with a Sunday bulletin protruding from beneath the front cover on the end table next to it. Two days' worth of sports sections and a half-finished crossword puzzle littered the cushion.

She sighed. Hadn't she just straightened this place up?

Madeline shuffled the paperwork into a neat pile at the corner of the desk and centered her laptop on the blotter. Reaching over to the couch, she tugged the order of worship from beneath the cover of the Bible and sent it twirling toward the wastebasket. A square of pastel pink paper fluttered to the floor when the tri-fold hit the rim. She bent to pick it up then drew up short.

Sally Morgan's name and phone number were printed on it.

A wave of heat shot to her forehead, and she began to crush the paper in her fist then stopped. Tightening her jaw, Madeline retrieved the bulletin from the trash can, replaced the note, and tucked them back into the Bible. She spun on her heel and stalked from the room.

Brendon had some explaining to do.

◈

*Ding!* "Ladies and gentlemen, this is the captain speaking. According to the altimeter, we've reached our cruising altitude of 28,000 feet, but I, for one, refuse to look down. It's a balmy minus 20 degrees Fahrenheit outside your window, and we're zipping along like a bat out of. . . well, we're making pretty good time. Anyway, I'm turning off the FASTEN SEATBELT sign, but don't take it seriously if you remain seated. If you do need to get up, unbuckle first, then please limit your activities to the inside of the aircraft. The FAA and your fellow passengers will be most appreciative."

Karen rolled her eyes as a wave of chuckling rose above the engine noise. Another comic who missed his calling. Her mother sat beside her, staring through delicate crystals of frost Mother Nature was busily tatting on the outer pane of her window. Her gaze appeared locked onto the layer of cumulus batting far below that stretched to the azure horizon like a puffy down comforter. Karen traced her stare, surrendering to an impulse that arose when-ever she flew above the clouds. She imagined herself with arms outstretched, soaring grace-fully through the air then bouncing on the fluffy mounds—despite the pilot's exhortation to remain inside the aircraft. She glanced again to the seat beside her, a slight smile tipping up her mouth. Did her even-tempered mother ever take similar flights of fancy?

She leaned forward and peered into the older woman's face. "Are you comfortable, Mother?"

"Yes, thank you."

"What are you thinking?—No, wait. Let me guess," Karen said with a teasing lilt. "You imagine frolicking on the soft clouds."

Her mother sniffed. "Don't be silly, dear."

Karen's shoulders sagged. So much for flights of fancy. "Then what are you thinking?"

"I was thinking. . .there should be mountains."

"Mountains?"

Her voice dropped to a near whisper. "Yes. I'm not certain why."

Karen studied her mother's pensive expression. "Are you nervous about. . .meeting your mother?"

The older woman shifted in her seat.

Karen laid a hand on her mother's arm. "You'll be glad we came. I promise."

Her mother's jaw twitched.

⊷∾

Madeline grumbled at the Arrivals board.

*Flight UA5354—Delayed.*

The new arrival time was exactly fifteen minutes after the original, which meant the airline had no idea when the plane would actually get there, so they were hedging a quarter-hour at a time.

She plopped onto a plastic seat in the baggage claim area, hunched over the purse on her lap, and stared at the floor. Plans B, C, and D gelled in her mind, each assigned to successively later arrival times. Brendon had arranged a few personal hours home from work this afternoon, so childcare was covered. He had promised under threat of violence to keep at least the downstairs neat, but if the plane was delayed very long, there was no telling what the place would look like when she and her guests arrived home. She shook away the worrisome image of her newly found aunt stumbling over building blocks scattered across the foyer the moment she walked in the door.

The sticky aroma of a hot cinnamon bun under vigorous attack by a robust lady two seats away switched Madeline's mental calculator into culinary mode. The lasagne would come out of the oven at five fifteen when the garlic bread would go in; croutons on the salad at the last minute; ice water to pour—oh! Did she remember to buy another bag of ice? An inward sigh; too late to worry about it now. The Chianti had already waited three years to be uncorked, so it shouldn't complain about another hour or two.

She blew a maverick curl from her forehead and glanced up at the clock over the Avis rental car counter. Three twenty-four. *Please, oh please. . .* The auburn ringlet rappelled back down her brow. She pushed it back with an impatient flick of her hand. It gleefully dropped again, just getting into the game.

To diffuse her annoyance, Madeline sat back and immersed herself in a favorite pastime: people-watching. Airports served as the best arena for the sport, providing a perfect backdrop for the entire gamut of human emotion, from screamingly blissful reunions to heartrending tearful partings.

She focused on a group of people waving little American flags and bobbing signs that read WELCOME HOME, TROOPS! at the exit from the concourse. A pretty young woman with a yellow ribbon affixed to her collar and a little boy squirming in her arms stood off to the side, her face drawn. The well-wishers exploded into cheers as the first of the desert-camouflaged soldiers sauntered into view. The lone woman shifted her stance and craned her neck to see past them. Five servicemen and two servicewomen stepped off the ramp into a joyful melee, backs slapped, necks hugged, children lifted over heads of parents absent too long. After a few minutes, the crowd loosened and gravitated toward the baggage carousels, leaving the woman to fidget alone. She shifted her son to the other hip and whispered something into his ear but didn't remove her gaze from the concourse. Even from 25 feet away, Madeline could see her chin quiver.

Unaccountably, Madeline's throat tightened. She entertained a notion to approach the woman, to offer whatever comfort she could, although she had no idea what to say. An airline crewmember exited the concourse and paused when the young woman addressed him. He shrugged and pointed behind himself. With a sympathetic nod, he continued on his way out the automatic doors of the terminal.

Madeline rose and took a couple tentative steps when the woman stiffened and covered her mouth with her hand. She turned her son and pointed. Two more uniformed figures approached then stopped in front of her. Tears streaming down her face, she lowered her son into the lap of the soldier in the wheelchair. A sob broke loose then muffled as she bent and buried her face into his neck. They embraced, their shoulders shaking, their son tugging playfully on his daddy's sleeve.

The soldier who had been pushing the wheelchair stepped back, hesitated, then quietly moved off with a pronounced limp toward baggage claim. Madeline made eye contact with him as he passed, briefly, but long enough for her to say, "Thank you."

He nodded.

She returned her attention to the newly reunited couple. An inclination prodded her to go to them, to tell them about Brendon's lost leg, to assure them things would work out, they'd see. But the young family's reunion was too precious, too fragile to disturb, so she turned and shuffled back toward her seat.

The entry on the Arrivals board startled her: *Flight UA5354—Landed.*

The Avis clock read three thirty-seven.

Madeline hurried toward the concourse and smiled at the tear-streaked beaming face of the lovely young wife wheeling her husband and son toward the baggage carousels. Halting at the spot where the woman had taken up her vigil, it suddenly occurred to her that she didn't know what Karen Donovan or Aunt Kammbrie looked like. She berated herself for not penning a sign with their names on it, one like the corporate limo driver standing to her left held. The next moment, though, quelled her fears.

A brown-haired woman holding the arm of a petite silver-haired lady stepped from the concourse, staying to the side of the mainstream traffic. Madeline and the younger woman met gazes, and the woman smiled. She smiled back then turned her attention to the older woman.

*Kammbrie Szpilmann, the lost twin!* She swallowed through a suddenly thick throat and blinked against the pressure behind her eyes.

"Madeline?" Karen asked as she and her mother approached.

Madeline nodded, her smile so broad it hurt. "Karen?"

Karen returned a more subdued smile. Madeline turned her gaze to her aunt's face and gasped. The only other time in her life she'd been so entranced at the color and clarity of a person's eyes was at her first encounter with Tante Katia in Berlin over six years ago. The German matron's eyes had reminded Madeline so much of the enigmatic crystalline hue of Alexandrite, and the comparison returned now with a vengeance.

Madeline covered her mouth and stared into her Aunt Kammbrie's face. She could add this moment to the very few times in her life she'd been struck speechless.

The woman's voice broke her stupor. "Why do you stare, young lady?"

Madeline reddened. "Tante—Aunt. . .Kammbrie?"

Aunt Kammbrie merely cocked her head.

Discomfited, Madeline's eyes flicked toward Karen. "I am. . .so pleased to meet you. . . both."

Karen patted her mother's arm. "Madeline wrote the article, Mother."

The older woman studied Madeline's face then stepped forward, Karen still at her side. She lifted a hand, touched Madeline's cheek, and searched her eyes. Her fingertips traced Madeline's jaw then drew back. "You have found my mother."

"Yes, ma'am."

"You are my. . .niece."

"Yes."

The crystalline chips softened; a gentle smile wavered at the corners of pale lips. Aunt Kammbrie leaned onto her tiptoes and placed a tender kiss on Madeline's cheek. Madeline's vision blurred, and her chest squeezed her heart. The older woman settled back, steadied by her daughter. "Young lady—"

Karen leaned toward her mother's ear. "Madeline, Mother."

"I know that." She cast a sideways frown at her daughter.

Madeline and Karen half stifled their laughs.

"Shall we go, please? I'm a bit tired."

Madeline took her aunt's other arm and led her guests to baggage claim.

# Chapter 43

Madeline cleared the last of the dessert dishes and coffee cups to the sink, reflecting over the evening. Dinner couldn't have gone better, but for one awkward moment. When her parents arrived, Ian McAllister hugged his half-sister and shared a quiet word of welcome. He'd barely told her how pleased he was to finally meet her when his wife engulfed Aunt Kammbrie in a bear hug, gushing with excitement at having a sister-in-law. She grasped Kammbrie's hand and led her to the sofa, barely releasing it long enough even at dinner for the poor woman to eat her lasagne. Ian shook his head and smiled then picked up the slack in conversation with Karen. Alone time with his half-sister could come later.

Brendon had done a marvelous job of keeping the house neat, watching over dinner—which would surely have been ruined by Madeline's distraction at all the excitement—and monitoring the twins' manners. She flashed him a smile of thanks as he herded the girls off to change into their pajamas after dessert. His partial nod weakened her smile.

Aunt Kammbrie kept her reserve, but her enthusiasm was unmistakable toward Katia and Maria. The instant Madeline introduced them in the foyer, Aunt Kammbrie clasped her hands together and knelt to their eye level. The twins peeked from behind Madeline's back with uncertain half smiles. Their great-aunt cooed and beckoned to them until they ventured out and shyly took her proffered hand. The older woman's eyes moistened as she hugged them, insisting they call her Auntie Kamm. Madeline smiled then paused as she recollected her phone call with Karen. Where was the Alzheimer's in the bright-eyed woman hugging her girls? The question would have to wait.

At dinner, Karen filled them in on life at the Donovan household, details of her family, what she had learned from the contents of Lilli-Anna's memory chest. There was much she couldn't relate, however, as the documents provided only fragmentary glimpses of her mother's life with Rósa Dudek. Aunt Kammbrie then took up the story and slowly filled in what she could recall from her young childhood.

That was when the one awkward moment occurred.

"I remember only a little of our first foster home. It was in Philadelphia with a Jewish family, the Oesterfelds. My sister and I were placed there together. Other refugee children were not so fortunate, and some siblings became separated by many miles. Mr. Oesterfeld wore very thick glasses, I recall. He was a cobbler, his wife a seamstress. They had one other child, a girl named Trina, but she was four years older than Lilli and I, and she would have little to do with us."

"Your first foster home? How many foster families did you have?" asked Madeline.

"I had three; Lilli-Anna, two. We stayed at the Oesterfelds for three years until scarlet fever took Trina's life. Mr. and Mrs. Oesterfeld were devastated. The household became quiet, cold. Mrs. Oesterfeld always had a ready smile, but not after Trina died. I have vague memories of loud arguments behind closed doors. Lilli and I covered our ears, but we could still hear the shouting. I think Mrs. Oesterfeld blamed her husband for Trina's death. I was still quite young. It's just what I remember."

Aunt Kammbrie paused to sip her iced water.

"What happened? Why did you leave?" Avery asked.

"I'm not sure. I only know a social worker came one afternoon and packed us up. We didn't see either Mr. or Mrs. Oesterfeld again; they never said good-bye. Perhaps they felt they could no longer keep us."

"Where did you go from there?"

"We stayed at a small orphanage for a short time, I don't remember exactly how long. Then Lilli was taken to a foster home in New Jersey. I was never so scared in my life as when Lilli and I were separated. Two days later, the social worker came back for me. She drove to a large house in Scranton. . ." Her voice faltered, and her eyes grew distant.

"Mother?" Karen leaned forward.

Aunt Kammbrie cleared her throat. "I was not there for very long. I don't remember much. The man and woman were not Jewish. I don't know what their faith was, if they had one. The wife worked in a war factory. The husband stayed at home. I remember he walked with a limp. He. . ." She went quiet.

Karen reached for her mother's hand.

"He. . . I remember. . ." She dropped her gaze.

"Mother, your hand is freezing."

Aunt Kammbrie stared at the tablecloth. "The man was. . .very affectionate. He looked at me. . .sometimes he. . ." Her cheek twitched, and she reached again for her water glass, her hand trembling.

Madeline paused with a forkful of salad halfway to her mouth. Her stomach cramped, and she returned the fork to her salad bowl. She glanced at her mother, who had also set her fork down, her face taut.

When Aunt Kammbrie resumed, her voice was barely audible. "One day, the wife came home from work, and I was hiding in the hallway closet. I remember not wanting to come out. A social worker came the next day. There was a policeman with her. I thought I was in trouble, but she just took me back to the orphanage."

"You never told me this," Karen whispered, her voice catching.

Aunt Kammbrie fell silent.

"Are you sad, Auntie Kamm?" asked Maria.

Madeline looked sharply at her daughter, a rebuke poised on her tongue, but she bit her lip when her aunt patted the young girl's hand and smiled. "No, dear. But thank you."

She took a deep breath and continued. "The next week the social worker brought the good news that the family who had taken Lilli, the Romanos, agreed to take me, too, so we could be together. They were a close family, devout Catholics."

"The Romanos," Karen repeated with a smile. Madeline looked at Aunt Kammbrie then at Karen, who returned a wink.

Aunt Kammbrie nodded. "Lilli and I stayed there until our eighteenth birthday. They were wonderful to us. Mr. Romano owned a plant that manufactured parts for trucks and automobiles. He had just come back from the war, a lieutenant colonel. Mrs. Romano said he could have gotten a deferment, since his factory supported the war effort, but he wanted to go, said that it was his duty. She cried for two days when he returned unharmed."

"Were you happy there?" asked Madeline.

"Oh, yes," replied her aunt. "They had four children of their own: three daughters and a son. Clara and Rose were younger, Helen our age. Lilli and I got along well with Clara and Rose, but Helen never warmed to us, even over the years. We tried to please her, but she seemed to resent us, although I don't know why."

"Let me guess," Karen broke in. "The son's name was Tony." Her smile widened.

Aunt Kammbrie nodded, a slight blush rising to her cheeks. "He was two years older than Lilli and I. He grew into a fine and handsome young man. I was very taken with him."

Madeline grinned.

"Lilli was also very taken with him."

Karen's smile dimmed. "Mother, is that why. . . ?"

"Yes. Lilli had always been more outgoing than I, but she was very shy in front of Tony. I was not so shy. He didn't know how she felt about him, but I let him know how I felt. When he asked me to his school dance just after we turned sixteen, Lilli was crushed. I tried to

283

console her, to tell her it was only a dance."

"Oh, Mother. . ." Karen squeezed her mother's hand.

Madeline creased her brow. "What?"

"Over the next two years, Tony and I drew closer. Lilli and I became more distant." Aunt Kammbrie's voice softened again. "She took a job at a soda fountain in a local drugstore. It took most of her time after school, time we used to spend together. I confess I barely noticed the distance between us increasing, I was so wrapped up in Tony. Neither did I realize the depth of feelings Lilli had for him until she left."

"Left?"

"When Lilli and I turned eighteen, we no longer fell under the foster program. The summer we graduated from high school, Tony asked me to marry him. I said yes. Early the next morning, Lilli packed her suitcase and left." She lowered her gaze to the table again.

"I haven't heard from her since."

# Chapter 44

After settling their guests into the master bedroom for the night, Brendon and Madeline made up beds on the sofas in the study and the living room. He'd just stretched out, when she poked her face around the corner of the doorway. "Umm, Bren?"

"Yeah."

"I need to check e-mail."

"You're kidding. It's eleven thirty. Today's been a big day, and tomorrow's even bigger."

"I know, but my column came out in this morning's edition of the *Times*, and I'm curious about any responses."

"Madeline—"

"Pretty please?" She stretched her lips into a cartoon grin.

He donned a wicked smile. "It'll cost you."

"Men! Is that all you think of?"

"What else is there?"

"Never mind. I'll take the laptop into the living room."

She strode to the desk, grabbed the computer, and jumped when his fingers tickled the hollow behind her right knee. "Hey! You're going to make me drop this thing."

"Pity."

She stuck her tongue out at him and scurried from the room, sidestepping another outstretched hand.

⁂

*Tap, tap, tap. . .tap, tap.*

Brendon shifted onto his side.

*Tap, tap, tap.*

He cracked open an eyelid to an eerie white glow bathing the wall outside the study door. Yawning, he pulled his left arm from under his pillow and squinted at the luminous dial of his sports watch. 12:55 a.m.

*What on earth. . . ?* He struggled onto an elbow and listened.

The tapping continued.

Still checking e-mail? He shoved the blanket aside and reached for his cane. Rising from the love seat, he hobbled to the door and peered into the living room.

Madeline lay on the couch, her shoulders propped up by a pillow, the computer balanced on her lap. She smiled then giggled.

Brendon set his jaw, limped back to the desk, grabbed the power cord to the wireless network router, and yanked it from the wall socket.

*Tap, tap, tap*—"Hey!"

Brendon went back to bed.

⁂

Madeline broke her blank stare at the floor, blurry-eyed. "What?"

"They're burning."

She peered through glazed eyes at the smoldering pancakes but didn't react until she caught the odor of scorched buckwheat. "Oh, no!" She thrust the spatula under one of the shriveled discs.

285

Brendon looked over her shoulder. "Those could pass quality-control inspection at a West Virginia coal mine, assuming coal mines have such a thing as quality control."

She flipped over another mortally wounded flapjack, and it wobbled on the griddle's surface. "Nuts!"

"We can always play Frisbee with them after breakfast—if we get breakfast."

"Ha ha." She glared at her husband, who turned and filled in the last of the glasses with orange juice.

He glanced at his watch. "Aunt Kammbrie and Karen should be down pretty soon. You want to mix up another batch of batter, or default to cereal?"

She sniffed and flipped the smoking hockey pucks from the griddle into the sink to cool. "There's plenty of batter. And speaking of defaults, something's wrong with our wireless network. It went down last night."

"Yeah, I noticed the problem this morning."

"What was it?"

"Power failure. I fixed it."

"Oh. Thanks."

"Sure."

"Mommy, what's that smell?"

Madeline switched the stove-hood fan onto HIGH. "Never mind, Katia. Did you wash your hands?"

"Yup."

Madeline yawned, applied another coating of nonstick spray onto the carbon-coated griddle, and ladled six more victims from the bowl of batter.

"You want me to take over?" Brendon set down the juice pitcher and nodded at the griddle.

She leveled her eyes at him and jammed a hand on her hip.

He held up his hands. "Just asking. You seem tired. How late did you stay up checking e-mail last night?"

"Not long."

"Anything interesting?"

"Not really. Some more responses to the column, the usual spam."

He searched her face then asked, "That's it?"

"Yeah. The network went down, remember?"

"Sure, but you can still read downloaded e-mail without the network."

"I know." She turned and began chucking dead pancakes from the sink into the trash can.

He studied her. "I heard you typing. Thought maybe you got something promising."

She pulled out the sprayer and rinsed charcoal dust down the drain. "I got a head start on next week's column."

"I see." His tone didn't support his words.

She pivoted around and eyed him. "Why all the questions?"

He shrugged. "No reason. Just wondered. You seem tired this morning. Thought maybe you stayed up late."

She stifled another yawn. "I'm fine."

"You also seem a bit distracted."

"Why do you say that?"

"Because they're burning again."

"What?—Oh, nuts!"

⧈

"Thank you, Madeline. Breakfast was delicious," Karen said as she set down her cereal spoon.

Madeline ignored Brendon's surreptitious grin. "Thanks. I meant to have pancakes, but

I didn't realize we were so short on batter mix." She glared at her husband when he snorted.

"So, today's the big day." Madeline smiled at Aunt Kammbrie, who sipped her coffee. "Are you excited?"

The older woman remained silent, her gaze fixed on the tablecloth. Karen smiled apologetically. "She's had some mixed emotions after discovering about her birth mother."

"I understand. I suppose I would, too. I told Grandpa everything so he could prepare for our visit, but we haven't said anything to Grandma. I wanted it to be a surprise." Madeline paused. "I only hope it's not too big of a shock. Her health is fragile, and—oh, excuse me. That's my cell phone."

Madeline hurried into the study, dabbing her mouth with her napkin.

Her voice filtered out into the kitchen. "Hi, Grandpa! We were just talking about you. . . . Oh, no. What happened? . . . Well, how is she? . . . Is it serious? Do you think we can still—. . . Okay, I understand. . . . No, it's better that we wait. Would you please keep me posted? . . . Thanks, Grandpa. Give her my love. Bye."

Madeline trudged back into the dining room and dropped into her chair. "Well, so much for today's plans."

"What's wrong?" Brendon asked.

"Grandma's back in the hospital. She had some chest pains and shortness of breath. Grandpa called an ambulance, and they're keeping her a couple of days for observation." She crumpled her napkin and tossed it on the table.

"Do you think it's serious?" Karen laid a hand on her mother's shoulder, who still gazed at the table.

"It's happened a couple of times before, but Grandpa seemed to think this episode was worse. We should know more later today."

"So, what do we do now?" asked Karen.

"Since you don't need me to watch the kids, I'm going on into work to save some vacation hours." Brendon picked up his cereal bowl and carried it to the dishwasher. "You could take Karen and Aunt Kammbrie shopping in Old Town, maybe take the kids for a picnic in Rust Park, or something."

Aunt Kammbrie looked up at the mention of a picnic with the children.

"How can we do that if you take the car to work?"

"The Sheldons have a van. Don's offered to let us borrow it anytime we need to. Why not ask Susan if it's available; or better yet, maybe she and Alisha would like to go along."

Madeline nodded. "Does that sound okay to you, Karen?"

"Sounds great."

"Okay. I guess I can afford a day away from my laptop."

"Yeah, that'll be the hard part," Brendon quipped on his way upstairs to change clothes.

# Chapter 45

Brendon pushed through the front door and tossed his jacket over the arm of the living-room couch. Halfway to the snack drawer in the kitchen he drew up short. *Oh, yeah, house guests.* With a sigh, he retrieved the jacket and hung it in the foyer closet. Now, for the snack drawer.

Munching a candy bar, he checked his watch. Five fifteen p.m. The women and kids weren't home yet. Was he supposed to get dinner started? He searched for a note from Madeline, but there was nothing on the kitchen counter. He leaned through the doorway of the study and scanned the desktop. Nothing.

His eyes rested on the closed laptop. A blinking green light signaled sleep mode. The memory of Madeline typing and giggling the night before, then her evasiveness at breakfast, rose, bringing with it a disturbing notion. Brendon moved around the desk. The drowsy green light beckoned. He eased himself into the chair and ran a finger along the front edge of the computer.

*She shouldn't have anything to hide, right?* Lifting the lid, he punched the ENTER button before his spotty conscience got the better of his curiosity. The monitor flashed to life, and the e-mail program's Inbox spread across the screen. Message headers filled the window, the oldest showing a date three months earlier. *Doesn't she ever file these things?*

He scanned the list, recognizing some addresses, others not. A fraction of a second before he clicked the first unfamiliar address, the front door thudded open and female chattering tripped through the living room into the study. Brendon slammed the lid closed and lurched up from the chair. He made it to the doorway just as Madeline passed, ushering a tearful Maria briskly toward the hallway bathroom.

She smiled. "Hi! When did you get home?"

"Umm, a few minutes ago."

"Good. Can you get everybody settled? Maria *really* needs to go."

"Yeah. Sure."

⌘

"Good news!" Madeline swooped in from the study. "That was Grandpa on the phone. Grandma's doing better. They want to keep her a little longer, but we can see her tomorrow. Visiting hours start at ten thirty in the morning, but they have a few more tests to run, and it's better if we wait until after lunch."

"Do you think it's too soon?" Karen asked. "Maybe she's not well enough."

"I think it'll be fine, and so does Grandpa. In fact, it may be the boost she needs. Besides, you guys have been here for two days now, probably bored to death. I'm sure the delay is killing you. I know it's killing me."

"We're not bored at all. You and Brendon are wonderful hosts. And," she gestured toward her mother sitting on the couch, the twins flanking her, all of them engrossed in a large story-book spread open on her lap, "Mother is in seventh heaven."

"I noticed." Madeline's eyes sparkled. "It's still so hard for me to believe she's here. I'm hoping we'll still find Lilli-Anna." She sobered. "The more time that passes, though, the worse our chances."

Karen nodded, her expression betraying little hope.

Brendon stumped down the stairs holding Oskar. "I changed his diaper. The rest is up to you."

Madeline settled into an easy chair as he handed her his son then draped a baby blanket over her shoulder. She fingered the top button of her blouse and glanced at Karen. "I hope this doesn't bother you."

"Of course not."

"Not everybody is comfortable with it. I get some interesting stares—and comments."

"So did I. To be fair, though, it doesn't come easily for everyone. I had more trouble getting my son to nurse than my daughter."

"Really? What was the problem?"

"It seemed to be—"

Brendon cleared his throat. "Ah, if you'll excuse me. This is obviously girl talk." He set a quick pace toward the study.

⟨⟨∙⟩⟩

Brendon settled onto the love seat with the newspaper. He pulled out the Sports section and began to scan the playoff statistics, when the paper lost its spine and the corner flopped forward, leaving him eye to eye with the laptop.

The green light blinked.

He gave it a frown.

It returned an alluring *wink. . .wink. . .wink.*

He shook the paper rigid and read about Detroit's latest excuse for their season record.

# Chapter 46

"Are you sure you don't want to come? We could still try to get a sitter." Madeline shrugged into her Michigan Wolverines Windbreaker.

Brendon shook his head. "You guys go on. It'll be too crowded in the VW, and Oskar's already asleep. No sense in waking him up."

"Okay."

Madeline opened the door for Karen and Aunt Kammbrie then turned around. When she rose on her tiptoes for her kiss, Brendon pecked her on the lips and turned away. She settled back onto her heels at the perfunctory gesture and watched him trudge across the living room toward the study. Unsettled, she stepped outside and clicked the door shut.

The ride to the hospital passed uneventfully, save a near collision with a taxi making a wide turn onto their street. Every mile tied another knot in Madeline's stomach at Brendon's coolness, at her grandmother's health, and in anticipation of the long-awaited reunion. Aunt Kammbrie rode in the front passenger seat, gazing silently out the side window. Through the rearview mirror, Madeline studied an equally thoughtful Karen staring at her lap.

She turned off South Washington into the parking lot of St. Mary's Hospital just after one o'clock. The three women entered the brightly lit entryway, their low heels clicking over the off-white tiles. Soft recessed lighting merged with sunlight streaming through the large front windows, bathing the main lobby in a warm glow. Despite the serenity, Madeline couldn't shake a nervous chill lodged at the base of her neck as she pushed the elevator's Up button.

"They normally limit visitors to two at a time, but Grandpa cleared us with the nursing staff. He said they're nearly as excited about the reunion as we are." She offered a smile but met only a sober expression on Karen's face and tension on Aunt Kammbrie's. She cleared her throat and turned toward the elevator when the door whispered open.

They entered, and Madeline selected her grandmother's floor. A quilted gray pad hung by metal grommets over the walls, apparently left behind by the maintenance department. From a hidden speaker, a nondescript instrumental rendition of a forgettable '90s tune seeped into the car. The padding absorbed the bass and treble, leaving little more than a bland stream of midrange notes that became background noise. The women huddled together in the center of the hushed elevator car, equally subdued. Aunt Kammbrie hugged her arms to her body. Karen rested her hand on her mother's arm and studied the older woman's countenance. No words mitigated the anesthetizing effect of their featureless environment, and Madeline's mind folded into itself until the elevator's electronic bell announced their floor.

The door slid open, and the sterile medicinal odor shared by every hospital ward in the civilized world swirled in on a waft of conditioned air. They exited into the long hallway and crossed to the nurses' station. The duty nurse gave them the room number then peered past Madeline, her smile lingering on Aunt Kammbrie. The nurse turned and whispered to another staff member behind the desk as Madeline thanked her and gestured down the hallway to Karen and her mother.

The women padded along the thin carpet, slowing as they approached the room. When they reached the door, Madeline paused. "Maybe it's better if I go in first to check and make sure she's ready. You know, that she's not getting medication or something."

Karen nodded. Aunt Kammbrie didn't respond, her gaze riveted on the name *McAllister* penned in heavy marker on a door placard. Madeline searched her pale face, worrying that this may not have been such a good idea after all. She took a deep breath. *Well, it's too late now.*

She tapped on the door. Her grandfather's muffled voice granted her entry. With one more nervous smile at her guests, she opened the door and stepped into the room.

Her grandmother lay slightly inclined on an adjustable bed, her eyes closed. Wires leading from beneath the covers drooped toward the floor then arced up to a portable monitor on a roll-around cart. A clear plastic bag hung from an IV stand at the head of the bed, its thin tube snaking down to a bandage covering her right hand. A nurse stood on the far side of the bed annotating a chart. Madeline flashed back to a similar scene in Berlin at Tante Katia's ICU bedside. The anxiety over that event, whether her dear aunt would recover from her coma, was now replaced by a similar anxiety over how her grandmother would react to the appearance of her lost daughter. Anxiety and hospitals just seemed to go together. She peered at the indecipherable monitor display, every flash of red and yellow unnerving her.

James McAllister rose from his chair and hugged his granddaughter. "She's resting, but everything's fine."

The nurse looked up from her work then toward the door. A slight smile touched her lips. "I'll stay, if you don't mind. It's probably better that a staff member be here in case she needs help." Her smile turned coy, and she lowered her voice. "Besides, we drew straws for who would get to be in the room. I won."

Madeline returned a half smile. "Thanks."

She stepped over to the bedside and studied her grandmother's face. She was more wan than the last time Madeline had seen her, the wrinkles around her eyes deeper. But her chest rose and fell with unlabored breathing, and she seemed peaceful.

Her grandfather caressed his wife's hand. "Maria, Madeline's here."

A full breath lifted her grandmother's blanket, then she released a soft sigh. Her eyelids flickered open, and a smile rose to her lips. "Madeline, it's so nice to see you."

Madeline leaned over the side of the bed and kissed her grandmother on the cheek. "You, too."

"Where are the children?"

"Brendon stayed home with them. They'll come to see you a little later."

Her grandmother threw a frown at the nurse. "Well, they'd better hurry. I have no intention of lying around here any longer than I have to."

The nurse kept to her work but chanced a smile.

Madeline fingered the bedrail. "Grandma, there's something I'd like to tell you."

Mrs. McAllister cocked her head then lifted it off the pillow. "You're pregnant again! That's it, isn't it? Oh, Madeline—"

Madeline burst into laughter. "No, I'm not pregnant. Whatever gave you that idea?"

Her grandmother sniffed. "The last time you used that sentence on me, little Oskar was the news."

"This is different—but just as exciting."

"What is it, then?"

Madeline took a deep breath. "Do you remember the *Times* column I've been writing about Tante Katia?"

"Of course. I've saved all of them—except the last one." She threw a teasing glare at her husband. "Somebody forgot to pick up a newspaper on the way home."

He smiled and shrugged.

"Do you remember the one about—" Her grandmother's sudden change of demeanor cut her short. The older woman was staring past her toward the doorway. Madeline looked at Grandfather McAllister, whose own gaze followed his wife's. She turned her head and stepped to the side.

Karen loomed in the open doorway, her hands resting lightly on her mother's shoulders. Aunt Kammbrie stood in front, wringing her hands, her gaze locked onto the hospital bed. When Madeline looked back at her grandmother, her eyes brimmed.

Maria Szpilmann-McAllister struggled onto an elbow and locked gazes with Kammbrie Szpilmann-Romano. Her eyes rounded.

The nurse broke her fixation on the unfolding drama and turned the portable equipment stand toward herself. Her alert eyes alternated their attention between her patient and the monitor.

Karen moved to her mother's side and gently urged her a couple of steps into the room. Aunt Kammbrie teetered on her feet then took two more steps on her own. Her eyes shone luminescent at the sight of her birth mother.

Grandmother McAllister lifted a hand to her mouth. Her husband steadied her arm.

Madeline glanced at the nurse, who studied the monitor.

Aunt Kammbrie slowly closed the gap between herself and the bed. After seventy years and countless miles, mother and daughter stood face-to-face with nothing but the moment and a stainless-steel bedrail between them. The room lay still, not a breath audible. Madeline jumped when the monitor suddenly beeped. Her gaze flitted to the nurse, who glanced up at her patient. "Mrs. McAllister, perhaps—"

"Don't even suggest it." Grandmother McAllister's voice resonated like the growl of a lioness. She extended a trembling hand, hesitated, then lightly touched Aunt Kammbrie's cheek. Her frail fingertips slid to her daughter's neck and brushed her hair behind her left ear, exposing the birthmark. Madeline's throat clogged as tears filled her grandmother's eyes.

"K–Kammbrie?" Her voice broke as she closed her eyes and whispered, "Oh, dearest Lord, have You brought me my baby?"

Aunt Kammbrie worked her jaw but managed no words. She reached up and covered her mother's hand with her own. Finally, she broke her silence with a choked sob. "Mama?"

Grandmother McAllister thrust herself into a sitting position and engulfed her daughter in her arms. A full cry broke from Aunt Kammbrie, and she returned the embrace, her shoulders shaking.

Grandmother McAllister's sudden move disconnected the IV from the needle in her hand. The nurse grabbed the dripping tube and pinched off the flow of fluid. When she reached over to pull back her patient's arm, Grandfather McAllister shook his head in warning. She paused then sighed.

Karen slipped over to Madeline's side and grasped her hand. They wiped tears from their own eyes, chuckling at themselves and each other.

After several minutes, Grandmother McAllister finally pulled back and held her daughter's face with both hands. Her voice shook. "But how did. . .where did. . .oh, I have too many questions!" She stroked her daughter's cheek and searched her eyes. "I had lost hope. I never thought I'd see you again." She peered over her daughter's shoulder. "Where's your sister? Where's Lilli-Anna?"

Aunt Kammbrie dropped her gaze.

# Chapter 47

Brendon released a heavy sigh when Madeline closed the front door. He dropped onto the living-room sofa, frustrated at her, at himself, at life in general. Every time he looked at her, his first inclination to sweep her off her feet suffocated under his second inclination to shake her silly. Her passion and single-focused zeal for life, two qualities that captured his heart their freshman year at the University of Michigan, now addled his heart. That notion turned his mind back to the day they met.

Framed, mounted, and eternally illuminated in his memory was the image of a lithe auburn beauty bursting wide-eyed through the door of the lecture hall two minutes after their history professor had begun class. Gasping for breath, face pink, and hair mussed—all likely the fault of the Frisbee still tucked under one arm—she dropped into the chair next to him, fumbling her canvas book bag from her shoulder. Horror froze her face as two thick textbooks slipped from the bag and slammed to the floor. She hunched in her seat and squeezed her eyes shut, as their impacts resounded through the hall like gunshots. In the ensuing hush, she cracked her eyes open to the professor's glare and the turned heads of two hundred snickering undergrads, Brendon excepted. He was already smitten.

When she leaned down to retrieve her books, he intercepted a third airborne tome a mere two inches from the floor. Her panicked expression melted into relief, and she looked up, brushed disheveled curls from her face, and smiled her gratitude. The world spun to a standstill as he stared into those deep hazel eyes. When she brushed her fingertips over his wrist and breathed a thank-you, his entire world imploded to the size of one auditorium seat. After who knew how long, a quiet giggle betrayed her awareness of his meltdown, and he snapped his attention back to his notes, silently cursing every hormone in his body. It just wasn't fair how quickly and completely the right woman could disassemble an innocent guy's constitution without even trying. And then giggle about it.

At that moment, Brendon's life changed forever. He just didn't count on the change never stopping.

The sound of the doorbell startled him from his reverie. The twins jumped up from the play table and raced each other to the foyer. He'd made it halfway across the room when Katia tugged open the door. Through the front window he glimpsed a taxi pulling away from the curb.

The girls squealed in unison, "Auntie Kamm!"

Aunt Kammbrie? They'd left for the hospital only a few minutes ago. He reached the foyer to see the girls clinging to a very surprised Aunt Kammbrie. She stared rigidly at the toddlers, her arms raised to her shoulders. Brendon stepped back. Wasn't she wearing a pale-green pantsuit when she left? Where did the blue dress come from?

She lifted her head.

His eyes widened. *It can't be—*

Brendon swallowed. "Girls, come back in the house."

They gave their great-aunt one more squeeze and ran back to the play table. Brendon stared at the woman.

"Let me guess: Lilli-Anna?"

She didn't respond.

He stared at Aunt Kammbrie's duplicate. Wispy silver-flaxen curls one trim shorter than her sister's, ice-blue eyes, delicate cheekbones. The only other difference between the two was her demeanor. Clearly ill at ease, Lilli-Anna had yet to make eye contact.

"Please come in." He moved away from the door, and she hesitantly stepped inside. He gestured toward the sofa.

She eased herself onto the edge of the cushion, purse clutched on her lap, shoulders stiff. She cast a furtive glance toward the hallway then at Brendon, who had settled into an easy chair next to the couch. "Is she here?"

"Do you mean Aunt Kammbrie?"

"Yes."

"No. You just missed her."

"She's gone home?"

"No, they've gone to see. . .your mother."

Lilli-Anna shifted her weight but returned no reply.

"How did you find us?" Brendon asked.

She reached into her bag and held up Madeline's most recent *Times* column. The phrase *flying to Saginaw* was underlined in red ink.

"You're in the white pages," she said simply, replacing the clipping in her purse. "I had been following the newspaper story. Then I read last week's article naming Kamm and me." She looked up from her purse but still avoided meeting his gaze. "Needless to say, it took me by surprise."

"I bet it did." He leaned forward. "Did you try to call or send an e-mail?"

She stiffened and tilted away from him. "I don't own a computer. I'm not sure why I didn't telephone when I arrived. I only thought to come."

"So, I'm sure you want to see your mother." Brendon sat back, and she straightened again. "I don't know. I think I do. I'm not sure."

"Why would you not want to?"

"I don't know if. . .if she wants to see me. And Kamm and I parted under. . .difficult terms."

"Of course she wants to see you." He paused. "And Aunt Kammbrie told us about Tony."

"Just about Tony?"

"Is there more?"

Her voice quieted. "Oh, yes."

Brendon pushed his sleeve back from his watch. "If we hurry, we can catch them at the hospital."

"Oh, I don't know—the hospital?"

"Grandmother was admitted yesterday. Just observation, though. She's okay."

She fingered a decorative button on her dress. "It's been so long."

Brendon ventured a smile. "Trust me. You want to be there. And they'll want you there."

He hurried to the kitchen telephone. His call to Madeline went immediately to voice mail, reminding him that most hospital wards request cell phones be turned off. He punched in the Sheldons' number.

"Hi, Susan? It's Brendon. Hey, something's come up. I wonder if you can watch Oskar and the girls for a little while. Sorry about the last-minute notice. . . . Yeah, I've got to chase Madeline down at the hospital. . . . Oh, wow, thanks. You're a gem. I was going to call a taxi, but if we can use the van, that'd be great. We won't be gone long. . . . Perfect! Thanks a lot, Susan. We'll be right over."

⁂

The elevator door slid open, and Brendon stepped onto the ward with Lilli-Anna. They crossed to the nurses' station.

"Excuse me, which room is Maria McAllister's, please?"

The nurse looked up from her chart. "The second door on the right. She already has some visitors, but—" She spotted Lilli-Anna, and her eyebrows drew together. "I thought. . ."

"Thank you." Brendon reached for Lilli-Anna's arm, but she drew back. He hesitated then gestured down the hallway.

As they approached the room, Lilli-Anna slowed and stopped a few paces short of the door. Her breathing had gone shallow, her face pale, and she appeared unsteady on her feet. When he took her arm in support, she stiffened.

"Are you okay?" he asked.

She inhaled deeply then gave a slight nod.

Brendon gently led her to the doorway and released her arm. Lilli-Anna's knuckles whitened in a viselike grip on her purse.

A burst of laughter echoed around the partially closed door, startling him. She didn't move.

Brendon knocked twice, pushed open the door, and the laughter died.

# Chapter 48

Grandmother McAllister inhaled sharply and held her breath. Grandfather McAllister covered her hand with his, both of their stares glued to the doorway.

Karen steadied her mother, who had turned then staggered backward against the side of the hospital bed.

The nurse shot another look at the monitor, which had beeped again. Twice.

Madeline's hushed voice broke the silence. "Brendon. . . ?"

He stepped forward. "Everybody, this is. . . well, I don't need to tell you who this is."

"Lilli?" Grandmother McAllister whispered, a catch in her voice.

Lilli-Anna stared at the floor.

"Please. . . dear. Come in."

Lilli-Anna lifted her head, but her eyes remained canted downward. She took a half step and halted, her shaking hands further twisting an already mangled purse strap. When Grandfather McAllister stepped forward and offered her his hand, Lilli-Anna stiffened and sidestepped him. He reddened but said nothing.

Aunt Kammbrie edged aside as her sister approached. When Lilli-Anna passed her, Kammbrie lifted a hand but dropped it back to her side without touching her sister. Madeline studied their faces. She wondered if Aunt Kammbrie had blinked once since Lilli-Anna entered the room.

Grandmother McAllister slipped her hand into Lilli-Anna's. The purse dropped to the floor. She drew her daughter closer then tipped up her chin. Lilli-Anna allowed her head to rise but kept her gaze downward. Then Grandmother McAllister caressed her daughter's cheek with her fingertips.

Lilli-Anna's eyes flicked up to meet her mother's. Grandmother McAllister pulled her into a tight embrace, a wave of tears flooding her eyes.

The nurse spoke quietly but urgently. "Mr. McAllister, her pulse and blood pressure. . . we need to slow down."

He nodded and took a step toward the bed then halted. He threw a helpless look at the nurse, who shook her head and frowned.

Grandmother McAllister freed an arm and beckoned to Aunt Kammbrie.

She didn't move.

The beckoning sharpened.

Kammbrie moved to her sister's side, her gaze locked on her mother, whose free arm enveloped her and pulled her into the hug. Kammbrie's right arm came up and hovered over Lilli-Anna's shoulder then dropped back.

Madeline threw a questioning look at Brendon, and he slipped to her side. "Aunt Lilli told me there's more to the story than Tony Romano," he whispered. "But she didn't say what."

Grandmother McAllister's quavering voice interrupted their exchange. "I never thought this day would come. My girls. My precious girls." She sat back and wiped the tears from her cheeks. Freed from the embrace, Lilli-Anna half stepped away from her sister.

The nurse asserted herself. "Mrs. McAllister, we really need to get this IV reconnected. And you need to rest."

"Nonsense. I'm fine."

"Yes, and if you want to stay that way, you'll listen to me." Her eyes sent a stern appeal to Grandfather McAllister.

"Okay." He held up his hands. "Maria, I know this seems far too short a reunion, but we'll have plenty of time to be together. We need to get you out of this hospital."

His wife huffed at him, but he only smiled. "The doctor said he can discharge you tomorrow morning if your test results are satisfactory. Let's plan to spend the day with. . .your children." He cast an awkward glance at Lilli-Anna and Kammbrie, his smile fading for an instant before he recovered. "There should be plenty of time," he repeated then faltered again.

Madeline filled the gap. "Absolutely! We can gather at our house, maybe go out for dinner, or something."

"*If* she's discharged," the nurse pointed out, earning another glare from her patient. The nurse ignored her and ushered everyone from the room.

Brendon led the way toward the elevator with Lilli-Anna and Kammbrie following, their eyes flitting to anything but each other. Madeline waited for her grandfather, who had stayed behind to kiss his wife good-bye.

"Are you okay?" she asked.

He nodded with a weak smile.

Madeline slipped her hand into the crook of his arm. "You always told me not to fib," she scolded in a tease.

Her grandfather half smiled. "I guess when I said the words for the first time, acknowledging your grandmother had children who weren't mine, it kind of hit me. I'm not sure why."

"I think I understand, Grandpa."

"Don't get me wrong. I'm thrilled for her—and very proud of you for finding them." He squeezed her hand. "But. . .it's hard to explain."

When they reached the elevator, she rose to her tiptoes and kissed his cheek. "Give it some time."

"Yeah."

# Chapter 49

The hiss of running water sputtered to silence, and Brendon appeared in the narrow doorway of the half bath, the overhead lamp casting a jaundiced halo around his head and bare shoulders.

"Bathroom's yours," he said through a yawn.

Madeline settled onto the edge of the sofa as Brendon headed for the study. "Bren?"

"Yeah." He squinted into the darkened front room.

"Got a minute?"

"Sure."

"This afternoon, when I left for the hospital, was something wrong?"

"Wrong?"

"You seemed, I don't know, a little distant."

He paused. The events of the past week chose that moment to crowd through his mind, refusing to sort themselves into any semblance of order, bumping into each other randomly like a poorly laid mosaic: an impatient Madeline furiously pounding the keys of her laptop, a sour Clive Ferguson and a lost account, Maria's scream in the front yard and Don Sheldon's awkwardness, Madeline's attack on Sally Morgan's perceived attentions. His chest tightened.

The images spanned an emotional chasm that yawned between Madeline and himself and wrenched it wider. Worse, though, than all the missteps, was that she seemed oblivious, even defensive, especially concerning the newspaper column. He tried to recall the last alone moment they shared—mentally, emotionally, and physically—but the turmoil in his mind obscured any memory of it. Then the niggling impression he'd been fighting that she might be tiring of him, of life with a "gimp," rose and crowded all the other images into the chasm.

*Self-pity, Sommers?* Self-pity or self-awareness?

The fact she wasn't oblivious, that she was asking the question, inviting the discourse, also disappeared into the chasm unacknowledged.

"Bren?"

"Nothing's wrong. I'm just tired."

He reached back and flicked off the bathroom light.

❧

Madeline slid the ham-and-macaroni casserole into the oven and closed the door. She set the timer and glanced into the living room.

Katia and Maria chattered in their play corner, slashing bright streaks across the creased page of a defenseless coloring book with washable-ink markers. Oskar kicked and cooed in his infant chair, honing his infantile charm to deploy on whatever unsuspecting adult—preferably female—might dare to come fuss over him.

Grandmother and Grandfather McAllister were due at noon, but her mother and father had already arrived with side dishes for lunch. Karen and Aunt Kammbrie had gone upstairs, much to Avery's disappointment. She kept glancing toward the staircase while she helped Madeline prepare lunch. In her distraction, she misjudged a third tumbler's location with the iced tea pitcher, soaking a place mat. Madeline took her by the shoulders.

"Mom, go sit in the living room while we still have something left in the house to drink."

Her mother blushed. "I'm sorry, dear. It's just so. . .I mean, a sister-in-law—*two* sisters-in-law!—I never knew I had."

"I know. Let me finish setting the table, then I'll go upstairs to see what's keeping them."

"Okay, if you're sure—"

"Trust me. It's less expensive this way."

Her mother nodded and shuffled toward the living room, stooping to gather up scattered doll clothes along the way.

Brendon emerged from the study and lifted his car keys from the hook on the kitchen wall, bound for Aunt Lilli-Anna's hotel.

"Don't be long, Bren." Madeline's shoulders drooped when the door clicked closed with no response.

She turned to see her mother regarding her with a puzzled frown.

❧

At the sound of the doorbell, Madeline hurried to the foyer to admit her grandmother and grandfather. She kissed them both on the cheek. "Sorry about the place. Don't twist your ankle on a toy."

Grandmother McAllister handed her sweater to her husband then scanned the living room. Avery held Aunt Kammbrie captive on the couch, deep in conversation, with Ian apparently trying to get a word in edgewise.

"Where's Lilli?"

"Brendon's picking her up at the hotel."

She nodded toward the sofa. "I see your mother and Kammbrie are getting along well."

Madeline grinned. "Yeah, I thought Mom was going to squeeze the stuffing out of her when they first met."

Grandmother McAllister laid a hand on Madeline's cheek. "You've done a wonderful thing. You know that, don't you?"

Madeline blushed. "I didn't really. I just wrote the column. God did the rest; I had no control over it."

Grandmother McAllister smiled. "Actually, God did it all. But you were obedient to his leading from the moment you packed for Berlin. You took on your Tante Katia's interview, followed up in your newspaper column, and more. And now you get to share in his blessing."

Madeline sputtered an embarrassed laugh. "Oh, believe me, I messed up so much along the way, I don't really think I helped very much."

"But God works with our messing up, doesn't he, dear? In doing so, he loves us into the knowledge of what you just confessed. Don't ever let 'messing up' become an excuse to quit. If you had," she gestured toward her newly united family, "we would never have witnessed this."

Madeline sobered, her thoughts flashing to Brendon. "Yes, ma'am."

Grandfather McAllister closed the closet door and followed his wife into the living room. He eased her onto the sofa beside her daughter and daughter-in-law. Karen and Madeline took seats in the easy chairs.

The women had just begun to chat when the door to the garage closed. Brendon appeared in the archway.

Madeline looked at him. "Where's Aunt Lilli?"

"I don't know. She checked out of her hotel early this morning."

# Chapter 50

Madeline shot to her feet. "Checked out?"

"That's what they said at the front desk."

"Well, where did she go?"

"I have no idea. She asked the receptionist to call a taxi then waited in the lobby until it arrived."

"Why didn't you *call* me?"

"I left my cell phone here. I didn't think I'd need it. I hurried back—"

Madeline strode across the room, her face taut. "Do you still have the hotel's phone number I gave you this morning?"

"Yeah." Brendon handed her a piece of paper.

"I don't believe you let her get away!" She snatched it from his fingers.

*"What?"*

"Madeline, that wasn't fair," interjected her mother, who had followed her from the living room.

Madeline yanked the phone off its wall mount and punched in the hotel's phone number. Brendon shook his head and stalked toward the study.

Avery paused in the hallway. "Brendon, she didn't mean that."

"Oh, yes she did," he muttered over his shoulder, as he threw his Windbreaker onto the sofa. "I give up."

"Brendon!"

He dropped onto the love seat and propped his head in his hands. Madeline's mother spun to face her daughter, who had just connected with the hotel.

"Hello, I'm trying to reach a guest of yours who checked out this morning. A Ms. Lilli-Anna—" she groaned and turned back toward the living room. "I don't even know her last name. Did she mention it to any of you?"

They shook their heads.

Madeline uncovered the phone. "I'm sorry. I don't have her last name. An elderly lady. You called a taxi for her this morning. . . . Szpilmann, yes, that would be it. Do you know where she went? . . . Airport taxi? Thanks so much." She jammed the phone back onto its cradle.

"She went to the airport. I'm going after her."

"Can I go, Mommy?

Madeline reached for her car keys. "Not this time, Katia."

"But I never get to—"

"I said no."

Katia's lip quivered.

Her mother stared at her. "Madeline! What's gotten into you?"

"Nothing! I can't. . .it's. . .oh, go ahead and eat lunch without me. I'll be back as soon as I can." She pushed through the door to the garage, and it slammed closed behind her.

❧

Madeline ground her teeth the entire forty minutes to the airport. Half the time she spent praying to God that he wouldn't let her aunt get away and the other half threatening her aunt telepathically that she'd better not even try. She'd expended too much effort and too many tears to settle for half a reunion, and there was no way she would let her eccentric aunt ruin everything, not now. She decelerated only long enough to swing off Garfield Road into the airport complex then hit the gas again. Speed limits were nowhere in her cognitive universe.

She screeched to a halt in the first open slot and raced to the terminal building, bemoaning not having changed out of her floppy bedroom slippers into her running shoes. She shoved through the doors into the terminal and jerked back when her pink and green *Kiss The Cook* apron snagged on the latch. She yanked it loose, fuming. *Don't I look great! I hope I find her before Security notices me.*

Lungs heaving, she skidded to a halt by the serpentine Security line, garnering a turned head from a nearby TSA agent. Her shoulders sagged at the seemingly endless stream of travelers shuffling through the checkpoint. She hovered on tiptoes and scanned the sea of heads for her aunt's curly silver hair. Oh, why did her relatives have to be so short?

Two minutes and half a lifetime later, she settled slowly back down onto her cramped arches. She squeezed her eyelids shut against the frustration.

"Can I help you, ma'am?"

She opened her eyes to the face of a half-concerned, half-suspicious security officer. "No. . .thank you. I. . .I just missed somebody." She sighed.

He nodded sympathetically. "I'm very sorry, but I'm going to have to ask you to step back from the line if you're not a ticketed passenger."

"Sure," Madeline murmured and turned away.

She rubbed the moisture from her eyes with the heel of her hands and plodded toward the exit doors. Refusing to admit defeat, she shook her hair back from her face and shifted her mind into problem-solving gear. Okay, when Aunt Lilli-Anna checked into the hotel, she'd have filled out a registration slip. Don't they still ask for a home address on those things? Hope began to rise then faltered. *Privacy laws won't let them tell you, Maddy.*

Maddy? When was the last time she called herself *that*?

Madeline slackened her pace on the sidewalk, her mind racing. Aunt Lilli probably used a credit card, but she'd encounter the same problem with getting information from those records. *Maybe if I told the police she owes me money, they'd help—*

A flash of bright red penetrated the glare on the plate-glass window to her right, pulling her attention. She peered through the window and halted. A diminutive silver-haired woman wearing a bright red pantsuit sat with her back to the window, a suitcase and a purse perched on the chair beside her. Madeline rushed back into the terminal. Her steps slowed as she approached the woman. "Aunt Lilli?"

The woman looked up, and Madeline's lungs deflated. "I'm sorry. I thought you were someone else."

She lowered her head, turned back toward the door, and ran headlong into someone carrying a paper beverage cup. Caught between them, the flimsy plastic lid popped off, dousing them with cold liquid.

Madeline gasped. "Oh, I'm so sorry!" She grabbed the sides of her apron and began dabbing the brown splotches from the person's blouse. She looked up, another apology poised on her lips.

"Aunt Lilli!" She instinctively threw her arms around the older woman and squeezed until a cold, wet feeling penetrated her apron. She pulled her head back and looked down. The cup wedged between them had flattened, soaking the remainder of its contents into their clothes. Aunt Lilli looked into Madeline's shocked face, her lips thinned.

"Oh! I'm so sorry. . .again!" Madeline stepped back, and the cup dropped to the floor. She renewed her efforts to dab at the spreading mocha stain on her aunt's blouse.

"What are you doing here?" Aunt Lilli asked quietly.

"Looking for you."

"Why?"

"Are you serious?"

Aunt Lilli hardened her eyes. "Don't be impertinent, young lady."

"That wasn't impertinent compared to what I felt like saying. C'mon, let's go."

"Where?"

"Where do you think? Home."

"I was going home."

"Huh-uh. My home. No way you're skipping out on me now."

"Now see here—"

"Ma'am, do you need my help any longer? I need to catch my flight." The woman in red rose from her chair.

Aunt Lilli nodded with a strained smile. "No, thank you very much for watching my suitcase. It was very kind of you."

"A pleasure."

The lady walked toward Security, and Madeline returned her attention to her aunt. "This is your bag?"

Aunt Lilli sniffed. "Yes. She was kind enough to mind it for me while I went for my. . . drink." She cast a brief look at her soggy blouse.

"You know you're not supposed to do that. The security rules are—"

"I know the security rules," Aunt Lilli snorted. "They announce the silly things over the loudspeaker every fifteen seconds."

Madeline softened her tone. "Can we sit a minute? Please?"

Her aunt released a heavy sigh and settled into the plastic chair the woman had vacated. Madeline took the seat next to her. She shifted toward her aunt and laid a hand over hers. Aunt Lilli stiffened but didn't pull away.

"Please explain."

"Explain what?"

"You know very well what I mean. I left behind a houseful of very anxious people wondering why you'd decided to leave without so much as a word."

"They've gotten along fine without me for this long. I doubt I'll be missed."

"You were missed the instant Brendon dropped you off at your hotel yesterday afternoon." Aunt Lilli's eyes flicked up momentarily then focused again on her lap.

Madeline stroked her aunt's wrist with her fingertip, a gesture she'd found so soothing during the many hours of interviewing Tante Katia in Berlin. Apparently, Aunt Lilli didn't view it quite the same way. She jerked her hand away and grasped it with her other hand, rubbing the spot Madeline's finger had caressed.

"What's wrong, Aunt Lilli? Talk to me. Please."

"It will never work. It's been too long, and too much has happened. It was nice of you to try, but it won't work."

Madeline shook her head. "It's already worked. You and your sister are here, reunited with your mother and each other. How can you just leave?"

Aunt Lilli fidgeted. "You wouldn't understand. You don't know what. . ."

"What?" Madeline reclaimed her aunt's hand, this time in a firm grip.

Aunt Lilli jerked but didn't pull away. "It was so many years ago. Mama—the mama I remember, who died—Kamm. . .Tony. . .so many others since, and now a mother I didn't know I had, who never came for me." She dropped her gaze. "When I left, nobody cared. Why should they now?"

"Oh, Aunt Lilli, of course your mother cared. She tried everything to find you, but you'd disappeared like so many other war children. The years, the miles, her illness, everything worked against her, worked against all of you. But that's over now. We want you back, more than you could ever know." Her tone firmed. "And I've come to take you home."

Aunt Lilli's hand trembled. "I didn't think anybody would."

"Would what?" asked Madeline. Then she paused. "Aunt Lilli, what time is your flight?"

Her aunt stared at the floor.

"Why haven't you checked in your baggage?"

Silence.

"You wanted. . .you hoped someone would come after you, didn't you?"

Aunt Lilli's shoulders sagged, and the wrinkles on her forehead deepened. She began to shake her head no, but the gesture fell flat.

Madeline drew her aunt close and whispered, "I love you so much. And I want you to come home."

# Chapter 51

They walked slowly to the car, where Madeline settled Aunt Lilli onto the passenger seat and stowed her bag in the trunk. She pulled into the exit lane from the parking lot toward the cashier booth then panicked as she realized she'd raced off from home without her purse. Reddening, she asked her aunt if she might have a dollar to spare. Aunt Lilli fished out a twenty but refused any change. The remainder of the drive home passed in silence.

When they pulled into the driveway, Madeline killed the engine and canted the rearview mirror toward her to survey the effects of her emotional morning. *Worse than I thought.* She combed her fingers through her disheveled hair and shook her head.

When the curtain behind the front window fluttered, Madeline reached for the door handle. She'd barely rounded the car and opened her aunt's door, when the door of the house banged open and her mother rushed down the sidewalk to the driveway. Avery engulfed her startled sister-in-law in a bear hug easily matching the one she smothered Aunt Kammbrie in two days earlier.

Madeline smiled. "Unlatch, Mom. She needs air."

Her mother laughed. She pulled back and held Lilli-Anna at arm's length, beaming into her face. "I can't believe it! My goodness, if I didn't know better, I'd think I was hugging Kammbrie again. You look identical."

Aunt Lilli remained stoic, but Avery carried on, her tone taking on a teasing scolding. "Now, just where did you think you were going, Sister?"

Color rose to Aunt Lilli's cheeks, and Madeline intervened with a gentle warning in her expression. "Mom, let's go inside."

Her mother glanced at her daughter then regrouped, a more dignified smile replacing the grin. "Of course. I'm sorry. Please. . ."

The three women entered the house to cheers. Brendon and Grandfather McAllister rose from their seats.

Aunt Lilli remained motionless when Grandmother McAllister stood and approached her. "I'm glad Madeline found you, Lilli," she said through an unrequited embrace. "This day would never have been complete without you. Please believe that."

Grandmother McAllister led her daughter by the arm to the sofa and indicated she should sit next to Aunt Kammbrie. Aunt Lilli hesitated then acquiesced, her focus still downward.

Maria and Katia wandered to the couch from their play table, hand in hand. They stared back and forth at their great-aunts' identical faces. Aunt Kammbrie smiled back; Aunt Lilli looked up momentarily then lowered her eyes again. Katia released her sister's hand and approached Aunt Lilli. She reached up and touched her older woman's face. Aunt Lilli flinched and lifted her head. Katia smiled and extended her arms. The older woman's eyes widened then softened. She helped the young girl onto her lap, and Katia laid her head on Aunt Lilli's shoulder. Maria climbed onto Aunt Kammbrie's lap and did likewise.

Grandfather McAllister's arm encircled his wife's waist, and they smiled at the two generations of twins cuddling on the sofa.

Madeline moved to Brendon's side and took his hand. "I'm sorry for the way I acted," she whispered. "I was just scared."

He nodded and squeezed her hand then released it. Madeline glanced up at him then slipped away to the kitchen, her steps leaden.

Mealtime passed with so much lively chatting it was a wonder anything got eaten. Even Aunt Lilli, though remaining serious, contributed a sentence or two. That Brendon contributed nothing didn't escape Madeline's notice.

After lunch, they retired to the living room, the buzz of their unabated conversation enveloping them like a verbal swarm of bees. Madeline settled into the chair next to the play corner to nurse Oskar and arbitrate a dispute between Maria and Katia over who got the last Little Mermaid sticker.

Karen excused herself and went upstairs then returned a moment later with an old shoe box. She set it on the coffee table and resumed her chair. Conversation dwindled until there was only silence, save the scratching of colored markers over recycled paper in the play corner. Madeline studied the scene across the room.

Aunt Lilli sat motionless, her stare fixed on the shoe box. Aunt Kammbrie remained equally still, but for a furtive glance or two at her sister. Karen shifted in her chair, folding and refolding her hands on her lap. Grandmother and Grandfather McAllister regarded the plain-looking box, their questioning eyes seeking out Karen's.

Finally, Aunt Lilli leaned forward and brushed the lid with her fingertips. Then she sat back.

Karen cleared her throat. "I brought this along, not knowing you'd be here, Aunt Lilli. I thought it might help fill in some of the gaps in Madeline's story. I believe it belongs to you."

"Did you read them?" Aunt Lilli asked, her voice as distant as her expression.

"No. I read the two letters and some documents—"

Aunt Lilli shook her head. "No. I mean did you read them?"

Karen hesitated, seeming puzzled.

Her mother shifted on the cushion. "No, Lilli. I never read them."

Madeline's pulse quickened at the first direct exchange between the estranged sisters. "Why?"

"They were yours. I was waiting for you to come back."

"And when I didn't?"

"Years went by before I gave up hope. Then it was too late; the desire was gone. They were remembrances from a hurtful past. I took the chest with me when Tony and I married, just in case this day would come and I could return them to you, but I never opened it."

"But it is open. This is not the chest."

"That's my fault," Karen interjected. "When I saw Madeline's column in the *Times*, I remembered the chest from Mother's attic. I thought there might be something in it that would help clarify things. I'm sorry if it was an intrusion. I didn't have the right. . . ."

Madeline buttoned her blouse under the nursing blanket then eased a sleeping Oskar into his playpen. She edged over to Brendon's easy chair and settled onto the overstuffed arm. When she propped her hand on the backrest behind his head, he shifted in the seat.

Aunt Kammbrie studied her sister's face. Her hand rested on the cushion halfway toward Lilli, fingers twitching on the loose-weave fabric.

"Why did you leave, Lilli? Where did you go?" asked Grandmother McAllister. She alternated her gaze between their faces. "What happened between you two?"

Madeline tried to fill the awkward silence. "Aunt Kammbrie, maybe it would help if you repeated the story you told us the other day at dinner, about your foster homes."

Her grandmother raised a silencing finger. "Thank you, dear, but we covered that while you were at the airport."

Aunt Lilli remained silent under her mother's gaze. Aunt Kammbrie fidgeted then lowered her head, too.

"Girls?" Grandmother McAllister's tone took on an edge.

"So, what did you tell them, Kamm?" murmured Aunt Lilli.

"The truth."

"Which was. . . ?"

"That you left the Romanos' without a word after Tony and I were engaged."

Aunt Lilli looked up and locked gazes with her sister for the first time. "That's it?"

Aunt Kammbrie lifted her chin. "Well, that's what happened. I had no idea where you went. You just left."

"And you couldn't fathom why I left?"

"I assumed it was because of Tony. I knew you had feelings for him, too, but you never said anything. He asked me to the dance; I didn't encourage it."

"Kamm, it had nothing to do with Tony asking you to the dance, or even your engagement to him."

"Then what was it?"

"Do you remember how close we were growing up?"

"Yes, of course."

"When did that change?"

"I don't know exactly."

"It changed when you came home from the dance. All you could talk about was Tony, which I understood, as disappointed as I was. But you began spending more time with him and less with me. I knew you were falling for him, but I didn't expect you to turn your back on me."

Aunt Kammbrie stiffened. "I didn't turn my back on you. You got that job at the soda fountain and weren't around as much."

"Kamm, the job didn't come until four months after the dance. I took it to fill in the time that you and I used to share. Tony became the focus of your life and I the third wheel." Her voice quieted. "I wasn't used to that."

"It wasn't that bad."

Aunt Lilli half turned on the cushion toward her sister. "Our seventeenth birthday, Kamm, do you remember it?"

Aunt Kammbrie's cheeks tinged pink. "Yes."

Silence ensued, each sister apparently waiting for the other to continue. Grandmother McAllister broke the deadlock. "What happened?"

"Lilli bought me a coral bracelet and hid it in our room. She left a card on my bed with a clue. I'd follow the clue to another clue, and then another, until I'd find the present. It's the way we always did each other's birthday gifts."

Avery smiled. "Sounds like fun."

"Only that year I completely forgot our birthday tradition. It fell on a Saturday, and Tony and I spent the afternoon together on a picnic. When I returned home, the birthday card from Lilli was on my bed. I'd done nothing in return. . . ."

Aunt Lilli gave a dismissive shrug. "It was just a birthday present—"

"No." Aunt Kammbrie shook her head. "It wasn't just a birthday present. I felt terrible." When her sister didn't respond, Aunt Kammbrie peered at her. "Is that why you left?"

"No, but it was when I realized that I would leave."

"Then why, Lilli?"

"Over the next six months, you slipped farther and farther away from me. You were the most important person in my entire life, the only person who. . ."

"Who what, Lilli?" asked Grandmother McAllister.

"Who wanted me," she whispered.

"Lilli, we all wanted you," objected Aunt Kammbrie.

"Like who?"

"Well, Mom and Dad Romano, for one example."

"They took me in because they felt sorry for me."

"That's not true—"

"It *is* true. The Oesterfelds sent us away, never even said good-bye. Tony liked you, and Helen hated me—"

"Tony never knew how you felt, and Helen didn't like either one of us."

Aunt Lilli shook her head, her face reddening. "I left to see if anyone would come after me, to see if anyone cared. They didn't. *You* didn't."

Aunt Kammbrie rose and crossed her arms over her chest. "That's not fair! You didn't tell us you were leaving or where you were going. No notes, no good-byes, nothing. You simply disappeared. We had no idea where to look."

Aunt Lilli stood and matched her sister's stance. "You could've found me if you wanted to. When did you even notice I was gone?"

"I saw your empty bed as soon as I got up that morning."

"Really?" Aunt Lilli scoffed. "Then how was it that I made it all the way to the bus station lugging my suitcase, waited for two and a half hours for the next bus, and still you never showed up?"

"I didn't know you'd gone anywhere until you didn't come down for breakfast. It was only then, when I went back up to our room, that I noticed your suitcase missing."

"Then what?"

"I don't remember exactly. We asked each other if anybody knew you were leaving, if you'd said anything to anyone."

"Hmph! You just talked about me? You didn't even guess I'd go to the bus station?"

"You could have gone to the bus station, the train station, a friend's house, any number of places."

"Face it, Kamm. You didn't care."

Aunt Kammbrie turned beet red. "I certainly did care! I was in shock after you left; we all were. I didn't know what to do."

Grandmother McAllister rose. "Girls, you need to calm down—"

Aunt Lilli spun on her. "Don't tell me to calm down! You were the first one to abandon me!"

The room went deathly still.

# Chapter 52

Grandmother McAllister teetered, face white, her breath shallow. Her husband rushed to her side and eased her into her chair. He narrowed his eyes at Aunt Lilli, his tone low and measured. "You have no idea what you're saying. No idea at all."

Aunt Lilli, chest heaving, stared at the floor.

Avery rose and moved to Aunt Lilli's side. "Lilli, it's okay," she said quietly. "Let's sit down."

Karen approached her mother and suggested the same. The Szpilmann twins settled back onto the couch, faces taut, the distance between them increased.

A thought struck Madeline, and she rose and headed toward the study. She stopped at the sight of her twins staring at the adults from across the room. Quietly, she stepped over to their play table and stooped low. "I need you girls to go upstairs and play for a little while," she whispered.

Maria stared at her mother. "Why is everybody mad?"

"Is Grammie crying?" asked Katia, eyes locked on her great-grandmother.

Madeline touched her forefinger to her lips. "I'll explain later."

"But—"

"No 'buts.' Upstairs, now," Madeline ordered but then softened at the tears welling in her daughters' eyes. "I'm sorry, girls. Please do as Mommy says. Everything is going to be fine, I promise."

Katia and Maria slipped from their chairs and trudged toward the staircase, their gaze glued to their great-grandmother's pale face. Another disgruntled pout at their mother and they clomped up the stairs.

Madeline slipped into the study. Returning with her draft copy of Tante Katia's memoir, she knelt at Aunt Lilli's feet and placed it on the coffee table. Lifting the cover, she flipped through the pages to a scanned image of a letter handwritten in German. An English translation appeared below the letter.

"I'd like you both to read something." She pointed to the translation.

Aunt Kammbrie glanced at her sister then slid closer. They leaned toward the page and read.

*Dearest Sister,*

*I know you received my first letter, as I have your reply here beside me. I was overjoyed to hear from you. There were days in Auschwitz and Bergen-Belsen that I believed I would never see any of my beloved family again. Praise God you survived the war! We must plan a reunion, whenever that may be.*

*My health continues to improve. Many of the women and children from the camp who have come to this hospital have not survived. There are burials every day. I was fortunate to be at Bergen-Belsen for only a few months. The typhus did not ravage me as it did so many others.*

*I have met a man, a Canadian soldier. I did not tell you in the first letter, because I was not sure how he felt about me, nor I about him. He is quiet, gentle, and very kind. He has hardly left my side, on or off duty. His name is Jim. This morning, he asked me to marry him, Anna! I said no, but not happily. Is it wrong to have such feelings for a man when I do not yet know the fate of my own husband? I feel as though I am being unfaithful, although Izaak and I did not see each other after leaving Ravensbrück. My gracious, that was five years ago! How do the days drag by so slowly, while the years race by so quickly?*

*I pray each day for Lilli-Anna and Kammbrie. They must be little ladies now, almost six years old. I pray they reached safety, now that you have told me of the Dudeks, praise God for them! It tore my heart from me when the Gestapo dragged us out the door, my baby girls asleep in the nursery. I hope yet to find them, but they were too young to remember me now. I wonder if they know, if they understand. Please pray with me that they understand.*

*I hope I will soon be strong enough to leave the hospital. Perhaps Jim can bring me to you. You will love him, too.*

*I must stop now. It is late, and they are calling for lights-out in the ward.*

*I remain always,*
*Your loving sister, Maria*

They leaned back, Aunt Lilli's focus still on the memoir. Madeline placed her hand over her aunt's.

"Anna Mahler received one letter from the Dudeks early in 1940 informing her of their intent to escape to Austria, but nothing more. As soon as possible after the war, she traveled to Salzburg to try to find you. She searched for days but only encountered one person who thought she remembered Mrs. Dudek and her twins. The woman only knew that they'd disappeared years before."

Madeline switched her focus to Aunt Kammbrie.

"Both your Aunt Anna and your mother wrote numerous letters to the European commission established to reunite families separated during the war. But there were hundreds of thousands of inquiries about lost children, and neither of them received replies. By that time, your mother was in Canada recovering from a near-fatal illness. Very few research avenues were open to her, and without any leads to go on, it was an impossible task."

Aunt Lilli shook her head. "There had to be some way, somebody—"

"Aunt Lilli, I spent hours upon hours scouring the Internet, telephoning organizations that maintain immigration records, researching database archives devoted to Holocaust victims and survivors, doing everything I could think of to find you. Remember, I'm a trained journalist with access to decades of documentation that neither your mother nor your aunt had available to them. And, even then, I couldn't find you. You found me."

Karen spoke up. "I'm so glad you're hearing this, Mother. Do you remember your first reaction to Madeline's newspaper article?"

Aunt Kammbrie nodded. "I didn't want to come. I didn't think. . . Well, I guess I felt much the way Lilli did."

Grandmother McAllister lifted her face, her hollow eyes half focused on her daughters. Her voice quavered. "I'm. . .so sorry, girls. . .for what I put you through. I. . .I should have fought when the soldiers came. . . . I should have forced them to—"

Silent until this moment, Ian shot to his feet. "Mother! You have absolutely nothing to apologize for. It took all your strength just to survive the concentration camps, and even while recovering from that, you did everything humanly possible to find your children."

She shook her head. "You must be willing to die for your children."

"Then you all would have died. You'd never have met Dad, had our family, your grandchildren and great-grandchildren." He gestured toward the sofa. "And this reunion would never have taken place."

"But the price. . ." She squeezed her eyelids too late against the tears.

❧

Silence enshrouded the living room, a suffocating ambiance that compressed the heart and mind. Madeline tugged at the collar of her blouse and shifted in her seat. Perhaps to open a window and release the pressure, but, no, the movement could smother words struggling for voice, sentiments poised for expression, both already suffering injury from pride, fear, and guilt.

She perked when Aunt Lilli shifted and stiffened her arms against the seat of the couch. She reached out and brushed a fingertip down the letter printed in the memoir. After a moment, Aunt Lilli turned her head and locked gazes with her sister. Madeline watched Aunt Kammbrie slide her hand across the cushion and intertwine her fingers with her sister's. Words tacit to the ear, but deafening to perception, flew between two identical sets of clear blue eyes. Aunt Lilli nodded almost imperceptibly, and Madeline backed away when, as one, the Szpilmann twins rose.

They approached their mother, who remained still, her eyes closed, her breathing light and irregular. Grandfather McAllister stepped behind his wife and watched his stepdaughters edge to the sides of the easy chair. They had risen as one, and as one they knelt.

Grandmother McAllister flinched at their simultaneous touch on her hands. She opened her eyes, releasing a cascade down her cheek, to her daughters' intent expressions. Tentative smiles gained hold, and the struggling words and poised sentiments blossomed in a single unison utterance.

"Mama..."

Her breath choked as her precious daughters laid their cheeks against her delicate forearms. Lilli's first tears dampened an ugly scar on her mother's cellophane skin, all that remained of the number tattooed onto her forearm at Auschwitz.

Grandfather McAllister rested his hands on his wife's shoulders, his gaze embracing his reunited family through glistening eyes.

Madeline caught his attention. She smiled.

He returned her smile then tipped his head and mouthed, *"Thank you."*

# Chapter 53

Dinner concluded, Madeline and her mother stowed the last of the silverware in the dishwasher. Grandmother and Grandfather McAllister had invited everyone to their house to look through some family mementos. Grandmother added that Lilli would spend the night with them, something about keeping an eye on her this time. Aunt Lilli, Aunt Kammbrie, and Karen gladly accepted the invitation, but Madeline declined, citing the need for the children to get to bed early for a change. Ian and Avery would follow along soon, after helping clean up the dinner dishes.

Madeline folded the dish towel and draped it over the handle of the oven door to dry. She turned and leaned her back against the counter.

"What are you thinking about?" asked her mother as she tucked a chair into its place at the table.

"Just the day, I guess. Everything has happened so fast since Karen e-mailed me; it's hard to believe it ever happened at all."

"It's wonderful. You should be proud."

Madeline shook her head and smiled. "Grandma put that one in perspective this afternoon."

"Where's Brendon?"

"Upstairs helping the girls with their pajamas." The tightening in Madeline's voice was palpable.

Avery folded her arms and faced her daughter. "What is it, Madeline?"

"What do you mean?"

"What's going on between you two?"

Madeline turned and began wiping down the already clean sink with a sponge. "Nothing."

"You know your dad and I have never pried into your marriage—"

"And I appreciate that."

Her mother's eyes narrowed at her daughter's back. "But then, you've never given us cause for concern before, have you?"

The wiping stopped. After a moment, Madeline's shoulders slackened and she laid the sponge back onto its tray.

"Look at me, Madeline."

Her daughter slowly turned and met her gaze, jaw set but eyes moist.

"I won't force you to talk about it, but I'm here if you need to."

"Talk about what?" The women started at Ian's voice coming from the entryway to the kitchen.

Madeline hugged her arms to her chest and stared at the floor. His wife beseeched him with her eyes. "Girl-talk, honey."

"Oh." He set his empty coffee mug on the counter, gave Madeline a serious look, then exited the room.

Avery allowed her daughter a moment to speak, but the silence only thickened. Finally, she said, "Okay. It's your life; it's your marriage. Just remember: your dad and I love you, and we love Brendon. That's the only reason we'd ever step in." She skirted the table and headed toward the living room.

"Mom?"

She paused at the entryway. When no further words came, she turned in time to see a tear trickle down her daughter's cheek. "Honey…?"

Madeline's hands went to her face.

Avery hurried back around the table and pulled Madeline into her arms. She shuddered through weak sobs, tears wetting her mother's shoulder.

"Oh, sweetheart. Can it be this bad?"

"I don't know…how bad it is," her daughter sniffled. "He won't talk to me."

"That's not like Brendon."

"He's been so tense. There was something about a problem at work; his prosthesis has suddenly become such an embarrassment; he seems insecure in his fatherhood—"

"Hmm, are you sure he doesn't want to talk? Sounds to me like he's been trying to tell you something."

"—and I found another woman's telephone number tucked in his Bible."

"*What?* Now that really doesn't sound like Brendon. Are you sure there's not a reasonable explanation for that?"

Madeline wiped her wet cheek with a sleeve. "How could *any* explanation for that be reasonable?"

"Have you asked him about it?"

"I shouldn't have to—"

"Have you *asked* him about it?"

Madeline jerked her head up. "No."

"Why?"

"I was going to, but Aunt Kammbrie was flying in that afternoon, and there was so much to do. Then it got lost in the visit, and—"

"Oh, Madeline." Avery touched her daughter's cheek. "The world stops for your husband."

Ian paused outside the kitchen doorway. His wife's voice resumed, but too softly to discern her words. He knit his brow at the recollection of his daughter's tight body language, affirming his impression that the air between her and Brendon had seemed thick today. Was that what the girl-talk was about? A thump on the ceiling pulled his attention to the staircase.

*So, maybe some guy-talk is in order.*

Upstairs, he poked his head into the twins' bedroom. They sat at the foot of their beds kicking a miniature soccer ball back and forth.

"Grandpa!" Maria slid down and ran to the doorway, Katia close behind her.

Ian knelt and swooped his granddaughters into his arms. "Have I told you young ladies how beautiful you are today?"

Maria disengaged and jammed her hands on her hips. "Yes, Grandpa." She rolled her eyes. "After lunch, before quiet time—"

"—and after supper!" Katia giggled and squeezed his neck.

"Oh. Well, you're still beautiful." He pulled Maria back into the embrace and tickled their ribs until they shrieked. "Where's your daddy?"

Maria pulled back, still giggling. "I don't know. He told us to get our jammies on and brush our teeth."

"We're waiting for story time," added Katia, then she sobered. "Daddy didn't look happy."

"Really? Why not?"

She shrugged.

"Tell you what: it's still early. Why don't you play for a few more minutes? I'll go find your daddy."

"'Kay."

Ian rose, and the girls scooted off toward their doll corner. He eased the door closed, then turned down the hallway.

The master bedroom lay in twilight, and he nearly walked past the doorway without spotting his son-in-law across the room. Dusky light hedging through the window framed Brendon's hunched silhouette, hands in pockets, head canted downward.

"Hey, Bren."

The silhouette jerked. "Hey, Dad."

"Got a minute?"

"Sure."

Ian stepped into the room, but remained by the door. "Lots going on, eh?"

"Yeah."

"Too much?"

Brendon half-turned toward the door. "What do you mean?"

"Not to pry, but when was the last chance you and Madeline had to be alone?"

The silhouette turned back toward the window.

Ian leaned against the wall. "She's a challenge, isn't she?"

"I love your daughter, sir." Brendon's voice came raspy.

"I know. And she loves you."

A breathy chuckle scraped across the room, and the silhouette rubbed the back of its neck. "Yeah."

"You doubt that?"

Silence.

"Not much satisfaction in talking to a man's back, Son."

Brendon sighed and turned around. Ian nodded toward the chair by the mirror. Brendon eased into it while his father-in-law perched onto the corner of the bed. He reached over to the nightstand and snapped on the lamp. Shadows streaked across the room, and Brendon blinked in the splay of light.

"Helps to talk sometimes," Ian offered.

"I don't know what to say."

"Or where to start?"

"I just…it's…"

"Lay it out, Bren."

Brendon leveled his gaze at his father-in-law. "Okay, I feel like I've been demoted from husband to facilitator."

"Go on."

"It's going to sound like I'm making excuses."

"No, it won't."

Brendon cleared his throat. "There are so many things I love about Madeline: her zeal for life, passion for the things she believes in. I've always been able to share her enthusiasm, even partner in her causes. I feel like she's dealt me out of this one, though."

"You mean finding her aunts?"

Brendon nodded. "She's glued to that laptop all hours of the day and night. If it's not the newspaper column, it's researching Web sites, or e-mailing. She joined a couple of social networking sites for information sources, and even now that she's found Aunt Kammbrie and Lilli, she hasn't slowed down. She spends more time with her virtual friends than her real ones."

"Tried hiding the computer?"

"Once. She threatened me with liver and onions for dinner."

Ian grimaced. "Swings hard, doesn't she?"

"And lima beans."

"Ouch."

"Yeah, that one was below the belt."

"I assume you've spoken with her about your frustration."

"Catch-22, Dad. I can't get her attention long enough to get her attention. It's been crazy. I'm trying to hold down a job, pick up the slack with the kids, keep up with church responsibilities. . . ."

Ian pursed his lips. "Bren, a moment ago when I said it wouldn't sound like you were making excuses. . . ?"

"Yeah?"

"I was wrong."

Brendon slumped his shoulders.

Ian propped his elbows on his knees. "Madeline can be hardheaded, but she understands the importance of family. I expect that's why she sank her teeth so deeply into the effort to find her aunts. Appeal to that, Bren, to her sense of loyalty and devotion to those she loves."

Brendon nodded.

His father-in-law continued. "Your wife is the fountainhead of your family; you are each other's greatest cause, and her first passion belongs to you. She needs to be reminded of that."

"I've tried to tell her—"

"Try harder, Son."

Brendon sighed. "No room for failure."

Ian smiled. "Even if it takes liver and onions."

# Chapter 54

Madeline dabbed her eyes with a dish towel while her mother brushed her daughter's bangs from her forehead. "Do you think—"

"Avery?" Madeline's father stood in the kitchen doorway. "Got a minute?"

"We're kind of in the middle of something, Ian."

"It won't take long."

"This really isn't the best time. Can't we—"

He cocked his head.

She paused then readdressed her daughter. "I'll be right back, dear."

Madeline nodded.

"What on earth can't wait until. . ." Avery's voice faded into the living room.

Madeline pressed her hands to her forehead, battling a fledgling headache. How could things be so right and so wrong at the same time? The joy surrounding her aunts' and grandmother's reunion seemed to suck the happiness from her own family, as though joyfulness were something to be rationed. Why did Brendon pick this, of all times, to be hypersensitive? Didn't he understand the significance of the reuniting of a family separated by tragedy and misunderstanding for seventy years? Why was he so into himself? Oh, and don't even think of Sally Morgan! Her temperature began to rise.

She perked at a scuffing across the room. Brendon stood in the doorway, hands in pockets, shoulders hunched. "Hey."

She dropped her gaze and brushed a strand of hair behind her ear. "Hey."

"You look a little tired."

"Thanks."

"C'mon, you know what I meant."

"Yeah. Sorry." She folded her arms at the waist.

"Sit?" He nodded toward the table.

She shrugged. He pulled out a chair. After a minute, she pushed away from the counter and sat, focusing on an imaginary hangnail. He took the chair next to her and clasped his hands on the table.

"I hate this."

Silence.

"We've never been this way before."

She met his gaze. "What way?"

"Madeline, please try."

She sighed. "Is this the part where it becomes my fault?"

"There is no fault. There's only us."

"There has to be fault."

"Why?"

"Cause and effect."

"But if we're both the cause, we cancel each other out. Then there's only the effect."

She refocused on the hangnail.

He laid his hand on her arm. "I don't know exactly when it happened, where we went wrong, but you're my whole life, Madeline. We need to fix this."

She looked up. "Your whole life?"

"Yes. I told you that in the car, remember?"

Her eyes darkened. "Then explain the phone number."

"Excuse me?"

"Sally Morgan."

He shook his head.

"Don't play dumb, Bren. I found the note."

"What note?"

"In your Bible. Sally Morgan's phone number."

The creases deepened. "I have no idea what you're talking about."

She rose and left the room. In a moment, she returned and flicked a piece of stationery onto the table.

He picked it up. "Madeline, I have no idea where this came from. I've never seen it before."

"Please."

"Seriously, I don't even recognize the handwriting. And if I were going to cheat on you—which is nowhere in my universe—does it make sense that I'd leave this lying around?"

Madeline stared at the note then again at her husband's puzzled expression. "You really didn't know about this?"

Shaking his head, he dropped the note on the table then took her hand in his. "Mrs. Sommers—" She lifted a finger, but he cut her off. "Don't interrupt. Follow me." He rose and led her to a framed mirror in the hallway. "Take a look."

She grimaced at her swollen eyes and streaked mascara. "What?"

"You're looking at my ideal of the perfect wife. How could I even think of looking elsewhere?"

Madeline lowered her gaze. He turned her toward him and raised her chin with his forefinger. "There is no one in this world more important to me than you. I wish I could get you to understand that."

"What about your children?"

"You gave me my children."

She searched his eyes. "Then why the distance the past couple of weeks?"

"I haven't gone anywhere, Madeline."

"But you have, Bren." They turned back toward the kitchen. "Okay, maybe I've been preoccupied with the *Times* column. I'll admit that. But when I do try to talk about things, you clam up."

They sat at the table.

"For example?"

"Your prosthesis, for one."

Brendon averted his gaze.

"There, you see?" She cupped her hands around his. "Why so sensitive all of the sudden?"

His jaw twitched. "There's nothing sudden about it. Did you know I still have nightmares about the accident?"

She shook her head, her eyes softening. "I knew you've had restless nights, but I didn't know why."

"I'm reminded of it everywhere I go, in whatever I try to do. I can't give horsey rides to my daughters." His voice tightened. "I'll never play football with Oskar."

"Why not?"

"Well, look what happened in the front yard."

"Bren, they do make athletic prostheses."

He choked back a laugh. "Do you have any idea how much those things cost?"

She squeezed his hands. "I would second-mortgage this house if it meant you playing football with Oskar."

He stared at her, his eyes taking on a sheen. Hers moistened in response.

Moments passed; then Brendon spoke. "And then there's. . . I guess I thought, with my leg, you know. . ."

"What?"

"We're in our seventh year of marriage. I thought maybe you felt an itch. . .or something."

"An itch?"

"You seemed to lose interest. All the e-mailing and social networking relationships replaced ours. It's been, well, how long has it been since we've been together?"

Madeline dipped her shoulders. "Oh, Bren. And you thought I was turned off by your leg."

He shrugged.

"That will never be true, Mr. Sommers." She searched his eyes. "I'm so sorry. I submerged myself in the project. Then when I did reemerge, there was Sally Morgan."

Brendon picked up the note and crumpled it. A flick of the wrist and the wad arced into the wastebasket by the back door.

She smiled. "Nice shot."

"I was motivated." He smiled back. "Is this really all it takes, a fifteen-minute conversation?"

"An honest fifteen-minute conversation."

"Stupid, huh? Two weeks lost for want of fifteen minutes."

Her mind flashed to her aunts' estrangement, then its cause. "Better than decades lost, I suppose."

"But just as stupid."

"Yeah."

They leaned forward and touched foreheads, then lips.

"When do you suppose they left?"

They stood on the porch, arms around each other's back, and surveyed the empty space where her parents' car had been parked.

"After they tucked the girls in, I guess."

He smiled. "You've got great parents."

"Yeah."

Madeline picked at a fingernail. "So, do you think the kids are asleep?"

"They were when I checked on them."

"Really?" She rose onto her tiptoes to nuzzle a lingering kiss on his neck.

He scrunched his shoulder. "Hey, that tickles."

She slipped her hand behind his head and twirled a dark curl with her fingertip. "You think *that* tickles. . .," she whispered.

He smiled. "What if Karen and Aunt Kammbrie come back early?"

"I don't think that'll happen. Like you said, I have great parents."

# Chapter 55

The adults sat in the living room on Sunday evening reminiscing the visit and nursing stomachs full of too much pizza—though Brendon argued that there is no such thing as too much pizza. The girls and Alisha Sheldon romped in the twins' bedroom, drawing Madeline upstairs more than once to find out what the last louder-than-necessary bump was. Inviting Alisha to sleep over allowed Don and Susan an unexpected date night, repayment for watching the kids and lending their van on Thursday afternoon.

*A most important afternoon.*

Madeline smiled as she righted the mattress and waived the obligatory scolding for jumping on Maria's bed.

When she and Brendon shared covert grins during dinner, her mother whispered her awareness of their antics and her joy at their reappearance. Madeline only smiled and kicked at Brendon's sock-clad toe nudging her ankle under the table.

Grandmother McAllister had brought along her copy of Tante Katia's memoirs, which now lay open on the coffee table. Aunt Kammbrie and Aunt Lilli paged through the tome, pausing with questions about the emerging faces and stories in their newly discovered heritage. Grandmother McAllister answered what she could, and Madeline filled in some of the gaps from her interview with their German cousin.

Aunt Lilli quietly told of her life after leaving the Romano household all those years ago. She'd never married, citing a growing fear of vulnerability planted by so unstable a childhood and nurtured at the hands of crass men in the years following. How she made her way from New Jersey to Los Angeles on her own she did not recount. Working odd jobs in California, she earned an associate's degree in accounting, then a bachelor's in economics, finally her CPA credentials. She shocked them all into laughter when she said, straight-faced, that, after landing her first real job with the IRS, a pang of conscience moved her up to organized crime. Aunt Kammbrie snickered her agreement, having kept the tax records for her husband's construction business. Grandmother McAllister smiled and shook her head at her daughters, her hand squeezing her husband's, her eyes rarely dry.

"So what now, Lilli?" Aunt Kammbrie asked.

"What now?"

"Yes, you're flying back home tomorrow. What will you do now?"

"I don't know. I hadn't given it much thought."

Aunt Kammbrie looked at Karen, who smiled and nodded. "Come to Texas."

"What?"

"You heard me. How can we separate again after so many years? Tony left me with insurance and a nice annuity from the business that supplement my Social Security checks. The cost of living is low in San Antonio. Maybe we could find an apartment. . .just the two of us." She peered hopefully into her sister's face.

Aunt Lilli returned a blank stare. "But it's hot in Texas."

Aunt Kammbrie chuckled then shrugged. "It'll be at least November by the time you close things up in California. We should be edging below 90 degrees by then."

Everyone laughed, and Aunt Lilli flashed a rare smile at her sister. "Let me think about it."

"Fair enough—but not too long."

They sealed the promise with what began as a shoulder hug but quickly turned into a prolonged embrace.

"Only if you promise to visit Michigan at least every other month," interjected Grandmother McAllister. Her husband seconded the motion.

"That can be arranged," said Aunt Kammbrie, grasping her sister's hand.

"I believe it can," affirmed Aunt Lilli.

❧

Aunt Lilli left to spend her final night in Michigan with her mother and stepfather, promising to keep in touch with everyone. Karen and her mother retired upstairs to pack for their flight home. Madeline followed to settle the girls into bed and check on Oskar. Brendon tossed his bedclothes onto the study sofa and went to the half bath to prepare for bed. Madeline returned just as he was buttoning up his pajama top.

He watched his wife lay her pillow at the head of the living-room couch. She tucked the edge of her thin blanket under the cushions then pecked him on the cheek on her way to the bathroom. He took the newspaper into the study, fluffed the pillow on the love seat, then stopped. Madeline's off-key voice penetrated the bathroom door, humming a tuneless stream of haphazard notes. He smiled.

When she returned to the living room, two pillows lay on the couch. Brendon's muscular arms enveloped her shoulders from behind.

"What could this be?" she asked.

"What do you think?" He nuzzled her ear.

"Isn't the sofa a little small for two of us?"

"Don't ask silly questions."

❧

The living room lay dark, but for the faint glow of a street lamp filtering through the window. Madeline lay on her side, head on her husband's chest, her fingertip playing with a curl at the base of his throat.

"Bren?"

No reply.

She plucked the hair.

"Ouch!"

"Are you awake?"

"Now I am. That hurt."

"Sorry." A sly smile toyed with her lips, and her fingertips searched out another hair. "Do you love me?"

"What do you think?—Ouch!"

"Wrong answer." She giggled.

"Stop that. Of course I love you."

Digging her elbow into her pillow, she propped her head onto her hand and peered into his face. "We are so blessed. Have you ever stopped to think about that?"

He kissed her on the nose. "Not often enough."

"When you think of everything Grandma went through in the camps, what Aunt Lilli and Aunt Kammbrie and so many children like them endured because of the war, it boggles the mind."

"Yeah, I can't imagine. Yet look at what they've become. They're wonderful."

"We're warm, well fed, safe, together." She kissed his nose in return. "Loved. Spoiled, really. And we don't appreciate it—or each other—nearly enough."

He drew his head back and focused into her eyes. "Trust me now?"

"Yup. And you forgive me?"

"Well. . ."

"Want to lose another chest hair?"

319

"Umm, of course I forgive you."

"That's better."

The next kiss wasn't on the nose, and it lingered. She laid her head down. He shifted on his pillow and closed his eyes.

"Bren?"

He sighed. "What?"

"The twins have so much fun together."

"Uh-huh."

"Oskar is all alone. Nobody to grow up with."

"What are you saying?"

"Have you ever thought about having another child?"

"Not really—ouch!"

"Wrong answer."

She giggled.

# Author's Note

It's widely known that over 6,000,000 Jews perished in Nazi concentration camps. Less widely known is that 1,500,000 of them were children.

From 1934–1945, one effort to rescue these endangered youth became known as the Kindertransport. Thousands of displaced children found refuge in Great Britain, the Americas, Palestine, and the Far East through the heroic efforts of individuals and organizations like those mentioned in Lilli-Anna and Kammbrie's story. Many thousands more did not. It is to them this book is dedicated.

During the summer of 1941, three groups of children journeyed from children's homes in Unoccupied (Vichy) France to America via Marseille, Spain, and Portugal. In creating Lilli-Anna and Kammbrie's journey from Montintin to Lisbon, I adapted some documented events from each of those transports.

For example, the story of the orphan girl in Marseille—my Angelique—appealing to the grace of a random woman on the street to avoid arrest is true.

Likewise, the heartrending event of the children's farewell stop at the internment camp at Gurs, including the young boy's birthday exclamation, is documented fact. The well-meaning stop occurred on the first transport in June, but due to the trauma it induced in the children, it was not repeated on the second and third transports.*

All characters in this story are fictitious, with two exceptions.

Anna Krakowskie was indeed the directress of La Chevrette in the summer of 1941. For the sake of authenticity, I wrote her into the story. As near as my research has enabled me, I've portrayed her accurately and in the positive light befitting her.

Vladimir Shach was the director of HICEM during this time, as well as a covert member of the French Underground. He risked life and fortune to rescue Jews from the clutches of the Nazis.

Although Hana and Noach Fuchs are fictitious characters, I've honored the memory of an actual couple by adopting their names. According to Yad Vashem records, Hana Hurvitz, born in Lodz, Poland, in 1904, married Noach Fuchs, an accountant from Wolkowisk, Poland, born the same year. Hana and Noach Fuchs perished at Auschwitz.

This was an emotionally exhausting novel to write. I hope it did not exhaust you, the reader, but still conveyed the stark essence of a little-known twentieth-century reality, one we should never forget. It's my prayer that this work will, even to a limited extent, help ensure it never happens again. Ever.

---

*There are two different accountings for the stop at Gurs. One has the train stopping at the railroad station at Oloron-Ste.-Marie, where the parents were trucked for a three-minute final reunion with their children. The second account has the train stopping at the railroad siding at the Gurs camp itself. I chose the latter venue for my story. The act of the children giving their food to their starving parents is present in both accounts.

# THE TRAIN BABY'S MOTHER

by Sharon Bernash Smith

# Dedication

For those who survived
and in honor of those who didn't.

# Introduction

It is impossible to summarize within the pages of one book the level of destruction perpetrated against humanity during the Holocaust when Europe became Adolf Hitler's hunting ground. Anyone possessing even a minute drop of Jewish blood was meant to be wiped off the face of the earth, along with those who dared interfere with his diabolical plan. He meant to exterminate them all, in order, he said, to create a "pure" race, worthy of preserving his chosen species.

Though all the stories can never be told (there are over six million), I've written a fictional account of one woman's imprisonment, survival, and fulfillment of her personal destiny. I've called her Hadassah.

My introduction to the Holocaust came when I discovered a book about Adolf Eichmann, a high-ranking officer in the German Army, in my high school library. Every page held the most hideous details of his evil involvement in the mass exterminations. This was only fifteen years after World War II had ended, yet not one of my history classes had mentioned this vast, debased atrocity.

I never forgot the book or the impact of its contents. Through the years, more and more information came to the forefront, and I began to glean a deeper insight, though I've yet to comprehend the evil behind it. I wonder, can anyone?

As an adult I saw *The Hiding Place*, a movie based on Corrie ten Boom's experience while hiding Jewish refugees in Holland during the German occupation. Tragically, her family was betrayed, and all were sent to prison. Corrie and her sister, Betsie, eventually ended up in Ravensbrück, a German prison camp for women. Betsie died there, but Corrie was miraculously released to become a worldwide speaker, called to "tramp for the Lord," until her death in her nineties.

After becoming a Christian myself, I read every book she wrote, and every book written about her. She became my mentor, and to this day I'm grateful for the life she lived and so graciously shared with others.

In 2008, I wrote a story called "The Train Baby,"* based on information from a friend (she is the *real* Ellie in this book) who grew up in Germany during the war. More than once her brothers took babies from Jewish captives held in cattle cars on the way to extermination camps. Each infant had been hidden in her family's basement and fed the only substance available. . .water from soaked bread. When it was safe, and arrangements were made, the infants were moved to the Jewish Underground by their sympathizers.

Later, I realized I wanted to tell a story about the train baby's *mother*. How did she die, or how did she live?

I am excited to share this story of God's plan and intimate participation in human destiny. I'm hoping and praying that the reality of God's grace will cause people to love Him with deep affection, honor Him more openly, and trust Him with gratitude. For just as the Jews have always been God's chosen people, so, dear reader, are you.

In His name,
Sharon Bernash Smith

---

*"The Train Baby" was first published in *Once Upon a Christmas*, coauthored by Sharon Bernash Smith, Rosanne Croft, and Linda Reinhardt (OakTara, 2010).

Comments from the U.S. Holocaust Museum

"I've been studying the Holocaust for many years, but today all my thoughts came to life. Everything I learned, everything I hated, became real."
Elenne, age 13, Maryland

"I saw my great-great grandfather's photograph in one of the halls. I knew it was him immediately, and it hit me so hard that, if it weren't for him, I wouldn't be here today."
Allie, New York

"The remembrance space here is beautifully haunting. It should be used as a space for quiet remembrance and contemplation for many years to come, or for as long as humans feel the need to hurt each other."
Felicity, Australia

*One past, one destiny!*
*Two women will soon discover they share both.*

*For I know the thoughts that I think toward you,*
*says the* LORD,
*thoughts of peace and not of evil,*
*to give you a future and a hope.*

JEREMIAH 29:11 NKJV

# *Prologue*

December 24, 1943
Germany

L isten!"

"I hear nothing, Ellie. Your imagination's once again getting the best of you."

"I tell you, I heard something, Fritz. What if it's a wounded animal caught in a hunter's trap?"

"They hunt only for food. How many times must I tell you this?"

"Tell me a thousand times, and I will still think it cruel."

Another sound rose from the direction of the rail tracks that ran through the back part of their grandparents' farm.

"Fritz!" Ellie's head jerked in the direction of the wail.

"I heard it. Maybe the train hit an animal."

They moved as fast as the knee-deep snow would allow, straining against the heavy restriction. Cousins brought together by misfortune, living in the country for safekeeping while their fathers fought for the homeland, they found comfort in the camaraderie that kept fears about war at a distance.

Fritz, whose long legs gave him an advantage over the younger Ellie, arrived first. "I see nothing here, Ellie. Winter plays a trick on us. See for yourself."

Ellie, her braids now loosed from a red wool stocking hat, grabbed her heaving sides. Misting breath almost crystallized in the fierce December cold. "Oh, Fritz, you are always so wise, far and above any boy in all the land." She waved her arm and bowed in mockery.

Suddenly the stillness collapsed with a cry, plaintive and intense.

They turned in unison toward the sound coming from the embankment directly on the other side from where they stood. Climbing up the bank for a better look brought them to a standstill. There, in the sooty snow, lay a half-buried bundle of reddish fur. It was moving.

"Ellie, quick. Take my hand. I'll help you down." A slippery slope made their progress slow. In places the drifts came to Ellie's waist. At the bottom, they nearly fell onto the pile that was still moving.

"Fritz," Ellie whispered, "it sounds like a..."

"A baby? Yes." He bent over, curiosity pushing aside fear. He picked up a corner, lifting it with utmost care.

"Ahhh," the cousins exhaled together. There, before them, lay an infant...tiny and pale, but alive, like a rose plucked from *Grossmütter's* summer garden.

"Pick it up, Fritz, before it freezes, for goodness' sake. Oh my, where could such a baby have come from?"

"The train."

"What?"

"From the train, Ellie. Someone threw this baby off when the engine slowed down to make the curve ahead."

With the child in his arms, Fritz looked closer. *Not very old*, he thought. But what did he know of babies? Calves, goats, and goslings, those he could tell you about, but a baby? This one was swaddled tight with blankets, snuggled inside a shabby remnant of ratty fur.

Some fierce emotion within the twelve-year-old boy emerged. Never had he understood the meaning of innocence until this very moment, staring into the face of something so fresh to the world. "Ellie, you are maybe too young to understand about this train. . .this baby." His words were a whisper.

"I'm about to be eight, may I remind you. Just because you're older doesn't mean I am stupid."

"Silly girl, listen. This baby is a Jew." A chill went through him. . .and not from the cold.

"And just how could you know that, Herr Fritz?"

"Because I know what this train carries inside the boarded cars that have been rolling through our backcountry."

Ellie stared at him, eyes wide. "Fritz, I've heard our mothers' whispered prayers in Grossmütter's kitchen. Those trains are filled with people, aren't they? They're being sent to work camps, are they not?"

Fritz, glanced at the infant's thin but cherubic face then quickly wrapped the baby's head beneath the coat again and turned toward home. He motioned for Ellie to follow. "Only the place to which they go is not a place of work at all, Ellie. What they say in the village is. . .is unspeakable."

"Fritz, please tell me. I'm not so little that you should have to protect me all the time."

He peeked again at the perfect face now sleeping in his arms and shuddered. He'd long ago lost his innocence when the war began. And now, if he told Ellie the truth, she would lose more of hers. But it was time.

"Ellie, the Jews are being taken away to die. Someone threw this little one from the train to save its life." There, he'd told her, but he couldn't look at her face.

She was silent for a moment, taking in the meaning of what she'd heard. "Poor baby. Poor, poor little baby," she cried in sympathy. "Fritz, maybe the baby is Jesus." She stumbled, falling to her knees.

He stopped and turned toward her. "Ellie, you just told me you were a big girl."

"Ja!" She picked herself up while he waited.

"Then think like a big girl. This is not Baby Jesus. Besides it's a girl. I saw a pink sweater."

Ellie began to sob. "Oh, Fritz, what if she got hurt in the fall? What if she dies after all?"

He, too, was worried. "She landed in a soft snowbank, and the train passed only minutes ago. See, she sleeps like a lamb, but soon she'll be hungry. Hurry, before it snows again."

He knew that his grandmother, mother, and Aunt Margot would help without question, but their neighbor, Herr Hoffman, hated the Jews with a passion. This might not go well. Fritz had no idea what somebody who hated Jews would do to a tiny baby, but he knew full well what happened to Jesus.

He fought back tears. He was much too old to cry, but this small bundle of blamelessness tied him to something bigger than himself. He didn't have a name for it, but the fierceness of the emotion made him feel old.

Welcoming lights from the farmhouse beckoned ahead, releasing a strong resolve within his very soul. Whatever it took to protect this little Jew baby, he would do.

∗

"Mein Gott, mein Gott!" His grandmother could hardly contain herself for the horror of what might have happened to this baby from the train. "Oh, how must the mother feel, tossing her own child to the wind? To the wind."

"Mama," Fritz's mother chided, "she had faith to believe that God would protect her baby. Perhaps she saw the children in the snow. Maybe that's when she made her decision."

Still, they all struggled with tears at the thought of such a desperate act. This child and that mother would never meet again this side of eternity. It was a horrible thought, but they could not take time to dwell on sentiment.

The women had the baby unwrapped and were looking her over for any injuries. Relieved she had none, they did discover she had a wet diaper.

"How old, do you suppose?" the grandmother wondered aloud.

"A few weeks, no more," offered Fritz's mother.

"Fritz, Ellie, bring me that pile of flour sacks behind the stove. We'll tear them up for *Windels*; she's soaking wet."

The children gladly obeyed.

"Now what do we feed you, mein *Schatz*? Cow's milk will not be good for you, but thank Gott we have a good goat."

His mother turned to Fritz, but he was already out the door, headed toward the barn to milk their sweet, productive nanny.

Herr Hoffman had been stopping by on a regular basis, and not out of unselfish motives, as far as Fritz could tell. Their neighbor flirted openly with his mother and Aunt Margot, despite their lack of reciprocation. Larger than life in his own mind because of all the land in his possession, he was arrogant and rude. The older man didn't care that his father and uncle were at war; he cared nothing for their honor. Fritz knew he was powerful and, therefore, dangerous.

Herr Hoffman was open about his hatred of the Jews, being a staunch supporter of Hitler, and made mention of the fact whenever he came. He brought game he'd killed and anything else he could think of, in order to gain access to the Schmidts' kitchen. Fritz was sure that, despite the extreme weather, Herr Hoffman would find a way to make a stop. How would they explain the baby to him?

Fritz focused on the task ahead when he reached the barn, preparing the stanchion and placing the goat on top. Rich milk sang into the bucket, causing comforting steam to rise against the boy's face. Still, his mind was on edge. Fritz leaned closer into Nanny's warm side; they'd have to have a plan, or Herr Hoffman would surely discover the train-baby secret.

After finishing, he turned the goat loose into a stall rich with hay. Grabbing the milk bucket again, he spotted a couple of brown nipples left over from when they had to bottle-feed an orphan lamb last spring. Relieved they at least had a way to feed the baby, he only hoped they'd be able to protect her from the living, breathing hatred residing a few kilometers away.

His grandmother was pacing when he arrived back at the house. "Thank Gott, Fritz, she is starving. Your *Mütter* has cleaned a bottle we found. Ja, I see you thought to bring the nipples. So big are they, but we will make them do."

After a few adjustments, the baby nursed with vigor, stopping only to burp.

"Oh, mein *Schatz*," his grandmother repeated over and over. "Mein Schatz."

Ellie stood as guardian. Fixed on the entire process, her eyes welled with fear. "Grossmütter, will she live?"

"Oh, I'm sure, Ellie," Fritz's mother, Gretchen, spoke up. "See how she eats? As long as she can tolerate Nanny's milk, she'll do just fine. Wait until your mother arrives from town. Won't she be in for a shock?"

Fritz came to attention at his place by the huge stone fireplace. "How's Aunt getting home, Mütter?"

"Well, she didn't want to, but she accepted a sleigh ride from Herr Hoffman. Otherwise, with the storm getting worse, she'd forced to stay in town. Who knows how long this could last?"

He thanked God for the information and for the old oak telephone that brought the news of his aunt's impending arrival. "But Herr Hoffman will surely come inside. He'll want to know about the child."

The room went silent except for the baby's hearty eating noises and Ellie's crying. "Herr Hoffman hates Jews, Auntie, even tiny ones. Fritz told me." Now her cries turned to sobs, and she buried her face in her aunt's shoulder.

Fritz's mother stood with the baby and began to pace in front of the living-room window, looking out at the foreboding sky. "They'll be here soon," she whispered. "We must be ready."

"I'll take her to the barn," offered Fritz. "She'll be safe and warm in the loft."

"*Nein*," said the grandmother. "What if he stays. . .invites himself to dinner besides? You and the baby could not be out in the barn too long. The cold would be dangerous. There has to be another way."

Suddenly, Fritz darted to the back door, grabbed his drying coat, and announced over his shoulder, "I'll be back in a moment. Pray while I'm gone."

Before his mother could question him, he was out the door and making his way back to the barn. Even since the last trip, snow had drifted higher, and he struggled to open the reluctant barn door.

He first took time to night-feed the animals held up inside. There was Nanny, a last-year's baby, and the surprise kid, born only weeks ago, now dubbed Gus.

Fritz threw grain down for the few chickens a marauding fox had missed then milked the cow, bawling for relief for her extended udder. He hated to take the time, but it needed to be done. Still, he shook with nervousness over the creeping darkness outside. His aunt would be home soon.

He prayed again out loud: "Dear Lord, help us protect the baby, and keep us safe from Herr Hoffman."

The cow must have thought he was talking to her, because she made a low response. His mouth watered and his stomach growled at the sight of the foaming bucket, half full of sweet Guernsey milk. He hoped dinner would be ready when he returned then chastised himself for the petty thought because he knew matters of life and death loomed before him.

With a pitchfork, he pulled hay down from overhead, filling all the racks double full, in case the storm got so bad he couldn't make it back in the morning.

Chores done, he looked around, grabbed another bottle, and picked up what he'd come for in the first place.

Head down against the wind, Fritz wrapped the protesting animal he carried inside his jacket. He could barely make out the lights from the house for the snow and ice pelting his head and face. Despite the noise of the wind and shutters banging against the house, he heard the familiar jingle of sleigh bells in the distance. He pushed harder against the elements and the pounding fear in his chest.

His feet slipped on the house stairs, tumbling him against the back door. The struggling animal protested the jostle with all four feet.

His mother opened the door to help him inside. "Fritz, have you gone mad? What were you thinking—" She stopped midsentence when she noticed what was under his coat. "Now I know. For sure, you are mad!"

"It's Gus."

"I recognized him immediately, son. What's this all about, Fritz?"

"I have a plan, Mütter. Here, take him." He handed the thrashing kid over to his bewildered mother, flung his coat over the back hook, and yanked off the barn boots filled with snow. The fire beckoned, but he checked first to make sure the baby was all right.

Ellie squealed when she saw the kid, and ran with delight to take it from her aunt. Frau Schmidt came from the back room carrying a quilt for the baby.

"What is that in my house? Another guest now, I suppose?"

"Nein, Grossmütter, he is part of my plan. Let me explain. He motioned for them all to sit while he retrieved the goat from Ellie. "Here's the idea. Please, there's not much time, so listen carefully."

Seconds after the explanation, cries from Herr Hoffman reached inside. "Whoa!"

The children grabbed the goat, lifted the baby from the couch, and headed for their sleeping loft directly above the living room. Ellie needed to use the bathroom, but Fritz shot her a look that said there wasn't time.

Fritz made a makeshift pen for the goat from an old blanket surrounded by leather suitcases pulled out of the wardrobe. He shoved a nursing bottle into its mouth, praying for cooperation.

Ellie looked as if she'd fall apart any second, but she'd have to be as strong as he needed her to be. He realized how much he loved her despite the difference in their ages. She was more like a sister than a cousin.

Down below, his mother was greeting her sister and Herr Hoffman. Just the sound of his voice frightened the children, but a scripture from Sunday school ran through Fritz's mind. *Ist er grosser, der in dir als er ist, her in der Welt ist." (Greater is he that is in you, than he that is in the world.)*

Immediately his aunt asked for Ellie. Up above, Ellie's face went pale, melting into what Fritz feared would become a big cry.

"Ellie," he whispered, "you are the bravest girl I know. God will give you strength to do this." He took her by the shoulders and knelt before her, looking into eyes the color of spring skies. "I know I've not always treated you with kindness, but I tell you now, I believe in you." He gave her a sound hug, which she returned with a deep sigh.

She sniffed, smoothed the front of her sweater, and swallowed. "I'm here, Mütter," she called downstairs. "Up here with Fritz." She touched the side of Fritz's face and mouthed, *"Thank you."* He watched her turn and go below, carefully placing stocking feet onto slippery rungs. As she descended, her face changed before him. *What was that look?*

Courage!

Fritz listened to the downstairs conversation, alert to any movement from the baby or the goat. So far they both slept, but he noticed the baby stirred in her sleep. Was she hungry again. . .so soon? Dreaming, perhaps. She stretched, rolled her perfect fuzzy head from side to side, and settled. He hadn't realized he was holding his breath. The reality of what could have happened to this child struck deep into his being. He reached over, stroked one hand resting out of the covers, before turning his attention back downstairs.

According to the plan, his mother and grandmother kept Aunt Margot and Herr Hoffman in the kitchen by the cookstove. Even a few feet away from the hiding place could mean the difference between life and death.

"Herr Hoffman, thank you so much for aiding my sister as you have." Fritz heard the strain in his mother's voice. Grossmütter was strangely silent. Praying, no doubt.

"It's no bother, Frau Miller. Anything to help out a lady." The loud voice startled the baby and the goat at the same time, but neither woke.

Herr Hoffman boomed on: "Such a storm, eh? I must press on to my own farm, or my animals will starve. All the servants but one are off for the holiday. Sorry to burden you with my problems, but with the war and the elements, I struggle. So much land brings great responsibilities."

"Yes, I imagine it is a weighty challenge." Fritz could hear the mock seriousness of his mother's comment. "You'll be on your way then?"

"Now, Frau Miller, surely you would not send a Good Samaritan on his way without some heated refreshment?"

Grossmütter ended her silence. "Herr Hoffman, I've some hot cider simmering here. I'll get you a cup. . .for the road." Fritz heard the tension in her high-pitched timbre.

"How very kind, Frau Schmidt." He paused then turned his attention to Ellie. "My, little girl, how lovely you are. Just like your mother, eh?"

Ellie did not respond.

"Well now, cat got your tongue. . .Ellie, is it?"

"No, Herr Hoffman. I. . .I mean yes." Ellie was flustered, and Fritz prayed for her resolve to return.

"Well now, which is it? Yes or no?" Herr Hoffman's laugh was short and edged with cruelty over Ellie's awkwardness.

"The cat does not have my tongue, and yes, my name is Ellie, Herr Hoffman."

"And where is your cousin, that boy?"

"Fritz is napping; he's not. . .uh. . ."

"Not well," interrupted his mother.

"Oh, my, sorry to hear that. . .so close to Christmas and all."

"Really?" said Aunt Margot. "He was fine this morning, was he not?"

Grossmütter interrupted now. "Herr Hoffman, sit, enjoy the cider."

"May I remove my fur, before I partake?"

"Of course. Here let me help y—"

Behind Fritz, the baby cried one long wail. He rushed over to pat her little back. She would not be comforted. He rolled her over and coaxed a warm bottle into her mouth. *Lord, please make her content.* He propped the bottle with a folded blanket and relaxed for a second when it seemed to work.

Below, silence screamed for an answer to the upstairs cry.

Herr Hoffman spoke first. "What was that?"

"It sounded like a baby." That was Aunt Margot.

"Oh, Mama," Ellie said, "Fritz and I have a secret."

"Ja?" It was Herr Hoffman. Fritz heard a chair scraping away from the table and heavy steps coming closer below. He jumped into action.

Glancing at the baby to make sure the bottle was stable, he reached down into the makeshift animal pen, grabbed the kid, and brought it up to his chest. He moved quickly to the stairs and was halfway down when the others met him at the bottom.

"This is your secret?" Aunt Margot laughed.

"I told you, Mama," Ellie jumped up and down, looking into Herr Hoffman's questioning face.

"Explain this animal in my house," Grossmütter scolded.

*Quite the actress*, Fritz thought admiringly.

"Oh Grossmütter, look at him. It was so cold in the barn when I did evening chores, I could not leave him. His cry means he's hungry, but I have a bottle upstairs. Please, may I keep him in for the night?"

Grossmütter nodded toward the loft. "Go."

"Hmmph, your boy is too soft," growled Herr Hoffman. "He needs a man's hand to his backside. When he's old enough to join the army, working in a Jew camp will toughen him up. A goat in the house, indeed." He turned in obvious disgust.

The family took a deep breath, but no one exhaled. Fritz looked at Ellie, and her lower lip was quivering like a leaf in the wind.

"Surely, the war will be finished before Fritz must serve, Herr Hoffman." Fritz's mother walked over to her son. She stroked the goat, winking at Fritz.

Worried the baby would finish her bottle any second, Fritz put a foot on the bottom rung of the ladder.

"Wait!" Herr Hoffman stomped toward him, and Fritz tightened his grip on the kid.

"Ja?"

"It's amazing how this kid sounded exactly like a human baby, eh?"

"Ja, amazing."

The goat bleated right on cue.

They all laughed, Herr Hoffman the loudest. "This creature reminds me of my animals at home. I must attend them immediately." He turned from Fritz and saluted to the others before making his way to the door.

Fritz tore up the ladder, arriving at the exact moment the baby finished nursing. Deftly, he lifted her to a shoulder. *Be calm, mein* Liebchen, *be calm.* He patted the tiny back and stifled a laugh when she burped in his ear. Her breath, like fluttering bird wings next to his cheek, caused a single tear to fall in compassion. *How cruel the world has already been to you. I'm so sorry.* In that moment, he knew something beyond explanation. . .a soul-knowledge.

Somehow he would be bonded to this child for the rest of his days. He knew it with the same certainty of faith that reminded him daily that God was real. He stayed put until he heard the sleigh bells fading into the distant night.

"Fritzie, come down." Grossmütter's voice was excited, but he heard relief as well.

He backed down the ladder, carrying the baby with great care.

Aunt Margot stood behind her mother, mouth agape with shock. "Is that a baby?" She walked over to her nephew with a look of wonder. "It is a baby! But. . . ?"

"Mama, we found her in the snow. She's a miracle—just like Jesus, Mama, because. . ." Ellie took a deep breath. "Because she's a Jew." The last part was a sigh. "Fritz and I want to keep her. Can we, please?"

"Children," Fritz's mother explained, "we will keep her until it is safe to let her go."

"What do you mean, Mütter?"

"Fritz, there are people in the village who will take this Liebchen and get her safely away from here."

"Sister, you know people in the Jewish Underground? This is extremely dangerous. You'll have to be careful, especially with Herr Hoffman sniffing around like some evil animal on the prowl."

"Ja, I know. But we cannot let him get his hands on this tiny one. Her life is worth any risk. How proud I am of our children." She walked over and hugged them both.

Frau Schmidt had the baby now, rocking before the blazing fire, singing close to one ear.

"What's that you're singing, Grossmütter?" Fritz asked.

"The same song I've sung to my grandchildren since they were born. . .see how it calms her?"

The clock struck the hour.

"Soon it will be Christmas Day, and we have a baby in the house. I cannot believe it," said Ellie's mother. She walked over to the fireplace, gazing down at the baby swaddled in one of her childhood quilts. "Remarkable, isn't it, how one so small can sleep through such trauma?"

"See," cried Ellie, "it's like when Jesus was born. He left his home and was born in the cold on Christmas. Oh, Mütter, a baby for Christmas. If Vater were here, he would help us save her, isn't that so?"

"You're right, of course, Ellie. Come over here, and let's take a closer look at our little Christmas surprise."

She unwrapped the sleeping infant, and in the glow of the fire they took turns admiring each and every delicate curve. The few strands of hair she possessed were dark and bound to be curly. Behind one ear they discovered a tiny birthmark in the shape of a star. Although a little on the thin side, they all agreed that she was quite the beauty.

"I think we should call her Star. What do you think, everyone?" Ellie looked around for approval. The agreement was unanimous.

"Ja." Frau Schmidt laughed. "She is our Christmas Star."

They carefully rewrapped her and prayed that God would pour out His blessing upon Star and the family who'd shown such faithful courage in letting go of their child.

Even though they had no idea what the future would hold for this tiny survivor, they took comfort in knowing there was One who kept them all in the palm of His hand, through this silent night. . .and beyond.

# Chapter 1

November 1965
New York City

D ead again! One by one the bodies piled on. She threw both hands over her face, unable to bear looking into the open eyes of the tormented dead. She couldn't move; both arms were now pinned by twisted bodies. The weight was crushing, the putrid odor unbearable. *No! No! Can't breathe! Can't breathe! . . .*

"Hadassah! Hadassah, it's okay. Wake up, sweetheart."

She sat straight up in bed, eyes still closed, clothing wet with sweat and reeking of fear. "Can't. . .breathe." Her arms flailed in the darkness. "I've got to get out." She threw off the winter covers. Gasping, her mind and eyes began to adjust to the familiar surroundings of her bedroom. There was the highboy in the corner with the dressing table to match. She lowered herself back onto the pillows. "Thanks for waking me, JD." The words came out a raspy whisper.

He kissed her on the cheek. "I'll get you some water."

"That'd be good," she managed.

He turned before leaving the room. "It's going to be okay, Haddie."

He hadn't called her Haddie for a long time. "I doubt that." She spoke to his back.

She wiped her face with a sheet, while one hand drifted to the stubble on her head. *"A woman's hair is her crowning glory, Hadassah."* Her mother's voice was clear, though her own thinking processes remained muddled from the dream and the effects of chemo. "Sure, Mama, it's my crowning glory all right."

"Talking to ghosts?" JD Jensen placed the glass of water into Hadassah's unsteady hands before lying down beside her.

"Mmm, you could say that. Thanks for the water, JD." She could tell he was already falling back to sleep, though she was now wide awake.

Hadassah eased out of bed, pulled on a robe, and walked the hallway to the kitchen, stopping to close her son Michael's bedroom door.

The ritual of making tea was grounding, like all rituals are supposed to be. Waiting for the kettle to boil, her thoughts returned to the nightmare. Always it was one of two: the one about being buried or. . . She shook her head to escape the suffocating memory of the other. The one that was real even in the daytime.

"Not tonight, Hadassah," she said to the rising steam. "Don't go there." The whistling kettle jarred her mind back, and she finished making the tea. *How much I'd love a* kinnish *right now. . .homemade.* She sat, remembering. A lot of time had been spent in memory-gathering these last months, ever since her diagnosis. . . .

*"It's not migraines, Mrs. Jensen."* So formal this doctor. *Hadn't he called her Hadassah before?*

*"Then what is it?"*

*"You have a brain tumor."*

*"Can you remove it?"*

*"No, it's inoperable."*

*"What does that mean. . .exactly?"*

*"It means, eventually, it will kill you. But with chemotherapy, you will have some time."*

*"Define 'some time,' please."*

*"Three to six months."*

# THE TRAIN BABY'S MOTHER

That had been two and a half months ago. She had no pain in her head now, but the rest of her had erupted from the chemo's side effects like a violent, narcissistic volcano, including vomiting and hives covering her entire body. And, of course, there was the inevitable hair loss.

It became the mark of the disease. . .the inevitable relinquishment to not only the demise of her body but also the death of all things feminine. When it first started falling out, she panicked. One morning, globs of it covered her pillow as well as the shower drain. Soon more lingered in the hairbrush than on her head, and in the mirror, the head reflection reminded her of a mange-infested dog she'd seen once in downtown Berlin. In protest, she ran to the drugstore, bought a bulky hair clipper, and shaved her entire head.

In the mirror, a strange, hairless, mocking alien stared back. "You're not me," she proclaimed to the foreign image. This wasn't the first time her head had been shaved. She wouldn't be a victim again. "You're not me, and you can't have me. I won't let it happen."

Of course it had already happened, but when her eyelashes and eyebrows disappeared, she gave up on the expensive wigs she'd been fitted for, tossed aside the silk scarves, and opted for the bold, bald look of every other patient at the clinic where she received chemotherapy.

JD had been wonderfully attentive, told her he'd secretly lusted after bald women. But he would say anything to make her feel better, even if it never remotely resembled the truth. She loved him for it.

Their twelve-year-old son, Michael, emulating his dad, found ways to compliment her daily. "Mom, you make the best cookies ever." He'd said that one day, knowing full well that Eunice Silverstone from next door had brought them over. Michael even read the paper to her every evening when the chemo had made it impossible for her to focus.

"Chemotherapy is buying me time, but what kind of time?" she asked the empty kitchen. *I should be grateful for every minute with JD and Michael.* One hand went to the top of her head again. A little fuzz. It felt just like it had in the camp. She shuddered and grabbed the teacup for an anchor. It didn't work. Giving up, she moved to the living-room couch and wrapped herself in a blanket. If she had energy, she'd have built a fire. *One more thing to give up.*

Many people at the cancer clinic had lists of things they wanted to do before death took them away. Instead, Hadassah had made a list of all the things she had to give up. Her list was never shared, but in the recesses of her mind, it grew longer and sadder each day.

*I'm not going to cave in. I won't.* Her eyes drifted around the familiar living room, gathering images like one gathers individual flowers to compose a fragrant bouquet. A wedding photo showed her and JD smiling into the camera. . .the only one of the ceremony. Even from the couch she could see the emptiness in her own eyes. Funny, she'd never noticed that before. Her eyes drifted to another frame that held a picture of Michael on his second birthday blowing out candles on his Howdy Doody cake. *I made that cake, just like my mama used to for me.*

So many memories, so little time to remember them all. *If I could recall only the things I want. . .* But she knew her memories weren't like a controllable faucet that dispensed water when required; instead, they flowed like a torrential river running swift and too deep for comfort. . .hence the still-frequent nightmares. *If I had a way to dam them up forever.* Her hands flew into the air for emphasis, causing the robe of her sleeve to slip down. There it was—the constant numerical memory she'd tried to hide all these years. An involuntary shudder ran through her entire body almost like a convulsion. Her eyes fell to the coffee table.

At the first visit to the chemo clinic, she'd been handed a journal—"good therapy," they'd said. It was lying in front of her, the blank pages inside the cheery flower cover, waiting for her to pour out her most profound thoughts, something monumental to leave for posterity. *What could I write that wouldn't reek of what I already know? I'm dying. Should I fill up the pages with just those two words?*

She thought about the word *posterity.* "Michael," she murmured, "you know nothing of who I was, or of my other family—*your* family." Picking up the journal, she found a pen tucked inside. Her hands ran over the pristine first page. *You deserve to know, my precious. But*

335

*will I be able to tell you everything?*

He was such a smart boy; he'd come to her one day when she was resting. "Mama, why are you in bed all the time?"

Hadassah had dreaded this conversation. "Michael, you know I have cancer. We told you." Her insides were shaking.

"Yes, I know," he said softly, while his incredible brown eyes filled to the brim. "But I thought the chemo was supposed to make you better." He used his sleeve to wipe the tears. "But you're not better, Mama."

She held his right hand, rubbed the scar on the back, then kissed it. "Michael, I'd love to kiss your hurt away like I did when you were little, but"—now her own tears formed—"that won't work this time. I'm not getting better, because I'm. . ."

He jerked his hand away and put it over her mouth. "No, no, don't say it, Mommy. Please don't say it." He was sobbing. "You can't die!"

She willed herself not to break down, though her very heart was ripping apart. "Mikey, listen to me. If I could will myself to get better, don't you think I would?" Her voice trembled with each word, but she had to stay strong for him, even though she was tired of being strong. She squeezed her eyes.

He sniffed then nodded, but wouldn't make eye contact.

"I want to see you grow up. . .to be a man like your father. But we cannot choose our own fate."

Michael's crying subsided, and Hadassah could tell he wanted to say something more. He lay on the bed with both arms around her and said softly into the crook of her neck, "Will it hurt when you. . .you. . .die?"

She squeezed him tightly. "There is powerful medicine to help with my pain." How could she assure him of something she wasn't sure of herself? "When the time comes, the doctors will be there for me."

They stayed like that, intertwined in their mother/child bond for a long time. "I love you, Mikey."

"I love you, too, Mommy."

Haddie believed she owed Michael the truth of who she was. . .all of it. . .regardless of the difficulty in telling it. Besides, though death was stalking her now, once long ago, at the bottom of that flowing river of memory, she'd been dead before. She picked up the journal, opened it to the first page, dated it, and began writing:

> *My dearest Michael:*
>
> *I'm writing this journal from a heart full of love. Well, nearly full, because sorrow has taken up a goodly portion of space. I should be having this conversation with you face-to-face, but I'm a coward. What, you didn't know that? Right now I am too cowardly to face you and speak the things I know I must before there is no more time for me to share.*
>
> *There are so many things about me, events, times, and people, I've not shared with you. There are countless reasons for this. For one, you took a lot of my energy growing up these past twelve years. Oh, do not misunderstand. I've loved every minute of every day with you, but somehow I've never had the strength to go to the place that contains the pieces of my past. It's like an ugly puzzle that I've never wanted (or had the courage) to put together.*
>
> *You see, that place is filled with so much darkness that when my mind drifts there, I am consumed by dread over the yawning abyss that waits. I'm sure you've wondered about your grandparents, my parents. So many times I wanted to gather you in my arms and tell you all about them. They were wonderful people and, more than that, wonderful parents.*
>
> *I remember the feel of my father's whiskers against my young cheek. I can hear the*

*singing of my mother while she worked in our farm kitchen. Although those pieces of my life puzzle are full of sunshine and warmth, fear has forced me to stay in the present. . . fear and a will of iron not to examine the dark, foreboding pieces that make up the rest.*

*You know how sick I am. There is little time to share anything, yet you have a right to know about your mother. Your real mother! I need to begin with complete honesty, and I will do so. It is not simply fear and my strong will that has kept me from sharing. Something else has held me back. Shame! Heavy, profound shame. At times I'm bent over with the weight of it. I've carried it so long and so far that it has become a parasite, more deadly than the tumor consuming my brain.*

*I wasn't always a woman of sorrows, even though you probably think that. (So serious I've been all your life, my boy.) Not like the other mothers I've heard about from your own lips.*

*"Samuel's mother loves Coney Island."*

*"Carrole Fauske's mom is the room mother."*

*Once I was as carefree as a child should be, living in a tiny village in the wide countryside of my homeland. My family was Jewish (yes, you are half Jewish), and our life was good. I would have thought it perfect if it had not been for my grandmother.*

*"Hadassah, you are lazy. Someday you will be fat because of it."*

*"But how do you know I'll be fat?" I asked. I knew sometimes I was lazy, but I was also so skinny that the thought of someday being fat was inconceivable. I tried over and over to conjure up such an image but never could do so.*

*"I'm an old woman; I know these things. Don't ask stupid questions, or people will think you are* naresh.*" As she hacked out the spiteful words, black spittle settled in the folds of her lips—testimony to the nasty tobacco she chewed. I wondered if she slept with it tucked somewhere in the cavity of a nearly toothless mouth.*

*At the time, we were peeling potatoes for supper, and she threw one at me for emphasis when she saw I rolled my eyes at her cruel remark. Bubbe's eyesight was not good, and she missed, but I knew my grandmother was not finished. She was never finished with me.*

*She squinted, her eyes becoming black slits, and pointed a bony finger in my direction. "You wait. You'll grow up and be a fat* alteh moid. *Ja, you'll see. . .a fat alteh moid."*

*I really did not care if I'd be an old maid. I was only six at the time and believed that God wasn't through with me yet. You see, then, before God died, I had hope. . . .*

"What are you writing?"

Hadassah jumped at the sound of her husband's voice. She hadn't heard him come in. "JD, you scared me." Closing the journal, she smiled. "I'm writing my life story. . .for Michael."

"All of it?" He sat next to her and rubbed one arm.

"I'm not sure how much I'll write. Do you mind that I'm doing this?" She looked into his honest eyes. He appeared strained; the worry lines on his rugged face were deeper each day. Her heart ached for the pain she saw.

"You know what I think, Hadassah?" He didn't wait for a response. "I think Michael deserves to know about his own mother." His gaze held hers.

She nodded and sighed. "I don't know if I can tell it all, JD." Her voice dropped. "I'm such a coward."

He moved closer and kissed one cheek, his voice going low and husky. "You're the bravest woman I know, Haddie, and your son believes the same." Both arms went around his wife.

She rested against his chest, receiving strength. "Thank you for loving me in this ugly state." Silent tears wet his shirt.

He pulled away to stand but kept hold of one hand and squeezed it. "Michael's in the shower. Tell him lunch is in the fridge." He grabbed his briefcase. "I'm meeting Steve this morning for a quick breakfast. Don't worry about dinner, either. I'll bring home some takeout. What sounds good?" He drew her to her feet to give one more hug.

"Pastrami on rye with a double side of potato salad." She laughed at the order, since she barely had an appetite. "Who knew a dying woman could eat so much?" *Yeah, right.*

JD gave the okay sign, picked up his keys, and left.

She heard Michael singing in the shower. . .a Beatles' song—"She loves you, yeah, yeah, yeah. . . ."

She grinned, picked up the journal, and stuck it on a high shelf. "What will become of my men, when I'm gone?" she asked aloud. It was Michael who stirred the most concern, because JD Jensen was probably the most independent, self-sufficient person she'd ever met. He was a survivor! Also, he'd been the reason she'd survived.

Indeed, JD would get along fine when the "thing" in her head finally stole the last breath from her withered body. Oh, the irony of surviving hell on earth, to then leave it so soon. Here and gone!

# Chapter 2

JD parked his Volvo at the train station, walked the short distance to the platform, and waited. Usually, he read copy from his employer, the *New York Times*, but not this morning. *She's getting weaker and weaker.* Some days he thought he could actually see the imploding process taking place before his eyes. It was insane because she'd survived the most brutal onslaught on the face of the earth. Somehow he'd believed that very fact to be his wife's guarantee for long life.

They were supposed to grow old together, bounce grandkids on their respective knees. Weren't they destined to sail around the world visiting the Seven Wonders of the World hand in hand? "Apparently not."

The man standing next to him glanced in his direction with a questioning look.

"Sorry, just talking to myself."

The man dropped his cigarette and ground it out before stepping toward the approaching train. JD followed and found his usual seat.

He was looking forward to this breakfast with his brother. They'd be going over the journalism contest his paper was sponsoring with one of Steve's professor friends, Fritz.

Steve and JD had been close growing up, along with their sister, but drifted apart like a lot of siblings when they became adults and went in different directions. When they'd both ended up in New York, it was fun to reconnect and get to know each other again.

About five years ago, Steve and his wife, Vikki, had become born-again Christians. JD feared the worst—long-winded discussions on hell and brimstone, etc.—but to date that hadn't happened.

The changes he'd seen in them spoke volumes about the value of "religion" in people's lives. It wasn't that Steve and Vikki had become radical, but some things had taken radical turns. Steve had been a two-pack-a-day smoker since sixteen, but since he'd been prayed for at his church, he'd never smoked another cigarette. At first, JD was the biggest skeptic, but over time, Steve hadn't resumed the habit.

Another change had been the way he treated his wife. Steve had always been part of a "good-ol'-boys" network of friends from college. Every weekend had been booked with poker parties, football games, or fishing trips. Whatever Vikki wanted to do was fine with him as long as she put up with his own agenda. And she did.

After becoming a Christian, he cut way back on the "boys" activities, making more time for family activities. One day JD was blown out of the water with his brother's off-the-wall declaration.

"Guess what, big brother? I'm now Crystal's coach." He was smiling from ear to ear.

"Of what?" had been JD's dry response. His brother looked totally goofy in his "coaching" outfit. . .shorts, a team shirt, and a baseball cap. He'd never even seen Steve in a hat unless it was the hot-orange one he wore hunting.

"Girls' softball, my brother, the sport of kings, uh, queens." His brother's enthusiasm was refreshing.

"Well, for your information, the sport of kings is horse racing," JD threw back at him.

"Whatever. Turns out, your niece is quite the pitcher, Uncle JD. Look, I don't know a thing about the sport, but Crystal's team coach is having a baby, so I raised my hand to take her place."

"To babysit a bunch of nine-year-olds?" JD had made little effort to hide his skepticism.

"Hey, they gave me a game book and a place to practice. How hard can it be?" Steve threw back his head and laughed then pounded his brother on the back. "Besides, if I get into a jam, I'll just call on you." He winked.

To the surprise of many, Crystal's team came in first that year, and every year after, but only because Steve had a way of motivating each girl to her full potential. In return, they played their hearts out for him.

The whole transformation was remarkable, and JD could see the effect of Steve and Vikki's conversion every time they were together. It wasn't like they didn't have problems. They'd had more than a fair share of "stuff" thrown their way. Their second baby, Luke, was born premature and nearly blind. Yet not once since the day Luke's blindness was discovered had JD heard a complaint, or a "why me?"

When Haddie was diagnosed with brain cancer, it was Steve and Vikki who bolstered the family when the world felt like it was tilting off its axis. Steve and JD's sister, Marjorie, had come for a week but spent the entire visit crying every time she looked at Hadassah. They then nicknamed her "Clara Barton," student-nurse/failure.

Hadassah was an extremely private person, but because of the respect her sister-in-law showed her, she'd let Vikki into the private hell she walked through every day. Vikki could love on Haddie and reach down inside to bring out the best of her, regardless of how many times her head had been in the toilet on any given day.

When Haddie's stomach went on shutdown for days at a time, Vikki made homemade custard, bringing it over any time of day or night. Somehow, that delicate ambrosia could be tolerated, and Haddie loved her even more for it. Once she'd scoured the entire city for the perfect tea to support Hadassah's precarious constitution.

The only thing Haddie turned away that Vikki offered was personal prayer, and Vikki never pushed. But whenever she was in the house cleaning or cooking, she'd be singing. . . mostly hymn-kind-of songs. Hadassah hadn't protested, and JD could tell that, for whatever reason, the songs soothed her spirit. Once he found her on the bed, tears streaming down both cheeks.

"Hadassah, are you in a lot of pain?"

She'd shaken her head.

"Then what's wrong?"

"Listen, JD." One finger went to her lips.

"Amazing Grace, how sweet the sound, that saved a wretch like me." It was Vikki singing in another part of the house.

"Nice," he'd said.

She whispered something he hadn't heard. He walked closer and sat on the bed. "What'd you say, honey?"

She put her mouth right next to his ear. "I'm the wretch. Only it's too late to save me, JD. . . ."

He could not imagine what he would do when his wife did die, but he had a strange kind of comfort knowing that his brother, Vikki, and their kids would be there for Michael and him. Poor Mike. Soon he'd have no mother and a father who was much more likely to be focused on what went on in the New York Times building than what concerned him.

JD could feel the change coming, like when he was a kid in the Midwest and one of those huge prairie storms could be seen in the distance. Something dark was waiting, and he could feel it. The pit of his stomach churned. *Poor Hadassah*, he thought. *You're being hit with a double whammy. You survived World War Two and Ravensbrück. . .for this.*

JD stared into the weakening darkness as the train hurtled toward the city. He'd grown up in about as normal a family that existed in Springfield, Missouri. A Norman Rockwell painting had nothing on his family. His dad had been a high school history teacher who kept family and students in the proper order. His father also wrote a regular column for their local newspaper—"Harry's Place"—anonymously because a lot of town gossip was exposed in that weekly exposition, and the editor/owner thought it best that Harry's name not be posted. JD had accidentally found out his father was the notorious "Harry" when he saw an unfinished piece in the Underwood typewriter his father had left on the dining-room table.

While most boys in his class hated English, JD's talent was apparent from the beginning. Encouraged by his dad and mother, he pushed himself and honed his skills right into college as a journalism major.

He'd barely finished college when he got drafted into the army in the middle of the war. But at least he could capitalize on his writing skills as a reporter for the *Army Times*. He cut his professional journalism teeth on the front lines in Europe, inspired by legends in the field, like Edward R. Morrow, Robert Trout, Eric Severied, and others. His style was gritty and to the point, unafraid to report what he saw exactly like it unfolded.

He'd seen wounded men wherever he went—men missing arms, legs; dead men without heads; human bodies unrecognizable lying in ditches, fields, and blood-filled puddles of water. But nothing he'd seen or heard had prepared him for what he saw when the death camps were liberated in 1945.

# *Chapter 3*

*Boring! Boring! Boring!* Scribbling out that honest sentiment across Star's notebook did little to relieve the frustration overflowing after an hour lecture from Professor Donovan. *"Grin and bear it, Liebchen."* That was her father's voice. She would have laughed out loud, but that might have awakened too many of the other students.

Even the way the professor dressed was boring. Did he not have a mirror, or a wife to explain the finer points of non-boring dress? Bow ties, each and every day—come on. How many bow ties could one man have anyway? She sketched a cartoon figure of him next to her notes then scratched through it.

When the buzzer went off, half the class was startled awake from their common doze. "Test coming up, class," Professor Donovan shouted above the din. There was an audible groan as the students exited.

"Are you ready?"

"For what?" Star quipped, flashing a perfect smile in the direction of Max Friesen, standing a little too close.

"Are you flirting with me, Miss Perfect Student?" He bowed in mock politeness.

"Uh, pretty sure not, Mr. Not-So-Perfect Student." She eased by him to get to the aisle.

He brushed off the remark and caught up with her in the hall. "Just want to know if you're ready for the testing of the boredom we've been subjected to these past weeks."

"Since I'm so perfect and all, then the answer is 'yes.' Yes, I'm ready." They were now outside, where the weather was freezing. "What about you?"

"Ready to quit. If I didn't need this class, I'd have done it already." He pulled a black stocking hat over his long, curly hair and hunched against the wind.

"Don't quit, Max. You're smart. Endure it one day at a time, and it'll all be over, my friend."

"Did you just call me 'friend'? Did the Ice Princess call me her friend? I think I detect a little thawing here." He ran a few circles around her, but she wasn't amused.

"Very funny." She turned away and headed toward the library, stopping to shout at his back, "Go study."

He waved over his shoulder.

*Maybe I did flirt. Ice Princess. . .did he say 'Ice Princess'? Well, no tall, dark, and handsome guy is going to ruin my plan. But Max can be quite the temptation.* She laughed out loud at her own drama.

Hurrying to get out of the wind, she took the library steps two at a time. Walking past the bulletin board inside the foyer, a posted flyer caught her eye.

## ATTENTION: CALLING ALL WOULD-BE WRITERS

*You could be published by the* New York Times *with your own byline.*

*Have a story to tell and want the chance to get published? Write it and submit it before the deadline.*

*Sponsored by the* New York Times *and NYU's Journalism Department, with Professors Fritz Miller, Steven Jensen, and Mr. JD Jensen,* Times *reporter, as judges.*

# THE TRAIN BABY'S MOTHER

*Final submission date: December 15*
*Requirements: Must be a current student.*
*Submissions must be at least 500 to 1,500 words in length.\**

*\*Submissions will not be returned unless a self-addressed, stamped envelope is provided.*

*Not much time left.* She dropped her book bag and jotted down the info on a piece of paper. *A byline in the* New York Times *would be a dream. My own byline. . .*
*Maybe it's time to tell my story. Would anyone want to hear it?*
Maybe, but who'd believe it?

# Chapter 4

*Hadassah's Journal*

My dearest Michael:

Why my grandmother treated me so badly was a mystery to me, but in those days adults never explained things to children. We weren't allowed even to ask, yet at times I desperately wondered. Did someone treat her mean? Had someone put a curse on her like the wicked witch of Endor the Bible told about?

Despite how she treated me, I still loved her. Such are the ways of a trusting child. Does this sound strange to you, my son?

How different was my *Tate*, her only child. He was to me the sun and the moon. Though he worked from early morning until late at night, Papa never put my brother and I to bed without a story, or our favorite. . .a treasured melody on his violin. Almost always those stories and songs revolved around the Torah because, of course, our home was centered on the Torah and all things Jewish.

To this day, I'm able to close my eyes and see him, smell him even. How vivid are those aromas still, rich with farm life. . .woodsy, verdantly mixed with the sweet, spicy tobacco he smoked nightly in a carved Bavarian pipe. Sitting on his lap, snuggled in all that comfort, I could have stayed forever.

Often he'd give us the gift of our own private concert in our tiny farmhouse living room. Song after song poured out from the center of his being.

We never knew, or thought to ask, how he learned to play the violin, but whenever Papa placed the instrument under his chin he was taken away by the power of those few narrow strings, and his tired, worn face transformed into profound peace.

Though we were present physically during those reveries, we knew he was being taken to a secret place that only he could enter. Oh, how I wanted to go there, to be with him in the hidden, peaceful spaces of his mind's vistas. At times I was jealous, like a sibling when another has taken a special place in the family.

It was this strong emotion that propelled me to master the violin myself. When I wasn't doing schoolwork or chores, I practiced. Most children would want to play childish games and such, but I was determined to enter my father's secret place. I never minded giving up the "foolish" things of my childhood, so I begged and begged Papa to teach me "one more piece." Though he worked harder than two men, he made the time to become my teacher and mentor. I learned quickly, holding the one material thing he treasured most. Playing it made me feel all the closer to him.

In the village I heard the word *prodigy* when people spoke of my playing. Yet in my mind I could never be the maestro my father had become. You see, it pleased me to play well only because it pleased him that one of his children loved what he loved. That alone was enough.

His own mother thought our playing an idle preoccupation and never once gave him, or me, credit for our efforts. I didn't care; I only wanted to please the man who brought to my life God's richest blessings. The man who, with my mother, made our home a place of refuge.

I loved him beyond words, Michael, and even as I write this, my eyes sting with tears at the reality of such innocence. Little did I know that those very memories would help keep me alive during the shadowed years of darkness that one day would blacken the whole earth. How could I know then that someday he'd disappear into a pit of death, the last sight of him etched in my mind and heart forever.

"Hadassah. . .my daughter, Hadassah." My name tore from his lips, one arm outstretched toward me, reaching to snatch his only daughter from the arms of evil.

The light of my life would be dead before his forty-fifth birthday. Killed by hatred bigger than all of us, an evil so rancid that imagination could never conjure up the depth of its power or the width of its annihilation. And he was not the only one.

# Chapter 5

*December 1965*
*New York City*

Fritz was looking forward to breakfast with Steve Jensen, one of his closest friends on staff. Besides both being professors, they attended the same Christian fellowship off campus. Steve was a true brother in the Lord, and they'd shared many hours in prayer for each other, their students, and respective families.

The writing contest they'd be judging together was a highlight of the academic year for Fritz. It always spurred him on to be a better teacher. Not that he wasn't good already. His class was full every semester, and many of his students had gone on to win accolades in the journalism field.

Last year, one of his graduates, Jerry Olson, had a huge spread in a national magazine when he wrote an exposé on drug use in the army. Ironically, he'd been killed in Vietnam while on another assignment, only months later.

Reflecting on how quickly time goes by, he was reminded of his own approaching birthday. *How could I be thirty-four?* He approached the staff cafeteria and spotted Steve waiting at one of the tables.

"Good to see you, man." Steve stood and gave Fritz a hearty hug.

"You're looking buff, Professor Jensen." Fritz smiled.

"You mean since you saw me on Sunday? Guess it's my new parka."

"Maybe so." He laughed and pulled out a chair. "How's your week going, by the way?"

"Not bad, but Vikki's been down with something. You know she's really sick when she goes to bed. That girl is tough. By the way, JD might be a little late."

"Hey, not a problem. How's his wife?"

"Not good, Fritz, not good at all." He traced circles on the tabletop. "Probably less than a month left for her." He looked at his friend. "Vikki and I have prayed and prayed for the opportunity to share the Lord with Hadassah, but she's simply not open." He shrugged. "It's so frustrating."

"What about JD?"

"You know my brother. He's a proficient writer, but not much for long conversations. . . more the strong, silent type."

"How's he taking all this sickness, do you think?"

"He's sharing a little more, maybe. I don't know. It's a heavy load right now, helping Hadassah and his son. I've got to hand it to him, though; he's really stepped up to the plate for them both. But," he exhaled, "it kills me to see him suffer. . .to see any of them suffer." His eyes brimmed with tears.

Fritz reached across the table and touched his friend's arm. "Maybe God will use this to draw them both to Himself."

"Hope so. How'd you ever put up with me before I finally gave in?" Steve chuckled.

"You were a hard nut to crack."

They both laughed.

JD now approached the table, and they stood to greet him.

"Hey, let's get some food before I starve." Steve hugged his brother.

"Yeah, you look like you might keel over any minute. Think you'll make it?" JD gave him a pat on the shoulder and greeted Fritz with a handshake. "Good to see you again."

"Thanks—you, too. Sorry about your wife, JD."

"Me, too."

After eating and small talk, the men got down to business about the contest, ironing out the final details, which took less than an hour.

"You really dig this whole thing, don't you, Fritz?" JD put on his coat.

"I do. Can't help myself. Comes with the job, I guess."

"Have to admit, I like this part of my job as well," JD said. "Hope you understand I'm overly distracted right now."

"Absolutely. Don't worry about anything." Fritz took the offered hand.

Steve walked over. "I love you, JD. And you know I'm. . ."

"Praying for me?" He coughed into his hand and eyed Steve. "Thanks, I appreciate it." His voice dropped. "I appreciate you. . .you and Vikki."

They walked out together into heavily falling snow.

"Wow, it's cold." Fritz wound his neck scarf tighter.

"What? You're a wimp! Aren't you supposed to be a Bavarian prince or something?" Steve slugged him on the shoulder. "Take it like a man."

"You're not very dignified for a professor." Fritz snickered.

"You've got that right. Never have been; never will be. That's why you have tenure and I don't, my friend." Steve laughed all the way down the stairs, waved, then took off running.

Fritz turned to JD and shrugged. "He's your brother!"

"Yeah, guess we're both stuck with him."

"Looking forward to seeing you soon, JD."

Fritz watched JD walk off. *I wonder what it's like to lose your wife. Maybe I'm glad to be single.* "Maybe not."

He hadn't intended *not* to marry, but with getting his doctorate, his personal life had been on the back burner. Though lately, he'd been feeling lonely for companionship and had actually dated a few women from church. Each one was attractive and articulate, but nothing other than friendship ever developed. He'd even talked to the pastor about it.

"Fritz, not everyone is meant to marry."

"I know that's true, Pastor, but then why do I have this kind of longing?"

His pastor had smirked. "Because you're a man, Fritz."

So much for sage advice. Now, with the contest coming up and semester finals approaching, his mind focused on other things.

# Chapter 6

## Hadassah's Journal

My dearest Michael:

I know all this must be a shock for you, especially since you won't be reading any of it until after the chemo has stopped working and my funeral is over. But I am compelled by the short number of my days, so I will continue while I still have my wits about me.

Tate never played favorites with my brother and me, though I'm sure we each thought we were his most prized offspring. Your uncle was Jacob. You remind me of him. Remember how you've made fun of me when sometimes you've caught me looking at you with tears? You see, Son, you're so like him. It's the subtle way you turn your head when you're working out a math problem, or how you frown when you've been misunderstood. It's those times I think of Jacob.

You'd have liked him. . .you, he would have adored. He was big and strong, and everyone loved him. . .a kind of magical boy, I believed. He was smart, too, a real leader at our school. We only went to *Schule* when the weather was good, so for winters we stayed at home. There, he was my tutor. Many of the country children stayed in town to attend during those long months, but our mother would not hear of it.

Although I was adventurous, at school I felt awkward and too shy to read aloud. Frau Minden would punish me for stuttering during the stand-up-read-aloud part of class, causing me to miss out on a lot of studies when she made me sit in the corner. Because of this, I didn't learn like the others. It was my Jacob who taught me to read.

Never did I read in front of the class without shaking knees, yet I mastered the skill nonetheless, devouring every book I could find. A fascinating world far from our farm and village magically opened up before me. From an early age, dreams of sailing ships and exotic places filled my growing imagination. There were no boundaries in those days of innocence. Looking back, no mind on the face of the earth could have imagined the horror that awaited me (us) in the years to come.

If I read indoors, Bubbe always found work for me, already hating the time I spent practicing the violin, so I was forced to secret myself away to the barn or one of the trees in the back of our apple orchard. Hidden away in the haymow, or balanced on a tree limb, I read and read. (Like you do now, Michael.) However, Bubbe was not easily deterred, and though she was old, tenacity pushed her forward in the pursuit of her wayward granddaughter. She'd beat the haymow with her cane, hoping to ferret me out with its fury.

"Come out, come out, you little *dummkopf!*" Pound, pound! "I will find you. It is work that builds character in a child. Work! Work! Work!"

But I was the master of my domain in that barn, and she never found my special spot. The hardest part was not to laugh, because I could see her through cracks in the barn boards. She'd pace around like an old biddy hen, with her head all tied up in a black wool kerchief, one arm flailing at her side while the other held the wicked cane. (Jacob and I named it *Gustav.*) When tiring of the hunt, she went back to the house to wait on her perch for the right opportunity to tell my parents of my errant, slothful ways.

As I got older, I became more and more adept at escaping her wrath and torment, but as the years passed, she only got meaner.

My mother's name was Esther. Such a woman I have always wanted to be, so patient and kind, always ready to help someone in need. She was our small village's midwife, but since there was never a doctor there, my mama was called on for all sorts of emergencies, sore throats, and "mysterious" ailments that otherwise eluded healing. In farm country, one's place only produced crops if the work animals were healthy, and, therefore, Mama was the local veterinarian as well.

"Frau Stein! Come quick—my mare is birthing, and her foal is stuck."

"Frau Stein, Mütter needs you! The baby's coming backwards, she thinks."

"Can you help me? My whole body burns like fire!"

A big cloth bag hung by our back door at all times, ready as needed for her "patients." In my child's mind, it was full of magic. Such a silly girl I was. I bet you think so, too, eh, Michael?

There was little money in those days, but my mother never turned down a single soul for lack of payment. Most paid with produce, jars of rainbow-colored food, or farm animals of every breed and size. Some alive, some ready to eat. Seldom did she come home empty-handed.

Often, when labor sitting, she'd be gone for hours. On her return, it was always a surprise to see what she'd been "paid." If late at night, Jacob and I would keep each other awake to witness her homecoming. Dancing thoughts of what treasures she might be carrying helped our sleepy eyes stay open.

One freezing winter's night, she came home covered with snow and empty-handed, or so we thought.

"Mütter, Mütter," we asked, "do you have nothing?"

"Were you not given a little something?"

"Children, you have no faith. Come closer. See."

We tiptoed down the stairs but saw nothing. Then there was a movement under her woolen shawl. We stepped back as a nearly hairless tail feebly moved back and forth.

"Look here, Liebchen. See what I've brought you."

It was a mongrel pup, skinny and covered with flea-ridden brownish fur, most of it missing. The pup piddled all down the side of Mütter's dress before being set on the floor. There could not have been a more pitiful, ugly dog in all of Germany.

Jacob and I could not believe our eyes. Was this a gift or punishment? "Ech!"

"Surely, Esther," my father had said, "she will not live the night. What were you thinking? Is this acceptable payment for all your hours of attendance?"

"*Nein*, Joseph. Silly man, I was actually given a fine share of food for our larder. . .in the wagon." She stood on tiptoe and kissed his stubbled cheek.

"But. . ."

"The dog I found in the snow, pitched there by who knows. Should I just have left her to die in the cold?" She did not wait for a response. "Surely, I could not. If she dies, she dies. So be it, then." She ended her declaration by kissing her hand and pointing toward heaven. (I can see that gesture in my mind as clear as if she stood before me now.)

The shivering puppy keeled over on the spot, but Jacob scooped her up and went to the fire. He began rubbing her pitiful body slowly and with great care. She licked his hand in response.

"See, Papa, she might make it. Please let us keep her."

Papa said nothing, winked at our mother, and returned to bed.

"Let's soak some bread in goat's milk and see if we can get this poor dog to eat. What do you think, Hadassah?"

"I think there's not much chance, Mütter, but I'll help." I walked to her side. "What about Grossmütter? She hates dogs."

"You leave the old woman to me, Haddie. This is still my house."

If you're wondering if the dog lived, she did and became our constant companion for over a decade. Even the old woman, who hated any and all dogs, could not resist the charms of

Tildy. We had one of her pups on the farm right up to the time the years of darkness began.

Your grandmother had a genius instinct for seeing beyond the obvious when dealing with her patients, be it the two-legged or four-legged variety. Never did she take credit for a healing of any kind. As the family midwives before her, always God received the glory. Though she was highly regarded in our small village and places beyond, we knew the place she loved the most was home. She was our rock, and God was her fortress.

Up to this point, Michael, I've told you of the happy years of my childhood, the life that barely knows me now. . .the before life that has disappeared into my memory like a ferry swallowed by fog on the Hudson.

There is more left to share of the good days. It is difficult to tell, not because of the pain but because of its beauty.

Your father knows this part, but I've sworn him to secrecy, and since he's an honorable man, I believe he's not shared this with anyone. I could have waited for him to tell you after I'm gone, but I, too, want to be known as a person of honor, so I'm choosing to reveal this to you now.

When I was fifteen, my parents surprised me with my very own violin. Ah, I cherished it like the younger sibling I never had. I spent hours polishing it, admiring the beauty of it even when it lay in the red-velvet-lined case that was its resting place.

I'd become proficient enough in my playing by then to perform for weddings, bar mitzvahs, and funerals. I also joined Papa in playing the songs for our weekly Shabbat and all the high holy days as well.

When I was nearly sixteen, one of my classmates had a sister who was marrying and asked Papa and me to perform the music. Playing for weddings was pretty much routine for me by then, but still I enjoyed every moment. . .all the celebration food, all the happy family members. And of course I was old enough to notice the euphoric state of the bride and groom.

"Soon, my Haddie, a handsome young man will sweep you off your feet, and you will leave your papa. Ech, it will break my heart." He winked at me and fiddled a lighthearted polka, challenging me to keep up his furious pace on my own instrument.

Flushed with performing and the festivities, we finished and took our bows in turn. That's when I felt someone staring at me. I turned, and there stood one of the tallest boys I had ever seen. Both hands were in his pockets, and he rocked back and forth with a silly lopsided grin. He removed one hand to wave but quickly shoved it back into a pocket. Not quite sure if he was waving at me, I ignored him. Tried to ignore him, that is, because my red face gave me away.

He strode over and offered to help me down from the stage. My face flushed even deeper over the invitation.

"*Danke,*" I said in my best German and held out my hand. He ignored it and put both his enormous hands around my waist, swinging me with little effort to the ground.

He threw back his head and laughed so loud, I jumped. Was he laughing at me? I didn't know and ducked my head, embarrassed by his outburst.

"Oh, please," he pleaded, "I was not laughing at you, *Fräulein.*" He bowed at the waist. "It's only that you are light as a feather."

I looked up to see if he was making fun of me. Our eyes met, and I saw only kindness. Well, kindness and something more. I could not breathe. You see, Michael, in that instant, I, your mother, fell in love for the first time.

Please don't think I was a brash girl. Nothing of the sort. I was as naive a young woman as ever lived in rural Germany. But so it happened.

"I am Avram, Avram Meyer," and he bowed at the waist again.

I was speechless. Never had my heart beat so in my chest; never had my knees been so weak. (Not even when I played the violin for the first time in front of an audience.)

"I loved your playing. Such heart you have for one so young."

"Th–thank you." I could not take my eyes off of his; they were the color of cornflowers. Could he see into my soul? If not, surely into my heart.

"I see the cat's got your tongue, Fräulein. . . . Uh, pardon me, but I've missed your name." He was standing too close. I stepped back, regained some of my composure, and told him my name.

"I love the name *Hadassah*." He smiled.

*"Danke,"* I managed again.

"Hadassah, might I perform with you? I have my own violin and was going to play a waltz or two later. Do you think your father would mind?"

"It is not necessary to ask my papa," I said a little defensively. I, after all, was not a child. I told him so.

"I see that you are not a child, my Hadassah." His eyes never left mine.

*My Hadassah!* Even though I thought him a rather brash infringement, I felt my cheeks blush crimson. What was wrong with me? Had I never heard my own name spoken before? Never in such a way!

"What do you wish to play, Herr Meyer?" I smiled and felt more relaxed with the prospect of performing.

"I happen to know that 'Clare de Lune' is the bride's favorite. Do you know it?"

"Indeed," I replied. "It's a favorite of mine, as well. You're the only other person I've met who plays it on strings."

"That pleases me." He walked over to a nearby chair and retrieved his own instrument. I was breathless when I looked upon the most exquisite violin I'd ever seen.

He stepped back onto the stage and helped me up, nodding for me to begin. I placed the violin under my chin and readied the bow. He glanced at me and did the same.

I closed my eyes and eased into the haunting familiar refrain of Claude Debussy. I was floating through the melody when, at just the right moment, Avram entered into the journey with perfect harmonies. Two musical voices intertwined. . .so intricately matched that every guest at the wedding stopped what they were doing. Tears slipped down their faces. . .and mine.

# Chapter 7

*December 1965*
*New York City*

O ne morning, Hadassah had been confined to bed because of intense nausea but was relishing the chicken broth her sister-in-law had made. Vikki was doing some cleaning, but in the afternoon, they'd ended up in an intense discussion about spiritual matters.

"Haddie, you can look around and see the goodness of God," Vikki said. "For instance, you have JD and Michael."

This was not an easy topic: why God allows suffering. But Vikki prayed daily for an opening to share the Lord with Hadassah and was grateful for this "divine" moment, regardless of the difficult content. *Give me wisdom to reach my sweet Hadassah.*

Vikki twisted a dust cloth in her hand. "I don't know all the biblical doctrine about why God allows things, like my son's blindness. But I do know I've seen Him work through Luke's birth and handicap in ways that are beyond marvelous."

"But, Vikki, wouldn't you have chosen to have Luke be sighted?"

"Yes, of course." She walked over and sat on the edge of the bed. "But I *don't* have the boy with 20/20 vision. I believe Luke is who he is *because* of his blindness. You know him, Haddie. Does he ever feel sorry for himself, or blame his shortcomings on his blindness?" Vikki stood and began straightening her sister-in-law's bedding.

"No, no, he does not," Hadassah said thoughtfully. "For sure, he does not. But. . ." She sat up straighter against the pillows. "I still don't understand how you can say that a God who allows such things is 'good.'"

Vikki stopped in the middle of stacking books on the nightstand. "I guess my accepting my son's limitations and calling the God who created him 'good' is because of my faith."

Haddie covered her face with both hands. "I knew you'd say that."

"Look, I'll never figure out the 'why' of God, Haddie. I can tell you, though, that the strength He's given Steve and me, and the grace He's poured out, in the midst of Luke's blindness, seem like very good things to us."

Hadassah shook her head.

Vikki sat on the bed again and hugged her sister-in-law with as much tenderness as possible. *Lord, help me reach Your child; give me the right words to speak.* She gazed tenderly into the eyes of the woman she loved like a sister. *I love her so much. I hate watching her die.* "I don't blame you for not understanding what I'm saying." She fiddled with the bedcovers. "If I'd seen the things, experienced the things you did in a concentration camp, I might believe just like you."

Hadassah rubbed the ugly row of numbers on her arm. "Really?"

"Really! Let me just say this: I believe that God knows your heart as well, if not better, than you. And I can say for certain He loves you and still has a plan for your life. I believe He has some unfinished business with you." *Where had that thought come from?* She couldn't believe she'd said that last part out loud.

Hadassah looked at her through half-closed eyes. "What do you mean?" She was fighting to stay awake.

Vikki leaned over to place a cheek against the side of her face and whispered in one ear, "I'm not sure exactly."

"What?" Hadassah settled more heavily into the newly fluffed pillows, evidently fighting for clarity against the impending sleep.

Vikki kissed the very top of her bald head. "We'll talk later, sweet lady. Okay?"

Hadassah nodded.

Vikki closed the door quietly and walked into the living room, where she fell on her knees in front of the winged-back chair. *Why did I say You had unfinished business with Haddie?* She grabbed a tissue from a pocket. That's when she heard a still, small voice in response. *"Because I do!"*

Vikki wept openly, muffling the sobs while petitioning the gates of heaven on behalf of the saddest person she'd ever met.

# Chapter 8

*Hadassah's Journal*

My dearest Michael:

I hope, my son, that you are not too shocked at the revelation of your mother's past. First, you must know that my former life in no way takes away from the life I've had with your father—or with you. But, I get ahead of myself.

I thought that God could only make one man as gentle and loving as my father, but I'd been wrong. He'd made one more, and that was Avram Meyer.

Avram was from a small village like mine, but when we met, he was studying at the university in Berlin. He'd come to the wedding because the bride was his cousin.

We spent the entire afternoon talking, though there was precious time left to do so. Rare moments in life often seem condensed into monumental capsules. Such was that day for the two of us. Avram treated me as an equal when we spoke of our dreams and goals in life. His was to be a doctor, and mine was to be a concert violinist. This I had not shared with another soul.

When Avram Meyer left that day, he took my address. . .and my heart.

The following seven days were the longest of my life. I struggled to be patient, hounding our mailman to death before Avram's first correspondence arrived. Bold handwriting addressed the stark white envelope. I carefully pried open the flap and retrieved the sheet of paper, unfolding it like the treasure I believed it to be.

"My dear Hadassah," he began, "I cannot tell you the delight just writing your name brings to me."

Thus began our correspondence, and the beginning of our future, as it turned out. His letters were full of all the exciting things happening on campus. My ramblings seemed mundane in comparison, but Avram testified he devoured every word I wrote and saved each letter I penned. I, the country girl, was elevated to the status of "interesting." But only because Avram thought me as such.

My Grossmütter was almost completely blind by then. Though her days of spying on me were over, her demands never ceased. Between her constant barrage, my Schule, farm chores, and performing, I had precious little time for writing but stole as many moments as I could.

Though Avram was three years older than me, and much more sophisticated, we seemed to complement one another, and not just on the surface. There was our love of the violin, of course, but Avram had been raised in a home like mine, where God, the Torah, and family took precedent.

His family was poor and could never pay for a higher education, but a substantial inheritance from his maternal grandfather made it possible. A bit of spending money, earned through his playing, provided "extra" funds for personal items, or an ale or two with other students, etc.

I did not know that the "etc." would mean a surprise for me.

My parents made Jacob's and my birthday celebrations wonderful occasions. . .not like our Jewish holy days, but special nonetheless. Mama made her best apple cake for me on my special day and a luscious chocolate one for Jacob on his.

It was my sixteenth birthday, and I noticed an air of something I could not put my finger on. There seemed to be a lot of whispering between Mama and Papa. What was it? Perhaps an unusual gift for me? Oh, how I hoped, but what could it be? A new outfit Mama had sewn in secret? A radio? I'd wanted a radio for months, loving the music sent magically dancing across the airwaves.

When the big day arrived, I was disappointed to see it raining buckets upon opening my eyes. Papa was out of the house when I awoke, while Grossmütter and Jacob still slept. I stood in the kitchen doorway in silence, watching my mother at work in her domain. Slim and trim, her fingers seemed to be filled with magic as they worked at putting my birthday cake together. Singing, she reached for the ingredients one by one—apples, cinnamon, butter, turning here and there, each culinary movement creating a domestic dance of the most graceful kind.

That memory of your grandmother is a gift that sometimes overshadows the final one of her, the one that haunts me. And sometimes, if I concentrate long and hard enough, I can almost smell the sweet, pungent aroma of that celebration cake. Almost.

I was hiding the disappointment I felt in not receiving a birthday greeting from Avram. Perhaps, I reasoned, some other girl, one far more sophisticated than one from a farm, had turned his head. I wouldn't let my family see me cry because I didn't want to spoil the day for them, but I'd lost all interest in the occasion. Even the smells from the kitchen could not brighten my mood.

Mama announced we would not be cutting my cake until afternoon tea. Despite my disappointment, I was determined to enjoy myself, but try as I might, I could not.

Our mid meal passed, and everyone but I (and of course Bubbe) seemed extra jovial.

"Hadassah, you seem so down today, Liebchen. It's not like you to not be excited about your birthday. Are you not feeling well?" Tate's questioning teasing only made me feel worse. I wanted to go to the top of the haymow and cry myself into oblivion.

Mama brought her wonderful cake to the table, and I carried a tray full of all the tea amenities, when a loud knocking sounded on our door.

"Who could be here?" Tate asked.

"I'm thinking perhaps Frau Haupt's baby is coming," Mütter chimed in. "Acht, my hands are full, Hadassah. Would you mind setting the tray down and answering the door, please?"

Although my hands were full as well, I went. At first, my brain refused to believe what my eyes were seeing. There, at my very own door, stood Avram, bearing flowers and a huge smile across his handsome face.

"I. . . I. . ." I was dumbstruck.

"Good afternoon to you, Hadassah," he said. And then did one of his courtly bows. "And a very happy birthday to you."

Besides the flowers, he carried a card addressed to me. I embarrassed myself with free-flowing tears. "I thought you'd forgotten me. . .uh, I mean, my birthday."

He was still standing outside. "May I come in, birthday girl?"

"Hadassah," Tate called, "invite the poor boy into our house before he changes his mind and returns to Berlin."

My entire family was laughing and clapping all at once. Even Bubbe had a toothless grin.

It was the best birthday of all. Avram was able to spend two days with us, and during that time our relationship was cemented and moved to another level. My parents could see exactly what was so evident from the first day we met: this was a man of high character and remarkable moral fiber. They began to love him as I did.

Although I had only turned sixteen, I knew in my heart of hearts that I wanted to spend the rest of my days with Avram. I was sure he felt the same about me.

But not until the day he left were the words spoken. The rain had stopped, and we went for a walk around our farm. I was able to show him all my "secret" places. . .the haymow, the tree in the woods, and a few other hiding places. When we were coming back to the house, he stopped.

"Hadassah, I enjoyed everything about today." He was holding both my hands in his.

"I feel the same, Avram. Thank you for coming all this way." My heart felt as though it would burst out of my chest.

"You know I have more school left at the university, but. . ." He struggled with the words. ". . .what I'm trying to say is, will you wait for me, Haddie?"

Deep in my spirit I knew what he was asking, but still I could hardly believe it. I was speechless, able only to stare into his riveting eyes.

"Hadassah, I'm so sorry. Have I spoken out too soon?" He backed away a couple steps, still holding my hands.

"Avram," I murmured, "I will wait for you until the day I die, if that is what it takes for us to be together."

He threw his head back and laughed out loud then picked me up in his arms and swung me around and around until I was dizzy. I could barely stand when he set me back onto the ground.

Before we'd returned to the house, we pledged ourselves to one another, promising that when I was finished with my school and he with college, we would get married. It was the longest two years of my life.

# Chapter 9

Entry for the *New York Times'* contest:

*"I Shouldn't Be Alive!"*
By Star Elisabeth Firstenberg

*The winter of 1943 saw the continued transportation of millions of German citizens to Nazi concentration camps. For anyone Jewish living in Germany, Hitler's cruel, demonic plan for the systematic destruction of them continued with a vengeance. Train after train swept the innocents from cities, towns, and obscure villages. Fueled by hatred, bigotry, and an enormous army of manpower, the wildfire "extermination" of every man, woman, and child of Jewish descent would eventually be carried to extremes never seen in the history of man.*

*"The final solution," as it was called, was of such magnitude, even now, after two decades, it is difficult to comprehend. Because I was once a passenger on one of those death trains, I intend to put a personal face to the enormity of the Holocaust. Some might find my story incomprehensible, but it is true nonetheless.*

*On December 24 of 1943, two German cousins were playing in the snow on their family farm, thirty miles north of Berlin and south of Ravensbrück, a Nazi prison camp for women. When one of the children heard an unfamiliar noise in the distance, they trekked through deep snow to investigate. What they found in a brown bundle lying next to the tracks would change all our lives. They had found me!*

*But how had I gotten there, and who had left me? The older cousin, a boy, understood immediately. He knew that freight trains carrying disposable human cargo came through on a regular basis. He knew I'd been thrown from one of the transport cars. The fall alone could have killed me, or the children could have easily missed my cry. How then did I survive?*

*I believe Divine intervention saved my life.*

*From the minute they took me out of the cold and into the safety of their warm home, my life was in as much danger as if I'd continued the journey to Ravensbrück. Nazi sympathizers lived everywhere. Yet my destiny was about to be altered forever in ways I've only heard about in stories told to me as I grew up.*

*Immediately, I had to be hidden with utmost discretion in order to keep me from being destroyed. Not only was my life at stake, but the entire family was in imminent danger. They would have been put to death if my small presence had been discovered.*

*My rescuers were three adult women living together with two children; therefore, they substituted prayer and cleverness for manpower and physical strength. Whom could they trust? It is my understanding that they never questioned a single soul without first praying. One misspoken word to the wrong person would have meant tragedy for us all.*

*Relying on faith alone, the women began making inquiries into the Jewish Underground but only from closest friends. Person by person received news of my arrival, until word of the Christmas Eve child, or the "train baby," eventually made it to the right contact people.*

*I'm told I became the symbol of a very large hope, hidden in a basket like Moses, sleeping in a barn like Jesus, and carried on skis in a snow pack. Isolated by mountainous terrain, my final destination was a village high in the Bavarian mountains, in a home set apart from prying eyes, nosy neighbors, and the Nazis. Because of this geographical isolation, the Firstenbergs, my adopted family, were seen only occasionally in the nearby village, and not at all during long German winters.*

*My mother shocked no one, therefore, when she arrived in the spring for Easter church services with a new baby. Instead Frau Firstenberg was greeted with the usual congratulations one would give any mother with her latest child. She had a ready answer for the full head of dark hair I bore that was so unlike my siblings or my parents.*

*"Came from one of her Grossmütters," was all she ever said. If anyone had doubts, they were never raised, at least not to my mother's face.*

*I thrived with the Firstenbergs, who loved me unconditionally as their own. They were brave, generous to a fault, and deeply loved by all their children.*

*Raised with five brothers and sisters, grandparents, and many aunts, uncles, and cousins, my childhood was wholesome and full of joy, despite the war years. When my mother told me the circumstances of how I came to them, I understood little in the beginning. It was only after I entered high school in America that I realized the enormity of my birth and rescue—the miraculous nature of it all.*

*I had not realized until then the enormity of the evil perpetrated against the descendants of my Jewish ancestors. What could these people have possibly done to enrage the German dictator, leading him to mastermind the despoliation of a single race of human beings?*

*For now, my most pressing questions surround my birth parents. What suffering had they already been through before making the decision to wrap me in an old brown coat and then throw me into the wind? I can only imagine their last thoughts in those final moments, the anguish that resulted from such a desperate act.*

*And what of the after? My mother would have been sent to Ravensbrück, the women's prison looming just ahead of where I was found. But what of her husband, my father? Was he on that same train? Perhaps there were other family members I don't know about.*

*I rarely allow myself to think of what happened to my birth family once they arrived at the extermination camps, but I've seen the pictures of ovens, smokestacks, and all the broken bodies. So, in my quiet reveries, I do wonder. Did they suffer long? Did they have tender last words for one another? When they died, were their final thoughts of their bundled little girl left in the snow?*

*I've read some camp survivor stories, and now I'm adding mine. I believe I've survived the horror of the Holocaust to remind others that we must stop all prejudice against all human beings. Can we now see that prejudice, as witnessed through the Holocaust, was perpetrated to its uttermost, consequential evil?*

*It must end with this generation.*

*Sincerely and with profound gratitude I am,*
*Star Elizabeth Firstenberg, Holocaust survivor*

Fritz had read through the first entries and was pleased with the response, feeling some pride at the enthusiasm of his students' work. Four had been dismissed and laid aside, but two others had promise.

The seventh entry got his attention immediately: "I Shouldn't Be Alive!" "Hmm, dramatic enough." He marked *Excellent* beside the title, and continued reading.

When Fritz read to the third paragraph, he jumped to his feet. His hands shook; his mind raced. *This can't be her. What are the chances? I simply cannot believe this.* He wanted to shout, but instead he wept. He read on: *"The older cousin, a boy, understood immediately."*

*Father God, all these years I've wondered, and wondered; now it's almost beyond my comprehension. You knew the minute we plucked her out of the freezing snow this day would come.*

He went from sitting to standing several times, reading and rereading the entry in his hand. From the moment he'd carried that small baby in his arms and hidden her from harm, a bond had formed, and now the years of wondering had been answered.

Wanting, no, *needing,* to tell someone, he thought of Steve, but it was too late for a phone call. Ellie! She was on the West Coast, and it was only eight there.

The phone rang three times before she answered. "Hello?"

"Ellie, it's Fritz."

"Fritz, who?" Her laugh was exactly the same as when she was a child.

"Funny. Ellie, I have something to tell you." He felt out of breath.

"You're getting married?" Another laugh.

"You'd better sit down." His tone was serious.

"Fritz, what's wrong? Are you all right? You're scaring me."

"I'm not sick. Let me start over." He paused to calm his thoughts. "Ellie, I think I've found Star." His voice quavered, and his words ran together.

"Wait a minute. You. . .you mean *our* Star?" His cousin's voice was high-pitched and breathy.

"Yes, yes, our baby girl. I believe she's the very same one." He went on to tell her of the contest and how he'd just read her entry letter.

"You mean to tell me, she's right on your campus? Have you spoken to her yet? Wow, now I *am* sitting down. This is amazing, Fritz. God's hand is on this whole thing. Honestly, I cannot believe it. And she still goes by 'Star'?"

"Yes, Star Elizabeth Firstenberg."

"Firstenberg? I will never forget that day we found her, Fritz."

"It's like it was yesterday, Cousin."

"When will you contact her?" Her excitement reverberated through the phone line.

"I'm not sure. I'm still in shock, I guess. I don't know if I should contact her in person or call. It's late here, and besides, I need to compose myself, or she'll think I'm a raving lunatic." He laughed. "Of course I sound like one, for sure."

"Oh, Fritzie, wait until our mothers hear about this. I wish Grossmütter were alive. She adored that baby girl." She squealed in absolute delight. "I love this. . . . I mean, I really love it."

"Me, too," he said softly. "Me, too. Listen, I'd better get off the phone and let you get back to your family. Tell them 'hi' for me."

"Oh, I surely will, Fritz, and I'll start praying as soon as I'm off the phone. Somehow I'm hoping I can meet her. Who knows, right?" She sighed.

"Right. Love you, Ellie. Bye."

"Love you, too. Call me the minute you talk with her. Bye."

"Okay." Crying, he hung up and knelt beside the bed in humble gratitude to the Lord God of the universe for answering the prayer of his heart after all these years. "Thank You for Your faithfulness." He climbed into bed, exhausted, falling into a restless sleep, with dreams of plaintive, distant cries, pristine snowbanks, and the feel of a newborn's breath on his cheek.

❧

Waking before six, Fritz made tea and scrambled eggs with toast, all the while reading Star's story over and over. It was only after showering and dressing for work that he realized it was Saturday. He laughed out loud. "Fritz, you're a basket case."

At the bottom of Star's entry was a phone number and address. She lived near campus. "I'll wait until eight before I call." *Or is that too early?* "Too early." He quickly threw on some running clothes and shoes, slammed a hat on his head, and left for a long run. Running always cleared his head and kept him in shape for skiing. *I wonder if she skis?*

It was below freezing, but he barely felt a thing. He had the nearby park to himself except for one other brave soul walking a dog. Fritz let the wonder of God's divine intervention play in his mind, while December 24, 1943, ran through his memory.

He'd never forgotten a single detail, from the moment they'd found that strange moving bundle in the snow, to the day they finally had to let her go. It had become the most profound memory of his childhood, remaining more prominent even than the day his family had arrived in the United States, some fifteen years ago.

He checked his watch: 8:45. He was nearly back to his apartment building. *Let her be home.*

# Chapter 10

*Hadassah's Journal*

My dearest Michael:

When the two years were up, we were married, and Avram began medical school. Even though I had barely ever been past the boundaries of my village, my determination to succeed at being his wife gave me purpose and courage to leave my family. I cried myself to sleep those first few weeks after moving to Berlin but only after Avram was sleeping because I didn't want to burden him with my childish homesickness. I was his biggest fan, and he was mine.

Our first home was small with a living room, kitchen, and bathroom. It came furnished with an ancient couch that made into a bed, an eating table with uneven legs (which doubled as Avram's study desk), and a floor lamp that sputtered and sparked if left on too long. At first, its sparseness made my homesickness worse. But the windows let in the morning sun, which stretched from wall to wall, expanding the space into a cozy, hospitable home.

My mother had sent some curtains—blue and white gingham with tiny embroidered red flowers—that had the lingering aroma of her kitchen. After hanging them, I surveyed my surroundings with renewed vision and liked what I saw: a few family photos (including one of our wedding) and a single wildflower in a chipped drinking glass. Avram had picked it for me one day after class. I was grateful, feeling grown up in that moment and very satisfied.

Although our home was barely large enough for the two of us, I began to give violin lessons to children in our apartment building. My life as a wife and teacher made me so happy that things around me went largely unnoticed for almost a full year.

One morning, I could barely make it to the bathroom down the hall before throwing up every bit of breakfast I'd eaten. I said nothing to Avram, but when the same thing happened the following day, I asked, "Avram, have you been feeling well?"

"Yes, perfectly well, except for never getting enough sleep in between class and studying. Why?"

"Because," I said, "I'm feeling queasy and haven't been able to hold my breakfast down the last few days; and if I could, I'd sleep the entire day away."

"Really?"

"Mmm, maybe I'm just a little sick."

"Perhaps, but I'm thinking that maybe you're a little pregnant." He was grinning from ear to ear.

"What? No! What?" When I recovered from the shock of his statement, I realized he was absolutely right. We were going to have a baby.

Despite the fact we were poor as church mice, the idea of having a child sent us to our knees in gratitude. Our parents were a little more apprehensive, since Avram had not finished school.

It was 1939, and although my personal world was full of contentment and wonderful joy, the city of Berlin was rumbling. Up to this point, I had been protected by my husband and my own ignorance of such evil matters, but a giant earthquake beyond the scope of imagination had begun, and there was no way to stop it. The foundation of our entire lives was about to be altered in ways only the devil could plan.

I'd read about the closing of shops and the burning of synagogues, but Berlin was large, and our neighborhood had been left out of the mayhem. We were more or less living communally, and the rhythm of that daily life remained intact. But slowly, like a fatal disease, the hatred crept over the city until we knew we had to make our escape or risk being sent to Dachau concentration camp where, just the year before, thousands of Jews had been delivered.

Avram had been allowed to continue in school only by some political fluke and the fact he was a brilliant student. There were several like him who had been protected by Christian professors who, by their conscience, could not eliminate them from the university. But when one prominent teacher was arrested and never heard from again, Avram knew we had to leave.

Since my family lived the greatest distance from the city, and therefore was the safest location, we made plans to go and stay until the war was over. We felt that the huge arm of the Third Reich would not find us there. After the war, perhaps we would return and Avram could finish getting his degree. Why would anyone care about a small village anyway? How ignorant we all were of the power or the extent of what evil's repercussions could reap.

Having been warned about trying to leave the city without proper papers, we made plans to escape in the dead of night. Many of our neighbors refused to accept what was going on all around us. Some even scoffed at the idea that anyone could even begin to believe it was possible to eliminate all the Jews from Berlin. Jewish business owners, Jewish doctors and lawyers, had been leaders in every aspect of the secular communities for years. Most did not realize the extent of the underlying hatred over their prosperity or the long-held prejudices that accompanied such success.

Our leaving was delayed by the birth of our son, Aaron. This was your brother, Michael, and he was every bit as beautiful and perfect as you.

Avram and I had planned on having my mother attend the birth to assist with the baby's delivery, but babies do not care about their parents' plans. He came, like all children before him, exactly when he was ready.

I woke with a nagging backache but assumed it was because of our lumpy mattress. Avram had gotten up early and left, which meant I was alone when I realized that indeed I was going to be delivering my child soon.

In between contractions, I gathered the things I'd been collecting for the birth. Though I'd been on births with my mother, and totally aware of the entire process, I passionately hoped my husband would return. I could not imagine giving birth without him. I did have a friend, Lydia, who lived down the hall. She came and paced with me, wiping my face of perspiration as the labor progressed. Her words of encouragement relieved any fear, allowing wonder and excitement over the entire process to flow over me.

Avram was shocked to find me in labor on his return. My confidence grew as I leaned on his strength and medical knowledge to help birth our child. "But Hadassah," he said, "don't forget it is you who are giving birth, and my assistance is merely an auxiliary arm to God's plan."

"Avram, God is not giving birth. . .I am!"

He hugged me and gave me all the backup I needed to endure. After several hours, your big brother made his entrance into our world. One look at him, and the primordial instinct of motherhood kicked in. I felt the dangerous weight of our situation like never before. I knew instantly we needed to get out of Berlin as soon as possible. By now, night raids on Jewish clusters were a daily given. It would only be a matter of time before the pounding would be upon our very own door.

We waited ten days for my recovery before making our exit. The night we left was moon-less and warm: two things we considered as divine intervention. We told no one in our build-ing of our plans beforehand, but after Aaron was born, we had many visitors. This made it difficult to keep our preparations hidden. We stuffed our packed goods behind the couch and into what little storage space we had for safekeeping.

I felt emotional over leaving the people we loved here behind, yet our need for survival now included our child, and his life and safety took precedence. All that day, Aaron had been fussy, and we prayed over and over that he was not getting sick. The day dragged on and on.

Each time someone came by, it was all I could manage to not break down into tears.

Lydia knew me well. "Hadassah," she said, "I can tell you seem down in the mouth. Do not worry, my friend; it is common after giving birth to have such feelings." She hugged me, and I hugged her back, knowing we'd probably never see one another again. I was right.

I fed Aaron around midnight, burped and changed him, hoping he'd sleep until the next feeding. Avram helped me wrap him into a sling so I could carry him in front with a pack on my back for his baby things. Diapers, a change of clothing for each of us, and some bread with sausages was all we had. Well, I did bring our wedding photo. How mightily things had changed since that perfect day, but each moment since had only brought us closer together as husband and wife. We'd need the strong bond we'd formed to survive.

Our building was totally quiet as we exited out the back entrance into the dark alley. There were no streetlights there, and the black midnight sky made me feel swallowed by the darkness. I was startled to see an old man leaning against the side of the brick apartments across from where we stood. He wore a dark hat with clothing to match. I'd only seen his form when he lit a cigarette. He put a finger to his lips and motioned for us to follow him. We did, but my legs were wobbly with apprehension.

We'd gone from alley to alley for about twenty minutes before the man stopped, giving me a moment to rearrange Aaron in his sling. I clung to Avram's sleeve while catching my breath. The man still had not spoken, but now he bent down and lifted a manhole cover with both hands, motioning with his head for Avram's help.

My heart pounded with fright when I realized where he was asking us to go. I knew the sewers were full of rats, other vermin, and the filthy remnants of our huge city. I shook my head in protest, but Avram took my arm and whispered, "Haddie, you've just given birth. Think about how much strength that took. You're stronger than anyone I know, a woman of substance. I believe you can do this."

If Avram believed I could do this, then I would believe it as well. He took Aaron from me and wrapped him onto his own body before leading me to the dark pit. Someone had left galoshes for us, and we helped one another get into them. The man went first then myself, my entire body shaking with fear as I descended into the gloom. I would be reminded of that pit years later.

We all had to bend over to negotiate through the water, but Avram was bent nearly in half. The intensity of the smell gagged me until I vomited. I tried to breathe through my mouth and focused on getting out as quickly as possible. We could not see a hand in front of our faces until the man lit a small lantern I'd not noticed before. The faint light flickered and danced up onto the damp walls, illuminating something scurrying away. Avram produced a handkerchief and tied it around my nose. It helped some.

The man spoke for the first time. "These tunnels will carry us out of the city, but the many twists and turns can be deceitful, so stay close together. You would not want to get separated."

I believed what he said, remaining as close as possible to him while we sloshed through God-knows-what to get out. Avram brought up the rear. The entire time we were in the sewer, he murmured words of encouragement behind me; other times I heard him praying words from the Torah.

Once the old man stopped, pointing overhead. We listened and could hear men yelling, followed by several rounds of gunfire. Sounds of running feet as they hit the grate above us echoed, bouncing off first one wall and then another. We heard a loud grunt, looked up, and saw the face of a man lying across the metal guard. Though he was staring right down at us, I realized in an instant that his eyes saw nothing. Avram moved forward and hid my face in his coat. My hand went to my mouth, and I feared I would vomit again.

The man motioned for us to be still. We stood frozen, but my sleeve was caught in the reflection from the streetlight above. Soon we heard more running feet and two soldiers arguing. Would they glance down and notice something out of the ordinary?

"Let's just throw the Jew rat into the sewer with the other city rats." The two of them pulled the dead man off the grate.

I fought against crying out as I heard more grunting. One of the soldiers began to swear. "This old thing will not budge. The metal is rusted shut."

"What shall we do with him, then?"

"Leave him. Let the rats bury their fellow rat." Their footsteps faded away down the street, but their laughter echoed behind them.

We moved away quickly. When I thought I could go no further, the man stopped, holding up his hand for us to do the same. It was then we heard a whistle. . .just two notes. . .a big pause. . .then two more notes.

Our guide answered with the exact same signal. We had made it to safety at a spot where the sewers emptied into a small river. We climbed up a ladder leading to the ground above. I'd never been more grateful for the clean smell of fresh air. The person at the other end greeted us in hushed tones and looked quite surprised when he saw we had a baby. His eyes brimmed with tears. He kissed his own hand before laying it on top of Aaron's sleeping head.

Our underground guide disappeared, leaving only our new aboveground leader, Ezra. He'd just turned sixteen, but we had great confidence in him because of his bravery. He was tall and looked strong as an ox.

"I have someone I'd like you to meet," he said quietly. Looking around, we saw no one. "Wait here." He motioned for us to stay put.

Avram shrugged, as confused as I.

In a minute, Ezra returned with a very small donkey pulling a cart three times the size of her diminutive body. "This is my little friend, Giezela. Don't let her size fool you; she's very strong and lovable besides." I must have looked skeptical, for Ezra chuckled lightly. "Trust me, she will get you to your destination much quicker than by foot, and since you will be taking back roads, you can count on her steady strength."

"I cannot pay you, friend," Avram said.

"Please, my father has raised these animals since before I was born. He believes soon the Third Reich will take them all for the army, and he's determined to use them for the good of as many Jews as possible. He asks only that if you're able, Giezela would have a good place to graze."

"I promise she'll have a good home," I said.

Avram helped me into the cart with Aaron, and we headed for the safety of my parents' farm with Ezra leading us until we could find our own way.

In a short amount of time, we became very fond of Ezra. When he heard that Avram wanted to be a doctor, he shared he had the same dream. "If God spares me, that is what I want to do with my life," he'd said.

"What if God does not spare your life? What then, Ezra?"

He waited several seconds then responded. "Then I should still be in His will." I shall never forget his smile and his absolute resoluteness.

It was early dawn when we came to a road that was familiar to us. We wished each other well, waved, and parted.

"Do you think he'll be okay, Avram?" I was feeding the baby, feeling sad at having to leave such a newly found ally.

Avram looked in the direction that Ezra had left us. "I'm praying that God would grant him the desires of his heart, Haddie."

"I hope that Aaron turns out like Ezra, don't you?" I gazed at my own child, finding it difficult to imagine him at sixteen.

Avram said nothing. I wondered if he was thinking about our survival.

My parents were shocked to see us. We hadn't had time to let them know we were coming. They were delighted especially to meet their grandson. But when they heard our story about why we left, they became distraught.

"We've heard some things," Tate said.

"What have you heard?" Avram asked.

"That hundreds of Jews have been imprisoned."

"It's true that Jews have been arrested, but the number is not hundreds." Avram paused. "It is thousands and thousands."

My head jerked up from feeding Aaron. "Thousands! How do you know this?"

"From where have they been arrested?" my father asked.

But Avram looked right into my eyes as he answered. "From all over Europe. From right in Berlin, under our very noses." He ran one hand through his hair. He needed a haircut.

I handed the now satisfied Aaron to my mother and went to stand in front of my husband. "Avram, why did you not tell me this before?"

He put his hands around my waist. "I wanted to protect you for as long as I could."

I hugged him close. "How many from Berlin?"

He sighed. "In June last year the roundups really began in earnest."

My father jumped to his feet and began to pace. "I've not heard from my cousin Saul since April of '38. Nothing from him or his family." He lit his pipe. "I thought it was because of the mail being interrupted." He sat back down, his face pale and sad. "I'm glad my mother is not here to hear such things."

Avram continued, "On the other side of the city, twelve thousand were arrested in one night last November."

"Mein Gott!" My mother hugged Aaron to her chest and cried into his downy hair. "To think we might have lost all of you. I can't bear the thought."

"Avram," I said, "how lucky we are to have gotten out when we did. I've been too naive, for sure."

"No, Hadassah, I didn't want you to worry, especially after you found out you were pregnant. I was trying to protect you."

"You are safe here with us," said Tate. "And I could use another pair of helping hands around here."

"I'm only too happy to earn our keep." Avram looked around. "Where's Jacob?"

"He's not often here." My mother lowered her head and brushed her lips across Aaron's forehead then wiped at her eyes.

"You might as well tell them, Esther," my father said.

Mama struggled with finding the words. "He's working with the Jewish Underground."

"The Underground? Then why do you not know what's going on in Berlin?" Avram sounded perplexed.

Tate's voice was low, concerned. "He shares nothing. . .to protect us, he says."

The room was silent, except for the *tick, tick, tick* of our heirloom clock. My mind was overwhelmed and full of what-ifs. Having a child changed everything, and because I had Aaron, I knew how much my mother's heart must ache over Jacob and his dangerous situation.

We did not see Jacob for several days after our arrival. When he walked into the house, I took him for a stranger. His hair was long and tangled, his face nearly hidden with a scruffy beard and mustache. He looked old beyond his years, while a peculiar weariness hung on him like the patched clothing worn over his too-thin body.

I threw myself against him when I finally recognized him. "Jacob, Jacob; how I've missed you!" I pushed myself away from him. "Let me look at you. I—I. . .don't think I would have known you on the street." I touched his face and tugged on his beard for emphasis. "Where have you been? Where do you go?"

He shook his head. "Hadassah, how beautiful you are. Motherhood becomes you, little sister." He pulled me into a tender embrace and spoke low into my ear. "I do not want our parents to know of my activities. Ask me later, and I will tell you. Promise me you will not ask in front of them."

I nodded before being released.

Despite the dark clouds gathering around us, we were still a family dedicated to staying strong in our love for one another.

I never did get to hear much more about Jacob's activities with the Underground because he came and went at longer and longer intervals. Each time he left, our mother seemed a little older. She continued her work in midwifery, now assisted by Avram on a regular basis. I filled in for him when my father needed help.

⁓

From the very beginning, Aaron loved the outdoors, and when he was older and could walk, he became Tate's shadow.

"Come along, my little *Schatten*. I might need your help."

Aaron never turned down the invitation whatever else he was doing. It was a joy to watch them together.

Over the next couple of years, even in our remote village, news of our fellow Jews continued to be heard. And though my mother and father had family history going back several generations in that very place, we began to see anti-Semitism rear its ugly head. Subtle at first, it crept upon us like an evil fog, silent and unnoticed in the beginning. But before long, its presence covered all it touched, seeping into places we'd never expected.

Mother got fewer and fewer calls for her expertise, and even her thriving home-birth practice dwindled to nothing. We went into town less and less, but thanks to the sustainability of the farm were able to thrive right up to the end.

Though the Third Reich's evil plan for us was getting closer and closer, we still had many non-Jewish friends in the village who kept the entire Jewish community informed. And Jacob would return with news off and on. For months, he'd been urging us to leave and follow him into hiding. There were thousands like him living in the woods all over Germany, he told us.

During the freezing weather of February 1943, he approached my father and Avram with the idea of moving us away.

"Things are far worse than you can imagine," he pleaded. "Please come with me. You'll have a better chance with me and the others than staying here. Trust me, I know this."

Tate smoked his pipe, listening. "This is my home, Jacob. Your mama's as well. We've worked hard, given our lives to this land. I could not abandon it now." He blew sweet-smelling smoke into the air; it lingered around his head.

"I agree, Jacob. Your father and I will stay," Mama said.

Jacob was pacing the floor, losing patience by the minute. "What about you, Avram? Will you risk your lives to stay here with them?" He waited for an answer.

Avram took my hand. "Haddie and I have discussed this, Jacob."

"And. . .?"

"And we cannot expose Aaron to the elements in the dead of winter. Surely he would not survive."

"Avram, none of you will survive if the SS comes knocking at your door." Jacob continued to pace, slapping one fist into his palm.

"Jacob, we live in the middle of nowhere. How will they find us out here?" Tate gestured with his pipe.

My brother's voice went very low. "They will find you because they want to find every last Jew who lives. They want every one of us—man, woman, and child—to be wiped off the face of the earth."

My mother took in a sharp breath. "But why, Jacob? What have we done to them that they should want us all dead?" Her voice quavered with emotion.

My brother knelt beside her chair. "They want us dead because the evil hatred of Adolf Hitler demands it, Mama. He wants a perfect Aryan race, and the Jews are not to be in it. This hatred is bigger than any of you can imagine. I know for certain that the 'work' camps the army has set up are mostly places to kill each and every person in them. There are gas chambers, firing squads, and..."

Shaking, I interrupted him. "There's another reason we must stay, Jacob. I am pregnant."

Only my mother's crying could be heard after my announcement. Avram hugged me, rocking back and forth to give me comfort.

Tate got up to stoke the fire, while Jacob found his hat, jacket, and gloves. He stepped out into the night without another word. We did not see him for nearly three months.

When he did return, he was emaciated, his eyes full of something I'd never seen. Hatred! My gentle, precious brother who nurtured me as a child had disappeared; instead a man I did not know had taken his place. It was frightening. I only spoke to Avram about it because I didn't want to further upset my mother and father. Yet I could see the concern and fear on their faces.

"Avram, I am so frightened for Jacob. What is happening to him?" I wanted to ask what would happen to all of us, but I knew Avram did not have an answer.

We were lying in bed, and Avram held me close, speaking in hushed tones in our little room tucked into the eaves of the house. "It's war, Haddie. It's what happens to a man's soul when he's a soldier. What we see in Jacob's face is what is taking place in his soul." He pulled me closer.

"I've never felt this much fear before. It's like a giant beast is waiting to devour us, and we are helpless to stop it." I wanted to discuss more with my husband, but I could tell by his breathing that he'd fallen to sleep. I lay there in the dark listening to him and Aaron breathing. Silent tears drenched my pillow.

Where was God in all of this? We were His chosen people, yet we were being taken like lambs to the slaughter. I could feel the hardness in my heart, and I welcomed it with open arms. I had to steel myself in order to protect us all. In that moment, I felt my unborn child move and wondered if I would live to see its face, feel the warmth of a newborn's breath, or hear a cry.

When spring arrived, it was easier to forget that around us the creeping death fog still existed, because life on the farm kept us all busy.

Aaron was thriving with the abundance of new life everywhere. He loved all of the outdoors and the incredible bounty it contained. I was amazed that one so young was not distracted away from the tedious side of farm life. It must have been bred in him from generations past because he was right there with Tate and Avram when the lambs were born.

Several calves were born that spring as well. Our oldest cow was trying to give birth, when her huge calf became stuck solid. To save mother and offspring, the two men put the mama into a headlock contraption and managed to get ropes around the feet of the calf. Aaron insisted on "helping," so he got behind his grandfather and his papa and began pulling with all of his might. It took some time but eventually the three of them pulled out a mammoth-sized bull calf. He flopped out, tongue lagging out of a slack mouth. It looked for sure that he was dead. My father grabbed it by the back legs and swung it around several times, and finally, with some vigorous rubbing and patting, the newborn began to come around.

Mama and I had been called to the barn to be part of the welcoming committee. Aaron was beside himself with happiness and excitement, which only grew when Tate told him he could name the new arrival anything he wanted. He hesitated a little while, taking time to look the calf over from stem to stern. He walked away, put both hands on his hips, and declared: "I'm calling him Aaron." This brought a round of laughter from everyone. Oh, the smile on my boy's face.

This laughter I still remember at times. And once in a while, on certain spring mornings when the earth is awakened from its last deep slumber, with my eyes closed and face to the sun, I see that sweet, perfect smile of indulgent innocence. What a stark contrast to what the near future held for us all.

We didn't see Jacob once during the spring or summer. But late in September, when we were working in our apple orchard, I looked up to wipe my forehead and saw a figure walking toward us.

"Jacob!" my mother cried. "Oh, Jacob, how good your face looks to me." She smothered him with tender kisses and would not let go of his hand.

We all dropped our work to rush and greet him ourselves. He was better groomed than the last time I'd seen him, but that desperate look of war was still upon him, and worse, he now carried a machine gun.

"Oh, Jacob, I thought the very worst after not hearing from you for so long. Please tell me you can stay for a few days." She was leading him back to the house.

I could tell by looking at him that he would not be staying, but he said nothing to our mother.

She prepared a wonderful meal, rich with the bounty of our harvest...smoked ham slices, browned with pungent sauerkraut and freshly dug potatoes. Bright shelled peas swam in a tangy cream sauce sprinkled with dill. And, of course, no one made better bread than our Mütter, smothered with ruby-red rhubarb jam and creamy butter. A feast! She did not take time to bake a cake, but we had chunky sweetened applesauce instead.

We laughed a lot during that meal, even over our memories of Bubbe, who had died in her sleep some six years before. Yet there was an uninvited guest as well. Fear had taken a chair at our dining-room table. We all felt it, but none of us wanted to address the subject, lest we have to admit it was there in the first place.

Finally, Avram spoke directly. "Tell us, Jacob, how long do you think we can last here before the army comes in and removes us?"

The question was hard and direct, but it needed to be asked. I didn't have the courage, but most of all I didn't want to know the answer. I wanted to take my son, my husband, my parents and return to the past of my innocent youth, to the country where I grew up full of love and contentment. I put both hands over my ears, not wanting to hear Jacob's reply. But I heard it anyway.

"Not long."

Both my parents regarded him incredulously. "Surely you are mistaken." Tate wiped his mouth with a napkin. "We've heard nothing."

Jacob looked intently at our father. "And tell me, Papa, when was the last time you've heard anything about the war and what our army is doing to the Jews?" Jacob blinked once, and his jaw went taut. I could see him clenching over and over.

"Well, I..."

"Whatever you've heard, whatever you *think* you know, it is most likely not accurate."

"But Jacob," my mother began. She started to get up, but Jacob motioned for her to stay. She sat back down with a sigh.

"I know, Mütter, because I've seen for myself exactly what happens to the Jews. I know where they are taken and what is done to them when they arrive. I told you this before. Oh, there are a few camps where the prisoners really do work in town factories. Yet even there, they labor twelve- to sixteen-hour days with little food. But trust me, they are the lucky ones. If you can call that 'luck.'" He threw his napkin down onto the table and placed his head in both hands.

Mütter got up, walked over, and stood behind him.

"Jacob," I said, "if we come with you now, how will we make it? I've still got several months to go before my delivery, and, of course, there's Aaron. We are strong people; perhaps together we could survive in one of those work camps."

He raised his head, slowly and deliberately, and stared into my eyes. I was frightened by what I saw. "Hadassah, you do not understand the depth of the evil that has been set against you."

I shuddered at the words.

He stood, excusing himself for the night. "I'll sleep in the barn." He turned before leaving and swept the room with a gesture. "Stay, or come with me; either way we could all die." He slammed the door but not before retrieving the huge gun.

Mama sat back down hard into her chair, saying nothing. The only sounds were Aaron's playing on the floor with a toy and Tate tapping his pipe ashes into a bowl.

Avram cleared his throat. "If Jacob is right, and I believe he is, we have to make a decision."

Tate shook his head. "I've been praying about this all along. I do not see how I can leave this land. It's been in my family by the Lord's benevolence. Can I just go, looking like an ungrateful man to the very God who gave it to me?" He stood and went to my mother's chair and embraced her from the back. She took hold of his hands and kissed each of them.

I looked at my husband. What would become of us?

We had no understanding that we wouldn't have long to wait. After that day, none of us stepped foot off the farm, but our tensions grew.

≈

The day our baby girl was born, we could hear gunfire resonating in the woods beyond our property.

Yes, Michael, you had a sister. Please, please forgive me for not telling you before now. I can only continue to ask your forgiveness and mercy, my sweet boy.

It was the dead of winter, and we continually fought the cold until it felt as dangerous as the enemy in the woods. It took brute strength to break water for the stock. And even though they were well fed, and despite Avram's and Papa's efforts, many of them died. All of us but Papa doubted our decision to stay when Jacob had advised us to leave.

"God lives here." Papa was pacing the floor with me as I walked out my labor. "Can you not feel Him in every inch of this farm?"

I paused long enough to give him a hug. "Papa, to tell you the truth, all I feel now is my body trying to deliver your grandchild."

"Oh, my girl, please forgive your Tate's rantings. . . . Continue. . .continue."

And so I did.

It was early morning when little Esther gave her first cry. Exhausted and fearful at the same time, we all gave thanks for her small, precious life. She had a head full of dark hair that, for sure, would be curly. Her skin was porcelain and perfect. She nursed with vigor and presented herself strong from the moment of her birth. What a dichotomy: here we were, surviving on the edge of disaster, when for one brief moment we felt the universal joy of new life in the precious breath of a newborn.

But oh, Michael, how short lived was our celebration. I had recovered quickly from Aaron's birth and expected the same after Esther was born, but the constant stress of our situation with the Nazis made me weak. I was disappointed in myself and felt I was letting my children down.

"Hadassah," Avram encouraged, "lean on me. Let me give you strength for today. Lean on God, that He might give us strength for tomorrow."

"But Avram, the gunfire comes closer each day. What will happen to us, to our children?"

He pulled me close and kissed my forehead then walked to the window in our attic room. Scraping ice from one pane, he spoke.

"What did you say Avram?"

He turned toward me with tears. ". . .therefore never send to know for whom the bell tolls; it tolls for thee."

Within a few days, right before Hanukkah, those words came true. The day dawned with temperatures way below freezing, and even with the roaring fire, we wore heavy clothing in the house. Our bedroom in the attic contained the most heat, so we slept warm and toasty, but descending to the kitchen was a shock each morning. The water pump on the sink had long been frozen, and we had to heat snow for our needs. That morning was no exception, and so all of us but the children were active with the day's preparations. It's what kept us from hearing the soldiers.

Mama was making an apple kuchen, as requested by Aaron, when the back door flew open. The rest happened in mere moments, but when I replay it in my mind, the action slows until every detail remains etched there as in stone.

Three SS soldiers were standing in the doorway, brandishing machine guns. In the background two more stood, one of them straining to hold back a huge German shepherd.

My mother's screams brought me from the other room, where I'd been nursing Esther. Aaron was frozen in place by the fire where he'd been playing Jacks. Papa had an armload of firewood, and Avram was putting it into the blaze.

One of the SS began shouting orders. "You're leaving, Jew pigs. Grab your things, immediately, or be shot where you stand." We were speechless. Avram went to step forward, but the soldier shoved a bayonet to his chest. "Come closer, and I will drop you like the pig that you are."

Tate dropped the firewood, and Aaron scrambled out of the way under the kitchen table. Mama ran to help him but was stopped by another soldier. She recognized him and was about to address him when he spoke first. "Speak to me, Frau Stein, and you risk being shot." My mother did as she was told but reached under the table to retrieve her grandson. Aaron was shaking uncontrollably by then and looked like a wild animal caught in a cruel trap.

The shouting continued as we were ordered to pack our things and prepare for "transport." Each of us was allowed one bag, nothing more. I will never forget the expression on my parents' faces as they prepared to leave what they'd worked for their entire married lives. Nothing mattered now. No pictures, no Hanukkah preparations, no violins, pipes, or family dishes. The air was filled with fear as well as our chilled breathing. The barking dog continued his protesting right outside the door.

It took no more than fifteen minutes for us to layer on clothing and pack our meager belongings into satchels. We had no time to think, but one thought kept running through my mind: *What about the children, my children?* We exchanged no words amongst ourselves, but the looks we passed back and forth said it all.

*I'm frightened for you.*

*I love you.*

*Say nothing.*

*We are together.*

They placed us in a wagon pulled by two oxen. "Stolen, no doubt," my father whispered as he helped me and Esther up into the back.

"Shut up, old man, or your next word will be your last." The soldier my mother had recognized walked over and spit on him where he stood. Tate only glared back, but I feared he might be shot right then and there.

My mother was next; then Avram helped Tate and handed him Aaron. My precious son was scared into shock, sucking his thumb, something I'd not seen him do since he was a year old. My heart was breaking into bits, and I was powerless to stop it.

The SS gave us no blankets, and despite the multilayering of our clothing, the morning freeze seeped into us as stinging sleet began to fall. Our hearts—no, our very souls—felt colder than the weather made our bodies feel. . .like death. How appropriate!

Soon night had come, and snow fell so heavily now that we could barely see the landscape around us. I had little Esther bundled in the old fur coat that Bubbe had kept from years past. I had grabbed it before we left the farm, so our newborn was probably the only one of us who was warm enough. She slept soundly, oblivious to the insanity unfolding.

Avram held tight to Aaron's hand so as not to get separated in the turmoil of over a hundred people at the rail station—people who'd been rounded up exactly like we had been. Oh, Michael, the air was filled with more than cold and snow; the stench of fear clung to every human forced to gather there, heavy enough to be tasted. It was all I could do to not vomit. I had wanted to be strong for my children's sake, but my knees trembled with terror.

Women wept silently, trying to bring calm to wailing children, while their men shuffled in the cold, talking in low voices. My mother looked around, desperately searching for Jacob. He was nowhere to be found. "Maybe he escaped," she murmured. "Some made it away from the woods, I've heard."

"Mama, there is no escape." I didn't tell her, but I feared him already dead.

"Hadassah, we must believe. That's all we have now. . .just our hope."

I longed to have even a glimmer of her hope, but that day, standing in the frigid air, weak from Esther's birth, I had none.

Just then a loud, single gunshot brought the crowd to a stunned silence. We looked around frantically to see what had happened. Heads jerked like puppets to watch as, in slow motion, Postmaster Heim fell next to the rail tracks. His wife threw herself onto the body, but she couldn't hide the fact that half his head was missing.

Avram grabbed Aaron's head to shield his son, but the effort was too late. I could tell by my little boy's expression that he'd already seen the horror. His innocence had been shattered with that gunshot.

"Hear this, Jew pigs," a Nazi SS soldier shouted, motioning with his rifle to where the body oozed blood onto the snow in a wider and wider circle. "This is what awaits any one of you who questions today's activities." He pointed again to the body of our kind and gentle postmaster. "That man had a question. Does anyone else have such an inquiry?"

No one moved at first. Then Mrs. Heim rose from the death spot, her tweed wool coat soaked crimson with the blood of her murdered husband.

The SS guard raised his rifle as a threat. No one in the crowd moved a muscle. "So, does the Jewess have a verboten question?" He cocked the gun, but still Mrs. Heim walked forward.

I wanted to scream for her to stop, but I was paralyzed when I realized what was unfolding before me. I braced myself for another shot.

When she had walked directly in front of the rifle muzzle, Frau Heim stopped, her breath creating shots of steam in the freezing cold. The soldier seemed shaken but pointed the gun directly at her chest. Her eyes never moved from his. In a flash, she slapped him hard in the face. Even in the roar of the howling wind, we heard it.

He recoiled in shock, but she never moved. In one lightning flash, he turned the gun around and smashed Mrs. Heim with the butt end. She dropped in a heap to her knees, falling forward onto her face exactly like a steer at slaughter.

The soldier went mad, first wildly touching his face then shooting in the air, ranting the entire time against the "Jew pigs." He shouted insults until he collapsed onto one knee from the maniacal outburst. Several other soldiers dragged him inside the rail station in order to end the tirade.

The instant he was gone, some men in the crowd rushed to the side of the fallen couple, but there was nothing anyone could do except wonder who would be next.

We must have stood at the station for over an hour with our pitiful possessions waiting for whatever diabolical plans the German soldiers had. Many of our village neighbors now wore SS armbands, signifying their solidarity against us. My mind could not comprehend what my heart knew as truth. People we'd grown up with, laughed and played with, had turned against us, aligning themselves with all the hatred of the German Army.

"But *we* are Germans," Papa whispered.

"Say nothing, Joseph, please," my mother pleaded.

"We've seen the writing on the wall, have we not?" Avram put his arms around them both, towering above their heads. "I am praying that my parents have escaped."

"We should try our best to stay together, wherever they are sending us," Papa said.

"Surely they would keep families together in these. . .camps?" My mother's eyes filled and spilled over onto her pale cheeks.

Even as she spoke the words, I knew in my heart that we were at the mercy of the devil, and apparently, the devil hated every living Jew in Germany. "Small and despised," it said of us in the Bible. That's what God had said of His own people: "small and despised."

My children, my children; how could I protect them? I leaned into my husband, feeling my weakness taking its toll. "We are going to die soon, Avram." I looked up into his rugged face and saw that he believed it as well. Our little Aaron was in a complete daze from it all, whimpering and talking to himself in a sing-songy way that was eerie and unfamiliar.

When he did speak, it was pitiful. "Poppy, I want to go home. Take me home, please. I am very cold." Avram picked him up, trying to bring some comfort and warmth. "Shhh, Aaron, we cannot go home today."

"Tomorrow, then. Are we going to go home tomorrow?"

Avram, unable to answer, regarded me with utter despair and sorrow. "Haddie, Haddie, I'm so sorry. I promised you the moon, and now I have nothing to give you." He drew me to his side, kissing the top of little Esther's head beneath the coat.

"Avram, you have been the moon and the stars to me. I could not have asked for more from you. You are my beloved." Just then a screeching train pulled into the station, belching thick black smoke into the pitiful collection of the hated.

I saw tears in my father's eyes as he gathered us around. "Whatever happens"—his voice cracked—"wherever they send us, we will always be together. Believe this." He looked each of us in the eye, and we nodded. Mama fell against his side, clinging to his jacket front.

A woman with seven children, all delivered by my mama, came up to her. Mama smiled until she saw what Frau Mueller was wearing on her coat sleeve. An armband. "Now we shall see who are the 'chosen people of God,' you filthy Jewess."

The shocked horror on my mother's face was beyond heartbreaking. "But Gertrude," she said, "I delivered your babies. . .every one. I know their names." She stepped closer. "I even remember their birth weights."

Gertrude Mueller stepped back. "And all the while you thought you were better than me." She spit on the ground. "You're only getting what you deserve." She looked around the milling throng of people, most of whom she'd known her entire life, and shouted at the top of her lungs, "You're all getting what you deserve. Tell me, cheating Jews, where has the Star of David gotten you now?" She spat again in Mütter's direction for emphasis and strode off.

Even though Avram and I had seen the anti-Semitism escalate in Berlin and had listened to the dire reports of my brother, I was shocked that this much hatred existed in my own special village. But why? I wondered. What had we done? What had my children done? I held my little Esther closer, knowing she would soon wake to eat. I was afraid to call attention to her, so I hoped she'd continue sleeping.

The lead boxcar was thrown open by soldiers, one of them holding a snarling dog like the one who'd been at our home. "Line up!" he shouted. "Line up in silence, or I will let my four-legged friend greet you in person." The dog continued to lunge, pulling at the chain holding him back.

A village man I did not know hoisted himself up into the car and reached down for another. Together, they lifted people inside the place meant to haul animals. The SS shoved others in far after the space was full. I could see bodies pressed against the inside while they loaded without ceasing. A loud cry of protest came from within when the door was slammed shut, like a coffin lid.

Mama hid her face. "God have mercy on our souls," she said into the blackness enveloping us. There was no time to respond because our family was next in line for the loading of the second car.

Avram jumped in first and pulled Papa up and inside. Next came my brave Aaron; mother and I were last, me still holding fast to Esther.

Suddenly, Jacob appeared in the crowd, but it was now too late for him to reach us. The soldiers pushed others before him, and he was shoved to the back of the throng. He jumped and waved like a wild man, shouting something we could not hear. The door slammed, plunging us into nearly total darkness.

"Jacob, Jacob," my mother and I sobbed together.

I would never again see my brother's face.

Misery reeked inside that car. People shrieked, pounding on the car sides to be released. I began to feel claustrophobic and faint. Just as my knees buckled, Avram caught me, and edged us toward the outside wall. There we found a small hole big enough to let in fresh air, even though it was freezing.

It was so crowded that a body could not even sit down, only lean on one another for support. An open bucket at one end was supposed to suffice as the toilet, but only those standing right next to it could use it.

One ancient man passed out, his face pinched and pale like a waning moon. His wife screamed, pleading for help, but no one could do a thing for them. Before our ride was finished, both had died. They were the lucky ones.

As soon as the train lurched forward, the wailing inside the cattle car became worse. Poor Aaron was nearly comatose by now, completely exhausted from fear and cold. Avram wrapped his overcoat around his son's little body and sang a favorite lullaby, *Sheyn vidi levone*:

*"Pretty like the moon*
*Bright like the stars*
*From heaven you were*
*Sent to me like a present."*

Surely you remember that song, Michael? How many times I've sung it to you. But your brother did not respond. Instead, he slipped deeper into some other place. At that moment, a vile thing began to rise within me, something I'd never experienced before. . .pure, unadulterated hatred. I didn't care what the Torah said about loving people. No God would expect me to love the very people who were destroying all of my family.

After leaving the outskirts of town, we saw no lights at all. Where were we going? We knew only the direction. Somehow through the misery, the hours passed until day began pushing its way into the car, as foreboding and miserable as the night had been. It had stopped snowing, but the cold clung to our bodies, like the awakened hatred clung to my soul.

While leaning against the side of the car, Avram discovered several boards around the small hole were loose. "Hadassah, don't say anything, just listen."

I nodded.

"I think I can pull enough boards loose so we might escape."

"No," I whispered, when I realized what he was suggesting. "No, no!"

"Just listen a minute," he said. "The train must slow down for turns since we are crossing the mountains now. You can go first. . . . The snow will be a soft landing. Then I will throw the children to you, and I'll come last."

"What about my parents?" Panic caused my heart to beat out of my chest, and I wanted to scream in protest.

"They are on the other side of the car." He looked deep into my eyes. "Do you understand what I'm saying? They could never make it over here."

I nodded but was unable to comprehend exactly what he said. How could we make it on foot? Where would we go, and who would help us?

By now the stench of human waste was unbearable, even with the small hole of fresh air where we stood. "Whatever you think is right, Avram," I finally said. I tried to relax to feed my baby again. She also needed to be changed. The most awful despair washed over me, despair so dark there were no words I knew that could describe it.

The train slowed, creaking and groaning as it made a turn. With one arm still holding Aaron, Avram began breaking off pieces of wood to make a hole. His fingers were nearly frozen even inside woolen gloves, but he continued.

The boards were much thicker than Avram first thought, and he made little progress. After two hours, the hole was only inches wide.

"Avram," I scolded, "this cannot work. Everyone will know what you're doing and crush us to death trying to get out. There has to be another plan."

My husband stopped and gazed at me. "Hadassah, then we will have to throw the children from the train." When he saw the shock on my face, he got right next to my ear. "It is the only way, my love, the only way to save them." Tears poured down his tired face. His awful suffering matched my own.

How I loved him.

"But Avram," I pleaded, "look at Aaron. He would never survive in the snow; already he is so fragile. He'd be too afraid to move, and besides, a wild animal might get him."

"We could wrap him in Bubbe's old coat with Esther."

"What if he tried to run after the train? I can't bear it. I can't even think of it." My hand went up in protest.

"We could take our chances with Aaron in the camp, then, and. . ."

"No, Avram, no! Don't make me throw my baby from the train. I couldn't; there has to be another way."

Just then the train lurched, and pandemonium broke out with more screaming and groaning. By now the old couple I'd observed when first we left was nowhere to be seen. Misery was sucking life from every passenger.

Avram put his mouth next to my ear again. "Haddie, I believe none of us has much of a chance. I heard that they separate the women and the men in those camps." I looked at him in utter panic, shaking my head in desperation. "Together, your father and I might be able to protect Aaron, but you. . .you are already so weak."

He was right, and I was getting worse. Thirst and hunger were making me weaker, and if not for my husband I would have collapsed to the place of the old couple. . .at the bottom of the railcar.

Avram continued to work on the boards. Although some around us shouted for him to stop because of the frosty air, others were grateful for some relief from the stench. Nearly all the inside of the railcar was encrusted with ice anyway, grim testimony to the outside temperatures.

All that day, Avram worked at making the hole big enough for our precious newborn to be thrown to what I was certain would be the end of her brief, cheerful life. I began to descend deeper and deeper into our hell. Mile by mile, my husband chipped away, his hands and fingers now bloodied for the effort. As each splinter came loose, I inched deeper into the depths of the pit that consumed me. Was I going mad?

Faintly, I could hear Tate praying above the din of moaning and groaning. In all the universe, there could be no consolation for me. As I nursed Esther for the last time, I touched the perfect small face of my daughter, ran my fingers through the dark mop of hair generously covering every inch of her precious head. I bent to kiss her tiny eyebrows, which were already pronounced, letting my lips linger there. Denying what was about to happen, I began to speak to her.

"Oh, my special girl, how wonderful your life will be. You will be raised in sunshine in the land of milk and honey. Golden fields will surround you, and your coffers will be full of treasured and bountiful blessings. You shall dance in green meadows and hear the song of the meadowlarks bidding you, 'Come, play,' in the midst of their wondrous harmonies.

"You shall be full of joy, dear Esther, so completely filled with light that you'll shine brighter than any star in the night sky."

Her eyes fluttered open, and for one brief, precise moment, she looked into my face. I believe, with all my heart, I saw her smile before returning to the secret place of slumber.

I felt Avram looking at us. I raised my head to see his shoulders shaking; anguish covered his pitiful face, a mirrored image of my own. He said only four sobbing words. "Hadassah. . . I. . .am. . .finished."

I wanted to die. There was no way I could do what now must be done. I shook my head over and over again, my mouth opening wide like an injured animal caught in a hunter's snare, fully aware of impending death. "I cannot do it, Avram. Please!" I continued to plead.

He said nothing but reached over and, with one hand, closed my eyes, then took Esther from my arms. I could only hope that my mother and father would not see what was about to happen. Avram slipped Aaron to me, his sleeping head resting on my shoulder; that sweet face turned toward mine. I felt his warm, sickly breath on my cheek.

Esther made a faint sound. My eyes flew open, and I wanted to grab her back, but she settled with a small burp, resting for the last time in her father's strong arms.

It was late afternoon, and soon it would be dark. I looked out the gaping, jagged hole into the placid countryside. Its beauty took my breath away in the crystal-clear loveliness. How pure. How ironic. We were riding to hell, but the world beyond looked like a frozen paradise. It was insane.

Just on the other side of the tracks ahead of the train, two children played in the snow. I pointed to them, and Avram nodded. I wanted to look away, but I could not. I needed to see where my daughter was about to die. Despite Avram's encouragement, I knew deep in my heart she had no chance for survival.

Watching in horror, the scene before me unraveled in slow motion. Avram wrapped Bubbe's old coat tighter and tighter around Esther's small body. He made a knot with the ragged sleeves and gripped it while she slept on, oblivious to her own demise. Finally satisfied, he lifted the little bundle to the opening and squeezed her through. Whispering a prayer over our daughter, Avram hung her into the air, stretching his arm as far away from the side as it would go.

On the inside his face was plastered against the wall. When he saw me watching, he turned it in the other direction so I could not see his expression. Waiting until the train slowed to a crawl for the curve ahead, he swung her back and forth, to and fro, gaining momentum, and then. . .

Then he brought his empty hand back into the car.

I pushed him aside, stood on tiptoes to stick my head out as far as I could until I saw the brown bundle lying beside the tracks. "My baby," I screamed into the uncaring wind. "Esther, Esther," I cried. "I love you, I love you, my girl."

The train finally negotiated the curve, and she was gone from sight, Michael. Your sister was gone from me forever. . . .

Now you know it all, Michael, the sum total of your mother's shame. I allowed your only sister to be thrown to a certain death. I know you probably now wonder what became of Aaron.

I love you, Michael, my precious, precious boy. All of your life I have tried to make up for my past by being the best mother I could to you. Yet I feel I have lacked still, perhaps because we can never really be free of the past. I've heard a Christian woman say once that Jesus can give this kind of freedom, but this is confusing to me, because after all, only God would have that kind of inclination and power. And like I said, for sure if God existed, He has died. When I tell you the rest of my story, I believe you will agree.

# Chapter 11

*December 1965*
*New York City*

She was stunning, with an ebony braid cascading down her back and little makeup. After removing a ski cap and wool neck scarf, her dark eyes darted nervously from his face to the paper lying in front of him.

They shook hands across the desk. "Sorry about my cold hands, Professor. Even with gloves they're never warm." Her accent was only slight.

He motioned for her to sit. "It's what we get for living in New York."

Fritz forced his mind to focus on what he was going to say instead of Star Firstenberg's beauty. "Miss Firstenberg, you must have noticed my accent."

She nodded.

"Of course, I am from Germany."

"Yes." She smiled politely. "It's not much different than mine."

He shifted in his seat. He hoped she didn't think he was rude, but he could not help staring at her. "First, I think your paper is excellent, and I. . ."

Star took a deep breath.

". . .I want you to know if it were just up to me, I'd give the *Times* spot to you, hands down."

She nodded but remained nervous, twirling the ski cap in her hands.

"But. . ."

She stared directly into his eyes. "But what, Professor?"

"Well, Miss Firstenberg, I must recuse myself from the judging." He propped his elbows on the desk.

"I'm sorry? I don't mean to appear obtuse, but I don't understand. Are you recusing yourself because of my paper?" She bit her lower lip.

"Yes."

"But why?"

"I know you."

"Of course, I'm a journalism major. But what difference does that make?"

Fritz stood and moved his office chair directly in front of hers then sat down again.

Now she was clearly very uncomfortable. He could see the question in her eyes: *What's going on? He doesn't seem like the type to hit on a student.*

"Miss Firstenberg," he said, "I am one of the people who found you in the snow." His words hung in the air, floating between them like fine vapor.

She clasped her hands together. "I beg your pardon. What did you just say?" Her eyes were riveted to his face, waiting for an answer.

"I know this is a shock. It was. . .it *is*. . .for me." He wanted to brush away the single tear that slipped down her cheek but restrained himself.

"I—I. . ." Star's eyes brimmed. "I simply cannot believe this. But how?"

Fritz forced his emotions aside. "I could tell by your paper that you believe in God's divine providence."

She nodded.

"I agree with you 100 percent, because there's absolutely no other explanation for how we've met after all of this time."

Now Star was openly weeping and laughing at the same time. "Oh my! Oh my!" was all she could utter. "Am I dreaming?"

When her head turned sideways, he saw the small birthmark she bore as a baby, shaped exactly like a star. Fritz leaned forward. "May I call you Star?"

She glanced up and smiled. "You may indeed. But what shall I call you?"

⁂

They talked for hours until a comfortable silence wrapped around them and they were able to leave one another. After saying good-bye, Fritz had a thousand thoughts running through his head. One of them was to call Steve.

The phone rang several times before his friend picked up. "Speak to me."

"How did you know it was me?" Fritz was laughing.

"Well, I didn't. But now that I know it's you, I'm going to hang up."

"No, don't, I have something to tell you."

"Like I said before, speak to me." Now Steve was laughing. "Sorry, Fritz, what's going on?"

"Are you sitting down?" Fritz was pacing, grateful for the extra-long phone cord.

"Hey, now you have my attention. Is everything all right?"

"Something incredible has happened. Have you read any of the contest entries?"

"Mmm, a few. None that excite me, though. Why?"

"I want you to read the one that says, 'I Shouldn't Be Alive!' Read it and call me back."

"This sounds mysterious. Mysterious and kind of bossy, Professor, Friend."

"Steve!" Fritz threw back, irritated.

"Okay, okay, Fritz, they're right here in front of me. Wait. . .yeah, I found it. Pretty intriguing title, I'll give it that. I'll call you right back when I'm finished." He hung up.

Fritz paced in the short interim. When the phone rang, he jumped and grabbed it on the first ring. "Well?"

"Do you think this story is legit? Pretty dramatic, don't you think?" Fritz could hear the doubt in Steve's voice and imagined him sucking on the end of a pencil.

"Steve, I know for a fact the entire thing is true." He sat down then stood again.

There was silence on the other end.

"Are you there?"

"I'm here, but tell me how you know this kid's story isn't made up?"

"Because. . ." Fritz began pacing again. ". . .because I was there."

"Get out of Dodge! What?"

"Steve, I was one of the children who found her in the snow. The other kid was my cousin, Ellie. I know it's hard to believe. I mean, I can hardly believe the whole thing."

"You mean you've known this and are just now telling me? Wow, you've got a lot of willpower. I'd have blabbed this all over campus by now."

Fritz lowered his voice. "I've met the writer, too."

"Wow. You know I'm rarely speechless, my friend, but this is unbelievable. God's hand is all over the entire thing." He whistled. "I know that JD hasn't read it, or he'd have called for sure, especially since his wife is a Holocaust survivor."

"I have to take myself out of the judging at this point. . .just too close to the author."

"Yeah, oh sure, but Fritz, hands down, her piece is the best I've read." He whistled again. "Listen, I'm on my way out the door to Crystal's Christmas program. Are you coming?"

"I totally forgot with all the excitement of meeting Star. I'll go to the next performance, I promise."

"Okay, man. I cannot wait to tell JD about this. Talk to you later."

Fritz hung up and walked to the window. It was snowing. . .just like the day he'd found her.

# Chapter 12

*Hadassah's Journal*

My dearest Michael:

Night fell shortly after we let Esther go. Never had a day ended in such blackness, swallowing me in its depths. Neither Avram nor I could keep from weeping. I thought I'd die from the pain, wanting more than anything to do just that. Poor Aaron now had a mother who was only half alive. What if he died, too? Would losing both my children be the end of my existence?

Sometime during the middle of that excruciating night, the train slowed. We paid no attention, thinking we were taking another sharp curve. Instead, we came to a halt. The engine belched, released a loud horn, and shuddered once. Murmurs and loud groaning could be heard all over the car.

"We've arrived," Avram said.

"God help us!" I heard my Tate cry.

"God, deliver us from evil," another man prayed.

I saw my own fear reflected in my husband's brave face. "Hadassah, whatever happens, I'll forever love you. Even in death, I am yours. You are my first love, my only love."

He put his big arms around both Aaron and me. At that instant I knew somehow that I would never see him again.

When the SS opened the car door, fresh air rushed in, and we gulped it like nectar. Huge lights split the darkness, and the brilliance blinded me. I felt Aaron being lifted from my arms and thought a soldier was taking him. I screamed as loudly as I could. The desperateness of my own voice made my blood curdle.

"Hadassah, it's just me." It was Avram. "I'll hold him until you're out of the car."

In back of me, I could hear my mother crying. How strange that, in the din of hell, I could recognize one familiar voice.

"Out," shouted a soldier in German. In the rush to exit, and blinded by the light, people tumbled over one another. A few stumbled and fell, causing those following to land on top of them. Pitiful cries rose from the pile, and one woman screamed her leg was broken. A soldier grabbed one arm and dragged her to the side. She was moaning in pain, but no one dared go to her aid.

"Women to the left, men to the right," shouted an armed guard.

Weak from our journey, many could barely stand and leaned on one another for support in order to obey the command. Avram let go of my hand, and the horror of our inevitable separation became real.

I saw my father kiss my mother tenderly before being jerked into line. She stumbled toward me, and we clung to one another. "Where is my Aaron?" she whispered with little strength.

I pointed to where Avram stood holding our son. "There." I began to shake uncontrollably, because I knew that, next, she would ask about Esther.

She looked all around and turned ashen white. "Hadassah, where is my granddaughter?"

I turned my face away.

"Where is Esther?" she repeated.

I fell to my knees in the snow and hid my face from my mother's questions.

When Avram saw me on the ground, he tried to leave his spot and come to me. "Move out of this line, and I will shoot you." One of the guards had a gun stuck under Avram's chin. He didn't move.

I longed to touch my husband one more time, to sing a lullaby into the ear of my sweet, sweet baby boy. But there, in the bitter cold with the sounds and smell of death all around, I mouthed good-bye to them both instead. "Good-bye, my loves, good-bye forever."

By now, all the cars were emptied out, including the ones filled before the stop at our village. There were several hundred of us standing around trying to keep warm. A whispered thread snaked through the group: we were in Ravensbrück. Only the women would stay here. All the men and boys were traveling further on to the men's prison. They were told to get back into the boxcars, but one teenaged young man broke loose from the others and tried to scramble under the train. He was dropped in his tracks by the same soldier who had threatened Avram. The entire crowd fell silent as the death crack of a rifle echoed off the railcars.

In that moment, my father cried out first to my mother and then to me. My name tore from his lips, both arms outstretched toward me, reaching to snatch me from the grasp of evil: "Hadassah. . .my daughter, Hadassah."

It was too late.

Some of the women and their daughters were wailing; others had been shocked into silence, caught in the grip of their own realities. My heart beat within me, threatening to explode, but I gritted my teeth and gripped my mother's hand. In that second, I made a decision: I would survive. I would survive this evil if only to tell the world of the perversity that insane hatred can bestow on those subjectively deemed unfit to share the planet with others.

My mother, once the vibrant strength of our family, was reduced to a woman overwhelmed by what she'd endured and the violent separation from my father. I feared she would not make it. But if I made her my "cause," I could will whatever strength I had to be hers as well.

Just then several female soldiers came forward, walking amongst the women, tapping some on the shoulder and shouting orders into their faces.

Soon we realized that a new separation was taking place—the young from the old—and another great, anguished cry went up. I will never forget the sheer terror on Mama's face. She clasped my hand so tightly I winced.

"I have loved every day as your mother, Hadassah," Mama murmured. Her voice became stronger as she spoke the last words I ever heard from her. "Do not forget me. Do not forget our God." She let go of my hand and walked with steady steps to take her place with the others her age. She did not turn around, not even when the train began to move the men and boys. I watched it pick up speed and disappear from view. *Good-bye, my loves!*

A very young woman began to lean against me, and I thought she'd soon collapse. "Are you ill?" I grabbed her around the waist. "Don't fall down," I said softly. "They might shoot you."

"I'm in labor." She spoke through clenched lips. "It's too early. My baby is too early." She began to weep silent tears.

"Can you walk at all?"

"Yes."

I grabbed the sleeve of another woman standing next to us, so that together we might give her support. Our group began moving forward, and I glanced over my shoulder to find Mama. She was nearly out of sight, marching into the night toward a huge building with a brick smokestack.

The crowd was pushed along through the cold until we came to a long building without windows. Even though I had no idea what was about to happen, I welcomed the possibility of being in a warmer place.

The pregnant girl, the other woman, who said her name was Miriam, and I, were in the middle of at least fifty others inside. Centered in the large, drafty room, a huge stack of clothing and shoes were piled nearly to the low ceiling. Around the edges of the stack, open suitcases lay everywhere.

"Line up single file and strip."

When the pregnant girl heard that, she stifled a groan.

"How will she make it?" Miriam asked me.

"I have to." The girl answered for herself, her face contorting with another contraction. They were getting closer.

Miriam looked at me, but I closed my eyes and shook my head then told the laboring girl, "We have to do as they say; maybe they'll have mercy on you because you're having a baby." Even as I said the words, I knew the possibility was slim.

We stripped down to our bare nakedness and stepped forward, where a half-dozen soldiers, all women except one man, stood with hair clippers. I began to shake, not just from the cold but from the shame of being totally exposed in front of all these people. I wanted more than anything to cover myself from head to toe. Many around me were weeping, but all of us knew by now to remain silent.

The man, barely as tall as me, grabbed a huge hunk of my hair and shoved the clippers to my scalp. This shedding of my "crowning glory" felt nearly as bad as standing naked in the midst of strangers.

After the head shaving, double doors in the distance opened and we were ordered to enter. Three walls were lined with showerheads. The floors were filthy, covered with slimy mold, but the thought of being able to take a shower and wash away the stench of the boxcar was encouraging, even though I could see my breath.

Miriam and I were helping our friend, when one of the soldiers hollered, "Halt." We stopped in our tracks.

"She must be able to walk on her own." The soldier walked closer, saw that the girl was pregnant, and to our shock, turned away.

"Oh, praise God," Miriam whispered.

"My name is Hildy," the pregnant girl said as she stepped under the shower. "I am nineteen and not married." She looked much younger. Another contraction bent her over, and she grabbed her barely bulging stomach. "I want to have a boy, so I can name him after his father. . .Frederick."

Miriam and I said nothing.

The water was cold, but we grabbed the small bar of lye soap, used it, and got out as quickly as possible. Immediately, we were doused with some kind of disinfectant that caused my body to burn like fire. Next, we hurried to the clothing pile. My dress was huge, but at least I was covered, and I managed to find a pair of shoes that almost fit. Who wore this dress before me? I wondered. Was she happy in her *real* life? Maybe she'd been a mother of two, like. . .like I had been.

When thoughts of my children ripped through me, I forced myself to set them aside. If I was to survive, I must keep those thoughts at bay, else I would die from the weight of the sorrow. No, survival meant things of the heart would no longer be allowed. . .ever. With that resolution, I could actually feel my emotions shutting down, like a huge fountain being turned off with my own hands, turning, twisting, until the flow stopped.

After all the women were clothed in dresses with a huge X on the front and back, each was handed a coat, some heavier than others, though none of them would prove adequate enough to hold off the bone-chilling freeze. Next we were handed a head scarf and woolen gloves. While marching on to the next building, Hildy began leaking large amounts of fluid.

She clung to me, the fear in her voice gut-wrenching. "What is happening, Hadassah?"

I grabbed her tighter. "Your bag of waters has broken, Hildy. It won't be long before your baby is born."

"Do you believe he will live?"

Despite my resolve of not feeling any more heart things, her pitiful expression tore at my resolve. I'd have to work harder on the containment of such things. *Certainly not!* I thought. Aloud, I said, "Yes, of course."

She smiled at me with renewed confidence.

After reaching building number 223, we stumbled in and found a small stove at one end that pumped some heat into the chill but only beyond a few feet from where it stood. The beds closest to the fire were taken first—not out of selfishness, but out of necessity for survival. Each woman there understood it was her fate whether or not you made it by the stove. The beds were actually platforms or piers stacked three high, each with a straw stuffed bag for a mattress with only one blanket.

"Five to a bed," the young soldier shouted.

"But they're filled with vermin!" came a cry from a woman who was lying on one of the bunks. It was true and horrifying. Even from a distance and in dim light, fleas could be seen jumping.

"That's why you were dusted with disinfectant, stupid Jew."

Immediately, Hildy begged me to bunk with her, and I could not refuse. Miriam stayed with us, as well as a woman named Sylvie, Miriam's cousin. Tall and frail looking, she appeared near collapse. Worse, she had the chills and shook so violently her teeth rattled. The fifth woman spoke only Polish and went away when she saw what was happening with the imminent birth.

I helped Hildy into a bottom bunk in time to hear her say, "Got to push."

"Already?" I was petrified. Not because I believed I couldn't help, but any hope of either mother or baby surviving this utter filth was slim to none.

"Oh, Gott, oh, Gott," she kept repeating as she began pushing. Each extreme effort left her exhausted. Soon beads of sweat broke out all over her young, innocent face, even in the cold.

"You're doing great, Hildy. You can do this, I know you can," I encouraged.

But I saw the hopelessness in her eyes. *She's still a child. She should be with her mother in a hospital, or in her own bed.* Suddenly, her eyes opened wide with surprise. Next, she held her breath and bore down with a mighty effort.

I looked onto the bed and saw a torrent of blood and water gush from her body. With it came a tiny body. . .totally still. I grabbed his mother's coat and began rubbing the frail baby's back with it. When I turned the tiny body over, I saw that Hildy had given birth to the son she wanted.

By now, a dozen or so women had gathered around, all of them silent, waiting for some sign of life from Hildy's baby boy. I continued to rub him vigorously and reached inside his mouth to pull out any mucous. His chest heaved as he struggled to breathe, and finally a small squeak came out. . .more like a mewing kitten than a human.

"Come on, my little Frederick, breathe for me. . .breathe for your mama."

He sucked in the cold air and gave out first one weak cry and then another. He lived!

Finding another dry spot on the coat, I rubbed all the white vernex from him, carefully.

"How old do you think he is?" Miriam asked softly.

"Not more than seven months, certainly."

His eyes were wide open now, and he turned his head to look around. So alert was he in the midst of such abject circumstances. How amazing. How sorrowful.

In the rush of his quick arrival, I'd not noticed how quiet his mother had become. "Look here, Hildy, you've got your. . ." That's when I noticed she wasn't moving. Her back was arched while her head tilted back onto the bed, eyes wide open. She looked surprised and serene at the same time.

"Hildy!" I straightened her head and put my cheek next to her mouth. Nothing. I handed the baby to Miriam and shook the young mother. It was then I noticed that the mattress was now completely soaked with blood.

Miriam spoke. "She's dead, isn't she?"

I choked back a sob. "Yes." I looked up to see that the women, who'd gathered before, had all moved away.

Dawn had broken through an eastern-facing window and found its way to our bed, resting on Hildy's young, perfect face. We closed her eyes and covered a once sweet, beautiful girl.

"What about *him*?" Miriam nodded toward the wiggling infant in her arms. "Surely now he'll die as well. I don't think I can watch him pass away right in front of us." She choked.

"I will feed him." I couldn't look her in the face.

"But how?" Miriam wiped her cheeks with the back of one hand and waited for an answer.

"I—I. . .just lost my own baby." The second I said it, I felt my milk let down. Without another word, Miriam handed him to me, and I put the newborn to my breast. His suckling was weak. Thoughts of Esther struck like lightning, and my heart quickened, but I would not let those images worm their way into the spot I'd determined to protect. The faucet handle wrenched tighter, and I focused on the task of keeping Hildy's baby boy alive. Cradling his too-small body next to mine, there was no way I would let myself get attached to him emotionally.

Less than an hour later, the same soldier who'd been there earlier threw open the door, allowing two prisoners inside. The first carried a large black kettle over to the stove and set it down. Behind her, the second woman carried a bucket full of eating utensils and set that on the floor.

Just as I was switching Frederick to the other breast, he let his presence be known with a rousing cry. The soldier strode down the narrow row of bunks, each heavy step echoing in the room that had gone totally silent. She stopped right in front of me. In the daylight I could see she was only a teenager.

"You're not the mother," she said, poking me with a nightstick.

I nodded to the covered body next to me, and the soldier's eyes followed my gesture. I might have seen a flicker of emotion on the young but hardened face.

"Get that out of here," she shrieked. Her eyes darted from one prisoner to another, finally settling on Miriam. "You," she pointed, "get someone to help you drag that body outside." Miriam and her cousin looked at one another in horror. The soldier started to walk away but turned. "And throw that mattress into the fire." Then she walked back and stood in front of me again. "I'm sure that squalling infant will die soon." She bent over to get a closer look. Looking me right in the eyes, she said, "But. . .if he lives and interferes with your work. . ." She straightened. ". . .I will dispose of him myself." You could hear the intake of breath all around us. She laid her stick right on top of my shoulder. "Do I make myself clear?"

"Yes, ma'am," I whispered.

Two women stepped forward to help Miriam drag Hildy off the bed. They carried her body down the long, narrow aisle and out the door. When they returned, the three women were crying and shaking with the effort.

"Remove the straw a little at a time and throw it in the fire," someone suggested.

Next, we all got in line for the food. . .turnip soup. It looked bad and smelled worse, but it was hot, and we wolfed it down like animals, grateful for every awful spoonful.

Rumors flew around the room as to what would happen to us next. Information was mostly nonexistent, hampered by the fact that we were a mixture of Germans, Dutch, Austrians, French, and Polish. The foreign women had mostly come from other camps in their respective countries, and only a few, mostly the Austrians, spoke German. There were lots of opinions and speculations, but it wouldn't be long before the reality of our individual fates became crystal clear.

# THE TRAIN BABY'S MOTHER

All the rest of that first day, one by one, women came to bring pieces of cloth for me to use as Windels for Frederick. They had torn the fabric from the back of their dresses so that, hidden beneath their coats, the missing pieces would not be noticed.

Only later, after my release, would I find out what happened to most of the children born in the camps. But for several days, things looked hopeful for our little barrack's baby. He became our symbol of hope, for if he survived, so might we.

The only way we could stay warm was to huddle together and use the only blanket to cover our bare legs. I kept Frederick next to my own skin and hoped that my milk would last. Despite my resolve to remain unattached to him, every time he moved, I felt my heart stir.

Our morning (and as it turned out, every morning thereafter) began at 4:00 a.m., in the pitch black. A loud, shrill blast from a whistle announced our wake-up. Those of us on the lower bunks were covered with straw and dust from the bunks above. More than once during that first full night, I heard a cracking sound as one of the upper beds collapsed and fell onto those below.

Regardless, when the whistle blew, we stampeded for the coffee and ration of bread left by the stove. . .the stove that had now gone cold. Those that tarried got nothing. Next we spilled out the door and into the bitter predawn that awaited Germany's stolen best. None of us were allowed to use the latrine beforehand. It was 4:40, precisely.

Outside, we were made to stand at attention for roll call. I was shocked at the number—thousands and thousands of women joined us. . .more than was possible to count, not that they could all be seen. The groups stretched out of sight in the faint light of tall lamps. When it began to snow, they were swallowed by a milky gray beast, bouncing falling flakes off its back. My mind echoed with early memories of winter's snow and how much I'd loved it then. Now it had become my enemy. The snow beast was just one of many who stalked in, and around, the evil grounds of Ravensbrück.

After roll call, work crews were snatched out of the first lines into another. Miriam, Sylvie, and I were sent together to a huge factory made up of mills and railcar tracks several miles from Ravensbrück.

We were marched out the huge iron gates and cement walls with electric wire fencing on top, past a frozen lake and trees laden to the ground with ice and snow. Though the air was unrelenting with its harsh cold, it was a relief from the stifling odors of the barracks and overflowing latrines.

Tucked beneath my coat, Frederick stayed quiet, but my instincts told me he was sleeping too much. Not a good sign. I refused to let my mind wander to how long he might survive. The day's work proved to be brutal enough to keep me distracted.

The factory was a miserable place, and we were made to work there eleven hours. I had to tie the baby to me to keep him hidden, but fear tore at me all day long. If discovered, the guards here would surely not be as lenient toward him as one young soldier at our barracks had been.

Despite childbirth and the horrific train ride, I was strong from years of farmwork. Others were not, and all that day they collapsed around me. One Polish woman seemed to go mad, screaming something few understood, and made a run for a back door. She got just beyond before a volley of shots rang out. I was grateful that I had not known her, or witnessed her murder.

When lunch came, I grabbed a potato, sneaking around a corner to devour it and nurse Frederick. He was difficult to rouse, and waves of sorrow washed over me. His hair, like peach fuzz, lay sweetly on a perfectly rounded head. His mouth formed a small flower bud, and despite his small size, Hildy's face was reflected in his own. I tried and tried to hold back my tears, but I could not. How could I let him die in this hellish place? Suddenly a brave thought came to me. If I'd been willing to let my own daughter go into the unknown, perhaps I could do the same for this orphaned boy. But how?

On our way to work, even in the dark, I had seen houses in the distance and a few villagers besides. Perhaps it was possible that good people still lived in Germany. And, I reasoned, it would only take one.

While an Austrian woman named Annika and I pushed a heavy cart full of metal parts to railcars all day, I formed a plan. When I shared it with her, she bravely agreed to help me. "I will pray that God gives us a way where there appears to be none," she said.

We were exhausted, hungry, and depleted, but I looked forward to our walk back to camp, hoping against all odds of finding someone on the road who might take Frederick.

"Let us make sure we're in the middle of the line back," she said. "There are fewer guards there."

It was only by sheer willpower and fear of being shot that kept my feet moving. They felt as heavy as lead. Twice I slipped on the packed snow.

About halfway back, Annika nudged me in the ribs when she spotted a man with a wagon coming toward us. A young girl about twelve, sat next to him holding a mutt dog in her lap. The back was filled with assorted sacks and a few bales of straw.

"Work your way to the outside of the line," she said.

I looked at her, unsure of what she wanted me to do.

She nodded toward the cart and mouthed the words, *"Follow me."*

Slowly we inched toward the outside, trying not to attract any attention in our direction. We had made it to the edge and saw the cart just ahead. When it was about to pass us, Annika slipped and fell, barely missing the front wheels of the wagon.

"Whoa," cried the driver. "Are you all right?" he shouted. Before the guards could run to where she lay, she motioned for me to help her. I ran over, and the driver jumped down. "Please, mister," she whispered, "would you help us save a life?" The man looked startled and glanced around in fear. "What?" He reached down to help Annika to her feet.

"Please take this baby." I opened my coat a fraction and showed him little Frederick's sleeping head. The man's face went ashen, and his eyes darted over my shoulder. The guard was coming. "Quick," he said, "give it to me." He grabbed Frederick, turned his back to thrust him into his coat. There was no hiding the bulge beneath.

At the same moment the guard arrived at the scene, the man had settled back onto the seat of the cart, where the ugly dog was squirming in his lap. . .a perfect foil for hiding the infant.

*Don't cry, my little man,* I pleaded in my mind.

"What happened here?" The guard's rifle pointed first to Annika and me, then to the man. It had a foot-long bayonet on the end.

"I slipped and fell, but this gentleman helped me," she said, not meeting the soldier's gaze.

"Ja, stupid woman, I nearly ran her down, and now I'm late for my supper. Ach!" Before the guard could respond, the man clucked to his horse, slapping the reins against its back, careful not to dislodge his dog. The girl looked over her shoulder at us for a second, and then they were gone.

Whether it was fate, or the cold, the guard ordered us back into line with only a warning and a whack each with a leather crop across our backs. "I could have shot you both, stupid Jews."

Annika stepped closer to me, with something of a smile on her angular face. "At least he *might* have a chance now, Hadassah. Ja?" My arms felt empty, but a tremendous sense of relief washed over me.

❧

All of January our routine remained the same, except the cold got colder, and our hunger increased with the intensity of the weather. Day after miserable day, we marched to the factory. The only ray of hope in that place was the fact that we had warmer temperatures when we were assigned work on the inside.

I felt my body turning against me, shrinking, day by day and pound by pound. Even if I hadn't recognized it in myself, the other women were reflections of me. Each and every face became hollowed-out versions of themselves, shriveling in the bleakness of our fate like tender spring plants, caught in the grip of winter's last blast.

Death stalked us all and had its way; every day dozens of women collapsed or were taken away. Rumors flew like flocks of hunted birds as to their fate. And every prisoner, within days of arrival, knew what the smokestack in the middle of the camp held. All its secrets were released twenty-four hours a day, seven days a week, carried skyward only to fall back on all who waited outside for roll call. At least in the winter the constant ash hid amongst falling snow. The worst work detail in the camp was that of the crematorium laborers. We'd heard that many of them went crazy, running from the place, only to be shot. They were the fortunate.

If death was better than life, then why did I retain such burning desire within me to survive? Did I have even a glimmer of hope for a sweet family reunion if I lived? Certainly not. My desires were reduced to the basest kind of animal instinct and nothing more. Though stripped of my femininity and every last bit of dignity, something gritty and feral remained. Something that was, though hardly recognizable, still human.

At the end of January, after the usual black dawn roll call, we were informed that we'd not be marching to the factory. Instead, we were taken just outside the gate and ordered to remove rocks and put them in the huge wheelbarrows provided. It was even more backbreaking than the previous work. My eyes scanned the hundreds of women who were scattered along the perimeters, looking for Annika. I spotted her, but she was much too far away for conversation.

We first had to dig through the snow to even get to the rocks below. Then, with crowbars, we were told to pry the stones from frozen ground. If it had not been for the effort expended, all of us would have died on the spot from the cold. When it began to snow so hard we could not see our hands in front of our faces, we were ordered back inside. It wasn't until night roll call that two women were noticed to be missing. They each had fallen unseen and froze where they dropped. It was weeks later I learned one of them had been Annika. We were not sent on that detail again until spring.

Winter's onslaught continued, of course, destroying the frailest in its wake. However, for every hundred women who died, there was always an equal number, if not more, to replace them. Where were they coming from? Wouldn't Hitler run out of places to find Jews?

When I'd first arrived at Ravensbrück, I was surprised to learn that not all the prisoners were Jewish. Indeed, many were Christians. What, I wondered, had they done?

The guards continually called out to the Jewish women, saying we were "killers of Jesus." Or, "Jesus haters." So why, then, were Christians living with us, some in my own barracks?

At first, only a few of them met in a group at the far end of our quarters for prayer. I was sure that must be against the rules of the camp, yet their numbers continued to grow. It was puzzling to me how their meeting together could even work well, since they did not all speak the same language. Often late at night I could hear them singing, and though we were the lowest of the low, housed more like animals in barracks number 223, the songs did not sound sad. Instead, they rang with life.

〰️

One morning, toward the end of winter, as we left the barracks for roll call, there was a paper tacked onto the door. Since we were sent to work right after, I had to wait until evening to read the notice. I'd nearly forgotten about it in my haste to collapse in my bed at the end of the day, but Miriam grabbed my sleeve as we walked in.

"Oh, how I wish I could play something. . .anything. At least I could escape work, perhaps."

"What do you mean?" I glanced at what she'd read. The camp director wanted to reward the guards for their faithful, dedicated service to the camp and, therefore, was putting together an orchestra for the pleasure and entertainment of them all.

The women began to rant over the idea. Especially because Herr Director was asking the very people considered to be vermin to step forward and volunteer for the said entertainment. It was a manipulative gesture, because which of us would not like an escape from the brutality of the work details?

"What will they do if someone hits a bad note. . .shoot them onstage?"

"Ja, will they ask us to play something Jewish?"

"Maybe they will want us to dance as well," laughed Sylvie.

"Wait," I said, "this could be good, could it not? Perhaps if we volunteered, it might go better for us." My heart raced. Maybe this was my way of survival, a ticket out of hell?

"Well, it's beside the point for me," a petite lady standing next to me said. "I know nothing about music."

It appeared only a few felt they played well enough to raise a hand—a celloist, two pianists, and one who played the flute. I said nothing about my ability to play because the women who had shared were instantly chastised.

"Would you sacrifice all of us for your own survival?" someone asked.

"You would do the same, if you had the ability, and you know it," the cello player screamed.

She was right; it was all about survival, whether it came to one more bite of food or an extra blanket left behind by someone who'd died. Every waking moment of every passing day had reduced us to nothing more than bodies trying to survive.

I had to get out of there alive. I'd made myself that promise, and I meant it. Finally, I stepped forward to stand with those who'd admitted they could play. "I play the violin," I said and signed my name on the paper.

We heard nothing after that, and my hope for a way out slipped into oblivion, every last drop of it.

One morning, we were told to wait in line after roll call. Every woman standing in a line knew what that meant. Some were about to be singled out, most likely for elimination. They'd be shot or gassed—either inside Ravensbrück or taken away in trucks to be killed somewhere else. Later, I found out many of the transportation trucks had the ability to gas passengers as they rode along, unsuspecting.

"You will step forward when you hear your number," shouted the guard.

Each time a number was called and a prisoner stepped forward, the tension in my body grew.

Eleven women walked out of line and were now standing directly in front of the guard. She read off the next series of numbers. . .they were mine. I joined the others, daring not to look at them for fear of retribution. I glanced down and saw that the woman next to me had wet herself.

Another guard came and ordered us to follow her. One of the women stumbled and fell, fear toppling her over, no doubt. I helped her to stand and murmured, "Stay on your feet, or you'll be killed for sure."

She nodded. "Danke."

Once past the crematorium, we sighed in relief. At least we'd escaped *that* fate. Dawn lightened the gray sky as we approached a huge building in the center quadrant of the camp. Warm air touched my face as we entered, and suddenly I remembered the paper I'd signed my name to a few weeks past.

Once assembled, several other groups joined us. Our relief filled the place, but we were not allowed to speak to one another while we waited.

"Remove your coats," came a command. We complied. "When I call out an instrument, you will raise your hand if you play it."

"Cello?"

Three hands went up.

"We only have one." The male soldier pointed at one of the women. "You will stay." He gestured to the two remaining. "Leave."

Their faces paled, and one began begging. "Please sir, I'm sure I'm able to play better than that woman. I am older and therefore have more experience."

The soldier slowly removed a pistol from the holder at his side and pointed it directly at her head. "Do you question my choice, Jew?"

The other prisoner who'd been rejected grabbed the woman's arm, pleading with her to stay silent.

She wouldn't. "Give me a chance. Listen to the both of us; then I will respect your choice if it is not me."

"Nein, nein, nein. I have made my decision, and it is final." He holstered the gun. "Remove her!" He turned back to the instruments.

The guard who'd been our escort removed both women, but we could hear their sobbing as they walked away. The selection continued.

There were four of us who played violin. We raised our hands with trepidation, but to our relief, there were actually four instruments. We gave knowing looks to one another, hoping we played well enough to remain.

The entire process of matching women to instruments took over an hour.

When I received mine, I was brought to tears over the pristine condition of the beautiful thing I held in my shaking hands. It was magnificent. Who had owned this wonderful thing of pleasure? Whose innocent arms had held it, revered it before it was snatched away? Truthfully, I didn't want to know. It was easier not to care that way. At least for the time being, I was free from the cold, free from backbreaking, spirit-crushing work, and. . .I was alive.

We were ordered to get our various instruments in tune. As I warmed up, the melodies rose from the violin and entered my soul. Though I'd willed myself to remain locked away from emotions, I cried, as did many others.

Our warm-up ended when a woman in her thirties entered the room. She wasn't wearing a uniform, and by the looks of her, there was no way she was a prisoner. All of us stared at the stunning creature before us who wore a gray flannel jacket over a black wool sweater. Perfectly pleated trousers exactly matched the jacket. She paused, letting a long gaze sweep the room, hand tapping a beat onto the side of one leg.

"I am assuming you all read music?" Another pause. "Because, if you are not able to read music"—she looked at the assembled collection before her—"you will not be allowed to participate." *Tap, tap, tap.* Her head moved from side to side, while she made little tch, tch sounds under her breath.

Who was this woman? We dared not ask, of course.

Orders were given to the forty of us. "You will get into positions, now. Winds, strings, piano, etc., all in their proper spots." Who had sent her?

"I am sure you have questions, do you not?"

Silence.

"Well, do you. . .have questions?" Her eyes scanned the room again. When those piercing eyes met mine, I was shocked at what I saw. Fear.

One hand went up in the back of the group.

"Speak."

"I. . .I want to say. . ."

"Yes, yes, speak up." The woman was now pacing, her arms folded across her chest.

". . .thank you," said the voice from the back.

The woman dropped her arms. "You might want to save your thanks, Fräulein, for we have a lot of work to do, I promise you." The tone of her voice had changed, if only a fraction.

It sounded softer.

The next two weeks we had practice every other day in the mornings after roll call. Coffee, good bread, and fresh cheese waited for us, and we were allowed to eat our fill. But how could this be? Who allowed such a thing?

During those first weeks the identity of our stern director remained a mystery. Only once during that time did she leave us alone. We whispered among ourselves, but again we did not all speak the same language. Our only common denominator was the music.

The director's communication was given in Deutsch, of course, but relayed around the room through various translations.

At the beginning of the third week, we had a visitor. Ravensbrück's highest-ranking officer entered the building. When the guard ordered us to stand, the only sound in the room was the scuffing of feet on the floor.

Our director placed her wand on a music stand and turned to face the older man. To our shock, he walked over and kissed both her cheeks.

"I hope my wife has chosen you well, ladies." His gaze went from side to side, reminding me of an animal about to pounce on its prey. "As you know, you will be playing for the guards' entertainment and pleasure, and of course, mine. I expect perfection." He turned to his wife. "They will be perfect, will they not, my dear?"

Our director forced a smile. "They will be ready." Was I the only one who saw the tension between them?

"Nein, perfect. They must be perfect," he corrected. Kissing her again, the commandant left the room.

We remained standing. Now that we knew the identity of our director, her presence went from mysterious to frightening.

She stood silent for a minute or two; her back turned. Facing us, she spoke. "Now you know who I am." I thought I saw her shiver. "Let's get back to work." Her hand tapped against one leg. "We have exactly one week before your performance."

There was a sharp intake of breath from each of us. Surely, she could not think our playing was even close to being the perfect presentation her husband demanded?

As if reading our minds, she said, "You will be ready."

We were ordered to practice every day that week. Every time we came together, she provided more food. As our playing improved, so did our physical bodies and our spirits as well. The positive impact was not bestowed on the players alone.

Her name was Amelia, and as the days of practice went on and our playing improved, we watched her demeanor soften, which increased her beauty. On the occasions her husband appeared unannounced, her posture and countenance would change dramatically.

Always, I detected the fear.

One day, she dismissed the guard who always stood in the back of the room. "I'm too cold," she said. "Get me my sweater." While he was gone, she opened her briefcase and took out something tied within a cloth bundle, releasing a most incredible aroma. Ginger. My mouth watered.

Amelia lifted the bundle, looking toward the door before coming closer. "I made it myself. . .this morning, while my husband. . .uh, the commandant, was in Berlin. You have worked very hard, and I must say that in the time given, and under these circumstances, your performance is remarkable."

These were the first words of kindness we'd heard since leaving our homes; yet none of us uttered a single word as Amelia walked around our chairs handing out the reward from her own hands. It was gingerbread, still a little warm.

It melted in my mouth, sweet and tangy all at once, exactly like my mama's. I ate it with my eyes closed, savoring every last morsel. We'd been given manna. I licked each one of my fingers.

Amelia stood in front of us again and laughed. "Eat up before you get caught, or it will be hell to pay." She gave a little giggle, like a child. "For all of us."

When the guard returned with the sweater, she thanked him and laid it on a chair over the empty briefcase. We immediately got back to work, invigorated by a small act of human empathy.

In the barracks, I was alienated for choosing the orchestra. I did not blame them, because I might have behaved exactly the same if I was working until I dropped from exhaustion while someone else escaped. Some days the intolerance hurt as much as the imprisonment, yet I wasn't sorry for my reprieve. I had no idea, at the time, how brief a time it would actually be.

As the performance date drew closer, Amelia managed to bring us more treats—once an entire bag of hard candy. We were like small children at a birthday party. . .all of us lifted from our plight for the minutes it took for the sweetness to melt in our mouths.

"Ladies, I have another surprise for each of you." She pulled a large box from a closet and set it on the floor in front of her.

My curiosity was piqued; I hoped it was more food.

It was clothing. The box contained forty dresses of various sizes and colors. They weren't made of cotton, but of fine silk and velvet. "Come, come," Amelia said, "come and see what I've brought you."

We formed a circle around the box, waiting for our turn to look. As we pulled dresses from the box, we passed them around until each person found one that fit relatively well.

Mine was royal-blue velvet, with a white lace collar. It was soothing against my chapped and wretched skin, but I was grateful I didn't have a mirror to see myself. With a nearly bald head, and winter galoshes, it wouldn't be a pretty sight.

Amelia seemed pleased enough, but her expression reflected what all forty of us must have looked like grouped together. A bizarre play scene from the pages of hell would have been my guess.

Regardless of what we looked like, it was our performance that would determine if the commandant was pleased or not. If he didn't like what he heard, chances were that our rag-tag orchestra would never play again. As it turned out, it would be our first and last performance anyway.

Before we played, we were ordered to clean the entire space where the performance was to be held. We scrubbed the floors, walls, and all the windows. The place sparkled, although it reeked of disinfectant.

Amelia came in as we finished. "It looks lovely, Fräuleins. Are you ready for this evening?"

Each of us nodded yes, and that seemed to please her. But when she turned away, that look of fear I'd seen when we first met had intensified. Agitated, she began to pace. "I want you to know. . ."

Just then two guards entered the building.

Her voice changed. "Very well," she shouted. "Get back to your barracks and wash yourselves."

❧

We had washed up as well as possible, changed into our new dresses, and took our seats in the cleaned-up barracks, still smelling of strong cleaning chemicals. But it was better than our own barracks, which were rarely cleaned.

When the guards began filing in, it was all I could do to remain seated. I wanted to run and refuse to play for this diabolical group. I recognized many of them, had been the brunt of their unmerciful brutality. The commandant came in last, escorting his wife on one arm.

She was breathtaking in an off-white full-length gown that swept the floor like a water-fall. Her hair had been pulled into a simple bun. The necklace and earrings matched each other and probably held real diamonds. I'd never seen anything quite like it.

Her husband walked her to the director's stand, holding her arm while she stepped up. He clicked his heels together before taking her hand to kiss it.

I wiped my hands on the folds of my dress before putting the violin under my chin. Amelia raised the baton. Our first piece was an excerpt from a Beethoven symphony, one of the commandant's favorites, we'd been told.

I had an intricate solo in which I imagined myself outside of the prison walls, playing for every man, woman, and child who'd suffered in absolute innocence. I looked up to see tears in Amelia's eyes.

We played two more pieces, each note performed with passion and skill. Amelia mouthed the words "thank you" when we finished. My heart pounded for what we'd accomplished. Truthfully, it had all been for her.

She turned to the audience and waited in a second of silence before a polite round of applause came from the group. One by one they rose from their seats, talking casually amongst themselves.

"Pigs!"

The commandant froze in the middle of a conversation with another officer. "Amelia?" His face turned scarlet. He ran to where she was now standing on the floor. "What's the meaning of this outburst?" He'd grabbed her arm, and she winced.

"I said, they...are...all...pigs, Herr Commandant. Ungrateful, fat pigs." She was shouting.

The commandant had grabbed both arms now. The red marks on her told of the force he was exerting.

"These women have been practicing for weeks and weeks, and all they get for their efforts is a small, weak applause?" Amelia pointed to the audience. "These guards have tormented each person sitting here, yet all of them poured themselves into this performance with grace and dignity." Her face went ashen as her anger spilled out.

I wanted her to stop, knowing great harm might come to her any minute.

"All of you, leave," the commandant screamed. His face contorted with rage while he kept clenched fists at his sides.

At first, no one moved. Had they turned into statues?

"I said, leave," he screamed again through gritted teeth. Jaw muscles twitched on both sides of his face.

Guards and prisoners alike stumbled over chairs and each other getting out of the building. I ran and hid in the shadows on the side rather than go back to the barracks. With no coat, the wind tore at my flesh, causing my teeth to chatter uncontrollably.

It was impossible to hear every word being said on the inside, but the intensity could not be mistaken amid the crashing of chairs.

Soon Amelia screamed but two words. "No, no!"

A shot rang out. Then an awful silence louder than the fighting crept into the darkness.

"Guards!" Two men ran back inside.

I crept close to the edge of the building and watched Amelia's body being dragged outside into the snow. A dark stain marred the entire front of the once pristine white gown. Though that beautiful face was hidden, I knew she was dead and put a hand over my mouth to stifle the outburst of my horror.

Amelia's orchestra never played again. Later we learned the instruments had been burned by order of the commandant. Within a week of returning to our backbreaking work, the entire episode became only another painful memory. Any weight I'd gained through Amelia's generosity fell off in mere days.

When typhus swept through the camp, not one barrack escaped its tirade. Already weak from the effects of daily survival, few had strength to recover, and the death tolls rose and rose until the disease ran its course. Because the accumulated bodies far exceeded the ability of the crematory to dispose of them, earth movers shoved the corpses into humongous ditches.

They lay exposed, sometimes for days, until mounds of excavated dirt covered them forever. For whatever reason, I escaped the ravages.

Since the labor force was depleted, more work went to the survivors, making each day even worse.

Near the one-year anniversary of my incarceration, in December 1944, I fell desperately ill. Dysentery consumed me, leaving a never-ending weakness that turned my limbs nearly useless. One morning, in the middle of roll call, I fainted. I felt myself being dragged across icy ground, certainly destined for the crematorium.

To my surprise, I woke in the infirmary. Though I received some care, including medication, my body remained weak and unable to work.

Every day, when daylight seeped through the frozen windowpanes, I expected to be removed and shot. However, on the days when I was able to get out of bed, I helped the nurses care for other inmates, most of whom died within days. By willing my body off the stinking mattress, I believed I would escape the inevitable. Or so I thought.

After the first of the year, the nurses talked of nothing else but the defeat of the German Army by Allied forces. The Russians were making headway, and in the whispered conversations, I heard the fear. What would happen when the contents of the prison was discovered? Would those in charge be shot? Certainly they'd be held accountable, as well as those who had worked so diligently alongside them.

I was sent back to my barracks and given "light" duty in one of the kitchens. Anyone caught eating food was shot, but still, a morsel or two could go undetected. My light duty lasted several months, until my ailment once again overtook my body with a vengeance. It was spring.

Back in the hospital, unable to even lift my head, word spread through the camp that the Russians were within days of our gates. My heart leapt with something I'd not felt in a year and a half. . .hope.

Afraid of what would happen when the state of the prisoners was discovered, any who could walk were ordered to leave. What must they have looked like. . .half-alive women streaming from the gates of hell? I wondered where they would all go.

When Allied nurses came to care for the remainder of us, I could not believe it. We were given fresh clothing, food, but more importantly, we were shown mercy and kindness. When they'd arrived, dead bodies were stacked in piles all around the compound. The horror of it must have been overwhelming, but the medical personnel began to remove them for decent burial outside the gates.

One morning, sunshine streamed through the window near my bed in the infirmary. Although I was still very weak, the light beckoned to me. Sitting up, I hung my legs over the side. The room spun around me, but I needed to feel fresh air and warmth on my face. If I was going to die, I didn't want it to be in that stifling, ugly room.

I managed to make it to the door before fainting. I don't know how long I was there, but when I woke, I was moving. Where was I?

When I opened my eyes, the horror of my reality crushed upon me like the bodies I was under. This was a morgue truck! I wanted to scream but couldn't. Pushing against the crushing weight caused the bodies to tumble onto the side. The stench overtook me, and I began retching, unable to stop.

Making my way to the back of the truck, I found fresh air. Just then the truck slowed to swerve around a rut in the road. That's when I rolled myself out.

The landing jarred my bones, but I was still breathing. Some feral instinct came alive, instantly giving me enough strength to crawl to the side of the road. I lay on my back while fluffy white clouds drifted overhead. *This must be a dream,* I thought, just before passing out.

When I woke, confusion overwhelmed my mind. Was anyone looking for me? Could I really be free? The Allies were there to help, but I knew they were not trustworthy. Many women had already been assaulted by the Russians. No, there was no going back.

That's when I heard running water in the distance, which meant there had to be a stream close by. I crawled inch after painful inch through grass and sharp rocks, driven by a terrible thirst. Death was closing in, stalking my every move, but still I managed to make the water's edge before drifting into darkness again.

I woke, shocked to be alive since every fiber in my body said I should be dead. That's when I saw or maybe heard someone splashing through the water. . .coming closer and closer. A soldier. I feared for the harm he might do and waited for the assault.

Instead, it was an American.

Of course, Michael, you know by now the man who found me was your father. He took me from death's door to life; no one could have been braver or kinder. He saw something in me I could not fathom in myself. His belief for my recovery is what saved me more than any care I received, though I was surrounded by kindness from generous souls.

Oh, my boy, I do not have the energy to fill in all the blanks for you, but hopefully this small journal will help. I have comfort, knowing you and your father will have each other.

I love you beyond what this earth can contain,

Mom

# Chapter 13

JD was in church only out of respect for Steve. This choir production was important to all of his family, especially Crystal. After all Steve and Vikki had done since Hadassah's illness had begun, JD could hardly say no. Michael came willingly when Steve had asked. Their neighbor lady, Eunice, was staying with Hadassah for the evening.

JD found it hard to stay focused in the stifling air of the sanctuary; his mind was with Hadassah. She was getting sicker and weaker by the day. He refused to believe there was nothing left to be done, and at her last doctor's appointment he'd embarrassed himself for the degree of anger he'd directed at the physician.

"Look, Doctor, my wife is suffering." He was pacing, slamming a fist into one palm. "Can't you do something? Another round of chemo might give her—us—more time." He was sweating profusely from the energy it took to deliver the diatribe.

The doctor placed both hands in his coat pockets. "I wish I were able to tell you something different, Mr. Jensen, to do something more, I mean." He dropped his head. "But"—he looked up to make eye contact—"your wife has little time left, and that's the bottom line."

JD felt like he'd been kicked in the gut, even though he'd watched the downhill slide, day after day, week after week. It was the inevitability of those words *little time left*, the finalized reality of what the "bottom line" really meant. Hadassah was going to die, and not his strong will, nor hers, could prevent it. Medicine couldn't stop it, and obviously God wasn't going to. His thoughts were interrupted when the lights went down.

"O, come, o come, Emanuel, and ransom captive Israel."

The choir walked in carrying individually lit candles. JD relaxed a little and focused on his niece, who was stunning in a burgundy dress with a silver bow. He smiled. She looked just like her mom with a definite imprint of Steve thrown in. . . .

When the production concluded, JD was surprised how much he'd enjoyed it. Apparently so did Mike, because he was applauding and grinning after Crystal's amazing solo during "Silent Night." Her voice had been strong and clear, stirring something within JD that he hadn't felt in years. Maybe it was the elusive Christmas spirit he could barely remember. Regardless, it was good for them both to be focused on something positive and uplifting. . .if even for an evening. He threw off a stab of guilt for being away from his wife.

When the concert finished, Steve's pastor came on stage. "We're here tonight not to draw attention to our talented choir—and they are talented—but to honor the reason for Christmas in the first place: our Lord Jesus Christ. It was no small thing for the King of the Universe to leave heaven for this earth. . .to leave heaven and be born of a virgin. And now, here's the most amazing part. He didn't come for all mankind, although for sure that is true. Jesus Christ came to earth specifically just for you."

JD noticed Michael sitting up straighter, his eyes fixed on the pastor.

"If you were the only person on earth, Jesus still would have come to earth in order to die for you thirty-three years after His humble birth. Amazing, isn't it, that the greatest gift ever given us is so often forgotten amidst the tinsel, paper, and ribbon? There might be people right here, right now, who are in despair. You're hurting, and it seems the lights of Christmas have gone out for you, at least in your heart, anyway."

JD's heartbeat quickened; his palms began to sweat.

"You came here tonight not because you wanted to celebrate anything, but because you felt obligated."

JD wanted to look at Steve but didn't want to draw attention to himself. He could see Michael out of the corner of one eye, still riveted to every word.

"I've got good news for you. Jesus knows you and the content of your heart. He sees the tears you weep in silence so no one around you will know. He feels your pain and wants to walk with you. He desires to relieve your burden and give you strength and hope. His Word, the Bible, says we are all sinners, but He came to take those sins upon Himself, and, in exchange, offers us a chance for a new and forgiven life, a life with Him. He is our hope. He is *your* hope. All a person needs to do is ask Him. The God of the Universe wants to be your Savior, to pour out His love and grace into your life. 'Amazing grace, how sweet the sound, that saved a wretch like me.'

"I'm asking all of you to please keep your head bowed." He paused. "If I'm speaking to you, will you just come forward now, and let me, or one of our prayer people, pray with you to accept this gift of salvation right now?" There was another pause. "Please don't be afraid. Come now."

Embarrassed, JD raised his head and looked around to see if anyone was going forward. At once he noticed Mike was gone. He saw him nearly running down the aisle. Steve saw him, too, and followed behind. When they arrived at the front, he tapped Mike on the shoulder. Mike turned around, and the two embraced. JD tried to choke back the tears. Steve held tight to Mike, whispering something in his ear. JD got out his handkerchief as about half a dozen more people walked forward.

Vikki slipped in beside him and took his hand, giving it a squeeze. He looked at her, but her eyes were fixed on Steve and Mike.

As JD watched his brother praying with Mike, he felt a warm breeze, like a delicate breath, blowing through the sanctuary. Funny, he hadn't noticed that before. Glancing around, no one else seemed aware of it.

What was happening? Then he heard someone speaking to him. . .a tender voice full of emotion. Again he looked around. A powerful force began to swirl around his head, and the warmth of the breeze pulsated down the length of his body. *God, are you calling me?* There wasn't an audible answer, but he was led by the "force" to let go of Vikki's hand and stand. He made his way out of the pew and walked on shaky legs down toward the front. He'd never felt so driven, so absolutely sure of his actions, or so loved in all his life.

Steve had finished praying with Michael when JD arrived beside them.

"Dad, Dad, I just prayed with Uncle Steve." His voice went lower. "Dad, Jesus is real." Tears streamed down his face.

Steve was wiping at his own cheeks.

"I know, Mike," JD said softly. He caught Steve's eye. "Will you pray with me?"

Steve grabbed JD by the shoulders and gave him a bear hug. "I've been waiting a long time to do that, big brother."

Time stood still while JD Jensen's destiny was impacted by his Maker for all eternity. That night in a small, candlelit church, the clever reporter, stalwart ex-soldier, the son, father, and devoted husband, became a follower of the living God.

⌘

JD and Michael talked all the way home about what had happened to them both. "Dad, I believed God was real before—I really did—but tonight I knew; I just knew." He began to hum "Away in a Manger."

JD understood what Mike was saying even if he didn't have words to express himself at the moment. Steve had given him his Bible and told him to read the book of John. For some reason, he couldn't wait to get home and do that. Although he lacked words for expression as to what had happened in his heart and soul, he knew for sure that his life had been changed for good. . .for good and for forever.

⊚∕∂⊚

Steve had been so distracted after praying with JD and Michael that he'd forgotten to say anything about the journalism entry. But, he reasoned, the most important thing had been taken care of. He'd call tomorrow.

⊚∕∂⊚

Just as JD turned down the last street before home, his mind froze. *Hadassah!* How would he tell his Jewish wife that not only was God alive, but also he'd just pledged a lifetime of allegiance to His Son, the Jewish Messiah?

In the guest room, equipped with a hospital bed, Hadassah was sleeping when the two walked in the house. JD followed Michael quietly down the hall to his room. They hugged for a long time. "Dad, even though Mom is sick, I feel something really special right here." He pointed to his heart. "Is it because Jesus lives there now?"

JD looked at his handsome, vulnerable twelve-year-old, and choked back emotion. "That's what the pastor and Uncle Steve told us, buddy. I have that same kind of feeling. I don't understand all of this, what happened to us tonight, I mean." He gave Mike another hug. "But I know it's real."

Mike squeezed him back and looked up into his face. "Dad, how's Mom going to take this whole Jesus thing?"

JD took a deep breath. "I don't know, but I guess we'll find out soon enough." He waited until Mike got into his pajamas and was under the covers. JD sat on the edge of the bed and couldn't stop smiling. "You're a great kid, you know that, Mike?"

"Thanks, Dad." He reached up and grabbed JD tight around the neck. They held that way for a long time. "I love you, Dad."

"Love you too, bud. Night."

Mike was asleep by the time JD shut the door.

He stopped in front of Hadassah's room down the hall. For the first time since her illness, he had a peace within that produced a new resolve. Regardless of what the future held, he knew he and Mike would have enough strength to make it through. *But what about you, Hadassah?*

His first prayer as a Christian was to ask God to bring that same kind of comforting strength to his wife.

Then he lit a fire in the living-room fireplace and settled in his lounger to read the book of the Bible Steve had mentioned. He was surprised that he remembered the names of the Gospels: Matthew, Mark, Luke, and John.

His fingers brushed against the page his brother had highlighted in yellow. "In the beginning was the Word, and the Word was with God. . . ."

He read through the entire thing as word after word and chapter after chapter came alive in his hands. All of this had been here all along. He felt a stab of remorse at not listening to Steve and Vikki, when they'd only wanted to share because they loved him.

When he at last closed the Bible, he listened to the crackle and pop of the fire. Though exhausted, he'd never been more awake, more alive, in his entire life. What a life he'd led, a "good" life by most people's standards.

Now, facing this uphill battle with Hadassah's cancer, he knew that *special* life he'd had with her was coming to a fast end. He rubbed his forehead. Twenty years now. . .twenty years.

395

# Chapter 14

*1945*
*Berlin*

JD had been sent to Berlin in 1945, when the war was over. The end had been long in coming, exhausting, and very ugly, but the troops and people in America wanted to know everything about the final days of Hitler's maniacal reign. Yet some things could not be put into words, regardless, like the devastation war had done to his very soul, emptying it of hope and filling it instead with disgust and rage. However, little did he know the worst revelations were to come.

He'd barely gotten to the outskirts of Berlin when the "camp" rumors started filtering through the ranks. They'd all heard things after the Russians got there first. The closest camp to the city was Ravensbrück. . .full of women, they'd heard.

Though he'd had his fill of war stories, JD felt compelled to check it out for himself. His "never take anyone's word for fact" motto had kicked in, and he was determined. He'd asked around for a Russian soldier who spoke English. He'd found several, but only one would speak of what he'd seen.

"There were walking dead. But the worst was the dead bodies everywhere, piled in ditches and stacked behind the buildings."

"How many people could be killed in one camp?" JD was a skeptic.

The soldier, no more than twenty, began to sob. "We'll probably never know." He looked right into JD's eyes. "I thought I knew what evil could do. I've seen my own troops commit atrocities. But until I entered the gates of Ravensbrück, I was an innocent. Someone needs to tell this story." He started to leave but hesitated and turned. "If you have the guts, that is."

JD watched him walk away and took a deep breath before looking for his superior officer.

"Good idea for a story, JD. We've been hearing these rumors for a while now, but mostly I think they're exaggerated." The commander pulled out two cigars, lit one, and passed the other to JD. "You can go, Jensen, but remember, if these stories are real, you better have the grit it's gonna take to tell 'em."

"You're the second person today who's told me that." He saluted and left.

The CO had no transportation for him, so he'd bummed rides as far as he could. Then he was on foot. The roads were strewn with abandoned military tanks, motorcycles, and cars. Most had been set on fire; some still smoldered.

The air was stagnant with the wastes of war, including hundreds of people walking all along the way. Each bore the burden of haunted nightmares, along with knapsacks filled with whatever could be salvaged from the ravages of the life they'd been forced to leave behind. He was reminded of an anthill he and his brother had once knocked apart in their backyard, scattering the living contents in all directions.

The children looked the worst. What had they suffered? What had their vacant eyes seen? JD wanted to ask but filed his questions away for another story. He knew there'd be hundreds.

Evidently there had been a heavy rain the night before, because soon the road became impassable, even for a bike he'd found abandoned. He ate his K-rations while lumbering through a roadside field the last five miles.

A side road had a white weathered sign with LAKE SCHWEDT and an arrow painted on it in faded green lettering. In the distance he saw large estates. He came upon a rise in the road, lifted his head, and took in a sharp breath. Ravensbrück! Nothing could have prepared him for its enormous size. Acres of barracks, stained by soot, stretched before him. Even from a distance he could see guard stations and the barbed wire that snaked on and on around the entire cement wall that contained the entire premises. Several huge smokestacks loomed above it all. And the camp was not empty, for he could see people walking back and forth. Were women still left inside?

By now the sun was high in the sky and nesting birds flitted from tree to tree. It was a beautiful day in the German countryside, a day for picnics and celebrations of life. . .birthdays, graduations, and christenings. Yet just ahead through a huge iron gate were the realities of Ravensbrück. It lay before him like a giant, evil entity, a dark, ugly scar carved on the face of the green landscape. What a dichotomy.

He was about to discover the magnitude of that thought.

Nearing the gate, he was forced to step aside for a huge white-canvassed truck bearing a red cross. Lumbering by, it belched black smoke as it geared down for the hill right behind him. JD glanced over his shoulder and saw in the shadows of the truck bed what looked like human beings, stacked on top of one another, nearly to the ceiling. The smell spilling out the back was like an overflowing cesspool. One hand went to his mouth, and he willed himself not to be sick. It didn't work. Instead, he vomited in projectile spurts until his gut felt like it was turning inside out. He walked several steps before collapsing onto the grass.

"Mister, mister, *are ni alla ratt? Behover du hjalp?*"

He opened his eyes and thought a child stood over him. But when JD sat up, he saw it was a very small woman dressed all in white, with a red-cross armband. A nun. He recognized what he thought was a Swedish accent, but he understood nothing except the "mister" part.

"Do you speak English?" He wiped his mouth.

She nodded. "Yes, I do, but not very well." She smiled and offered him a hand up.

"Oh, thank you, but no." He was embarrassed. "I'm JD Jensen."

"I'm Sister Anna Clare, and I am very much stronger than I look, sir." She fingered the carved wooden cross hanging around her neck.

Nevertheless, he got to his feet without help. He would have killed for a shot of anything stronger than water but took a big swig from his nearly empty canteen. He rinsed his mouth and turned away from the nun to spit.

"I'm sorry," he apologized. "It was just the truck. . .the smell. . . ."

"Sir, I understand. I myself am a nurse, and I am not used to it. That truck is taking the dead to bury them outside of this camp in a real cemetery. It is the least we can do for them. . . now." She wiped her hands on the stained apron tied around her petite frame. "Please, come with me. We have a place you can sit if you like."

"Uh, no. No, thank you, Sister. I'm a reporter, and I wanted to see what was really going on up here." He showed her his identification and notebook.

"Oh, yes, now I see, you come for the story." She looked up at him with soulful eyes. "It is very tragic and ugly, I'm afraid."

He shrugged. "Isn't all war ugly?"

"Ja, but this. . .this is the most ugly. It is vile. . .evil"—she struggled with an adjective—"personified."

Her accent was thick, but he understood every word. For the first time since coming to Europe, he wanted to run as far as his legs could take him, to try and forget what he'd seen and smelled in the back of that truck. Instinct told him there would be more vehicles carrying the exact same cargo.

"Mister, are you a brave man?" Her gaze was steady.

"I thought I was. . .until today." He couldn't take his eyes from hers. They were big and pitifully old, having seen more than any person should, he imagined.

"Perhaps today will be one of the greatest tests of your courage, then." Her voice dropped to a whisper. "Ravensbrück has been my testing place." She looked down at her tiny feet, covered with well-worn laced boots.

"Are you passing or failing?" She was so small and young. For sure younger than him; he'd bet maybe still a teenager. He wondered what her real name was before she became the "bride of Christ."

"Both." Her hands flew up. "One minute I'm passing. . .coping. . .and then, then I see one more tortured soul, one more stack of bodies, and I can only cry out to God." She adjusted her habit and cleared her throat, obviously embarrassed by the outburst.

"You mean you've cursed God?" Had he heard right? Wasn't she a woman of faith?

Looking up sharply, she said, "Oh no, I don't curse Him. I cry to Him for strength. For understanding. But mostly, I cry out to him for courage." She took a step closer. "You see, I am a weak person." One hand rested on JD's arm for emphasis.

Suddenly he wanted to take this young girl and hide her from any more evil. Something had changed in him. From the inside out, he felt different. This, he found confusing, and more than a little upsetting. He tried to pull himself together; there was, after all, still a story to tell. What words would he use to describe what he'd seen even *before* going inside this German hellhole?

He nodded toward the barracks. "Who's left inside there?" His voice sounded awkward and strained because his insides were still churning.

"Only the weakest of the weak. . .those too sick to leave when the Germans forced the others to march away before the Russians came." She paused. "And, of course, as you saw, the dead. We have only one doctor, I'm afraid, and several more nurses to care for maybe three thousand women."

"Three thousand! That can't be. But how?" He felt his knees grow weak. There had been rumors that such things were happening all over Europe, but few believed the extent of what he was discovering. Now he wondered how many knew the truth and chose to look away. The thought of that reality caused him to burn with an even deeper anger.

"It was the Swedish Red Cross who initiated a rescue in March. Nearly eight thousand were taken from here then. That's when I arrived to help sort out our women. The Nazis sent all others who could walk on what became a death march." She exhaled loudly.

JD could only shake his head in response. He followed her inside the gates but stopped. The minute they entered he'd felt something palpable. The hair on the back of his neck stood, causing a shudder through his entire body. His head jerked in her direction.

"You are feeling the evil, are you not?"

JD stared at her with unbelief. What was she saying?

"It is real, believe me." She stepped close to him again. "Are you a praying man, Mister Soldier-Reporter?"

"Not really." He felt ashamed.

She crossed herself with the sign of the cross. "Well, now might be a good time to become one."

She was right. She gave him some potent menthol to smear under his nose and a hand-kerchief to cover his face, but it did not alleviate the smell of death that permeated every inch of breathing space. His brain continually refused to process what he was seeing. Barrack after barrack was filled with dying women of all ages. He assumed they were all ages, because he was not able to tell the young from the not-so-young, or the old from not-so-old. Truth was, they all looked old. Most had little hair, and every bone in their wasted bodies protruded like they were trying to escape the sickly, abused skin that barely held them together.

The worst were the ones whose eyes were open; each orb a deep pool of horror and degradation. He had to remind himself that this was not a nightmare but the reality of hatred churned into insanity.

At one point he turned to Sister Anna Clare. "Will any of them live?" He was shaking, while sweat sent steady rivulets running down his neck to soak his entire shirt.

"Perhaps." Her voice dropped, and she looked up into his face. "But what kind of life might they have after?" Her mouth contorted with grief over the reality of those words, and she turned her face.

"Then why are you here, Sister? What's the point?"

She didn't speak for a moment, gathering her thoughts. "We," she gestured toward the others, "are here to give comfort to the dying and to bury the dead. That is all." Tears streamed down her face, wetting the chin cloth of her habit.

"How long will you stay?"

"As long as it takes, JD. And you, fine reporter, how long will you stay?"

He stayed less than two hours, the longest two hours of his entire life. He left feeling like the coward he now knew himself to be. How could a teenaged nun with eyes like a doe be stronger than a grown man? Every fiber of his being screamed for release from the pictures in his head—the smells that followed him. When he got out of sight of Ravensbrück, he broke into a run across a nearby field. It wasn't easy because the plentiful grass hid rocks and ruts. He stumbled twice, falling flat against the verdant earth, but scrambled to his feet. When he reached the forest, JD crashed through like a wild thing. Branches continually assaulted his face, until he couldn't tell if what dripped down his face was blood or sweat. It couldn't be tears. He had none left.

He ran until completely void of breath, the sound of running water drawing him deeper into the woods. When he reached the fairly good-sized stream, he threw himself facedown on the bank, lapping its cool contents like a wild animal. Rolling onto his back, he saw that the sky was filled with billowy white clouds. Their pristine presence mocked what he'd left behind in Ravensbrück.

"God," he shouted, "how could You create such beauty up there and allow this much evil down here?" With one arm over his face, he lay there with no answers then slept with fitful visions flitting through his mind like a macabre play.

The crying woke him—faint moans. Were they from his dreams? He sat up and turned to look across the water. There was a pile of something lying very near the edge. He squinted. Had it moved?

Now he was up and on his feet. What was it? Maybe that's what he'd heard in his sleep. Maybe it wasn't a dream after all. "Hello!"

No response.

The water was swift but not deep. He removed both boots and rolled up his pant legs. Though the water was icy, he couldn't turn back. Walking swiftly across, he slowed when the "something" on the bank lifted its head. A woman! At least he thought it was a woman. With no hair, he couldn't be sure.

He approached slowly, not wanting to frighten whoever it was. Closer now, he definitely could see the person was a woman. . .what was left of one. Just like the women in the barracks, this one looked old and about to die. But what was she doing out here?

Still in the water, he felt his heart breaking into little pieces like slivered shards of glass over what remained on the bank. Finally, the body stirred and spoke something in German. He couldn't understand at first. With one feeble move, she pointed at the water and then touched her lips.

"Oh, you must be thirsty." He took his canteen, emptied the stale contents, and filled it full with the crystal stream water. When he stepped toward her, she flinched; one arm going across her face in defense.

"It's okay, okay. . ." He pointed to himself and said, "American. . .USA," then handed her the canteen.

She tried to take it, but her hands and arms shook so hard, it knocked against her teeth. She whimpered over the failed effort.

"Let me help." He held the canteen to her lips, and she drank until exhausted.
"Danke" came out barely audible.

"I have food." Did she understand? He pulled a can of K-rations from his pack, opened it, and dug around until he found the spoon. She was lying back in the grass again, and he was afraid she might have passed out. He clinked the metal spoon against the can. Her eyes flew open, and she rolled her head to look at him but didn't speak. Yet the eyes said it all. *Help me.*

He sat beside her and supported her head, letting her lean against his chest. He reached around and held a spoonful of meat to her mouth. She could only lick at it. He offered her water again, and she took more than before. The next bite of food was substantial, but she threw it up. He wiped her mouth with his shirt, and she fell back to sleep with her head in his lap. He removed his jacket carefully and covered as much of her as possible.

He dozed off and woke with a start. It was late afternoon, and the sun was listing to the western sky. *We need shelter for the night.* He strained to see through the woods. Nothing. He lifted her head and placed it on the ground so he could reconnoiter a little.

Walking away from the water, he looked to make sure she was still sleeping. JD's mind wrestled with where she'd come from, but he knew the minute he'd spotted the body exactly where she'd been. . .Ravensbrück. But, if she'd been marched away earlier, then why was she still this close? He froze. She must have been on the truck that left the camp earlier. His stomach lurched! The thought of that little waiflike body being mistaken for dead and put in the back of a truck with several dozen actual dead made him run. He ran until he felt his lungs might burst, but he couldn't stop.

In the density of the forest, he nearly missed the large overgrown stone barn. He could barely breathe, but at least his head felt clearer. It took what remaining strength he had to push the heavy door open. In the darkened rafters overhead, something large took wing, and he cried out.

A miserly stream of light forced its way through a green-encrusted window, casting a prism of light into the barn's interior. He saw that the inside was dry, still clinging to the heady, musty smells of its past life. He spotted a lantern; it sloshed with some remaining fuel. *Hope my matches are still dry.*

A sudden hissing and a low growl caused him to jump again. A momma cat and four kittens ran in all directions as he walked by. Grateful for the shelter, JD found some clean hay as well as a worn, but fairly intact, woolen horse blanket. He spread the hay and shook out the blanket before laying it on top. He fluffed the makeshift bed as best as he could and turned to get the woman. "God, You know I haven't prayed since I was a kid, but if You're listening, help me get this woman to safety. Amen."

When he hurried back to her, she was in the exact spot he'd left her. What if now she *was* actually dead? He knelt beside her and put one hand on a shoulder. Her eyes flew open and then fluttered shut again. As deftly as possible, he picked her up and found she weighed next to nothing. Tears he thought were spent streamed down his face. He was powerless to stop them.

Though she appeared to be unconscious, he began to talk anyway. "You're going to be okay. I'll see to it; you can count on me. I'm John David Jensen, but everyone calls me JD." He was afraid they'd get caught in the dark before making it back to the barn, but just as early night songs of the forest began, he spotted it.

He laid her down on the makeshift bed, dug out his two remaining matches, and lit the kerosene lantern. It sputtered at first but, with a little adjustment, flared to life. There was no sign of the cats, but overhead a protesting owl made its presence known. Despite the chaos of war, nature's heartbeat continued. What irony.

He sat as a sentinel, watching the woman. Should he try to wake her or let her sleep? He wrestled with the decision, but after an hour she woke on her own. Her lips were cracked and bleeding, but they moved to speak. "Danke," she whispered.

"Do you want more water?" He held up the canteen.

She nodded with closed eyes, accepting JD's help to drink. She licked her lips and looked at him. Laying one bony hand against her chest, she said, "Hadassah." The effort to speak sent her back to a prone position.

"Hadassah. Never met anyone with that name." He smiled. "I'm JD, JD Jensen." Her eyes were closed again, and he thought she'd fallen back to sleep.

"I. . .I. . .got. . .out." Her voice was such a low raspy whisper, JD had to lean very close to hear. Though heavy with German accent, he had no trouble understanding the English.

"Yes, I know, I found you by the water." He pulled the jacket closer around her.

"I. . .got out. . .of. . .truck." She opened her eyes, and he could see the lantern flame reflected in them. "Every. . .one. . .dead. . ." Big pause. ". . .but. . .me." Tears rolled down the ravaged face, pooling on the coat before being absorbed. Her body began to shake with silent sobs.

JD wasn't sure if he should touch her, but in sympathy he couldn't hold back. Scooting as close as he could, he lifted her into his lap and cradled the frailness of her just like he would a child. She clung to him while the horror of her memory spent itself against him. "Shhh now. Shhh, Hadassah. I'm sorry, so sorry."

When she finally settled, he asked her if she could eat something. The first response was no, but after a little coaxing, he got her to eat several more bites of the K-rations. This time they stayed down. In the bottom of his pack he discovered an overaged orange, but when Hadassah tried to eat it, the citric acid stung her lips, and she whimpered a little.

Before he blew out the lantern, he thought she looked improved, if only a little. Although he wanted to keep vigil overnight, he fell into a restless sleep, all night dreaming of huge owls sweeping down to devour whomever dared enter the barn where they kept an ancient vigil.

⟡

When JD woke, dawn was pushing into the shadowy recesses of their shelter. Hadassah was still asleep, her breathing even and steady.

He stood and walked around the barn to warm up and get rid of some body kinks. In one stall, he found a metal bin nearly full of oats. He picked out some black specs, ignoring repugnant thoughts of mice droppings, or worse yet, a rat's remnants. If he could find a metal container, perhaps he could build a fire and make oatmeal. Poking around in another bin, he found an old coffee tin that would hold water. At one end of the building a pile of dry alder sticks and a couple rotting barn boards made elements for a good fire.

With his one remaining match he built a fire in the middle of the dirt floor away from where they'd slept. Soon the water from his canteen boiled, and he sprinkled in the oats a little at a time, stirring them with his metal spoon. How many mornings had he eaten an oatmeal breakfast growing up? His mother's kitchen was always open to everyone, and all his friends loved her. The "gruel" she served was steaming hot with huge slabs of butter melting right in the middle, always accompanied by raisins and brown sugar on the side, and a full plate of toast. "You boys will eat me out of house and home someday."

The owl above stirred the air with beating wings, bringing his thoughts to the present. While the oats thickened, he left to check on Hadassah. When he returned to where'd they'd slept, her spot was empty, the jacket thrown aside. He panicked.

"I'm here." She stood in the doorway, clinging to one side for support. "I had to go."

It took him a second before he understood what she meant.

"I'm glad you're on your feet, but I would have helped you."

Her knees buckled. He caught her just in time. "I found some oats, and they're cooking. Could you maybe eat some?" He helped her back to the hay bed.

She nodded and licked her dry lips. "More water first. . .please."

He brought the canteen to her lips and was pleased when she held it by herself. *What must this woman have suffered already?* He was forming a plan to get them away from here, but he'd need some help. She was too weak to walk back to the road, and he couldn't carry her all the way to Berlin.

He put the leftover meat from the K-rations into the oatmeal, and she managed to eat twice more than yesterday. "Would you be all right here, for an hour or so?"

"Where are you going?" He heard panic in the question as she pushed up on one elbow.

"Just looking around for some kind of transportation to get you and me out of here. I promise I'll get back as soon as possible." He made strong eye contact. "I'm a man of my word, Hadassah." She eased down onto the hay again, closed her eyes, saying nothing.

He stole one last look at her before walking out the barn. Never had he felt such purpose or resolve for any one duty in his entire life. She needed some serious medical help. . .would probably not survive without it.

The house that went with the barn had been burned to the ground, but maybe whoever lived here had neighbors. He walked in the direction of the rising sun. After fifteen minutes or so, he thought he heard someone singing. A lilting melody streamed through the trees, drifting round and round his head. He slowed down, not wanting to frighten anyone, especially if they had a gun. Just ahead a young girl had a cow tethered to a pole in the middle of a fenced pasture. Her golden head pressed against its side, while rhythmically pulling milk from a huge udder. She was the one singing.

His stomach growled at the prospect of fresh milk. Quietly he stepped out of the woods and into the clearing. The cow gave him away with a long, low bellow. The startled girl jumped to her feet, knocking over the milking stool and bucket. In turn the cow began hopping around the pole until it broke free, making a loping run back toward its barn.

The young girl stamped her foot in disgust and turned her attention to him. She put out her hand in a warning for him to stay back. Her head shook back and forth, while she shouted, "Nein, nein," at the top of her lungs.

In seconds a woman came running from the barn with a rifle braced against one shoulder. "Halt or I'll shoot!" She spoke German, but he understood every word, raising both arms as far as possible.

"Nein, don't shoot." He hoped she understood his poor German. "American, American," he repeated slowly. The mother walked closer, slowly lowering the gun. Her hand went to her heart. She looked up at him, and he saw tears filling her eyes. "Thank Gott," she whispered.

"English? Do you speak English?" He hoped beyond hope that she would be the answer to his prayer for help with Hadassah.

"Ja." She smiled. "I speak quite well." She pointed to herself and curtsied. "I am Frau Handberg. . .Lotte."

He was relieved to hear English spoken so well and walked forward to hold out his hand. "JD Jensen."

She took his hand then looked around. "Are you without others?"

"Not exactly." By now the little girl he'd first seen was back with four other children of various sizes and ages. The oldest, a boy about fifteen, glared at him and approached his mother's side to throw a protective arm around her. She said something too low for JD to hear, but the boy relaxed some. The other children seemed more curious than afraid, and JD buoyed a little.

"Hungry?" Frau Handberg asked.

"No, uh, nein. But thank you."

She looked puzzled, and waited.

He took a couple steps toward the family, causing the tall boy to bristle. JD held up one hand and stopped. "I do have someone with me. She. . .needs help." He gestured behind him. "She's sick, very sick."

The woman glanced at her children then back at him. "From the camp?"

He nodded.

Frau Handberg sighed. "We have others here. You bring her here, please. We will help her, Mister American." She pushed the tall boy forward. "This is Lutz. He is good and strong. Come, and we will get you our wagon. There's been no doctor here for years and years, but I will do what I can."

JD said nothing, following behind the Handberg family, grateful he'd been greeted with such hospitality. When they approached the barn, for a second he feared that perhaps Herr Handberg might be waiting with another gun, but no such person appeared.

On the house porch he caught sight of three other women. Frau Handberg noticed his glances and explained, "From Ravensbrück." She said something in German under her breath then clamped a hand over her mouth. He thought she might have been swearing. "I apologize to you, JD." She smiled, and he relaxed.

"No need to apologize." He saluted. It made him feel good to know that there were people left in Germany who spoke against the camp and were willing to help. Before the liberation, he knew this family would have been helpless against the Nazi Gestapo. Only later would he discover what had happened when one family member had protested.

Turned out, the frisky cow he'd seen earlier was as helpful pulling a cart as it was giving sustenance. Lutz was as strong as his mother claimed and had the bovine hooked up to a wagon with wooden wheels in only minutes. He grabbed a stick, jumped up on the seat, and motioned for JD to do the same. "Sit with me, Soldier. . .less bumps up here." He patted the place beside him.

JD was amazed at how well the kid spoke English. He smiled and hopped up. "Thanks."

Frau Handberg and all four remaining children waved them off like they were leaving on holiday. Lutz glanced at JD but said nothing for several minutes. "When the camp is empty, I wish to burn it to the ground." He never flinched when he said it, even though his voice quavered with emotion.

"I feel the same, Lutz, and I only spent a few hours there." JD was curious about the man of the family, Lutz's father. Maybe he was still trying to get home from service, or perhaps he'd been taken a prisoner of war.

They rode in silence some more before Lutz spoke again. "My father tried to help some women who escaped two years ago."

JD waited.

"We hid them for three days before the Nazis came and found them. They were dragged from our barn and stripped of their clothing." The boy's face went crimson with the memory. He cleared his throat. "Then the guards told them to run for the woods. They had almost made it there before dogs were turned on them. The screaming was unbearable, but all of us were made to watch." He wiped his face with the back of a sleeve. "When there were no more screams, one soldier marched my father over to where the women were laying, mutilated with torn flesh but still alive. 'Shoot them!' he ordered. My father refused and was smashed in the head with the butt of a rifle and staggered. He was given the order once more. Still he refused and was hit again. This time he dropped like a slaughtered animal to his knees. He looked at us and mouthed final words of love." Lutz's tears could not be stopped.

"Then the guard touched my father's head with the rifle barrel and shot him. Quickly he turned the gun on the women before grabbing the dogs. We believed we would be next, but instead he only walked back to us. My sisters and brothers were hysterical, but my mother refused to let them see her cry.

"The soldier lifted his gun once more. 'I could shoot you all like the pigs you are.' He spit in our direction and acted as if he was going to release the snarling dogs. 'But,' the guard paused to light a cigarette, 'I think it would be delicious to have all of you remember this day for the rest of your lives.' He threw back his head and laughed like the devil was living inside him. The other soldiers joined in, and then they left us, left us there to bury the women and my father...." Sobs ripped from Lutz's body. "A man so good he gave his own life to save the lives of innocent women he barely knew."

JD was stunned at the eloquent revelation. He, the award-winning reporter, was at a complete loss for words. It was crazy. Here was a kid who had every right to the innocence of youth, yet it had been stolen from him with the crack of an army rifle. JD placed one hand on the boy's shoulder and gave it a squeeze. His mind was overwhelmed with the suffering he'd witnessed in such a short time. He'd never be able to tell all the stories. Yet wasn't he still a journalist?

An abrupt dip jarred him back to attention. It wasn't easy maneuvering the cart along the rut-filled road, but Lutz was good at coaxing the cow, and JD finally spotted the place where he'd entered the woods the previous day. He could only hope Hadassah would be fit to travel in the back of the hard wagon.

Lutz stayed with the cow, while JD trekked back into the woods, forded the creek, and found the barn. Hadassah was sitting up, wrapped in his jacket and the horse blanket. When he entered, she smiled then covered her cracked lips with one hand.

"You look better." He smiled in return.

"Yes, though I am very weak. Thank you for the food. . .and the coat." Her voice was raspy.

He knelt beside her. "I brought help."

She stiffened.

"It's okay, Hadassah. I found a family ready to help us. They live just down the road. There's a cart for you if you're up to that."

She shrugged. He helped her stand, lifting her into his arms to carry her through the woods and to the waiting boy.

With Lutz's help, JD propped her against one side, placing the blanket behind her head for comfort. "Will you be warm enough without the blanket?"

She nodded and stared at Lutz.

"Oh, sorry for the bad manners. Hadassah, this is Lutz Handberg, a new friend, but a very good one."

The two acknowledged each other.

The cart bounced so hard on the way back to the farm, JD feared Hadassah's bones might break, but she made it without further damage.

Lotte Handberg walked from the porch to the wagon when they pulled in.

"Hadassah, this is Frau Handberg, Lutz's mother."

Hadassah gazed at the woman, whose eyes were full of compassion. She tried to speak, but her mouth barely moved.

"Say nothing, little bird. Soon you'll be strong, and we'll have time for talk. Come, there is a real bed for you inside. After you rest in it, I have clothes and some good food for those skinny bones. You can trust us. . . . You are safe here."

Hadassah nodded, licked her lips, and scratched at her head.

"Ach, I have a good old-fashioned remedy for those lice. When they're gone, you will feel like a new woman, I promise, Liebchen."

Lotte spoke something to Lutz that JD didn't understand and then climbed into the back of the wagon, lifted her new patient to her feet, and helped her down to the ground. All the way up the porch steps, she talked to the grown woman in German, soft and low like a mother speaks to a child. JD only understood a few of the words, but Lotte's tone said it all. When they got to the door Hadassah's head was resting on her new friend's shoulder.

Hadassah did not come to the supper table that evening, but the other three "guests" were seated with the family and JD. That made ten in all.

Lotte's children were well mannered, bowing their heads when their mother gave thanks. "Lord, we ask You to bless this food from Your bounty. Help us to aid the new friends You have brought here today. In Jesus' name, we pray." When she finished, "amens" repeated all around the table.

Each of the camp women looked hauntingly alike with their shorter hair. But they at least had color and some meat on their bones, unlike Hadassah. As a reporter, JD wanted to ask details of their imprisonment. Had they come to Ravensbrück by themselves, or did they have other family? Why did they make it when thousands did not? However, he could not bring himself to say anything. He wanted to ask the same questions of Hadassah, but only time would tell if that would happen.

Steaming bowls of succulent venison stew full of potatoes and heaps of peppered cabbage were served with yeasty, thick-crusted bread. It was a feast for JD, but he felt more than a twinge of guilt for eating from this family's table when he was sure that they could ill afford to feed one more mouth.

Embarrassed by his own appetite, JD made a mental note to reward them in some way. "This stew is delicious, Lotte. You are quite the cook."

She beamed. "Thank God and thank Lutz. God created the deer, and Lutz shot and dressed it. Eat up."

When JD said he wanted to check on Hadassah, Lotte assured him that she would take food to her later. "I'll mash it good like for a baby." She winked. "Don't worry; I will coax her back to good health." She motioned her head in the direction of the three women from camp. "When they came here, they were as sickly as I'd ever seen, maybe close to death." She pointed to one of them. "Plus, Miriam had lice and fleas so bad that every inch of her body was scratched and bleeding."

"The women are alive now because of you, no doubt," he said. "Tell me, Lotte, how is it that you and Lutz speak English so well?"

She put her spoon down and sighed. "My husband grew up with English-speaking neighbors in Berlin, where he lived as a boy. By the time we married, my Dietrich spoke fluent English, and I learned from him through the years. When the children came, we taught them what we knew." Her face lit up when she spoke of her husband. "Dietrich would have liked you," she said wistfully. "It was his dream to live in America. . .someday."

"Lutz told me what happened to him. I'm so sorry for your loss. That kind of bravery is rare in a man. In anyone."

"Tell me, JD, what are you doing way out here?" She made a sweeping motion with her hands.

"I'm a reporter. . .for the army. Just got to Berlin a week ago." It seemed like a lifetime, after what he'd experienced the last two days. He cleared his throat and set his spoon down. "Uh, I was sent here to see if what we'd heard about the camps was true." Suddenly, his appetite was gone.

"Ach!" Lotte's voice rose with emotion. "You could write a hundred books, and they would not begin to touch the surface of the evil that those walls have contained." Silent tears slid down her face, and the entire table stopped eating.

One of the camp girls went to her side and hugged her. The younger woman looked over at JD. That's when he saw the bright pink scar on her neck that ran from one ear to the other like a macabre, twisted necklace. She said, "Mister American, you were right when you said we were only alive because of Lotte." Her voice cracked, and she returned to her seat. "The Germans had us on march away from Ravensbrück, but we"—she gestured to the other two—"we were too weak. Anyone who fell on road was killed where they landed." She swallowed hard. "We stole away to hide in woods. Lutz was the one who found us." She smiled at him. "He is brother now. We love this family like own family." Her hands were shaking as she touched the shoulders of the companions on either side. They lowered their eyes but not before JD saw their anguish.

He had no words in response but pushed away from the table. "I'll sleep in the barn with that horse blanket." He motioned for them all to stay seated. "I'll check on Hadassah before I go out; you can bring the food later." He turned back to face them. "I'm not sure what I'll write, but whatever story I tell, it will include all of you." He saluted the entire room.

Hadassah was curled up on one side, sleeping soundly, reminding him of a vulnerable child. He walked to the side of the bed. Wanting to caress her face, he restrained himself. He wanted to take her in his arms with assurances that she would be safe with him for the rest of her life. *I don't even know you, Hadassah, but I'll try with all my might to protect you, so help me, God.* JD backed out of the room.

On the way to the barn, the night sky tumbled with overflowing stars. He stared for a long time in awe and wonder. *God please.* Too tired for a longer prayer, he found a spot to lie down in one corner, heard the cow low once, and then fell to sleep in seconds.

# Chapter 15

Something brushed against JD's face, and he sat up with a jolt. "What the heck?" He heard giggling and caught movement out of the corner of one eye. JD stretched and yawned. "Guess I missed breakfast." More giggles from behind a mound of hay. "Hmm, maybe I'll look around and see what I can find to eat." He stood and stomped the dirt floor, making loud noises.

Two bright faces peeked out at him. "*Guten Morgen*," said a lilting voice. It was the older of the two. She curtsied and grinned at him, showing a distinct dimple on either side of a perfect rosebud mouth. "I am Isolde." She pulled another girl to her side. "And this is Silke." They shared identical smiles and the same nearly white hair. The brilliance of the new morning streamed through the barn and bounced off each head like sunlight on water.

JD bowed dramatically. "So nice to see you again. You two scared me, you know."

Hiding something behind their backs, both giggled some more.

"What's that you've got?" He took a step in their direction. This sent them shrieking off in a run.

They stopped and turned around. "We have your breakfast, Mr. Soldier."

JD felt guilty for sleeping so long. He didn't want to be a bother to Lotte; she'd already done so much. The girls walked back to him and held out the food they'd brought: more of last night's thick bread, this time accompanied with huge chunks of homemade cheese.

He accepted it and took a large bite of the bread. "Wow, this is delicious. Thank you, girls."

"We helped make the cheese." Isolde rocked back and forth on her heels.

"*And* the bread," added Silke, playing with a ringlet of hair.

"I'm sure you girls are a big help around here." He ate another bite. "How old are you?"

"Five and six," they answered in unison. Walking closer, Isolde spoke in a low melodic voice. "We have to help because we do not have a Vater." Her English was nearly perfect.

"We don't remember him either," said Silke.

JD could barely swallow the rest of the food. "I've heard from Lutz that he was a fine, brave man. How proud he'd be of you two."

"A hero, would you say?"

"Yes, no doubt. Your father was a hero."

"Will you write about him, then?" Both looked up into his face with eyes the color of sapphires.

"I will. I promise."

They each took one hand. "Mama says to tell you that the lady you brought is awake."

❦

He found Hadassah sitting up in bed wearing clean clothes. A bright blue and yellow scarf was wrapped around her head. Though her eyes were sunken, they at least contained a hint of brightness.

"Guten Morgen," he said in his best German, bowing at the foot of the bed. "You look rested."

"Yes." She met his gaze. "Though I might be dreaming."

"Pardon me?"

Her voice was still weak. "Surely this place. . .you. . .must be a dream."

He sat on the end of the bed, careful not to touch her. "This is not a dream, Hadassah. This place is real." His eyes swept the room. "You're safe now."

She flinched. "I cannot believe I will ever be safe. . .anywhere. . .ever." Both hands went to her head to adjust the kerchief before saying something else.

JD missed it. He leaned forward. "I'm sorry, Hadassah. What did you say?"

"Why am I alive?"

"You are alive, Hadassah, because God meant you to be." Both JD and Hadassah jumped at the sound of Frau Handberg, standing in the doorway. She carried some kind of hot beverage on a wooden tray into the room.

Hadassah was about to protest, but the older woman interrupted. "I know you have suffered unspeakable horrors, dear woman, but please do not question why you remain on this earth." Hadassah would not look at her. "God has a plan," Lotte said, setting the tray down beside the bed. "I've made you some tea." Holding the cup to Hadassah's lips she waited for her to sip. "We have no sugar, but I found a squeeze of honey left in my cupboard." She smiled. Hadassah took several long swallows. "I think you've had enough activity for now, Miss." She stood, leaving the teacup on its tray. "Ja, enough for this morning." She motioned for JD to leave.

He backed out, saying he'd return. Outside the bedroom door he heard Lotte continue the one-way conversation with Hadassah. He needed to clear his head and make plans for the return to Berlin.

Outside, he found Lutz chopping wood. He wanted to do something to earn his keep, so he made an offer to chop while the boy split and stacked. They worked without speaking for over an hour before taking a break.

"Won't you have to leave soon?"

"Yes." JD wiped his face.

"Are you taking the woman?"

"Not yet. She's not strong enough. I'll go back to Berlin and make some arrangements to get her there. I need to talk with your mother about it."

"She will never turn you down; my mother never refuses anyone's need." Lutz began working on the woodpile again.

JD stared at the young man for a minute. He was very tall and would probably be well over six feet sometime in the not-too-distant future. He'd had to grow up too fast, yet JD saw no bitterness in him, only a lingering sadness that made him too old and too serious before his time. He should be thinking about girls and school instead of all this manly responsibility.

"Lutz." The boy turned. "Do you ever think about the future?"

"Not much." He went on chopping the wood.

"Well, if you and your family ever get to the U.S., I want you to look me up."

He received a huge grin in return for the offer. JD went back in the house to talk with Lotte. Lotte graciously agreed to keep Hadassah as long as needed, but when he left the next day, JD was riddled with guilt. With only a boy for protection, the women and children were vulnerable, yet the situation dictated no other choice.

*1945*
*Berlin*

He'd walked nearly one full day before finally hitching a ride back to Berlin. His CO was livid.

"For crying out loud, Jensen, I thought you might have gotten yourself killed or some such stupid thing." He put his hand out. "Where's the piece I sent you to write?" He was chomping on a well-chewed cigar that looked like it might burn his lips with one more puff.

"Uh, sir, I. . .I don't have it done yet." JD fingered his army cap, waiting for the man's reaction.

The CO's voice softened. "That bad, huh?" He smashed the stogie out in an ashtray.

JD locked eyes with the CO. "Sir, I am a reliable journalist. You know my work."

The CO blinked.

"I promise to write a report, but, sir, I, uh, have a huge request."

The officer waved his hand in JD's direction. "Son, take all the time you need." He walked forward to shake JD's hand. "I've heard plenty since you've been gone."

"Well, sir," he took the offered handshake, "I do need time, but I'd also like to take some leave."

The CO stood right in front of him. "What for?" His gaze never wavered.

"I–I've met someone. . .from the camp. She's survived hell, Captain, and I need to, make that *have* to, help her."

"Where's she now?"

"In a safe place with a family near Ravensbrück."

"Since you left, the streets have been filling up with people returning to their homes in Berlin. All the talk is about the camp refugees. Makes me sick." He struck one fist into the other hand. "What do you need, Jensen?"

JD relaxed when he heard the sympathetic tones of the tough officer. "For starters, she needs some medical help. There's a better chance of finding that here, because for sure there's none in the countryside."

"Get some rest, and let me see what I can do about that leave. The *Army Times* is not going to be thrilled with you taking time off." He fished around in his desk and pulled out another cigar." "There's a convent right outside the city that's got a reputation for helping the Jewish refugees. I've already met the mother superior. The old gal's tough as nails and won't take 'no' for an answer when she comes asking for help. Maybe she'd be the one to talk to."

"Thank you, sir." JD gave a salute and sighed before walking out the door. His shoulders slumped with fatigue, but at least now he had more hope for the woman he barely knew.

*I don't know you, Hadassah, but a promise is a promise. You will be safe.*

Tired as he was, when he hit the barracks, his mind wouldn't turn off when he tried to sleep. All his thoughts were of the frail human being who had turned his life and heart upside down.

❧

Just like Sister Anna Clare, Sister Eloise, the mother superior, was dedicated to her calling. Though much older than the first nun he'd met, Sister Eloise had the same heart of compassion for taking care of the suffering, particularly the Jewish survivors of the camps.

Her English was good, and although just as tough as the captain had said, she was totally given over to helping the "least of these," as she called the camp survivors.

"So tell me, Mr. Jensen, what do you know about this Hadassah person? What should I expect when she gets here?" Sister Eloise sat behind a huge oak desk weighed down with stacks of papers and yellow manila folders.

She brushed some aside and offered JD a cup of coffee when he sat down across from her.

As he held the cup, his mind spun with how he'd answer her very direct question about Hadassah. The coffee was strong and hot. He raised it in her direction as a toast. "To tell you the truth, Sister, I don't know a thing except her first name and the fact that she fell off a truck full of dead women."

The nun took in a sharp breath but said nothing.

"You see, I found her out in the woods just beyond the camp, and she was in such bad shape there wasn't much talk." He took another sip of coffee.

"I see. Well, it would be nice to know *something* about her." She refilled his cup. "By the way, you can thank your captain for the coffee." When she smiled, JD realized she wasn't as old as he'd first thought.

He lifted the cup in her direction again. "And thank you for sharing, Sister." He continued. "Even though I do not really *know* Hadassah, something about her makes me want to protect her." He couldn't believe he was exposing his deepest feelings to a complete stranger.

The nun was silent for a moment before speaking. "JD, love rarely makes much sense."

"Love?"

"It's obvious that you have deep affection for this woman. What would you call it, if it is not 'love'?"

She had spoken the words his heart knew all along. "But Sister, we've just met." He set the cup down and felt his cheeks flush.

"Yes, I understand that; but war and its aftermath tear at our being and change us in ways we'd never planned, like an unexpected windstorm. Is that not so?"

"Sister, I thought I'd seen everything this war could show me." He gripped the cup tighter. "But that camp, that place. . ." He couldn't go on.

"That place is hell on earth. Is that what you wanted to say?"

"Yes," he whispered. "Even though I know nothing about her, can she still come?" His eyes misted over, but he wouldn't cry.

She stood and addressed him. "JD, it will be my honor to help you—that is, Hadassah—as much as possible." She walked around the desk to shake his hand.

It took nearly two weeks to make all the arrangements to bring her to Berlin because the convent was full. He had to wait for at least one person to leave in order for Hadassah to have a bed. He hoped the empty bed was because someone left on her own accord, rather than being carried out on a morgue stretcher.

He didn't ask how the bed was vacated when he arrived at the convent for the second time.

"How long will it take you to get there and back?" Sister Eloise asked.

"Depends on how bad the roads are and if I can get a ride there." He looked worried. "And, of course, I'll have to find a ride back here."

Sister Eloise looked surprised. "Didn't the captain tell you?"

JD shrugged. "Tell me what?"

"He's procured a jeep for you." She smiled again.

His breath caught. "I hadn't a clue. Was this your doing?"

"Afraid not, JD, but I believe God is in the business of helping these survivors more than we know." She walked out with him.

There was something very calming about the convent despite the hum of activity in all corners. "I think Hadassah will do okay here, Sister. Maybe better than okay. Thank you for making a place for her."

"You are very welcome, Mr. Jensen. I'm looking forward to meeting this woman who has captured your heart so quickly." Someone approached with a request, and she said her good-byes. After walking away a couple steps, she called out, "God bless you." Then she turned the corner and was gone.

# Chapter 16

JD could hardly contain his excitement over the "luxury" transportation when leaving the next morning. Besides a tank full of gas and two extra cans for the return trip, the back was also filled with food. When word got around about Hadassah and the family who had taken her in, some of the guys in his barracks threw together a special "care package." He was proud of these soldiers who even gathered some toys for the children. One man had given up his own watch for Lutz, after JD told him about the hardworking kid with so much responsibility.

Night stars still twinkled as the late spring morning began with promise. He watched while the sun rose from its rest to gift the entire countryside with shimmering light. Though signs of war's destruction lay everywhere, nature would not be denied the glory of its June display.

His heart felt like it might jump out of his chest with thoughts of seeing Hadassah. *What if she got sicker after I left? What if the family ran out of food?* He tried singing to keep his mind free of dire thoughts. It didn't work.

He was grateful for fewer ruts in the road this trip and fewer people. But the sides were still cluttered with left-behind objects thrown aside like forgotten memories, including chamber pots lying beside empty satchels, jewelry boxes, and other former "necessities." Mountains of clothing were strewn about everywhere like drab ghosts. . .haunting reminders of former lives. What would happen to all the people who had tossed these things? How do you put a life together after war has torn it to shreds? How would she?

The weather remained perfect for the final leg of his journey, and he was surprised at how quickly the miles gave way. When he slowed for the turn into the Handbergs' roadway, he was excited but still apprehensive. For fun, he parked a distance from the farmhouse and headed the rest of the way on foot to maintain an element of surprise.

He spotted the friendly front porch about the same time he heard the music. A record playing? No, the melody swept away from the house, drifting with sound so full of melancholy it stopped him in his tracks. Laying down the bundles he carried, he propped himself against an ancient apple tree and listened.

It was a violin, played by someone nearby. Replicating the human voice, pure melodic tones rose and fell with emotions released from deep within the recesses of a longing soul. It became a cry in the wind, pulsing with the sorrow of deep-abiding loss. He heard—no, he felt—the emotion of its confession. . .perfect and haunting. Hadassah!

Suddenly he was an eavesdropper, or a time traveler interloping on another's sacred journey. Yet he was a captive, unable to move from the influence. He forced himself to stand and was about to make a retreat when the music stopped. She'd seen him.

He watched as Hadassah rose from a chair on the porch, wearing a pale yellow dress that revealed the weight she'd gained. Though she wore a head scarf, dark hair peeked from beneath. Barefoot, she descended the stairs one at a time, holding the rail for support. She shaded her eyes as he approached but said nothing.

When they were within feet of each other, he found his voice. "The music. . .I—I had no idea you played. . ."

"How could you?" She didn't move closer. "You know nothing of me."

Her voice was clearer, and the raspy tone was gone. She was frail, but it was obvious she'd regained some strength. Maybe it was her eyes; they seemed more alive now. He was encouraged.

He took one step closer. "You're wrong, Hadassah. . . ."

She frowned.

". . .I do know something of you."

One eyebrow raised in question.

"I know you're a survivor."

Tears filled her eyes, and she lowered her gaze from his. Taking one more step toward him, she asked, "Why?"

He smiled. "Why do I know you're a survivor? Isn't that obvious?"

She shook her head. "No. Why did you come back?" She stared up at him, the tears gone.

"I came to help you." He wanted to enclose her in his arms, promise to steal the moon from the sky as a gift just for her. "I told you I'd come back. I made you a promise."

"But. . .why?"

"Because I. . ." *I care more about you than any other person in my life.* ". . .because I want you to be well and. . ."

Her hand went up in protest. "I'm going to say something, even though I believe you will not want to hear it." Her voice matched the timbre of the music she'd played.

He nodded. "Go ahead."

"When I first arrived at the camp, I made a decision to live, but later, after so much happened, I never wanted to live." She paused to gather more words. "Yet I have, but I don't believe I will ever be 'well,' so I don't see how you can help me." She shifted her weight from one leg to another.

*She's tired. How vulnerable she looks.* "You know what, Hadassah? Let's get you back inside, and I'll tell you about a plan I've come up with. I can't force you to accept my help, but maybe you'll change your mind when you hear what it is."

She didn't protest and let him guide her toward the house.

Lotte was ecstatic when she saw JD, rushing to embrace him. "Oh, praise Gott, I knew you'd come back. See, did I not tell you the soldier would return, Miss Hadassah? Oh, wait until the children see you. They've talked about you every day since you left." She gave him another hearty hug, and he returned it with as much enthusiasm. "Want some tea, Mister Soldier?"

"Yes, please."

The house smelled of yeast and boiled cabbage. It was comforting. Lotte disappeared into the kitchen, but he could hear her fussing about and found comfort in that as well. Hadassah had collapsed at one end of the couch.

"Do you want tea, Hadassah?"

She nodded, but her eyes were closed.

"You're still fragile. You need help."

"I'm eating well, but I have so little strength." Her voice sounded weak.

He pulled a chair next to the couch. "Hadassah, I want you to come to Berlin with me." Her eyes fluttered open.

"My commanding officer and I found you a place to live." She turned her head in his direction. He continued. "There's this nunnery. . .I guess it's called a convent. Anyway, nuns run the place, and they have a bed for you in their infirmary." He waited for a response, but nothing in her eyes indicated an interest. "Look, I know you're Jewish and all, but these women are really. . ."

She placed one finger on his lips to stop his talking. "I've no doubt they are good women; it's not that."

"Then what, what is it?" She'd removed her touch, yet the warmth lingered.

"I don't deserve it. There must be many others besides me who need help." Her eyes closed again, and she shuddered.

Lotte returned with a tray heavy with tea and all the fixings. The aroma of freshly baked bread escaped from under a cloth napkin, and JD's stomach growled in anticipation.

"Sorry," Lotte said. "I'm afraid the children used the last of the butter this morning. We won't have more until after milking." She set the tray in front of them both.

"Lotte, you're too generous. How well I remember your cooking. Thank you; the butter won't be missed." He poured tea for all of them and handed Hadassah a generous portion of bread. To his surprise, she ate the entire piece.

He'd finished telling Lotte and Hadassah the particulars surrounding the convent when all four of the younger children ran into the living room.

"Mama, there's an auto in the driveway!" They stopped short when they saw JD. Suddenly shy, they said nothing.

"Hey, cat got your tongues? Come look at what I brought you. . .and there's more in that 'auto.'"

"We saw," they cried, jumping up and down with excitement.

"Children," their mother scolded, "don't be impolite."

Isolde said, "We prayed every night for you. Didn't we, Mütter?"

The next day, loaded down with food and amid promises to write, JD and Hadassah left for Berlin. She had only the dress on her back and a few toiletries that Lotte had gifted her, and one other thing. . .a special treasure.

They were saying the last of their "good-byes" when Lutz ran out of the house carrying a cracked leather case. The violin!

"Wait!" he cried, running up to the jeep. "I, that is, we, want you to take this, Hadassah." He caught his breath. "My father would have wanted you to have it. . .he played it often and well." He placed it in Hadassah's lap. She ran both hands over the entire case and hugged it to her chest, looking up at him with misty eyes.

"Dear Lutz, *my* father gave me my first violin. I am honored to have the one that belonged to yours. Such a just man for you to emulate, thank you." She reached up and pulled his face to hers and softly kissed one cheek. He blushed.

"Good-bye, good-bye," they cried. Lotte ran a ways beside them. "Write to us, Liebchen. Our address is in your satchel, Hadassah. Godspeed."

They made only one stop and had little conversation except polite comments made about the food Lotte had sent. It didn't matter, JD told himself; they could talk later.

# Chapter 17

After settling Hadassah in the convent, JD's army life kept him in the city for nearly a week, though daily his mind drifted to her. Would she ever recover from the horrors of imprisonment and torture? He was sure she'd lost family members, but who and how many he had no idea.

His first visit started out hot. He was sweating profusely upon arrival, like an awkward teenager on prom night. On the way he'd stopped and picked wildflowers from a vacant field. The juxtaposition of finding fresh new life in the middle of a bombed building lot was not lost on him.

As he finished the drive, he struggled with the scope of what he'd experienced since going to Ravensbrück. He was obliged to put words to it (it's what the army paid him to do), but none even came close. He couldn't stall the *Army Times* much longer. He even thought of blowing them off since he'd be out of the service soon, but JD prided himself on being an honorable, dependable reporter. Therein lay the dilemma: the horrors of reality pounding against the need to forget and his sense of duty. Which would win out? At this point, he wasn't sure, but he needed to make a decision.

When he turned down the road leading to the convent, it seemed as though the entire property existed in another realm of veracity, all of it left untouched by the ravages of Russian tanks and warfare. Surreal!

Garden plots were laid out in symmetrical squares, each pristine with greenery and the promise of an abundant harvest in a few months. Several nuns and four or five others were busy watering or weeding. It all looked so "normal." But would the world ever be "normal" again? He doubted it.

A younger version of the mother superior escorted him to a waiting room while she went to check on Hadassah. He scanned the sparsely furnished reception area. A statue of a man dressed in robes stood in one corner, his face looking upward with a small bird held in an outstretched hand. Against one wall, a chair pushed into a very small desk upon which sat a fountain pen, black leather Bible, and several sheets of paper. He cleared his throat, and the sound echoed off the decrepit stone walls.

From a distance, hollowed footsteps approached. His heart sank; there was only one set. He stood when the nun entered. "I'm sorry to have kept you waiting," she said, her English thick with an accent he didn't recognize. "Mrs. Meyer is still in the infirmary, I'm afraid."

He was puzzled. He'd never heard, nor asked, Hadassah's last name. *She's married?* "The infirmary. . .still?"

"Yes, she has a stubborn case of some parasite and remains quite weak."

His stomach rolled. "Is she all right?"

"The doctor assures us she will recover. . .in time." She shook her head in sympathy. "Such a sad lady." Immediately her hand went over her mouth. "I'm sorry to have said that." She curtsied in apology.

"What did she say when you told her I was here?"

She curtsied again. "That she'd very much like to see you."

He breathed a sigh of relief. "Good."

The infirmary held a dozen beds; all but two were occupied. His eyes searched the room until he saw her sitting up, supported with pillows, reading a book. She didn't see him. The air smelled of alcohol and disinfectant, despite fresh breezes blowing in through several open windows. Still, the room was cheerful enough with midday light bouncing off pristine walls, while casting mysterious dancing shadows all around.

Some of the patients were sleeping. A few had visitors who talked in hushed tones. JD approached Hadassah's bed, taking in the uniqueness of her beauty. *She's stronger.* She tugged on one ear, focused on the book in her lap.

He cleared his throat to announce his presence, and she jumped in response, causing the book to fall. "Oh, you startled me." Then she smiled, patting the bed.

It was a million-dollar invitation. "You look fantastic. How are you feeling?" He thought he saw a slight blush.

"Every day, a little stronger." She looked pleased to see him and nodded. "Yes, a little bit each day."

He wanted to touch her hand, to give some assurance that he believed she would recover. Instead, she reached out and brushed his arm with one hand. "Thank you, JD." Her hand lingered for a moment.

"Hadassah, you don't need to thank me."

She put a finger to her lips. "Shhh, please, let me tell you something."

He waited.

"That day you found me, the day by the water?"

He nodded.

Her voice quavered, but she continued. "I'd made up my mind that I was going to die. Even though I'd escaped from the truck of the dead, I believed that death would finally have me, and soon." She looked deep into his eyes. "When you came, I was actually angry to still be alive. But now I see that I was meant to live after all." She gestured around the room. "The sisters here have convinced me of that. But in all honesty, JD, I still do not know why."

"I can tell you what I believe," he said slowly, his voice unsteady. "I believe it's your destiny to live, just as it was mine to find you."

Hadassah shook her head. "Such drama you speak. Is this coming from the writer now?"

"This," he paused for emphasis, "comes from the man."

She reached for him again, and this time he took her hand in his.

JD cleared his throat. "Hadassah, I found out today that you were married."

Her face contorted with pain.

"I'm sorry; I don't mean to upset you."

"No, it's all right." He handed her a handkerchief, and she twisted it around one hand before speaking. "I *was* married, to Avram Meyer." She swallowed hard. "The day our train arrived at Ravensbrück, the women were left there, but the men. . .the men continued on." Her hands went up in a desperate gesture. "That was the last time I saw my husband. And. . ."

He hated to see her confront more pain. "Tell me, Hadassah, who else was taken from you?"

She was weeping into both hands now, shaking with the emotion of remembering. "My, my son."

JD was holding her in his arms now; he felt the wetness of her tears drenching the front of his shirt. "My precious boy called to me, over and over. Aaron had barely spoken a word the entire train ride, but when the railroad car pulled away, I could hear his voice above all the others. My father was on that train and went with Avram as well. My mother stayed with me." She began to shudder and collapsed back onto the bed.

"Sister, Sister!" The nun he'd met at the front door came immediately. "I think she's fainted." JD was frantic.

"Too much visiting, sir; your time is over for today." She was bent over Hadassah.

"I'm so sorry, I never meant to. . ."

"She'll be fine. Right now, she's exhausted. You'll have to leave."

He touched the foot of the bed and left. Once outside he let go of pent-up emotions, walking around the jeep to kick all four tires with a vengeance. He didn't want to go, but clearly he'd made her situation worse. "You're an idiot, Jensen."

"She needs more time."

JD jumped. He hadn't seen the mother superior approaching. "Have I made things worse?"

"No, you are exactly who she needs right now."

"How do you know that?" He wanted to run back inside and apologize.

"I know this, Mr. Jensen, because as far as I can tell, she has no one else."

On the way back to the base, the nun's words rang in his mind. If what she'd said was true, he had an even deeper responsibility than he realized. *I need some help here. A lot of help.*

That week, he wrote his story and submitted it. He was surprised, but pleased, at the notoriety he received when it was published.

JD needed some counsel. He wished he could talk with his dad. He knew he loved Hadassah, but was it based on pity or something more? It was more than simply feeling responsible for her. . .way more. Anyone who knew him would say that JD Jensen would always do the responsible thing, regardless. Yet, deep in the recesses of his mind and heart, the feelings he had for Hadassah went beyond "responsibility."

There wasn't anyone in the barracks he felt close to except the CO, but even then, they didn't know each other that well. On a sweltering day in July, not far from his mustering out, he went to the captain's office and waited for a chance to talk with him.

"So, Jensen, you're about done being GI Joe?"

"Yes, sir."

"Got a job?" He was sitting with his feet up on his desk, squinting through cigar smoke winding round his head.

"Yes, sir, I do. The *New York Times* has taken me on." JD couldn't help but smile.

The CO whistled and dropped his feet to the floor. "Congratulations, JD. No doubt, the piece you wrote about Ravensbrück secured you that honor."

JD shrugged. "Think so?"

"At ease, Soldier, have a seat."

JD removed his hat, moving it around in his hands. "Uh. . ."

"Is this about the woman you found. . .what's her name?"

"Hadassah's her name, and yes, sir, it is about her."

"Gonna marry her?" His stare made JD squirm.

"That's what I'd like to talk about."

"Talk away. I'm married myself. Did you know that?"

"No, sir, I didn't." JD wanted to leave and forget about any private conversation but knew he needed some advice.

"Never mind, talk." He pounded the cigar into an ashtray, folded his hands on the desk, and waited.

"There's no doubt in my mind that I love Hadassah, but she's been through a lot, and I. . ."

"Afraid her situation might be too much?" He was squinting.

"No, sir, I'm afraid I might not be enough for her. How will I be able to help her forget the horror she's seen? Maybe I'd fail her in a million ways."

"I'm not one to give out a lot of marital wisdom, Jensen, but I'll tell you this much. Anyone, married or not, is going to fail. . .it's a given."

"But. . ."

"Look, marriage is hard work, and since we're not perfect, we screw up. . .daily. Doesn't mean you're a failure. Means you're human." He pushed back from the desk and walked around to stand in front of JD. "That woman needs someone, and looks like, to me, that someone is you, Jensen."

"Then you think it's okay if I ask her to marry me? You don't think it's too soon. . .for her, I mean?"

"Why don't you ask her and let the chips fall where they may? If she says no, it's a done deal." He reached to shake JD's hand, pulling him to his feet. "But if she says yes, I'll be your best man."

"Thanks, Captain Marsh, I really appreciate it. . .you, that is."

"Jensen, go talk to that woman. Get outta here."

⤜⤛

Watching Hadassah blossom in his frequent visits had taken JD's breath away. She became more beautiful with each passing day. The first time she laughed, she instantly broke down. "Oh my," she said. "What a foreign sound that is to my ears." She'd looked at him, touched his face with the back of one hand. "I never thought I'd laugh again." She hugged him. "It's only because of you, dear friend."

But there were often dark moments. Some small word would trigger an erupting volcano of pain and fear, exploding into a memory. She'd excuse herself to walk away. Sometimes she'd be gone for a couple minutes; other times she never returned. That's when he doubted himself the most. What could he say to make her better? Should he prod her into talking, or be a good listener? In the end, he concluded, there was nothing he could do or say to make her, or any of it, *better*. He'd always heard that time is a healer, but without a doubt he knew all the time in the universe would never be enough to heal one human soul from the damages inflicted at Ravensbrück.

Hadassah had told him she believed God had died. Regardless, he believed that only the power God Himself possessed would be enough to make a dent in the healing she needed.

After his talk with the captain, JD was encouraged, yet the idea of being rejected made him wary, so he waited awhile before asking Hadassah to marry him.

⤜⤛

"I can't marry again, JD. Not you, not anyone." She choked on the words and tried to run from him, but he caught her by both arms and walked her to a nearby tree in the yard where they'd been talking.

"Hadassah, I know you feel something for me. Tell me you don't." She tried to look away, but he pulled her close. They had never kissed, but at this moment he never wanted anything more in his life.

Her head went back and forth, flinging tears in his direction. "You won't want me, no one will want me, when I. . ." She couldn't go on and collapsed at his feet.

He knelt beside her. "Hadassah, what do you mean? I just told you I want you. I want you forever."

"But you don't know." Through the wracking sobs, he was barely able to understand what she was saying.

"Don't know what? Please tell me. There is nothing you could say that would make me not want to marry you. Listen, we'll have a good life in New York." He got close to one ear and murmured, "When you're ready, maybe we could have our own children."

She threw herself away from him and beat both fists into the ground. "No, no, no! I don't deserve to have more children."

"But Hadassah, it wasn't your fault your son died. You couldn't have done anything."

Then she said something he couldn't hear.

"Tell me what you said, sweetheart; let me help you."

She sat up, blew her nose into a hankie, and looked right into his eyes. Her voice sounded strange. "Aaron was not my only child."

JD said nothing, but despite the heat, a chill ran up his spine.

417

"I—I had a baby girl. Her name was Esther, and I killed her."

"What? What are you saying?" He was sitting beside her, one arm draped around her shoulders. He helped Hadassah to her feet and found a shady spot with a bench. He tugged her gently down next to him, rubbing one hand, hoping to bring some kind of comfort.

She began to tell him the entire story of what had led up to the day she and Avram made the decision to throw their daughter from the train. Word by word the story unraveled like a huge ball of tangled yarn. The chronicle of sadness took over an hour to release, and when she finished she collapsed against him, limp as a rag. He was emotionally drained as well.

"Hadassah," he whispered, "you saw two children there that day, right?"

"Yes, in the snow."

"Don't you think they might have found her?"

"Maybe." She looked at him, eyes wide.

"Yes, maybe; because they were so close they must have seen it all happen."

"But they were just children. Children miss a lot."

"Of course, but consider this: they must have been the adventuresome type. You know, because they were out playing in all that snow in the dead of winter."

"Do you think if they found her, they might have kept her?" Hadassah seemed encouraged by this possibility and sat up straighter.

He touched her chin, making her look into his eyes. "Of course."

She went silent for a moment then stated dully, "Or she died on the spot."

# Chapter 18

When JD left Berlin, he was discharged from the army and headed for New York. Hadassah was not well enough to travel, but all the arrangements had been made for her when she was strong enough. Thanks to his CO, they had a wedding ceremony and even an overnight honeymoon of sorts in one of the few hotels still standing and open.

Lotte had brought all of the children for a visit before he left, and the reunion did wonders for Hadassah's spirits. Lotte insisted she stay with the family before her big move to the States, and she agreed. He didn't want to leave Hadassah at all but knew she couldn't have been in better hands. So when he left, his mind was set in forward motion, focused on his new job and new life with the frail, but hauntingly lovable, woman who was now his wife.

As a way of introduction to his new post, the managing editor, Frank Josephs, insisted on printing his last story for the *Army Times*.

*Hell!*
*By JD Jensen*

*War is hell! We all know it, but what I didn't know was this: hell has different levels of degradation within its boundaries.*

*It's been a season since this reporter has posted a story and for good reason. I've been shaken to the bottom of my government-issued boots. I'm writing now from Berlin, where my assignment began over a month ago. We'd all heard stories of the Nazi death camps, and the closer we came to Berlin, the more prolific the stories became. Millions of Jews and political prisoners had been put to death in camps all across Europe, they said. How many millions? I asked. No one knew. But I had to find out.*

*After my arrival, my CO allowed me the chance to see for myself what the inside of a death camp actually looked like, which is how I ended up at the gates of Ravensbrück, fifty miles north of Berlin.*

*The day was warm, and the road wound up a hill before I saw the sign indicating my arrival. Who knew hell had buildings? But there they were, stretching before me, row after row on acres and acres of land, surrounded by huge barbed-wire fences. Did you know that hell contained huge smokestacks situated directly in its center? I couldn't miss it and felt my gut roll in response to the clear intent of its purpose.*

*Hell had a lot of outside visitors that day—those in the process of rescuing the leftovers from the Nazis' heinous attempt at annihilating every Jew they could find. Ravensbrück had been reserved for women, where now only the sick and dying remained.*

*Did you know that hell had a smell? Everywhere the air was consumed with what remained behind after the Germans had sent thousands of prisoners out before the Russians liberated the camp. Immediately I succumbed and became violently ill but, fortunately, was rescued by a tiny young Swedish woman named Sister Anna Clare.*

*She was my tour guide for hell that day. I saw women so skinny that at any moment it appeared their bones might pierce the sickly, paper-thin skin that hung from all of them. Their heads had been shaved and every last bit of femininity stripped from them, stripped away like the lives they'd led before this place. Sister Anna Clare and the others were there to comfort the dying and bury the dead, a monumental task.*

*Most of those who'd been slaughtered at Ravensbrück were either gassed, starved to death, or shot. After, they were thrown into huge open pits, many of which had been sloshed with gasoline and set on fire. I was told by the tiny nun that not all who entered the pits were actually dead. Get the picture?*

*To say that looking into these atrocities is necessary is an understatement, but we must not, cannot, forget. The numbers are staggering, but each and every one represents a man, or woman, or worse yet, a child. A husband, father, mother, son, or daughter, all destroyed while the rest of the world looked away. "We didn't know," we claim. Maybe, but now we do.*

*Can any good come from visiting hell? This reporter says yes, because we can come together to never let this kind of inhumane prejudice rear its evil head again. As a society, we must ensure that the atrocities that took place at Ravensbrück and all the other places of hell never be repeated. How will this be accomplished? From shared knowledge, and thereafter, a deep conscientious resolve to never forget the millions of innocents who died because of one man's annihilating hatred. Never!*

*Reporting just outside of hell, I am, JD Jensen*

"This is the gritty kind of journalism our paper stands for, Jensen." JD's new boss was showing him to his desk. "Don't have an office for you yet, but keep up this kind of work, and I'll see what I can do. Found a place to live yet?"

"Nope, got a hotel room for now. My wife wasn't well enough to travel, so I'm waiting for her before I find something more permanent." JD set a battered briefcase down on the office chair.

Within a month, JD had not only an office but also his name on the door.

# Chapter 19

December 1965
New York City

The fire's embers were barely glowing when Hadassah called him. JD hurried down the hall to find her sitting up in bed. "You're still awake."

"Yes," he said softly, "but how come you're up?" He sat down beside her on the bed. "Bad dream?"

"No, I'm lonely." She leaned on him, resting her head on a shoulder.

He took off his shoes and scooted next to her in the narrow bed. "Better?"

"Mmm." She took a couple of deep breaths. "JD?"

"What?" he murmured into her hair.

"I love you."

He inched a little closer.

⸙

He awoke at dawn and knew he'd never go back to sleep, so he got up, showered, and made coffee.

JD thrived on deadlines; it kept his adrenaline pumping. . .well, that and coffee, lots and lots of coffee. But with Hadassah's rapidly declining health, he'd not been as diligent as he needed to be. . .expected himself to be. One of the things he'd postponed was the journalism contest. With the deadline looming for the promised winner's publication, he hadn't read one entry.

Opening his briefcase, he took out the top one, read it through while the coffee perked, and set it aside. "Not this time, kid." The story line was okay, but it was redundant and not well executed.

His coffee was ready, and he poured a large cup. This was going to be a long day. . .maybe he'd just stay home. "Nope." There was an important staff meeting at nine, and it was imperative that he be there. He took the stack of journalism entries and set them on the chair at the end of the table, promising himself that he'd finish them that evening. Hadassah used to love to help him do the choosing in years back. Maybe, just maybe she might feel like it this time. *There's always hope. Right, Lord?*

⸙

Fritz and Star had spent every evening together since the startling revelation of their previous relationship had brought them together. Of course, Star had dozens of questions about what had happened *after* the miraculous rescue that had saved her life, and Fritz looked forward to every conversation.

"Surprisingly, I have lots of information about you, Miss Star." Every time they were together, Fritz felt the same sense of destiny he'd experienced the day he and Ellie had picked her out of the snow.

"How do you know all of this, Fritz?"

"Our little village was small, and your story is what legends are made of."

She laughed. "I think you're just being melodramatic now. You're teasing me."

"Not really. Truthfully, your story is part of our family history. Really, how many babies are ever found in the snow in one's lifetime?"

421

And so they drank coffee as he told her more of the story. . . .

❧

*1945*
*Fritz's Story*

My cousin Ellie and I wanted to keep you, of course, but because of the close proximity of Herr Hoffman, that was out of the question. Our plan was to inquire discreetly in the village as to who might know of how to contact the Jewish Underground in order to get you to a safer place.

Had we known exactly how dangerous it was, we might have been deterred, but as it turned out, God was on our side all along. . .and, of course, on yours, Star.

There was a little bakery in the village that had become a gathering place, especially during the war. Frau Willert, the baker's wife and assistant, made the best apple strudel in the country, according to the sign in the window. They had been in the baking business for two decades and, as we found out, were faithful partners with the Jewish Underground.

We were not the only family to have taken a baby into our home. At least a dozen children were hidden for safekeeping in our village alone.

The Willerts had three sons, and it was the oldest who had brought home the first baby from a train. This one was handed off, not dropped in the snow like you were. Eric had a wagon full of flour and had stopped to water the old horse pulling it. The stream where it drank followed along beside the railroad tracks, and on that day, the train was stopped. Eric heard wailing coming from each and every car. He knew exactly the direction they were going and took the time to offer water to as many as he could before the train pulled away.

"Mister!" he heard someone calling from inside. "Mister, take my child. Please, if he's with you, I can die in peace." Eric said a young man handed him a baby no more than weeks old through a hole in the side of the car. The father was weeping, and from somewhere inside a woman sobbed the child's name over and over. "Be careful," the father cautioned, "be careful, friend. You'll be shot if the Nazis catch you."

When the train continued, he heard the father crying out more gratitude, but as the train picked up speed, his words were lost in the wind.

The baby seemed robust enough, but Eric was worried for its immediate safety. Where would he be able to hide an infant when the SS routinely drove through town? "There has to be a way, Liebchen," he told the little boy. "I will help you; God will help me find a way."

He needed time to form a plan, so in the beginning he had no choice but to return home with his "surprise."

"What in heaven's name will we do with a baby?" his mother scolded. She fell in love, of course, just like my grandmother did with you when I brought you into our house. Still, it would be too dangerous to hide a human hated and hunted by the Führer's minions for very long. The Willerts began to pray.

They were a large family, trusted by one another and others. Though their bakery was small, its reputation was well spread around the surrounding area, and even during wartime, their business prospered. Since many households were without the men, women had to tend to their own fields and farm animals, which left little time for household chores like baking. The bakery charged fair prices, but when families couldn't afford to pay in cash, the Willerts took bartered goods.

Like Eric, the other brothers had wagons for hauling. They not only picked up the flour from a small mill but also delivered it to other bakeries in the surrounding villages on a regular basis. Thus their networking capabilities were built-in and quite large. This they took advantage of in order to find a safe escape for baby number one.

It was on one of the hauling trips that Eric heard a whispered account of the Jewish

Underground's activity. Two men, teenaged boys really, were taking a break, sitting on the flour mill's loading dock.

"They'd be shot in a heartbeat, if caught."

"Shhh." The younger one looked around, and Eric pretended to be busy with the cart. "How many do you think there are in the group?"

"I've met five or six men and at least that many women." He looked toward Eric and lowered his voice. "But I know there are more. They say hundreds are living in the woods."

"Women? There are women involved?"

"Yes my Mütter and sister are part of it."

"What? But you're not Jewish. That's crazy!" He stood.

"Of course we're not Jewish, but Mütter says it's time Christians stood up to help the helpless."

"I still think it's crazy." The younger boy lowered his voice. "And you should be very careful who you tell this to; you never know who might turn you in." He walked back inside, leaving the other young man alone.

Eric made his move, striding over to the remaining teen. "I heard you talking."

The boy's face went white with fear, and he hopped up to leave.

"Wait." Eric lowered his voice. "You're safe with me, but I need your help."

The boy jumped down and walked out of sight of the dock, motioning Eric to follow. Hidden behind a huge piece of machinery, Eric told him the story of how he'd rescued the baby from the train.

And that's how the Jewish Underground connection was made to my village. But the line was complicated and took some time to complete, so that first boy—Willem, they called him—took several weeks.

The Willerts lived directly behind the bakery in connected quarters, so Frau Willert was able to attend to her little houseguest quite well, at least for the first few days. One morning her husband became ill, complaining of a bellyache. He couldn't work. Could he watch the baby, then? "Nein. What if I gave my sickness to him?" had been the reply.

"Ach, very well, I'll just have to keep him with me." She tied him sling-fashion to her very plump body and went out front to work. She'd carried her own children around that very same way and had the uttermost confidence in the method. It nearly worked out.

The morning had gone well, and the only time she stopped the bakery work was to feed and change her little man. How very happy he was, contented being carried from worktable to oven, clinging to the nice soft chest of his surrogate mother. She was humming while working and did not hear two men enter the bakery. They rapped on the counter, causing her to turn. That's when she saw the SS soldiers.

"Guten Morgen," one of them said. "We've heard good things about your bakery, Frau Willert." He removed his hat and smoothed his hair. "You *are* Frau Willert?"

She nodded, keeping silent. The first one to speak was not very old, but she knew he could be deadly, regardless.

The second soldier asked, "You are the baker's wife, are you not?"

She shivered and gathered her wits. "Yes, yes, that's me." She was not afraid to make eye contact. Silently she prayed that the little one would not wake and reveal his deep brown eye color to the soldiers. . .a possible giveaway to his heritage.

One of them walked behind the counter and reached out to touch the infant's nearly bald head. "Hmm, this child appears to be sprouting some very dark hair, Frau Willert."

She raised her eyebrows. "Now how can you tell such a thing, young man?" She willed her voice to be strong.

"I'm wondering also what color are his eyes? Ja, I'd like to know that for sure."

"Would you wake him to find out?" she answered with an indignant tone. "He looks like all my others, hair a little darker, maybe, but all with eyes the color of a spring sky."

"Ja, well you appear quite old to have such a young child."

"And you appear to have left your manners somewhere else, young man. If you worked as hard as I did in this bakery, you would look just as old." Her knees knocked together, and she grabbed the countertop for support, praying all the conversation would not wake her little charge." She swayed him back and forth to keep him pacified.

"We have heard that some around here have taken the Jews' baby rats off the camp trains. Would you know anything about that?" He began to walk along the length of the enclosed bakery display. She hoped he was more hungry than curious.

"Well, as you can see, I am much too busy to care for any other baby." Her heart beat so fast; she feared they would see it, or hear it, pounding in her chest. The baby began to stir. Frau Willert grabbed a couple of hot pads and walked toward the huge brick oven at the back of the bakery.

"Halt!"

She froze.

"Turn around!"

She moved as in slow motion, inhaling a deep breath.

"We want to try your apple strudel."

She exhaled slowly, swallowed, and walked back to the counter. "How many would you like?"

Undeterred by that encounter with the SS, Frau Willert continued to care for train-car babies until the end of the war. However, she never brought another one of them into the store.

❧

Star stretched. "Do you think I was one of her babies?"

"I happen to know that you were. . .eventually," Fritz said.

"Eventually?"

And Fritz went on with the story.

❧

The Werners were another village family. With twelve children, they ran an enormous dairy farm. A large portion of their milk was used to make cheese for the soldiers, so the older Werner, Karl, had been exempt from the army. The Werners had been supportive of the war initially, but when word spread of the atrocities being carried out through Hitler's elite SS troops, they became enraged. Isolated from the outside, they, like many, had felt helpless to come against the powerful evil of the Third Reich. That is, until Jewish babies began to be lifted from the death cars.

What better place to hide a child than in the middle of twelve others? If they often had trouble keeping count of their rambunctious tribe, surely others would if push ever came to shove.

However, spies were everywhere, and people like Herr Hoffman made any rescue plans life-threatening.

Ellie and I found you on Christmas Eve, as you already know, so because of the holiday and the continuing snow, we felt safe keeping you for a while. But all of us knew that your stay with us would be limited, for your own safety and, as you stated in your contest letter, for our own lives as well.

It was another three days before my aunt could return to the village and make an inquiry into how we could safely move you.

She worked for the town's only doctor, Dr. Schlotfeldt. Too old to enter the army, he was a pillar of strength in our community. A strong Christian man, he prayed daily for those who were being carted away all over Germany. My aunt often warned him of his outspoken opinions, but he would not be silenced.

"God did not put me on this earth to keep quiet about His truth," he'd declared often.

His sister was Frau Willert, and so from the very beginning, he became ally number one in saving the lives of the train babies. But although Aunt Margot knew of the Underground activity and had heard rumors that Dr. Schlotfeldt was involved, she was totally surprised to discover that her employer, mentor, and friend was not only a part of it but also deeply committed as the Underground liaison. It was her conversations with him that started you in the direction of a new and safe life.

She, my mother, and grandmother had all prayed and, as one, felt she should seek advice from Dr. Schlotfeldt. It was late in the afternoon, when the two of them were having tea, that the good doctor actually began the conversation with my aunt.

"Margot, I'm sensing that you're preoccupied with something. Is it your husband?" He reached over and touched her arm for emphasis.

She lowered her head.

"Oh, I hope I'm not being too personal. . .too forward perhaps." He blushed.

"No, no, Doctor, it's not my husband."

"Your daughter, then?"

"Nein, it's not her either." She sipped her tea. "I need to ask you something."

"Please, Margot, if you need anything and it's at my disposal, I will give it."

"It's not for me." She lowered her voice even though they were alone. "I have heard. That is, there's talk in the village that you. . ."

"That I'm a spy for the Underground?" He watched her intently, and she nodded. He set his cup down on the table between them and looked over his spectacles. "Tell me why you bring this up."

She hesitated.

"Do you believe I am trustworthy, Margot?"

She stared at him. After her own family, this man was her rock, a surrogate father even. "I would trust you with my very life, dear friend, but it's not for me that I have need."

She told him all about you, how we'd found that strange bundle in the snow. And of course, she told him of the near exposure of our secret, when Herr Hoffman had insisted on coming into our home.

"He's a very dangerous man, Margot, and I've noticed his unhealthy interest in you. He could pose the biggest threat to the Liebchen's safety."

"I agree."

"It will take me a few days to make arrangements to get her away from here, but first we need to move her out of your house immediately. We cannot risk an encounter with Hoffman."

"Move her to where?" Margot's mind reeled with the dangerous possibility of someone discovering you.

"The Werners' farm."

"But they have so many children already." She was confused.

"Exactly." He laughed. "What better place, my dear? I don't think even Herr Hoffman keeps track of how many children the Werners have at any given time." He laughed again. "Since I delivered every one of them, I am probably the only one, besides the family themselves, who knows the exact number."

"I have to admit it's a brilliant idea."

"Since the phone lines are working again, I want you to stop by the Werners' farm and give them a message to call me and say one of the children is sick."

"I don't understand. Why don't you call them yourself?"

"Too dangerous, and too many opportunities for eavesdroppers; we simply cannot risk it."

"Yes, yes, of course. I will leave early so as not to get caught in the dark."

My aunt was delighted at the happy chaos she found at the Werners'. A dozen children of various sizes were at play or work, all of them seeming to be talking at once.

"Margot, what a surprise to see you. Come in. Do you have time for some cider?" Mrs. Werner greeted her with warmth.

"I don't have much time before dark, but Dr. Schlotfeldt wants you to call and ask him to visit one of your children."

"Ah," she winked, "yes indeed, my Giselle has a stubborn cough."

"I cannot tell you the entire story right now, Dorthea, but we have a little one at our place who needs a home." She gave her friend a tender hug.

"Oh my, my, I so want to hear about it all, but do get back into your truck before night falls. There's still so much snow, and you shouldn't be out after dark. Perhaps we will all be able to make church on Sunday, and we can catch up then."

"You are precious and very, very brave. Hug all the children for me."

Within two days you had left our home, spent a night with the Werners', and then were whisked away from us forever. . . .

<hr />

"Not forever. Here I am, remember?" Star was smiling.

He looked at her long and hard. "You're pretty hard to forget, you know."

She blushed. "I want to hear the rest."

"Well, the next part was pieced together from bits and pieces we heard in town, and from what Aunt Margot learned from Dr. Schlotfeldt."

Fritz continued the story.

<hr />

Your rescuers came in the safety of late night at the Werners. . .on skis. A teenaged boy and his mother. There could be no chance of someone on the roads seeing two strangers skiing across the countryside in the dark. They approached the Werners' home at 2:00 a.m. from the woods in back, making their appearance during the milking activity.

Frau Werner carried you from the house into the barn underneath a long wool coat. She said your slumber was sweet and fast like you knew you needed to be extra quiet for the long journey ahead.

The mother and son were waiting for you in the warm barn. They were Germans committed to helping the Jews in whatever way they could.

Frau Werner said she'd been totally prepared to let you go, but when the moment came, she was overcome with emotion.

"You can trust us," said the mother. "We will keep her safe, I promise."

"Oh, I do trust you; it's just that she's so small and has been through so much already."

"Trust me; I know exactly what could happen to this child. It is why I am here, and why I will do all I possibly can to save her. This is my oldest son, Jan. He feels like I do."

"Where will you take her, then?" Frau Werner removed you from her coat, placing you in a woolen knapsack.

"Dear lady, I cannot tell you this." The woman lifted the knapsack and strapped you to her own body inside of her jacket. "It is safer for you not to know. Can you understand?"

Frau Werner nodded, gazing into the woman's eyes, and saw nothing but loving-kindness. "Lord, we pray for Your hand of protection to be upon this child and the people who now have her. May You make a way where there appears to be none. Amen."

So there in that warm barn, surrounded by lowing cattle and another family who cared for you, you began the third part of your journey.

At my home we missed you terribly, but we, too, were praying.

The two people on skis traveled effortlessly the first several miles and had just cleared the Werners' property, when the boy, who was in front, stopped abruptly. His mother did the same.

They saw nothing but heard voices in the distance. Who could possibly be out in the dead of night? Soldiers! They'd been searching the woods with the advantage of moonlight, looking for Jewish squatters.

As soon as your rescuers stopped, you began to stir within the safety of the knapsack's cocoon. The woman rocked you back and forth and you settled, but soon you'd need to eat. The soldiers' voices were moving closer.

Time to make a decision! Stay where they were and choose a tree to hide behind, or backtrack swiftly. They'd be moving targets out in the open and their tracks easily followed. Directly in front of them, two trees stood close together. They'd barely have time to reach them and would hardly be hidden because their shadows would be cast across the moonlit snow. They were grateful for a small cloud cover just then and made a dash for the trees.

The closer the men got to them, the more you began to stretch. . .a sure sign you were hungry. The woman unbuttoned her jacket and put a finger into your mouth. You greedily began sucking. But how long could you be pacified?

The men were within twenty yards when they stopped for a cigarette break. All five of them complained of the cold and the length of the war. Suddenly, they went silent and in unison looked over just as the clouds parted and the entire area of where your rescuers stood was highlighted with the full light of winter's moon. The ground sparkled and danced in the reflected light from millions upon millions of minute frozen mirrors. The woman and boy held their breath, fully expecting gunshots to ring out. But within minutes, the men turned and went their way.

What had blinded the soldiers' eyes to what was so plainly before them? Only God knows for sure, because there was no earthly explanation as to why they didn't spot you in the center of all that spectacular light. As soon as the men could no longer be seen, the woman fed you a bottle, and you nursed greedily. This marked another milestone overcome in completing your long passage to safety.

❧

"I wonder what happened to that mother and son? Did anyone ever know?"

"We never heard another thing about them, but I've often wondered, too."

"Is this when I ended up at the Willerts' bakery?" Star asked.

"Yes."

"How long was I there?"

"Not long, maybe forty-eight hours. You remained there until one of her sons was ready to make a visit to the mill. There could be no suspicious trips because it was known that the SS were getting desperate and had been seen patrolling the railroad tracks. This put them right on the main road leading to and from our village."

"Was it Eric who took me away, Fritz?"

"As I remember, yes."

And Fritz shared more of what he knew.

❧

Eric was stopped about five miles outside the village by three soldiers on foot blocking the road in front of the wagon.

"Where are you going?" they demanded.

"Where I go every week—to deliver flour." The driver watched cautiously as one of the soldiers walked around the wagon, raising his rifle with a bayonet attached. He lowered it over the side and poked around the flour sacks.

"Be careful there, or you'll puncture one and make a mess." Eric forced his voice to be calm.

"Don't tell me what I can or cannot do," came the sharp retort.

You were hidden within a wooden crate, well fed and, up to this point, sound asleep, aided by a mild sedative from Dr. Schlotfeldt.

"Are you one of the Willerts?" a soldier asked.

"I am Eric." By now Eric was sweating, even though the temperature was very cold.

"We have noticed that you and your brothers make a lot of trips around the countryside. Do you not?"

"Ja, it is part of the job." He became more nervous, not knowing how long you would stay asleep.

"Say," one of the soldiers asked, "you wouldn't happen to have any of your mother's strudel hidden back there, would you?"

"No, but I have some up front with me." Eric handed them a generous gift of Frau Willert's handiwork before being waved on.

Eric traveled around the bend before stopping to check on you. He was relieved to find you still sleeping. On down the road he pulled the wagon into an empty barn, shut the door, and waited.

Within the hour a side door opened and a very tall man entered. "You are Eric Willert?"

"Ja."

"Where is my precious cargo?" The tall man removed his snowshoes and stomped his feet free of ice and snow.

Together they lifted you from the hiding place and carefully placed you in yet another front pack for warmth and safekeeping.

"How much longer will she sleep?"

"She's going to be hungry very soon," Eric replied.

"Hopefully, I can reach the river before that happens. There's a small fishing cabin waiting for us."

Eric shook his head. "I wish we could save them all." He choked back tears and anger as he prepared to leave. "I must be going, or I'll be late with my delivery. Godspeed." He took one last look at you, pulled your cap down over your head, and exited the barn.

The man with the snowshoes traveled on another five miles or so before making it to the cabin. He built a fire and heated up the bottle he'd been given. This big, rough-and-tumble man held you, fed and burped you, before making preparations to leave.

❧

"Preparations?" Star got up and stretched. "Well, you know I've got to know the rest." She made them each another cup of coffee before settling back down to hear more.

She noticed that Fritz's eyes looked particularly blue in the ski sweater he wore. She dismissed the thought while adding milk and sugar to her drink.

❧

Once you were fed, burped, and changed, the man nestled you back into the front pack, dampened the fire, and headed for the river. There, hidden in a designated spot, he pulled out a boat, pushed it to the water, and began rowing. The wind had picked up, and the current was strong. Knowing you'd never survive a spill into the freezing river, he prayed over every stroke taken. There could be no turning back, or he'd miss the connections on the other side.

Once there, he pulled the boat onshore and put his snowshoes back on. By now, you were wide awake and looking all around. He said he'd never forget your trusting expression and the contentment you bore. At that moment, he vowed to pray for you the rest of his life.

He had directions to move into the woods and find a particular growth of trees. Once there, he was met by two women, more members of the Underground. These people were the ones who carried you to your home and the Firstenbergs.

Star was in tears. "I've always wondered, and now that I know, I'm humbled beyond words that God would spare my life when so many thousands died. I cannot wrap my mind around it all."

"There's something more," Fritz said.

"About me. . . ?"

". . .about the man who crossed the river with you. On his way back home, he stopped once more at the cabin where he tended you. He did not know that the place was being watched by the SS, who'd been tipped off by a traitor to the Underground.

"The man had just rebuilt the fire, intending to spend the night, when the soldiers stormed in and confronted him. They found one of your diapers and demanded to know where the Jew baby was being hidden. The man refused to say a word despite intense torture. Eventually, they took him to the riverbank where, just hours before, he'd been your hero. In an instant, the flowing vessel of your rescue became his grave."

Star sobbed before collapsing against Fritz. "So many people involved, Fritz, so many people."

He gave her an encouraging hug. "I believe more than we'll ever know for sure, Star. From the very beginning, God had a plan for your life."

"I've heard that my entire life." She looked at him and shrugged. "But until this moment, I've never fully understood the depth of it."

# Chapter 20

*December 1965*
*New York City*

Today, despite some questions about the commitment he'd made the night before, JD felt completely different on the inside. According to the Bible passages Steve had given him, he *was* a "new creation." He'd read that "old things had passed away." The words said, *"If any man be in Christ, he is a new creature: old things are passed away; behold, all things are become new."*

JD clung to those words, because he wanted to be able to lay aside the past. He had a long list of things he'd like to change. The thought was refreshing and overwhelming at the same time.

Even in the midst of Hadassah's last days on earth, this morning felt peaceful. Never in his life had he understood the meaning of that word in regard to a human soul. Should he feel guilty? Was he in denial about the inevitability of what was racing toward them? She was paper-thin. He swallowed hard against the lump in his throat. *How many "good" days could there be left?* Yet in the midst of the sadness was God, giving him the same kind of peace Steve said he and Vikki had in the midst of dealing with Luke's blindness. *How will I tell her about what happened to Michael and me?*

Soul peace is what he longed to give his wife. *Lord, let her see the truth of Your love for her like You've been showing it to me. Thank You.*

⟨≫⟩

Hadassah was enjoying a good morning without dizziness. She paused on the edge of the bed, listening to JD in the kitchen making coffee. She loved the everyday sounds. It gave her courage to ignore the dying face reflected in the mirror across the room. Even though today's energy might be something of a fluke, it would be embraced for the unique gifting of its presence.

The raised bedroom blind let in the morning sun to bathe her face in winter warmth, spreading the elixir from head to toe, pushing aside the ravages of cancer. . .at least for the moment. "Ah, glorious!"

"Did you say something, Hadassah?" JD was standing in the doorway.

She grabbed the walker and made her way to him. "I was just enjoying the sun and the fact that I have some energy this morning. Care to walk me to the kitchen for some morning sustenance?"

"Hey, you're in a good mood." He placed a hand on each shoulder and kissed her forehead.

Walking to the kitchen took a lot of effort, but it was worth it to her to be out of the hospital bed. She sat, watching her husband make scrambled eggs like she liked them.

He was humming. *Humming?* JD never hummed, although once in a while he'd whistle the latest tune from the Hit Parade. She didn't recognize the song.

"What's that you're humming, JD?"

He looked up and smiled. "Something I heard in church last night. The concert was great, and Crystal did a good job on her solo." He continued making the eggs. "You know, Hadassah, a lot of people there are. . ."

". . .praying for me?" She closed her eyes and took a deep breath. "Well, JD, how do you think the prayers are working?"

430

He winced. "I'm not exactly sure about all this prayer business, but maybe it's those prayers that gave you the extra strength today." He set the plate of food on the table, sat down, and reached for her hand. "I love you, Hadassah."

She gazed at him with mist in her eyes. "I love you, too, JD. Thank you for the eggs; they're perfect."

After a few bites, she began moving the food around on the plate, a sure sign she was finished, her appetite spent.

He wanted to grab her tight and never let go. "Hadassah?"

"Mmm?"

"Just how much energy do you have today?" He picked up some papers from the chair where he'd left them.

"Why? Do you want to go dancing after work?" She smirked and laid down her fork.

"Funny. No, I've procrastinated so long on the paper's journalism contest that I've run out of time." He set the manuscripts in front of her.

"How many this year?"

"Haven't counted them, but I'd say seven or eight. You don't have to read them all, but it would be helpful if you could do a couple, anyway." He kissed the top of her head.

She thumbed through the papers. "Let me see how I feel after Michael leaves. Thanks for asking me to do this, JD. Makes me feel human and, you know, useful."

"Do you want help back to the bedroom?"

"No, but you could pour me another cup of coffee with extra cream please. Michael can help me if I need it."

He poured the coffee before grabbing his briefcase and coat. He kissed Hadassah on the lips. "You're the best, you know?" He winked.

The door slammed, and she could hear him humming again, all the way to the car.

Michael's alarm went off down the hall, and she pushed herself up from the chair to make her way to his bedroom. He was still sleeping like a baby. She could not imagine having to say good-bye to him. *I love you, Mikey.* She crossed the room and lay down on the bed, enfolding him from behind.

Michael stirred and leaned into his mother's embrace. "Morning, Mom."

"Time to get up, Mike; you don't want to be late for school."

He nodded. "Mom, I've got something to tell you."

"What? You know you can tell me anything, right?" They sat up and propped themselves against the headboard. She brushed a lock of hair from his forehead.

"Do you remember how excited I always am on the morning of my birthday?"

"Sure."

"Well, that's how I'm feeling this morning." He turned to face her.

"Really?" She was puzzled.

"Really, because last night, at Uncle Steve's church"—big pause—"I asked Jesus into my heart."

Hadassah tried to hide her feelings and control her shaky voice. "Wow, Michael. That's pretty big news."

"It is Mom; it really is. And Mom?"

"Yes?" She felt like she was losing him somehow.

"Dad prayed, too." He was staring right into her eyes.

She closed hers. She had to think. What was happening? *No, no, no!* "Your dad didn't say anything to me this morning when I saw him."

"No? Well, he came right down front after I did." He placed one hand over his heart. His eyes scanned her face. "It's true, Mom. Dad's a Christian, too." When she didn't respond, he asked, "Can I pray for you?"

"Why do you want to pray for me? I'm too sick." She could count the freckles on his face.

"Uncle Steve said nothing's too hard for God, Mom." He touched her face. "Can I please pray for you, Mommy?"

Huge tears trickled down his cheeks. *I love you so much, Michael, but. . .* Her own tears wouldn't stop. "Sure." She closed her eyes and waited while Michael's breathing slowed and he sighed. Hadassah peeked and saw his eyes were closed.

"Dear God, it's me, Michael."

Hadassah chocked back sobs.

"I'm sort of new at this, but I do believe You're real. And I do believe You're listening to me now. Please help my mom; I love her and don't want her to d. . ." He broke down and threw his arms around Hadassah, sobbing into her neck.

He helped her back to the kitchen, and she watched while he ate breakfast. They didn't talk any more about what happened at church, but she could tell Michael was different.

She glanced at the stack of papers JD had left. *I used to be good at this.* She picked up the top one, caught the title, and set it aside. She did the same for the next, and the one after.

Michael came over and kissed her on the cheek. "See you later."

"Love you, Mikey."

"Oh, Mom," he called over his shoulder, "please, not *Mikey*."

She laughed, picked up the rest of the papers, and rose to the call of the whistling teakettle. Passing the phone, she took it off the hook. "Don't have strength to talk *and* read."

# Chapter 21

JD grabbed the phone on the first ring. "Jensen."

"JD, how's it going this morning, big brother?"

"Good. I haven't messed up anything thus far." He lowered his voice. "We need to talk, though, Steve. I'm not quite sure how to process all that happened last night."

"JD, I know this whole 'Christian' thing is new and may be overwhelming right now. Believe me, I know how you feel."

"Sounds good to me. I do need to tell you something." He suddenly felt very emotional and turned his face to the wall so no one in the newsroom could see.

"Shoot."

"For the first time since Hadassah got sick, I feel. . .a strange kind of. . .I guess you'd call it peace." He cleared his throat.

"JD, that's the power of God already at work in your life. Hey, don't try to analyze it with that superior mind of yours. Just accept it, because for sure it's a gift."

"Okay." He took out his handkerchief.

"Listen, JD, I called for another reason. Have you read the contest entries?"

JD felt a stab of guilt. "Not yet."

"Well, I talked to Fritz last night; and I really meant to share this with you after the concert, but I didn't get the chance. You're not going to believe what he discovered."

JD could hear the excitement in Steve's voice. "Spill it."

"Do you have the entries with you, by any chance?"

"No."

"That's okay; I'll make this brief. One of the entries was written by a student who survived the Holocaust. The whole story is amazing in itself, but that's not the most incredible part." He paused to catch his breath.

JD put the handkerchief back into his pocket and sat straighter in his chair. "Yes?"

"She, the writer, was only a baby when someone left her in the snow. . .threw her there, really. . .off a prison train on the way to one of those death camps." Steve waited for a response. "Still there, JD?"

JD took a sharp breath and tried to stop his hands from shaking. "I'm here."

"Okay, here's the part you won't believe. There were two kids playing by the train tracks, in the dead of winter mind you, and they found that baby. . .found the girl who wrote the story. I can't believe it!"

JD began to weep but covered the phone so Steve couldn't hear.

"And. . .there's more! JD, one of those kids in the snow was Fritz. *Our* Fritz! For sure, this is God's hand, God's amazing hand! I'm pumped! Can't believe you haven't read it. It's a miracle!"

JD was unable to speak.

"So, what do you think?"

JD's mind was racing. Hadassah! She had the entries, maybe was reading them as they spoke. "Steve, you're right; this is God's hand. I know you'd like to talk more, but do me a favor."

"Anything. Are you all right? You sound stressed? Is it Hadassah?"

"Yes, but I don't have time to explain." The pitch of his voice rose. "I need you to pray. . . don't have time to explain, but I've got to hang up." His mouth was as dry as cotton.

"Sure, call me when you can. And. . .JD?"

"Yes?"

"Love you."

"Love you, too." JD punched the phone for a dial tone and called home. He drummed his fingers on the desktop. All he got was a busy tone! He slammed the phone back into the cradle. "God, Hadassah needs you."

❧

Thumbing through the entries again, the fourth one caught Hadassah's eye. "I Shouldn't Be Alive!" *Me neither*, she thought. Intrigued by the title, she lifted it from the pile.

❧

JD tried the phone again, in case he might have made a mistake with the number. . .busy still. He flipped through the huge Rolodex on the desk until he found his neighbor Eunice's number. No answer. JD slapped the desktop; he'd forgotten they were out of town. He'd have to leave work. Hadassah would be beyond shocked, and he needed to be there for her.

He was shocked! *God, I believe this is a miracle, but how will it all play out? Hadassah's baby girl is alive; she's alive.* Stifling the emotion that overtook him, he struggled into his coat and hat. *This is what "destiny" means. God, You've reached down from heaven for this one.*

All the way home on the train, he could only imagine Hadassah's response to finding out that her only daughter survived. All those years of guilt, and now she'd know the decision she'd made in utter desperation had been the right one after all. *Who can wrap their mind around this one?*

"Who indeed?"

❧

Making tea had sapped the last bit of energy from Hadassah, and carrying it to the table had been an enormous accomplishment. When finished with the tea, she'd nearly dismissed the task of reading the paper with the fascinating title but decided to take it back to the bedroom with her. A nap might renew some strength. . .maybe. . . .

Glancing at the clock, Hadassah realized the quick nap she meant to take had lasted over an hour. *I'm more tired by the day.* She yawned, debating whether to go back to sleep or read. Laying aside the covers, she made it to the bathroom, did her business and returned to bed, propped a pillow behind her the best she could, and began reading.

Immediately, unbelievable words bounced off the paper. The exact moment Avram threw their baby from the train struck her mind like thunder. *Can't pass out.* Bright twinkling stars pulsed around the edges of her vision, while she fought against wavering darkness.

Maybe her mind was playing cruel tricks. *Breathe, breathe.* No, here it was in black and white: a story of a tiny life rescued from certain death in the German countryside in 1943. If this was true, and Esther had really survived, then. . .then this Star person was her daughter. "My daughter is alive!" *Avram, our daughter lives!*

She was blinded by a flood of emotion that would not stop. Years and years of guilt were contained in each drop that fell like cleansing rain, washing away years of the worst inhumane burden of her life. Exhausted, she toppled onto her side, unable to move.

❧

JD found her on her side when he rushed into the room. He spoke before moving to the bedside, fearing the worst. "Hadassah?"

She lifted her head in his direction. For an instant his mind flew back to the first time he'd seen her lying beside the stream near Ravensbrück.

"I didn't kill her; I didn't kill her, JD. Esther is not dead!" She tried to sit but hadn't the strength and reached for him.

He lifted her up and held on, unwilling to let go. "I know, Hadassah, I know." He rocked gently. "Your baby girl is alive." He pulled back to look at her, grabbing some tissues from the bedside to wipe her face.

She was hoarse from crying. "I can't believe this, JD. Am I dreaming?" She clung to him.

"You're not dreaming, Hadassah. The story you've read is true." He held her gaze. "Your daughter will be in as much shock as you when she finds out her birth mother survived the death camp. There are gaps in both your stories that you'll be able to fill in now."

"Yes, but I'm so scared of what she'll think." She wiped at her nose and took the tissues away. "JD!" she screamed.

He looked down. The tissues were stained bright red. Running to the bathroom, he grabbed a hand towel and rushed back to Hadassah. She was pale and breathing rapidly. "Hold this to your nose, and tip your head back. I'm calling an ambulance."

The medics were there in less than ten minutes, enough time for JD to write a note to Michael and bundle up Hadassah in a warm blanket. He tried calling Steve and Vikki but didn't get an answer.

All the way to the hospital, Hadassah was silent except to say "I love you." Her eyes were sunk back into her head, and JD was again reminded of how she looked the day he'd found her all those years ago. *Please, please God.* He pleaded for her now, just like he'd pleaded for her then.

Once at the hospital, Hadassah was checked in, hooked up to IVs, and made as comfortable as possible in a dull room on the third floor. JD felt like a fish out of water, dodging nurses or doctors, always in their way. Most frustrating to him was that while each of the staff went about their business, no one spoke a word to him.

It was three hours before Hadassah's primary doctor got there. He examined Hadassah briefly, read her chart, and caught JD by the elbow to lead him outside and into the hallway. He stood, hands in his pockets, head down. "Mr. Jensen, this is the time we talked about awhile back."

*"Time?"* JD asked the question, even though he knew exactly what the doctor was alluding to.

"It's time we make her as comfortable as possible." He looked up. "This is when you need to gather your family and friends. This—"

JD interrupted, one hand raised in protest. "Okay, I get it." He lowered his voice. "How long before. . ."

Now it was the doctor who interrupted. "There's no way to know for sure, but probably no more than a week, two at the most."

JD's heart raced as his face stung with a hot, prickly sweat. He leaned against the green wall for support, closing his eyes. When he opened them, the doctor was gone, replaced by a pretty candy striper who was saying something to him. "I beg your pardon, were you speaking to me?"

"Uh, yes, your wife is asking for you, Mr. Jensen."

"Thank you." He sighed.

Hadassah smiled when she saw him walking to the bed. He took the hand without the IV, squeezed it, and pressed it to his lips.

"You always were a true romantic." Her voice was weak, but she held up her arms for a hug. "Could you please roll up my bed?"

He did and plumped the pillow behind her. "Okay?"

She nodded, fingering the blanket covering her failing body. "JD, I want to meet the girl. . .the one who wrote that paper." She was fighting sleep.

He would have given her anything within his power. He smiled. "Well, she'll be easy to find." He let go of her hand.

Her eyebrows went up with question.

"Because she's a journalism major, as you know, and Steve's friend Fritz has already been talking to her."

Hadassah sighed deeply and began shaking her head from side to side.

"What's wrong, Haddie?"

"I–I'm scared." She rubbed both hands over her face. "What if she's angry?"

"You read the letter; she only wonders what happened to you. I didn't see a bit of anger in one word she wrote. It's your destiny to meet, Hadassah."

"You mean God meant for it to happen, don't you?" She looked away, avoiding eye contact.

JD leaned very close to her. "Hadassah, I have another surprise. . .there's more to tell."

"More? What more could there be?"

"I told you that Fritz, Steve's friend, had been talking with the girl, with Star."

"Hmm." A look of fright passed over her face.

"Hadassah, Fritz is from Germany. He's one of the children who found Star in the snow."

She was speechless, her mouth moving but unable to utter a word.

"Only God could have brought this whole thing to this place at this time."

"Oh my, oh my." JD could see that her hands were shaking.

He wanted to talk more, but a nurse came in and asked him to leave. Bending over the bed, he kissed Hadassah on the lips and promised to return soon. She only nodded.

He left the room, quietly shutting the door, scanning for a telephone. He needed to call Steve then check to see if Mike had gotten home.

Steve's phone at work rang five times before he answered. "Speak to me."

"Steve."

"What's wrong, JD? I can tell by your voice, something's up."

"It's Hadassah, she. . .she's in the hospital."

"What happened; are you all right?"

"I'm fine, but it looks like. . ." He didn't want to speak the words. "Steve, it looks like Haddie won't be leaving here. The doctor says it's 'her time.'"

"Wow!" Steve was silent for a moment. "JD, I'm so sorry. Look, I need to finish up some stuff here at work before I can leave, but I'll call Vikki. What can we do?"

"I need you here, little brother." JD's voice cracked. "But could you pick up Mike first?"

"Will do, JD."

"I'll call Mike and tell him you guys are coming. See you soon."

JD hung up the receiver and dialed the hardest phone call of his life. Mike picked up on the first ring. "Hello?"

"Mike."

"Dad, I just found your note. What happened to Mom?" His voice was high-pitched and breathy.

It took all JD had not to break down at the sound of his son's anguish. "She's stable for now, kiddo."

"Oh, good!"

JD heard the relief in his son's voice. "Uncle Steve will be there in a couple of hours to bring you here."

"Sure, Dad, I'm just eating some cereal, but I'll be ready." He took a deep breath. "And Dad?"

"Yeah, Son?"

"Don't worry about me, okay? I'm all right." His voice dropped. "I'll be praying. Tell Mom I'll see her in a little while."

"Sure, Mike, bye."

"Bye, Dad."

JD put his head against the wall next to the phone. *What an incredible kid*. He was surprised that his hands were shaking. Turning, he saw a bright red Exit sign and walked toward it. Once in the stairwell, JD sat on the steps and put his head in both hands. Wracking sobs tore from his body, echoing off the pale walls like strange mourners weeping with him. He covered his ears, but the echoed grieving continued.

Steve hung up the phone. *Lord, give me wisdom and discernment to be the kind of support JD and his family need.* He dialed Fritz's office number.

"Professor Schmidt."

"Oh, good, I caught you, Fritz."

"Hey, you sound stressed."

"I just got a call from JD. Hadassah's back in the hospital."

"Sorry, Steve."

His voice cracked. "Thanks. Uh, looks like this will be the last hospital stay, too."

"How are JD and Mike holding up?"

"I'll find out when I get to the hospital. I called so you could be praying for them. . .for all of us."

"Sure thing, Steve; thanks for calling me. Keep me posted."

"Will do. Thanks, my brother." Next he called Vikki.

JD slept in a chair in Hadassah's room. He woke with a start at a soft knocking and saw Mike, with Steve and Vikki, standing in the doorway. Glancing at Hadassah, he got up to greet his son, who threw himself into JD's arms. His sobs came in short bursts, with little choking sounds. JD held on with as much comfort as he could, patting Mike with reassurance. "It's okay, buddy. It's okay."

Steve and Vikki could not hold back their own tears. They walked over to Mike and JD, enclosing both into their arms.

"Hey, people." It was Hadassah. "There'll be no more of those tears, unless they're mine." She motioned for them to come closer. Michael reached her first and climbed in the bed. JD started to say something, but Hadassah put up her hand. "It's okay, JD."

Michael didn't cry; he simply hugged his mother. Steve and Vikki backed out of the room, closing the door behind them.

In a little while, JD came out. "They're both sleeping."

"Will the hospital let Mike stay in there?" Vikki asked.

JD exhaled. "I guess we'll find out." Suddenly he realized he hadn't eaten since breakfast. "Could you two eat something?"

"Sure," Steve said. "How risky is the food here?"

"I don't know, but I'm willing to find out at this point."

After they'd eaten, JD fingered the silverware piece by piece. "I'm glad the two of you are sitting down because what I have to say would knock you off your feet otherwise."

Steve and Vikki looked at each other then back to him. They waited.

"You know that incredible journalism entry you called me about?"

"Yes." Steve turned to his wife. "He's talking about the train baby story."

"Well, there's even more." JD looked at first one then the other. "When you told me on the phone the circumstances of this kid's story, I didn't have time to respond."

"Yeah, I wondered about that." Steve stole a glance at his wife. "Go on."

"I had to get home to Hadassah, because I'd asked her to go over the entries for me. I needed to prepare her for what you told me was in the entry from the Firstenberg girl." He couldn't go on.

Steve reached across the table and touched JD on the arm. "What are you trying to tell us?"

"The baby who was thrown from the train and Fritz found. . .was Hadassah's child."

"What?" Vikki jumped up from the table, knocking the chair over. Steve just stared at his brother.

"Oh, Lord!" Vikki clapped her hands together in astonishment.

Steve stood and walked around to JD, pulling him to his feet. He waited for words to come. They didn't; instead tears stained his entire face.

"Steven," Vikki laughed, "I believe this is the first time in your life you've ever been speechless." She ran to them both.

Finally Steve regained his composure. "Fritz is not going to believe this," was all he could manage to say.

"Oh, I think he will," Vikki said. "After meeting Star, I'll just bet you he will. Now, for her, it might be more of a stretch."

"I can hardly believe it myself," JD said.

"So Haddie knows?" Vikki was still too excited to sit.

"Yes, I found her at home right after she'd read the entry. Then she got this terrible nose-bleed that wouldn't stop, and we came here."

"What an emotional roller coaster," Steve said. "Look, I can't tell this to Fritz on the phone; I'll go see him first thing in the morning."

"I've got to call my office and tell them I won't be in for a while. Good thing I've got a lot of time off coming. I don't want to leave Hadassah alone."

"Look," Vikki said, "I'll take Mike home with us. School will be out for Christmas break in a few days; our kids will love it." She kissed JD on the cheek. "Love you, brother. Hope you know how much I love Haddie."

"Thanks, Vikki. I do know how much she means to you. Your connection is special." He winked.

"It's a God thing, for sure," she said.

When he got back to the room, Mike was just waking up.

"Dad, can I stay here with you and Mom?" He rubbed his eyes.

"Uncle Steve and Aunt Vikki are taking you home with them for a few days, bud."

"Oh." He was trying to hide his disappointment. "I guess that's okay, but I really want to stay here." He glanced down at his mother. "Are *you* staying with Mom?"

"Yeah, you know how she hates hospitals." They made their way to the hallway. "Right now I've got to run home and get some things. I'll grab clothes for you, too, how's that?" He put his arm around Michael's shoulders.

"Okay." Mike took hold of JD's sleeve. "Would you mind praying with me, Dad? I'm having a hard time."

"I've never prayed out loud with anyone before." JD felt his face flush.

"That's okay, Dad. God won't care."

JD walked to the EXIT sign again. Placing one arm around Mike, JD prayed, "God, only You and Mike know how hard it is on him having his mother sick. Please help him during this time, and please help his mother as well."

Mike gave his dad a long hug before he headed back to his mother's room. At the exact moment he did, a thought struck JD: *Mike has a sister.*

# Chapter 22

Fritz enjoyed every minute he was able to spend with Star, still amazed at how they'd been brought together after all these years. Even his cousin Ellie had been able to talk with her on the phone several times.

Star didn't know it, but Fritz was fairly certain she'd won the journalism contest, hands down. He was waiting to hear what JD thought but had little doubt that he would agree with Steve and himself.

He'd found her to be bright and focused, with a deep commitment to the Lord. Their relationship felt like the most natural thing in the world to him, even though he had some concerns about the age difference.

"Fritz, you're not that much older than me. And besides, I'm not a child after all."

They'd been walking around a local park, having a discussion about the propriety of him dating a student. . .a much younger student.

"So are we?" she'd asked.

"Are we what?"

"Dating?" She laughed and ran ahead of him to a steaming hotdog stand.

"Well, I'm pretty sure this is a date, and to prove it, I'll even buy you dinner." He held up two fingers to the hotdog vendor.

"Wow, you're a big spender," she teased him.

"Truthfully, I've spent less."

This sent her into spasms of laughter. "You know, Fritz, that's the first joke I've heard you crack. That was really funny."

"Thanks for the compliment. And because of it, I'll even buy you dessert. What do you say to a fancy ice-cream cone. . .double scoop?" He handed her a dog and then bowed.

She laughed even harder. "I'll take that double scoop, mister."

Earlier, he'd gotten an early morning call from Steve. He'd heard a lot of concern in his voice over his sister-in-law's condition, but there seemed to be something else he wanted to say. Now Fritz wondered what it was.

⟡

JD was stiff from sleeping in the hospital chair all night but didn't regret the chance to be there for Hadassah whenever she woke. The first time, she was clawing at the air, trying to run from the nightmares that plagued her.

He'd climbed into bed, patted her back just like he used to do, until she fell back to sleep. She continued to whimper throughout the night and slept fitfully. Between his vigil with her and all the medical interruptions, he felt like a tank had run over him when daylight pushed itself through the slats of the metal blinds.

Stretching, he crossed the room in a desperate quest for a cup of coffee. Even a machine concoction would do. He stepped into the hallway.

"Can I help you, Mr. Jensen?" It was the night nurse about to check out of her shift.

"Yes, you could. I'd do anything for a hot cup of strong coffee." He realized he must look a mess and tried to pat down the cowlick on top of his head.

"Wait here. I'll get you some."

He tucked in his shirt and realized he was shoeless. The nurse—her name tag said JENN—came back with a large cup of coffee, brimming to the top. He sipped gratefully. "Thank you, Jenn." She started to walk toward the elevators, and he followed her. "How long have you been a nurse?"

She turned to answer. "Going on fifteen years, now. Yup, in January, it will be that long."

He heard the elevator stop and waited for the doors to open. He watched her get on and waved as the doors closed, lifting his cup in a kind of toast. "Thank you, for what you do." She nodded and smiled.

Walking down to an empty waiting area, he sat in a worn, overstuffed chair, careful not to spill the hot coffee. *How do I tell Mike about his newfound sister? Maybe Hadassah should tell him.* His head spun with the reality and the irony of the entire situation. *Why did God choose now for this whole thing to unfold? Why now, when. . .in a few short days, Hadassah will be dead?* He looked down at his stocking feet and watched his own tears dripping onto the tops of them.

Fritz whistled, staring at Steve in disbelief. He couldn't speak.

"I was speechless myself, Fritz. The whole thing is miraculous. I mean, I don't know what else to call it." He picked up the half-empty coffee cup in front of him.

Fritz was weeping. Pulling out a handkerchief, he wiped his face. "All I can say is praise Him. I praise Him, and I thank Him." He continued to dab his eyes, ignoring the people around him who stared.

"What an incredible time of year for this all to take place. . .you know, Christmas and all. You found Star on Christmas Eve, right?"

Fritz cleared his throat. "That's right. How appropriate for mother and daughter to meet so close to that anniversary. I'm glad we're on Christmas break now, too; at least Star will be free to spend more time with Hadassah." He paused. "I *hope* they have some time, Steve. How bad is it?"

"Bad. The doctor's saying not more than a couple of weeks at the most. It makes me sick. . .so close to death and now she finds out her daughter's alive. The irony of it all could wipe me out if I thought about it too long."

"I'll tell you this, Steve: I'm more than grateful that God is in control."

"Amen. So"—he touched Fritz on the arm—"when will you tell Star?"

"We're going ice-skating. I'll tell her then." He smiled. "What a Christmas gift for her."

# Chapter 23

Mike's eyes were wide, and for a moment he didn't say a word. Hadassah shot a glance to JD, who mouthed, *"Just wait."*

"I have a *sister?*" He rubbed both hands on his pant legs. "You mean, I have a sister who lives right *here?*" He was grinning ear to ear. "Wow, right *here!*" He pointed to the floor for emphasis then ran over and grabbed JD around the waist.

"Mikey," Hadassah said, "this is a very long story, and at home I've explained it all in that journal I've been writing in."

"Does it have to do with the prison camp where you lived during the war?" He looked soulfully at Hadassah.

She nodded. "I—I thought that my daughter was dead, even though I did something I thought might save her life." Her eyes closed.

Mike shrugged and shot a confused look at his dad.

"Let's let Mom rest, and I'll fill in some blanks for you," JD said.

Hadassah mumbled, "Thanks."

Out in the hallway, Mike paced. "I thought I'd be an only child my whole life." He stopped, frowning at JD. "Dad, how do you feel about this?"

"I knew about your sister, but it was only a day or so ago I found out she was alive and right here in New York. I'm very happy all this has happened."

"I think this is one of those 'God things' Uncle Steve and Aunt Vikki are always talking about. What do you think?"

"I agree with you 100 percent, buddy. . .100 percent."

Mike walked over to stand in front of JD. "I have two questions for you, Dad." His voice was playful.

"What are they?" JD couldn't help but smile.

"Number one: When do I get to meet her? And number two: Will you buy me lunch?" He turned his baseball cap around backward. "I'm starving."

⁂

Close to the same time Michael Jensen found out he had a sister, Star Firstenberg was learning she had a mother.

"Fritz, you're awfully jumpy. Don't tell me you're afraid of skating after all this time? I'm a little rusty myself, so relax." She tossed her braid off of one shoulder.

He was lacing up the last skate and stalling. It wasn't fear that held him back, but a sheer lack of experience to broach the subject. How do you share this kind of life-changing news with someone? Beginning with his words, Star's life would change in a way she'd only dreamt about. It would be thrilling for her to meet Hadassah, that was a given, but how difficult would it become when they had to say good-bye so soon after?

"Come on, slow poke, I'll race you. Let's see if that age difference you're worrying about proves true." She was laughing, holding out one hand to him. He took it, and they glided out onto the ice. "I'm Dreaming of a White Christmas" streamed from loudspeakers, while they made their way around the first time. He felt his courage level rising as they skated and put one arm around Star's waist, gliding around the rink several times before leading her to a wooden bench on the side.

She looked at him. "You look awfully serious; are you all right?"

Fritz sat, tugging her down beside him. He took one hand. "I've got something to tell you, Star."

"Are you ill?"

He could see the fear on her face. "No, it's not anything about me, truly." He took a deep breath. "You know how from the very beginning of our meeting again that we've said God brought us together?"

She nodded. "Yes."

"There's more to God's plan, Star. . .more than I could ever have foreseen. Perhaps more than you ever dreamt possible."

Star said nothing.

Taking both her hands, he held them tight and maintained eye contact. "I've found out that your mother is alive."

"My mother?" She gasped. "You mean my *birth* mother?" She sat motionless.

"Yes."

She collapsed against him, and he felt her shiver from head to toe.

They sat like that for a long time while he told her all the details and answered what questions he could. The one thing he didn't share was the part about Hadassah's terminal illness.

"How I praise Him. First I found you, and now my mother." She lifted her face to his, and for the first time since they'd met, he kissed her lightly on the lips. She kissed him back, pulled away, and looked at him. "There is something more for you to tell me, isn't there?"

He nodded but couldn't speak. How wonderful that, at this dramatic moment, he realized he deeply loved Star Elizabeth Firstenberg. As a child, he had loved her before; but now, now he was *in* love. *Thank You, God.*

Drawing her into another embrace, he whispered in one ear, "Star, your mother is very ill." He heard her draw a deep breath.

"How ill?"

"Right now, she's in the hospital."

"Oh, Fritz, no, no! How cruel this seems to be. Now I'm confused."

"I'll be there for you, Star."

"Thank you," she said and reached up to lay a hand on the side of his face. "How difficult this has been for you. I'm more than happy that it was you who told me, Fritz. . .so happy."

"There is one more thing I need to share, Star. . .a very good thing."

She regarded him with wide-eyed anticipation.

"You have a brother as well. I believe his name is Michael. Yes, that's it, Michael. He's around twelve, I think."

"A brother, a *little* brother? How perfect! Did you know I'm the youngest in the Firstenberg clan?" She got up and turned to pull him to his feet. "My, won't Mama Firstenberg be surprised. . .surprised, but happy for me, of course. I'll call her when I get back to the dorm. Right now, I'm freezing."

When they'd gotten their street shoes on and were leaving the ice rink, Star stopped. "When can my mother and I meet, do you think?"

Fritz shook his head. "I'll call Steve right away and then let him take it from there." He put up one finger in front of her and said, "Oh."

"Goodness, don't tell me there's someone else for me to meet."

"No, it's not that." He laughed. "But I do have more good news." He was helpless to stop a huge grin from spreading across his face. "You won the journalism contest."

"What? Oh my goodness, I almost forgot about that. Wow, what if I hadn't written that piece, Fritz?"

"Well, you did, and you've indeed won your own byline in the *New York Times.*"

"When will it be published, do you know?" Although she was smiling, huge tears threatened to spill over, and her hands shook when she took one of his. He gave it a squeeze for assurance.

"Maybe next Sunday. Steve will let us know for sure."

# Chapter 24

Hadassah had been dreaming of a baby bundled in pink, lying against her breast. She could taste her freshness in a kiss, smell her intoxicating fragrance. "Esther," she whispered.

She jerked awake, surprised at where she was. She licked her lips and reached for a glass next to the bed. Both hands shook with the effort. *So weak. So weak.*

A perky nurse's aide with vibrant strawberry-blond hair stuck her head in the door. "Good morning. How would you like to feel like a new woman?"

Hadassah shrugged. "Is that even possible at this point?"

"Well, I'm betting that a nice hot shower, a clean gown, and brushed teeth might help some. Whaddya say?"

Her Brooklyn accent matched her looks to a T, Hadassah thought. "Why not? Maybe I'll have a hot date tonight." She smiled.

"Sure, you just never know, hon. Besides, I saw your husband earlier; he's very handsome. You been married long?" She was assembling all the shower amenities while she talked.

"Mmm, a wonderful long time." Hadassah swallowed against the lump forming in her throat.

"Kids, you've got kids, I'll bet."

"Uh, yes we do." *I've had three children altogether.* "We have a son, Michael, and I. . ." *I have a daughter raised from the dead.* Hadassah changed the subject. "How is this shower thing going to work exactly?"

"Well, hon, I've got a chair, and I'll help ya get in it. How's that sound?" She oozed confidence, which in turn, gave her patient some. . .a little anyway. She'd need all she could muster in order to face the living, breathing past.

Mostly, all the confrontations from the past occurred at night in the darkest depths of her mind, but when she was pregnant with Michael, the past came leaping at her on the steps of the public library. When she was about eight months along and feeling cumbersome, the steps leading to the building were taking their toll. . . .

*"Hadassah Meyer!" Someone below shouted her name. And they had said* Meyer. *She stopped but did not turn, her heart beating too fast.*

*"I know it's you. Do not pretend I do not." The voice was shrill, filled with anger, and getting closer.*

*Someone tapped her hard on the right shoulder. Hadassah turned to see a woman about her age, eyes blazing with hatred. Something about her seemed familiar, yet no name came to mind.*

*"Hah, I see you do not recognize me." A fat finger waved in front of Hadassah's face, and suddenly a name popped into her mind.* Helga Franklin. *But how. . .*

*"Ach, now I see you know me. Good!" She continued to wave the finger. "Do you also remember I know the despicable thing you did?"*

*For a minute, Hadassah had feared the woman would strike her. Instead, she stepped right up next to her face and spit. Hadassah felt it slipping down her cheeks and thought she'd vomit.*

*"I. . . I. . ." Hadassah was speechless and felt faint. No, that couldn't happen, because then she'd tumble down the stairs and hurt the baby. Trying to escape the tirade, she turned to continue her climb up the stairs.*

*"I'm not finished!" Helga Franklin screamed. "You killed your baby! You're a baby killer! What kind of a mother throws her own baby from a moving train?" She now had a death grip on Hadassah's arm.*

*Soon library patrons were staring at the scene unfolding on the steps. One young man with long hair and a multicolored headband approached them. "Do you need help, ma'am?" he said to Hadassah, standing between her and the still shouting Helga Franklin.*

*Hadassah could barely speak. "Yes, that would be good." He escorted her up the stairs and through the door. Even inside, Helga could still be heard. "May God curse your womb with the most pain a woman ever felt."*

*"Man, you must have really done something to tick her off." He acted like she was going to give him an explanation, but Hadassah said, "I don't know that woman."*

*It was a lie, of course, but she thanked the young man and made her way out of the vestibule. As quickly as possible, she went to the first room off the long hallway and made her way to the farthest wall. Checking that no one was watching, she squatted down and leaned her head against a shelf. Covering her mouth with both hands, Hadassah tried to muffle the agony spilling from the recesses of her being. She knew Helga Franklin all right. They'd been on the death train together. . . .*

Alone in the shower, she let the hot water wash the painful thoughts away, but immediately, new ones took their place. *What will I say to you, Esther? Have you forgiven me?*

# Chapter 25

Across town, Star awoke, stretched, and looked at the clock. *In only a few hours, I'll come face-to-face with my mother.* Suddenly, she was a little girl in Germany, maybe seven or eight, staring at herself in the old mirror over her dresser. *Who do I look like? Who has this face? I wonder, how tall was my father?* When her mama had asked her why she spent so much time in front of the mirror, Star didn't confess the truth because never would she want to hurt her parents' feelings. She knew they loved her, yet the questions about her identity often haunted the reflection in the glass.

Today, there would be an answer. Hopefully there would be *many* answers. She stood in front of the reflective glass, turning around slowly in the bath towel. "What does one wear to meet one's mother for the first time?"

Just then the phone rang.

"Hello?"

"Eleven o'clock."

"To meet her, you mean? Oh, Fritz!" She began to tremble.

"Yes, are you excited?"

"I can't quite identify my feelings. I'm mostly nervous out of my skin, I'd say." Her voice dropped. "Could you come a little earlier maybe. . .to pray with me?"

He laughed. "I'll pick you up a half hour before, how's that?" He paused. "Star, it's going to be all right. Remember, this is your destiny. . .and hers. God has brought you together, and He won't let you go."

"But. . ." She started to cry. "But we aren't getting much time, Fritz. The burden of her illness is overwhelming, to say the least."

"Look, try to focus on what time you *will* have." He cleared his throat. "I don't mean to give you any advice, Star. Forgive me, please. Who am I to offer sage words for a time such as this?"

"There's nothing to forgive," she murmured. "I know your heart, Fritz. I'm hanging up so I can get dressed. See you soon. Bye."

As soon as she hung up, she began to pray.

⁂

JD had been up since before dawn, sipping lukewarm coffee from a machine. He'd been surprised to see snow on the window ledge of Hadassah's room. She'd had a good night, which made his sleep better on the cot brought in for him beside her.

Her decline appeared visible almost an hour at a time. With little or no appetite, her flesh seemed to be melting away. But, since finding out about the existence of one Star Firstenberg, a new fierceness possessed his wife. There was a brightness in her beautiful brown eyes he'd not seen for years. Despite the condition of her body, Hadassah's spirits had been revived.

She'd awakened only once last night, around three. "JD, are you sleeping?"

"Barely."

She was whispering. "Do you think she'll look like me?" Her voice reminded him of Mike when he was little on Christmas Eve. *"Do you think Santa got my letter, Dad?"*

He smiled in the darkness, despite the hour. "Well, it won't be long, Hadassah, before you'll find out."

"Could you come in bed with me for a while?"

He slid in beside her, careful not to put any pressure on the frailness he felt through the covers.

In that moment, even though he still had a desperate sadness, that strange, wonderful peace he'd felt since becoming a Christian won out, and he was able to hold her until she slept again. *Sweet dreams, sweet Hadassah.*

❧

After the shower Hadassah felt refreshed with a real sense of renewal. She'd gotten into a beautiful teal brocade robe that Vikki had brought for the occasion and a splendid silk head scarf to match. With some blush and lipstick, the reflection in the hand mirror looked somewhat familiar. *But I'll be a stranger to her.*

❧

"Hey, beautiful!" JD walked into the room, nearly hidden by a huge bouquet of flowers.

"I wondered where you went, mister. Wow, those are beautiful."

Though she was smiling and radiant, JD saw fear in her eyes. "This is a big day, Haddie. I thought these were appropriate for the occasion." He kissed her on the forehead before placing the vase down.

"I'd like to be sitting in a chair when my. . .when Star gets here. And, if you don't mind, I'd like for us to meet alone for a while." She adjusted the head scarf a little. "I don't want her to be overwhelmed with all of us. Do you know what I mean?"

"Good idea. Fritz is bringing her here at eleven. That way you two can have some time together, and then, if you feel like it, maybe we could all have lunch together." She was looking at the window. "What are you thinking, Hadassah?"

Fingering the sleeves of her robe, she said. "I was just thinking that it was snowing the last time I saw her. . .that *last* day." When she looked up, her eyes were misty. He handed her a tissue. "I'm not going to cry, JD." She glanced at the clock.

❧

"Fritz, I don't want to be late. Do the roads feel slippery? They should have been sanded by now." She fingered her hair, trying to make it stay under the white stocking cap she wore.

"The roads are good, Star. This will probably melt off in a few hours." He glanced in her direction. "What will be the first thing you ask Hadassah?"

She thought for a moment. "I'd like to know what she named me." She paused. "Maybe I was named after someone in the family. What do you think?"

"That's probably the first thing I'd ask myself, if I were you. I'm still amazed that your adoptive family kept the name *we* gave you." He smiled.

"Truthfully, I've a head full of questions, but I'm sure she has some as well."

"Steve told me she read your letter, so at least she knows you had a good childhood."

Star glanced at him. "I've read there are generally two kinds of Holocaust survivors. . . those who want to talk of every detail to whoever will listen, and those who say little or nothing." She paused. "I wonder which category my mother falls into."

A sign along the highway read HOSPITAL NEXT RIGHT. Star took in a deep breath and exhaled slowly. "Oh, Fritz," she whispered, "we're almost there."

He caught her eye and winked.

❧

"Aunt Vikki, do I look all right; should I wear a baseball hat, or not?"

"I say wear it backward, sport." Steve interrupted and poked his nephew in the shoulder.

"Steven, stop teasing." Vikki turned to Mike. "Mike, I think you should wear whatever you feel most comfortable in. . .and don't listen to your Uncle Steve."

Mike walked over and gave her a hug. "I'll wear the hat. . .the right way." He looked in the mirror by the Jensens' front door. "Do you think there's any chance we look alike?"

"I think there's a good chance." Steve was standing behind Michael and hugged his neck. "You and your mom have the same eyes."

"Really?" Michael blinked, stepping closer to the mirror. "Hey, I think you're right." He put on his jacket. "Okay, people, let's go."

"Want to pray before we leave?" Steve asked.

"Good idea, Uncle Steve."

They formed a circle of three. "Dear Lord, how we thank You for who You are in our lives. We thank You that today marks the beginning of a whole new, exciting chapter in Mike's life, and it's not just meeting his sister; it's a new chapter with You. Please help Hadassah and her daughter as they come together after all this time. Make it a holy time, and may You be glorified in all of this. In Jesus' name, we pray. Amen."

They all said "amen" in response.

"Okay, Michael, my man, we're ready to roll."

# Chapter 26

*10:48 a.m.*

"Mom, please, can't I be in here when you meet my sister?" Mike stood by her chair, holding one hand. "I won't say a word, I promise."

"That would be a first." Hadassah kissed the back of Mike's hand. "You can come in after a little while, Mikey, but I'd like just a few minutes alone with Star. Please do this for me." She smiled up at him.

Mike shuffled his feet a little before speaking. "Okay, but don't wait too long." He looked at JD. "Will you buy me a soda, Dad?"

"Sure." JD kissed Hadassah on the cheek and opened the door, waiting for Mike.

"Mom, I know you don't like it when I say this, but I'm praying for you. . .big-time. Okay?"

She motioned for him to leave but said nothing. Her hands were sweaty, and she wiped them on the front of her new robe. *So long, it's been. So long, and I never once thought I'd see her again. I guess she couldn't hate me, or she wouldn't have wanted to meet.*

<hr style="width:20%" />

Once in the elevator, Star's mouth went dry while she clung tight to a sleeve of Fritz's overcoat. The doors opened, and they stepped out into the hallway. Fritz took her elbow and guided her down and around to the far end, until they stood before a door that read HADASSAH JENSEN. Star looked at Fritz and mouthed the words, *"I'm scared."*

On the other side, Hadassah forced her mind to focus. She felt weak but determined. A knock on the door startled her. She went to speak, but words refused to come out. Swallowing hard, she tried again. "Come in."

Fritz opened the door, gave Star a squeeze, and stepped aside. Three steps and she was inside. The door closed behind her. There, sitting in a wheelchair, was her mother. . .her *mother*. She couldn't move.

Hadassah's hand went to her mouth while years of sorrow fell as silent tears into her lap. No doubt this was her daughter. Thrown back in time, Star looked exactly like her namesake, Esther. And, for sure, the resemblance of mother and daughter was apparent.

Star took a couple more steps toward Hadassah. Even though she knew how sick this woman looked, she was still able to see the physical connection between them. . .their eyes, for one. Yet the burning eyes of her very ill mother held something Star had never seen before. . . intense suffering. Still, she moved forward.

"Hello," she whispered, feeling exactly like that little girl in Germany who'd stood in front of the mirror so many times in search of an unknown identity. Now that she knew, she had more courage.

Hadassah grabbed a tissue and held it to her face. "Hello, Star. I'm Hadassah." *I'm your mother, the one who wanted to die when I threw you to the wind.*

Star couldn't stifle a little nervous laugh. "I was pretty sure that's who you were."

Hadassah thought, *Even her voice is like my mother's.* She motioned for Star to sit in front of her, unable to take her eyes from the beautiful face. *Am I dreaming, Avram?*

They sat facing each other in a silence both comforting and awkward.

It was Hadassah who spoke next. "Thank you for coming." *I never thought I'd see you again, my precious.* "When I read your entry for the paper, I knew I had to meet you, but I wasn't sure if you would really want to. . .meet me."

Now it was Star who was weeping, choking back sobs. "I. . . I. . ." She wiped her cheeks. "I've wondered about you my whole life." Her voice quavered. "I love my family, I really do, but somehow I knew there must be someone out there who looked like me." Timidly, she put one hand on Hadassah's arm.

Hadassah covered her face with both hands and held them there awhile. "I never wanted. . . I never wanted to let you go." She put her hand over Star's. "I wanted you to live more than *I* wanted to live. I—I. . ." She felt dizzy and closed her eyes against it.

"Do you need to get back into bed?" Star asked, standing. "I've upset you, haven't I?" She wrung her hands in anguish.

"No, no, please, just help me, and I'll be fine. I've not been out of bed for a while, that's all."

"Should I ring the nurse?"

Hadassah shook her head no and tried to stand. Star stood in front of the chair and offered both hands for support. Slowly, she pulled Hadassah to her feet. Although they looked alike, Star was much taller.

Hadassah looked up and smiled.

"You are tall like your father." *You were his special treasure.* They worked her back into bed where Hadassah lay on top of the covers, her head resting on several propped pillows.

"Better?" Star offered a drink.

"Much." *I can't believe how beautiful you are.* "There are so many things I want to share with you about why. . .why we let you go, but I want you to ask me whatever you want."

"There are many questions, as you can imagine." She stood by Hadassah's bed with a concerned expression. Hadassah held out her hand, and Star took it readily, smiling. "Okay, here goes. I guess what I'd like to ask first is: What did you name me?"

"Funny you mentioned that, because you look just like your namesake."

"Really?" She was still smiling.

"I, *we*, named you Esther. . .for your grandmother. . .my Mütter." Hadassah paused. "Esther translated into Hebrew is *Hadassah.* I was named after my mother, and you also."

Star took in a sharp breath and placed one hand over her heart, excited over the revelation of her name. "Do you know what Esther means in English?"

Puzzled, Hadassah shook her head. "I don't think I do." She waited.

Leaning over the bed, Star whispered, "Esther means star. Can you believe it? Fritz's family saw my birthmark and named me Star." Noticing Hadassah's eyelids were drifting shut, she leaned closer again. "Do you want to rest, now?"

Hadassah's eyes flew open. "No, I was just listening to the sound of your voice and remembering my mother. This Fritz you mentioned, he's one of the children who found you in the snow?"

"Yes, it was him and a younger cousin, Ellie."

Hadassah quietly said something Star could not understand.

"I'm sorry, I couldn't hear you."

Hadassah spoke a little louder. "I saw them that day. . .playing in the snow, though we could not see whether they were girls or boys."

"We?"

"Yes, it was your father and I who made the decision that day, but in the end it was he who. . ." A wave of sorrow washed over Hadassah. Trying to sit up, she failed. "Could you raise the head of my bed a little?"

In a better position, she began to weep openly. Star stepped closer and patted one shoulder.

"You know about Michael, of course." Hadassah sighed. "Well, you had another brother as well."

Star gasped in surprise.

"His name was Aaron, and I swear to you, there was never a happier child born on this earth. He was born in Berlin but spent the years before you were born in the countryside with my parents. Times were difficult, but Aaron's sweet nature made it all bearable somehow."

Star could not hold back the question. "What happened to him?"

Hadassah steeled herself before answering. "He died with your father in a camp. He survived the transport on the train, but when we arrived at Ravensbrück, he was taken away, and I never saw him again." Her hands rubbed across the sheet and blanket on the bed while Star tried to hide her disappointment.

Hadassah spoke again. "You know that I'm very sick, right?"

Star nodded.

"Well, I have lots to tell you, all I can right now, but after. . .well, after I'm gone, I've left something I want you to read." She struggled against the drowsiness. "At my house is a journal with most of my history." She paused. "And yours. I wrote it for Michael." She reached for her daughter's hands. "Of course, I did not know about you, or that we would ever meet, Star. But now the words are meant for your eyes as well." Tears of joy and relief released themselves, and this time, Hadassah made no attempt to stop them.

Hadassah fell into a sleep that could no longer be resisted. Star watched for a minute before brushing Hadassah's forehead with a kiss. "Sleep, my Mütter, sleep and rest."

⟨⟩

Once Star was outside, she collapsed into Fritz's arms, unable to let go. She looked into his face and whispered, "My name is Esther." They stood that way for a long while. He stroked her hair while she gained composure.

Finally someone cleared his throat. Turning, she saw a man standing near them.

"I'm sorry to interrupt, but I have a young man who will jump out of his skin if he cannot meet you in the next five seconds." He reached out and took Star's outstretched hand. "I'm JD Jensen, Hadas. . .uh, your mother's husband."

"Oh, my, yes," she stammered, "I recognize you. . .from the paper." Any awkwardness melted away with the enthusiastic handshake. She looked over his shoulder, expecting to see Michael.

"Uh, I've got Mike stashed away in the waiting room with my brother."

"Thank you. I am very ready, Mr. Jensen."

⟨⟩

Her dazzling smile was so like Hadassah's before the cancer that JD was taken aback for a second as they walked toward the waiting room.

Steve and Vikki got up as soon as JD entered, while Mike continued writing his name on a steamed-up window. JD smiled and called, "Mike!"

Michael jerked around with both hands by his side, looking first at his dad then the beautiful young woman standing by the door, the beautiful woman with his mother's eyes. . . his eyes.

She took two steps toward him and held out her arms. He practically flew across the room.

"Hi, I'm Michael." Despite his efforts not to, he was crying.

"I'm Star, Michael. I'm your sister." He threw his arms around her waist before looking up into her face. "You look just like my mom." He corrected himself. "I mean, *our* mom."

There wasn't a dry eye in the waiting room, including a couple sitting at the far end.

"I've just spent some time with her, Michael, and I believe you are right. Tell me how old you are."

"Hey, call me Mike. I'm twelve." Wiping his eyes, he said, "But, please, whatever you do, do *not* call me Mikey." This made everyone laugh.

Steve and Vikki walked over and introduced themselves. "We're so happy to meet you,"

Vikki said. "This is the best Christmas gift Hadassah could ever have."

Fritz spoke up. "Frankly, Star's the best present *I've* ever had. . .twice." He looked at her and smiled. She rested her head against his shoulder.

"I—I am speechless," was all she could manage. "I think I could use a drink of water."

"I'll get it," Michael offered. "I know where everything is on this floor by now."

When he was out of sight, JD said, "Just so you know, Star, Mike knows exactly how sick his mother is, but I'm not sure if you do." He lowered his head then lifted it again, making eye contact.

"I'm afraid I do, JD; Fritz has told me everything." She dabbed at her eyes. "The irony of it all is overwhelming at times, but I know that whatever time we have left is in God's hands." She swallowed hard. "I will be more than thankful for every minute."

"What does your family think about all of this, Star?" JD asked.

"They can hardly believe it, but they're very happy for me. If Hadassah was not so ill, they would like to meet her, I know. But I do have some pictures of me growing up. . .for later, I think."

Michael returned with a cup of water.

"Thank you, Mike. What a helpful boy you are. I can tell your parents have done a good job raising you." Star reached out and put a hand on one of her brother's shoulders. "Tell me what you like to do for fun?"

"Hey," Steve interrupted, "can we have this get-acquainted talk over lunch? I'm starving!"

"Let me check on Haddie, first," JD said. "This morning we'd talked about maybe everyone eating together, but I don't know how she's feeling right now. Wait here a minute; and I'll look in on her."

<hr>

Hadassah looked peaceful, her mouth slightly open with a tear stain still on one cheek. She didn't stir, so JD left. At the nurses' station he told them where he'd be if she woke up and asked.

"I'll let her know, Mr. Jensen. She's been talking to me about the entire situation. I'm so happy for her. It's quite a remarkable story, isn't it?"

"There's no doubt about it."

"For sure, it's God's hand, wouldn't you agree?"

"There's no doubt in my mind whatsoever." He winked, and she smiled in return.

<hr>

"I mostly love to play baseball, but I'm also a good skater. Well, not good enough for professional hockey or anything, but I almost never fall anymore."

JD sat across the table from Mike and Star, who were turned to each other. Mike's face had not been this animated since last Christmas, when he discovered his new Spyder bike hidden behind the Christmas tree. JD could tell that Star was as interested in her brother as Mike was in her. *They will have each other after. . .*

Fritz spoke up. "Star's a good skater as well, Mike. She grew up on skates and skis."

Steve leaned over to his wife and murmured just loud enough for JD to hear, "I'm thinking that Professor Fritz is quite smitten with the grown-up child he found in the snow. What do you think?"

Vikki punched him in the arm. "It doesn't take a rocket scientist to figure that out. I'm still amazed every time I think about how this has all unfolded, Steve. Two women, one destiny."

"Hmm," Steve agreed.

They'd been at lunch for nearly forty minutes when JD heard his name being paged over the loudspeaker. Everyone stood in unison.

"I'm going on up ahead of you and see what's happened. See you there."

They each nodded, and then he was gone. Star sat down slowly, and Fritz took her hand.

❧

Upstairs, Hadassah had awakened from a nightmare and became disoriented to the point of panic. Had her meeting with Esther all been a dream as well? She shook her head. *Can't think straight. . .so confused.* That's when she'd rung the nurse and asked for her husband.

JD pushed open the door, out of breath. "What's wrong?"

She smiled. "I'm sorry, sweetheart. . .just a little panicked for a moment." She turned her face for a kiss, and JD relaxed. "Well, what do you think of my daughter? Is she not beautiful, JD?"

"I'm very impressed with your daughter, and wait until you hear what Mike thinks of his sister. He hasn't stopped talking since they met." He chuckled. "They've got a lot in common. . . pretty amazing, I'd say."

"I think *you're* amazing," she whispered. "Sorry I interrupted your lunch."

"No problem. Do you feel like seeing Star and Mike together?"

"That would be the best medicine ever."

A knock on the door brought Mike inside. "Mom, are you okay?"

She smiled and waved him closer. Star followed behind, face aglow. There were no words to describe how full Hadassah's heart felt at this very moment. In one brief second the past took a giant step into oblivion, taking with it the long list of tragedies that had haunted her mind for decades. She delighted in the release, like a volcano had finally spewed its last bit of residue.

"Come, children, let me look at you. The two of you are a magnificent couple."

Mike perched himself on the bed and kissed Hadassah on the cheek. "Do you think we look alike, Mom? Do we?" His grin went from ear to ear. Before his mother could answer, he rushed on. "And guess what? Star likes to skate, and Fritz, that's her boyfriend, Fritz said she was really good." He took a deep breath. "Besides skating, she's also a very good skier, and later we're going skiing together, Mom."

Hadassah said, "Mike, slow down a little. I'm so happy you two are finding so much in common. It makes me *more* than happy to see you together." *After all this time. If only Aaron were here.* She refused to let her mind wander to that thought. . .not now.

That night after the family left, Hadassah was alone with her thoughts, and for once they were all good. Everyone kept remarking throughout the day that God had brought this reunion with Star to pass. Could it be so? Was God alive after all? She fell into a peaceful rest.

# Chapter 27

On the way home from the hospital, Michael was as animated as JD had ever seen him, his face glowing with enthusiasm. Not since before Haddie's illness had his boy shown this much energy. "Dad, this whole thing with my sister, Mom, and Fritz is a top-of-the-line miracle. Wouldn't you say so, Dad?" He went right on talking without waiting for JD's response. "I mean, Dad, what else could you call it?" He started humming.

"You know what, Mike? From the first day I met your mother, I've believed in miracles. And I agree with you 100 percent that this whole thing is truly one of them." He smiled at the recognition.

Suddenly Mike was quiet. "Dad," he said softly, "I'm praying for another miracle, just so you know."

JD took a deep breath. He knew what Mike was going to say.

"I want God to heal Mom." His voice cracked.

"Me too, Mike, me too."

❧

Star leaned her head back into the seat of the car.

"A penny for your thoughts," Fritz said.

"I'm thinking how grateful I am. . .so grateful. Never in my life did I think this day would come."

"Do I hear a 'but. . .'?" He glanced in her direction.

She sat upright. "I guess. To find my mother after all these years is beyond my comprehension, even now. Yet my heart hurts thinking about how sick she really is. We've just said hello, and soon we'll be saying good-bye."

Fritz pulled the car to the curb and turned to face her. "You know I'm here for you, Star." She nodded. "But I'm just a man. The God of the Universe has brought you and your mother to this place. Surely that God will not abandon either of you at this point."

"Oh, Fritz, of course you're right, and I believe it with all my heart. It's just sad. . .not only for my mother and me, but of course there's JD and precious Michael." She smiled, thinking about him.

"I feel bad for all of you." He reached over and touched her hand then pulled the car back out into traffic. "Did I tell you that both Michael and his father prayed to become Christians?"

"No, you didn't, but thank you, thank you so much for telling me this. It's a burden lifted from me, Fritz."

"I knew you'd be pleased."

"What about my mother? What about Hadassah?"

"Steve and Vikki have tried lots of times to share their faith with her, but she said she believes God is dead."

"Truthfully, Fritz, if I'd lived through what happened to her in Germany, I might believe the same thing."

❧

After getting Mike settled, it was late, but JD was not the least bit sleepy. The house felt empty without Hadassah. "I feel you here, Haddie." *She'll never live here again.* The thought hit him in the gut, making him want to run back to the hospital. He'd only left in the first place at her insistence, "so Mike could sleep in his own bed."

After building a fire and making tea, he picked up the Bible and settled before the fireplace. Steve had given him more scriptures to read, and he looked them up. It took him awhile to find the first one, since he was still unfamiliar with where all the books were located. It was in Matthew.

*"Blessed are they that mourn: for they shall be comforted."*

JD already knew this to be true. Every time his mind wandered to the what-ifs, and the if-onlys, that special comforting peace showed up. Sometimes it came like a flood, other times as a trickle. It seemed whatever he needed for any one moment, God provided.

Steve had written a cross-reference in Revelation 21:4: *"And God shall wipe away all tears from their eyes; and there shall be no more death, neither sorrow, nor crying, neither shall there be any more pain: for the former things are passed away."*

He took this as a promise for the future and found it refreshing. *But God, we've still got to walk this path with our Hadassah. Thank You for sending us Star. Already I feel better knowing how much comfort she brings to her mother. But I also ask that You would bring my wife into fellowship with You. Thank You for what You've done for us so far. Amen.*

After praying, JD grabbed a blanket from the back of his chair and wrapped himself in it. Within seconds he was sleeping, his dreams full of scenes from the German countryside. Pieces of violin music floated in his mind while snippets of Hadassah's stay at the convent infirmary came and went.

❧

Singing! Hadassah thought she'd been dreaming, but when she opened her eyes, the voices could still be heard. Was it someone's radio? No, the melody came from the hallway and was getting closer. Christmas carolers.

*"Deck the halls with boughs of holly,*
*Fa la la la la la la la la!*
*'Tis the season to be jolly,*
*Fa la la la la la la la la!"*

Their voices faded after passing by the door. Despite the fact that she felt weaker today, her spirits lifted, and Hadassah found herself humming the tune when a candy striper came in with breakfast.

"Good morning, Mrs. Jensen. Did you enjoy the carolers?" She set the tray in front of Hadassah, removing the cover on a steaming bowl of oatmeal.

"Yes, I did, thank you." She smiled at the young girl, whose name tag read SHEILA.

Sheila left, and Hadassah took one bite of the cold toast that came with the oatmeal. It tasted like cardboard, but she forced herself to eat for the strength she wanted to have when Star returned. The coffee was hot, which buoyed her spirits almost as much as the carolers.

❧

Star was getting ready for a trip back to the hospital when the phone rang. It was Fritz.

"Almost ready," she said when she heard his voice.

"Well, get ready for notoriety." He laughed.

"What? What are you talking about?"

"Your story. . .it's in the paper this morning. It's Sunday, remember?"

"I can't believe I forgot all about it, with everything else going on. Well, how does it look?"

"Amazing, Star."

"Wow, here I am a published journalist, and truthfully it means so little to me now. I mean, compared to finding my mother and Michael. Does that make sense, Fritz?"

"Of course it does. Hey, I'll be there in a few minutes; you can see the article then."

Across town JD was showing Star's *Time* entry to Michael. "Wow, my sister's famous. Wait until my friends at school see it." He looked at JD. "I'm so happy about all of this, Dad. It's like the best Christmas present I've ever had."

"I think it's the best present your mom's ever had," JD laughed, "other than you, of course." He ruffled Mike's head. "We'd better get moving. Mom expects us up at the hospital bright and early."

"Okay, Dad. Wait till she sees this. . .she'll be so excited."

JD headed to the coat closet when the phone rang.

"Jensen." It was Pete Betker from the paper.

"What's up, Betker?"

"I wouldn't have called you at home. . .you being on leave and all. . .but I just got a phone call I think you'll want to hear about."

"Shoot, man." JD felt his heartbeat increase as he listened. He could barely respond. "Wow, Pete, that's incredible news. Give me that number." He jotted down a name and phone number and thanked his coworker.

"You're welcome, JD."

JD hung up the phone and said a silent prayer. *Lord, every day I'm amazed at what You do.* He clicked the phone, listened for the tone, and dialed. A woman answered.

"Hello, this is JD Jensen."

# Chapter 28

Hadassah's mind kept playing over and over the conversations with Star. Sometimes she had trouble believing the entire thing. Wanting to hang on to every second, she let the sweetness of their reunion float through her mind like fine dandelion dust on a late spring morning. She'd found a listening ear in her favorite nurse, who had become a confidant of sorts, and had shared with her the entire saga of events.

"Mrs. Jensen, I don't know how you feel about how you were brought back together with your daughter, but in my book, I think it's miraculous."

She hadn't wanted to hurt the woman's feelings over spiritual matters, so she'd said nothing in response, but thinking about it now caused something within to shift. . .it was a gentle move, but a shift no less. What if God wasn't dead? *Well, if He's still alive, I've got a lot of questions.*

She tried to stay awake. . .she'd wanted to get back into her new robe, but just the thought of expending that much effort was exhausting. Instead, she gave in to the sleep that continually claimed more of her time. *Precious, precious time. . .how I love you now.*

❧

JD and Mike walked into the lobby of the hospital, right as Star and Fritz entered. They greeted one another with handshakes and hugs. Mike could not keep his eyes off of Star. "You're even prettier today," he said. In that instant he could feel his face flush bright red, and he stared at his feet in embarrassment.

"Mike, you're so sweet. Thank you for the compliment. But just so you know, I was quite a fright when I was your age." They walked to the elevator.

JD held the door while they all got in. "I'll be up in a few minutes."

"Are you okay, Dad?"

"I'm fine, Mike. See you up there."

The door closed, and Mike turned to Star. "Were you really not good-looking as a kid?"

"No, I was not." She winked at Fritz. "My hair was very curly, and I hated to take care of it. Whenever my mother approached me with the hairbrush, I'd run and hide."

Mike laughed. "That sounds like me, only it's my mom trying to get me in the shower that makes me run and hide." He stepped closer to his sister and slipped his hand into hers. She squeezed it tight.

❧

Downstairs in the lobby, JD's eyes watched every person coming in the double doors. In a few minutes he saw a woman in her sixties come down the sidewalk with a younger man. They looked alike.

JD walked toward them once they stepped inside. "Are you the Bakers?"

"Ja, and you must be Mr. Jensen." She was a handsome woman with beautiful silver hair knotted into a bun. She removed a glove before taking his outstretched hand. "I never thought in a million years this day would come." Her eyes welled with tears. "Oh goodness, excuse my bad manners." She turned to the man beside her. "This is my son, Jan."

JD shook his hand.

"Thank you, Mr. Jensen, for calling us. I'm visiting my mother for the holidays, like she told you on the phone."

"I can only imagine your shock when you read Star's piece in the paper this morning. It's a good thing my friend at the paper took your call, because he knows the whole story." JD shook his head. "It still boggles my mind when I think of how this has come about after all these years."

The mother spoke. "Mr. Jensen, I've prayed for that little girl since the day we met in the dark of night so long ago. To know she lived is. . ." She took a hankie from her purse. "To know that not only did she survive but also her mother lives is beyond anything I could have ever wished or prayed for. Maybe I didn't have that much faith." She wiped at her eyes. "Thank you for filling in the blanks about Star's mother. . .your wife."

Jan began to speak with perfect English, accented by only a hint of his German heritage. "It's my mother's habit to read the paper very early in the morning, so it was barely daylight when she woke me." He laughed softly. "Neither of us could believe what we read, yet somehow we knew this was the baby we'd helped; there were just too many similarities to not be the same child." He shook his head with disbelief. "But now to be here, about to meet her. . ." He shrugged. "Words escape me, I'm afraid."

JD led them to a group of generic chairs near the elevators. "Please, tell me, what part did you have in Star's journey?"

Jan deferred to Frau Baker. "I was a mother, left behind with three children after my husband was drafted into the army. He was very proud to serve. . .in the beginning. But as the war continued, he wrote home of the atrocities being carried out everywhere around us in the name of our homeland. Soon we at home heard of what was being done to our Jewish neighbors." She wrung her hands. "And, of course, that brought about the trains. . . ." Her voice trembled. "Those evil trains.

"I am a simple farm woman, born and raised, Mr. Jensen, but my heart burned with desire to help the helpless. What could I do while still keeping a home and my children's welfare? Could I even make a small difference against the Third Reich? I began to pray and ask God to help me contribute something. No matter what it would be, I'd be willing to do it if He'd only provide the opportunity."

JD listened with fascination at the story of this humble country woman, who stepped away from her own safety and risked her life to defend the defenseless.

"At first, we only heard vague rumors of the Jewish Underground. But I'm a very good listener, and soon I had gathered more and more information."

Jan leaned forward in his chair to interject. "You have to realize, Mr. Jensen, just how dangerous this was at the time. Any Jewish sympathizer was considered an instant traitor, and many were shot on the spot. There was no opportunity for defending oneself."

His mother continued. "Once I understood what was going on with the babies being handed off those trains, I knew I had my answered prayer. One day I approached our village doctor while in his office with one of my own children. It was that good doctor who made contact with the Underground." She sighed. "And that's how we came to transport Star."

Jan spoke again. "The baby was at the second destination in her rescue when we were sent in the dead of night to transport her on skis to the next contact. Once our part was completed, of course, we had no way to know whatever became of her." He choked up and couldn't continue.

JD's emotions were raw. "I have to tell you that as long as I live, I will never forget meeting the two of you. Like I told you on the phone, my wife suffered untold horrors, but the worst was losing her children. When she and her husband let Star go that day in the countryside, she believed they'd thrown their daughter to a certain death."

Frau Baker reached over and touched JD's arm. "I don't want to interrupt you, but could you please tell me what her birth name was?"

"Her parents named her Esther, after my wife's mother." He stood, and they did as well. "There is another twist to this story that I haven't shared with you yet."

The mother and son regarded him with anticipation.

"You probably already knew before reading Star's story that she was found by two children playing in the snow?"

"Ja!" They nodded in unison.

"One of those children emigrated to the U.S. and now lives right here in New York."

Frau Baker gasped, and her son put an arm around her.

"His name is Fritz, and he teaches journalism at the university. Not only that, but he's one of my paper's contest judges. When he read Star's account, he was the first to contact her and brought this story full circle to the rest of us."

Jan placed a hand over his heart and shook his head in disbelief. "Amazing, Mr. Jensen. It's God-amazing."

They walked to the elevators and punched the up button. "Jan, there's no doubt in my mind that you are absolutely right." The doors opened, and JD held them while the other two entered. "Well, are you ready to meet your baby girl and her mother?"

Mother and son looked at each other and smiled. "We're ready," Jan said.

∽∾

Upstairs, JD asked the Bakers to wait while he checked on Hadassah. He was surprised to see her alone.

"Hey lady, where's your fan club?" He walked over and kissed her on the forehead. He was startled to see an oxygen cannula in her nose.

She smiled, but when she spoke her voice was low and breathy. "Lately your son seems to have a hollow leg, so they all went to the cafeteria to fill him up." Hadassah looked at JD. "What's on your mind? Something's up; what is it?"

Now it was his turn to smile. "Think you know me pretty well, don't you?" He took one of her hands. "Are you up to more company?"

"Who?"

"Well, it's no one you've ever met." He placed her hand back on the covers and winked.

She squinted. "JD, you're confusing me."

"Did anyone show you Star's entry in this morning's paper?"

"Sure, first thing." With a puzzled look, Hadassah sat up a little straighter. "I'm still confused."

"You don't know all the details of Star's rescue yet, but there's some people who were involved who are right here in the city."

"And...?"

"I just met them, and they'd like to meet you and Star."

Both of Hadassah's hands went to cover her face, and she shook her head before speaking. Her voice sounded stronger. "All of this has happened so fast. I—I..." She shook her head in disbelief. "But of course I want to meet them. Bring them in, JD, then please, let's get Star, uh, Esther, back here."

JD ushered the Bakers into Hadassah's room and left for the cafeteria.

∽∾

Frau Baker offered her hand first. "Mrs. Jensen, I cannot tell you what it means to me to meet you. I..." She choked on her tears and couldn't finish.

Hadassah kissed the back of the older woman's hand. "If it had not been for your bravery, this day would have never happened." She placed another kiss on the hand she couldn't release. " 'Thank you' does not seem enough for what you did for my daughter."

Frau Baker stepped a little closer before speaking. "May I call you Hadassah?"

Hadassah nodded.

"Hadassah, I want you to know that you are the bravest woman I know."

Hadassah shook her head no but didn't speak.

458

"Madame, let me tell you why I believe this. Surely you must know what happened to most of the children who went to Ravensbrück?"

Hadassah winced.

"Of course, you know." She took both of Hadassah's hands into her own. "Hadassah, that one act of bravery saved your daughter's life. There is no doubt in my mind for that fact." Frau Baker continued in a low, soothing voice. "I myself am a mother; I know how much courage it took to let Star go from your arms that day."

Unstoppable tears streamed down their faces. Frau Baker let go of Hadassah's hands and bent even closer to give a long, tender hug.

"Danke, sweet, sweet woman," Hadassah whispered. "If I could, I'd give you a million dollars for *your* bravery."

"Oh, for sure, my reward is this mighty act of God unfolding before my very eyes." She wiped at her face with the back of a hand. "But I've gone on too long. I want you to meet my son, Jan. He was with me the night we carried your daughter away."

Jan and Hadassah were shaking hands just as JD returned with the others. He took Star by the elbow and guided her to where the Bakers stood next to Hadassah.

Frau Baker's hands went to her mouth, so it was Jan who spoke first. "Miss Firstenberg, I am Jan Baker, and once before we have met." He was grinning from ear to ear.

"Oh Herr Baker, I have heard. It is my deepest pleasure to meet you and to. . .to thank you for saving my life." They embraced.

Star reached for the woman, who held out her arms to her. "Let me look at you, Miss Firstenberg; how beautiful you are. . .the picture of your mother." She touched Star's cheek like she was made of glass.

JD made introductions all around and pulled some chairs from the hallway for everyone. The Bakers had a wonderful story to tell, and he didn't want any of his family to miss hearing this chapter of Star's rescue.

# Chapter 29

When the Bakers left, it was obvious Hadassah was exhausted. "Haddie, I think you've had enough excitement for one day."

She started to protest, but JD put a finger to his lips. "Shhh, we'll come back in the evening. . .after you've rested."

Hadassah nodded. "But I'd like Esther to stay until I fall asleep, if that's okay?"

Star smiled. "Mütter, I am here, and I will stay as long as you need me." She brushed a kiss on Hadassah's cheek. It felt dry and feverish, but she said nothing. *There won't be much time left for kisses.*

Fritz said good-bye to Hadassah before giving Star a hug. "I'll be in the waiting room; take your time."

"Thank you."

Steve and Vikki said their good-byes as well and left the room. Michael and JD were the last to leave, promising to return later.

When only the two remained, Hadassah patted the bed and asked Star to come closer. "What a day we've had, Liebchen." Her eyes were drifting closed.

"I think maybe you've had too much company for one day."

Hadassah shook her head. "It's my best medicine. No," she corrected herself, "*you're* my best medicine." She scooted over and motioned for Star to lie beside her.

Star lowered the side of the bed and scrunched in. Even with the covers between them, she could feel the frailness of her mother's body. They stayed that way for a while, each relishing the presence of the other.

Hadassah spoke first. "When you were born, you slept with your father and me because it was so cold. Even way up in the rafters of the farmhouse, we were afraid you might freeze in a crib." When she paused, Star thought she'd fallen to sleep, but she continued. "Of course, your brother, Aaron, would not be left out, and he slept with us, as well. All of us in a single bed not much bigger than this one." Hadassah turned her head. "I believe Aaron would look a lot like you. . .or maybe your father."

"Was he handsome? My father, I mean." Star was fighting back powerful emotions and bit her lower lip to keep from breaking down.

"Oh, not like a movie star, or anything, if that's what you mean. But he had solid good looks." She paused to remember. "And I loved everything about his face. . .everything about. . . *him.* So tall was your father, Esther, and kind. His way of gentleness is not found in many men."

Sweet thoughts of what Hadassah had shared ran though Star's mind like a drifting summer cloud until she felt Hadassah's breathing change into the rhythm of sleep. Silent tears wet her face, but surprisingly, they were not for herself, not even for Hadassah. No, this sorrow coming like a torrent was for two people she'd never met. . .her big brother and her loving father.

⊷❧⊷

When thirty minutes had passed and Star hadn't come out, JD tiptoed into the room and found both women sleeping in each other's arms—another memory to keep, like a precious etching on fine glass.

Michael was waiting with Fritz when JD returned. "Mike, you were supposed to go home with Uncle Steve and Aunt Vikki," JD scolded.

"Mom wants you to sleep in your own bed, and I think you shouldn't be alone."

He ruffled Mike's hair. "I could use your company."

"Is Star coming?" Fritz asked, looking down the hall.

"They're sleeping. I didn't want to wake them."

"Aw," Michael said. "Mom must be so happy. She is, don't you think, Dad?"

"I know she is, Mike."

"Dad?"

"Yeah?"

"Will you buy me and Fritz a pepperoni pizza?"

They all laughed. "Your mother's right, Mike," JD said. "You do have a hollow leg."

The three of them got on the elevator.

"Hollow leg? What the heck does that mean?"

When Fritz, JD, and Michael got back to the hospital, Star was sitting in the waiting room. She stood to greet them.

"We brought you back some pizza," Michael offered.

"Thanks, Mike; you're thoughtful." Star took the pizza.

"How was Hadassah when you left?" JD asked.

"Sleeping well. We had a wonderful visit." Star regarded him with a melancholy smile. "Thank you for giving me that time." Her face contorted with grief. "I cannot wrap my mind around what she must have gone through." She shook her head. "My poor mother."

JD spoke while Fritz held Star. "Hadassah never talked much about what happened in Ravensbrück. Of course it was all bad, but these last few days with you have been the best medicine she could ever have. Meeting you has erased her deepest sadness over those years. I never believed it was possible."

Star dabbed at both eyes. "She told me the same thing—that I'm her *best* medicine. But all the medicine in the world isn't enough to keep her alive, is it?"

Michael walked over and patted his sister on the back.

JD felt helpless to bring them any comfort when the reality of Hadassah's condition, the number of her days, wore just as heavy on him. *Lord, help us.*

The night nurse, Miss Santella, apologized for waking her. "I'm sorry to disturb you, Mrs. Jensen, but I need to take your vitals."

"Oh, it's okay, what time is it?" Hadassah yawned.

"A little after midnight. How's your pain level?"

"I feel like my head belongs to someone else." She studied the kind woman who, night after night, tended to her needs, giving her a special dignity somehow. "What made you want to be a nurse, Miss Santella?"

"Oh, please call me Jenn." She gently rolled Hadassah to one side and straightened her rumpled gown then fluffed her pillow before rearranging the covers. "Well, I didn't grow up in a home where much talk was given to the future; we struggled just to get by."

"Really?"

"See, my parents were alcoholics, and my brother and I ended up in foster care off and on the whole time we were little. Sometimes my grandma took us in, but she died when I was ten." She finished with the bedding and checked Hadassah's pulse before giving her a dose of morphine.

"*Somebody* must have been a good influence on you. Look how far you've come." Talking seemed a huge effort for some reason.

"*Somebody* did. The last foster home I was in belonged to a very special family. They were Christians. I arrived there about as confused and mean as a fourteen-year-old could be." She smiled.

"What happened? Did they let you stay?" Hadassah wanted to hear more.

"Yes, they not only let me stay, but they requested the state to let my brother come as well."

"How often does that happen?"

"I have no idea, but that single act of kindness began a change in me. These people, the O'Malleys, weren't like any family I'd ever been around. They showed so much love to their foster kids that most never wanted to leave. Can you imagine not wanting to leave a foster home?" She laughed. "Are you sure you want to hear all of this, Mrs. Jensen? You need your rest."

Hadassah was wide awake and squirming, waiting for the pain medication to kick in. "Please, tell me more." *For some reason, I need to hear.*

"My healing didn't happen overnight. I guess you could say my anger and hurt were peeled away. . .one painful layer at a time. See, one rule all the kids in the O'Malley house had to follow centered on going to church. At first I refused, but I soon learned it wasn't an option. Oh, I made it as unpleasant as possible in the beginning. Teenagers can be nasty." She chuckled.

"Anyway, once I realized how friendly people were at the O'Malleys' church, something inside me began to melt. In Sunday school class I kept hearing that Jesus loved me. *Yeah right,* I said to myself. I knew that if I'd been the least bit lovable, my parents wouldn't drink, and I wouldn't have ended up living with people I didn't even know."

Hadassah began to drift into the morphine, but she fought against it, wanting to hear what Nurse Santella had to say.

"I also heard that Jesus had died for me. How unbelievable was that!"

Hadassah shrugged.

"I didn't buy any of it. Then, one Sunday, my brother ran up to me. His face looked different. Turns out he *was* different. . .from the inside out."

"What happened to him?" She was drifting. . . .

⟨⟨∙⟩⟩

The young woman bent down close to Hadassah's ear. "Mrs. Jensen, how 'bout I tell you the rest of the story tomorrow night?"

Hadassah was in a deep, morphine-induced sleep.

Laying a hand on her patient's head, Nurse Santella could no longer hold back the emotion that flooded her entire being. "Lord, thank You for allowing me to care for this wounded woman. Please give me another chance to share Your love with her. In Jesus' name, amen."

# Chapter 30

Star had asked Michael if he might like to come home with her for the night, and he'd said yes.

"Will you be okay without me, Dad?"

"Sure, Mike. I would stay here with Mom, but I need a shower. I'm so tired I'll probably just go home and crash anyway."

Mike hugged his dad and left with Fritz and Star.

❧

"Your apartment is nice, Star," Mike said.

"Pretty small, don't you think?" She took his coat and hung it on the rack by the front door. "Do you want something to drink before bed? Hot chocolate sounds good to me."

"Sure, I'll have some." He walked over to a bookshelf in the corner of the living room while she made their drinks. "Hey, I had this book when I was a kid." He pulled a ragged copy of *The Pokey Little Puppy* from the middle shelf. "Mine looks just like this. . .all beat up."

Star walked in with two steaming cups of cocoa and set them on the coffee table. "My mother used to read me that when I was little. All my brothers and sisters and I had it memorized by the time we started school."

"So did I. Even though we didn't know about each other, we still have stuff in common." He sipped from the steaming cup then leaned back on the sofa.

She studied him. "Would it make you sad to talk about our mom?"

He thought for a minute. "Mmm, not really. Sometimes it makes me feel *better*. Can I tell you one of the worst things about my mom being sick?"

She nodded.

"You know how when you first wake up in the morning and things are kind of groggy in your head?" He was looking at the ceiling. "There's a second or two before all the thoughts from before snap back into your mind." He lowered his head. "Then, when you remember all the bad stuff again, that's when I'm the saddest. Because that's when I remember how sick my mom really is." He gazed at Star; tears fringed his lashes.

Her heart broke for him. He was so young. She got up, moved next to him, and put one arm around his shoulders. "I know that moment, Mike. It happened to me just this morning." Star gave him a little squeeze. "I'm so happy I have you."

They sat in silence, sipping the hot chocolate.

"Mike, do you know what the word *irony* means?"

He shook his head no. "Not really. Why?"

"Well, this whole incredible story of my survival and finding Hadassah when. . .when she's so sick is a blatant case of irony."

Mike looked puzzled.

"It almost feels like a cruel joke, doesn't it?"

"Yes," he said and set his cup down.

"That's what irony means. I've thought about this a lot the last few days. See, God is not cruel. . .men are cruel. The war and the Holocaust—those were cruel happenings. But none of that was God's idea. Do you see what I'm getting at?"

"People are cruel, but God isn't?"

"Exactly! But in the middle of man's worst, most cruel ideas, God is still sovereign and has a plan."

"And...?"

"And"—she pointed at Mike—"even though I found my mother, and she's dying, I have you."

He passed her a wistful smile. "And that's no joke."

She hugged him as tight as she could. "You're so right, little brother. That's no joke."

"Hey, I have a question for you."

"What's that?"

"Are you going to marry Fritz?"

She could feel her cheeks turn pink. "I believe we love each other."

"Well, then, doesn't it just make sense you should get married?" Mike was looking quite smug.

Star poked him in the shoulder. "I think, Mr. Smarty Pants, that a woman does not consider marriage until she's asked. True?"

"Oh, trust me, he's going to ask." Mike finished off the cocoa and wiped his mouth on one sleeve.

"Michael, you make me laugh." She glanced at her watch. "Enough family talk for the night. Let's go to bed."

Star found him a pillow, sleeping bag, and an extra toothbrush before getting him settled on the sofa.

When they had said their good nights and turned out the lights, the apartment was quiet. *Lord*, Star prayed, *You know I do love Fritz. You have brought us this far, and I trust You for our future. Please help my mother as she faces her eternal future.*

She smiled to herself, thinking about her biological brother now sleeping under her very own roof.

"Star, are you still awake?"

"Yes."

"I love you, Star." Short pause. "I'm glad you're my sister."

"I love you, too, Mike, and I'm more than glad you're my brother."

❦

JD was wide awake at 5:10 in the dark of morning, staring at the ceiling. Reality weighed on him like a huge rock sitting in the middle of his chest. He sat up for a minute or two, shook his head, and fell back onto the bed. "God, I don't know much, but I know You're real, and I believe You hear me now. Please help me be a comfort to my wife in these last days. I want to be the best husband for her. Make me strong enough for...for what lies ahead. Amen."

❦

Hadassah was having a strange dream. She was moving on a...no, not the death train again. It was the train all right, but this time the awful dread of what was about to happen with Esther wasn't there. It was like watching a movie you've seen before, and you know the ending. But how could this be? In the past, this dream had been one of the worst nightmares in her life. Why, she wondered, was this time different? She watched as Avram peeled the last bits of wood away from the opening he'd worked on until his fingers were bloodied. Watched as they exchanged children; Avram now held Esther. She saw him lift their baby girl to the opening, and, as if in slow motion, he released her.

Immediately, there was a huge flash of light right beside the railcar. It moved and swirled, full of power and something more. She squinted and looked again. Directly in the center of the swirling light was an incredible being. Though the dazzling light was nearly blinding, she could tell it was a man. His clothing was aflame with the brilliance of a summer sunrise, and he held something in his arms. Esther! The heavenly being was holding Esther....

Hadassah woke with a start. At first the surroundings looked unfamiliar, but soon she recognized the hospital room. She blinked several times, allowing her eyes to adjust to the dimness. Then, like a lightning bolt, she remembered the dream.

Was it real? Was what she saw in her dream the reality of how Esther survived? Did some creature from heaven intervene the very second Esther was thrown from the train? Hadassah's mind reeled with the possibility.

Nurse Santella came in and walked to the side of Hadassah's bed. "Oh, you're awake."

Hadassah tried to smile.

"Are you in a lot of pain, Hadassah?"

She shook her head.

"But something's bothering you, right?"

"I had a dream." Tears formed in her eyes.

Jenn patted one arm and adjusted the covers. "Do you want to tell me?"

"I don't want to keep you, Jenn. It's time for you to leave."

"Hey, I've finished my paperwork." She leaned forward. "I'm all yours."

Word for word, Hadassah shared the dream. She'd already shared with her new friend about the train incident, so Jenn knew the background story.

When Hadassah finished, Jenn began to sob. She rested her head on the side of the hard metal hospital bed, unable to stop the flow of tears.

Hadassah reached over to touch the younger woman's head. "Shhh, sweet Jenn. I didn't mean to upset you. . .please. . .I'm sorry."

Jenn lifted her head. "Hadassah, I'm not upset. I'm moved to tears because of the awesome thing God showed you."

"You believe it was God who gave me this dream?" She rubbed the top of her head, puzzled.

"Listen to me. The Bible is full of times when God spoke to people in dreams. Surely you remember those stories from the Old Testament?"

"Yes, yes, I do, but. . ."

"Please, listen to me. You told me how for years you felt such horrible guilt about throwing your daughter from a train, yet here she is, alive and well." She swiped at her eyes. "I believe God showed you in this dream exactly how Esther survived."

"You mean," Hadassah said slowly, "it was an. . .angel." She stared into Jenn's face. "It *was* an angel, wasn't it, Jenn?"

"Oh, Hadassah, I believe it. I believe it with my whole heart. It all fits together: those children right next to the train tracks, Esther being found uninjured. It was God all along." She offered her patient a sip of water.

"Jenn, for so many years, my heart has been closed to God, and now"—it was difficult to speak—"my family tells me they all believe in Y'shua." Chills began to wrack her body, and she clenched her teeth against the onslaught. "I. . ."

Jenn interrupted, "Hadassah, I'm giving you more pain medication so you'll be up to having visitors. I'm working again tonight, and we can talk more then. Okay?"

In the midst, Hadassah could only nod and give a weak smile.

⁂

Jenn left the room to get the medication but first leaned heavily on the wall next to Hadassah's door. "Oh Lord," she whispered, "thank You for who You are. Thank You from the bottom of my heart."

# Chapter 31

Hadassah was sleeping when JD got to the hospital, so he waited for Mike, Star, and Fritz in a big chair by a window in the waiting room. Snow was falling, and Bing Crosby sang "White Christmas" over the hospital speakers, jolting him with the realization that Christmas was only days away. Time had never slipped by like this ever. A huge clock inside his head ticked off the days, minutes, every second, making him feel old.

In the beginning, when Hadassah was first diagnosed, he'd not spent much of that ticking time thinking about the reality of life after she was actually gone. But now he understood that when a puzzle is thrown into the air, it never lands put together. Instead it's scattered and. . .

The next thought was one of absolute clarity. *"Peace I give you. . . . "* There was that word again. *God, You know I've felt Your peace in so many ways in just a short time, and for sure, Mike and I will need all You can give.*

The elevator hummed and stopped. Mike stepped out on a run toward him. "Hi, Dad. How's Mom?" They hugged.

"Sleeping when I got here, but I'll see if she's awake." He shook hands with Fritz and gave Star a squeeze and winked. "I hope your brother was a gracious guest at your place, Star."

"Yes, he was, except he kept me up too late."

Mike laughed. "That's not true. I was a perfect gentleman. I even put my hot chocolate cup in the sink."

JD turned Mike's baseball cap backward. "I think it's evident these two are related. What do you think, Fritz?"

Fritz gazed first at Star then at Mike. "I think you're absolutely right, JD."

They were at Hadassah's door. JD entered first. The minute he stepped inside, he could hear Hadassah's breathing; it was labored. He shivered. *I need to collect myself.* He found it hard to breathe and couldn't move. *God help me.* His breath returned to normal, and he touched her arm. "Haddie."

She stirred at his voice and mouthed *"hello."*

He bent down to kiss her cheek, finding her skin to be like fine parchment paper. "Your kids are here," he said right next to one ear.

Both eyes fluttered open, and she smiled. "Water, please."

He held a cup with a straw to her mouth, and she took a couple sips.

"Thank you."

"Do you want me to get Mike and Star?"

"Wait. . .a minute. . .please." She reached out for him.

He took one of her hands and placed it to his lips. "I'd take your place, if I could, Haddie." He wasn't going to cry.

Her gaze was tender. "I know you would, JD, and I love you for it." She sipped more water. "I need you to do me a favor. I want to add some things to that journal I've been keeping. It's on the bookshelf in the living room. Would you bring it to me, please?"

"If you promise to write nice things about me." He kissed her lips this time.

"I'll do my best. Now I'd like to get myself presentable before the children come in."

JD helped her change into a fresh hospital gown, trying to ignore how much weight had been eaten away since she'd been in the hospital.

"I think I'll put on a scarf today. What do you think?" She was wiping at her face with a washcloth he'd warmed.

"I like the yellow one," he said.

"Then the yellow one it is." She tried to make a bow, but her arms were too weak, so JD did his best. When it was tied, she lay back on the pillows. "I feel like I've just run a marathon."

"Haddie, you *are* running a marathon." His eyes misted.

"But at the end, I don't win, JD. Ironic, isn't it? All this effort and pain, and in the end, I lose."

He was about to say something about the Lord when a knock at the door interrupted. Michael came in, followed by Star.

"Oh, I've missed both of you. Come sit by me."

Star took both Hadassah's hands.

"Mom, I spent the night with Star." Mike gave his mother a quick hug then gestured at his sister. "We're so much alike. Can you believe it?"

"Oh, I do believe it. Stand next to each other; let me see you side by side."

They complied, laughing with the effort. JD watched Hadassah's face as she looked on. It was glowing. He had to look away.

"JD, I had Vikki bring me a camera. . .please take their picture. I want one of them together."

The fact that the pictures would never be developed before she died was lost on Hadassah, but JD found the camera and took the picture anyway. It made her happy. Next, she wanted one of herself with Mike and Star together and then one alone with each child.

There was another knock on the door, and Vikki and Steve entered. Vikki carried a huge poinsettia that nearly hid her face.

"Vikki, you remembered!" Hadassah exclaimed.

"Of course, I did, silly. You never have Christmas without one, right?" She put the plant next to the bed and hugged Hadassah.

"Wait a minute," Steve said, "how do you know it was Vikki who bought that. Maybe it was me?"

Mike hugged his aunt and uncle. "Sure you did, Uncle Steve."

Steve picked Mike up from the floor in a bear hug. "Missed you, bud." His voice was husky.

"Missed you guys, too." He looked up into his uncle's face. "I had fun hanging out at my sister's place."

"I'm sure you did, Mike."

JD noticed Hadassah biting her lower lip and suspected she was in pain. He knew she held off as long as possible because the morphine made her sleepy, and she was trying her best to avoid it. He made his way next to the bed. "How are you doing, Haddie? Do you need more pain meds?"

"No, I'm fine, JD." But her eyes said otherwise. "Vikki, is it still snowing?"

"Dumping gobs."

Hadassah leaned into the pillows. "I used to love the snow at the farm."

"What farm, Mom?" Michael was standing right next to her.

She didn't answer, and for a second JD thought she'd fallen asleep. Then her eyes opened slowly, and she smiled. "Oh, Mikey, I once lived on a perfect farm, with animals and people who loved me, except my Bubbe. I never figured out why she was so mean to me. There was even an apple orchard where I had a secret place and a huge barn with a hay mow. . . . Sorry, I'm not making sense, am I?" Hadassah took his hand, pressing it between her own. "You'll understand when you read the journal I'm writing for you and Star."

"You can tell me more if you want, Mom." His voice fought back tears.

Hadassah winced and a moan escaped from her lips.

JD punched the call button for a nurse.

"Yes," came a voice floating from the intercom.

"Mrs. Jensen needs some pain meds."

"I'll be right in."

Steve asked JD if he wanted him to pray, and JD nodded. They all gathered around the hospital bed and held hands. "Dear Lord, please touch Hadassah with Your comfort and peace. Please let her know how much she is loved and appreciated. In Jesus' name, we pray, amen."

When they opened their eyes, Hadassah's were closed. JD pulled the blankets up to cover her shoulders. She'd fallen asleep even without medication.

⊰⊱

In the hallway, JD spotted Hadassah's primary care physician, walking toward him. They shook hands, and he braced himself for what the doctor would say.

"It won't be long, Mr. Jensen." He made eye contact. "Your wife has held on longer than most people might."

"That's because she's a survivor." Instantly JD realized how ridiculous that sounded. He looked at the doctor. "You know what I mean."

"Of course I do." He started to walk away but turned back. "If you haven't already, it would be good to make the final arrangements, Mr. Jensen."

JD heard the words, but his mind reeled in anger at what they meant. "Yes, Doctor, I will do that." He spoke so loud that Mike walked over from the rest who were waiting to leave.

"Dad, are you all right?"

Mike looked just like he did at five, grabbing JD by the heart. "I'm fine, Mike, just feeling sad for Mom. It hurts, that's all."

Mike clutching at the sleeves of his dad's coat. "Me, too. Even my bones hurt sometimes." He looked up. "But I have you and Star and"—he sniffed—"and I feel like I'm going to be okay. Does that make any sense?"

"It makes perfect sense, Mike. Our situation is not perfect, but we do have each other and Star and a whole lot of other people who love us." He changed the subject. "I could eat a horse. What do you say we let Mom rest awhile and I'll treat everyone to the best burgers in town."

"Sounds good to me," Mike said. They joined the others. "But you better order your own fries, because I'm not sharing mine with anyone." He laughed and put a hand inside one of JD's. . .something he'd not done for a long time.

Mike was trying so hard to be grown up, but JD was painfully aware of his vulnerability. JD fought to stay in control for Michael's sake, but his mind was reeling with thoughts he could not hold back. He was climbing on that roller coaster of what-ifs and if-onlys again, and his stomach lurched with the descent of the elevator.

Star gave him a sympathetic gaze. "We're going to be okay, JD."

Had she read his mind? The second she said the words, he believed her. She began talking softly to Mike about something, and the gentle way she spoke caused his stomach to settle. She'd be a great support for his son. He had no doubt that Mike would be hers as well.

⊰⊱

Mike went back to the hospital with Fritz and Star, while JD ran home to get the journal Hadassah wanted. He was grateful for the small window of solitude, because it helped his mind focus. He needed to make the "final" plans the doctor had mentioned. As difficult as it would be, it needed to be done, and it was his responsibility.

The phone was ringing when he stepped through the front door. "Jensen."

"JD, it's Steve."

"What's up?"

"After lunch today, Vikki and I talked, and we'd like you to let us do something for you."

"I'm listening." JD sat down near the phone.

"We'd like to make the arrangements for Hadassah's. . .you know, her final arrangements."

"I can't let you guys do that, Steve. I'm the husband; it's my job."

"Look, I know it's your job, and no doubt you could do it all, but we feel so helpless, and this way, we'd at least feel useful."

"I don't know. . . ."

"Look, Vikki wants to talk with you. . . . Here she is."

"Hi, JD. Please listen for a minute. You know how much we love Hadassah, right?"

"Yes, of course." Vikki loved his wife like her very own sister.

"Then, please, let this be a gift to you and her, from us. I've prayed a lot before asking you, and if you'll sit down with us first, we can do the rest."

JD sighed.

"Are you still there?"

"Yeah, I'm here, Vikki. I guess if you guys did that, I'd have more time to give Mike." He paused again. "Okay. . .thanks, Vikki."

"I'm glad you said yes. Love you, JD."

"Love you, too, Vikki. Tell Steve thanks for me."

"Will do. Bye."

When he hung up, a weight had lifted. He exhaled slowly. "What a family I have." He scanned the living room, which still held Hadassah's lingering presence, grabbed her journal, and left.

# Chapter 32

Hadassah's breathing seemed steady, but a bit labored, when Star entered the room. Fritz and Mike were playing gin rummy while she visited with her mother.

Heavy emotions threatened to overwhelm her, and she prayed silently for the strength to be the daughter she wanted to be. *"I can do all things through Christ which strengtheneth me."*

"Mother." Star touched Hadassah's arm and received no response. She leaned down farther. "Mama?"

Hadassah jumped. "Oh, have you been here long?" Eyes barely open, she reached for Star. "Every time I see you, I want to touch your beautiful face. Please sit." She patted the bed.

Star maneuvered the side rail down and sat on the edge of the bed.

"What time is it?"

"After lunch."

"Are you here alone?"

"Mike and Fritz are here. . .playing cards outside."

"You know," Hadassah said, "I have not met that young man who rescued you. Do you think he might want to meet me?"

Star smiled. "I'm sure he'd like nothing more. I'll get him."

❧

In a few minutes Hadassah watched Star return, followed by a tall, very handsome man with striking blond hair. She had no trouble imagining him as the young boy she'd seen decades before.

His brilliant blue eyes were full of compassion. "Mrs. Jensen, I am Fritz."

She took the offered hand and didn't let go. "Yes," she whispered, "yes, I know." Silent tears slipped down her cheeks, but she was not embarrassed by them.

He, too, began to cry.

"Please, please, call me Hadassah," she asked. Wiping her face on the bedsheets, she gazed up at him. "I have no words for what you did back then, Fritz. I possess none that are able to express the gratitude contained in my heart."

"None are needed, Hadassah." He looked up at Star then back to Hadassah. He leaned very close to her. "I'd like to tell you something."

"Yes?"

"That day in the snow. . .the day I found your daughter. . .is sealed in my memory. I can close my eyes and recall every detail. . .the feel of the cold and even the sound of her cries carried on the wind like a haunting echo. But there's something more."

She waited, never losing eye contact.

"I also remember thinking that the mother who let her go must have been the bravest person in the world." He lowered his head as more tears slipped down and stained his shirtfront.

"Thank you, Fritz, for sharing. I only wish I could have more time. There's so much I'd like to know about you. . .your family."

Star came closer and laid a hand on Fritz's shoulder. "We have another thing to tell, and you're the first."

Fritz took Star's hand. "We love each other."

"Oh my!" Hadassah said. She smiled weakly. "I'm not really surprised, but I am happy for you."

"And one more thing. . ."

Both women waited.

Fritz reached into an overcoat pocket and pulled out a small black box. He turned to Star. "I know God brought us together again, Star. And, though we've only been reunited a short time, I believe our hearts are one." He began to choke up. "I would have waited to ask this question, but I wanted your mother to be a part of it."

His eyes locked with Hadassah's. "Traditionally, a man asks a woman's father for permission to marry, but I'm asking you, Hadassah. Would you give your blessing to me? I want to ask Star to be my wife."

Hadassah looked first at Star then Fritz. How perfect they seemed together. *Oh, Avram, how I wish you were here for this moment.* "You have my permission," she said, her voice cracking.

Fritz took both of Star's hands into his own and pulled her close. "Star, would you marry me?"

Her face flushed before speaking the two words he wanted to hear. "I will."

They embraced.

"Are you happy, Mother?" Star asked.

"More than happy," Hadassah said with passion. "I know you will take good care of this girl and keep her safe, Fritz. Just like the day you plucked her from the snow." So much talk had sapped her energy, and she began to drift. "Be happy. . .be happy. . .children."

⁂

Star and Fritz were leaving the room when she stopped in front of the door. "Aren't you forgetting something?" she whispered to Fritz.

He shrugged.

"What about the ring you pulled from your pocket?"

He nudged her out the door and into the hallway. His face flushed as he held out the ring box. "Well, this is embarrassing."

"Don't worry about it. I'm very grateful you included my mother." *I'm so grateful God brought me back to you.*

"I know it's soon, Star, but in a way I've been waiting a very long time for this moment." He removed the ring, taking her left hand, and placed a solitaire diamond on her finger. "I didn't mean to rush this at all, but we have lots of time, and your mother doesn't."

Star nodded in agreement. "You're right, Fritz." She reached up to stroke his face. "We have our entire future." She stood on her toes and brushed his cheek with a kiss. "Should we tell Mike?"

"If you want to."

"Let's go find him."

Star and Fritz returned to the waiting area, where Mike was now playing cards with his dad. "I'm beating Dad all to pieces."

"Remind me never to play cards with you, little brother."

"How's Hadassah?" JD asked.

"She seems to tire more easily now. Even short conversation wears her out."

Silence reigned in the room until Michael said softly, "It won't be long, will it?" He was looking at JD.

"Mike, I've never lied to you, and I won't start now." He stood and reached for his son, pulling him to his feet, tipping his face upward. "No, Mike, it won't be long. . .for sure."

Mike said nothing for several minutes, clinging to JD's side.

Star broke the sadness. "Mike, come here. There's something I have to show you."

He looked up. "What is it?"

"Just come over here. . .please."

Curious, Mike went and stood by Star and Fritz. "So?"

"Give me your hand."

471

Mike stuck his hand out in her direction, and Star laid her left one on top.

"Is this some kind of new handshake I don't know about?"

"Mike," JD said, "look at what she's wearing on her finger." He couldn't help but smile.

"Yeah, I see a ring. . .so what?"

Fritz spoke up. "What the ring means is: I've asked Star to marry me."

"No! You mean I'll have a new brother?" His eyes went back and forth between Fritz and Star. "Wow. . .how cool is that! Does Mom know?"

"We told her first," Star said.

"Well, when are you getting married?" His face lit up with a thought. "Hey, can I be in your wedding?"

Star couldn't help but laugh at the enthusiasm. "We're not getting married for a while, but whenever it happens, Mike, you will most certainly have an important part in it." She hugged and kissed him. He hugged her back.

❧

JD spoke his congratulations then excused himself to take Hadassah's journal to her. There was little daylight left in the already dim room, but a soft lamp glow cast long shadows across the floor. Something was changing; he could feel it. She was leaving him one breath at a time, entering into the shadow land of her last hours. A now familiar feeling totally encompassed his being. God was preparing him.

He hung his coat on the back of a chair. With great care, JD scooted Hadassah's nearly weightless body to the other side of the bed. She stirred but didn't wake. He cradled the body of his dying wife, listening. . .for what, he wasn't sure. *Are you dreaming, Hadassah? Is God bringing you comfort like we prayed?*

He woke when Mike touched his arm. "Did I sleep long?"

Mike shook his head. "I was just checking on you, Dad." He walked to the other side of the bed and touched his mother. She didn't wake. One single tear slipped down his face. He looked up at JD. "Mom's favorite nurse is outside, and she wants to talk with you."

❧

JD was surprised to see Jenn Santella in the hall. "Aren't you on the night shift?"

"Usually," she said. "But I know your wife's time is short, and I wanted to come and sit with her."

JD could see she was fighting to contain her feelings.

She smiled. "Mrs. Jensen is very special to me, and I want to be here, if you don't mind."

"That's very nice of you. Thank you for. . ."

"Please, no need to thank me." She took JD's arm and led him down the hall a bit, away from Michael. "If the rest of the family wants to say good-bye, they need to do it now. According to the doctor, she won't make it through another night."

JD lowered his head. "I think the doctor's right."

"If you want to go get coffee or something, I'll stay with her."

"That would be good." He started to go to the waiting room but turned. "I almost forgot. Hadassah had me bring her journal from home. I can't see her able to write in it, but she said she wanted to have it. I left it by her bed."

"Hopefully, I can help her. I've seen people rally sometimes, right before"—tears welled— "right before they pass."

# Chapter 33

Hadassah woke when she heard footsteps near the bed. Star was waiting at the foot. Unlike earlier, Hadassah's mind felt crystal clear. "Would you mind raising my head? I can see you better that way."

Star cranked the head of the bed.

"Come closer, Leibchen."

Star smiled. "That's what my Mütter used to call me—her little dark-eyed Liebchen."

"Tell me about her. Were you happy in her house?"

"Yes, very. Her family was everything, and she loved us every day we lived under her roof." She pulled a chair next to the bed and lowered the rail. "Her favorite love gift to us was her baking. When we came home from school, our afternoon treat would be something fresh from the oven—sometimes snickerdoodles, sometimes pastry made from apples or plums from our orchard."

Hadassah's eyes drifted shut.

"Are you in pain, Mother?" Star rested a hand on one of Hadassah's.

"No, I'm just listening. Strange, isn't it? About the pain, I mean. I have no pain, and my mind is clear. Even though I'm dying, I've never felt happier." She smiled at her daughter. "Oh, I don't want to leave any of my family, but finding you, having these days together is like giving birth to you all over again." Her eyes closed again. "Except your father's not here."

Star struggled, her mind and heart holding on to every last minute, like trying to catch wind in a glass jar. "Growing up, my Mütter sang me lots of songs. When I was older, I wondered if my other family ever sang to me."

"Oh, yes, we did. Your father had a song he sang to you and Aaron from your first breath." Eyes half closed, she began.

*"Pretty like the moon*
*Bright like the stars*
*From heaven you were*
*Sent to me like a present."*

The room echoed with haunting melodic memories for the singer. Each note carrying a loving caress for the listener.

"What's it called?"

"*Sheyn vidi levone*. . .that's Yiddish." She looked wistful. "I sang it to Mike when he was little. Sometimes, I'd pretend I was singing to you. . .and Aaron."

"I'll never forget it. . .ever." Star's voice broke with emotion.

"Promise?"

"I promise. I will sing it to my own children someday."

"That makes. . .me happy." She swallowed visibly. "I'd like to see Mike now."

Star went to the waiting room and found Michael sitting quietly with JD and Fritz. They looked up in expectation.

"Mother wants to see you, Mike." She went to sit by Fritz.

Michael stood, his face ashen and questioning. He looked at his dad.

"I'll go with you." JD placed both hands on Mike's shoulders. "I'm here for you, bud."

"Thanks, Dad," he murmured.

When they got to Hadassah's room, they thought she was sleeping. "I'm awake," she said.

Mike lost his voice, and she patted him tenderly. "I love you, Mikey."

"I love you, too, Mommy." He wiped at his cheeks. "Guess what?"

"What?"

"It's almost Christmas."

"Really?" She winked. "You've. . .always loved. . .Christmas."

"Yeah. This year Star's my best present."

"You're so right."

JD took one of Hadassah's hands. "I'm taking these guys downstairs to eat, but there's someone here who'd like to stay with you, if you want."

She mouthed the word *"Who."*

"Your new friend." He kissed her hand.

"Jenn is here? She's not due back until late."

"I know, but she's here and said she'll help with your journal if you want."

". . .just a few more things to say."

"I'll send her in, and then we'll go." He paused. "Unless you want me to stay?"

"No," she said. "Come back when you're done. I'll be fine with Jenn."

Mike looked torn.

"Look, Mikey, Jenn takes good care of me." She motioned toward the door. "Go."

Jenn was waiting in the hall when they came out. "Page me if you need to, Jenn," JD said. "We'll be downstairs in the cafeteria."

"I will, Mr. Jensen."

<hr>

The cafeteria was packed, and they'd waded through the line with little patience. Each ate quietly, the weight of sorrow leaving them to their own thoughts. When JD's name was paged, they left the food and hurried to the elevators.

Jenn stood outside Hadassah's room holding the door.

Fritz said, "I'll wait out here for you, Star," then kissed her. "I'm praying."

<hr>

"Hadassah, can you hear me?" JD asked.

Her breathing was shallow. "Mmm."

"We love you, Hadassah. Star and Mike are here." First he touched a cheek then her forehead.

Mike's sobs broke the silence.

"Come closer, Mike. Mom can still hear you." *He looks so small.*

"I love you. I love you, Mom."

Hadassah nodded.

JD turned to Star. "Maybe you should take him out for a few minutes." Star agreed but first took Hadassah's hand and put it to her lips. "I love you, too, Mama."

Hadassah smiled.

Mike shuffled alongside his sister, taking one long look in Hadassah's direction before leaving.

"I'm still here, Haddie," JD said.

She stirred, turning her head slightly in his direction, and mouthed, *"I love you."*

"I love you, too, Hadassah." He kissed the side of her face before climbing in next to her.

She was struggling to speak, but no sound came out. JD shifted closer and put his ear right next to her mouth. "Take. . .good care. . .of. . .Mikey. . . ." Mike's name came with one long exhale.

JD propped himself onto an elbow, placing a hand under her nose. Nothing. His heart skipped several beats. In that instant he knew his wife had taken her last breath and entered into eternity.

He got up, straightened his clothing, standing for a couple minutes, staring. Thoughts of their life ran together in vivid color, and although the weight of reality of the moment felt heavy, he smiled.

It had all been good.

He stepped into the hall and found Jenn, clutching Hadassah's journal. She smiled through tears and handed it to him. "You'll want to read the last entry, Mr. Jensen."

# Chapter 34

Fritz and Star were the last ones at the grave site. Though the sun had broken through, it did nothing to ease the bone-chilling cold. Star wrapped her neck scarf tighter against the assault. She yearned to touch the coffin one last time, and stepped closer. That's when she noticed an envelope lying beneath a spray of white roses and an ancient violin. She laid one gloved hand on it before turning to Fritz. "Look what I found."

"Must be a card JD missed. Pick it up, Star; we shouldn't leave it here." He walked over to where she stood.

She lifted it and read *Hadassah* on the front. "It's addressed to my mother; what should I do with it?"

Fritz shrugged. "I don't know, Star."

She held it close to her chest. "I know this sounds strange, but I feel I'm *supposed* to open it."

He nodded toward the envelope. "Then open it."

Carefully, she ran a nail under the flap, her hands trembling a bit. Inside was a single sheet of paper. Removing it, she shoved the envelope into a pocket. In an instant, her face went ashen, and she stumbled against the casket. Fritz stepped forward, but she raised a hand to indicate it was okay.

Her head snapped up with a sharp gasp, and she began to scan the distance, searching for something below. One hand went to her throat. Dropping the letter, she began running toward a very tall man in a gray overcoat and hat. When he saw Star coming toward him, he walked in her direction. He used a cane.

"Star," Fritz called out, "who is that man?"

She yelled over one shoulder. "My father!"

He watched, shaking his head in amazement as they embraced, then bent to pick up the piece of paper at his feet. Smoothing it out, he read:

> *My dearest Hadassah,*
>
> *I have searched for you since the day we parted in the hellish place of Ravensbrück. Though I know you no longer walk this earth; you shall be with me always. . .in the cherished spot created for you alone.*
>
> *When the men's camp was liberated, I waited outside the gates of your prison for days, searching every face leaving, hoping you were still alive. Hunger, thirst, and a terrible illness dragged me away from that place, but not from you.*
>
> *I read in your obituary that our daughter lives. And, because she survived, a part of you will as well. How grateful I am for such an incredible blessing.*
>
> *I will always be devoted to you and to our brief, but unforgettable, memories.*
>
> *Love always, Avram*

Fritz could barely see through his tears, watching Star living out another predestined meeting, one that only God could have created and brought about.

She looked up and waved, her laughter floating toward him on winter's breath. He waved back, folded the note, and began walking into the brilliant sunshine that marked the pathway into his own destiny, thanking God each step of the way.

# Epilogue

My dearest Michael and Esther (My Star!):

How sweet it is for me to write this word: *children*. I asked for my journal because I wanted to say good-bye here. But now, I have something more to share with you.

You will notice this new entry is not my writing. I am weak, so my special friend is lending me her hands. How grateful I am for this moment.

A very long time ago, I declared to myself that God was dead. How could a God with all the power of the universe let so many suffer? I still do not have the answer to that question, but I have a truth I never possessed before, one that the two of you already know. God is not dead!

In the dark of these hospital nights, when I was unable to sleep, God brought me an angel. She doesn't have wings, but she is heaven-sent, regardless. As Jenn tended to this failing body, she recognized the longing of a desperate soul.

You see, your faith did not go unrecognized by me. Michael, I saw the changes of your heart written all over your sweet, innocent face...your father's as well. I could have been kinder.

Oh, and my darling Esther, how your face glowed with love and forgiveness when we met. At first, I did not believe that you would be able to forgive me for leaving you. Yet the minute you walked into my presence I saw it. But where, I wondered, did that kind of power come from? Even though my mind formed the question, in my heart, I knew it had to be divinely sent.

When I look back, I see God's hand on my life in many ways. The fact I survived Ravensbrück at all is more than remarkable. Only JD knows what it took to bring me back to life. And, of course, Esther's rescue and the entire story of our reunion makes me see so clearly how wrong I've been.

And then, Jenn shared her story with me. Life had been cruel to her, but she wasn't blaming God. How was that possible?

"God did not create evil," she told me. In an instant, I realized the truth of what she'd spoken. I still do not understand it all. Can anyone? Yet, when I heard Jenn's complete story, I felt my brokenness falling away. In my dying state, I am fully alive for the first time. That can only be God.

When Jenn read from an Isaiah scripture, in the Old Testament, word after word described the Messiah. You see, I knew them all. Even in my frailty, I remembered the words from my childhood. The precious scripture your grandfather had read to me was about to live with new truth.

I'd never looked at a New Testament, but when Jenn opened it today, there it was—the history of Jesus, the completion of all the promises of my Jewish heritage. Oh, how I understood. Our Messiah came, and His name is Y'shua. I have prayed. He is mine, and I am His. I'm at peace with no fear.

So tired now. Hope I will have enough strength to share this with you, my loves; but if I don't, I will be waiting...watching...complete and whole with Y'shua.

Until then, I love you.

# About the Authors

**BRUCE JUDISCH**, a senior analyst on contract to the Department of Defense, has been writing for many years. He is the author of *Katia*, *For Maria*, and the A Prophet's Tale series (*The Journey Begun* and *The Word Fulfilled*), as well as *Ben Amittai: First Call*, the prequel—a trilogy on the story of Jonah—and also more than eighteen Bible study booklets, as well as topical studies on the Seven Churches of Revelation, the Resurrection, and Discerning God's Will.

Bruce participated in the events surrounding the opening of the Berlin Wall while stationed in the city from 1989–1992 with the U.S. Air Force. He witnessed a scene near Checkpoint Charlie that inspired *Katia* and is featured as a prominent scene in the novel. KENS Channel 5, San Antonio's local CBS affiliate, interviewed Bruce concerning the "fall of the Wall," and featured *Katia* on November 9, 2010, the twenty-first anniversary of that historic event. More information, including a gallery of photos, can be viewed on his website at www.brucejudisch.com/katia.htm.

*For Maria* is the story of two minor characters from the prequel, *Katia*. As Bruce researched the arc of the story, the work of the OSE and of the Kindertransport came to light and led to alumni of the Kindertransport, some of whom he had the unlimited joy of befriending. It was an honor to tell their story.

Bruce holds an MA in information systems and computer resources management; an MA in management; a BA in Russian; and an AA in communications processing management. He lives in Texas.

www.brucejudisch.com
www.oaktara.com

**SHARON BERNASH SMITH** wore many hats while raising two sons in rural Washington State—preschool owner/teacher, midwife's assistant in a home-birth practice, and a Pregnancy Resource Center volunteer for twenty-five years. Now as a writer, Sharon desires to touch lives for Christ through the written word and her own life experiences.

"Reality Fiction™ *Faith Meets Imagination* is my commitment to address the real-life struggles we all face," Sharon says. "There are no pat answers in life, and you won't find them in my books; however, God is just, and I will always portray Him as such."

Sharon is also the author of *The Short Life of Moths*, a young-adult novel; *Old Sins, Long Shadows*, book 2 in The McLeod Family Saga; and coauthor, with Rosanne Croft and Linda Reinhardt, of the historical novel *Like a Bird Wanders*, book 1 in The McLeod Family Saga; and the Christmas classics, *Once Upon a Christmas*, *Always Home for Christmas*, and *Starry Starry, Christmas Night* (all OakTara). She has also been published by Focus on the Family and AMG Publishers.

Sharon enjoys watercolor painting, land-sailing around the Pacific Northwest, and spending as much time as possible with friends and family, especially her three granddaughters. Sharon and her husband attend a large church in Washington State.

See her on Facebook and at sharonbernashsmith.blogspot.com
www.oaktara.com

F
JUD

Judisch, Bruce
The lost loves of
World War II collection

AMHERST PUBLIC LIBRARY
221 SPRING STREET
AMHERST, OHIO 44001